W9-BMA-508

HENRY JAMES

HENRY JAMES

NOVELS 1901–1902

The Sacred Fount
The Wings of the Dove

THE LIBRARY OF AMERICA

The paper used in this publication meets the
minimum requirements of the American National Standard for
Information Sciences—Permanence of Paper for Printed
Library Materials, ANSI Z39.48—1984.

Distributed to the trade
in the United States by Penguin Putnam Inc.
and in Canada by Penguin Books Canada Ltd.

Library of Congress Catalog Number: 2005049443
For cataloging information, see end of Notes.
ISBN 1–931082–88–x

―――――

First Printing
The Library of America—162

Manufactured in the United States of America

LEO BERSANI
WROTE THE NOTES FOR THIS VOLUME

Contents

THE SACRED FOUNT

I

IT WAS an occasion, I felt—the prospect of a large party—to look out at the station for others, possible friends and even possible enemies, who might be going. Such premonitions, it was true, bred fears when they failed to breed hopes, though it was to be added that there were sometimes, in the case, rather happy ambiguities. One was glowered at, in the compartment, by people who on the morrow, after breakfast, were to prove charming; one was spoken to first by people whose sociability was subsequently to show as bleak; and one built with confidence on others who were never to reappear at all—who were only going to Birmingham. As soon as I saw Gilbert Long, some way up the platform, however, I knew him as an element. It was not so much that the wish was father to the thought as that I remembered having already more than once met him at Newmarch. He was a friend of the house—he wouldn't be going to Birmingham. I so little expected him, at the same time, to recognise me that I stopped short of the carriage near which he stood—I looked for a seat that wouldn't make us neighbours.

I had met him at Newmarch only—a place of a charm so special as to create rather a bond among its guests; but he had always, in the interval, so failed to know me that I could only hold him as stupid unless I held him as impertinent. He was stupid in fact, and in that character had no business at Newmarch; but he had also, no doubt, his system, which he applied without discernment. I wondered, while I saw my things put into my corner, what Newmarch could see in him—for it always had to see something before it made a sign. His good looks, which were striking, perhaps paid his way—his six feet and more of stature, his low-growing, tight-curling hair, his big, bare, blooming face. He was a fine piece of human furniture— he made a small party seem more numerous. This, at least, was the impression of him that had revived before I stepped out again to the platform, and it armed me only at first with surprise when I saw him come down to me as if for a greeting. If he had decided at last to treat me as an acquaintance made, it was none the less a case for letting him come all the way. That, accordingly, was what he did, and with so clear a conscience, I hasten to add, that at the end of a minute we were talking together quite as with the tradition of prompt intimacy. He was good-looking enough, I now again saw, but not such a model of it as I had seemed to remember; on the other hand his manners had distinctly gained in ease. He referred to our previous encounters and common contacts—he was glad I was going; he peeped into my compartment and thought it better than his own. He called a porter, the next minute, to shift his things, and while his attention was so taken I made out some of the rest of the contingent, who were finding or had already found places.

This lasted till Long came back with his porter, as well as with a lady unknown to me and to whom he had apparently mentioned that our carriage would pleasantly accommodate her. The porter carried in fact her dressing-bag, which he put upon a seat and the bestowal of which left the lady presently free to turn to me with a reproach: "I don't think it very nice of you not to speak to me." I stared, then caught at her identity through her voice; after which I reflected that she might easily have thought me the same sort of ass as I had thought Long. For she was simply, it appeared, Grace Brissenden. We had, the three of us, the carriage to ourselves, and we journeyed together for more than an hour, during which, in my .corner, I had my companions opposite. We began at first by talking a little, and then as the train—a fast one—ran straight and proportionately bellowed, we gave up the effort to compete with its music. Meantime, however, we had exchanged with each other a fact or two to turn over in silence. Brissenden was coming later—not, indeed, that that was such a fact. But his wife was informed—she knew about the numerous others; she had mentioned, while we waited, people and things: that Obert, R.A., was somewhere in the train, that her husband was to bring on Lady John, and that Mrs. Froome and Lord Lutley were in the wondrous new fashion—and their servants too, like a single household—starting, travelling, arriving together. It came back to me as I sat there that when she mentioned Lady John as in charge of Brissenden the other member of our trio had expressed interest and surprise—

expressed it so as to have made her reply with a smile: "Didn't you really know?" This passage had taken place on the platform while, availing ourselves of our last minute, we hung about our door.

"Why in the world *should* I know?"

To which, with good nature, she had simply returned: "Oh, it's only that I thought you always did!" And they both had looked at me a little oddly, as if appealing from each other. "What in the world does she mean?" Long might have seemed to ask; while Mrs. Brissenden conveyed with light profundity: "*You* know why he should as well as I, don't you?" In point of fact I didn't in the least; and what afterwards struck me much more as the beginning of my anecdote was a word dropped by Long after someone had come up to speak to her. I had then given him his cue by alluding to my original failure to place her. What in the world, in the year or two, had happened to her? She had changed so extraordinarily for the better. How could a woman who had been plain so long become pretty so late?

It was just what he had been wondering. "I didn't place her at first myself. She had to speak to me. But I hadn't seen her since her marriage, which was—wasn't it?—four or five years ago. She's amazing for her age."

"What then *is* her age?"

"Oh—two or three-and-forty."

"She's prodigious for that. But can it be so great?"

"Isn't it easy to count?" he asked. "Don't you remember, when poor Briss married her, how immensely she was older? What was it they called it?—a case of child-stealing. Everyone made jokes. Briss isn't yet thirty." No, I bethought myself, he wouldn't be; but I hadn't remembered the difference as so great. What I had mainly remembered was that she had been rather ugly. At present she was rather handsome. Long, however, as to this, didn't agree. "I'm bound to say I don't quite call it beauty."

"Oh, I only speak of it as relative. She looks so well—and somehow so 'fine.' Why else shouldn't we have recognised her?"

"Why indeed? But it isn't a thing with which beauty has to do." He had made the matter out with an acuteness for which

I shouldn't have given him credit. "What has happened to her is simply that—well, that nothing has."

"Nothing has happened? But, my dear man, she has been married. That's supposed to be something."

"Yes, but she has been married so little and so stupidly. It must be desperately dull to be married to poor Briss. His comparative youth doesn't, after all, make more of him. He's nothing but what he is. Her clock has simply stopped. She looks no older—that's all."

"Ah, and a jolly good thing too, when you start where she did. But I take your discrimination," I added, "as just. The only thing is that if a woman doesn't grow older she may be said to grow younger; and if she grows younger she may be supposed to grow prettier. That's all—except, of course, that it strikes me as charming also for Brissenden himself. *He* had the face, I seem to recall, of a baby; so that if his wife did flaunt her fifty years——!"

"Oh," Long broke in, "it wouldn't have mattered to him if she had. That's the awfulness, don't you see? of the married state. People have to get used to each other's charms as well as to their faults. He wouldn't have noticed. It's only you and I who do, and the charm of it is for *us*."

"What a lucky thing then," I laughed, "that, with Brissenden so out of it and relegated to the timetable's obscure hereafter, it should be you and I who enjoy her!" I had been struck in what he said with more things than I could take up, and I think I must have looked at him, while he talked, with a slight return of my first mystification. He talked as I had never heard him—less and less like the heavy Adonis who had so often "cut" me; and while he did so I was proportionately more conscious of the change in him. He noticed in fact after a little the vague confusion of my gaze and asked me—with complete good nature—why I stared at him so hard. I sufficiently disembroiled myself to reply that I could only be fascinated by the way he made his points; to which he—with the same sociability—made answer that he, on the contrary, more than suspected me, clever and critical as I was, of amusement at his artless prattle. He stuck none the less to his idea that what we had been discussing was lost on Brissenden. "Ah, then I hope," I said, "that at least Lady John isn't!"

"Oh, Lady John——!" And he turned away as if there were either too much or too little to say about her.

I found myself engaged again with Mrs. Briss while he was occupied with a newspaper-boy—and engaged, oddly, in very much the free view of him that he and I had just taken of herself. She put it to me frankly that she had never seen a man so improved: a confidence that I met with alacrity, as it showed me that, under the same impression, I had not been astray. She had only, it seemed, on seeing him, made him out with a great effort. I took in this confession, but I repaid it. "He hinted to me that he had not known you more easily."

"More easily than you did? Oh, nobody does that; and, to be quite honest, I've got used to it and don't mind. People talk of our changing every seven years, but they make me feel as if I changed every seven minutes. What will you have, at any rate, and how can I help it? It's the grind of life, the wear and tear of time and misfortune. And, you know, I'm ninety-three."

"How young you must feel," I answered, "to care to talk of your age! I envy you, for nothing would induce me to let you know mine. You look, you see, just twenty-five."

It evidently too, what I said, gave her pleasure—a pleasure that she caught and held. "Well, you can't say I dress it."

"No, you dress, I make out, ninety-three. If you *would* only dress twenty-five you'd look fifteen."

"Fifteen in a schoolroom charade!" She laughed at this happily enough. "Your compliment to my taste is odd. I know, at all events," she went on, "what's the difference in Mr. Long."

"Be so good then, for my relief, as to name it."

"Well, a very clever woman has for some time past——"

"Taken"—this beginning was of course enough—"a particular interest in him? Do you mean Lady John?" I inquired; and, as she evidently did, I rather demurred. "Do you call Lady John a very clever woman?"

"Surely. That's why I kindly arranged that, as she was to take, I happened to learn, the next train, Guy should come with her."

"You arranged it?" I wondered. "She's not so clever as you then."

"Because you feel that *she* wouldn't, or couldn't? No doubt she wouldn't have made the same point of it—for more than one reason. Poor Guy hasn't pretensions—has nothing but his youth and his beauty. But that's precisely why I'm sorry for him and try whenever I can to give him a lift. Lady John's company *is*, you see, a lift."

"You mean it has so unmistakably been one to Long?"

"Yes—it has positively given him a mind and a tongue. *That's* what has come over him."

"Then," I said, "it's a most extraordinary case—such as one really has never met."

"Oh, but," she objected, "it happens."

"Ah, so very seldom! Yes—I've positively never met it. Are you very sure," I insisted, "that Lady John *is* the influence?"

"I don't mean to say, of course," she replied, "that he looks fluttered if you mention her, that he doesn't in fact look as blank as a pickpocket. But that proves nothing—or rather, as they're known to be always together, and she from morning till night as pointed as a hat-pin, it proves just what one sees. One simply takes it in."

I turned the picture round. "They're scarcely together when she's together with Brissenden."

"Ah, that's only once in a way. It's a thing that from time to time such people—don't you know?—make a particular point of: they cultivate, to cover their game, the appearance of other little friendships. It puts outsiders off the scent, and the real thing meanwhile goes on. Besides, you yourself acknowledge the effect. If she hasn't made him clever, what has she made him? She has given him, steadily, more and more intellect."

"Well, you may be right," I laughed, "though you speak as if it were cod-liver oil. Does she administer it, as a daily dose, by the spoonful? or only as a drop at a time? Does he take it in his food? Is he supposed to know? The difficulty for me is simply that if I've seen the handsome grow ugly and the ugly handsome, the fat grow thin and the thin fat, the short grow long and the long short; if I've even, likewise, seen the clever, as I've too fondly, at least, supposed them, grow stupid: so have I *not* seen—no, not once in all my days—the stupid grow clever."

It was a question, none the less, on which she could perfectly stand up. "All I can say is then that you'll have, the next day or two, an interesting new experience."

"It *will* be interesting," I declared while I thought—"and all the more if I make out for myself that Lady John *is* the agent."

"You'll make it out if you talk to her—that is, I mean, if you make *her* talk. You'll see how she *can*."

"She keeps her wit then," I asked, "in spite of all she pumps into others?"

"Oh, she has enough for two!"

"I'm immensely struck with yours," I replied, "as well as with your generosity. I've seldom seen a woman take so handsome a view of another."

"It's because I like to be kind!" she said with the best faith in the world; to which I could only return, as we entered the train, that it was a kindness Lady John would doubtless appreciate. Long rejoined us, and we ran, as I have said, our course; which, as I have also noted, seemed short to me in the light of such a blaze of suggestion. To each of my companions—and the fact stuck out of them—something unprecedented had happened.

II

THE DAY was as fine and the scene as fair at Newmarch as the party was numerous and various; and my memory associates with the rest of the long afternoon many renewals of acquaintance and much sitting and strolling, for snatches of talk, in the long shade of great trees and through the straight walks of old gardens. A couple of hours thus passed, and fresh accessions enriched the picture. There were persons I was curious of—of Lady John, for instance, of whom I promised myself an early view; but we were apt to be carried away in currents that reflected new images and sufficiently beguiled impatience. I recover, all the same, a full sequence of impressions, each of which, I afterwards saw, had been appointed to help all the others. If my anecdote, as I have mentioned, had begun, at Paddington, at a particular moment, it gathered substance step by step and without missing a link. The links, in fact, should I count them all, would make too long a chain. They formed, nevertheless, the happiest little chapter of accidents, though a series of which I can scarce give more than the general effect.

One of the first accidents was that, before dinner, I met Ford Obert wandering a little apart with Mrs. Server, and that, as they were known to me as agreeable acquaintances, I should have faced them with confidence had I not immediately drawn from their sequestered air the fear of interrupting them. Mrs. Server was always lovely and Obert always expert; the latter straightway pulled up, however, making me as welcome as if their converse had dropped. She was extraordinarily pretty, markedly responsive, conspicuously charming, but he gave me a look that really seemed to say: "Don't—there's a good fellow—leave me any longer alone with her!" I had met her at Newmarch before—it was indeed only so that I had met her—and I knew how she was valued there. I also knew that an aversion to pretty women—numbers of whom he had preserved for a grateful posterity—was his sign neither as man nor as artist; the effect of all of which was to make me ask myself what she could have been doing to him. Making love, possibly—yet from that he would scarce have appealed. She wouldn't, on the other hand, have given him her company only to be inhuman. I joined them, at all events, learning from Mrs. Server that she had come by a train previous to my own; and we made a slow trio till, at a turn of the prospect, we came upon another group. It consisted of Mrs. Froome and Lord Lutley and of Gilbert Long and Lady John—mingled and confounded, as might be said, not assorted according to tradition. Long and Mrs. Froome came first, I recollect, together, and his lordship turned away from Lady John on seeing me rather directly approach her. She had become for me, on the spot, as interesting as, while we travelled, I had found my two friends in the train. As the source of the flow of "intellect" that had transmuted our young man, she had every claim to an earnest attention; and I should soon have been ready to pronounce that she rewarded it as richly as usual. She was indeed, as Mrs. Briss had said, as pointed as a hat-pin, and I bore in mind that lady's injunction to look in her for the answer to our riddle.

The riddle, I may mention, sounded afresh to my ear in Gilbert Long's gay voice; it hovered there—before me, beside, behind me, as we all paused—in his light, restless step, a nervous animation that seemed to multiply his presence. He became really, for the moment, under this impression, the thing I was most conscious of; I heard him, I felt him even while I exchanged greetings with the sorceress by whose wand he had been touched. To be touched myself was doubtless not quite what I wanted; yet I wanted, distinctly, a glimpse; so that, with the smart welcome Lady John gave me, I might certainly have felt that I was on the way to get it. The note of Long's predominance deepened during these minutes in a manner I can't describe, and I continued to feel that though we pretended to talk it was to him only we listened. He had us all in hand; he controlled for the moment all our attention and our relations. He was in short, as a consequence of our attitude, in possession of the scene to a tune he couldn't have dreamed of a year or two before—inasmuch as at that period he could have figured at no such eminence without making a fool of himself. And the great thing was that if his eminence was now so perfectly graced he yet knew less than any of us what was the matter with him. He was unconscious of how he had "come out"—which was exactly what sharpened my wonder. Lady John, on her side, was thoroughly conscious, and I had a fancy that she looked at me to measure how far *I* was. I cared, naturally, not in the least what she guessed; her interest for me was all in the operation of her influence. I am afraid I watched to catch it in the act—watched her with a curiosity of which she might well have become aware.

What an intimacy, what an intensity of relation, I said to myself, so successful a process implied! It was of course familiar enough that when people were so deeply in love they rubbed off on each other—that a great pressure of soul to soul usually left on either side a sufficient show of tell-tale traces. But for Long to have been so stamped as I found him, how the pliant wax must have been prepared and the seal of passion applied! What an affection the woman working such a change in him must have managed to create as a preface to her influence! With what a sense of her charm she must have paved the way for it! Strangely enough, however—it was even rather irritating—there was nothing more than usual in Lady John to assist my view of the height at which the pair so evoked must move. These things—the way other people could feel about each other, the power not one's self, in the given instance, that made for passion—were of course at best the mystery of mysteries; still, there were cases in which fancy, sounding the depths or the shallows, could at least drop the lead. Lady John, perceptibly, was no such case; imagination, in her presence, was but the weak wing of the insect that bumps against the glass. She was pretty, prompt, hard, and, in a way that was special to her, a mistress at once of "culture" and of slang. She was like a hat—with one of Mrs. Briss's hat-pins—askew on the bust of Virgil. Her ornamental information—as strong as a coat of furniture-polish—almost knocked you down. What I felt in her now more than ever was that, having a reputation for "point" to keep up, she was always under arms, with absences and anxieties like those of a celebrity at a public dinner. She thought too much of her "speech"—of how soon it would have to come. It was none the less wonderful, however, that, as Grace Brissenden had said, she should still find herself with intellect to spare—have lavished herself by precept and example on Long and yet have remained for each other interlocutor as fresh as the clown bounding into the ring. She cracked, for my benefit, as many jokes and turned as many somersaults as might have been expected; after which I thought it fair to let her off. We all faced again to the house, for dressing and dinner were in sight.

I found myself once more, as we moved, with Mrs. Server, and I remember rejoicing that, sympathetic as she showed herself, she didn't think it necessary to be, like Lady John, always "ready." She was delightfully handsome—handsomer than ever; slim, fair, fine, with charming pale eyes and splendid auburn hair. I said to myself that I hadn't done her justice; she hadn't organised her forces, was a little helpless and vague, but there was ease for the weary in her happy nature and her peculiar grace. These last were articles on which, five minutes later, before the house, where we still had a margin, I was moved to challenge Ford Obert.

"What was the matter just now—when, though you were so fortunately occupied, you yet seemed to call me to the rescue?"

"Oh," he laughed, "I was only occupied in being frightened!"

"But at what?"

"Well, at a sort of sense that she wanted to make love to me."

I reflected. "Mrs. Server? Does Mrs. Server make love?"

"It seemed to me," my friend replied, "that she began on it to *you* as soon as she got hold of you. Weren't you aware?"

I debated afresh; I didn't know that I had been. "Not to the point of terror. She's so gentle and so appealing. Even if she took one in hand with violence, moreover," I added, "I don't see why terror—given so charming a person—should be the result. It's flattering."

"Ah, you're brave," said Obert.

"I didn't know you were ever timid. How can you be, in your profession? Doesn't it come back to me, for that matter, that—only the other year—you painted her?"

"Yes, I faced her to that extent. But she's different now."

I scarcely made it out. "In what way different? She's as charming as ever." As if even for his own satisfaction my friend seemed to think a little. "Well, her affections were not then, I imagine, at her disposal. I judge that that's what it must have been. They were fixed—with intensity; and it made the difference with *me*. Her imagination had, for the time, rested its wing. At present it's ready for flight—it seeks a fresh perch. It's trying. Take care."

"Oh, I don't flatter myself," I laughed, "that I've only to hold out my hand! At any rate," I went on, "*I* sha'n't call for help."

He seemed to think again. "I don't know. You'll see."

"If I do I shall see a great deal more than I now suspect." He wanted to get off to dress, but I still held him. "Isn't she wonderfully lovely?"

"Oh!" he simply exclaimed.

"Isn't she as lovely as she seems?"

But he had already broken away. "What has that to do with it?"

"What has anything then?"

"She's too beastly unhappy."

"But isn't that just one's advantage?"

"No. It's uncanny." And he escaped.

The question had at all events brought us indoors and so far up our staircase as to where it branched towards Obert's room. I followed it to my corridor, with which other occasions had made me acquainted, and I reached the door on which I expected to find my card of designation. This door, however, was open, so as to show me, in momentary possession of the room, a gentleman, unknown to me, who, in unguided quest of his quarters, appeared to have arrived from the other end of the passage. He had just seen, as the property of another, my unpacked things, with which he immediately connected me. He moreover, to my surprise, on my entering, sounded my name, in response to which I could only at first remain blank. It was in fact not till I had begun to help him place himself that, correcting my blankness, I knew him for Guy Brissenden. He had been put by himself, for some reason, in the bachelor wing and, exploring at hazard, had mistaken the signs. By the time we found his servant and his lodging I had reflected on the oddity of my having been as stupid about the husband as I had been about the wife. He had escaped my notice since our arrival, but I had, as a much older man, met him—the hero of his odd union—at some earlier time. Like his wife, none the less, he had now struck me as a stranger, and it was not till, in his room, I stood a little face to face with him that I made out the wonderful reason.

The wonderful reason was that I was *not* a much older man; Guy Brissenden, at any rate, was not a much younger. It was he who was old—it was he who was older—it was he who was oldest. That was so disconcertingly what he had become. It was in short what he would have been had he been as old as he looked. He looked almost anything—he looked quite sixty. I made it out again at dinner, where, from a distance, but opposite, I had him in sight. Nothing could have been stranger than the way that, fatigued, fixed, settled, he seemed to have piled up the years. They were there without having had time to arrive. It was as if he had discovered some miraculous short cut to the common doom. He had grown old, in fine, as people you see after an interval sometimes strike you as having grown rich—too quickly for the honest, or at least for the straight, way. He had cheated or inherited or speculated. It took me but a minute then to add him to my little gallery—the small collection, I mean, represented by his wife and by Gilbert Long, as well as in some degree doubtless also by Lady John: the museum of those who put to me with such intensity the question of what had happened to them. His wife, on the same side, was not out of my range, and now, largely exposed, lighted, jewelled, and enjoying moreover visibly the sense of these things —his wife, upon my honour, as I soon remarked to the lady next me, his wife (it was too prodigious!) looked about twenty.

"Yes—isn't it funny?" said the lady next me.

It was so funny that it set me thinking afresh and that, with the interest of it, which became a positive excitement, I had to keep myself in hand in order not too publicly to explain, not to break out right and left with my reflections. I don't know why—it was a sense instinctive and unreasoned, but I felt from the first that if I was on the scent of something ultimate I had better waste neither my wonder nor my wisdom. I *was* on the scent—that I was sure of; and yet even after I was sure I should still have been at a loss to put my enigma itself into words. I was just conscious, vaguely, of being on the track of a law, a law that would fit, that would strike me as governing the delicate phenomena—delicate though so marked—that my imagination found itself playing with. A part of the amusement they yielded came, I daresay, from my exaggerating them—grouping them into a larger mystery (and thereby a larger "law") than the facts, as observed, yet warranted; but that is the common fault of minds for which the vision of life is an obsession. The obsession pays, if one will; but to pay it has to borrow. After dinner, but while the men were still in the room, I had some talk again with Long, of whom I inquired if he had been so placed as to see "poor Briss."

He appeared to wonder, and poor Briss, with our shifting of seats, was now at a distance. "I think so—but I didn't particularly notice. What's the matter with poor Briss?"

"That's exactly what I thought you might be able to tell me. But if nothing, in him, strikes you——!"

He met my eyes a moment—then glanced about. "Where is he?"

"Behind you; only don't turn round to look, for he knows——" But I dropped, having caught something directed toward me in Brissenden's face. My interlocutor remained blank, simply asking me, after an instant, what it was he knew. On this I said what I meant. "He knows we've noticed."

Long wondered again. "Ah, but I *haven't*!" He spoke with some sharpness.

"He knows," I continued, noting the sharpness too, "what's the matter with him."

"Then what the devil is it?"

I waited a little, having for the moment an idea on my hands. "Do you see him often?"

Long disengaged the ash from his cigarette. "No. Why should I?"

Distinctly, he was uneasy—though as yet perhaps but vaguely—at what I might be coming to. That was precisely my idea, and if I pitied him a little for my pressure my idea was yet what most possessed me. "Do you mean there's nothing in him that strikes you?"

On this, unmistakably, he looked at me hard. "'Strikes' me—in that boy? Nothing in him, that I know of, ever struck me in my life. He's not an object of the smallest interest to me!"

I felt that if I insisted I should really stir up the old Long, the stolid coxcomb, capable of rudeness, with whose redemption, reabsorption, supersession—one scarcely knew what to call it—I had been so happily impressed. "Oh, of course, if you haven't noticed, you haven't, and the matter I was going to speak of will have no point. You won't know what I mean." With which I paused long enough to let his curiosity operate if his denial had been sincere. But it hadn't. His curiosity never operated. He only exclaimed, more indulgently, that he didn't know what I was talking about; and I recognised after a little that if I had made him, without intention, uncomfortable, this was exactly a proof of his being what Mrs. Briss, at the station, had called cleverer, and what I had so much remarked while, in the garden before dinner, he held our small company. Nobody, nothing could, in the time of his inanity, have made him turn a hair. It was the mark of his aggrandisement. But I spared him —so far as was consistent with my wish for absolute certainty; changed the subject, spoke of other things, took pains to sound disconnectedly, and only after reference to several of the other ladies, the name over which we had just felt friction. "Mrs. Brissenden's quite fabulous."

He appeared to have strayed, in our interval, far. "'Fabulous'?"

"Why, for the figure that, by candle-light and in cloth-of-silver and diamonds, she is still able to make."

"Oh dear, yes!" He showed as relieved to be able to see what I meant. "She has grown so very much less plain."

But that wasn't at all what I meant. "Ah," I said, "you put it the other way at Paddington—which was much more the right one."

He had quite forgotten. "How then did I put it?"

As he had done before, I got rid of my ash. "She hasn't grown very much less plain. She has only grown very much less old."

"Ah, well," he laughed, but as if his interest had quickly dropped, "youth is—comparatively speaking—beauty."

"Oh, not always. Look at poor Briss himself."

"Well, if you like better, beauty is youth."

"Not always, either," I returned. "Certainly only when it *is* beauty. To see how little it may be either, look," I repeated, "at poor Briss."

"I thought you told me just now not to!" He rose at last in his impatience.

"Well, at present you can."

I also got up, the other men at the same moment moved, and the subject of our reference stood in view. This indeed was but briefly, for, as if to examine a picture behind him, the personage in question suddenly turned his back. Long, however, had had time to take him in and then to decide. "I've looked. What then?"

"You don't see anything?"

"Nothing."

"Not what everyone else must?"

"No, confound you!"

I already felt that, to be so tortuous, he must have had a reason, and the search for his reason was what, from this moment, drew me on. I had in fact half guessed it as we stood there. But this only made me the more explanatory. "It isn't really, however, that Brissenden has grown less lovely—it's only that he has grown less young."

To which my friend, as we quitted the room, replied simply: "Oh!"

The effect I have mentioned was, none the less, too absurd. The poor youth's back, before us, still as if consciously presented, confessed to the burden of time. "How old," I continued, "did we make out this afternoon that he would be?"

"That who would?"

"Why, poor Briss."

He fairly pulled up in our march. "Have you got him on the brain?"

"Don't I seem to remember, my dear man, that it was you yourself who knew? He's thirty at the most. He can't possibly be more. And there he is: as fine, as swaddled, as royal a mummy, to the eye, as one would wish to see. Don't pretend! But it's all right." I laughed as I took myself up. "I must talk to Lady John."

I did talk to her, but I must come to it. What is most to the point just here is an observation or two that, in the smoking-room, before going to bed, I exchanged with Ford Obert. I forbore, as I have hinted, to show all I saw, but it was lawfully open to me to judge of what other people did; and I had had before dinner my little proof that, on occasion, Obert could see as much as most. Yet I said nothing more to him for the present about Mrs. Server. The Brissendens were new to him, and his experience of every sort of facial accident, of human sign, made him just the touchstone I wanted. Nothing, naturally, was easier than to turn him on the question of the fair and the foul, type and character, weal and woe, among our fellow-visitors; so that my mention of the air of disparity in the couple I have just named came in its order and produced its effect. This effect was that of my seeing—which was all I required—that if the disparity was marked for him this expert observer could yet read it quite the wrong way. Why had so fine a young creature married a man three times her age? He was of course astounded when I told him the young creature was much nearer three times Brissenden's, and this led to some interesting talk between us as to the consequences, in general, of such association on such terms. The particular case before us, I easily granted, sinned by over-emphasis, but it was a fair, though a gross, illustration of what almost always occurred when twenty and forty, when thirty and sixty, mated or mingled, lived together in intimacy. Intimacy of course had to be postulated. Then either the high number or the low always got the upper hand, and it was usually the high that succeeded. It seemed, in other words, more possible to go back than to keep still, to grow young than to remain so. If Brissenden had been of his wife's age and his wife of Brissenden's, it would thus be he who must have redescended the hill, it would be she who would have been pushed over the brow. There was really a touching truth in it, the stuff of—what did people call such things?—an apologue or a parable. "One of the pair," I said, "has to pay for the other. What ensues is a miracle, and miracles are expensive. What's a greater one than to have your youth twice over? It's a second wind, another 'go'—which isn't the sort of thing life mostly treats us to. Mrs. Briss had to get her new blood, her extra allowance of time and bloom, somewhere; and from whom could she so conveniently extract them as from Guy himself? She *has*, by an extraordinary feat of legerdemain, extracted them; and he, on his side, to supply her, has had to tap the sacred fount. But the sacred fount is like the greedy man's description of the turkey as an 'awkward' dinner dish. It may be sometimes too much for a single share, but it's not enough to go round."

Obert was at all events sufficiently struck with my view to

throw out a question on it. "So that, paying to his last drop, Mr. Briss, as you call him, can only die of the business?"

"Oh, not yet, I hope. But before *her*—yes: long."

He was much amused. "How you polish them off!"

"I only talk," I returned, "as you paint; not a bit worse! But one must indeed wonder," I conceded, "how the poor wretches feel."

"You mean whether Brissenden likes it?"

I made up my mind on the spot. "If he loves her he must. That is if he loves her passionately, sublimely." I saw it all. "It's in fact just because he does so love her that the miracle, for her, is wrought."

"Well," my friend reflected, "for taking a miracle coolly——!"

"She hasn't her equal? Yes, she does take it. She just quietly, but just selfishly, profits by it."

"And doesn't see then how her victim loses?"

"No. She can't. The perception, if she had it, would be painful and terrible—might even be fatal to the process. So she hasn't it. She passes round it. It takes all her flood of life to meet her own chance. She has only a wonderful sense of success and well-being. The *other* consciousness——"

"Is all for the other party?"

"The author of the sacrifice."

"Then how beautifully 'poor Briss,'" my companion said, "must have it!"

I had already assured myself. He had gone to bed, and my fancy followed him. "Oh, he has it so that, though he goes, in his passion, about with her, he dares scarcely show his face." And I made a final induction. "The agents of the sacrifice are uncomfortable, I gather, when they suspect or fear that you see."

My friend was charmed with my ingenuity. "How you've worked it out!"

"Well, I feel as if I were on the way to something."

He looked surprised. "Something still more?"

"Something still more." I had an impulse to tell him I scarce knew what. But I kept it under. "I seem to snuff up——"

"*Quoi donc?*"

"The sense of a discovery to be made."

"And of what?"

"I'll tell you to-morrow. Good-night."

III

I DID on the morrow several things, but the first was not to redeem that vow. It was to address myself straight to Grace Brissenden. "I must let you know that, in spite of your guarantee, it doesn't go at all—oh, but not at all! I've tried Lady John, as you enjoined, and I can't but feel that she leaves us very much where we were." Then, as my listener seemed not quite to remember where we had been, I came to her help. "You said yesterday at Paddington, to explain the change in Gilbert Long—don't you recall?—that that woman, plying him with her genius and giving him of her best, is clever enough for two. She's not clever enough then, it strikes me, for three—or at any rate for four. I confess I don't see it. Does she really dazzle *you*?"

My friend had caught up. "Oh, you've a standard of wit!"

"No, I've only a sense of reality—a sense not at all satisfied by the theory of such an influence as Lady John's."

She wondered. "Such a one as whose else then?"

"Ah, that's for us still to find out! Of course this can't be easy; for as the appearance is inevitably a kind of betrayal, it's in somebody's interest to conceal it."

This Mrs. Brissenden grasped. "Oh, you mean in the lady's?"

"In the lady's most. But also in Long's own, if he's really tender of the lady—which is precisely what our theory posits."

My companion, once roused, was all there. "I see. You call the appearance a kind of betrayal because it points to the relation behind it."

"Precisely."

"And the relation—to do that sort of thing—must be necessarily so awfully intimate."

"*Intimissima.*"

"And kept therefore in the background exactly in that proportion."

"Exactly in that proportion."

"Very well then," said Mrs. Brissenden, "doesn't Mr. Long's tenderness of Lady John quite fall in with what I mentioned to you?"

I remembered what she had mentioned to me. "His making her come down with poor Briss?"

"Nothing less."

"And is that all you go upon?"

"That and lots more."

I thought a minute—but I had been abundantly thinking. "I know what you mean by 'lots.' Is Brissenden in it?"

"Dear no—poor Briss! He wouldn't like that. *I* saw the manœuvre, but Guy didn't. And you must have noticed how he stuck to her all last evening."

"How Gilbert Long stuck to Lady John? Oh yes, I noticed. They were like Lord Lutley and Mrs. Froome. But is that what one can call being tender of her?"

My companion weighed it. "He must speak to her *sometimes*. I'm glad you admit, at any rate," she continued, "that it does take what you so prettily call some woman's secretly giving him of her best to account for him."

"Oh, that I admit with all my heart—or at least with all my head. Only, Lady John has none of the signs——"

"Of being the beneficent woman? What then *are* they—the signs—to be so plain?" I was not yet quite ready to say, however; on which she added: "It proves nothing, you know, that *you* don't like her."

"No. It would prove more if she didn't like *me*, which—fatuous fool as you may find me—I verily believe she does. If she hated me it would be, you see, for my ruthless analysis of her secret. She *has* no secret. She would like awfully to have—and she would like almost as much to be believed to have. Last evening, after dinner, she could feel perhaps for a while that she *was* believed. But it won't do. There's nothing in it. You asked me just now," I pursued, "what the signs of such a secret would naturally be. Well, bethink yourself a moment of what the secret itself must naturally be."

Oh, she looked as if she knew all about *that*! "Awfully charming—mustn't it?—to act upon a person, through an affection, so deeply."

"Yes—it can certainly be no vulgar flirtation." I felt a little like a teacher encouraging an apt pupil; but I could only go on with the lesson. "Whoever she is, she gives all she has. She keeps nothing back—nothing for herself."

"I see—because *he* takes everything. He just cleans her out." She looked at me—pleased at last really to understand—with the best conscience in the world. "Who *is* the lady then?"

But I could answer as yet only by a question. "How can she possibly be a woman who gives absolutely nothing whatever; who scrapes and saves and hoards; who keeps every crumb for herself? The whole show's there—to minister to Lady John's vanity and advertise the business—behind her smart shop-window. You can see it, as much as you like, and even amuse yourself with pricing it. But she never parts with an article. If poor Long depended on *her*——"

"Well, what?" She was really interested.

"Why, he'd be the same poor Long as ever. He would go as he used to go—naked and unashamed. No," I wound up, "he deals—turned out as we now see him—at another establishment."

"I'll grant it," said Mrs. Brissenden, "if you'll only name me the place."

Ah, I could still but laugh and resume! "He doesn't screen Lady John—she doesn't screen herself—with your husband or with anybody. It's she who's herself the screen! And pleased as she is at being so clever, and at being thought so, she doesn't even know it. She doesn't so much as suspect it. She's an un-mitigated fool about it. 'Of course Mr. Long's clever, because he's in love with me and sits at my feet, and don't you see how clever *I* am? Don't you hear what good things I say—wait a little, I'm going to say another in about three minutes; and how, if you'll only give him time too, he comes out with them after me? They don't perhaps sound so good, but you see where he has got them. I'm so brilliant, in fine, that the men who admire me have only to imitate me, which, you observe, they strikingly do.' Something like that is all her philosophy."

My friend turned it over. "You do sound like her, you know. Yet how, if a woman's stupid——"

"Can she have made a man clever? She can't. She can't at least have begun it. What we shall know the real person by, in the case that you and I are studying, is that the man himself will have made her what she has become. She will have done just what Lady John has not done—she will have put up the shutters and closed the shop. She will have parted, for her friend, with her wit."

"So that she may be regarded as reduced to idiocy?"

"Well—so I can only see it."

"And that if we look, therefore, for the right idiot——"

"We shall find the right woman—our friend's mystic Egeria? Yes, we shall be at least approaching the truth. We shall 'burn,' as they say in hide-and-seek." I of course kept to the point that the idiot would have to *be* the right one. *Any* idiot wouldn't be to the purpose. If it was enough that a woman was a fool the search might become hopeless even in a house that would have passed but ill for a fools' paradise. We were on one of the shaded terraces, to which, here and there, a tall window stood open. The picture without was all morning and August, and within all clear dimness and rich gleams. We stopped once or twice, raking the gloom for lights, and it was at some such moment that Mrs. Brissenden asked me if I then regarded Gilbert Long as now exalted to the position of the most brilliant of our companions. "The cleverest man of the party?"—it pulled me up a little. "Hardly that, perhaps—for don't you see the proofs I'm myself giving you? But say he *is*"—I considered —"the cleverest but one." The next moment I had seen what she meant. "In that case the thing we're looking for ought logically to be the person, of the opposite sex, giving us the maximum sense of depletion for his benefit? The biggest fool, you suggest, *must*, consistently, be the right one? Yes again; it would so seem. But that's not really, you see, the short cut it sounds. The biggest fool is what we want, but the question is to discover who *is* the biggest."

"I'm glad then *I* feel so safe!" Mrs. Brissenden laughed.

"Oh, you're not the biggest!" I handsomely conceded. "Besides, as I say, there must be the other evidence—the evidence of relations."

We had gone on, with this, a few steps, but my companion again checked me, while her nod toward a window gave my attention a lead. "Won't *that*, as it happens, then do?" We could just see, from where we stood, a corner of one of the rooms. It was occupied by a seated couple, a lady whose face was in sight and a gentleman whose identity was attested by his back, a back somehow replete for us, at the moment, with a guilty significance. There *was* the evidence of relations. That we had suddenly caught Long in the act of presenting his receptacle at the sacred fount seemed announced by the tone in which Mrs. Brissenden named the other party—"Mme. de Dreuil!" We looked at each other, I was aware, with some elation; but our triumph was brief. The Comtesse de Dreuil, we quickly felt—an American married to a Frenchman—wasn't at all the thing. She was almost as much "all there" as Lady John. She was only another screen, and we perceived, for that matter, the next minute, that Lady John was also present. Another step had placed us within range of her; the picture revealed in the rich dusk of the room was a group of three. From that moment, unanimously, we gave up Lady John, and as we continued our stroll my friend brought out her despair. "Then he has nothing *but* screens? The need for so many does suggest a fire!" And in spite of discouragement she sounded, interrogatively, one after the other, the names of those ladies the perfection of whose presence of mind might, when considered, pass as questionable. We soon, however, felt our process to be, practically, a trifle invidious. Not one of the persons named could, at any rate—to do them all justice—affect us as an intellectual ruin. It was natural therefore for Mrs. Brissenden to conclude with scepticism. "She may exist—and exist as you require her; but what, after all, proves that she's here? She mayn't have come down with him. Does it necessarily follow that they always go about together?"

I was ready to declare that it necessarily followed. I had my idea, and I didn't see why I shouldn't bring it out. "It's my belief that he no more goes away without her than you go away without poor Briss."

She surveyed me in splendid serenity. "But what have we in common."

"With the parties to an abandoned flirtation? Well, you've in common your mutual attachment and the fact that you're thoroughly happy together."

"Ah," she good-humouredly answered, "we don't flirt!"

"Well, at all events, you don't separate. He doesn't really suffer you out of his sight, and, to circulate in the society you adorn, you don't leave him at home."

"Why shouldn't I?" she asked, looking at me, I thought, just a trifle harder.

"It isn't a question of why you shouldn't—it's a question of whether you do. You don't—do you? That's all."

She thought it over as if for the first time. "It seems to me I often leave him when I don't want him."

"Oh, when you don't want him—yes. But when don't you want him? You want him when you want to be right, and you want to be right when you mix in a scene like this. I mean," I continued for my private amusement, "when you want to be happy. Happiness, you know, is, to a lady in the full tide of social success, even more becoming than a new French frock. You have the advantage, for your beauty, of being admirably married. You bloom in your husband's presence. I don't say he need always be at your elbow; I simply say that you're most completely yourself when he's not far off. If there were nothing else there would be the help given you by your quiet confidence in his lawful passion."

"I'm bound to say," Mrs. Brissenden replied, "that such help is consistent with his not having spoken to me since we parted, yesterday, to come down here by different trains. We haven't so much as met since our arrival. My finding him so indispensable is consistent with my not having so much as looked at him. Indispensable, please, for what?"

"For your not being without him."

"What then do I do *with* him?"

I hesitated—there were so many ways of putting it; but I gave them all up. "Ah, I think it will be only *he* who can tell you! My point is that you've the instinct—playing in you, on either side, with all the ease of experience—of what you are to each other. All I mean is that it's the instinct that Long and *his* good friend must have. They too perhaps haven't spoken to each other. But where he comes she does, and where she comes he does. That's why I know she's among us."

"It's wonderful what you know!" Mrs. Brissenden again laughed. "How can you think of them as enjoying the facilities of people in *our* situation?"

"Of people married and therefore logically in presence? I don't," I was able to reply, "speak of their facilities as the same, and I recognise every limit to their freedom. But I maintain, none the less, that so far as they *can* go, they do go. It's a relation, and they work the relation: the relation, exquisite surely, of knowing they help each other to shine. Why are they not, therefore, like you and Brissenden? What I make out is that when they do shine one will find—though only after a hunt, I admit, as you see—they must both have been involved. Feeling their need, and consummately expert, they will have managed, have arranged."

She took it in with her present odd mixture of the receptive and the derisive. "Arranged what?"

"Oh, ask *her*!"

"I would if I could find her!" After which, for a moment, my interlocutress again considered. "But I thought it was just your contention that *she* doesn't shine. If it's Lady John's perfect repair that puts that sort of thing out of the question, your image, it seems to me, breaks down."

It did a little, I saw, but I gave it a tilt up. "Not at all. It's a case of shining as Brissenden shines." I wondered if I might go further—then risked it. "By sacrifice."

I perceived at once that I needn't fear: her conscience was too good—she was only amused. "Sacrifice, for mercy's sake, of what?"

"Well—for mercy's sake—of his time."

"His time?" She stared. "Hasn't he all the time he wants?"

"My dear lady," I smiled, "he hasn't all the time *you* want!"

But she evidently had not a glimmering of what I meant. "Don't I make things of an ease, don't I make life of a charm, for him?"

I'm afraid I laughed out. "That's perhaps exactly it! It's what Gilbert Long does for *his* victim—makes things, makes life, of an ease and a charm."

She stopped yet again, really wondering at me now. "Then it's the woman, simply, who's happiest?"

"Because Brissenden's the man who is? Precisely!"

On which for a minute, without her going on, we looked at each other. "Do you really mean that if you only knew *me* as I am, it would come to you in the same way to hunt for my confederate? I mean if he weren't made obvious, you know, by his being my husband."

I turned this over. "If you were only in flirtation—as you

reminded me just now that you're not? Surely!" I declared. "I
should arrive at him, perfectly, after all eliminations, on the
principle of looking for the greatest happiness——"

"Of the smallest number? Well, he may be a small number,"
she indulgently sighed, "but he's wholly content! Look at him
now there," she added the next moment, "and judge." We
had resumed our walk and turned the corner of the house, a
movement that brought us into view of a couple just round
the angle of the terrace, a couple who, like ourselves, must
have paused in a sociable stroll. The lady, with her back to us,
leaned a little on the balustrade and looked at the gardens;
the gentleman close to her, with the same support, offered us
the face of Guy Brissenden, as recognisable at a distance as the
numbered card of a "turn"—the black figure upon white—at a
music-hall. On seeing us he said a word to his companion,
who quickly jerked round. Then his wife exclaimed to me—
only with more sharpness—as she had exclaimed at Mme. de
Dreuil: "By all that's lovely—May Server!" I took it, on the
spot, for a kind of "Eureka!" but without catching my friend's
idea. I was only aware at first that this idea left me as unconvinced as when the other possibilities had passed before us.
Wasn't it simply the result of this lady's being the only one
we had happened not to eliminate? She had not even occurred
to us. She was pretty enough perhaps for any magic, but she
hadn't the other signs. I didn't believe, somehow—certainly
not on such short notice—either in her happiness or in her
flatness. There was a vague suggestion, of a sort, in our having
found her there with Brissenden: there would have been a pertinence, to our curiosity, or at least to mine, in this juxtaposition of the two persons who paid, as I had amused myself with
calling it, so heroically; yet I had only to have it marked for me
(to see them, that is, side by side,) in order to feel how little—
at any rate superficially—the graceful, natural, charming
woman ranged herself with the superannuated youth.

She had said a word to him at sight of us, in answer to his
own, and in a minute or two they had met us. This had given
me time for more than one reflection. It had also given Mrs.
Brissenden time to insist to me on her identification, which I
could see she would be much less quick to drop than in the
former cases. "We have her," she murmured; "we have her; it's

she!" It was by her insistence in fact that my thought was quickened. It even felt a kind of chill—an odd revulsion—at the touch of her eagerness. Singular perhaps that only then—yet quite certainly then—the curiosity to which I had so freely surrendered myself began to strike me as wanting in taste. It was reflected in Mrs. Brissenden quite by my fault, and I can't say just what cause for shame, after so much talk of our search and our scent, I found in our awakened and confirmed keenness. Why in the world hadn't I found it before? My scruple, in short, was a thing of the instant; it was in a positive flash that the amusing question was stamped for me as none of my business. One of the reflections I have just mentioned was that I had not had a happy hand in making it so completely Mrs. Brissenden's. Another was, however, that nothing, fortunately, that had happened between us really signified. For what had so suddenly overtaken me was the consciousness of this anomaly: that I was at the same time as disgusted as if I had exposed Mrs. Server and absolutely convinced that I had yet *not* exposed her.

While, after the others had greeted us and we stood in vague talk, I caught afresh the effect of their juxtaposition, I grasped, with a private joy that was quite extravagant—as so beyond the needed mark—at the reassurance it offered. This reassurance sprang straight from a special source. Brissenden's secret was so aware of itself as to be always on the defensive. Shy and suspicious, it was as much on the defensive at present as I had felt it to be—so far as I was concerned—the night before. What was there accordingly in Mrs. Server—frank and fragrant in the morning air—to correspond to any such consciousness? Nothing whatever—not a symptom. Whatever secrets she might have had, she had not *that* one; she was not in the same box; the sacred fount, in her, was not threatened with exhaustion. We all soon re-entered the house together, but Mrs. Brissenden, during the few minutes that followed, managed to possess herself of the subject of her denunciation. She put me off with Guy, and I couldn't help feeling it as a sign of her concentration. She warmed to the question just as I had thrown it over; and I asked myself rather ruefully what on earth I had been thinking of. I hadn't in the least had it in mind to "compromise" an individual; but an individual would be compromised if I didn't now take care.

IV

I HAVE said that I did many things on this wonderful day, but perhaps the simplest way to describe the rest of them is as a sustained attempt to avert that disaster. I succeeded, by vigilance, in preventing my late companion from carrying Mrs. Server off: I had no wish to see her studied—by anyone but myself at least—in the light of my theory. I felt by this time that I understood my theory, but I was not obliged to believe that Mrs. Brissenden did. I am afraid I must frankly confess that I called deception to my aid; to separate the two ladies I gave the more initiated a look in which I invited her to read volumes. This look, or rather the look she returned, comes back to me as the first note of a tolerably tight, tense little drama, a little drama of which our remaining hours at Newmarch were the all too ample stage. She understood me, as I meant, that she had better leave me to get at the truth—owing me some obligation, as she did, for so much of it as I had already communicated. This step was of course a tacit pledge that she should have the rest from me later on. I knew of some pictures in one of the rooms that had not been lighted the previous evening, and I made these my pretext for the effect I desired. I asked Mrs. Server if she wouldn't come and see them with me, admitting at the same time that I could scarce expect her to forgive me for my share in the invasion of the quiet corner in which poor Briss had evidently managed so to interest her.

"Oh, yes," she replied as we went our way, "he *had* managed to interest me. Isn't he curiously interesting? But I hadn't," she continued on my being too struck with her question for an immediate answer—"I hadn't managed to interest *him*. Of course you know why!" she laughed. "No one interests him but Lady John, and he could think of nothing, while I kept him there, but of how soon he could return to her."

These remarks—of which I give rather the sense than the form, for they were a little scattered and troubled, and I helped them out and pieced them together—these remarks had for me, I was to find, unexpected suggestions, not all of which was

I prepared on the spot to take up. "And is Lady John interested in our friend?"

"Not, I suppose, given her situation, so much as he would perhaps desire. You don't know what her situation *is*?" she went on while I doubtless appeared to be sunk in innocence. "Isn't it rather marked that there's only one person she's interested in?"

"One person?" I was thoroughly at sea.

But we had reached with it the great pictured saloon with which I had proposed to assist her to renew acquaintance and in which two visitors had anticipated us. "Why, here he is!" she exclaimed as we paused, for admiration, in the doorway. The high frescoed ceiling arched over a floor so highly polished that it seemed to reflect the faded pastels set, in rococo borders, in the walls and constituting the distinction of the place. Our companions, examining together one of the portraits and turning their backs, were at the opposite end, and one of them was Gilbert Long.

I immediately named the other. "Do you mean Ford Obert?"

She gave me, with a laugh, one of her beautiful looks. "Yes!"

It was answer enough for the moment, and the manner of it showed me to what legend she was committed. I asked myself, while the two men faced about to meet us, why she was committed to it, and I further considered that if Grace Brissenden, against every appearance, was right, there would now be something for me to see. Which of the two—the agent or the object of the sacrifice—would take most precautions? I kept my companion purposely, for a little while, on our side of the room, leaving the others, interested in their observations, to take their time to join us. It gave me occasion to wonder if the question mightn't be cleared up on the spot. There *was* no question, I had compunctiously made up my mind, for Mrs. Server; but now I should see the proof of that conclusion. The proof of it would be, between her and her imputed lover, the absence of anything that was not perfectly natural. Mrs. Server, with her eyes raised to the painted dome, with response charmed almost to solemnity in her exquisite face, struck me at this moment, I had to concede, as more than ever a person to have a lover imputed. The place, save for its pictures of later date, a triumph of the florid decoration of two centuries ago, evidently met her special taste, and a kind of profane piety had dropped on her, drizzling down, in the cold light, in silver, in crystal, in faint, mixed delicacies of colour, almost as on a pilgrim at a shrine. I don't know what it was in her—save, that is, the positive pitch of delicacy in her beauty—that made her, so impressed and presented, indescribably touching. She was like an awestruck child; she might have been herself—all Greuze tints, all pale pinks and blues and pearly whites and candid eyes—an old dead pastel under glass.

She was not too reduced to this state, however, not to take, soon enough, her own precaution—if a precaution it was to be deemed. I was acutely conscious that the naturalness to which I have just alluded would be, for either party, the only precaution worth speaking of. We moved slowly round the room, pausing here and there for curiosity; during which time the two men remained where we had found them. She had begun at last to watch them and had proposed that we should see in what they were so absorbed; but I checked her in the movement, raising my hand in a friendly admonition to wait. We waited then, face to face, looking at each other as if to catch a strain of music. This was what I had intended, for it had just come to me that one of the voices was in the air and that it had imposed close attention. The distinguished painter listened while—to all appearance—Gilbert Long did, in the presence of the picture, the explaining. Ford Obert moved, after a little, but not so as to interrupt—only so as to show me his face in a recall of what had passed between us the night before in the smoking-room. I turned my eyes from Mrs. Server's; I allowed myself to commune a little, across the shining space, with those of our fellow-auditor. The occasion had thus for a minute the oddest little air of an æsthetic lecture prompted by accidental, but immense, suggestions and delivered by Gilbert Long.

I couldn't, at the distance, with my companion, quite follow it, but Obert was clearly patient enough to betray that he was struck. His impression was at any rate doubtless his share of surprise at Long's gift of talk. This was what his eyes indeed most seemed to throw over to me—"What an unexpected demon of a critic!" It was extraordinarily interesting—I don't mean the special drift of Long's eloquence, which I couldn't, as I say, catch; but the phenomenon of his, of all people, dealing in that article. It put before me the question of whether, in these strange relations that I believed I had thus got my glimpse of, the action of the person "sacrificed" mightn't be quite out of proportion to the resources of that person. It was as if these elements might really multiply in the transfer made of them; as if the borrower practically found himself—or herself—in possession of a greater sum than the known property of the creditor. The surrender, in this way, added, by pure beauty, to the thing surrendered. We all know the French adage about that *plus belle fille du monde* who can give but what she has; yet if Mrs. Server, for instance, *had* been the heroine of this particular connection, the communication of her intelligence to her friend would quite have falsified it. She would have given much more than she had.

When Long had finished his demonstration and his charged voice had dropped, we crossed to claim acquaintance with the work that had inspired him. The place had not been completely new to Mrs. Server any more than to myself, and the impression now made on her was but the intenser vibration of a chord already stirred; nevertheless I was struck with her saying, as a result of more remembrance than I had attributed to her, "Oh yes,—the man with the mask in his hand!" On our joining the others I expressed regret at our having turned up too late for the ideas that, on a theme so promising, they would have been sure to produce, and Obert, quite agreeing that we had lost a treat, said frankly, in reference to Long, but addressing himself more especially to Mrs. Server: "He's perfectly amazing, you know—he's perfectly amazing!"

I observed that as a consequence of this Long looked neither at Mrs. Server nor at Obert; he looked only at me, and with quite a penetrable shade of shyness. Then again a strange thing happened, a stranger thing even than my quick sense, the previous afternoon at the station, that he was a changed man. It was as if he were still more changed—had altered as much since the evening before as during the so much longer interval of which I had originally to take account. He had altered almost like Grace Brissenden—he looked fairly distinguished. I said to myself that, without his stature and certain signs in his dress, I should probably not have placed him. Engrossed an instant with this view and with not losing touch of the uneasiness that I conceived I had fastened on him, I became aware only after she had spoken that Mrs. Server had gaily and gracefully asked of Obert why in the world so clever a man should *not* have been clever. "Obert," I accordingly took upon myself to remark, "had evidently laboured under some extraordinary delusion. He must literally have doubted if Long *was* clever."

"Fancy!" Mrs. Server explained with a charming smile at Long, who, still looking pleasantly competent and not too fatuous, amiably returned it.

"They're natural, they're natural," I privately reflected; "that is, he's natural to *her*, but he's not so to me." And as if seeing depths in this, and to try it, I appealed to him. "Do, my dear man, let us have it again. It's the picture, of all pictures, that most needs an interpreter. *Don't* we want," I asked of Mrs. Server, "to know what it means?" The figure represented is a young man in black—a quaint, tight black dress, fashioned in years long past; with a pale, lean, livid face and a stare, from eyes without eyebrows, like that of some whitened old-world clown. In his hand he holds an object that strikes the spectator at first simply as some obscure, some ambiguous work of art, but that on a second view becomes a representation of a human face, modelled and coloured, in wax, in enamelled metal, in some substance not human. The object thus appears a complete mask, such as might have been fantastically fitted and worn.

"Yes, what in the world does it mean?" Mrs. Server replied. "One could call it—though that doesn't get one much further —the Mask of Death."

"Why so?" I demanded while we all again looked at the picture. "Isn't it much rather the Mask of Life? It's the man's own face that's Death. The other one, blooming and beautiful——"

"Ah, but with an awful grimace!" Mrs. Server broke in.

"The other one, blooming and beautiful," I repeated, "is Life, and he's going to put it on; unless indeed he has just taken it off."

"He's dreadful, he's awful—that's what I mean," said Mrs. Server. "But what does Mr. Long think?"

"The artificial face, on the other hand," I went on, as Long now said nothing, "is extremely studied and, when you carefully look at it, charmingly pretty. I don't see the grimace."

"I don't see anything else!" Mrs. Server good-humouredly insisted. "And what does Mr. Obert think?"

He kept his eyes on her a moment before replying. "He thinks it looks like a lovely lady."

"That grinning mask? What lovely lady?"

"It does," I declared to him, really seeing what he meant—"it does look remarkably like Mrs. Server."

She laughed, but forgivingly. "I'm immensely obliged. You deserve," she continued to me, "that I should say the gentleman's own face is the image of a certain other gentleman's."

"It isn't the image of yours," Obert said to me, fitting the cap, "but it's a funny thing that it should really recall to one some face among us here, on this occasion—I mean some face in our party—that I can't think of." We had our eyes again on the ominous figure. "We've seen him yesterday—we've seen him already this morning." Obert, oddly enough, still couldn't catch it. "Who the deuce is it?"

"I know," I returned after a moment—our friend's reference having again, in a flash, become illuminating. "But nothing would induce me to tell."

"If *I* were the flattered individual," Long observed, speaking for the first time, "I've an idea that you'd give me the benefit of the compliment. Therefore it's probably not me."

"Oh, it's not you in the least," Mrs. Server blandly took upon herself to observe. "This face is so bad——"

"And mine is so good?" our companion laughed. "Thank you for saving me!"

I watched them look at each other, for there had been as yet between them no complete exchange. Yes, they were natural. I couldn't have made it out that they were not. But there was something, all the same, that I wanted to know, and I put it immediately to Long. "Why do you bring against me such an accusation?"

He met the question—singularly enough—as if his readiness had suddenly deserted him. "I don't know!"—and he turned off to another picture.

It left the three of us all the more confronted with the conundrum launched by Obert, and Mrs. Server's curiosity remained. "*Do* name," she said to me, "the flattered individual."

"No, it's a responsibility I leave to Obert."

But he was clearly still at fault; he was like a man desiring, but unable, to sneeze. "I see the fellow—yet I don't. Never mind." He turned away too. "He'll come to me."

"The resemblance," said Long, on this, at a distance from us and not turning, "the resemblance, which I shouldn't think would puzzle anyone, is simply to 'poor Briss'!"

"Oh, of course!"—and Obert gave a jump round.

"Ah—I do see it," Mrs. Server conceded with her head on one side, but as if speaking rather for harmony.

I didn't believe she saw it, but that only made her the more natural; which was also the air she had on going to join Long, in his new contemplation, after I had admitted that it was of Brissenden I myself had thought. Obert and I remained together in the presence of the Man with the Mask, and, the others being out of earshot, he reminded me that I had promised him the night before in the smoking-room to give him to-day the knowledge I had then withheld. If I had announced that I was on the track of a discovery, pray had I made it yet, and what was it, at any rate, that I proposed to discover? I felt now, in truth, more uncomfortable than I had expected in being kept to my obligation, and I beat about the bush a little till, instead of meeting it, I was able to put the natural question: "What wonderful things was Long just saying to you?"

"Oh, characteristic ones enough—whimsical, fanciful, funny. The things he says, you know."

It was indeed a fresh view. "They strike you as characteristic?"

"Of the man himself and his type of mind? Surely. Don't *you*? He talks to talk, but he's really amusing."

I was watching our companions. "Indeed he is—extraordinarily amusing." It was highly interesting to me to hear at last of Long's "type of mind." "See how amusing he is at the present moment to Mrs. Server."

Obert took this in; she was convulsed, in the extravagance always so pretty as to be pardonable, with laughter, and she even looked over at us as if to intimate with her shining, lingering eyes that we wouldn't be surprised at her transports if we suspected what her entertainer, whom she had never known for such a humourist, was saying. Instead of going to find out, all the same, we remained another minute together. It was for me, now, I could see, that Obert had his best attention. "What's the matter with them?"

It startled me almost as much as if he had asked me what was the matter with myself—for that something *was*, under this head, I was by this time unable to ignore. Not twenty minutes had elapsed since our meeting with Mrs. Server on the terrace had determined Grace Brissenden's elation, but it was a fact that my nervousness had taken an extraordinary stride. I had perhaps not till this instant been fully aware of it—it was really brought out by the way Obert looked at me as if he fancied he had heard me shake. Mrs. Server might be natural, and Gilbert Long might be, but I should not preserve that calm unless I pulled myself well together. I made the effort, facing my sharp interlocutor; and I think it was at this point that I fully measured my dismay. I had grown—that was what was the matter with me—precipitately, preposterously anxious. Instead of dropping, the discomfort produced in me by Mrs. Brissenden had deepened to agitation, and this in spite of the fact that in the brief interval nothing worse, nothing but what was right, had happened. Had I myself suddenly fallen so much in love with Mrs. Server that the care for her reputation had become with me an obsession? It was of no use saying I simply pitied her: what did I pity her for if she wasn't in danger? She *was* in danger: that rushed over me at present—rushed over me while I tried to look easy and delayed to answer my friend. She *was* in danger—if only because she had caught and held the search-light of Obert's attention. I took up his inquiry. "The matter with them? I don't know anything but that they're young and handsome and happy—children, as who should say, of the world; children of leisure and pleasure and privilege."

Obert's eyes went back to them. "Do you remember what I said to you about her yesterday afternoon? She darts from flower to flower, but she clings, for the time, to each. You've been feeling, I judge, the force of my remark."

"Oh, she didn't at all 'dart,'" I replied, "just now at me. I darted, much rather, at *her*."

"Long didn't then," Obert said, still with his eyes on them.

I had to wait a moment. "Do you mean he struck you as avoiding her?"

He in turn considered. "He struck me as having noticed with what intensity, ever since we came down, she has kept alighting. She inaugurated it, the instant she arrived, with *me*, and every man of us has had his turn. I dare say it's only fair, certainly, that Long should have."

"He's lucky to get it, the brute! She's as charming as she can possibly be."

"That's it, precisely; and it's what no woman ought to be—as charming as she possibly can!—more than once or twice in her life. This lady is so every blessed minute, and to every blessed male. It's as if she were too awfully afraid one wouldn't take it in. If she but knew how one does! However," my friend continued, "you'll recollect that we differed about her yesterday—and what does it signify? One should of course bear lightly on anything so light. But I stick to it that she's different."

I pondered. "Different from whom?"

"Different from herself—as she was when I painted her. There's something the matter with her."

"Ah, then, it's for me to ask *you* what. I don't myself, you see, perceive it."

He made for a little no answer, and we were both indeed by this time taken up with the withdrawal of the two other members of our group. They moved away together across the shining floor, pausing, looking up at the painted vault, saying the inevitable things—bringing off their retreat, in short, in the best order. It struck me somehow as a retreat, and yet I insisted to myself, once more, on its being perfectly natural. At the high door, which stood open, they stopped a moment and looked back at us—looked frankly, sociably, as if in consciousness of our sympathetic attention. Mrs. Server waved, as in temporary farewell, a free explanatory hand at me; she seemed to explain that she was now trying somebody else. Obert moreover added *his* explanation. "That's the way she collars us."

"Oh, Long doesn't mind," I said. "But what's the way she strikes you as different?"

"From what she was when she sat to me? Well, a part of it is that she can't keep still. She was as still then as if she had been paid for it. Now she's all over the place." But he came back to something else. "I like your talking, my dear man, of what you 'don't perceive.' I've yet to find out what that remarkable quantity is. What you do perceive has at all events given me so much to think about that it doubtless ought to serve me for the present. I feel I ought to let you know that you've made me also perceive the Brissendens." I of course remembered what I had said to him, but it was just this that now touched my uneasiness, and I only echoed the name, a little blankly, with the instinct of gaining time. "You put me on them wonderfully," Obert continued, "though of course I've kept your idea to myself. All the same it sheds a great light."

I could again but feebly repeat it. "A great light?"

"As to what may go on even between others still. It's a jolly idea—a torch in the darkness; and do you know what I've done with it? I've held it up, I don't mind telling you, to just the question of the change, since this interests you, in Mrs. Server. If you've got your mystery I'll be hanged if I won't have mine. If you've got your Brissendens I shall see what I can do with *her*. You've given me an analogy, and I declare I find it dazzling. I don't see the end of what may be done with it. If Brissenden's paying for his wife, for her amazing second bloom, who's paying for Mrs. Server? Isn't *that*—what do the newspapers call it?—the missing word? Isn't it perhaps in fact just what you told me last night you were on the track of? But don't add now," he went on, more and more amused with his divination, "don't add now that the man's obviously Gilbert Long—for I won't be put off with anything of the sort. She collared him much too markedly. The real man must be one she doesn't markedly collar."

"But I thought that what you a moment ago made out was that she so markedly collars all of us." This was my immediate reply to Obert's blaze of ingenuity, but I none the less saw more things in it than I could reply to. I saw, at any rate, and saw with relief, that if he should look for the missing word, as he happily enough called it, on the principle suggested to him by the case of the Brissendens, there would be no danger at all of his finding it. If, accordingly, I was nervous for Mrs. Server, all I had to do was to keep him on this false scent. Since it was not she who was paid for, but she who possibly paid, his fancy might harmlessly divert him till the party should disperse. At the same time, in the midst of these reflections, the question of the "change" in her, which he was in so much better a position than I to measure, couldn't help having for me its portent, and the sense of that was, no doubt, in my next words. "What makes you think that what you speak of was what I had in my head?"

"Well, the way, simply, that the shoe fits. She's absolutely not the same person I painted. It's exactly like Mrs. Brissenden's having been for you yesterday not the same person you had last seen bearing her name."

"Very good," I returned, "though I didn't in the least mean to set you digging so hard. However, dig on your side, by all means, while I dig on mine. All I ask of you is complete discretion."

"Ah, naturally!"

"We ought to remember," I pursued, even at the risk of showing as too sententious, "that success in such an inquiry may perhaps be more embarrassing than failure. To nose about for a relation that a lady has her reasons for keeping secret——"

"Is made not only quite inoffensive, I hold"—he immediately took me up—"but positively honourable, by being confined to psychologic evidence."

I wondered a little. "Honourable to whom?"

"Why, to the investigator. Resting on the *kind* of signs that the game takes account of when fairly played—resting on psychologic signs alone, it's a high application of intelligence. What's ignoble is the detective and the keyhole."

"I see," I after a moment admitted. "I did have, last night, my scruples, but you warm me up. Yet I confess also," I still added, "that if I do muster the courage of my curiosity, it's a little because I feel even yet, as I think you also must, altogether destitute of a material clue. If I had a material clue I should feel ashamed: the fact would be deterrent. I start, for my part, at any rate, quite in the dark—or in a darkness lighted, at best, by what you have called the torch of my analogy. The analogy too," I wound up, "may very well be only half a help. It was easy to find poor Briss, because poor Briss is here, and it's always easy moreover to find a husband. But say Mrs. Server's poor Briss—or his equivalent, whoever it may be —*isn't* here."

We had begun to walk away with this, but my companion pulled up at the door of the room. "I'm sure he is. She tells me he's near."

" 'Tells' you?" I challenged it, but I uncomfortably reflected that it was just what I had myself told Mrs. Brissenden.

"She wouldn't be as she is if he weren't. Her being as she is is the sign of it. He wasn't present—that is he wasn't present in her life at all—when I painted her; and the difference we're impressed with is exactly the proof that he is now."

My difficulty in profiting by the relief he had so unconsciously afforded me resided of course in my not feeling free to show for quite as impressed as he was. I hadn't really made out at all what he was impressed *with*, and I should only have spoiled everything by inviting him to be definite. This was a little of a worry, for I should have liked to know; but on the other hand I felt my track at present effectually covered. "Well, then, grant he's one of us. There are more than a dozen of us—a dozen even with you and me and Brissenden counted out. The hitch is that we're nowhere without a primary lead. As to Brissenden there *was* the lead."

"You mean as offered by his wife's bloated state, which was a signal——?"

"Precisely: for the search for something or other that would help to explain it. Given his wife's bloated state, his own shrunken one was what was to have been predicated. I knew definitely, in other words, what to look for."

"Whereas we don't know here?"

"Mrs. Server's state, unfortunately," I replied, "is not bloated."

He laughed at my "unfortunately," though recognising that I spoke merely from the point of view of lucidity, and presently remarked that he had his own idea. He didn't say what it was, and I didn't ask, intimating thereby that I held it to be in this fine manner we were playing the game; but I indulgently questioned it in the light of its not yet having assisted him. He answered that the minutes we had just passed were what had made the difference; it had sprung from the strong effect produced on him after she came in with me. "It's but now I really see her. She did and said nothing special, nothing striking or extraordinary; but that didn't matter—it never does: one saw how she *is*. She's nothing but *that*."

"Nothing but what?"

"She's all *in* it," he insisted. "Or it's all in *her*. It comes to the same thing."

"Of course it's all in her," I said as impatiently as I could, though his attestation—for I wholly trusted his perception—left me so much in his debt. "That's what we start with, isn't it? It leaves us as far as ever from what we must arrive at."

But he was too interested in his idea to heed my question. He was wrapped in the "psychologic" glow. "I *have* her!"

"Ah, but it's a question of having *him*!"

He looked at me on this as if I had brought him back to a mere detail, and after an instant the light went out of his face. "So it is. I leave it to you. I don't care." His drop had the usual suddenness of the drops of the artistic temperament. "Look for the last man," he nevertheless, but with more detachment, added. "I daresay it would be he."

"The last? In what sense the last?"

"Well, the last sort of creature who could be believed of her."

"Oh," I rejoined as we went on, "the great bar to that is that such a sort of creature as the last won't *be* here!"

He hesitated. "So much the better. I give him, at any rate, wherever he is, up to you."

"Thank you," I returned, "for the beauty of the present! You do see, then, that our psychologic glow doesn't, after all, prevent the thing——"

"From being none of one's business? Yes. Poor little woman!" He seemed somehow satisfied; he threw it all up. "It isn't any of one's business, is it?"

"Why, that's just what I was telling you," I impatiently exclaimed, "that *I* feel!"

V

T HE first thing that happened to me after parting with him was to find myself again engaged with Mrs. Brissenden, still full of the quick conviction with which I had left her. "It *is* she—quite unmistakably, you know. I don't see how I can have been so stupid as not to make it out. I haven't your cleverness, of course, till my nose is rubbed into a thing. But when it *is*——!" She celebrated her humility in a laugh that was proud. "The two are off together."

"Off where?"

"I don't know where, but I saw them a few minutes ago most distinctly 'slope.' They've gone for a quiet, unwatched hour, poor dears, out into the park or the gardens. When one knows it, it's all there. But what's that vulgar song?—'You've got to know it first!' It strikes me, if you don't mind my telling you so, that the way *you* get hold of things is positively uncanny. I mean as regards what first marked her for you."

"But, my dear lady," I protested, "nothing at all first marked her for me. She *isn't* marked for me, first or last. It was only you who so jumped at her."

My interlocutress stared, and I had at this moment, I remember, an almost intolerable sense of her fatuity and cruelty. They were all unconscious, but they were, at that stage, none the less irritating. Her fine bosom heaved, her blue eyes expanded with her successful, her simplified egotism. I couldn't, in short, I found, bear her being so keen about Mrs. Server while she was so stupid about poor Briss. She seemed to recall to me nobly the fact that *she* hadn't a lover. No, she was only eating poor Briss up inch by inch, but she hadn't a lover. "I don't," I insisted, "see in Mrs. Server any of the right signs."

She looked almost indignant. "Even after your telling me that you see in Lady John only the wrong ones?"

"Ah, but there are other women here than Mrs. Server and Lady John."

"Certainly. But didn't we, a moment ago, think of them all and dismiss them? If Lady John's out of the question, how can Mrs. Server possibly *not* be in it? We want a fool——"

43

"Ah, *do* we?" I interruptingly wailed.

"Why, exactly by your own theory, in which you've so much interested me! It was you who struck off the idea."

"That we want a fool?" I felt myself turning gloomy enough. "Do we really want anyone at all?"

She gave me, in momentary silence, a strange smile. "Ah, you want to take it back now? You're sorry you spoke. My dear man, you may be——" but that didn't hinder the fact, in short, that I had kindled near me a fine, if modest and timid, intelligence. There did remain the truth of our friend's striking development, to which I had called her attention. Regretting my rashness didn't make the prodigy less. "You'll lead me to believe, if you back out, that there's suddenly someone you want to protect. Weak man," she exclaimed with an assurance from which, I confess, I was to take alarm, "something has happened to you since we separated! Weak man," she repeated with dreadful gaiety, "you've been squared!"

I literally blushed for her. "Squared?"

"Does it inconveniently happen that you find you're in love with her yourself?"

"Well," I replied on quick reflection, "do, if you like, call it that; for you see what a motive it gives me for being, in such a matter as this wonderful one that you and I happened to find ourselves for a moment making so free with, absolutely sure about her. I *am* absolutely sure. There! She won't do. And for your postulate that she's at the present moment in some sequestered spot in Long's company, suffer me without delay to correct it. It won't hold water. If you'll go into the library, through which I have just passed, you'll find her there in the company of the Comte de Dreuil."

Mrs. Briss stared again. "Already? She *was*, at any rate, with Mr. Long, and she told me on my meeting them that they had just come from the pastels."

"Exactly. They met there—she and I having gone together; and they retired together under my eyes. They must have parted, clearly, the moment after."

She took it all in, turned it all over. "Then what does that prove but that they're afraid to be seen?"

"Ah, they're *not* afraid, since both you and I saw them!"

"Oh, only just long enough for them to publish themselves

as not avoiding each other. All the same, you know," she said, "they do."

"Do avoid each other? How is your belief in that," I asked, "consistent with your belief that they parade together in the park?"

"They ignore each other in public; they foregather in private."

"Ah, but they *don't*—since, as I tell you, she's even while we talk the centre of the mystic circle of the twaddle of M. de Dreuil; chained to a stake if you *can* be. Besides," I wound up, "it's not only that she's not the 'right fool'—it's simply that she's not a fool at all. We want the woman who has been rendered most inane. But this lady hasn't been rendered so in any degree. She's the reverse of inane. She's in full possession."

"In full possession of what?"

"Why, of herself."

"Like Lady John?"

I had unfortunately to discriminate here. "No, not like Lady John."

"Like whom then?"

"Like anyone. Like me; like you; like Brissenden. Don't I satisfy you?" I asked in a moment.

She only looked at me a little, handsome and hard. "If you wished to satisfy me so easily you shouldn't have made such a point of working me up. I daresay I, after all, however," she added, "notice more things than you."

"As for instance?"

"Well, May Server last evening. I was not quite conscious at the time that I did, but when one has had the 'tip' one looks back and sees things in a new light."

It was doubtless because my friend irritated me more and more that I met this with a sharpness possibly excessive. "She's perfectly natural. What I saw was a test. And so is he."

But she gave me no heed. "If there hadn't been so many people I should have noticed of myself after dinner that there was something the matter with her. I should have seen what it was. She was all over the place."

She expressed it as the poor lady's other critic had done, but this didn't shut my mouth. "Ah, then, in spite of the people, you did notice. What do you mean by 'all over the place'?"

"She couldn't keep still. She was different from the woman

one had last seen. She used to be so calm—as if she were always sitting for her portrait. Wasn't she in fact always being painted in a pink frock and one row of pearls, always staring out at you in exhibitions, as if she were saying 'Here they are again'? Last night she was on the rush."

"The rush? Oh!"

"Yes, positively—from one man to another. She was on the pounce. She talked to ten in succession, making up to them in the most extraordinary way and leaving them still more crazily. She's as nervous as a cat. Put it to any man here, and see if he doesn't tell you."

"I should think it quite unpleasant to put it to any man here," I returned; "and I should have been sure you would have thought it the same. I spoke to you in the deepest confidence."

Mrs. Brissenden's look at me was for a moment of the least accommodating; then it changed to an intelligent smile. "How you *are* protecting her! But don't cry out," she added, "before you're hurt. Since your confidence has distinguished me—though I don't quite see why—you may be sure I haven't breathed. So I all the more resent your making me a scene on the extraordinary ground that I've observed as well as yourself. Perhaps what you don't like is that my observation may be turned on *you*. I confess it is."

It was difficult to bear being put in the wrong by her, but I made an effort that I believe was not unsuccessful to recover my good humour. "It's not in the least to your observation that I object, it's to the extravagant inferences you draw from it. Of course, however, I admit I always want to protect the innocent. What does she gain, on your theory, by her rushing and pouncing? Had she pounced on Brissenden when we met him with her? Are you so very sure he hadn't pounced on *her*? They had, at all events, to me, quite the air of people settled; she was not, it was clear, at that moment meditating a change. It was we, if you remember, who had absolutely to pull them apart."

"Is it your idea to make out," Mrs. Brissenden inquired in answer to this, "that she has suddenly had the happy thought of a passion for my husband?"

A new possibility, as she spoke, came to me with a whirr of wings, and I half expressed it. "She may have a sympathy."

My interlocutress gazed at space. "You mean she may be sorry for him? On what ground?"

I had gone too far indeed; but I got off as I could. "You neglect him so! But what is she, at any rate," I went on, "nervous—as nervous as you describe her—*about*?"

"About her danger; the contingency of its being fixed upon them—an intimacy so thoroughgoing that they can scarcely afford to let it be seen even as a mere acquaintance. Think of the circumstances—*her* personal ones, I mean, and admit that it wouldn't do. It would be too bad a case. There's everything to make it so. They must live on pins and needles. Anything proved would go tremendously hard for her."

"In spite of which you're surprised that I 'protect' her?"

It was a question, however, that my companion could meet. "From people in general, no. From me in particular, yes."

In justice to Mrs. Brissenden I thought a moment. "Well, then, let us be fair all round. That you don't, as you say, breathe is a discretion I appreciate; all the more that a little inquiry, tactfully pursued, would enable you to judge whether any independent suspicion does attach. A little loose collateral evidence *might* be picked up; and your scorning to handle it is no more than I should, after all, have expected of you."

"Thank you for 'after all'!" My companion tossed her head. "I know for myself what I scorn to handle. Quite apart from that there's another matter. You must have noticed yourself that when people are so much liked——"

"There's a kind of general, amiable consensus of blindness? Yes—one can think of cases. Popularity shelters and hallows—has the effect of making a good-natured world agree not to see."

My friend seemed pleased that I so sufficiently understood. "This evidently has been a case then in which it has not only agreed not to see, but agreed not even to look. It has agreed in fact to look straight the other way. They say there's no smoke without fire, but it appears there may be fire without smoke. I'm satisfied, at all events, that one wouldn't in connection with these two find the least little puff. Isn't that just what makes the magnificence of their success—the success that reduces us to playing over them with mere moonshine?" She thought of it; seemed fairly to envy it. "I've never *seen* such luck!"

"A rare case of the beauty of impunity *as* impunity?" I laughed. "Such a case puts a price on passions otherwise to be deprecated. I'm glad indeed you admit we're 'reduced.' We *are* reduced. But what I meant to say just now was that if you'll continue to join in the genial conspiracy while I do the same—each of us making an exception only for the other—I'll pledge myself absolutely to the straight course. If before we separate I've seen reason to change my mind, I'll loyally let you know."

"What good will that do me," she asked, "if you *don't* change your mind? You won't change it if you shut your eyes to her."

"Ah, I feel I can't do that now. I *am* interested. The proof of that is," I pursued, "that I appeal to you for another impression of your own. I still don't see the logic of her general importunity."

"The logic is simply that she has a terror of appearing to encourage anyone in particular."

"Why then isn't it in her own interest, for the sake of the screen, just to *do* that? The appearance of someone in particular would be exactly the opposite of the appearance of Long. Your own admission is that that's *his* line with Lady John."

Mrs. Brissenden took her view. "Oh, she doesn't want to do anything so like the real thing. And, as for what he does, they don't feel in the same way. He's not nervous."

"Then why does he go in for a screen?"

"I mean"—she readily modified it—"that he's not so nervous as May. He hasn't the same reasons for panic. A man never has. Besides, there's not so much in Mr. Long to show——"

"What, by my notion, has taken place? Why not, if it was precisely by the change in him that my notion was inspired? Any change in *her* I know comparatively little about."

We hovered so near the case of Mr. and Mrs. Brissenden that it positively excited me, and all the more for her sustained unconsciousness. "Oh, the man's not aware of his own change. He doesn't see it as we do. It's all to his advantage."

"But *we* see it to his advantage. How should that prevent?"

"We see it to the advantage of his mind and his talk, but not to that of——"

"Well, what?" I pressed as she pulled up.

She was thinking how to name such mysteries. "His delicacy.

His consideration. His thought *for* her. He would think for her if he weren't selfish. But he *is* selfish—too much so to spare her, to be generous, to realise. It's only, after all," she sagely went on, feeding me again, as I winced to feel, with profundity of my own sort, "it's only an excessive case, a case that in him happens to show as what the doctors call 'fine,' of what goes on whenever two persons are so much mixed up. One of them always gets more out of it than the other. One of them—you know the saying—gives the lips, the other gives the cheek."

"It's the deepest of all truths. Yet the cheek profits too," I more prudently argued.

"It profits most. It takes and keeps and uses all the lips give. The cheek, accordingly," she continued to point out, "is Mr. Long's. The lips are what we began by looking for. We've found them. They're drained—they're dry, the lips. Mr. Long finds his improvement natural and beautiful. He revels in it. He takes it for granted. He's sublime."

It kept me for a minute staring at her. "So—do you know? —are *you*!"

She received this wholly as a tribute to her acuteness, and was therefore proportionately gracious. "That's only because it's catching. You've *made* me sublime. You found me dense. You've affected me quite as Mrs. Server has affected Mr. Long. I don't pretend I show it," she added, "quite as much as he does."

"Because that would entail *my* showing it as much as, by your contention, *she* does? Well, I confess," I declared, "I do feel remarkably like that pair of lips. I feel drained—I feel dry!" Her answer to this, with another toss of her head, was extravagant enough to mean forgiveness—was that I was impertinent, and her action in support of her charge was to move away from me, taking her course again to the terrace, easily accessible from the room in which we had been talking. She passed out of the window that opened to the ground, and I watched her while, in the brighter light, she put up her pink parasol. She walked a few paces, as if to look about her for a change of company, and by this time had reached a flight of steps that descended to a lower level. On observing that here, in the act to go down, she suddenly paused, I knew she had been checked by something seen below and that this was what made her turn the next moment to give me a look. I took it as an invitation to rejoin her, and I perceived when I had done so what had led her to appeal to me. We commanded from the point in question one of the shady slopes of the park and in particular a spreading beech, the trunk of which had been inclosed with a rustic circular bench, a convenience that appeared to have offered, for the moment, a sense of leafy luxury to a lady in pale blue. She leaned back, her figure presented in profile and her head a little averted as if for talk with someone on the other side of her, someone so placed as to be lost to our view.

"There!" triumphed Mrs. Brissenden again—for the lady was unmistakably Mrs. Server. Amusement was inevitable— the fact showed her as so correctly described by the words to which I had twice had to listen. She seemed really all over the place. "I thought you said," my companion remarked, "that you had left her tucked away somewhere with M. de Dreuil."

"Well," I returned after consideration, "that *is* obviously M. de Dreuil."

"Are you so sure? I don't make out the person," my friend continued—"I only see she's not alone. I understood you moreover that you had lately left them in the house."

"They *were* in the house, but there was nothing to keep them from coming out. They've had plenty of time while we've talked; they must have passed down by some of the other steps. Perhaps also," I added, "it's another man."

But by this time she was satisfied. "It's *he*!"

"Gilbert Long? I thought you just said," I observed, "that you can make nobody out."

We watched together, but the distance was considerable, and the second figure continued to be screened. "It *must* be he," Mrs. Brissenden resumed with impatience, "since it was with him I so distinctly saw her."

"Let me once more hold you to the fact," I answered, "that she had, to my knowledge, succumbed to M. de Dreuil afterwards. The moments have fled, you see, in our fascinating discussion, and various things, on your theory of her pounce, have come and gone. Don't I moreover make out a brown shoe, in a white gaiter, protruding from the other side of her dress? It must be Lord Lutley."

Mrs. Brissenden looked and mused. "A brown shoe in a white gaiter?" At this moment Mrs. Server moved, and the next—as if it were time for another pounce—she had got up. We could, however, still distinguish but a shoulder and an out-stretched leg of her gentleman, who, on her movement, ap-peared, as in protest, to have affirmed by an emphatic shift of his seat his preference for their remaining as they were. This carried him further round the tree. We thus lost him, but she stood there while we waited, evidently exhorting him; after a minute of which she came away as in confidence that he would follow. During this process, with a face more visible, she had looked as charming as a pretty woman almost always does in rising eloquent before the apathetic male. She hadn't yet no-ticed us, but something in her attitude and manner particularly spoke to me. There were implications in it to which I couldn't be blind, and I felt how my neighbour also would have caught them and been confirmed in her certitude. In fact I felt the breath of her confirmation in another elated "There!"—in a "Look at her *now*!" Incontestably, while not yet aware of us, Mrs. Server confessed with every turn of her head to a part in a relation. It stuck out of her, her part in a relation; it hung before us, her part in a relation; it was large to us beyond the breadth of the glade. And since, off her guard, she so let us have it, with whom in the world could the relation—so much of one as that—be but with Gilbert Long? The question was not settled till she had come on some distance; then the pro-ducer of our tension, emerging and coming after her, offered himself to our united, to our confounded, anxiety once more as poor Briss.

That we should have been confounded was doubtless but a proof of the impression—the singular assurance of intimacy borne toward us on the soft summer air—that we had, how-ever delusively, received. I should myself have been as ready as my neighbour to say "Whoever he is, they're in deep!"— and on grounds, moreover, quite as recklessly, as fantastically constructive as hers. There was nothing to explain our impres-sion but the fact of our already having seen them figure to-gether, and of this we needed breathing-time to give them the natural benefit. It was not indeed as an absolute benefit for either that Grace Brissenden's tone marked our recognition. "Dear Guy *again*?"—but she had recovered herself enough to laugh. "I should have thought he had had more than his turn!" She had recovered herself in fact much more than I; for somehow, from this instant, convinced as she had been and turning everything to her conviction, I found myself dealing, in thought, with still larger material. It was odd what a difference was made for me by the renewed sight of dear Guy. I didn't of course analyse this sense at the time; that was still to come. Our friends meanwhile had noticed us, and something clearly passed between them—it almost produced, for an instant, a visible arrest in their advance—on the question of their having perhaps been for some time exposed.

They came on, however, and I waved them from afar a greeting, to which Mrs. Server alone replied. Distances were great at Newmarch and landscape-gardening on the grand scale; it would take them still some minutes to reach our place of vantage or to arrive within sound of speech. There was accordingly nothing marked in our turning away and strolling back to the house. We had been so intent that we confessed by this movement to a quick impulse to disown it. Yet it was remarkable that, before we went in, Mrs. Brissenden should have struck me afresh as having got all she wanted. Her recovery from our surprise was already so complete that her high lucidity now alone reigned. "You don't require, I suppose, anything more than *that*?"

"Well, I don't quite see, I'm bound to say, just where even 'that' comes in." It incommoded me singularly little, at the point to which I had jumped, that this statement was the exact reverse of the truth. Where it came in was what I happened to be in the very act of seeing—seeing to the exclusion of almost everything else. It was sufficient that I might perhaps feel myself to have done at last with Mrs. Brissenden. I desired, at all events, quite as if this benefit were assured me, to leave her the honours of the last word.

She was finely enough prepared to take them. "Why, this invention of using my husband——!" She fairly gasped at having to explain.

"Of 'using' him?"

"Trailing him across the scent as she does all of you, one after the other. Excuse my comparing you to so many red herrings. You each have your turn; only *his* seems repeated, poor dear, till he's quite worn out with it."

I kept for a little this image in my eye. "I can see of course that his whole situation must be something of a strain for him; for I've not forgotten what you told me yesterday of his service with Lady John. To have to work in such a way for two of them at once"—it couldn't help, I admitted, being a tax on a fellow. Besides, when one came to think of it, the same man couldn't be *two* red herrings. To show as Mrs. Server's would directly impair his power to show as Lady John's. It would seem, in short, a matter for his patronesses to have out together.

Mrs. Brissenden betrayed, on this, some annoyance at my levity. "Oh, the cases are not the same, for with Lady John it amuses him: he thinks he knows."

"Knows what?"

"What she wants him for. He doesn't know"—she kept it wonderfully clear—"that she really doesn't want him for anything; for anything except, of course"—this came as a droll second thought—"himself."

"And he doesn't know, either"—I tried to remain at her level—"that Mrs. Server does."

"No," she assented, "he doesn't know what it's her idea to do with him."

"He doesn't know, in fine," I cheerfully pursued, "the truth about anything. And of course, by your agreement with me, he's not to learn it."

She recognised her agreement with me, yet looked as if she had reserved a certain measure of freedom. Then she handsomely gave up even that. "I certainly don't want him to become conscious."

"It's his unconsciousness," I declared, "that saves him."

"Yes, even from himself."

"We must accordingly feed it." In the house, with intention, we parted company; but there was something that, before this, I felt it due to my claim of consistency to bring out. "It wasn't, at all events, Gilbert Long behind the tree!"

My triumph, however, beneath the sponge she was prepared to pass again over much of our experience, was short-lived. "Of course it wasn't. We shouldn't have been treated to the scene if it *had* been. What could she possibly have put poor Briss there for but just to show it wasn't?"

VI

I SAW other things, many things, after this, but I had already so much matter for reflection that I saw them almost in spite of myself. The difficulty with me was in the momentum already acquired by the act—as well as, doubtless, by the general habit—of observation. I remember indeed that on separating from Mrs. Brissenden I took a lively resolve to get rid of my ridiculous obsession. It was absurd to have consented to such immersion, intellectually speaking, in the affairs of other people. One had always affairs of one's own, and I was positively neglecting mine. Such, for a while, was my foremost reflection; after which, in their order or out of it, came an inevitable train of others. One of the first of these was that, frankly, my affairs were by this time pretty well used to my neglect. There were connections enough in which it had never failed. A whole cluster of such connections, effectually displacing the centre of interest, now surrounded me, and I was —though always but intellectually—drawn into their circle. I did my best for the rest of the day to turn my back on them, but with the prompt result of feeling that I meddled with them almost more in thinking them over in isolation than in hovering personally about them. Reflection was the real intensity; reflection, as to poor Mrs. Server in particular, was an indiscreet opening of doors. She became vivid in the light of the so limited vision of her that I already possessed—try positively as I would not further to extend it. It was something not to ask another question, to keep constantly away both from Mrs. Brissenden and from Ford Obert, whom I had rashly invited to a degree of participation; it was something to talk as hard as possible with other persons and on other subjects, to mingle in groups much more superficial than they supposed themselves, to give ear to broader jokes, to discuss more tangible mysteries.

The day, as it developed, was large and hot, an unstinted splendour of summer; excursions, exercise, organised amusement were things admirably spared us; life became a mere arrested ramble or stimulated lounge, and we profited to the full

by the noble freedom of Newmarch, that overarching ease
which in nothing was so marked as in the tolerance of talk.
The air of the place itself, in such conditions, left one's powers
with a sense of play; if one wanted something to play at one
simply played at being there. I did this myself, with the aid, in
especial, of two or three solitary strolls, unaccompanied dips,
of half an hour apiece, into outlying parts of the house and the
grounds. I must add that while I resorted to such measures
not to see I only fixed what I *had* seen, what I did see, the
more in my mind. One of these things had been the way that,
at luncheon, Gilbert Long, watching the chance given him by
the loose order in which we moved to it, slipped, to the visible
defeat of somebody else, into the chair of conspicuity beside
clever Lady John. A second was that Mrs. Server then occupied a place as remote as possible from this couple, but not
from Guy Brissenden, who had found means to seat himself
next her while my notice was engaged by the others. What I
was at the same time supremely struck with could doubtless
only be Mrs. Server's bright ubiquity, as it had at last come to
seem to me, and that of the companions she had recruited for
the occasion. Attended constantly by a different gentleman,
she was in the range of my vision wherever I turned—she kept
repeating her picture in settings separated by such intervals
that I wondered at the celerity with which she proceeded from
spot to spot. She was never discernibly out of breath, though
the associate of her ecstasy at the given moment might have
been taken as being; and I kept getting afresh the impression
which, the day before, had so promptly followed my arrival,
the odd impression, as of something the matter with each party,
that I had gathered, in the grounds, from the sight of her advance upon me with Obert. I had by this time of course made
out—and it was absurd to shut my eyes to it—what *that* particular something, at least, was. It was that Obert had quickly
perceived something to be the matter with *her*, and that she,
on her side, had become aware of his discovery.

I wondered hereupon if the discovery were inevitable for
each gentleman in succession, and if this were their reason for
changing so often. Did everyone leave her, like Obert, with an
uneasy impression of her, and were these impressions now
passed about with private hilarity or profundity, though with-

out having reached me save from the source I have named? I affected myself as constantly catching her eye, as if she wished to call my attention to the fact of who was with her and who was not. I had kept my distance since our episode with the pastels, and yet nothing could more come home to me than that I had really not, since then, been absent from her. We met without talk, but not, thanks to these pointed looks, without contact. I daresay that, for that matter, my cogitations—for I must have bristled with them—would have made me as stiff a puzzle to interpretative minds as I had suffered other phenomena to become to my own. I daresay I wandered with a tell-tale restlessness of which the practical detachment might well have mystified those who hadn't suspicions. Whenever I caught Mrs. Server's eye it was really to wonder how many suspicions *she* had. I came upon her in great dim chambers, and I came upon her before sweeps of view. I came upon her once more with the Comte de Dreuil, with Lord Lutley, with Ford Obert, with almost every other man in the house, and with several of these, as if there had not been enough for so many turns, two or three times over. Only at no moment, whatever the favouring frame, did I come upon her with Gilbert Long. It was of course an anomaly that, as an easy accident, I was not again myself set in the favouring frame. That I consistently escaped being might indeed have been the meaning most marked in our mute recognitions.

Discretion, then, I finally felt, played an odd part when it simply left one more attached, morally, to one's prey. What was most evident to me by five o'clock in the afternoon was that I was too preoccupied not to find it the best wisdom to accept my mood. It was all very well to run away; there would be no effectual running away but to have my things quickly packed and catch, if possible, a train for town. On the spot I had to *be* on it; and it began to dawn before me that there was something quite other I possibly might do with Mrs. Server than endeavour ineffectually to forget her. What was none of one's business might change its name should importunity take the form of utility. In resisted observation that was vivid thought, in inevitable thought that was vivid observation, through a succession, in short, of phases in which I shall not pretend to distinguish one of these elements from the other, I found

myself cherishing the fruit of the seed dropped equally by Ford
Obert and by Mrs. Briss. What was the matter with *me?*—so
much as that I had ended by asking myself; and the answer had
come as an unmistakable return of the anxiety produced in me
by my first seeing that I had fairly let Grace Brissenden loose.
My original protest against the flash of inspiration in which she
had fixed responsibility on Mrs. Server had been in fact, I now
saw, but the scared presentiment of something in store for myself. This scare, to express it sharply, had verily not left me
from that moment; and if I had been already then anxious it
was because I had felt myself foredoomed to be sure the poor
lady herself would be. Why I should have minded this, should
have been anxious at her anxiety and scared at her scare, was a
question troubling me too little on the spot for me to suffer it
to trouble me, as a painter of my state, in this place. It is sufficient that when so much of the afternoon had waned as to
bring signs of the service of tea in the open air, I knew how far
I was gone in pity for her. For I had at last had to take in what
my two interlocutors had given me. Their impression, coin-
ciding and, as one might say, disinterested, couldn't, after a
little, fail in some degree to impose itself. It had its value. Mrs.
Server *was* "nervous."

It little mattered to me now that Mrs. Briss had put it to
me—that I had even whimsically put it to myself—that I was
perhaps in love with her. That was as good a name as another
for an interest springing up in an hour, and was moreover a decent working hypothesis. The sentiment had not indeed asserted itself at "first sight," though it might have taken its
place remarkably well among the phenomena of what is known
as second. The real fact was, none the less, that I was quite too
sorry for her to be anything except sorry. This odd feeling was
something that I may as well say I shall not even now attempt
to account for—partly, it is true, because my recital of the rest
of what I was to see in no small measure does so. It was a force
that I at this stage simply found I had already succumbed to.
If it was not the result of what I had granted to myself was
the matter with her, then it was rather the very cause of my
making that concession. It was a different thing from my first
prompt impulse to shield her. I had already shielded her—
fought for her so far as I could or as the case immediately re-

quired. My own sense of how I was affected had practically cleared up, in short, in the presence of this deeper vision of her. My divinations and inductions had finally brought home to me that in the whole huge, brilliant, crowded place I was the only person save one who was in anything that could be called a relation to her. The other person's relation was concealed, and mine, so far as she herself was concerned, was unexpressed—so that I suppose what most, at the juncture in question, stirred within me was the wonder of how I might successfully express it. I felt that so long as I didn't express it I should be haunted with the idea of something infinitely touching and tragic in her loneliness—possibly in her torment, in her terror. If she was "nervous" to the tune I had come to recognise, it could only be because she had grounds. And what might her grounds more naturally be than that, arranged and arrayed, disguised and decorated, pursuing in vain, through our careless company, her search for the right shade of apparent security, she felt herself none the less all the while the restless victim of fear and failure?

Once my imagination had seen her in this light the touches it could add to the picture might be trusted to be telling. Further observation was to convince me of their truth, but while I waited for it with my apprehension that it would come in spite of me I easily multiplied and lavished them. I made out above all what she would most be trying to hide. It was not, so to speak, the guarded primary fact—it could only be, wretched woman, that produced, that disastrous, treacherous consequence of the fact which her faculties would exhibit, and most of all the snapped cord of her faculty of talk. Guy Brissenden had, at the worst, his compromised face and figure to show and to shroud—if he were really, that is, as much aware of them as one had suspected. She had her whole compromised machinery of thought and speech, and if these signs were not, like his, external, that made her case but the harder, for she had to create, with intelligence rapidly ebbing, with wit half gone, the illusion of an unimpaired estate. She was like some unhappy lady robbed of her best jewels—obliged so to dispose and distribute the minor trinkets that had escaped as still to give the impression of a rich *écrin*. Was not that embarrassment, if one analysed a little, at the bottom of her having been all day, in the vulgar phrase and as the three of us had too cruelly noted, all over the place? *Was* indeed, for that matter, this observation confined to us, or had it at last been irrepressibly determined on the part of the company at large? This was a question, I hasten to add, that I would not now for the world have put to the test. I felt I should have known how to escape had any rumour of wonder at Mrs. Server's ways been finally conveyed to me. I might from this moment have, as much as I liked, my own sense of it, but I was definitely conscious of a sort of loyalty to her that would have rendered me blank before others: though not indeed that—oh, at last, frankly, quite the contrary!—it would have forbidden me to watch and watch. I positively dreaded the accident of my being asked by one of the men if I knew how everyone was talking about her. If everyone was talking about her, I wanted positively not to know. But nobody was, probably—they scarcely could be as yet. Without suggestive collateral evidence there would be nobody in the house so conscientiously infernal as Mrs. Brissenden, Obert and I.

Newmarch had always, in our time, carried itself as the great asylum of the finer wit, more or less expressly giving out that, as invoking hospitality or other countenance, none of the stupid, none even of the votaries of the grossly obvious, need apply; but I could luckily at present reflect that its measurements in this direction had not always been my own, and that, moreover, whatever precision they possessed, human blandness, even in such happy halls, had not been quite abolished. There was a sound law in virtue of which one could always—alike in privileged and unprivileged circles—rest more on people's density than on their penetrability. Wasn't it their density too that would be practically nearest their good nature? Whatever her successive partners of a moment might have noticed, they wouldn't have discovered in her reason for dropping them quickly a principle of fear that they might notice her failure articulately to keep up. My own actual vision, which had developed with such affluence, was that, in a given case, she could keep up but for a few minutes and was therefore obliged to bring the contact to an end before exposure. I had consistently mastered her predicament: she had at once to cultivate contacts, so that people shouldn't guess her real concentration, and to make them a literal touch and go, so that they shouldn't suspect the enfeeblement of her mind. It was obviously still worth everything to her that she was so charming. I had theorised with Mrs. Brissenden on her supposititious inanity, but the explanation of such cynicism in either of us could only be a sensibility to the truth that attractions so great might float her even a long time after intelligence pure and simple should have collapsed.

Was not my present uneasiness, none the less, a private curiosity to ascertain just how much or how little of that element she had saved from the wreck? She dodged, doubled, managed, broke off, clutching occasions, yet doubtless risking dumbnesses, vaguenesses and other betrayals, depending on attitudes, motions, expressions, a material personality, in fine, in which a plain woman would have found nothing but failure; and peace therefore might rule the scene on every hypothesis but that of her getting, to put it crudely, worse. How I remember saying to myself that if she didn't get better she surely *must* get worse!—being aware that I referred on the one side to her occult surrender and on the other to its awful penalty. It became present to me that she possibly might recover if anything should happen that would pull her up, turn her into some other channel. If, however, that consideration didn't detain me longer the fact may stand as a sign of how little I believed in any check. Gilbert Long might die, but not the intensity he had inspired. The analogy with the situation of the Brissendens here, I further considered, broke down; I at any rate rather positively welcomed the view that the sacrificed party to *that* union might really find the arrest of his decline, if not the renewal of his youth, in the loss of his wife. Would this lady indeed, as an effect of *his* death, begin to wrinkle and shrivel? It would sound brutal to say that this was what I should have preferred to hold, were it not that I in fact felt forced to recognise the slightness of such a chance. She would have loved his youth, and have made it her own, in death as in life, and he would have quitted the world, in truth, only the more effectually to leave it to her. Mrs. Server's quandary—which was now all I cared for—was exactly in her own certitude of every absence of issue. But I need give little more evidence of how it had set me thinking.

As much as anything else, perhaps, it was the fear of what one of the men might say to me that made me for an hour or two, at this crisis, continuously shy. Nobody, doubtless, would have said anything worse than that she was more of a flirt than ever, that they had all compared notes and would accordingly be interested in some hint of another, possibly a deeper, experience. It would have been almost as embarrassing to have to tell them how little experience I had had in fact as to have had to tell them how much I had had in fancy—all the more that I had as yet only my thin idea of the line of feeling in her that had led her so to spare me. Tea on the terraces represented, meanwhile, among us, so much neglect of everything else that my meditations remained for some time as unobserved as I could desire. I was not, moreover, heeding much where they carried me, and became aware of what I owed them only on at last finding myself anticipated as the occupant of an arbour into which I had strolled. Then I saw I had reached a remote part of the great gardens, and that for some of my friends also secluded thought had inducements; though it was not, I hasten to add, that either of the pair I here encountered appeared to be striking out in any very original direction. Lady John and Guy Brissenden, in the arbour, were thinking secludedly together; they were together, that is, because they were scarce a foot apart, and they were thinking, I inferred, because they were doing nothing else. Silence, by every symptom, had definitely settled on them, and whatever it was I interrupted had no resemblance to talk. Nothing—in the general air of evidence —had more struck me than that what Lady John's famous intellect seemed to draw most from Brissenden's presence was the liberty to rest. Yet it shook off this languor as soon as she saw me; it threw itself straight into the field; it went, I could see, through all the motions required of it by her ladyship's fallacious philosophy. I could mark these emotions, and what determined them, as behind clear glass.

I found, on my side, a rare intellectual joy, the oddest secret exultation, in feeling her begin instantly to play the part I had attributed to her in the irreducible drama. She broke out in a manner that could only have had for its purpose to represent to me that mere weak amiability had committed her to such a predicament. It was to humour her friend's husband that she had strayed so far, for she was somehow sorry for him, and—good creature as we all knew her—had, on principle, a kind little way of her own with silly infatuations. His *was* silly, but it was unmistakable, and she had for some time been finding it, in short, a case for a special tact. That he bored her to death I might have gathered by the way they sat there, and she could trust me to believe—couldn't she?—that she was only musing as to how she might most humanely get rid of him. She would lead him safely back to the fold if I would give her time. She seemed to ask it all, oddly, of *me*, to take me remarkably into her confidence, to refer me, for a specimen of his behaviour, to his signal abandonment of his wife the day before, his having waited over, to come down, for the train in which poor *she* was to travel. It was at all events, I felt, one of the consequences of having caught on to so much that I by this time found myself catching on to everything. I read into Lady John's wonderful manner—which quite clamoured, moreover, for an interpretation—all that was implied in the lesson I had extracted from other portions of the business. It was distinctly poor she who gave me the lead, and it was not less definite that she put it to me that I should render her a service either by remaining with them or by inventing something that would lure her persecutor away. She desired him, even at the cost of her being left alone, distracted from his pursuit.

Poor he, in his quarter, I hasten to add, contributed to my picking out this embroidery nothing more helpful than a sustained detachment. He said as little as possible, seemed heedless of what was otherwise said, and only gave me on his own account a look or two of dim suggestiveness. Yet it was these looks that most told with me, and what they, for their part, conveyed was a plea that directly contradicted Lady John's. I understood him that it was he who was bored, he who had been pursued, he for whom perversity had become a dreadful menace, he, in fine, who pleaded for my intervention. He was so willing to trust me to relieve him of his companion that I think he would simply have bolted without deferring to me if I had not taken my precautions against it. I had, as it happened, another momentary use for him than this: I wished on the one hand not to lose him and on the other not to lose Lady John, though I had quickly enough guessed this brilliant woman's real preference, of which it in fact soon became my lively wish to see the proof. The union of these two was too artificial for me not already to have connected with it the service it might render, in her ladyship's view, to that undetected cultivation, on her part, of a sentiment for Gilbert Long which, through his feigned response to it, fitted so completely to the other pieces in my collection. To see all this was at the time, I remember, to be as inhumanly amused as if one had found one could create something. I had created nothing but a clue or two to the larger comprehension I still needed, yet I positively found myself overtaken by a mild artistic glow. What had occurred was that, for my full demonstration, I needed Long, and that, by the same stroke, I became sure I should certainly get him by temporising a little.

Lady John was in love with him and had kicked up, to save her credit, the dust of a fictive relation with another man—the relation one of mere artifice and the man one in her encouragement of whom nobody would believe. Yet she was also discoverably divided between her prudence and her vanity, for if it was difficult to make poor Briss figure at all vividly as an insistent satellite, the thankless tact she had to employ gave her exactly, she argued, the right to be refreshingly fanned with an occasional flap of the flag under which she had, as she ridiculously fancied, truly conquered. If she was where I found her because her escort had dragged her there, she had made the best of it through the hope of assistance from another quarter. She had held out on the possibility that Mr. Long—whom one *could* without absurdity sit in an arbour with—might have had some happy divination of her plight. He had had such divinations before—thanks to a condition in him that made sensibility abnormal—and the least a wretched woman could do when betrayed by the excess of nature's bounty was to play admirer against admirer and be "talked about" on her own terms. She would just this once have admitted it, I was to gather, to be an occasion for pleading guilty—oh, so harmlessly!—to a consciousness of the gentleman mutely named between us. Well, the "proof" I just alluded to was that I had not sat with my friends five minutes before Gilbert Long turned up.

I saw in a moment how neatly my being there with them played *his* game; I became in this fashion a witness for him that he could almost as little leave Lady John alone as—well, as other people could. It may perfectly have been the pleasure of this reflection that again made him free and gay—produced in him, in any case, a different shade of manner from that with which, before luncheon, as the consequence perhaps of a vague *flair* for my possible penetration, I had suspected him of edging away from me. Not since my encounter with him at Paddington the afternoon before had I had so to recognise him as the transfigured talker. To see Lady John with him was to have little enough doubt of *her* recognitions, just as this spectacle also dotted each "i" in my conviction of his venial— I can only call it that—duplicity. I made up my mind on the spot that it had been no part of his plan to practise on her, and that the worst he could have been accused of was a good-natured acceptance, more apparent than real, for his own purposes, of her theory—which she from time to time let peep out —that they would have liked each other better if they hadn't been each, alas! so good. He profited by the happy accident of having pleased a person so much in evidence, and indeed it was tolerably clear to me that neither party was duped. Lady John didn't want a lover; this would have been, as people say, a larger order than, given the other complications of her exis-tence, she could meet; but she wanted, in a high degree, the appearance of carrying on a passion that imposed alike fearless realisations and conscious renouncements, and this circum-stance fully fell in with the convenience and the special situa-tion of her friend. Her vanity rejoiced, so far as she dared to let it nibble, and the mysteries she practised, the dissimulations she elaborated, the general danger of detection in which she flattered herself that she publicly walked, were after all so much grist to the mill of that appetite.

By just so much, however, as it could never come up be-tween them that there was another woman in Gilbert's history, by just so much would it on the other hand have been an ar-ticulate axiom that as many of the poor Brisses of the world as she might care to accommodate would be welcome to figure in her own. This personage, under that deeper induction, I suddenly became aware that I also greatly pitied—pitied almost as much as I pitied Mrs. Server; and my pity had doubtless something to do with the fact that, after I had proposed to him that we should adjourn together and we had, on his prompt, even though slightly dry response, placed the invidious arbour at a certain distance, I passed my hand into his arm. There were things I wanted of him, and the first was that he should let me show him I could be kind to him. I had made of the circumstance of tea at the house a pretext for our leaving the others, each of whom I felt as rather showily calling my attention to their good old ground for not wishing to rejoin the crowd. As to what Brissenden wished I had made up my mind; I had made up my mind as to the subject of his thoughts while they wandered, during his detention, from Lady John; and if the next of my wishes was to enter into his desire, I had decided on giving it effect by the time we reached the shortest of the vistas at the end of which the house reared a brave front.

VII

I STAYED him there while I put it to him that he would probably in fact prefer to go back.

"You're not going then yourself?"

"No, I don't particularly want tea; and I may as well now confess to you that I'm taking a lonely, unsociable walk. I don't enjoy such occasions as these," I said, "unless I from time to time get off by myself somewhere long enough to tell myself how much I do enjoy them. That's what I was cultivating solitude for when I happened just now to come upon you. When I found you there with Lady John there was nothing for me but to make the best of it; but I'm glad of this chance to assure you that, every appearance to the contrary notwithstanding, I wasn't prowling about in search of you."

"Well," my companion frankly replied, "I'm glad you turned up. I wasn't especially amusing myself."

"Oh, I think I know how little!"

He fixed me a moment with his pathetic old face, and I knew more than ever that I was sorry for him. I was quite extraordinarily sorry, and I wondered whether I mightn't without offence or indiscretion really let him see it. It was to this end I had held him and wanted a little to keep him, and I was reassured as I felt him, though I had now released him, linger instead of leaving me. I had made him uneasy last night, and a new reason or two for my doing so had possibly even since then come up; yet these things also would depend on the way he might take them. The look with which he at present faced me seemed to hint that he would take them as I hoped, and there was no curtness, but on the contrary the dawn of a dim sense that I might possibly aid him, in the tone with which he came half-way. "You 'know'?"

"Ah," I laughed, "I know everything!"

He didn't laugh; I hadn't seen him laugh, at Newmarch, once; he was continuously, portentously grave, and I at present remembered how the effect of this had told for me at luncheon, contrasted as it was with that of Mrs. Server's desperate, exquisite levity. "You know I decidedly have too much of that dreadful old woman?"

There was a sound in the question that would have made me, to my own sense, start, though I as quickly hoped I had not done so to Brissenden's. I couldn't have persuaded myself, however, that I had escaped showing him the flush of my effort to show nothing. I had taken his disgusted allusion as to Mrs. Brissenden, and the action of that was upsetting. But nothing, fortunately, was psychologically more interesting than to grasp the next moment the truth of his reference. It was only the fact of his himself looking so much older than Lady John that had blinded me for an instant to the propriety of his not thinking of her as young. She wasn't young as *he* had a right to call people, and I felt a glow—also, I feared, too visible—as soon as I had seen whom he meant. His meaning Lady John did me somehow so much good that I believed it would have done me still more to hear him call her a harridan or a Jezebel. It was none of my business; how little was anything, when it came to that, my business!—yet indefinably, unutterably, I felt assuaged for him and comforted. I verily believe it hung in the balance a minute or two that in my impulse to draw him out, so that I might give him my sympathy, I was prepared to risk overturning the edifice of my precautions. I luckily, as it happened, did nothing of the sort; I contrived to breathe consolingly on his secret without betraying an intention. There was almost no one in the place save two or three of the very youngest women whom he wouldn't have had a right to call old. Lady John was a hag, then; Mrs. Server herself was more than on the turn; Gilbert Long was fat and forty; and I cast about for some light in which I could show that I—*à plus forte raison*—was a pantaloon. "Of course you can't quite see the fun of it, and it really isn't fair to you. You struck me as much more in your element," I ventured to add, "when, this morning, more than once, I chanced to observe you led captive by Mrs. Server."

"Oh, that's a different affair," he answered with an accent that promised a growth of confidence.

"Mrs. Server's an old woman," I continued, "but she can't seem to a fellow like you as old as Lady John. She has at any rate more charm; though perhaps not," I added, "quite so much talk."

On this he said an extraordinary thing, which all but made me start again. "Oh, she hasn't any *talk*!"

I took, as quickly as possible, refuge in a surprised demurrer. "Not *any*?"

"None to speak of."

I let all my wonder come. "But wasn't she chattering to you at luncheon?" It forced him to meet my eyes at greater length, and I could already see that my experiment—for insidiously and pardonably such I wished to make it—was on the way to succeed. I had been right then, and I knew where I stood. He couldn't have been "drawn" on his wife, and he couldn't have been drawn, in the least directly, on himself, but as he could thus easily be on Lady John, so likewise he could on other women, or on the particular one, at least, who mattered to me. I felt I really knew what I was about, for to draw him on Mrs. Server was in truth to draw him indirectly on himself. It was indeed perhaps because I had by this time in a measure expressed, in terms however general, the interest with which he inspired me, that I now found myself free to shift the ground of my indiscretion. I only wanted him to know that on the question of Mrs. Server I was prepared to go as far with him as he should care to move. How it came to me now that he was *the* absolutely safe person in the house to talk of her with! "I was too far away from you to hear," I had gone on; "and I could only judge of her flow of conversation from the animated expression of her face. It was extraordinarily animated. But that, I admit," I added, "strikes one always as a sort of *parti pris* with her. She's never *not* extraordinarily animated."

"She has no flow of conversation whatever," said Guy Brissenden.

I considered. "Really?"

He seemed to look at me quite without uneasiness now. "Why, haven't you seen for yourself——?"

"How the case stands with her on that head? Do you mean haven't I talked with her? Well, scarcely; for it's a fact that every man in the house *but* I strikes me as having been deluged with that privilege: if indeed," I laughed, "her absence of topics suffers it to be either a privilege or a deluge! She affects me, in any case, as determined to have nothing to do with me. She walks all the rest of you about; she gives you each your turn; me only she skips, she systematically ignores. I'm half consoled for it, however," I wound up, "by seeing what short innings any individual of you has. You personally strike me as having had the longest."

Brissenden appeared to wonder where I was coming out, yet not as if he feared it. There was even a particular place, if I could but guess it, where he would have liked me to come. "Oh, she's extremely charming. But of course she's strikingly odd."

"Odd?—really?"

"Why, in the sense, I mean, that I thought you suggested you've noticed."

"That of extravagant vivacity? Oh, I've had to notice it at a distance, without knowing what it represents."

He just hesitated. "You haven't any idea at all what it represents?"

"How should I have," I smiled, "when she never comes near me? I've thought *that*, as I tell you, marked. What does her avoidance of *me* represent? Has she happened, with you, to throw any light on it?"

"I think," said Brissenden after another moment, "that she's rather afraid of you."

I could only be surprised. "The most harmless man in the house?"

"*Are* you really?" he asked—and there was a touch of the comic in hearing him put it with his inveterate gravity.

"If you take me for anything else," I replied, "I doubt if you'll find anyone to back you."

My companion, on this, looked away for a little, turned about, fixed his eyes on the house, seemed, as with a drop of interest, on the point of leaving me. But instead of leaving me he brought out the next moment: "I don't want anyone to back me. I don't care. I didn't mean just now," he continued, "that Mrs. Server has said to me anything against you, or that she fears you because she dislikes you. She only told me she thought you disliked *her*."

It gave me a kind of shock. "A creature so beautiful, and so—so——"

"So what?" he asked as I found myself checked by my desire to come to her aid.

"Well, so brilliantly happy."

I had all his attention again. "Is that what she *is*?"

"Then don't you, with your opportunities, know?" I was conscious of rather an inspiration, a part of which was to be jocose. "What are you trying," I laughed, "to get out of me?"

It struck me luckily that, though he remained as proof against gaiety as ever, he was, thanks to his preoccupation, not disagreeably affected by my tone. "Of course if you've no idea, I can get nothing."

"No idea of what?"

Then it was that I at last got it straight. "Well, of what's the matter with her."

"Is there anything particular? If there *is*," I went on, "there's something that I've got out of *you*!"

"How so, if you don't know what it is?"

"Do you mean if you yourself don't?" But without detaining him on this, "Of what in especial do the signs," I asked, "consist?"

"Well, of everyone's thinking so—that there's something or other."

This again struck me, but it struck me too much. "Oh, everyone's a fool!"

He saw, in his queer wan way, how it had done so. "Then you *have* your own idea?"

I daresay my smile at him, while I waited, showed a discomfort. "Do you mean people are talking about her?"

But he waited himself. "Haven't they shown you——?"

"No, no one has spoken. Moreover I wouldn't have let them."

"Then there you *are*!" Brissenden exclaimed. "If you've kept them off, it must be because you differ with them."

"I shan't be sure of that," I returned, "till I know what they think! However, I repeat," I added, "that I shouldn't even then care. I don't mind admitting that she much interests me."

"There you are, there you are!" he said again.

"That's all that's the matter with her so far as *I*'m concerned. You see, at any rate, how little it need make her afraid of me. She's lovely and she's gentle and she's happy."

My friend kept his eyes on me. "What is there to interest you so in that? Isn't it a description that applies here to a dozen other women? You can't say, you know, that you're interested in *them*, for you just spoke of them as so many fools."

There was a certain surprise for me in so much acuteness,

which, however, doubtless admonished me as to the need of presence of mind. "I wasn't thinking of the ladies—I was thinking of the men."

"That's amiable to *me*," he said with his gentle gloom.

"Oh, my dear Brissenden, I except 'you.'"

"And why should you?"

I felt a trifle pushed. "I'll tell you some other time. And among the ladies I except Mrs. Brissenden, with whom, as you may have noticed, I've been having much talk."

"And will you tell me some other time about that too?" On which, as I but amicably shook my head for no, he had his first dimness of pleasantry. "I'll get it then from my wife."

"Never. She won't tell you."

"She has passed you her word? That won't alter the fact that she tells me everything."

He really said it in a way that made me take refuge for an instant in looking at my watch. "Are you going back to tea? If you are, I'll, in spite of my desire to roam, walk twenty steps with you." I had already again put my hand into his arm, and we strolled for a little till I threw off that I was sure Mrs. Server was waiting for him. To this he replied that if I wished to get rid of him he was as willing to take that as anything else for granted—an observation that I, on my side, answered with an inquiry, though an inquiry that had nothing to do with it. "Do you also tell everything to Mrs. Brissenden?"

It brought him up shorter than I had expected. "Do you ask me that in order that I shan't speak to her of this?"

I showed myself at a loss. "Of 'this'——?"

"Why, of what we've made out——"

"About Mrs. Server, you and I? You must act as to that, my dear fellow, quite on your own discretion. All the more that what on earth *have* we made out? I assure you I haven't a secret to confide to you about her, except that I've never seen a person more unquenchably radiant."

He almost jumped at it. "Well, that's just it!"

"But just what?"

"Why, what they're all talking about. That she *is* so awfully radiant. That she's so tremendously happy. It's the question," he explained, "of what in the world she has to make her so."

I winced a little, but tried not to show it. "My dear man, how do *I* know?"

"She *thinks* you know," he after a moment answered.

I could only stare. "Mrs. Server thinks I know what makes her happy?" I the more easily represented such a conviction as monstrous in that it truly had its surprise for me.

But Brissenden now was all with his own thought. "She *isn't* happy."

"You mean that that's what's the matter with her under her appearance——? Then what makes the appearance so extraordinary?"

"Why, exactly what I mention—that one doesn't see anything whatever in her to correspond to it."

I hesitated. "Do you mean in her circumstances?"

"Yes—or in her character. Her circumstances are nothing wonderful. She has none too much money; she has had three children and lost them; and nobody that belongs to her appears ever to have been particularly nice to her."

I turned it over. "How you *do* get on with her!"

"Do you call it getting on with her to be the more bewildered the more I see her?"

"Isn't to say you're bewildered only, on the whole, to say you're charmed? That always—doesn't it?—describes more or less any engrossed relation with a lovely lady."

"Well, I'm not sure I'm so charmed." He spoke as if he had thought this particular question over for himself; he had his way of being lucid without brightness. "I'm not at all easily charmed, you know," he the next moment added; "and I'm not a fellow who goes about much after women."

"Ah, that I never supposed! Why in the world *should* you? It's the last thing!" I laughed. "But isn't this—quite (what shall one call it?) innocently—rather a peculiar case?"

My question produced in him a little gesture of elation—a gesture emphasised by a snap of his forefinger and thumb. "I knew you knew it was special! I knew you've been thinking about it!"

"You certainly," I replied with assurance, "have, during the last five minutes, made me do so with some sharpness. I don't pretend that I don't now recognise that there *must* be something the matter. I only desire—not unnaturally—that there *should* be, to put me in the right for having thought, if, as you're so sure, such a freedom as that can be brought home to me. If Mrs. Server is beautiful and gentle and strange," I speciously went on, "what are those things but an attraction?"

I saw how he had them, whatever they were, before him as he slowly shook his head. "They're not an attraction. They're too queer."

I caught in an instant my way to fall in with him; and not the less that I by this time felt myself committed, up to the intellectual eyes, to ascertaining just *how* queer the person under discussion might be. "Oh, of course I'm not speaking of her as a party to a silly flirtation, or an object of any sort of trivial pursuit. But there are so many different ways of being taken."

"For a fellow like you. But not for a fellow like me. For me there's only one."

"To be, you mean, in love?"

He put it a little differently. "Well, to be thoroughly pleased."

"Ah, that's doubtless the best way and the firm ground. And you mean you're *not* thoroughly pleased with Mrs. Server?"

"No—and yet I want to be kind to her. Therefore what's the matter?"

"Oh, if it's what's the matter with *you* you ask me, that extends the question. If you want to be kind to her, you get on with her, as we were saying, quite enough for my argument. And isn't the matter also, after all," I demanded, "that you simply feel she desires you to be kind?"

"She does that." And he looked at me as with the sense of drawing from me, for his relief, some greater help than I was as yet conscious of the courage to offer. "It *is* that she desires me. She likes it. And the extraordinary thing is that *I* like it."

"And why in the world shouldn't you?"

"Because she terrifies me. She has something to hide."

"But, my dear man," I asked with a gaiety singularly out of relation to the small secret thrill produced in me by these words—"my dear man, what woman who's worth anything hasn't?"

"Yes, but there are different ways. What *she* tries for is this false appearance of happiness."

I weighed it. "But isn't that the best thing?"

"It's terrible to have to keep it up."

"Ah, but if you don't *for* her? If it all comes on herself?"

"It doesn't," Guy Brissenden presently said. "I do—'for' her—help to keep it up." And then, still unexpectedly to me, came out the rest of his confession. "I want to—I try to; that's what I mean by being kind to her, and by the gratitude with which she takes it. One feels that one doesn't want her to break down."

It was on this—from the poignant touch in it—that I at last felt I had burnt my ships and didn't care how much I showed I was with him. "Oh, but she won't. You must keep her going."

He stood a little with a thumb in each pocket of his trousers, and his melancholy eyes ranging far over my head—over the tops of the highest trees. "Who am *I* to keep people going?"

"Why, you're just the man. Aren't you happy?"

He still ranged the tree-tops. "Yes."

"Well, then, you belong to the useful class. You've the where-withal to give. It's the happy people who should help the others."

He had, in the same attitude, another pause. "It's easy for *you* to talk!"

"Because I'm not happy?"

It made him bring his eyes again down to me. "I think you're a little so now at my expense."

I shook my head reassuringly. "It doesn't cost you anything if—as I confess to it now—I do to some extent understand."

"That's more, then, than—after talking of it this way with you—I feel that *I* do!"

He had brought that out with a sudden sigh, turning away to go on; so that we took a few steps more. "You've nothing to trouble about," I then freely remarked, "but that you *are* as kind as the case requires and that you do help. I daresay that you'll find her even now on the terrace looking out for you." I patted his back, as we went a little further, but as I still pre-ferred to stay away from the house I presently stopped again. "Don't fall below your chance. *Noblesse oblige.* We'll pull her through."

"You say 'we,'" he returned, "but you do keep out of it!"

"Why should you wish me to interfere with you?" I asked. "I wouldn't keep out of it if she wanted me as much as she wants you. That, by your own admission, is exactly what she doesn't."

"Well, then," said Brissenden, "I'll make her go for you. I think I want your assistance quite as much as she can want mine."

"Oh," I protested for this, "I've really given you already every ounce of mine I can squeeze out. And you know for yourself far more than I do."

"No, I don't!"—with which he became quite sharp; "for you know *how* you know it—which I've not a notion of. It's just what I think," he continued, facing me again, "you ought to tell me."

"I'm a little in doubt of what you're talking of, but I suppose you to allude to the oddity of my being so much interested without my having been more informed."

"You've got some clue," Brissenden said; "and a clue is what I myself want."

"Then get it," I laughed, "from Mrs. Server!"

He wondered. "Does she know?"

I had still, after all, to dodge a little. "Know what?"

"Why, that you've found out what she has to hide."

"You're perfectly free to ask her. I wonder even that you haven't done so yet."

"Well," he said with the finest stroke of unconsciousness he had yet shown me—"well, I suppose it's because I'm afraid of her."

"But not too much afraid," I risked suggesting, "to be hoping at this moment that you'll find her if you go back to where most of our party is gathered. You're not going for tea—you're going for Mrs. Server: just of whom it was, as I say, you were thinking while you sat there with Lady John. So what is it you so greatly fear?"

It was as if I could see through his dim face a sort of gratitude for my making all this out to him. "I don't know that it's anything that she may do to *me*." He could make it out in a manner for himself. "It's as if something might happen to her. It's what I told you—that she may break down. If you ask me how, or in what," he continued, "how can I tell you? In whatever it is that she's trying to do. I don't understand it." Then he wound up with a sigh that, in spite of its softness, he imperfectly stifled. "But it's something or other!"

"What would it be, then," I asked, "but what you speak of as what I've 'found out'? The effort you distinguish in her is the effort of concealment—vain, as I gather it strikes you both, so far as *I*, in my supernatural acuteness, am concerned."

Following this with the final ease to which my encouragement directly ministered, he yet gave me, before he had quite arrived, a queer sidelong glance. "Wouldn't it really be better if you were to tell me? I don't ask her myself, you see. I don't put things to her in that way."

"Oh, no—I've shown you how I do see. That's a part of your admirable consideration. But I must repeat that nothing would induce me to tell you."

His poor old face fairly pleaded. "But I want so to know."

"Ah, there it is!" I almost triumphantly laughed.

"There what is?"

"Why, everything. What I've divined, between you and Mrs. Server, as the tie. Your wanting so to know."

I felt as if he were now, intellectually speaking, plastic wax in my hand. "And her wanting me not to?"

"Wanting *me* not to," I smiled.

He puzzled it out. "And being willing, therefore——"

"That you—you only, for sympathy, for fellowship, for the wild wonder of it—*should* know? Well, for all those things, and in spite of what you call your fear, *try* her!" With which now at last I quitted him.

VIII

I'M AFRAID I can't quite say what, after that, I at first did, nor just how I immediately profited by our separation. I felt absurdly excited, though this indeed was what I had felt all day; there had been in fact deepening degrees of it ever since my first mystic throb after finding myself, the day before in our railway-carriage, shut up to an hour's contemplation and collation, as it were, of Gilbert Long and Mrs. Brissenden. I have noted how my first full contact with the changed state of these associates had caused the knell of the tranquil mind audibly to ring for me. I have spoken of my sharpened perception that something altogether out of the common had happened, independently, to each, and I could now certainly flatter myself that I hadn't missed a feature of the road I had thus been beguiled to travel. It was a road that had carried me far, and verily at this hour I *felt* far. I daresay that for a while after leaving poor Briss, after what I may indeed call launching him, this was what I predominantly felt. To be where I was, to whatever else it might lead, treated me by its help to the taste of success. It appeared then that the more things I fitted together the larger sense, every way, they made—a remark in which I found an extraordinary elation. It justified my indiscreet curiosity; it crowned my underhand process with beauty. The beauty perhaps was only for *me*—the beauty of having been right; it made at all events an element in which, while the long day softly dropped, I wandered and drifted and securely floated. This element bore me bravely up, and my private triumph struck me as all one with the charm of the moment and of the place.

There was a general shade in all the lower reaches—a fine clear dusk in garden and grove, a thin suffusion of twilight out of which the greater things, the high tree-tops and pinnacles, the long crests of motionless wood and chimnied roof, rose into golden air. The last calls of birds sounded extraordinarily loud; they were like the timed, serious splashes, in wide, still water, of divers not expecting to rise again. I scarce know what odd consciousness I had of roaming at close of day in the grounds of some castle of enchantment. I had positively encountered nothing to compare with this since the days of fairy-tales and of the childish imagination of the impossible. *Then* I used to circle round enchanted castles, for then I moved in a world in which the strange "came true." It was the coming true that was the proof of the enchantment, which, moreover, was naturally never so great as when such coming was, to such a degree and by the most romantic stroke of all, the fruit of one's own wizardry. I was positively—so had the wheel revolved —proud of my work. I had thought it all out, and to have thought it was, wonderfully, to have brought it. Yet I recall how I even then knew on the spot that there was something supreme I should have failed to bring unless I had happened suddenly to become aware of the very presence of the haunting principle, as it were, of my thought. This was the light in which Mrs. Server, walking alone now, apparently, in the grey wood and pausing at sight of me, showed herself in her clear dress at the end of a vista. It was exactly as if she had been there by the operation of my intelligence, or even by that—in a still happier way—of my feeling. My excitement, as I have called it, on seeing her, was assuredly emotion. Yet what *was* this feeling, really?—of which, at the point we had thus reached, I seemed to myself to have gathered from all things an invitation to render some account.

Well, I knew within the minute that I was moved by it as by an extraordinary tenderness; so that this is the name I must leave it to make the best of. It had already been my impression that I was sorry for her, but it was marked for me now that I was sorrier than I had reckoned. All her story seemed at once to look at me out of the fact of her present lonely prowl. I met it without demur, only wanting her to know that if I struck her as waylaying her in the wood, as waiting for her there at eventide with an idea, I shouldn't in the least defend myself from the charge. I can scarce clearly tell how many fine strange things I thought of during this brief crisis of her hesitation. I wanted in the first place to make it end, and while I moved a few steps toward her I felt almost as noiseless and guarded as if I were trapping a bird or stalking a fawn. My few steps brought me to a spot where another perspective crossed our own, so that they made together a verdurous circle with an evening sky above and great lengthening, arching recesses in which the twilight thickened. Oh, it was quite sufficiently the castle of enchantment, and when I noticed four old stone seats, massive and mossy and symmetrically placed, I recognised not only the influence, in my adventure, of the grand style, but the familiar identity of this consecrated nook, which was so much of the type of all the bemused and remembered. We were in a beautiful old picture, we were in a beautiful old tale, and it wouldn't be the fault of Newmarch if some other green *carrefour*, not far off, didn't balance with this one and offer the alternative of niches, in the greenness, occupied by weather-stained statues on florid pedestals.

I sat straight down on the nearest of our benches, for this struck me as the best way to express the conception with which the sight of Mrs. Server filled me. It showed her that if I watched her I also waited for her, and that I was therefore not affected in any manner she really need deprecate. She had been too far off for me to distinguish her face, but her approach had faltered long enough to let me see that if she had not taken it as too late she would, to escape me, have found some pretext for turning off. It was just my seating myself that made the difference—it was my being so simple with her that brought her on. She came slowly and a little wearily down the vista, and her sad, shy advance, with the massed wood on either side of her, was like the reminiscence of a picture or the refrain of a ballad. What made the difference with *me*—if any difference had remained to be made—was the sense of this sharp cessation of her public extravagance. She had folded up her manner in her flounced parasol, which she seemed to drag after her as a sorry soldier his musket. It was present to me without a pang that this was the person I had sent poor Briss off to find—the person poor Briss would owe me so few thanks for his failure to have found. It was equally marked to me that, however detached and casual she might, at the first sight of me, have wished to show herself, it was to alight on poor Briss that she had come out, it was because he had not been at the house and might therefore, on his side, be wandering, that she had taken care to be unaccompanied. My demonstration was complete from the moment I thus had them in the act of seeking each other, and I was so pleased at having gathered them in that I cared little what else they had missed. I neither moved nor spoke till she had come quite near me, and as she also gave no sound the meaning of our silence seemed to stare straight out. It absolutely phrased there, in all the wonderful conditions, a relation already established; but the strange and beautiful thing was that as soon as we had recognised and accepted it this relation put us almost at our ease. "You must be weary of walking," I said at last, "and you see I've been keeping a seat for you."

I had finally got up, as a sign of welcome, but I had directly afterwards resumed my position, and it was an illustration of the terms on which we met that we neither of us seemed to mind her being meanwhile on her feet. She stood before me as if to take in—with her smile that had by this time sunk quite to dimness—more than we should, either of us, after all, be likely to be able to say. I even saw from this moment, I think, that, whatever she might understand, she would be able herself to say but little. She gave herself, in that minute, more than she doubtless knew—gave herself, I mean, to my intenser apprehension. She went through the form of expression, but what told me everything was the way the form of expression broke down. Her lovely grimace, the light of the previous hours, was as blurred as a bit of brushwork in water-colour spoiled by the upsetting of the artist's glass. She fixed me with it as she had fixed during the day forty persons, but it fluttered like a bird with a broken wing. She looked about and above, down each of our dusky avenues and up at our gilded tree-tops and our painted sky, where, at the moment, the passage of a flight of rooks made a clamour. She appeared to wish to produce some explanation of her solitude, but I was quickly enough sure that she would never find a presentable one. I only wanted to show her how little I required it. "I like a lonely walk," I went on, "at the end of a day full of people: it's always, to me, on such occasions, quite as if something has happened that the mind wants to catch and fix before the vividness fades. So I mope by myself an hour—I take stock of my impressions. But there's one thing I don't believe you know. This is the very first time, in such a place and at such an hour, that it has ever befallen me to come across a friend stricken with the same perversity and engaged in the same pursuit. Most people, don't you see?"—I kept it up as I could—"don't in the least know what has happened to them, and don't care to know. That's one way, and I don't deny it may be practically the best. But if one does care to know, that's another way. As soon as I saw you there at the end of the alley I said to myself, with quite a little thrill of elation, 'Ah, then it's *her* way too!' I wonder if you'll let me tell you," I floundered pleasantly on, "that I immediately liked you the better for it. It seemed to bring us more together. That's what I sat straight down here to show you. 'Yes,' I wished you to understand me as frankly saying, 'I *am*, as well as you, on the mope, or on the muse, or on whatever you call it, and this isn't half a bad corner for such a mood.' I can't tell you what a pleasure it is to me to see you do understand."

I kept it up, as I say, to reassure and soothe and steady her; there was nothing, however fantastic and born of the pressure of the moment, that I wouldn't have risked for that purpose. She was absolutely on my hands with her secret—I felt that from the way she stood and listened to me, silently showing herself relieved and pacified. It was marked that if I had hitherto seen her as "all over the place," she had yet nowhere seemed to me less so than at this furthermost point. But if, though only nearer to her secret and still not in possession, I felt as justified as I have already described myself, so it equally came to me that I was quite near enough, at the pass we had reached, for what I should have to take from it all. She was on my hands—it was she herself, poor creature, who was: this was the thing that just now loomed large, and the secret was a comparative detail. "I think you're very kind," she said for all answer to the speech I have reported, and the minute after this she had sunk down, in confessed collapse, to my bench, on which she sat and stared before her. The mere mechanism of her expression, the dangling paper lantern itself, was now all that was left in her face. She remained a little as if discouraged by the sight of the weariness that her surrender had let out. I hesitated, from just this fear of adding to it, to commiserate her for it more directly, and she spoke again before I had found anything to say. She brought back her attention indeed as if with an effort and from a distance. "What is it that has happened to you?"

"Oh," I laughed, "what is it that has happened to *you*?" My question had not been in the least intended for pressure, but it made her turn and look at me, and this, I quickly recognised, was all the answer the most pitiless curiosity could have desired —all the more, as well, that the intention in it had been no greater than in my words. Beautiful, abysmal, involuntary, her exquisite weakness simply opened up the depths it would have closed. It was in short a supremely unsuccessful attempt to say nothing. It said everything, and by the end of a minute my chatter—none the less out of place for being all audible—was hushed to positive awe by what it had conveyed. I saw as I had never seen before what consuming passion can make of the marked mortal on whom, with fixed beak and claws, it has settled as on a prey. She reminded me of a sponge wrung dry and with fine pores agape. Voided and scraped of everything, her shell was merely crushable. So it was brought home to me that the victim could be abased, and so it disengaged itself from these things that the abasement could be conscious. That was Mrs. Server's tragedy, that her consciousness survived— survived with a force that made it struggle and dissemble. This consciousness was all her secret—it was at any rate all mine. I promised myself roundly that I would henceforth keep clear of any other.

I none the less—from simply sitting with her there—gathered in the sense of more things than I could have named, each of which, as it came to me, made my compassion more tender. Who of us all could say that his fall might not be as deep?—or might not at least become so with equal opportunity. I for a while fairly forgot Mrs. Server, I fear, in the intimacy of this vision of the possibilities of our common nature. She became such a wasted and dishonoured symbol of them as might have put tears in one's eyes. When I presently returned to her—our session seeming to resolve itself into a mere mildness of silence —I saw how it was that whereas, in such cases in general, people might have given up much, the sort of person this poor lady was could only give up everything. She was the absolute wreck of her storm, accordingly, but to which the pale ghost of a special sensibility still clung, waving from the mast, with a bravery that went to the heart, the last tatter of its flag. There are impressions too fine for words, and I shall not attempt to say how it was that under the touch of this one I felt how nothing that concerned my companion could ever again be

present to me but the fact itself of her admirable state. This
was the source of her wan little glory, constituted even for
her a small sublimity in the light of which mere minor identifi-
cations turned vulgar. I knew who *he* was now with a vengeance, because I had learnt precisely from that who *she* was; and
nothing could have been sharper than the force with which it
pressed upon me that I had really learnt more than I had bargained for. Nothing need have happened if I hadn't been so
absurdly, so fatally meditative about poor Long—an accident
that most people, wiser people, appeared on the whole to have
steered sufficiently clear of. Compared with my actual sense,
the sense with which I sat there, that other vision was gross,
and grosser still the connection between the two.

Such were some of the reflections in which I indulged while
her eyes—with their strange intermissions of darkness or of
light: who could say which?—told me from time to time that
she knew whatever I was thinking of to be for her virtual advantage. It was prodigious what, in the way of suppressed
communication, passed in these wonderful minutes between
us. Our relation could be at the best but an equal confession,
and I remember saying to myself that if she had been as subtle
as I—which she wasn't!—she too would have put it together
that I had dreadfully talked about her. She would have traced
in me my demonstration to Mrs. Briss that, whoever she was,
she must logically have been idiotised. It was the special poi-
gnancy of her collapse that, so far at least as I was concerned,
this was a ravage the extent of which she had ceased to try to
conceal. She had been trying, and more or less succeeding, all
day: the little drama of her public unrest had had, when one
came to consider, no other argument. It had been terror that
had directed her steps; the need constantly to show herself detached and free, followed by the sterner one not to show herself, by the same token, limp and empty. This had been the
distinct, ferocious logic of her renewals and ruptures—the anxious mistrust of her wit, the haunting knowledge of the small
distance it would take her at once, the consequent importance
of her exactly timing herself, and the quick instinct of flight
before the menace of discovery. She couldn't let society alone,
because that would have constituted a symptom; yet, for fear of
the appearance of a worse one, she could only mingle in it with

a complex diplomacy. She was accordingly exposed on every side, and to be with her a while thus quietly was to read back into her behaviour the whole explanation, which was positively simple to me now. To take up again the vivid analogy, she had been sailing all day, though scarce able to keep afloat, under the flag of her old reputation for easy response. She had given to the breeze any sad scrap of a substitute for the play of mind once supposed remarkable. The last of all the things her still-ness said to me was that I could judge from so poor a show what had become of her conversability. What I did judge was that a frantic art had indeed been required to make her pretty silences pass, from one crisis to another, for pretty speeches. Half this art, doubtless, was the glittering deceit of her smile, the sublime, pathetic overdone geniality which represented so her share in any talk that, every other eloquence failing, there could only be nothing at all from the moment it abandoned its office. There *was* nothing at all. That was the truth; in accor-dance with which I finally—for everything it might mean to myself—put out my hand and bore ever so gently on her own. Her own rested listlessly on the stone of our seat. Of course, it had been an immense thing for her that she was, in spite of everything, so lovely.

All this was quite consistent with its eventually coming back to me that, though she took from me with appreciation what was expressed in the gesture I have noted, it was certainly in quest of a still deeper relief that she had again come forth. The more I considered her face—and most of all, so permittedly, in her passive, conscious presence—the more I was sure of this and the further I could go in the imagination of her beautiful duplicity. I ended by divining that if I was assuredly good for her, because the question of keeping up with me had so com-pletely dropped, and if the service I so rendered her was not less distinct to her than to myself—I ended by divining that she had none the less her obscure vision of a still softer ease. Guy Brissenden had become in these few hours her positive need—a still greater need than I had lately amused myself with making out that he had found her. Each had, by their unprece-dented plight, something for the other, some intimacy of un-speakable confidence, that no one else in the world could have for either. They had been feeling their way to it, but at the end of their fitful day they had grown confusedly, yet beneficently sure. The explanation here again was simple—they had the sense of a common fate. They hadn't to name it or to phrase it—possibly even couldn't had they tried; peace and support came to them, without that, in the simple revelation of each other. Oh, how I made it out that if it was indeed very well for the poor lady to feel thus in *my* company that her burden was lifted, my company would be after all but a rough substitute for Guy's! He was a still better friend, little as he could have told the reason; and if I could in this connection have put the words into her mouth, here follows something of the sense that I should have made them form.

"Yes, my dear man, I do understand you—quite perfectly now, and (by I know not what miracle) I've really done so to some extent from the first. Deep is the rest of feeling with you, in this way, that I'm watched, for the time, only as you watch me. It has all stopped, and *I* can stop. How can I make you understand what it is for me that there isn't at last a creature any more in sight, that the wood darkens about me, that the sounds drop and the relief goes on; what can it mean for you even that I've given myself up to not caring whether or no, amongst others, I'm missed and spoken of? It does help my strange case, in fine, as you see, to let you keep me here; but I should have found still more what I was in need of if I had only found, instead of you, him whom I had in mind. He is as much better than you as you are than everyone else." I finally felt, in a word, so qualified to attribute to my companion some such mute address as that, that it could only have, as the next consequence, a determining effect on me—an effect under the influence of which I spoke. "I parted with him, some way from here, some time ago. I had found him in one of the gardens with Lady John; after which we came away from her together. We strolled a little and talked, but I knew what he really wanted. He wanted to find you, and I told him he would probably do so at tea on the terrace. It was visibly with that idea—to return to the house—that he left me."

She looked at me for some time on this, taking it in, yet still afraid of it. "You found him with Lady John?" she at last asked, and with a note in her voice that made me see what—as there was a precaution I had neglected—she feared.

The perception of this, in its turn, operated with me for an instant almost as the rarest of temptations. I had puzzled out everything and put everything together; I was as morally confident and as intellectually triumphant as I have frankly here described myself; but there was no objective test to which I had yet exposed my theory. The chance to apply one—and it would be infallible—had suddenly cropped up. There would be excitement, amusement, discernment in it; it would be indeed but a more roundabout expression of interest and sympathy. It would, above all, pack the question I had for so many hours been occupied with into the compass of a needle-point. I was dazzled by my opportunity. She had had an uncertainty, in other words, as to whom I meant, and that it kept her for some seconds on the rack was a trifle compared to my chance. She would give herself away supremely if she showed she suspected me of placing my finger on the spot—if she understood the person I had not named to be nameable as Gilbert Long. What had created her peril, of course, was my naming Lady John. Well, how can I say in any sufficient way how much the extraordinary beauty of her eyes during this brevity of suspense had to do with the event? It had everything—for it was what caused me to be touched beyond even what I had already been, and I could literally bear no more of that. I therefore took no advantage, or took only the advantage I had spoken with the intention of taking. I laughed out doubtless too nervously, but it didn't compromise my tact. "Don't you know how she's perpetually pouncing on him?"

Still, however, I had not named him—which was what prolonged the tension. "Do you mean—a—do you mean——?" With which she broke off on a small weak titter and a still weaker exclamation. "There are so *many* gentlemen!"

There was something in it that might in other conditions have been as trivial as the giggle of a housemaid; but it had in fact for my ear the silver ring of poetry. I told her instantly whom I meant. "Poor Briss, you know," I said, "is always in her clutches."

Oh, how it let her off! And yet, no sooner had it done so and had I thereby tasted on the instant the sweetness of my wisdom, than I became aware of something much more extraordinary. It let her off—she showed me this for a minute, in spite of herself; but the next minute she showed me something quite different, which was, most wonderful of all, that she wished me to see her as not quite feeling why I should so much take for granted the person I *had* named. "Poor Briss?" her face and manner appeared suddenly to repeat—quite, moreover (and it was the drollest, saddest part), as if all our friends had stood about us to listen. Wherein did poor Briss so intimately concern her? What, pray, was my ground for such free reference to poor Briss? She quite repudiated poor Briss. She knew nothing at all about him, and the whole airy structure I had erected with his aid might have crumbled at the touch she thus administered if its solidity had depended only on that. I had a minute of surprise which, had it lasted another minute as surprise pure and simple, might almost as quickly have turned to something like chagrin. Fortunately it turned instead into something even more like enthusiasm than anything I had yet felt. The stroke *was* extraordinary, but extraordinary for its nobleness. I quickly saw in it, from the moment I had got my point of view, more fine things than ever. I saw for instance that, magnificently, she wished not to incriminate him. All that had passed between us had passed in silence, but it was a different matter for what might pass in sound. We looked at each other therefore with a strained smile over any question of identities. It was as if it had been one thing—to her confused, relaxed intensity—to give herself up to me, but quite another thing to give up somebody else.

And yet, superficially arrested as I was for the time, I directly afterwards recognised in this instinctive discrimination—the last, the expiring struggle of her native lucidity—a supremely convincing bit of evidence. It was still more convincing than if she had done any of the common things—stammered, changed colour, shown an apprehension of what the person named might have said to me. She had had it from me that he and I had talked about her, but there was nothing that she accepted the idea of his having been able to say. I saw—still more than this—that there was nothing to my purpose (since my purpose was to understand) that she would have had, as matters stood, coherence enough to impute to him. It was extremely curious to me to divine, just here, that she hadn't a glimmering of the real logic of Brissenden's happy effect on her nerves. It was the effect, as coming from him, that a beautiful delicacy forbade her as yet to give me her word for; and she was certainly herself in the stage of regarding it as an anomaly. Why, on the contrary, I might have wondered, shouldn't she have jumped at the chance, at the comfort, of seeing a preference trivial enough to be "worked" imputed to her? Why shouldn't she have been positively pleased that people might helpfully couple her name with that of the wrong man? Why, in short, in the language that Grace Brissenden and I had used together, was not that lady's husband the perfection of a red herring? Just because, I perceived, the relation that had established itself between them *was*, for its function, a real relation, the relation of a fellowship in resistance to doom.

Nothing could have been stranger than for *me* so to know it was while the stricken parties themselves were in ignorance; but nothing, at the same time, could have been, as I have since made out, more magnanimous than Mrs. Server's attitude. She moved, groping and panting, in the gathering dusk of her fate, but there were calculations she still could dimly make. One of these was that she must drag no one else in. I verily believe that, for that matter, she had scruples, poignant and exquisite, even about letting our friend himself see how much she liked to be with him. She wouldn't, at all events, let another see. I saw what I saw, I felt what I felt, but such things were exactly a sign that I could take care of myself. There was apparently, I was obliged to admit, but little apprehension in her of her unduly showing that *our* meeting had been anything of a blessing to her. There was no one indeed just then to be the wiser for it; I might perhaps else even have feared that she would have been influenced to treat the incident as closed. I had, for that matter, no wish to prolong it beyond her own convenience; it had already told me everything it could possibly tell. I thought I knew moreover what she would have got from it. I preferred, none the less, that we should separate by my own act; I wanted not to see her move in order to be free of me. So I stood up, to put her more at her ease, and it was while I remained before her that I tried to turn to her advantage what I had committed myself to about Brissenden.

"I had a fancy, at any rate, that he was looking for you—all the more that he didn't deny it."

She had not moved; she had let me take my hand from her own with as little sign as on her first feeling its touch. She only kept her eyes on me. "What made you have such a fancy?"

"What makes me ever have any?" I laughed. "My extraordinary interest in my fellow-creatures. I have more than most men. I've never really seen anyone with half so much. That breeds observation, and observation breeds ideas. Do you know what it has done?" I continued. "It has bred for me the idea that Brissenden's in love with you."

There was something in her eyes that struck me as betraying —and the appeal of it went to the heart—the constant dread that if entangled in talk she might show confusion. Nevertheless she brought out after a moment, as naturally and charmingly as possible: "How can that be when he's so strikingly in love with his wife?"

I gave her the benefit of the most apparent consideration. "Strikingly, you call it?"

"Why, I thought it was noticed—what he does for her."

"Well, of course she's extremely handsome—or at least extremely fresh and attractive. He *is* in love with her, no doubt, if you take it by the quarter, or by the year, like a yacht or a stable," I pushed on at random. "But isn't there such a state also as being in love by the day?"

She waited, and I guessed from the manner of it exactly why. It was the most obscure of intimations that she would have liked better that I shouldn't make her talk; but obscurity, by this time, offered me no more difficulties. The hint, none the less, a trifle disconcerted me, and, while I vaguely sought for some small provisional middle way between going and not going on, the oddest thing, as a fruit of my own delay, occurred. This was neither more nor less than the revival of her terrible little fixed smile. It came back as if with an audible click—as a gas-burner makes a pop when you light it. It told me visibly that from the moment she must talk she could talk only with its aid. The effect of its aid I indeed immediately perceived. "How do I know?" she asked in answer to my question. "I've never *been* in love."

"Not even by the day?"

"Oh, a day's surely a long time."

"It is," I returned. "But I've none the less, more fortunately than you, been in love for a whole one." Then I continued, from an impulse of which I had just become conscious and that was clearly the result of the heart-breaking facial contortion—heart-breaking, that is, when one knew what I knew—by which she imagined herself to represent the pleasant give-and-take of society. This sense, for me, was a quick horror of forcing her, in such conditions, to talk at all. Poor Briss had mentioned to me, as an incident of his contact with her, his apprehension of her breaking down; and now, at a touch, I saw what he had meant. She *would* break down if I didn't look out. I found myself thus, from one minute to the other, as greatly dreading it for her, dreading it indeed for both of us, as I might have dreaded some physical accident or danger, her fall from an unmanageable horse or the crack beneath her of thin ice. It was impossible—that was the extraordinary impression—to come too much to her assistance. We had each of us all, in our way, hour after hour, been, as goodnaturedly as unwittingly, giving her a lift; yet what was the end of it but her still sitting there to assure me of a state of gratitude—that she couldn't even articulate—for every hint of a perch that might still be held out? What could only, therefore, in the connection, strike me as indicated was fairly to put into her mouth—if one might do so without showing too ungracefully as alarmed—the words one might have guessed her to wish to use were she able to use any. It was a small service of anticipation that I tried to render her with as little of an air as possible of being remedial. "I daresay you wonder," I remarked on these lines, "why, at all, I should have thrust Brissenden in."

"Oh, I *do* so wonder!" she replied with the refined but exaggerated glee that is a frequent form in high companies and light colloquies. I *did* help her—it was admirable to feel it. She liked my imposing on her no more complex a proposition. She liked my putting the thing to her so much better than she could have put it to me. But she immediately afterwards looked away as if—now that we *had* put it, and it didn't matter which of us best—we had nothing more to do with it. She gave me a hint of drops and inconsequences that might indeed have opened up abysses, and all the while she smiled and smiled. Yet whatever she did or failed of, as I even then observed to myself, how she remained lovely! One's pleasure in that helped one somehow not to break down on one's own side—since breaking down was in question—for commiseration. I didn't know what she might have hours of for the man—whoever he was—to whom her sacrifice had been made; but I doubted if for any other person she had ever been so beautiful as she was for me at these moments. To have kept her so, to have made her more so—how might that result of their relation not in fact have shone as a blinding light into the eyes of her lover? What would he have been bound to make out in her after all but her passion and her beauty? Wasn't it enough for such wonders as these to fill his consciousness? If they didn't fill mine—even though occupying so large a place in it—was that not only because I had not the direct benefit of them as the other party to the prodigy had it? They filled mine too, for that matter, just at this juncture, long enough for me to describe myself as rendered subject by them to a temporary loss of my thread. What *could* pass muster with her as an account of my reason for evoking the blighted identity of our friend? There came constantly into her aspect, I should say, the strangest alternatives, as I can only most conveniently call them, of presence and absence—something like intermissions of intensity, cessations and resumptions of life. They were like the slow flickers of a troubled flame, breathed upon and then left, burning up and burning down. She had really burnt down—I mean so far as her sense of things went—while I stood there.

I stood long enough to see that it didn't in the least signify whether or no I explained, and during this interval I found myself—to my surprise—in receipt of still better assistance than any I had to give. I had happened to turn, while I awkwardly enough, no doubt, rested and shifted, to the quarter from which Mrs. Server had arrived; and there, just at the end of the same vista, I gathered material for my proper reply. Her eyes at this moment were fixed elsewhere, and that gave me still a little more time, at the end of which my reference had all its point. "I supposed you to have Brissenden in your head," I said, "because it's evidently what he himself takes for granted. But let him tell you!" He was already close to us: missing her at the house, he had started again in search of her and had successfully followed. The effect on him of coming in sight of us had been for an instant to make him hang back as I had seen Mrs. Server hang. But he had then advanced just as she had done; I had waited for him to reach us; and now she saw him. She looked at him as she always looked at all of us, yet not at either of us as if we had lately been talking of him. If it was vacancy it was eloquent; if it was vigilance it was splendid. What was most curious, at all events, was that it was now poor Briss who was disconcerted. He had counted on finding her, but not on finding her with me, and I interpreted a certain ruefulness in him as the sign of a quick, uneasy sense that he must have been in question between us. I instantly felt that the right thing was to let him know he had been, and I mentioned to him, as a joke, that he had come just in time to save himself. We had been talking of him, and I wouldn't answer for what Mrs. Server had been going to say. He took it gravely, but he took everything so gravely that I saw no symptom in that. In fact, as he appeared at first careful not to meet my eyes, I saw for a minute or two no symptom in anything—in anything, at least, but the way in which, standing beside me and before Mrs. Server's bench, he received the conscious glare of her recognition without returning it and without indeed giving her a look. He looked all about—looked, as she herself had done after our meeting, at the charming place and its marks of the hour, at the rich twilight, deeper now in the avenues, and at the tree-tops and sky, more flushed now with colour. I found myself of a sudden quite as sorry for him as I had been for Mrs. Server, and I scarce know how it was suggested to me that during the short interval since our separation something had happened that made a difference in him. Was the difference a consciousness still more charged than I had left it? I couldn't exactly say, and the question really lost itself in what soon came uppermost for me—the desire, above all, to spare them both and to spare them equally.

The difficulty, however, was to spare them in some fashion that would not be more marked than continuing to observe them. To leave them together without a decent pretext would be marked; but this, I eagerly recognised, was none the less what most concerned me. Whatever they might see in it, there was by this time little enough doubt of how it would indicate for my own mind that the wheel had completely turned. That

was the point to which I had been brought by the lapse of a
few hours. I had verily travelled far since the sight of the pair
on the terrace had given its arrest to my first talk with Mrs.
Briss. I was obliged to admit to myself that nothing could very
well have been more singular than some of my sequences. I
had come round to the opposite pole of the protest my companion had then drawn from me—which was the pole of
agreement with herself; and it hung sharply before me that I
was pledged to confess to her my revolution. I couldn't now
be in the presence of the two creatures I was in the very act of
finally judging to be not a whit less stricken than I had originally imaged them—I couldn't do this and think with any
complacency of the redemption of my pledge; for the process
by which I had at last definitely inculpated Mrs. Server was
precisely such a process of providential supervision as made me
morally responsible, so to speak, for her, and thereby intensified my scruples. Well, my scruples had the last word—they
were what determined me to look at my watch and profess
that, whatever sense of a margin Brissenden and Mrs. Server
might still enjoy, it behoved me not to forget that I took, on
such great occasions, an hour to dress for dinner. It was a fairly
crude cover for my retreat; perhaps indeed I should rather say
that my retreat was practically naked and unadorned. It formulated their relation. I left them with the formula on their hands,
both queerly staring at it, both uncertain what to do with it.
For some passage that would soon be a correction of this,
however, one might surely feel that one could trust them. I
seemed to feel my trust justified, behind my back, before I had
got twenty yards away. By the time I had done this, I must
add, something further had befallen me. Poor Briss had met
my eyes just previous to my flight, and it was then I satisfied
myself of what had happened to him at the house. He had met
his wife; she had in some way dealt with him; he had been with
her, however briefly, alone; and the intimacy of their union had
been afresh impressed upon him. Poor Briss, in fine, looked
ten years older.

IX

I SHALL never forget the impressions of that evening, nor the way, in particular, the immediate effect of some of them was to merge the light of my extravagant perceptions in a glamour much more diffused. I remember feeling seriously warned, while dinner lasted, not to yield further to my idle habit of reading into mere human things an interest so much deeper than mere human things were in general prepared to supply. This especial hour, at Newmarch, had always a splendour that asked little of interpretation, that even carried itself, with an amiable arrogance, as indifferent to what the imagination could do for it. I think the imagination, in those halls of art and fortune, was almost inevitably accounted a poor matter; the whole place and its participants abounded so in pleasant-ness and picture, in all the felicities, for every sense, taken for granted there by the very basis of life, that even the sense most finely poetic, aspiring to extract the moral, could scarce have helped feeling itself treated to something of the snub that affects—when it does affect—the uninvited reporter in whose face a door is closed. I said to myself during dinner that these were scenes in which a transcendent intelligence had after all no application, and that, in short, any preposterous acuteness might easily suffer among them such a loss of dignity as over-takes the newspaperman kicked out. We existed, all of us to-gether, to be handsome and happy, to be really what we looked —since we looked tremendously well; to be that and neither more nor less, so not discrediting by musty secrets and aggres-sive doubts our high privilege of harmony and taste. We were concerned only with what was bright and open, and the ex-pression that became us all was, at worst, that of the shaded but gratified eye, the air of being forgivingly dazzled by too much lustre.

Mrs. Server, at table, was out of my range, but I wondered if, had she not been so, I shouldn't now have been moved to recognise in her fixed expressiveness nothing more than our common reciprocal tribute. Hadn't everyone my eyes could at present take in a fixed expressiveness? Was I not very possibly

myself, on this ground of physiognomic congruity, more physiognomic than anyone else? I made my excellence, on the
chance, go as far as it would to cover my temporary doubts. I
saw Mrs. Brissenden, in another frock, naturally, and other
jewels from those of the evening before; but she gave me,
across the board, no more of a look than if she had quite done
with me. It struck me that she felt she *had* done—that, as to
the subject of our discussion, she deemed her case by this time
so established as to offer comparatively little interest. I could-
n't come to her to renew the discussion; I could only come to
her to make my submission; and it doubtless appeared to
her—to do her justice—more delicate not to triumph over me
in advance. The profession of joy, however, reigned in her
handsome face none the less largely for my not having the
benefit of it. If I seem to falsify my generalisation by acknowl-
edging that her husband, on the same side, made no more
public profession of joy than usual, I am still justified by the
fact that there was something in a manner decorative even in
Brissenden's wonted gloom. He reminded me at this hour
more than ever of some fine old Velasquez or other portrait—
a presentation of ugliness and melancholy that might have
been royal. There was as little of the common in his dry, distinguished patience as in the case I had made out for him.
Blighted and ensconced, he looked at it over the rigid conven-
tion, his peculiar perfection of necktie, shirt-front and waistcoat, as some aged remnant of sovereignty at the opera looks
over the ribbon of an order and the ledge of a box.

I must add, however, that in spite of my sense of his wife's
indulgence I kept quite aware of the nearer approach, as course
followed course, of my hour of reckoning with her—more and
more saw the moment of the evening at which, frankly amused
at last at having me in a cleft stick, she would draw me a little
out of the throng. Of course, also, I was much occupied in
asking myself to what degree I was prepared to be perjured.
Was I ready to pretend that my candour was still unconvinced?
And was I in this case only instinctively mustering my argu-
ments? I was certainly as sorry that Mrs. Server was out of my
view as if I proposed still to fight; and I really felt, so far as that
went, as if there might be something to fight for after the lady
on my left had given me a piece of news. I had asked her if she

happened to know, as we couldn't see, who was next Mrs. Server, and, though unable to say at the moment, she made no scruple, after a short interval, of ascertaining with the last directness. The stretch forward in which she had indulged, or the information she had caused to be passed up to her while I was again engaged on my right, established that it was Lord Lutley who had brought the lovely lady in and that it was Mr. Long who was on her other side. These things indeed were not the finest point of my companion's communication, for I saw that what she felt I would be really interested in was the fact that Mr. Long had brought in Lady John, who was naturally, therefore, his other neighbour. Beyond Lady John was Mr. Obert, and beyond Mr. Obert Mrs. Froome, not, for a wonder, this time paired, as by the immemorial tradition, so fairly comical in its candour, with Lord Lutley. Wasn't it too funny, the kind of grandmotherly view of their relation shown in their always being put together? If I perhaps questioned whether "grandmotherly" were exactly the name for the view, what yet at least was definite in the light of this evening's arrangement was that there did occur occasions on which they were put apart. My friend of course disposed of this observation by the usual exception that "proved the rule"; but it was absurd how I had thrilled with her announcement, and our exchange of ideas meanwhile helped to carry me on.

My theory had not at all been framed to embrace the phenomenon thus presented; it had been precisely framed, on the contrary, to hang together with the observed inveteracy of escape, on the part of the two persons about whom it busied itself, from public juxtaposition of more than a moment. I was fairly upset by the need to consider at this late hour whether going in for a new theory or bracing myself for new facts would hold out to me the better refuge. It is perhaps not too much to say that I should scarce have been able to sit still at all but for the support afforded me by the oddity of the separation of Lord Lutley and Mrs. Froome; which, though resting on a general appearance directly opposed to that of my friends, offered somehow the relief of a suggestive analogy. What I could directly clutch at was that if the exception did prove the rule in the one case it might equally prove it in the other. If on a rare occasion one of these couples might be divided, so, by as uncommon a chance, the other might be joined; the only difference being in the gravity of the violated law. For which pair was the betrayal greatest? It was not till dinner was nearly ended and the ladies were about to withdraw that I recovered lucidity to make out how much more machinery would have had to be put into motion consistently to prevent, than once in a way to minimise, the disconcerting accident.

All accidents, I must add, were presently to lose themselves in the unexpectedness of my finding myself, before we left the dining-room, in easy talk with Gilbert Long—talk that was at least easy for *him*, whatever it might have struck me as necessarily destined to be for me. I felt as he approached me—for he did approach me—that it was somehow "important"; I was so aware that something in the state of my conscience would have prevented me from assuming conversation between us to be at this juncture possible. The state of my conscience was that I knew too much—that no one had really any business to know what I knew. If he suspected but the fiftieth part of it there was no simple spirit in which he could challenge me. It would have been simple of course to desire to knock me down, but that was barred by its being simple to excess. It wouldn't even have been enough for him merely to ground it on a sudden fancy. It fitted, in fine, with my cogitations that it was so significant for him to wish to speak to me that I didn't envy him his attempt at the particular shade of assurance required for carrying the thing off. He would have learned from Mrs. Server that I was not, as regarded them, at all as others were; and thus his idea, the fruit of that stimulation, could only be either to fathom, to felicitate, or—as it were—to destroy me. What was at the same time obvious was that no one of these attitudes would go quite of itself. The simple sight of him as he quitted his chair to take one nearer my own brought home to me in a flash—and much more than anything had yet done—the real existence in him of the condition it was my private madness (none the less private for Grace Brissenden's so limited glimpse of it,) to believe I had coherently stated. Is not this small touch perhaps the best example I can give of the intensity of amusement I had at last enabled my private madness to yield me? I found myself owing it, from this time on and for the rest of the evening, moments of the highest concentration.

Whatever there might have been for me of pain or doubt was washed straight out by the special sensation of seeing how "clever" poor Long not only would have to be, but confidently and actually *was*; inasmuch as this apprehension seemed to put me in possession of his cleverness, besides leaving me all my own. I made him welcome, I helped him to another cigarette, I felt above all that I should enjoy him; my response to his overture was, in other words, quickly enough to launch us. Yet I fear I can do little justice to the pleasant suppressed tumult of impression and reflection that, on my part, our ten minutes together produced. The elements that mingled in it scarce admit of discrimination. It was still more than previously a deep sense of being justified. My interlocutor was for those ten minutes immeasurably superior—superior, I mean, to himself—and he couldn't possibly have become so save through the relation I had so patiently tracked. He faced me there with another light than his own, spoke with another sound, thought with another ease and understood with another ear. I should put it that what came up between us was the mere things of the occasion, were it not for the fine point to which, in my view, the things of the occasion had been brought. While our eyes, at all events, on either side, met serenely, and our talk, dealing with the idea, dealing with the extraordinary special charm, of the social day now deepening to its end, touched our companions successively, touched the manner in which this one and that had happened to be predominantly a part of that charm; while such were our immediate conditions I wondered of course if he had not, just as consciously and essentially as I, quite another business in mind. It was not indeed that our allusion to the other business would not have been wholly undiscoverable by a third person.

So far as it took place it was of a "subtlety," as we used to say at Newmarch, in relation to which the common register of that pressure would have been, I fear, too old-fashioned a barometer. I had moreover the comfort—for it amounted to that—of perceiving after a little that we understood each other too well for our understanding really to have tolerated the interference of passion, such passion as would have been represented on his side by resentment of my intelligence and on my side by resentment of his. The high sport of such intelligence—between

gentlemen, to the senses of any other than whom it must
surely be closed—demanded and implied in its own intimate
interest a certain amenity. Yes, accordingly, I had promptly got
the answer that my wonder at his approach required: he had
come to me for the high sport. He would formerly have been
incapable of it, and he was beautifully capable of it now. It was
precisely the kind of high sport—the play of perception, expression, sociability—in which Mrs. Server would a year or
two before have borne as light a hand. I need scarcely add how
little it would have found itself in that lady's present chords.
He had said to me in our ten minutes everything amusing she
couldn't have said. Yet if when our host gave us the sign to adjourn to the drawing-room so much as all this had grown so
much clearer, I had still, figuratively speaking, a small nut or
two left to crack. By the time we moved away together, however, these resistances had yielded. The answers had really only
been waiting for the questions. The play of Long's mind
struck me as more marked, since the morning, by the same
amount, as it might have been called, as the march of poor
Briss's age; and if I had, a while before, in the wood, had my
explanation of this latter addition, so I had it now of the
former—as to which I shall presently give it.

When music, in English society, as we know, is not an accompaniment to the voice, the voice can in general be counted
on to assert its pleasant identity as an accompaniment to music;
but at Newmarch we had been considerably schooled, and this
evening, in the room in which most of us had assembled, an
interesting pianist, who had given a concert the night before at
the near county town and been brought over during the day to
dine and sleep, would scarce have felt in any sensitive fibre that
he was not having his way with us. It may just possibly have
been an hallucination of my own, but while we sat together
after dinner in a dispersed circle I could have worked it out
that, as a company, we were considerably conscious of some
experience, greater or smaller from one of us to the other, that
had prepared us for the player's spell. Felicitously scattered
and grouped, we might in almost any case have had the air of
looking for a message from it—of an imagination to be flattered, nerves to be quieted, sensibilities to be soothed. The
whole scene was as composed as if there were scarce one of us

but had a secret thirst for the infinite to be quenched. And it was the infinite that, for the hour, the distinguished foreigner poured out to us, causing it to roll in wonderful waves of sound, almost of colour, over our receptive attitudes and faces. Each of us, I think, now wore the expression—or confessed at least to the suggestion—of some indescribable thought; which might well, it was true, have been nothing more unmentionable than the simple sense of how the posture of deference to this noble art has always a certain personal grace to contribute. We neglected nothing of it that could make our general effect ample, and whether or no we were kept quiet by the piano, we were at least admonished, to and fro, by our mutual visibility, which each of us clearly desired to make a success. I have little doubt, furthermore, that to each of us was due, as the crown of our inimitable day, the imputation of having something quite of our own to think over.

We thought, accordingly—we continued to think, and I felt that, by the law of the occasion, there had as yet been for everyone no such sovereign warrant for an interest in the private affairs of everyone else. As a result of this influence, all that at dinner had begun to fade away from me came back with a rush and hovered there with a vividness. I followed many trains and put together many pieces; but perhaps what I most did was to render a fresh justice to the marvel of our civilised state. The perfection of that, enjoyed as we enjoyed it, all made a margin, a series of concentric circles of rose-colour (shimmering away into the pleasant vague of everything else that didn't matter,) for the so salient little figure of Mrs. Server, still the controlling image for me, the real principle of composition, in this affluence of fine things. What, for my part, while I listened, I most made out was the beauty and the terror of conditions so highly organised that under their rule her small lonely fight with disintegration could go on without the betrayal of a gasp or a shriek, and with no worse tell-tale contortion of lip or brow than the vibration, on its golden stem, of that constantly renewed flower of amenity which my observation had so often and so mercilessly detached only to find again in its place. This flower nodded perceptibly enough in our deeply stirred air, but there was a peace, none the less, in feeling the spirit of the wearer to be temporarily at rest.

There was for the time no gentleman on whom she need pounce, no lapse against which she need guard, no presumption she need create, nor any suspicion she need destroy. In this pause in her career it came over me that I should have liked to leave her; it would have prepared for me the pleasant after-consciousness that I had seen her pass, as I might say, in music out of sight.

But we were, alas! all too much there, too much tangled and involved for that; every actor in the play that had so unexpectedly insisted on constituting itself for me sat forth as with an intimation that they were not to be so easily disposed of. It was as if there were some last act to be performed before the curtain could fall. Would the definite dramatic signal for ringing the curtain down be then only—as a grand climax and *coup de théâtre*—the due attestation that poor Briss had succumbed to inexorable time and Mrs. Server given way under a cerebral lesion? Were the rest of us to disperse decorously by the simple action of the discovery that, on our pianist's striking his last note, with its consequence of permitted changes of attitude, Gilbert Long's victim had reached the point of final simplification and Grace Brissenden's the limit of age recorded of man? I could look at neither of these persons without a sharper sense of the contrast between the tragedy of their predicament and the comedy of the situation that did everything for them but suspect it. They had truly been arrayed and anointed, they had truly been isolated, for their sacrifice. I was sufficiently aware even then that if one hadn't known it one might have seen nothing; but I was not less aware that one couldn't know anything without seeing all; and so it was that, while our pianist played, my wandering vision played and played as well. It took in again, while it went from one of them to the other, the delicate light that each had shed on the other, and it made me wonder afresh what still more delicate support they themselves might not be in the very act of deriving from their dim community. It was for the glimmer of this support that I had left them together two or three hours before; yet I was obliged to recognise that, travel between them as my fancy might, it could detect nothing in the way of a consequent result. I caught no look from either that spoke to me of service rendered them; and I caught none, in particular, from one of them to the other, that I could read as a symptom of their having compared notes. The fellow-feeling of each for the lost light of the other remained for me but a tie supposititious—the full-blown flower of my theory. It would show here as another flower, equally mature, for me to have made out a similar dim community between Gilbert Long and Mrs. Brissenden—to be able to figure them as groping side by side, proportionately, towards a fellowship of light overtaken; but if I failed of this, for ideal symmetry, that seemed to rest on the general truth that joy brings people less together than sorrow.

So much for the course of my impressions while the music lasted—a course quite consistent with my being prepared for new combinations as soon as it was over. Promptly, when that happened, the bow was unbent; and the combination I first seized, amid motion and murmur and rustle, was that, once more, of poor Briss and Lady John, the latter of whom had already profited by the general reaction to endeavour to culti- vate afresh the vainest of her sundry appearances. She had laid on him the same coercive hand to which I owed my having found him with her in the afternoon, but my intervention was now to operate with less ceremony. I chanced to be near enough to them for Brissenden, on seeing me, to fix his eyes on me in silence, but in a manner that could only bring me im- mediately nearer. Lady John never did anything in silence, but she greeted me as I came up to them with a fine false alarm. "No, indeed," she cried, "you shan't carry him off this time!" —and poor Briss disappeared, leaving us face to face, even while she breathed defiance. He had made no joke of it, and I had from him no other recognition; it was therefore a mere touch, yet it gave me a sensible hint that he had begun, as things were going, to depend upon me, that I already in a fashion figured to him—and on amazingly little evidence after all—as his natural protector, his providence, his effective om- niscience. Like Mrs. Server herself, he was materially on my hands, and it was proper I should "do" for him. I wondered if he were really beginning to look to me to avert his inexorable fate. Well, if his inexorable fate was to be an unnameable cli- max, it had also its special phases, and one of these I *had* just averted. I followed him a moment with my eyes and I then ob- served to Lady John that she decidedly took me for too simple a person. She had meanwhile also watched the direction taken by her liberated victim, and was the next instant prepared with a reply to my charge. "Because he has gone to talk with May Server? I don't quite see what you mean, for I believe him really to be in terror of her. Most of the men here *are*, you know, and I've really assured myself that he doesn't find her any less awful than the rest. He finds her the more so by just the very marked extra attention that you may have noticed she has given him."

"And does that now happen to be what he has so eagerly gone off to impress upon her?"

Lady John was so placed that she could continue to look at our friends, and I made out in her that she was not, in respect to them, without some slight elements of perplexity. These were even sufficient to make her temporarily neglect the defence of the breach I had made in her consistency. "If you mean by 'impressing upon' her speaking to her, he hasn't gone —you can see for yourself—to impress upon her anything; they have the most extraordinary way, which I've already observed, of sitting together without sound. I don't know," she laughed, "what's the matter with such people!"

"It proves in general," I admitted, "either some coldness or some warmth, and I quite understand that that's not the way *you* sit with your friends. You steer admirably clear of every extravagance. I don't see, at any rate, why Mrs. Server is a terror——"

But she had already taken me up. "If she doesn't chatter as *I* do?" She thought it over. "But she does—to everyone but Mr. Briss. I mean to every man she can pick up."

I emulated her reflection. "Do they complain of it to you?"

"They're more civil than you," she returned; "for if, when they flee before it, they bump up against me in their flight, they don't explain that by intimating that they're come from bad to worse. Besides, I see what they suffer."

"And do you hear it?"

"What they suffer? No, I've taken care not to suffer myself. I don't listen. It's none of my business."

"Is that a way of gently expressing," I ventured to ask, "that it's also none of mine?"

"It might be," she replied, "if I had, as you appear to, the imagination of atrocity. But I don't pretend to so much as conceive what's your business."

"I wonder if it isn't just now," I said after a moment, "to convict you of an attempt at duplicity that has not even had the saving grace of success! Was it for Brissenden himself that you spoke just now as if you believed him to wish to cling to you?"

"Well, I'm kind enough for anything," she good-naturedly enough laughed. "But what," she asked more sharply, "are you trying to find out?"

Such an awful lot, the answer to this would politely have been, that I daresay the aptness of the question produced in my face a shade of embarrassment. I felt, however, the next moment that I needn't fear too much. What I, on approaching Lady John, had found myself moved to test, using her in it as a happy touchstone, was the degree of the surrounding, the latent, sense of things: an impulse confirmed by the manner in which she had momentarily circled about the phenomenon of Mrs. Server's avidity, about the mystery of the terms made with it by our friend. It was present to me that if I could catch, on the part of my interlocutress, anything of a straight scent, I might take that as the measure of a diffused danger. I mentally applied this term to the possibility of diffusion, because I suddenly found myself thinking with a kind of horror of any accident by which I might have to expose to the world, to defend against the world, to share with the world, that now so complex tangle of hypotheses that I have had for convenience to speak of as my theory. I could toss the ball myself, I could catch it and send it back, and familiarity had now made this exercise—in my own inner precincts—easy and safe. But the mere brush of Lady John's clumsier curiosity made me tremble for the impunity of my creation. If there had been, so to speak, a discernment, however feeble, of *my* discernment, it would have been irresistible to me to take this as the menace of some incalculable catastrophe or some public ugliness. It wasn't for me definitely to image the logical result of a verification by the sense of others of the matter of my vision; but the thing had only to hang before me as a chance for me to feel that I should utterly object to it, though I may appear to weaken this statement if I add that the opportunity to fix the degree of my

actual companion's betrayed mystification was almost a spell.
This, I conceive, was just by reason of what was at stake. How
could I happily tell her what I was trying to find out?—tell her,
that is, not too much for security and yet enough for relief?
The best answer seemed a brave jump. I was conscious of a
certain credit open with her in my appearance of intellectual
sympathy.

"Well," I brought out at last, "I'm quite aching to ask you if
you'll forgive me a great liberty, which I owe to your candid
challenge my opportunity to name. Will you allow me to say
frankly that I think you play a dangerous game with poor Briss,
in whom I confess I'm interested? I don't of course speak of
the least danger to yourself; but it's an injustice to any man to
make use of him quite so flagrantly. You don't in the least
flatter yourself that the poor fellow is in love with you—you
wouldn't care a bit if he were. Yet you're willing to make him
think you like him, so far as that may be necessary to explain
your so frequently ingenious appropriation of him. He doesn't
like you *too* much, as yet; doesn't even like you quite enough.
But your potency may, after all, work on him, and then, as
your interest is so obviously quite elsewhere, what will happen
will be that you'll find, to your inconvenience, that you've
gone too far. A man never likes a woman enough unless he
likes her *more* than enough. Unfortunately it's what the inveterate ass is sure sooner or later to do."

Lady John looked just enough interested to look detached
from most of the more vulgar liabilities to offence. "Do I
understand that to be the pretty name by which you describe
Mr. Briss?"

"He has his share of it, for I'm thinking of the idiots that we
every one of us are. I throw out a warning against a contingency."

"Are you providing for the contingency of his ceasing to
care for his wife? If you are"—and Lady John's amusement
took on a breadth—"you may be said to have a prudent mind
and to be taking time by the forelock."

At this I pricked up my ears. "Do you mean because of his
apparently incorruptible constancy?"

"I mean because the whole thing's so before one. She has
him so in hand that they're neither of them in as much danger
as would count for a mouse. It doesn't prevent his liking to

dally by the way—for *she* dallies by the way, and he does everything she does. Haven't I observed her," Lady John continued, "dallying a little, so far as that goes, with *you*? You've the tact to tell me that he doesn't think me good enough, but I don't require, do I?—for such a purpose as his—to be very extraordinarily good. You may say that you wrap it up immensely and try to sugar the dose! Well, all the same, give up, for a quiet life, the attempt to be a providence. You can't be a providence and not be a bore. A real providence *knows*; whereas you," said Lady John, making her point neatly, "have to find out—and to find out even by asking 'the likes of' *me*. Your fine speech meanwhile doesn't a bit tell me what."

It affected me again that she could get so near without getting nearer. True enough it was that I wanted to find out; and though I might expect, or fear, too much of her, I wondered at her only seeing this—at her not reading deeper. The peril of the public ugliness that haunted me rose or fell, at this moment, with my varying view of her density. Or rather, to be more exact, I already saw her as necessarily stupid because I saw her as extravagantly vain. What I see now of course is that I was on my own side almost stupidly hard with her—as I may also at that hour have been subject to her other vice. Didn't I perhaps, in proportion as I felt how little she saw, think awfully well of myself, as we said at Newmarch, for seeing so much more? It comes back to me that the sense thus established of my superior vision may perfectly have gone a little to my head. If it was a frenzied fallacy I was all to blame, but if it was anything else whatever it was naturally intoxicating. I really remember in fact that nothing so much as this confirmed presumption of my impunity had appeared to me to mark the fine quality of my state. I think there must fairly have been a pitch at which I was not sure that not to partake of that state was, on the part of others, the sign of a gregarious vulgarity; as if there were a positive advantage, an undiluted bliss, in the intensity of consciousness that I had reached. *I* alone was magnificently and absurdly aware—everyone else was benightedly out of it. So I reflected that there would be almost nothing I mightn't with safety mention to my present subject of practice as an acknowledgment that I was meddlesome. I could put no clue in her hand that her notorious acuteness would make of the

smallest use to her. The most she could do would be to make
it of use to myself, and the clue it seemed best to select was
therefore a complete confession of guilt.

"You've a lucidity of your own in which I'm forced to
recognise that the highest purity of motive looks shrivelled and
black. You bring out accordingly what has made me thus beat
about the bush. Have you really such a fund of indulgence for
Gilbert Long as we most of us, I gather—though perhaps in
our blindness—seem to see it stick out again that he supposes?
May he fondly feel that he can continue to count on it? Or, if
you object to my question in that form, is it not, frankly, to
making his attitude—after all so thoroughly public—more convenient to each of you that (without perhaps quite measuring
what you're about,) you've gone on sacrificing poor Briss? I
call it sacrificing, you see, in spite of there having been as yet
no such great harm done. And if you ask me again what business of mine such inquiries may represent, why, the best thing
will doubtless be to say to you that, with a smaller dose of irrepressible irony in my composition than you have in yours, I
can't make so light as you of my tendency to worry on behalf
of those I care for. Let me finally hasten to add that I'm not
now including in that category either of the two gentlemen
I've named."

I freely concede, as I continue my record, that to follow me
at all, at this point, gave proof on Lady John's part of a faculty
that should have prevented my thinking of her as inordinately
backward. "Then who in the world *are* these objects of your
solicitude?"

I showed, over and above my hesitation, my regret for the
need of it. "I'm afraid I can't tell you."

At this, not unnaturally, she fairly scoffed. "Asking me
everything and telling me nothing, you nevertheless look to
me to satisfy you? Do you mean," she pursued, "that you
speak for persons whose interest is more legitimately founded
than the interest you so flatteringly attribute to myself ?"

"Well, yes—let them be so described! Can't you guess," I
further risked, "who constitutes at least *one* of my preoccu-
pations?"

The condescension of her consent to think marked itself
handsomely enough. "Is it your idea to pretend to me that I'm

keeping Grace Brissenden awake?" There was consistency enough in her wonder. "She has not been anything but nice to me; she's not a person whose path one crosses without finding it out; and I can't imagine what has got into her if any such grievance as that is what she has been pouring out to you in your apparently so deep confabulations."

This toss of the ball was one that, I saw quickly enough, even a taste for sport wouldn't justify my answering, and my logical interest lay moreover elsewhere. "Dear no! Mrs. Brissenden certainly feels her strength, and I should never presume to take under my charge any personal situation of hers. I had in my mind a very different identity."

Lady John, as if to be patient with me, looked about at our companions for a hint of it, wondering which of the ladies I might have been supposed to "care for" so much as to tolerate in her a preference for a rival; but the effect of this survey was, I the next instant observed, a drop of her attention from what I had been saying. Her eye had been caught by the sight of Gilbert Long within range of us, and then had been just visibly held by the fact that the person seated with him on one of the small sofas that almost of necessity made conversation intimate was the person whose name, just uttered between us, was, in default of the name she was in search of, still in the air. Gilbert Long and Mrs. Briss were in familiar colloquy—though I was aware, at the first flush, of nothing in this that should have made my interlocutress stare. That is I was aware of nothing but that I had simultaneously myself been moved to some increase of sharpness. What *could* I have known that should have caused me to wonder at the momentary existence of this particular conjunction of minds unless it were simply the fact that I hadn't seen it occur amid the many conjunctions I had already noticed—*plus* the fact that I had a few minutes before, in the interest of the full roundness of my theory, actually been missing it? These two persons had met in my presence at Paddington and had travelled together under my eyes; I had talked of Mrs. Briss with Long and of Long with Mrs. Briss; but the vivid picture that their social union forthwith presented stirred within me, though so strangely late in the day, it might have seemed, for such an emotion, more than enough freshness of impression. Yet—now that I did have it there—why

should it be vivid, why stirring, why a picture at all? Was *any*
temporary collocation, in a house so encouraging to sociability, out of the range of nature? Intensely prompt, I need scarcely
say, were both my freshness and my perceived objections to it.
The happiest objection, could I have taken time to phrase it,
would doubtless have been that the particular effect of this
juxtaposition—to my eyes at least—was a thing not to have
been foreseen. The parties to it looked, certainly, as I felt that
I hadn't prefigured them; though even this, for my reason, was
not a description of their aspect. Much less was it a description
for the intelligence of Lady John—to whom, however, after
all, some formulation of what she dimly saw would not be so
indispensable.

We briefly watched, at any rate, together, and as our eyes
met again we moreover confessed that we had watched. And
we could ostensibly have offered each other no explanation of
that impulse save that we had been talking of those concerned
as separate and that it was in consequence a little odd to find
ourselves suddenly seeing them as one. For that was it—they
were as one; as one, at all events, for *my* large reading. My large
reading had meanwhile, for the convenience of the rest of my
little talk with Lady John, to make itself as small as possible. I
had an odd sense, till we fell apart again, as of keeping my finger rather stiffly fixed on a passage in a favourite author on
which I had not previously lighted. I held the book out of
sight and behind me; I spoke of things that were not at all in
it—or not at all on that particular page; but my volume, none
the less, was only waiting. What might be written there hummed
already in my ears as a result of my mere glimpse. Had *they* also
wonderfully begun to know? Had *she*, most wonderfully, and
had they, in that case, prodigiously come together on it? This
was a possibility into which my imagination could dip even
deeper than into the depths over which it had conceived the
other pair as hovering. These opposed couples balanced like
bronze groups at the two ends of a chimney-piece, and the
most I could say to myself in lucid deprecation of my thought
was that I mustn't take them equally for granted merely *because* they balanced. Things in the real had a way of not bal-
ancing; it was all an affair, this fine symmetry, of artificial
proportion. Yet even while I kept my eyes away from Mrs. Briss

and Long it was vivid to me that, "composing" there beautifully, they could scarce help playing a part in my exhibition. The mind of man, furthermore—and my generalisation pressed hard, with a quick twist, on the supersubtlety as to which I had just been privately complacent—the mind of man doubtless didn't know from one minute to the other, under the appeal of phantasmagoric life, what it would profitably be at. It had struck me a few seconds before as vulgarly gross in Lady John that she was curious, or conscious, of so small a part; in spite of which I was already secretly wincing at the hint that these others had begun to find themselves less in the dark and perhaps even directly to exchange their glimmerings.

My personal privilege, on the basis of the full consciousness, had become, on the spot, in the turn of an eye, more than questionable, and I was really quite scared at the chance of having to face—of having to see *them* face—another recognition. What did this alarm imply but the complete reversal of my estimate of the value of perception? Mrs. Brissenden and Long had been hitherto magnificently without it, and I was responsible perhaps for having, in a mood practically much stupider than the stupidest of theirs, put them gratuitously and helplessly *on* it. To be without it was the most consistent, the most successful, because the most amiable, form of selfishness; and why should people admirably equipped for remaining so, people bright and insolent in their prior state, people in whom this state was to have been respected as a surface without a scratch is respected, be made to begin to vibrate, to crack and split, from within? Wasn't it enough for *me* to pay, vicariously, the tax on being absurd? Were we all to be landed, without an issue or a remedy, in a condition on which that tax would be generally levied? It was as if, abruptly, with a new emotion, I had wished to unthink every thought with which I had been occupied for twenty-four hours. Let me add, however, that even had this process been manageable I was aware of not proposing to begin it till I should have done with Lady John.

The time she took to meet my last remark is naturally not represented by this prolonged glance of mine at the amount of suggestion that just then happened to reach me from the other quarter. It at all events duly came out between us that Mrs. Server was the person I did have on my mind; and I remember that it had seemed to me at the end of a minute to matter comparatively little by which of us, after all, she was first designated. There is perhaps an oddity—which I must set down to my emotion of the moment—in my not now being able to say. I should have been hugely startled if the sight of Gilbert Long had appeared to make my companion suddenly think of her; and reminiscence of that shock is not one of those I have found myself storing up. What does abide with me is the memory of how, after a little, my apprehensions, of various kinds, dropped—most of all under the deepening conviction that Lady John was not a whit less agreeably superficial than I could even at the worst have desired. The point established for me was that, whereas she passed with herself and so many others as taking in everything, she had taken in nothing whatever that it was to my purpose she should not take. Vast, truly, was the world of observation, that we could both glean in it so actively without crossing each other's steps. There we stood close together, yet—save for the accident of a final dash, as I shall note—were at opposite ends of the field.

It's a matter as to which the truth sounds priggish, but I can't help it if—yes, positively—it affected me as hopelessly vulgar to have made any induction at all about our companions *but* those I have recorded, in such detail, on behalf of my own energy. It was better verily not to have touched them— which was the case of everyone else—than to have taken them up, with knowing gestures, only to do so little with them. That I felt the interest of May Server, that May Server felt the interest of poor Briss, and that my feeling incongruously presented itself as putting up, philosophically, with the inconvenience of the lady's—these were, in fine, circumstances to which she clearly attached ideas too commonplace for me to judge it useful to gather them in. She read all things, Lady John, heaven knows, in the light of the universal possibility of a "relation "; but most of the relations that she had up her sleeve could thrust themselves into my theory only to find themselves, the next minute, eliminated. They were of alien substance—insoluble in the whole. Gilbert Long had for her no connection, in my deeper sense, with Mrs. Server, nor Mrs. Server with Gilbert Long, nor the husband with the wife, nor the wife with the husband, nor I with either member of either pair, nor anyone with anything, nor anything with anyone. She was thus exactly where I wanted her to be, for, frankly, I became conscious, at this climax of my conclusion, that I a little wanted her to be where she had distinctly ended by betraying to me that her proper inspiration had placed her. If I have just said that my apprehensions, of various kinds, had finally and completely subsided, a more exact statement would perhaps have been that from the moment our eyes met over the show of our couple on the sofa, the question of any other calculable thing than *that* hint of a relation had simply known itself superseded. Reduced to its plainest terms, this sketch of an improved acquaintance between our comrades was designed to make Lady John think. It was designed to make me do no less, but we thought, inevitably, on different lines.

I have already so represented my successions of reflection as rapid that I may not appear to exceed in mentioning the amusement and philosophy with which I presently perceived it as unmistakable that she believed in the depth of her new sounding. It visibly went down for her much nearer to the bottom of the sea than any plumb I might be qualified to drop. Poor Briss was in love with his wife—that, when driven to the wall, she had had to recognise; but she had not had to recognise that his wife was in love with poor Briss. What was then to militate, on that lady's part, against a due consciousness, at the end of a splendid summer day, a day on which occasions had been so multiplied, of an impression of a special order? What was to prove that there was "nothing in it" when two persons sat looking so very exceptionally *much* as if there were everything in it, as if they were for the first time—thanks to finer opportunity—doing each other full justice? Mustn't it indeed at this juncture have come a little over my friend that Grace had lent herself with uncommon good nature, the previous afternoon, to the arrangement by which, on the way from town, her ladyship's reputation was to profit by no worse company, precisely, than poor Briss's? Mrs. Brissenden's own was obviously now free to profit by my companion's remembering —if the fact had reached her ears—that Mrs. Brissenden had meanwhile had Long for an escort. So much, at least, I saw Lady John as seeing, and my vision may be taken as representing the dash I have confessed myself as making from my end of our field. It offers us, to be exact, as jostling each other just sensibly—though *I* only might feel the bruise—in our business of picking up straws. Our view of the improved acquaintance was only a straw, but as I stooped to it I felt my head bump with my neighbour's. This might have made me ashamed of my eagerness, but, oddly enough, that effect was not to come. I felt in fact that, since we had even pulled against each other at the straw, I carried off, in turning away, the larger piece.

X

IT WAS in the moment of turning away that I somehow learned, without looking, that Mrs. Brissenden had also immediately moved. I wanted to look and yet had my reasons for not appearing to do it too quickly; in spite of which I found my friends, even after an interval, still distinguishable as separating for the avoidance of comment. Gilbert Long, rising directly after his associate, had already walked away, but this associate, lingering where she stood and meeting me with it, availed herself of the occasion to show that she wished to speak to me. Such was the idea she threw out on my forthwith going to her. "For a few minutes—presently."

"Do you mean alone? Shall I come with you?"

She hesitated long enough for me to judge her as a trifle surprised at my being so ready—as if indeed she had rather hoped I wouldn't be; which would have been an easy pretext to her to gain time. In fact, with a face not quite like the brave face she had at each step hitherto shown me, yet unlike in a fashion I should certainly not have been able to define on the spot; with an expression, in short, that struck me as taking refuge in a general reminder that not my convenience, but her own, was in question, she replied: "Oh, no—but before it's too late. A few minutes hence. Where shall you be?" she asked with a shade, as I imagined, of awkwardness. She had looked about as for symptoms of acceptance of the evening's end on the part of the ladies, but we could both see our hostess otherwise occupied. "We don't go up quite yet. In the morning," she added as with an afterthought, "I suppose you leave early."

I debated. "I haven't thought. And you?"

She looked at me straighter now. "I haven't thought either." Then she was silent, neither turning away nor coming to the point, as it seemed to me she might have done, of telling me what she had in her head. I even fancied that her momentary silence, combined with the way she faced me—as if that might speak for her—was meant for an assurance that, whatever train she should take in the morning, she would arrange that it shouldn't be, as it had been the day before, the same as mine.

I really caught in her attitude a world of invidious reference to
the little journey we had already made together. She had sym-
pathies, she had proprieties that imposed themselves, and I was
not to think that any little journey was to be thought of again
in those conditions. It came over me that this might have been
quite a matter discussed by her, discussed and settled, with her
interlocutor on the sofa. It came over me that if, before our
break-up for the night, I should happen also to have a minute's
talk with that interlocutor, I would equally get from it the
sense of an intention unfavourable to our departing in the same
group. And I wondered if this, in that case, wouldn't affect
me as marking a change back to Long's old manner—a forfei-
ture of the conditions, whatever view might be taken of them,
that had made him, at Paddington, suddenly show himself as
so possible and so pleasant. If *he* "changed back," wouldn't
Grace Brissenden change by the same law? And if Grace Brissenden did, wouldn't her husband? Wouldn't the miracle take
the form of the rejuvenation of that husband? Would it, still by
the same token, take the form of *her* becoming very old, becoming if not as old as her husband, at least as old, as one
might say, as herself? Would it take the form of her becoming
dreadfully plain—plain with the plainness of mere stout matu-
rity and artificial preservation? And if it took this form for the
others, which would it take for May Server? Would she, at a
bound as marked as theirs, recover her presence of mind and
her lost equipment?

The kind of suspense that these rising questions produced
for me suffered naturally no drop after Mrs. Briss had cut everything short by rustling voluminously away. She had something
to say to me, and yet she hadn't; she had nothing to say, and
yet I felt her to have already launched herself in a statement.
There were other persons I had made uncomfortable without
at all intending it, but she at least had not suffered from me,
and I had no wish that she should; according to which she had
no pressure to fear. My suspense, in spite of this, remained—
indeed all the more sensibly that I had suddenly lost my discomfort on the subject of redeeming my pledge to her. It had
somehow left me at a stroke, my dread of her calling me, as by
our agreement, to submit in respect to what we had talked of
as the identification of the woman. That call had been what I

looked for from her after she had seen me break with Lady
John; my first idea *then* could only be that I must come, as it
were, to time. It was strange that, the next minute, I should
find myself sure that I was, as I may put it, free; it was at all
events indisputable that as I stood there watching her recede
and fairly studying, in my preoccupation, her handsome affirmative back and the special sweep of her long dress—it was indisputable that, on some intimation I could, at the instant,
recognise but not seize, my consciousness was aware of having
performed a full revolution. If I was free, that was what I had
been only so short a time before, what I had been as I drove,
in London, to the station. Was this now a foreknowledge that,
on the morrow, in driving away, I should feel myself restored
to that blankness? The state lost was the state of exemption
from intense obsessions, and the state recovered would therefore logically match it. If the foreknowledge had thus, as by
the stir of the air from my friend's whisk of her train, descended upon me, my liberation was in a manner what I was
already tasting. Yet how I also felt, with it, something of the
threat of a chill to my curiosity! The taste of its being all over,
that really sublime success of the strained vision in which I had
been living for crowded hours—was this a taste that I was sure
I should particularly enjoy? Marked enough it was, doubtless,
that even in the stress of perceiving myself broken with I ruefully reflected on all the more, on the ever so much, I still
wanted to know!

Well, something of this quantity, in any case, would come,
since Mrs. Briss did want to speak to me. The suspense that remained with me, as I have indicated, was the special fresh one
she had just produced. It fed, for a little, positively, on that
survey of her fine retreating person to which I have confessed
that my eyes attached themselves. These seconds were naturally few, and yet my memory gathers from them something
that I can only compare, in its present effect, to the scent of a
strange flower, passed rapidly under my nose. I seem in other
words to recall that I received in that brush the very liveliest
impression that my whole adventure was to yield—the impression that is my reason for speaking of myself as having at the
juncture in question "studied" Mrs. Brissenden's back. Study
of a profound sort would appear needed in truth to account

for it. It was as handsome and affirmative that she at once met and evaded my view, but was not the affirmation (as distinguished from the handsomeness, which was a matter of stature and mass,) fairly downright and defiant? Didn't what I saw strike me as saying straight *at* me, as far as possible, "I *am* young—I am and I *will* be; see, *see* if I'm not; there, there, there!"—with "there's" as insistent and rhythmical as the undulations of her fleeing presence, as the bejewelled nod of her averted brow? If her face had not been hidden, should I not precisely have found myself right in believing that it looked, exactly, for those instants, dreadfully older than it had ever yet had to? The answer ideally cynical would have been: "Oh, any woman of your resources can look young with her back turned! But you've had to turn it to make that proclamation." She passed out of the room proclaiming, and I did stand there a little defeated, even though with her word for another chance at her. Was this word one that she would keep? I had got off—yes, to a certainty. But so too had not she?

Naturally, at any rate, I didn't stay planted; and though it seemed long it was probably for no great time after this that I roamed in my impatience. I was divided between the discourtesy of wishing the ladies would go to bed and the apprehension that if they did too soon go I might yet lose everything. Was Mrs. Briss waiting for more privacy, or was she only waiting for a complete escape? Of course, even while I asked myself that, I had to remember how much I was taking for granted on her part in the way of conscious motive. Still, if she had not a motive for escaping, why had she not had one, five minutes before, for coming to the point with me? This inquiry kept me hovering where she might at any instant find me, but that was not inconsistent with my presently passing, like herself, into another room. The first one I entered—there were great chains of them at Newmarch—showed me once more, at the end opposite the door, the object that all day had been, present or absent, most in my eyes, and that there now could be no fallacy in my recognising. Mrs. Server's unquenchable little smile had never yet been so far from quenched as when it recognised, on its own side, that I had just had time to note how Ford Obert was, for a change, taking it in. These two friends of mine appeared to have moved together, after the music, to the corner in which I should not have felt it as misrepresenting the matter to say that I surprised them. They owed nothing of the harmony that held them—unlike my other couple—to the constraint of a common seat; a small glazed table, a receptacle for minute objects of price, extended itself between them as if it had offered itself as an occasion for their drawing toward it a pair of low chairs; but their union had nevertheless such an air of accepted duration as led it slightly to puzzle me. This would have been a reason the more for not interrupting it even had I not peculiarly wished to respect it. It was grist to my mill somehow that something or other had happened as a consequence of which Obert had lost the impulse to repeat to me his odd invitation to intervene. He gave me no notice as I passed; the notice was all from his companion. It constituted, I felt, on her part, precisely as much and precisely as little of an invitation as it had constituted at the moment—so promptly following our arrival—of my first seeing them linked; which is but another way of saying that nothing in Mrs. Server appeared to acknowledge a lapse. It was nearly midnight, but she was again under arms; everything conceivable—or perhaps rather inconceivable—had passed between us before dinner, but her face was exquisite again in its repudiation of any reference.

Any reference, I saw, would have been difficult to *me*, had I unluckily been forced to approach her. What would have made the rare delicacy of the problem was that blankness itself was the most direct reference of all. I had, however, as I passed her by, a comprehension as inward as that with which I had watched Mrs. Briss's retreat. "*What* shall I see when I next see you?" was what I had mutely asked of Mrs. Briss; but "God grant I don't see *you* again at all!" was the prayer sharply determined in my heart as I left Mrs. Server behind me. I left her behind me for ever, but the prayer has not been answered. I did see her again; I see her now; I shall see her always; I shall continue to feel at moments in my own facial muscles the deadly little ache of her heroic grin. With this, however, I was not then to reckon, and my simple philosophy of the moment could be but to get out of the room. The result of that movement was that, two minutes later, at another doorway, but opening this time into a great corridor, I found myself arrested by a combination that should really have counted for me as the least of my precious anomalies, but that—as accident happened to protect me—I watched, so long as I might, with intensity. I should in this connection describe my eyes as yet again engaging the less scrutable side of the human figure, were it not that poor Briss's back, now presented to me beside his wife's—for these were the elements of the combination—had hitherto seemed to me the most eloquent of his aspects. It was when he presented his face that he looked, each time, older; but it was when he showed you, from behind, the singular stoop of his shoulders, that he looked oldest.

They had just passed the door when I emerged, and they receded, at a slow pace and with a kind of confidential nearness, down the long avenue of the lobby. Her head was always high and her husband's always low, so that I couldn't be sure—it might have been only my fancy—that the contrast of this habit was more marked in them than usual. If I had known nothing about them I should have just unimaginatively said that talk was all on one side and attention all on the other. I, of course, for that matter, *did* know nothing about them; yet I recall how it came to me, as my extemporised shrewdness hung in their rear, that I mustn't think anything too grossly simple of what might be taking place between them. My position was, in spite of myself, that of my having mastered enough possibilities to choose from. If one of these might be—for her face, in spite of the backward cock of her head, was turned to him—that she was looking her time of life straight *at* him and yet making love to him with it as hard as ever she could, so another was that he had been already so thoroughly got back into hand that she had no need of asking favours, that she was more splendid than ever, and that, the same poor Briss as before his brief adventure, he was only feeling afresh in his soul, as a response to her, the gush of the sacred fount. Presumptuous choice as to these alternatives failed, on my part, in time, let me say, to flower; it rose before me in time that, whatever might be, for the exposed instant, the deep note of their encounter, only one thing concerned me in it: its being wholly their own business. So for that I liberally let it go, passing into the corridor, but proceeding in the opposite sense and aiming at an issue which I judged I should reach before they would turn in their walk. I had not, however, reached it before I

caught the closing of the door furthest from me; at the sound
of which I looked about to find the Brissendens gone. They
had not remained for another turn, but had taken their course,
evidently, back to the principal drawing-room, where, no less
presumably, the procession of the ladies bedward was even
then forming. Mrs. Briss would fall straight into it, and I *had*
accordingly lost her. I hated to appear to pursue her, late in the
day as it may appear to affirm that I put my dignity before my
curiosity.

Free again, at all events, to wait or to wander, I lingered a
minute where I had stopped—close to a wide window, as it
happened, that, at this end of the passage, stood open to the
warm darkness and overhung, from no great height, one of the
terraces. The night was mild and rich, and though the lights
within were, in deference to the temperature, not too numerous, I found the breath of the outer air a sudden corrective to
the grossness of our lustre and the thickness of our medium,
our general heavy humanity. I felt its taste sweet, and while I
leaned for refreshment on the sill I thought of many things.
One of those that passed before me was the way that Newmarch and its hospitalities were sacrificed, after all, and much
more than smaller circles, to material frustrations. We were all
so fine and formal, and the ladies in particular at once so little
and so much clothed, so beflounced yet so denuded, that the
summer stars called to us in vain. We had ignored them in our
crystal cage, among our tinkling lamps; no more free really to
alight than if we had been dashing in a locked railway-train
across a lovely land. I remember asking myself if I mightn't
still take a turn under them, and I remember that on appealing
to my watch for its sanction I found midnight to have struck.
That then was the end, and my only real alternatives were bed
or the smoking-room. The difficulty with bed was that I was in
no condition to sleep, and the difficulty about rejoining the
men was that—definitely, yes—there was one of them I desired
not again to see. I felt it with sharpness as I leaned on the sill;
I felt it with sadness as I looked at the stars; I felt once more
what I had felt on turning a final back five minutes before, so
designedly, on Mrs. Server. I saw poor Briss as he had just
moved away from me, and I knew, as I had known in the other
case, that my troubled sense would fain feel I had practically

done with him. It would be well, for aught I could do *for* him, that I should have seen the last of him. What remained with me from that vision of his pacing there with his wife was the conviction that his fate, whatever it was, held him fast. It wouldn't let him go, and all I could ask of it now was that it should let *me*. I *would* go—I was going; if I had not had to accept the interval of the night I should indeed already have gone. The admonitions of that moment—only confirmed, I hasten to add, by what was still to come—were that I should catch in the morning, with energy, an earlier train to town than anyone else was likely to take, and get off alone by it, bidding farewell for a long day to Newmarch. I should be in small haste to come back, for I should leave behind me my tangled theory, no loose thread of which need I ever again pick up, in no stray mesh of which need my foot again trip. It was on my way to the place, in fine, that my obsession had met me, and it was by retracing those steps that I should be able to get rid of it. Only I must break off sharp, must escape all reminders by forswearing all returns.

That was very well, but it would perhaps have been better still if I had gone straight to bed. In that case I *should* have broken off sharp—too sharp to become aware of something that kept me a minute longer at the window and that had the instant effect of making me wonder if, in the interest of observation, I mightn't snap down the electric light that, playing just behind me, must show where I stood. I resisted this impulse and, with the thought that my position was in no way compromising, chanced being myself observed. I presently saw moreover that I was really not in evidence: I could take in freely what I had at first not been sure of, the identity of the figure stationed just within my range, but just out of that of the light projected from my window. One of the men of our company had come out by himself for a stroll, and the man was Gilbert Long. He had paused, I made out, in his walk; his back was to the house, and, resting on the balustrade of the terrace with a cigarette in his lips, he had given way to a sense of the fragrant gloom. He moved so little that I was sure—making no turn that would have made me draw back; he only smoked slowly in his place and seemed as lost in thought as I was lost in my attention to him. I scarce knew what this told me; all I felt was that, however slight the incident and small the evidence, it essentially fitted in. It had for my imagination a value, for my theory a price, and it in fact constituted an impression under the influence of which this theory, just impatiently shaken off, perched again on my shoulders. It was of the deepest interest to me to see Long in such detachment, in such apparent concentration. These things marked and presented him more than any had yet done, and placed him more than any yet in relation to other matters. They showed him, I thought, as serious, his situation as grave. I couldn't have said what they proved, but I was as affected by them as if they proved everything. The proof simply acted from the instant the vision of him alone there in the warm darkness was caught. It was just with all that was in the business that he *was*, that he had fitfully needed to be, alone. Nervous and restless after separating, under my eyes, from Mrs. Briss, he had wandered off to the smoking-room, as yet empty; *he* didn't know what to do either, and was incapable of bed and of sleep. He had observed the communication of the smoking-room with the terrace and had come out into the air; this was what suited him, and, with pauses and meditations, much, possibly, by this time to turn over, he prolonged his soft vigil. But he at last moved, and I found myself startled. I gave up watching and retraced my course. I felt, none the less, fairly humiliated. It had taken but another turn of an eye to re-establish all my connections.

I had not, however, gone twenty steps before I met Ford Obert, who had entered the corridor from the other end and was, as he immediately let me know, on his way to the smoking-room.

"Is everyone then dispersing?"

"Some of the men, I think," he said, "are following me; others, I believe—wonderful creatures!—have gone to array themselves. Others still, doubtless, have gone to bed."

"And the ladies?"

"Oh, they've floated away—soared aloft; to high jinks—isn't that the idea?—in their own quarters. Don't they too, at these hours, practise sociabilities of sorts? They make, at any rate, here, an extraordinary picture on that great staircase."

I thought a moment. "I wish I had seen it. But I do see it. Yes—splendid. Is the place wholly cleared of them?"

"Save, it struck me, so far as they may have left some 'black plume as a token'——"

"Not, I trust," I returned, "of any 'lie' their 'soul hath spoken!' But not one of them lingers?"

He seemed to wonder. "'Lingers?' For what?"

"Oh, I don't know—in this house!"

He looked at our long vista, still lighted—appeared to feel with me our liberal ease, which implied that unseen powers waited on our good pleasure and sat up for us. There is nothing like it in fact, the liberal ease at Newmarch. Yet Obert reminded me—if I needed the reminder—that I mustn't after all presume on it. "Was one of them to linger for *you?*"

"Well, since you ask me, it was what I hoped. But since you answer for it that my hope has not been met, I bow to a superior propriety."

"You mean you'll come and smoke with me? Do then come."

"What, if I do," I asked with an idea, "will you give me?"

"I'm afraid I can promise you nothing more that *I* deal in than a bad cigarette."

"And what then," I went on, "will you take from me?"

He had met my eyes, and now looked at me a little with a smile that I thought just conscious. "Well, I'm afraid I *can't* take any more——"

"Of the sort of stuff," I laughed, "you've already had? Sorry stuff, perhaps—a poor thing but mine own! Such as it is, I only ask to keep it for myself, and that isn't what I meant. I meant what flower will you gather, what havoc will you play——?"

"Well?" he said as I hesitated.

"Among superstitions that I, after all, cherish. *Mon siège est fait*—a great glittering crystal palace. How many panes will you reward me for amiably sitting up with you by smashing?"

It might have been my mere fancy—but it *was* my fancy—that he looked at me a trifle harder. "How on earth can I tell what you're talking about?"

I waited a moment, then went on: "Did you happen to count them?"

"Count whom?"

"Why, the ladies as they filed up. Was the number there?"

He gave a jerk of impatience. "Go and see for yourself!"

Once more I just waited. "But suppose I should find Mrs. Server——?"

"Prowling there on the chance of you? Well—I thought she was what you wanted."

"Then," I returned, "you *could* tell what I was talking about!" For a moment after this we faced each other without more speech, but I presently continued: "You didn't really notice if any lady stayed behind?"

"I think you ask too much of me," he at last brought out. "Take care of your ladies, my dear man, yourself! Go," he repeated, "and see."

"Certainly—it's better; but I'll rejoin you in three minutes." And while he went his way to the smoking-room I proceeded without more delay to assure myself, performing in the opposite sense the journey I had made ten minutes before. It was extraordinary what the sight of Long alone in the outer darkness had done for me: my expression of it would have been that it had put me "on" again at the moment of my decidedly feeling myself off. I believed that if I hadn't seen him I could now have gone to bed without seeing Mrs. Briss; but my renewed impression had suddenly made the difference. If that was the way he struck me, how might not, if I could get at her, she? And she might, after all, in the privacy at last offered us by empty rooms, be waiting for me. I went through them all, however, only to find them empty indeed. In conformity with the large allowances of every sort that were the law of Newmarch, they were still open and lighted, so that if I had believed in Mrs. Briss's reappearance I might conveniently, on the spot, have given her five minutes more. I am not sure, for that matter, that I didn't. I remember at least wondering if I mightn't ring somewhere for a servant and cause a question to be sent up to her. I didn't ring, but I must have lingered a little on the chance of the arrival of servants to extinguish lights and see the house safe. They had not arrived, however, by the time I again felt that I must give up.

XI

I GAVE up by going, decidedly, to the smoking-room, where several men had gathered and where Obert, a little apart from them, was in charmed communion with the bookshelves. They are wonderful, everywhere, at Newmarch, the book shelves, but he put a volume back as he saw me come in, and a moment later, when we were seated, I said to him again, as a recall of our previous passage, "Then you *could* tell what I was talking about!" And I added, to complete my reference, "Since you thought Mrs. Server was the person whom, when I stopped you, I was sorry to learn from you I had missed."

His momentary silence appeared to admit the connection I established. "Then you find you *have* missed her? She wasn't there for you?"

"There's no one 'there for me'; so that I fear that if you weren't, as it happens, here for me, my amusement would be quite at an end. I had, in fact," I continued, "already given it up as lost when I came upon you, a while since, in conversation with the lady we've named. At that, I confess, my prospects gave something of a flare. I said to myself that since *your* interest hadn't then wholly dropped, why, even at the worst, should mine? Yours *was* mine, wasn't it? for a little, this morning. Or was it mine that was yours? We exchanged, at any rate, some lively impressions. Only, before we had done, your effort dropped or your discretion intervened: you gave up, as none of your business, the question that had suddenly tempted us."

"And you gave it up too," said my friend.

"Yes, and it was on the idea that it was mine as little as yours that we separated."

"Well then?" He kept his eyes, with his head thrown back, on the warm bindings, admirable for old gilt and old colour, that covered the opposite wall.

"Well then, if I've correctly gathered that you're, in spite of our common renunciation, still interested, I confess to you that I am. I took my detachment too soon for granted. I haven't been detached. I'm not, hang me! detached now. And it's all because you were originally so suggestive."

"Originally?"

"Why, from the moment we met here yesterday—the moment of my first seeing you with Mrs. Server. The look you gave me then was really the beginning of everything. Everything"— and I spoke now with real conviction—"was traceably to spring from it."

"What do you mean," he asked, "by everything?"

"Well, this failure of detachment. What you said to me as we were going up yesterday afternoon to dress—what you said to me then is responsible for it. And since it comes to that," I pursued, "I make out for myself now that you're not detached either—unless, that is, simply detached from *me*. I had indeed a suspicion of that as I passed through the room there."

He smoked through another pause. "You've extraordinary notions of responsibility."

I watched him a moment, but he only stared at the books without looking round. Something in his voice had made me more certain, and my certainty made me laugh. "I see you *are* serious!"

But he went on quietly enough. "You've extraordinary notions of responsibility. I deny altogether mine."

"You *are* serious—you *are*!" I repeated with a gaiety that I meant as inoffensive and that I believe remained so. "But no matter. You're no worse than I."

"I'm clearly, by your own story, not half so bad. But, as you say, no matter. I don't care."

I ventured to keep it up. "Oh, don't you?"

His good nature was proof. "I don't care."

"Then why didn't you so much as look at me a while ago?"

"Didn't I look at you?"

"You know perfectly you didn't. Mrs. Server did—with her unutterable intensity; making me feel afresh, by the way, that I've never seen a woman compromise herself so little by proceedings so compromising. But though you saw her intensity, it never diverted you for an instant from your own."

He lighted before he answered this a fresh cigarette. "A man engaged in talk with a charming woman scarcely selects that occasion for winking at somebody else."

"You mean he contents himself with winking at *her*? My dear fellow, that wasn't enough for you yesterday, and it wouldn't have been enough for you this morning, among the impressions that led to our last talk. It was just the fact that you did wink, that you *had* winked, at me that wound me up."

"And what about the fact that you had winked at *me*? *Your* winks—come"—Obert laughed—"are portentous!"

"Oh, if we recriminate," I cheerfully said after a moment, "we agree."

"I'm not so sure," he returned, "that we agree."

"Ah, then, if we differ it's still more interesting. Because, you know, we didn't differ either yesterday or this morning."

Without hurry or flurry, but with a decent confusion, his thoughts went back. "I thought you said just now we did—recognising, as you ought, that you were keen about a chase of which I washed my hands."

"No—I wasn't keen. You've just mentioned that you remember my giving up. I washed my hands too."

It seemed to leave him with the moral of this. "Then, if our hands are clean, what are we talking about?"

I turned, on it, a little more to him, and looked at him so long that he had at last to look at me; with which, after holding his eyes another moment, I made my point. "Our hands are not clean."

"Ah, speak for your own!"—and as he moved back I might really have thought him uneasy. There was a hint of the same note in the way he went on: "I assure you I decline all responsibility. I see the responsibility as quite beautifully yours."

"Well," I said, "I only want to be fair. You were the first to bring it out that she was changed."

"Well, she isn't changed!" said my friend with an almost startling effect, for me, of suddenness. "Or rather," he immediately and incongruously added, "she *is*. She's changed back."

"'Back'?" It made me stare.

"Back," he repeated with a certain sharpness and as if to have done at last, for himself, with the muddle of it.

But there was that in me that could let him see he had far from done; and something, above all, told me now that he absolutely mustn't have before I had. I quickly moreover saw that I must, with an art, make him want not to. "Back to what she was when you painted her?"

He had to think an instant for this. "No—not quite to that."

"To what then?"

He tried in a manner to oblige me. "To something else."

It seemed so, for my thought, the gleam of something that fitted, that I was almost afraid of quenching the gleam by pressure. I must then get everything I could from him without asking too much. "You don't quite know to *what* else?"

"No—I don't quite know." But there was a sound in it, this time, that I took as the hint of a wish to know—almost a recognition that I might help him.

I helped him accordingly as I could and, I may add, as far as the positive flutter he had stirred in me suffered. It fitted—it fitted! "If her change is to something other, I suppose then a change back is not quite the exact name for it."

"Perhaps not." I fairly thrilled at his taking the suggestion as if it were an assistance. "She isn't at any rate what I thought her yesterday."

It was amazing into what depths this dropped for me and with what possibilities it mingled. "I remember what you said of her yesterday."

I drew him on so that I brought back for him the very words he had used. "She was so beastly unhappy." And he used them now visibly not as a remembrance of what he had said, but for the contrast of the fact with what he at present perceived; so that the value this gave for me to what he at present perceived was immense.

"And do you mean that that's gone?"

He hung fire, however, a little as to saying so much what he meant, and while he waited he again looked at me. "What do *you* mean? Don't you think so yourself?"

I laid my hand on his arm and held him a moment with a grip that betrayed, I daresay, the effort in me to keep my thoughts together and lose not a thread. It betrayed at once, doubtless, the danger of that failure and the sharp foretaste of success. I remember that with it, absolutely, I struck myself as knowing again the joy of the intellectual mastery of things unamenable, that joy of determining, almost of creating results, which I have already mentioned as an exhilaration attached to some of my plunges of insight. "It would take long to tell you what I mean."

The tone of it made him fairly watch me as I had been watching him. "Well, haven't we got the whole night?"

"Oh, it would take more than the whole night—even if we had it!"

"By which you suggest that we haven't it?"

"No—we haven't it. I want to get away."

"To go to bed? I thought you were so keen."

"I *am* keen. Keen is no word for it. I don't want to go to bed. I want to get away."

"To leave the house—in the middle of the night?"

"Yes—absurd as it may seem. You excite me too much. You don't know what you do to me."

He continued to look at me; then he gave a laugh which was not the contradiction, but quite the attestation, of the effect produced on him by my grip. If I had wanted to hold him I held him. It only came to me even that I held him too much. I felt this in fact with the next thing he said. "If you're too excited, then, to be coherent now, will you tell me to-morrow?"

I took time myself now to relight. Ridiculous as it may sound, I had my nerves to steady; which is a proof, surely, that for real excitement there are no such adventures as intellectual ones. "Oh, to-morrow I shall be off in space!"

"Certainly we shall neither of us be here. But can't we arrange, say, to meet in town, or even to go up together in such conditions as will enable us to talk?"

I patted his arm again. "Thank you for your patience. It's really good of you. Who knows if I shall be alive to-morrow? We *are* meeting. We *do* talk."

But with all I had to think of I must have fallen, on this, into the deepest of silences, for the next thing I remember is his returning: "We don't!" I repeated my gesture of reassurance, I conveyed that I should be with him again in a minute, and presently, while he gave me time, he came back to something of his own. "My wink, at all events, would have been nothing for any question between us, as I've just said, without yours. That's what I call your responsibility. It was, as we put the matter, the torch of your analogy——"

"Oh, the torch of my analogy!"

I had so groaned it—as if for very ecstasy—that it pulled him up, and I could see his curiosity as indeed reaffected. But he went on with a coherency that somewhat admonished me: "It was your making me, as I told you this morning, think over what you had said about Brissenden and his wife: it was *that*——"

"That made you think over"—I took him straight up—"what you yourself had said about our troubled lady? Yes, precisely. That *was* the torch of my analogy. What I showed you in the one case seemed to tell you what to look for in the other. You thought it over. I accuse you of nothing worse than of *having* thought it over. But you see what thinking it over does for it."

The way I said this appeared to amuse him. "I see what it does for *you*!"

"No, you don't! Not at all yet. That's just the embarrassment."

"Just whose?" If I had thanked him for his patience he showed that he deserved it. "Just yours?"

"Well, say mine. But when you do——!" And I paused as for the rich promise of it.

"When I do see where you are, you mean?"

"The only difficulty is whether you *can* see. But we must try. You've set me whirling round, but we must go step by step. Oh, but it's all in your germ!"—I kept that up. "If she isn't now beastly unhappy——"

"She's beastly happy?" he broke in, getting firmer hold, if not of the real impression he had just been gathering under my eyes, then at least of something he had begun to make out that my argument required. "Well, that *is* the way I see her difference. Her difference, I mean," he added, in his evident wish to work with me, "her difference from her other difference! There!" He laughed as if, also, he had found himself fairly fantastic. "Isn't *that* clear for you?"

"Crystalline—for *me*. But that's because I know why."

I can see again now the long look that, on this, he gave me. I made out already much of what was in it. "So then do I!"

"But how in the world——? I know, for myself, *how* I know."

"So then do I," he after a moment repeated.

"And can you tell me?"

"Certainly. By what I've already named to you—the torch of your analogy."

I turned this over. "You've made evidently an admirable use of it. But the wonderful thing is that you seem to have done so without having all the elements."

He on his side considered. "What do you call all the elements?"

"Oh, it would take me long to tell you!" I couldn't help laughing at the comparative simplicity with which he asked it. "That's the sort of thing we just now spoke of taking a day for. At any rate, such as they are, these elements," I went on, "I believe myself practically in possession of them. But what I don't quite see is how *you* can be."

Well, he was able to tell me. "Why in the world shouldn't your analogy have put me?" He spoke with gaiety, but with lucidity. "I'm not an idiot either."

"I see." But there was so much!

"Did you think I *was*?" he amiably asked.

"No. I see," I repeated. Yet I didn't, really, fully; which he presently perceived.

"You made me think of your view of the Brissenden pair till I could think of nothing else."

"Yes—yes," I said. "Go on."

"Well, as you had planted the theory in me, it began to bear fruit. I began to watch them. I continued to watch them. I did nothing but watch them."

The sudden lowering of his voice in this confession—as if it had represented a sort of darkening of his consciousness—again amused me. "You too? How then we've been occupied! For I, you see, have watched—or had, until I found you just now with Mrs. Server—everyone, everything *but* you."

"Oh, I've watched *you*," said Ford Obert as if he had then perhaps after all the advantage of me. "I admit that I made you out for myself to be back on the scent; for I thought I made you out baffled."

To learn whether I really had been was, I saw, what he would most have liked; but I also saw that he had, as to this, a scruple about asking me. What I most saw, however, was that to tell him I should have to understand. "What scent do you allude to?"

He smiled as if I might have fancied I could fence. "Why, the pursuit of the identification that's none of our business— the identification of her lover."

"Ah, it's as to that," I instantly replied, "you've judged me baffled? I'm afraid," I almost as quickly added, "that I must admit I *have* been. Luckily, at all events, it *is* none of our business."

"Yes," said my friend, amused on his side, "nothing's our business that we can't find out. I saw you hadn't found him. And what," Obert continued, "does he matter now?"

It took but a moment to place me for seeing that my companion's conviction on this point was a conviction decidedly to respect; and even that amount of hesitation was but the result of my wondering how he had reached it. "What, indeed?" I promptly replied. "But how did you see I had failed?"

"By seeing that I myself had. For I've been looking too. He isn't here," said Ford Obert.

Delighted as I was that he should believe it, I was yet struck by the complacency of his confidence, which connected itself again with my observation of their so recent colloquy. "Oh, for you to be so sure, has Mrs. Server squared you?"

"*Is* he here?" he for all answer to this insistently asked.

I faltered but an instant. "No; he isn't here. It's no thanks to one's scruples, but perhaps it's lucky for one's manners. I speak at least for mine. If you've watched," I pursued, "you've doubtless sufficiently seen what has already become of mine. He isn't here, at all events," I repeated, "and we must do without his identity. What, in fact, are we showing each other," I asked, "but that we *have* done without it?"

"*I* have!" my friend declared with supreme frankness and with something of the note, as I was obliged to recognise, of my own constructive joy. "I've done perfectly without it."

I saw in fact that he had, and it struck me really as wonderful. But I controlled the expression of my wonder. "So that if you spoke therefore just now of watching them——"

"I meant of course"—he took it straight up—"watching the Brissendens. And naturally, above all," he as quickly subjoined, "the wife."

I was now full of concurrence. "Ah, naturally, above all, the wife."

So far as was required it encouraged him. "A woman's lover doesn't matter—doesn't matter at least to anyone but himself, doesn't matter to you or to me or to her—when once she has given him up."

It made me, this testimony of his observation, show, in spite of my having by this time so counted on it, something of the vivacity of my emotion. "She *has* given him up?"

But the surprise with which he looked round put me back on my guard. "Of what else then are we talking?"

"Of nothing else, of course," I stammered. "But the way you see——!" I found my refuge in the gasp of my admiration.

"I do see. But"—he *would* come back to that—"only through your having seen first. You gave me the pieces. I've but put them together. You gave me the Brissendens—bound hand and foot; and I've but made them, in that sorry state, pull me through. I've blown on my torch, in other words, till, flaring and smoking, it has guided me, through a magnificent chiaroscuro of colour and shadow, out into the light of day."

I was really dazzled by his image, for it represented his personal work. "You've done more than I, it strikes me—and with less to do it with. If I gave you the Brissendens I gave you all I had."

"But all you had was immense, my dear man. The Brissendens are immense."

"Of course the Brissendens are immense! If they hadn't been immense they wouldn't have been—*nothing* would have been—anything." Then after a pause, "Your image is splendid," I went on—"your being out of the cave. But what is it exactly," I insidiously threw out, "that you *call* the 'light of day'?"

I remained a moment, however, not sure whether I had been too subtle or too simple. He had another of his cautions. "What do *you*——?"

But I was determined to make him give it me all himself, for it was from my not prompting him that its value would come. "You tell me," I accordingly rather crudely pleaded, "first."

It gave us a moment during which he so looked as if I asked too much, that I had a fear of losing all. He even spoke with some impatience. "If you really haven't found it for yourself, you know, I scarce see what you *can* have found."

Then I had my inspiration. I risked an approach to roughness, and all the more easily that my words were strict truth. "Oh, don't be afraid—greater things than yours!"

It succeeded, for it played upon his curiosity, and he visibly imagined that, with impatience controlled, he should learn what these things were. He relaxed, he responded, and the next moment I was in all but full enjoyment of the piece wanted to make all my other pieces right—right because of that special beauty in my scheme through which the whole depended so on each part and each part so guaranteed the whole. "What I call the light of day is the sense I've arrived at of her vision."

"Her vision?"—I just balanced in the air.

"Of what they have in common. *His*—poor chap's—extraordinary situation too."

"Bravo! And you see in that——?"

"What, all these hours, has touched, fascinated, drawn her. It has been an instinct with her."

"Bravissimo!"

It saw him, my approval, safely into port. "The instinct of sympathy, pity—the response to fellowship in misery; the sight of another fate as strange, as monstrous as her own."

I couldn't help jumping straight up—I stood before him. "So that whoever may have *been* the man, the man *now*, the actual man——"

"Oh," said Obert, looking, luminous and straight, up at me from his seat, "the man now, the actual man——!" But he stopped short, with his eyes suddenly quitting me and his words becoming a formless ejaculation. The door of the room, to which my back was turned, had opened, and I quickly looked round. It was Brissenden himself who, to my supreme surprise, stood there, with rapid inquiry in his attitude and face. I saw, as soon as he caught mine, that I was what he wanted, and, immediately excusing myself for an instant to Obert, I anticipated, by moving across the room, the need, on poor Briss's part, of my further demonstration. My whole sense of the situation blazed up at the touch of his presence, and even before I reached him it had rolled over me in a prodigious wave that I had lost nothing whatever. I can't begin to say how the fact of his appearance crowned the communication my interlocutor had just made me, nor in what a bright confusion of many things I found myself facing poor Briss. One of these things was precisely that he had never been so much poor Briss as at this moment. That ministered to the confusion as well as to the brightness, for if his being there at all renewed my sources and replenished my current—spoke all, in short, for my gain—so, on the other hand, in the light of what I had just had from Obert, his particular aspect was something of a shock. I can't present this especial impression better than by the mention of my instant certitude that what he had come for was to bring me a message and that somehow—yes, indubitably—this circumstance seemed to have placed him again at the very bottom of his hole. It was down in that depth that he let me see him—it was out of it that he delivered himself. Poor Briss! poor Briss!—I had asked myself before he spoke with what kindness enough I could meet him. Poor Briss! poor Briss!—I am not even now sure that I didn't first meet him by *that* irrepressible murmur. It was in it all for me that, thus, at midnight, he had traversed on his errand the length of the great dark house. I trod with him, over the velvet and the marble, through the twists and turns, among the glooms and glimmers and echoes, every inch of the way, and I don't know what humiliation, for him, was constituted there, between us, by his long pilgrimage. It was the final expression of his sacrifice.

"My wife has something to say to you."

"Mrs. Briss? Good!"—and I could only hope the candour of my surprise was all I tried to make it. "Is she with you there?"

"No, but she has asked me to say to you that if you'll presently be in the drawing-room she'll come."

Who could doubt, as I laid my hand on his shoulder, fairly patting it, in spite of myself, for applause—who could doubt where I would presently be? "It's most uncommonly good of both of you."

There was something in his inscrutable service that, making him almost august, gave my dissimulated eagerness the sound of a heartless compliment. *I* stood for the hollow chatter of the vulgar world, and he—oh, he was as serious as he was conscious; which was enough. "She says you'll know what she wishes—and she was sure I'd find you here. So I may tell her you'll come?"

His courtesy half broke my heart. "Why, my dear man, with all the pleasure——! So many thousand thanks. I'll be with her."

"Thanks to *you*. She'll be down. Good-night." He looked round the room—at the two or three clusters of men, smoking, engaged, contented, on their easy seats and among their popped corks; he looked over an instant at Ford Obert, whose eyes, I thought, he momentarily held. It was absolutely as if, for me, he were seeking such things—out of what was closing over him—for the last time. Then he turned again to the door, which, just not to fail humanly to accompany him a step, I had opened. On the other side of it I took leave of him. The passage, though there was a light in the distance, was darker than the smoking-room, and I had drawn the door to.

"Good-night, Brissenden. I shall be gone tomorrow before you show."

I shall never forget the way that, struck by my word, he let his white face fix me in the dusk. "'Show'? *What* do I show?"

I had taken his hand for farewell, and, inevitably laughing, but as the falsest of notes, I gave it a shake. "You show nothing! You're magnificent."

He let me keep his hand while things unspoken and untouched, unspeakable and untouchable, everything that had been between us in the wood a few hours before, were between us again. But so we could only leave them, and, with a short, sharp "Good-bye!" he completely released himself. With my hand on the latch of the closed door I watched a minute his retreat along the passage, and I remember the reflection that, before rejoining Obert, I made on it. I seemed perpetually, at Newmarch, to be taking his measure from behind.

Ford Obert has since told me that when I came back to him there were tears in my eyes, and I didn't know at the moment how much the words with which he met me took for granted my consciousness of them. "He looks a hundred years old!"

"Oh, but you should see his shoulders, always, as he goes off! *Two* centuries—ten! Isn't it amazing?"

It was so amazing that, for a little, it made us reciprocally stare. "I should have thought," he said, "that he would have been on the contrary——"

"Visibly rejuvenated? So should I. I must make it out," I added. "I *shall*."

But Obert, with less to go upon, couldn't wait. It was wonderful, for that matter—and for all I had to go upon—how I

myself could. I did so, at this moment, in my refreshed intensity, by the help of confusedly lighting another cigarette, which
I should have no time to smoke. "I should have thought," my
friend continued, "that he too might have changed back."

I took in, for myself, so much more of it than I could say!
"Certainly. You wouldn't have thought he would have changed
forward." Then with an impulse that bridged over an abyss of
connections I jumped to another place. "Was what you most
saw while you were there with *her*—was this that her misery,
the misery you first phrased to me, has dropped?"

"Dropped, yes." He was clear about it. "I called her beastly
unhappy to you though I even then knew that beastly unhap-
piness wasn't quite all of it. It was part of it, it was enough of
it; for she was—well, no doubt you could tell *me*. Just now, at
all events"—and recalling, reflecting, deciding, he used, with
the strongest effect, as he so often did in painting, the simplest
term—"just now she's all right."

"All right?"

He couldn't know how much more than was possible my
question gave him to answer. But he answered it on what he
had; he repeated: "All right."

I wondered, in spite of the comfort I took, as I had more
than once in life had occasion to take it before, at the sight of
the painter-sense deeply applied. My wonder came from the
fact that Lady John had also found Mrs. Server all right, and
Lady John had a vision as closed as Obert's was open. It didn't
suit my book for both these observers to have been affected in
the same way. "You mean you saw nothing whatever in her
that was the least bit strange?"

"Oh, I won't say as much as that. But nothing that was
more strange than that she *should* be—well, after all, all right."

"All there, eh?" I after an instant risked.

I couldn't put it to him more definitely than that, though
there was a temptation to try to do so. For Obert to have
found her all there an hour or two after I had found her all absent, made me again, in my nervousness, feel even now a trifle
menaced. Things *had*, from step to step, to hang together, and
just here they seemed—with all allowances—to hang a little
apart. My whole superstructure, I could only remember, reared
itself on my view of Mrs. Server's condition; but it was part of

my predicament—really equal in its way to her own—that I couldn't without dishonouring myself give my interlocutor a practical lead. The question of her happiness was essentially subordinate; what I stood or fell by was that of her faculty. But I couldn't, on the other hand—and remain "straight"—insist to my friend on the whereabouts of this stolen property. If he hadn't missed it in her for himself I mightn't put him on the track of it; since, with the demonstration he had before my eyes received of the rate at which Long was, as one had to call it, intellectually living, nothing would be more natural than that he should make the cases fit. Now my personal problem, unaltered in the least particular by anything, was for me to have worked to the end without breathing in another ear that Long had been her lover. That was the only thing in the whole business that was simple. It made me cling an instant the more, both for bliss and bale, to the bearing of this fact of Obert's insistence. Even as a sequel to his vision of her change, almost everything was wrong for her being all right except the one fact of my recent view, from the window, of the man un-named. I saw him again sharply in these seconds, and to notice how he still kept clear of our company was almost to add certi-tude to the presumption of his rare reasons. Mrs. Server's being now, by a wonderful turn, all right would at least decidedly offer to these reasons a basis. It would be something Long's absence would fit. It would supply ground, in short, for the possibility that, by a process not less wonderful, he himself was all wrong. If he *was* all wrong my last impression of him would be amply accounted for. If he was all wrong—if he, in any case, felt himself going so—what more consequent than that he should have wished to hide it, and that the most immediate way for this should have seemed to him, markedly gregarious as he usually was, to keep away from the smokers? It came to me unspeakably that he *was* still hiding it and *was* keeping away. How, accordingly, must he not—and must not Mrs. Briss—have been in the spirit of this from the moment that, while I talked with Lady John, the sight of these two seated to-gether had given me its message! But Obert's answer to my guarded challenge had meanwhile come. "Oh, when a woman's so clever——!"

That was all, with its touch of experience and its hint of

philosophy; but it was stupefying. She was already then positively again "so clever"? This was really more than I could as
yet provide an explanation for, but I was pressed; Brissenden
would have reached his wife's room again, and I temporised.
"It was her cleverness that held you so that when I passed you
couldn't look at me?"

He looked at me at present well enough. "I knew you were
passing, but I wanted precisely to mark for you the difference.
If you really want to know," the poor man confessed, "I was a
little ashamed of myself. I had given her away to you, you
know, rather, before."

"And you were bound you wouldn't do it again?"

He smiled in his now complete candour. "Ah, there was no
reason." Then he used, happily, to right himself, my own expression. "She was all there."

"I see—I see." Yet I really didn't see enough not to have for
an instant to turn away.

"Where are you going?" he asked.

"To do what Brissenden came to me for."

"But I don't *know*, you see, what Brissenden came to you
for."

"Well, with a message. She was to have seen me this
evening, but, as she gave me no chance, I was afraid I had lost
it and that, so rather awkwardly late, she didn't venture. But
what he arrived for just now, at her request, was to say she
does venture."

My companion stared. "At this extraordinary hour?"

"Ah, the hour," I laughed, "is no more extraordinary than
any other part of the business: no more so, for instance, than
this present talk of yours and mine. What part of the business
isn't extraordinary? If it *is*, at all events, remarkably late, that's
her fault."

Yet he not unnaturally, in spite of my explanation, continued
to wonder. "And—a—where is it then you meet?"

"Oh, in the drawing-room or the hall. So good-night."

He got up to it, moving with me to the door; but his mystification, little as I could, on the whole, soothe it, still kept me.
"The household sits up for you?"

I wondered myself, but found an assurance. "She must have

squared the household! And it won't probably take us very long."

His mystification frankly confessed itself, at this, plain curiosity. The ground of such a conference, for all the point I had given his ingenuity, simply baffled him. "Do you mean you propose to discuss with her——?"

"My dear fellow," I smiled with my hand on the door, "it's *she*—don't you see?—who proposes."

"But what in the world——?"

"Oh, *that* I shall have to wait to tell you."

"With all the other things?" His face, while he sounded mine, seemed to say that I must then take his expectation as serious. But it seemed to say also that he was—definitely, yes—more at a loss than consorted with being quite sure of me. "Well, it will make a lot, really——!" But he broke off. "You do," he sighed with an effort at resignation, "know more than I!"

"And haven't I admitted that?"

"I'll be hanged if you *don't* know who he is!" the poor fellow, for all answer, now produced.

He said it as if I had, after all, not been playing fair, and it made me for an instant hesitate. "No, I really don't know. But it's exactly what I shall perhaps now learn."

"You mean that what she has proposed is to *tell* you?"

His darkness had so deepened that I saw only now what I should have seen sooner—the misconception that, in my excessive estimate of the distance he had come with me, I had not at first caught. But it was a misconception that only enriched his testimony; it involved such a conviction of the new link between our two sacrificed friends that it immediately constituted for me the strongest light he would, in our whole talk, have thrown. Yes, he had not yet thrown so much as in this erroneous supposition of the source of my summons. It took me of course, at the same time, but a few seconds to remind myself again of the innumerable steps he had necessarily missed. His question meanwhile, rightly applied by my own thought, brought back to that thought, by way of answer, an immense suggestion, which moreover, for him too, was temporarily answer enough. "She'll tell me who he *won't* have been!"

He looked vague. "Ah, but *that*——"

"That," I declared, "will be luminous."

He made it out. "As a sign, you think, that he must be the very one she denies?"

"The very one!" I laughed; and I left him under this simple and secure impression that my appointment was with Mrs. Server.

XII

I WENT from one room to the other, but to find only, at first, as on my previous circuit, a desert on which the sun had still not set. Mrs. Brissenden was nowhere, but the whole place waited as we had left it, with seats displaced and flowers dispetalled, a fan forgotten on a table, a book laid down upon a chair. It came over me as I looked about that if she *had* "squared" the household, so large an order, as they said, was a sign sufficient of what I was to have from her. I had quite rather it were her doing—not mine; but it showed with eloquence that she had after all judged some effort or other to be worth her while. Her renewed delay moreover added to my impatience of mind in respect to the nature of this effort by striking me as already part of it. What, I asked myself, could be so much worth her while as to have to be paid for by so much apparent reluctance? But at last I saw her through a vista of open doors, and as I forthwith went to her—she took no step to meet me—I was doubtless impressed afresh with the "pull" that in social intercourse a woman always has. She was able to assume on the spot by mere attitude and air the appearance of having been ready and therefore inconvenienced. Oh, I saw soon enough that she was ready and that one of the forms of her readiness would be precisely to offer herself as having acted entirely to oblige me—to give me, as a sequel to what had already passed between us, the opportunity for which she had assured me I should thank her before I had done with her. Yet, as I felt sure, at the same time, that she had taken a line, I was curious as to how, in her interest, our situation could be worked. What it had originally left us with was her knowing I was wrong. I had promised her, on my honour, to be candid, but even if I were disposed to cease to contest her identification of Mrs. Server I was scarce to be looked to for such an exhibition of gratitude as might be held to repay her for staying so long out of bed. There were in short elements in the business that I couldn't quite clearly see handled as favours to me. Her dress gave, with felicity, no sign whatever of preparation for the night, and if, since our last words, she had stood with

any anxiety whatever before her glass, it had not been to remove a jewel or to alter the place of a flower. She was as much
under arms as she had been on descending to dinner—as fresh
in her array as if that banquet were still to come. She met me
in fact as admirably—that was the truth that covered every
other—as if she had been able to guess the most particular curiosity with which, from my end of the series of rooms, I advanced upon her.

A part of the mixture of my thoughts during these seconds
had been the possibility—absurd, preposterous though it looks
when phrased here—of some change in her person that would
correspond for me to the other changes I had had such keen
moments of flattering myself I had made out. I had just had
them over in the smoking-room, some of these differences,
and then had had time to ask myself if I were not now to be
treated to the vision of the greatest, the most wonderful, of all.
I had already, on facing her, after my last moments with Lady
John, seen difference peep out at me, and I had seen the impression of it confirmed by what had afterwards happened. It
had been in her way of turning from me after that brief passage; it had been in her going up to bed without seeing me
again; it had been once more in her thinking, for reasons of her
own, better of that; and it had been most of all in her sending
her husband down to me. Well, wouldn't it finally be, still more
than most of all——? But I scarce had known, at this point,
what grossness or what fineness of material correspondence to
forecast. I only had waited there with these general symptoms
so present that almost any further development of them occurred to me as conceivable. So much as this was true, but I
was after a moment to become aware of something by which I
was as strongly affected as if I had been quite unprepared. Yes,
literally, that final note, in the smoking-room, the note struck
in Obert's ejaculation on poor Briss's hundred years, had
failed to achieve for me a worthy implication. I was forced, after
looking at Grace Brissenden a minute, to recognise that my
imagination had not risen to its opportunity. The full impression took a minute—a minute during which she said nothing;
then it left me deeply and above all, as I felt, discernibly conscious of the prodigious thing, *the* thing, I had not thought
of. This it was that gave her such a beautiful chance not to

speak: she was so quite sufficiently occupied with seeing what I hadn't thought of, and with seeing me, to make up for lost time, breathlessly think of it while she watched me.

All I had at first taken in was, as I say, her untouched splendour; I don't know why that should have impressed me—as if it had been probable she would have appeared in her dressing-gown; it was the only thing to have expected. And it in fact plumed and enhanced her assurance, sustained her propriety, lent our belated interview the natural and casual note. But there was another service it still more rendered her: it so covered, at the first blush, the real message of her aspect, that she enjoyed the luxury—and I felt her enjoy it—of seeing my perception in arrest. Amazing, when I think of it, the number of things that occurred in these stayed seconds of our silence; but they are perhaps best represented by the two most marked intensities of my own sensation: the first the certitude that she had at no moment since her marriage so triumphantly asserted her defeat of time, and the second the conviction that I, losing with her while, as it were, we closed, a certain advantage I should never recover, had at no moment since the day before made so poor a figure on my own ground. Ah, it may have been only for six seconds that she caught me gaping at her renewed beauty; but six seconds, it was inevitable to feel, were quite enough for every purpose with which she had come down to me. She might have been a large, fair, rich, prosperous person of twenty-five; she was at any rate near enough to it to put me for ever in my place. It was a success, on her part, that, though I couldn't as yet fully measure it, there could be no doubt of whatever, any more than of my somehow paying for it. Her being there at all, at such an hour, in such conditions, became, each moment, on the whole business, more and more a part of her advantage; the case for her was really in almost any aspect she could now make it wear to my imagination. My wealth of that faculty, never so stimulated, was thus, in a manner, her strength; by which I mean the impossibility of my indifference to the mere immense suggestiveness of our circumstances. How can I tell now to what tune the sense of all these played into my mind?—the huge oddity of the nameless idea on which we foregathered, the absence and hush of everything except that idea, so magnified in consequence and yet still, after all, altogether fantastic. There remained for her, there spoke for her, too, her vividly "unconventional" step, the bravery of her rustling, on an understanding so difficult to give an account of, through places and times only made safe by the sleep of the unsuspecting. My imagination, in short, since I have spoken of it, couldn't do other than work for her from the moment she had, so simply yet so wonderfully, not failed me. Therefore it was all with me again, the vision of her reasons. They were in fact sufficiently in the sound of what she presently said. "Perhaps you don't know—but I mentioned in the proper quarter that I should sit up a little. They're of a kindness here, luckily——! So it's all right." It was all right, obviously—she made it so; but she made it so as well that, in spite of the splendour she showed me, she should be a little nervous. "We shall only take moreover," she added, "a minute."

I should perhaps have wondered more what she proposed to do in a minute had I not felt it as already more or less done. Yes, she might have been twenty-five, and it was a short time for *that* to have taken. However, what I clutched at, what I clung to, was that it was a nervous twenty-five. I might pay for her assurance, but wasn't there something of mine for which *she* might pay? I was nervous also, but, as I took in again, with a glance through our great chain of chambers, the wonderful conditions that protected us, I did my best to feel sure that it was only because I was so amused. That—in so high a form— was what it came to in the end. "I supposed," I replied, "that you'd have arranged; for, in spite of the way things were going, I hadn't given you up. I haven't understood, I confess," I went on, "why you've preferred a conference so intensely nocturnal —of which I quite feel, however, that, if it has happened to suit you, it isn't for me to complain. But I felt sure of you— that was the great thing—from the moment, half an hour ago, you so kindly spoke to me. I gave you, you see," I laughed, "what's called 'rope.'"

"I don't suppose you mean," she exclaimed, "for me to hang myself!—for that, I assure you, is not at all what I'm prepared for." Then she seemed again to give me the magnificence of her youth. It wasn't, throughout, I was to feel, that she at all had abysses of irony, for she in fact happily needed none. Her triumph was in itself ironic enough, and all her point in her sense of her freshness. "Were you really so impatient?" But as I inevitably hung fire a little she continued before I could answer; which somewhat helped me indeed by showing the one flaw in her confidence. More extraordinary perhaps than anything else, moreover, was just my perception of this; which gives the value of all that each of us so visibly felt the other to have put together, to have been making out and gathering in, since we parted, on the terrace, after seeing Mrs. Server and Briss come up from under their tree. We *had*, of a truth, arrived at our results—though mine were naturally the ones for me to believe in; and it was prodigious that we openly met not at all where we had last left each other, but exactly on what our subsequent suppressed processes had achieved. We hadn't named them—hadn't alluded to them, and we couldn't, no doubt, have done either; but they were none the less intensely there between us, with the whole bright, empty scene given up to them. Only she had her shrewd sense that mine, for reasons, might have been still more occult than her own. Hadn't I possibly burrowed the deeper—to come out in some uncalculated place behind her back? That was the flaw in her confidence. She had in spite of it her firm ground, and I could feel, to do her justice, how different a complacency it was from such smug ignorance as Lady John's. If I didn't fear to seem to drivel about my own knowledge I should say that she had, in addition to all the rest of her "pull," the benefit of striking me as worthy of me. She was *in* the mystic circle—not one of us more; she knew the size of it; and it was our now being in it alone together, with everyone else out and with the size greater than it had yet been at all—it was this that gave the hour, in fine, so sharp a stamp.

But she had meanwhile taken up my allusion to her having preferred so to wait. "I wanted to see you quietly; which was what I tried—not altogether successfully, it rather struck me at the moment—to make you understand when I let you know about it. You stared so that I didn't quite know what was the matter. Nothing could be quiet, I saw, till the going to bed was over, and I felt it coming off then from one minute to the other. I didn't wish publicly to be called away for it from this putting of our heads together, and, though you may think me absurd, I had a dislike to having our question of May up so

long as she was hanging about. I knew of course that she
would hang about till the very last moment, and that was what
I perhaps a little clumsily—if it was my own fault!—made the
effort to convey to you. She may be hanging about still," Mrs.
Briss continued, with her larger look round—her looks round
were now immense; "but at any rate I shall have done what I
could. I had a feeling—perfectly preposterous, I admit!—
against her seeing us together; but if she comes down again, as
I've so boldly done, and finds us, she'll have no one but herself
to thank. It's a funny house, for that matter," my friend ram-
bled on, "and I'm not sure that anyone *has* gone to bed. One
does what one likes; I'm an old woman, at any rate, and *I* do!"
She explained now, she explained too much, she abounded,
talking herself stoutly into any assurance that failed her. I had
meanwhile with every word she uttered a sharper sense of the
pressure, behind them all, of a new consciousness. It was full
of everything she didn't say, and what she said was no representation whatever of what was most in her mind. We had indeed taken a jump since noon—we had indeed come out
further on. Just this fine dishonesty of her eyes, moreover—
the light of a part to play, the excitement (heaven knows what
it struck me as being!) of a happy duplicity—may well have
been what contributed most to her present grand air.

It was in any case what evoked for me most the contrasted
image, so fresh with me, of the other, the tragic lady—the image that had so embodied the unutterable opposite of everything actually before me. What was actually before me was the
positive pride of life and expansion, the amplitude of conscious
action and design; not the arid channel forsaken by the stream,
but the full-fed river sweeping to the sea, the volume of water,
the stately current, the flooded banks into which the source
had swelled. There was nothing Mrs. Server had been able to
risk, but there was a rich indifference to risk in the mere carriage of Grace Brissenden's head. Her reference, for that
matter, to our discussed subject had the effect of relegating to
the realm of dim shades the lady representing it, and there was
small soundness in her glance at the possibility on the part of
this person of an anxious prowl back. There was indeed—there
could be—small sincerity in any immediate demonstration from
a woman so markedly gaining time and getting her advantages

in hand. The connections between the two, certainly, were indirect and intricate, but it was positive to me that, for the spiritual ear, my companion's words had the sound of a hard bump,
a contact from the force of which the weaker vessel might have
been felt to crack. At last, merciful powers, it was in pieces! The
shock of the brass had told upon the porcelain, and I fancied
myself for an instant facing Mrs. Briss over the damage—a
damage from which I was never, as I knew, to see the poor
banished ghost recover. As strange as anything was this effect
almost of surprise for me in the freedom of her mention of
"May." For what had she come to me, if for anything, but to
insist on her view of May, and what accordingly was more to
the point than to mention her? Yet it was almost already as if
to mention her had been to get rid of her. She was mentioned,
however, inevitably and none the less promptly, anew—even as
if simply to receive a final shake before being quite dropped.
My friend kept it up. "If you were so bent on not losing what
I might have to give you that you fortunately stuck to the ship,
for poor Briss to pick you up, wasn't this also"—she roundly
put it to me—"a good deal because you've been nursing all
day the grievance with which I this morning so comfortably
furnished you?"

I just waited, but fairly for admiration. "Oh, I certainly had
my reasons—as I've no less certainly had my luck—for not indeed deserting our dear little battered, but still just sufficiently
buoyant vessel, from which everyone else appears, I recognise,
to *s'être sauvé*. She'll float a few minutes more! But (before she
sinks!) do you mean by my grievance——"

"Oh, you know what I mean by your grievance!" *She* had no
intention, Mrs. Briss, of sinking. "I was to give you time to
make up your mind that Mrs. Server was our lady. You so resented, for some reason, my suggesting it that I scarcely believed you'd consider it at all; only I hadn't forgotten, when I
spoke to you a while since, that you had nevertheless handsomely promised me that you would do your best."

"Yes, and, still more handsomely, that if I changed my mind,
I would eat, in your presence, for my error, the largest possible
slice of humble pie. If you didn't see this morning," I continued, "quite why I should have cared so much, so I don't quite
see why, in your different way, *you* should; at the same time

that I do full justice to the good faith with which you've given me my chance. Please believe that if I *could* candidly embrace that chance I should feel all the joy in the world in repaying you. It's only, alas! because I cling to my candour that I venture to disappoint you. If I cared this morning it was really simple enough. You didn't convince me, but I should have cared just as much if you had. I only didn't see what *you* saw. I needed more than you could then give me. I knew, you see, what I needed—I mean before I struck! It was the element of collateral support that we both lacked. I couldn't do without it as you could. This was what I, clumsily enough, tried to show you I felt. You, on your side," I pursued, "grasped admirably the evident truth that that element *could* be present only in such doses as practically to escape detection." I kept it up as she had done, and I remember striking myself as scarce less excitedly voluble. I was conscious of being at a point at which I should have to go straight, to go fast, to go it, as the phrase is, blind, in order to go at all. I was also conscious—and it came from the look with which she listened to me and that told me more than she wished—I felt sharply, though but instinctively, in fine, that I should still, whatever I practically had lost, make my personal experience most rich and most complete by putting it definitely to her that, sorry as I might be not to oblige her, I had, even at this hour, no submission to make. I doubted in fact whether my making one *would* have obliged her; but I felt that, for all so much had come and gone, I was not there to take, for her possible profit, any new tone with her. She would sufficiently profit, at the worst, by the old. My old motive—old with the prodigious antiquity the few hours had given it—had quite left me; I seemed to myself to know little now of my desire to "protect" Mrs. Server. She was certainly, with Mrs. Briss at least, past all protection; and the conviction had grown with me, in these few minutes, that there was now no rag of the queer truth that Mrs. Briss hadn't secretly—by which I meant morally—handled. But I none the less, on a perfectly simple reasoning, stood to my guns, and with no sense whatever, I must add, of now breaking my vow of the morning. I had made another vow since then—made it to the poor lady herself as we sat together in the wood; passed my word to *her* that there was no approximation I pretended even to myself to have made. How then was I to pretend to Mrs. Briss, and what facts *had* I collected on which I could respectably ground an acknowledgment to her that I had come round to her belief? If I had "caught" our incriminated pair together—really together—even for three minutes, I would, I sincerely considered, have come round. But I was to have performed this revolution on nothing less, as I now went on to explain to her. "Of course if you've got new evidence I shall be delighted to hear it; and of course I can't help wondering whether the possession of it and the desire to overwhelm me with it aren't, together, the one thing you've been nursing till now."

Oh, how intensely she didn't like such a tone! If she hadn't looked so handsome I would say she made a wry face over it, though I didn't even yet see where her dislike would make her come out. Before she came out, in fact, she waited as if it were a question of dashing her head at a wall. Then, at last, she charged. "It's nonsense. I've nothing to tell you. I feel there's nothing in it and I've given it up."

I almost gaped—by which I mean that I looked as if I did—for surprise. "You agree that it's not she——?" Then, as she again waited, "It's *you* who've come round?" I insisted.

"To your doubt of its being May? Yes—I've come round."

"Ah, pardon me," I returned; "what I expressed this morning was, if I remember rightly, not at all a 'doubt,' but a positive, intimate conviction that was inconsistent with *any* doubt. I was emphatic—purely and simply—that I didn't see it."

She looked, however, as if she caught me in a weakness here. "Then why did you say to me that if you should reconsider——"

"You should handsomely have it from me, and my grounds? Why, as I've just reminded you, as a form of courtesy to you—magnanimously to help you, as it were, to feel as comfortable as I conceived you naturally would desire to feel in your own conviction. Only for that. And now," I smiled, "I'm to understand from you that, in spite of that immense allowance, you *haven't*, all this while, felt comfortable?"

She gave, on this, in a wonderful, beautiful way, a slow, simplifying headshake. "Mrs. Server isn't in it!"

The only way then to take it from her was that her concession was a prelude to something still better; and when I had given her time to see this dawn upon me I had my eagerness and I jumped into the breathless. "You've made out then who *is*?"

"Oh, I don't make out, you know," she laughed, "so much as you! *She* isn't," she simply repeated.

I looked at it, on my inspiration, quite ruefully—almost as if I now wished, after all, she were. "Ah, but, do you know? it really strikes me you make out marvels. You made out this morning quite what I couldn't. I hadn't put together anything so extraordinary as that—in the total absence of everything—it *should* have been our friend."

Mrs. Briss appeared, on her side, to take in the intention of this. "What do you mean by the total absence? When I made my mistake," she declared as if in the interest of her dignity, "I didn't think everything absent."

"I see," I admitted. "I see," I thoughtfully repeated. "And do you, then, think everything now?"

"I had my honest impression of the moment," she pursued as if she had not heard me. "There were appearances that, as it at the time struck me, fitted."

"Precisely"—and I recalled for her the one she had made most of. "There was in especial the appearance that she was at a particular moment using Brissenden to show whom she was not using. You felt *then*," I ventured to observe, "the force of that."

I ventured less than, already, I should have liked to venture; yet I none the less seemed to see her try on me the effect of the intimation that I was going far. "Is it your wish," she inquired with much nobleness, "to confront me, to my confusion, with my inconsistency?" Her nobleness offered itself somehow as such a rebuke to my mere logic that, in my momentary irritation, I might have been on the point of assenting to her question. This imminence of my assent, justified by my horror of her huge egotism, but justified by nothing else and precipitating everything, seemed as marked for these few seconds as if we each had our eyes on it. But I sat so tight that the danger passed, leaving my silence to do what it could for my manners. She proceeded meanwhile to add a very handsome account of her own. "You should do me the justice to recognise how little I need have spoken another word to you, and how little, also, this amiable explanation to you is in the interest of one's natural pride. It seems to me I've come to you here altogether in the interest of *yours.* You talk about humble pie, but I think that, upon my word—with all I've said to you —it's I who have had to eat it. The magnanimity you speak of," she continued with all her grandeur—"I really don't see, either, whose it is but mine. I don't see what account of anything I'm in any way obliged to give."

I granted it quickly and without reserve. "You're not obliged to give any—you're quite right: you do it only because you're such a large, splendid creature. I quite feel that, beside you"—I did, at least, treat myself to the amusement of saying —"I move in a tiny circle. Still, I won't have it"—I could also, again, keep it up—"that our occasion has nothing for you but the taste of abasement. You gulp your mouthful down, but hasn't it been served on gold plate? You've had a magnificent day—a brimming cup of triumph, and you're more beautiful and fresh, after it all, and at an hour when fatigue would be almost positively graceful, than you were even this morning, when you met me as a daughter of the dawn. That's the sort of sense," I laughed, "that must sustain a woman!" And I wound up on a complete recovery of my good-humour. "No, no. I thank you—thank you immensely. But I don't pity you. You can afford to lose." I wanted her perplexity—the proper sharp dose of it—to result both from her knowing and her not knowing sufficiently what I meant; and when I in fact saw how perplexed she could be and how little, again, she could enjoy it, I felt anew my private wonder at her having cared and dared to meet me. Where *was* enjoyment, for her, where the insolence of success, if the breath of irony could chill them? Why, since she was bold, should she be susceptible, and how, since she was susceptible, could she be bold? I scarce know what, at this moment, determined the divination; but everything, the distinct and the dim alike, had cleared up the next instant at the touch of the real truth. The certitude of the source of my present opportunity had rolled over me before we exchanged another word. The source was simply Gilbert Long, and she was there because he had directed it. This connection hooked itself, like a sudden picture and with a click that fairly resounded through our empty rooms, into the array of the other connections, to the immense enrichment, as it was easy to feel, of the occasion, and to the immense confirmation of the very idea that, in the course of the evening, I had come near dismissing from my mind as too fantastic even for the rest of the company it should enjoy there. What I now was sure of flashed back, at any rate, every syllable of sense I could have desired into the suggestion I had, after the music, caught from the juxtaposition of these two. Thus solidified, this conviction, it spread and spread to a distance greater than I could just then traverse under Mrs. Briss's eyes, but which, exactly for that reason perhaps, quickened my pride in the kingdom of thought I had won. I was really not to have felt more, in the whole business, than I felt at this moment that by my own right hand I had gained the kingdom. Long and she were together, and I was alone thus in face of them, but there was none the less not a single flower of the garden that my woven wreath should lack.

I must have looked queer to my friend as I grinned to myself over this vow; but my relish of the way I was keeping things together made me perhaps for the instant unduly rash. I cautioned myself, however, fortunately, before it could leave her —scared a little, all the same, even with Long behind her—an advantage to take, and, in infinitely less time than I have needed to tell it, I had achieved my flight into luminous ether and, alighting gracefully on my feet, reported myself at my post. I had in other words taken in both the full prodigy of the *entente* between Mrs. Server's lover and poor Briss's wife, and the finer strength it gave the last-named as the representative of their interest. I may add too that I had even taken time fairly not to decide which of these two branches of my vision—that of the terms of their intercourse, or that of their need of it— was likely to prove, in delectable retrospect, the more exquisite. All this, I admit, was a good deal to have come and gone while my privilege trembled, in its very essence, in the scale. Mrs. Briss had but a back to turn, and everything was over. She had, in strictness, already uttered what saved her honour, and her revenge on impertinence might easily be her withdrawing with one of her sweeps. I couldn't certainly in that case hurry after her without spilling my cards. As my accumulations of lucidity, however, were now such as to defy all leakage, I

promptly recognised the facilities involved in a superficial sacrifice; and with one more glance at the beautiful fact that she
knew the strength of Long's hand, I again went steadily and
straight. She was acting not only for herself, and since she had
another also to serve and, as I was sure, report to, I should sufficiently hold her. I knew moreover that I held her as soon as I
had begun afresh. "I don't mean that anything alters the fact
that you lose gracefully. It *is* awfully charming, your thus giving
yourself up, and yet, justified as I am by it, I can't help regretting a little the excitement I found it this morning to pull a different way from you. Shall I tell you," it suddenly came to me
to put to her, "what, for some reason, a man feels aware of?"
And then as, guarded, still uneasy, she would commit herself
to no permission: "That pulling against you also had its thrill.
You defended your cause. Oh," I quickly added, "I know—
who should know better?—that it was bad. Only—what shall I
say?—*you* weren't bad, and one had to fight. And then there
was what one was fighting for! Well, you're not bad now, either; so that you may ask me, of course, what more I want." I
tried to think a moment. "It isn't that, thrown back on the
comparative dullness of security, I find—as people have been
known to—my own cause less good: no, it isn't that." After
which I had my illumination. "I'll tell you what it is: it's the
come-down of ceasing to work with you!"

She looked as if she were quite excusable for not following
me. "To 'work'?"

I immediately explained. "Even fighting was working, for
we struck, you'll remember, sparks, and sparks were what we
wanted. There we are then," I cheerfully went on. "Sparks are
what we still want, and you've not come to me, I trust, with a
mere spent match. I depend upon it that you've another to
strike." I showed her without fear all I took for granted. "Who,
then, *has*?"

She was superb in her coldness, but her stare was partly blank.
"Who then has what?"

"Why, done it." And as even at this she didn't light I gave
her something of a jog. "You haven't, with the force of your
revulsion, I hope, literally lost our thread." But as, in spite of
my thus waiting for her to pick it up, she did nothing, I offered
myself as fairly stooping to the carpet for it and putting it back

in her hand. "Done what we spent the morning wondering at. Who then, if it isn't, certainly, Mrs. Server, *is* the woman who has made Gilbert Long—well, what you know?"

I had needed the moment to take in the special shade of innocence she was by this time prepared to show me. It was an innocence, in particular, in respect to the relation of anyone, in all the vast impropriety of things, to anyone. "I'm afraid I know nothing."

I really wondered an instant how she could expect help from such extravagance. "But I thought you just recognised that you do enjoy the sense of your pardonable mistake. You knew something when you knew enough to see you had made it."

She faced me as with the frank perception that, of whatever else one might be aware, I abounded in traps, and that this would probably be one of my worst. "Oh, I think one generally knows when one has made a mistake."

"That's all then I invite you—*a* mistake, as you properly call it—to allow me to impute to you. I'm not accusing you of having made fifty. You made none whatever, I hold, when you agreed with me with such eagerness about the striking change in him."

She affected me as asking herself a little, on this, whether vagueness, the failure of memory, the rejection of nonsense, mightn't still serve her. But she saw the next moment a better way. It all came back to her, but from so very far off. "The change, do you mean, in poor Mr. Long?"

"Of what other change—except, as you may say, your own —have you met me here to speak of? Your own, I needn't remind you, is part and parcel of Long's."

"Oh, my own," she presently returned, "is a much simpler matter even than that. My own is the recognition that I just expressed to you and that I can't consent, if you please, to your twisting into the recognition of anything else. It's the recognition that I know nothing of any other change. I stick, if you'll allow me, to my ignorance."

"I'll allow you with joy," I laughed, "if you'll let me stick to it *with* you. Your own change is quite sufficient—it gives us all we need. It will give us, if we retrace the steps of it, everything, everything!"

Mrs. Briss considered. "I don't quite see, do I? why, at this hour of the night, we should begin to retrace steps."

"Simply because it's the hour of the night you've happened, in your generosity and your discretion, to choose. I'm struck, I confess," I declared with a still sharper conviction, "with the wonderful charm of it for our purpose."

"And, pray, what do you call with such solemnity," she inquired, "our purpose?"

I had fairly recovered at last—so far from being solemn—an appropriate gaiety. "I can only, with positiveness, answer for mine! That has remained all day the same—to get at the truth: not, that is, to relax my grasp of that tip of the tail of it which you so helped me this morning to fasten to. If you've ceased to *care* to help me," I pursued, "that's a difference indeed. But why," I candidly, pleadingly asked, "*should* you cease to care?" It was more and more of a comfort to feel her imprisoned in her inability really to explain her being there. To show herself as she was explained it only so far as she could express that; which was just the freedom she could least take. "What on earth is between us, anyhow," I insisted, "but our confounded interest? That's only quickened, for me, don't you see? by the charming way you've come round; and I don't see how it can logically be anything less than quickened for yourself. We're like the messengers and heralds in the tale of Cinderella, and I protest, I assure you, against any sacrifice of our *dénoûment*. We've still the glass shoe to fit."

I took pleasure at the moment in my metaphor; but this was not the case, I soon enough perceived, with my companion. "How can I tell, please," she demanded, "what you consider you're talking about?"

I smiled; it was so quite the question Ford Obert, in the smoking-room, had begun by putting me. I hadn't to take time to remind myself how I had dealt with *him*. "And you knew," I sighed, "so beautifully, you glowed over it so, this morning!" She continued to give me, in every way, her disconnection from this morning, so that I had only to proceed: "You've not availed yourself of this occasion to pretend to me that poor Mr. Long, as you call him, is, after all, the same limited person——"

"That he always was, and that you, yesterday, so suddenly discovered him to have ceased to be?"—for with this she had waked up. But she was still thinking how she could turn it. "You see too much."

"Oh, I know I do—ever so much too much. And much as I see, I express only half of it—so you may judge!" I laughed. "But what will you have? I see what I see, and this morning, for a good bit, you did me the honour to do the same. I returned, also, the compliment, didn't I? by seeing something of what *you* saw. We put it, the whole thing, together, and we shook the bottle hard. I'm to take from you, after this," I wound up, "that what it contains is a perfectly colourless fluid?"

I paused for a reply, but they were not to come so happily as from Obert. "You talk too much!" said Mrs. Briss.

I met it with amazement. "Why, whom have I told?"

I looked at her so hard with it that her colour began to rise, which made me promptly feel that she wouldn't press that point. "I mean you're carried away—you're abused by a fine fancy: so that, with your art of putting things, one doesn't know where one is—nor, if you'll allow me to say so, do I quite think *you* always do. Of course I don't deny you're awfully clever. But you build up," she brought out with a regret so indulgent and a reluctance so marked that she for some seconds fairly held the blow—"you build up houses of cards."

I had been impatient to learn what, and, frankly, I was disappointed. This broke from me, after an instant, doubtless, with a bitterness not to be mistaken. "Long *isn't* what he seems?"

"Seems to whom?" she asked sturdily.

"Well, call it—for simplicity—to *me*. For you see"—and I spoke as to show *what* it was to see—"it all stands or falls by that."

The explanation presently appeared a little to have softened her. If it all stood or fell only by *that*, it stood or fell by something that, for her comfort, might be not so unsuccessfully disposed of. She exhaled, with the swell of her fine person, a comparative blandness—seemed to play with the idea of a smile. She had, in short, her own explanation. "The trouble with you is that you over-estimate the penetration of others. How can it approach your own?"

"Well, yours had for a while, I should say, distinct moments of keeping up with it. Nothing is more possible," I went on, "than that I do talk too much; but I've done so—about the question in dispute between us—only to *you*. I haven't, as I conceived we were absolutely not to do, mentioned it to anyone else, nor given anyone a glimpse of our difference. If you've not understood yourself as pledged to the same reserve, and have consequently," I went on, "appealed to the light of other wisdom, it shows at least that, in spite of my intellectual pace, you must more or less have followed me. What am I *not*, in fine, to think of your intelligence," I asked, "if, deciding for a resort to headquarters, you've put the question to Long himself?"

"The question?" She was straight out to sea again.

"Of the identity of the lady."

She slowly, at this, headed about. "To Long himself?"

XIII

I HAD felt I could risk such directness only by making it extravagant—by suggesting it as barely imaginable that she could so have played our game; and during the instant for which I had now pulled her up I could judge I had been right. It was an instant that settled everything, for I saw her, with intensity, with gallantry too, surprised but not really embarrassed, recognise that of course she must simply lie. I had been justified by making it so possible for her to lie. "It would have been a short cut," I said, "and even more strikingly perhaps—to do it justice—a bold deed. But it would have been, in strictness, a departure—wouldn't it?—from our so distinguished little compact. Yet while I look at you," I went on, "I wonder. Bold deeds are, after all, quite in your line; and I'm not sure I don't rather want not to have missed so much possible comedy. 'I have it for you from Mr. Long himself that, every appearance to the contrary notwithstanding, his stupidity is unimpaired'—isn't that, for the beauty of it, after all, what you've veraciously to give me?" We stood face to face a moment, and I laughed out. "The beauty of it would be great!"

I had given her time; I had seen her safely to shore. It was quite what I had meant to do, but she now took still better advantage than I had expected of her opportunity. She not only scrambled up the bank, she recovered breath and turned round. "Do you imagine he would have told me?"

It was magnificent, but I felt she was still to better it should I give her a new chance. "Who the lady really is? Well, hardly; and that's why, as you so acutely see, the question of your having risked such a step has occurred to me only as a jest. Fancy indeed"—I piled it up—" your saying to him: 'We're all noticing that you're so much less of an idiot than you used to be, and we've different views of the miracle'!"

I had been going on, but I was checked without a word from her. Her look alone did it, for, though it was a look that partly spoiled her lie, it—by that very fact—sufficed to my confidence. "I've not spoken to a creature."

It was beautifully said, but I felt again the abysses that the mere saying of it covered, and the sense of these wonderful things was not a little, no doubt, in my immediate cheer. "Ah, then, we're all right!" I could have rubbed my hands over it. "I mean, however," I quickly added, "only as far as that. I don't at all feel comfortable about your new theory itself, which puts me so wretchedly in the wrong."

"Rather!" said Mrs. Briss almost gaily. "Wretchedly indeed in the wrong!"

"Yet only—equally of course," I returned after a brief brooding, "if I come within a conceivability of accepting it. Are you conscious that, in default of Long's own word—equivocal as that word would be—you press it upon me without the least other guarantee?"

"And pray," she asked, "what guarantee had *you*?"

"For the theory with which we started? Why, our recognised fact. The change in the man. You may say," I pursued, "that I was the first to speak for him; but being the first didn't, in your view, constitute a weakness when it came to your speaking yourself for Mrs. Server. By which I mean," I added, "speaking against her."

She remembered, but not for my benefit. "Well, you then asked me *my* warrant. And as regards Mr. Long and your speaking against *him*——"

"Do you describe what I say as 'against' him?" I immediately broke in.

It took her but an instant. "Surely—to have made him out horrid."

I could only want to fix it. "'Horrid'——?"

"Why, having such secrets." She was roundly ready now. "Sacrificing poor May."

"But *you*, dear lady, sacrificed poor May! It didn't strike you as horrid *then*."

"Well, that was only," she maintained, "because you talked me over."

I let her see the full process of my taking—or not taking—this in. "And who is it then that—if, as you say, you've spoken to no one—has, as I may call it, talked you under?"

She completed, on the spot, her statement of a moment before. "Not a creature has spoken to me."

I felt somehow the wish to make her say it in as many ways

as possible—I seemed so to enjoy her saying it. This helped me to make my tone approve and encourage. "You've communicated so little with anyone!" I didn't even make it a question.

It was scarce yet, however, quite good enough. "So little? I've not communicated the least mite."

"Precisely. But don't think me impertinent for having for a moment wondered. What I should say to you if you had, you know, would be that you just accused me."

"Accused you?"

"Of talking too much."

It came back to her dim. "Are we accusing each other?"

Her tone seemed suddenly to put us nearer together than we had ever been at all. "Dear no," I laughed—"not each other; only with each other's help, a few of our good friends."

"A few?" She handsomely demurred. "But one or two at the best."

"Or at the worst!"—I continued to laugh. "And not even those, it after all appears, very much!"

She didn't like my laughter, but she was now grandly indulgent. "Well, I accuse no one."

I was silent a little; then I concurred. "It's doubtless your best line; and I really quite feel, at all events, that when you mentioned a while since that I talk too much you only meant too much to *you*."

"Yes—I wasn't imputing to you the same direct appeal. I didn't suppose," she explained, "that—to match your own supposition of *me*—you had resorted to May herself."

"You didn't suppose I had asked her?" The point was positively that she didn't; yet it made us look at each other almost as hard as if she did. "No, of course you couldn't have supposed anything so cruel—all the more that, as you knew, I had not admitted the possibility."

She accepted my assent; but, oddly enough, with a sudden qualification that showed her as still sharply disposed to make use of any loose scrap of her embarrassed acuteness. "Of course, at the same time, you yourself saw that your not admitting the possibility would have taken the edge from your cruelty. It's not the innocent," she suggestively remarked, "that we fear to frighten."

"Oh," I returned, "I fear, mostly, I think, to frighten *any* one. I'm not particularly brave. I haven't, at all events, in spite of my certitude, interrogated Mrs. Server, and I give you my word of honour that I've not had any denial from her to prop up my doubt. It still stands on its own feet, and it was its own battle that, when I came here at your summons, it was prepared to fight. Let me accordingly remind you," I pursued, "in connection with that, of the one sense in which you were, as you a moment ago said, talked over by me. I persuaded you apparently that Long's metamorphosis was not the work of Lady John. I persuaded you of nothing else."

She looked down a little, as if again at a trap. "You persuaded me that it was the work of somebody." Then she held up her head. "It came to the same thing."

If I had credit then for my trap it at least might serve. "The same thing as what?"

"Why, as claiming that it *was* she."

"Poor May—'claiming'? When I insisted it wasn't!"

Mrs. Brissenden flushed. "You didn't insist it wasn't anybody!"

"Why should I when I didn't believe so? I've left you in no doubt," I indulgently smiled, "of my beliefs. It was somebody —and it still is."

She looked about at the top of the room. "The mistake's now yours."

I watched her an instant. "Can you tell me then what one does to recover from such mistakes?"

"One thinks a little."

"Ah, the more I've thought the deeper I've sunk! And that seemed to me the case with you this morning," I added, "the more *you* thought."

"Well, then," she frankly declared, "I must have stopped thinking!"

It was a phenomenon, I sufficiently showed, that thought only could meet. "Could you tell me then at what point?"

She had to think even to do that. "At what point?"

"What in particular determined, I mean, your arrest? You surely didn't—launched as you were—stop short all of yourself."

She fronted me, after all, still so bravely that I believed her for an instant not to be, on this article, without an answer she could produce. The unexpected therefore broke for me when she fairly produced none. "I confess I don't make out," she simply said, "why you seem so little pleased that I agree with you."

I threw back, in despair, both head and hands. "But, you poor, dear thing, you don't in the *least* agree with me! You flatly contradict me. You deny my miracle."

"I don't believe in miracles," she panted.

"So I exactly, at this late hour, learn. But I don't insist on the name. Nothing *is*, I admit, a miracle from the moment one's on the track of the cause, which was the scent we were following. Call the thing simply my fact."

She gave her high head a toss. "If it's yours it's nobody else's!"

"Ah, there's just the question—if we could know all! But my point is precisely, for the present, that you do deny it."

"Of course I deny it," said Mrs. Briss.

I took a moment, but my silence held her. "Your 'of course' would be what I would again contest, what I would denounce and brand as the word too much—the word that spoils, were it not that it seems best, that it in any case seems necessary, to let all question of your consistency go."

On that I had paused, and, as I felt myself still holding her, I was not surprised when my pause had an effect. "You do let it go?"

She had tried, I could see, to put the inquiry as all ironic. But it was not all ironic; it was, in fact, little enough so to suggest for me some intensification—not quite, I trust, wanton—of her suspense. I should be at a loss to say indeed how much it suggested or half of what it told. These things again almost violently moved me, and if I, after an instant, in my silence, turned away, it was not only to keep her waiting, but to make my elation more private. I turned away to that tune that I literally, for a few minutes, quitted her, availing myself thus, superficially, of the air of weighing a consequence. I wandered off twenty steps and, while I passed my hand over my troubled head, looked vaguely at objects on tables and sniffed absently at flowers in bowls. I don't know how long I so lost myself, nor quite why—as I must for some time have kept it up—my companion didn't now really embrace her possible alternative of rupture and retreat. Or rather, as to her action in this last matter, I am, and was on the spot, clear: I knew at that moment how much *she* knew she must not leave me without having got

from me. It came back in waves, in wider glimpses, and produced in so doing the excitement I had to control. It could
not but be exciting to talk, as we talked, on the basis of those
suppressed processes and unavowed references which made
the meaning of our meeting so different from its form. We
knew ourselves—what moved me, that is, was that she knew
me—to mean, at every point, immensely more than I said or
than she answered; just as she saw me, at the same points,
measure the space by which her answers fell short. This made
my conversation with her a totally other and a far more interesting thing than any colloquy I had ever enjoyed; it had even
a sharpness that had not belonged, a few hours before, to my
extraordinary interview with Mrs. Server. She couldn't afford
to quarrel with me for catechising her; she couldn't afford not
to have kept, in her way, faith with me; she couldn't afford,
after inconceivable passages with Long, not to treat me as an
observer to be squared. She had come down to square me;
she was hanging on to square me; she was suffering and stam-
mering and lying; she was both carrying it grandly off and letting it desperately go: all, all to square me. And I caught
moreover perfectly her vision of her way, and I followed her
way even while I judged it, feeling that the only personal privilege I could, after all, save from the whole business was that of
understanding. I couldn't save Mrs. Server, and I couldn't save
poor Briss; I *could*, however, guard, to the last grain of gold,
my precious sense of their loss, their disintegration and their
doom; and it was for this I was now bargaining.

It was of giving herself away just enough not to spoil for me
my bargain over my treasure that Mrs. Briss's bribe would
consist. She would let me see as far as I would if she could feel
sure I would *do* nothing; and it was exactly in this question of
how much I might have scared my couple into the sense I *could*
"do" that the savour of my suspense most dwelt. I could have
made them uneasy, of course, only by making them fear my intervention; and yet the idea of their being uneasy was less
wonderful than the idea of my having, with all my precautions,
communicated to them a consciousness. This was so the last
thing I had wanted to do that I felt, during my swift excursion,
how much time I should need in the future for recovery of the
process—all of the finest wind-blown intimations, woven of

silence and secrecy and air—by which their suspicion would have throbbed into life. I could only, provisionally and sketchily, figure it out, this suspicion, as having, little by little—not with a sudden start—felt itself in the presence of my own, just as my own now returned the compliment. What came back to me, as I have said, in waves and wider glimpses, was the marvel of their exchange of signals, the phenomenon, scarce to be represented, of their breaking ground with each other. They both had their treasure to guard, and they had looked to each other with the instinct of help. They had felt, on either side, the victim possibly slip, and they had connected the possibility with an interest discernibly inspired in me by this personage, and with a relation discoverably established by that interest. It wouldn't have been a danger, perhaps, if the two victims hadn't slipped together; and more amazing, doubtless, than anything else was the recognition by my sacrificing couple of the opportunity drawn by my sacrificed from being conjoined in my charity. How could they know, Gilbert Long and Mrs. Briss, that actively to communicate a consciousness to my other friends had no part in my plan? The most I had dreamed of, I could honourably feel, was to assure myself of their independent possession of one. These things were with me while, as I have noted, I made Grace Brissenden wait, and it was also with me that, though I condoned her deviation, she must take it from me as a charity. I had presently achieved another of my full revolutions, and I faced her again with a view of her overture and my answer to her last question. The terms were not altogether what my pity could have wished, but I sufficiently kept everything together to have to see that there were limits to my choice. "Yes, I let it go, your change of front, though it vexes me a little—and I'll in a moment tell you why—to have to. But let us put it that it's on a condition."

"Change of front?" she murmured while she looked at me. "Your expressions are not of the happiest."

But I saw it was only again to cover a doubt. My condition, for her, was questionable, and I felt it would be still more so on her hearing what it was. Meanwhile, however, in spite of her qualification of it, I had fallen back, once and for all, on pure benignity. "It scarce matters if I'm clumsy when you're practically so bland. I wonder if you'll understand," I continued, "if I make you an explanation."

"Most probably," she answered, as handsome as ever, "not."

"Let me at all events try you. It's moreover the one I just promised; which was no more indeed than the development of a feeling I've already permitted myself to show you. I lose"—I brought it out—"by your agreeing with me!"

" 'Lose'?"

"Yes; because while we disagreed you were, in spite of that, on the right side."

"And what do you call the right side?"

"Well"—I brought it out again—"on the same side as my imagination."

But it gave her at least a chance. "Oh, your imagination!"

"Yes—I know what you think of it; you've sufficiently hinted how little that is. But it's precisely because you regard it as rubbish that I now appeal to you."

She continued to guard herself by her surprises. "Appeal? I thought you were on the ground, rather," she beautifully smiled, "of dictation."

"Well, I'm that too. I dictate my terms. But my terms are in themselves the appeal." I was ingenious but patient. "See?"

"How in the world can I see?"

" *Voyons*, then. Light or darkness, my imagination rides me. But of course if it's all wrong I want to get rid of it. You can't, naturally, help me to destroy the faculty itself, but you can aid in the defeat of its application to a particular case. It was because you so smiled, before, on that application, that I valued even my minor difference with you; and what I refer to as my loss is the fact that your frown leaves me struggling alone. The best thing for me, accordingly, as I feel, is to get rid altogether of the obsession. The way to do that, clearly, since *you've* done it, is just to quench the fire. By the fire I mean the flame of the fancy that blazed so for us this morning. What the deuce have you, for yourself, poured on it? Tell me," I pleaded, "and teach me."

Equally with her voice her face echoed me again. "Teach you?"

"To abandon my false gods. Lead me back to peace by the steps *you've* trod. By so much as they must have remained traceable to you, shall I find them of interest and profit. They must in fact be most remarkable: won't they even—for what *I* may find in them—be more remarkable than those we should now be taking together if we hadn't separated, if we hadn't pulled up?" That was a proposition I could present to her with candour, but before her absence of precipitation had permitted her much to consider it I had already followed it on. "You'll just tell me, however, that since I do pull up and turn back with you we shall just have *not* separated. Well, then, so much the better—I see you're right. But I want," I earnestly declared, "not to lose an inch of the journey."

She watched me now as a Roman lady at the circus may have watched an exemplary Christian. "The journey has been a very simple one," she said at last. "With my mind made up on a single point, it was taken at a stride."

I was all interest. "On a single point?" Then, as, almost excessively deliberate, she still kept me: "You mean the still commonplace character of Long's—a—consciousness?"

She had taken at last again the time she required. "Do you know what I think?"

"It's exactly what I'm pressing you to make intelligible."

"Well," said Mrs. Briss, "I think you're crazy."

It naturally struck me. "Crazy?"

"Crazy."

I turned it over. "But do you call that intelligible?"

She did it justice. "No: I don't suppose it *can* be so for you if you *are* insane."

I risked the long laugh which might have seemed that of madness. "'If I am' is lovely!" And whether or not it was the special sound, in my ear, of my hilarity, I remember just wondering if perhaps I mightn't be. "Dear woman, it's the point at issue!"

But it was as if she too had been affected. "It's not at issue for me now."

I gave her then the benefit of my stirred speculation. "It always happens, of course, that one is one's self the last to know. You're perfectly convinced?"

She not ungracefully, for an instant, faltered; but since I really would have it——! "Oh, so far as what we've talked of is concerned, perfectly!"

"And it's actually what you've come down then to tell me?"

"Just exactly what. And if it's a surprise to you," she added, "that I *should* have come down—why, I can only say I was prepared for anything."

"Anything?" I smiled.

"In the way of a surprise."

I thought; but her preparation was natural, though in a moment I could match it. "Do you know that's what I was too?"

"Prepared——?"

"For anything in the way of a surprise. But only *from* you," I explained. "And of course—yes," I mused, "I've got it. If I *am* crazy," I went on—"it's indeed simple."

She appeared, however, to feel, from the influence of my present tone, the impulse, in courtesy, to attenuate. "Oh, I don't pretend it's simple!"

"No? I thought that was just what you did pretend."

"I didn't suppose," said Mrs. Briss, "that you'd like it. I didn't suppose that you'd accept it or even listen to it. But I owed it to you——" She hesitated.

"You owed it to me to let me know what you thought of me even should it prove very disagreeable?"

That perhaps was more than she could adopt. "I owed it to myself," she replied with a touch of austerity.

"To let me know I'm demented?"

"To let you know I'm *not*." We each looked, I think, when she had said it, as if she had done what she said. "That's all."

"All?" I wailed. "Ah, don't speak as if it were so little. It's much. It's everything."

"It's anything you will!" said Mrs. Briss impatiently. "Good-night."

"Good-night?" I was aghast. "You leave me on it?"

She appeared to profess for an instant all the freshness of her own that she was pledged to guard. "I must leave you on something. I couldn't come to spend a whole hour."

"But do you think it's so quickly done—to persuade a man he's crazy?"

"I haven't expected to persuade you."

"Only to throw out the hint?"

"Well," she admitted, "it would be good if it could work in you. But I've told you," she added as if to wind up and have done, "what determined me."

"I beg your pardon"—oh, I protested! "That's just what you've not told me. The reason of your change——"

"I'm not speaking," she broke in, "of my change."

"Ah, but *I* am!" I declared with a sharpness that threw her back for a minute on her reserves. "It's your change," I again insisted, "that's the interesting thing. If I'm crazy, I must once more remind you, you were simply crazy *with* me; and how can I therefore be indifferent to your recovery of your wit or let you go without having won from you the secret of your remedy?" I shook my head with kindness, but with decision. "You mustn't leave me till you've placed it in my hand."

The reserves I had spoken of were not, however, to fail her. "I thought you just said that you let my inconsistency go."

"Your moral responsibility for it—perfectly. But how can I show a greater indulgence than by positively desiring to enter into its history? It's in that sense that, as I say," I developed, "I do speak of your change. There must have been a given moment when the need of it—or when, in other words, the truth of my personal state—dawned upon you. That moment is the key to your whole position—the moment for us to fix."

"Fix it," said poor Mrs. Briss, "when you like!"

"I had much rather," I protested, "fix it when *you* like. I want—you surely must understand if I want anything of it at all—to get it absolutely right." Then as this plea seemed still not to move her, I once more compressed my palms. "You *won't* help me?"

She bridled at last with a higher toss. "It wasn't with such views I came. I don't believe," she went on a shade more patiently, "I don't believe—if you want to know the reason—that you're really sincere."

Here indeed was an affair. "Not sincere—*I?*"

"Not properly honest. I mean in giving up."

"Giving up what?"

"Why, everything."

"Everything? Is it a question"—I stared—"of *that?*"

"You would if you *were* honest."

"Everything?" I repeated.

Again she stood to it. "Everything."

"But is that quite the readiness I've professed?"

"If it isn't then, what is?"

I thought a little. "Why, isn't it simply a matter rather of the renunciation of a confidence?"

"In your sense and your truth?" This, she indicated, was all she asked. "Well, what is that but everything?"

"Perhaps," I reflected, "perhaps." In fact, it no doubt was. "We'll take it then for everything, and it's as so taking it that I renounce. I keep nothing at all. Now do you believe I'm honest?"

She hesitated. "Well—yes, if you say so."

"Ah," I sighed, "I see you don't! What can I do," I asked, "to prove it?"

"You can easily prove it. You can let me go."

"Does it strike you," I considered, "that I should take your going as a sign of your belief?"

"Of what else, then?"

"Why, surely," I promptly replied, "my assent to your leaving our discussion where it stands would constitute a very different symptom. Wouldn't it much rather represent," I inquired, "a failure of belief on my own part in *your* honesty? If you can judge me, in short, as only pretending——"

"Why shouldn't you," she put in for me, "also judge *me*? What have I to gain by pretending?"

"I'll tell you," I returned, laughing, "if you'll tell me what *I* have."

She appeared to ask herself if she could, and then to decide in the negative. "If I don't understand you in any way, of course I don't in that. Put it, at any rate," she now rather wearily quavered, "that one of us has as little to gain as the other. I believe you," she repeated. "There!"

"Thanks," I smiled, "for the way you say it. If you don't, as you say, understand me," I insisted, "it's because you think me crazy. And if you think me crazy I don't see how you *can* leave me."

She presently met this. "If I believe you're sincere in saying you give up I believe you've recovered. And if I believe you've recovered I don't think you crazy. It's simple enough."

"Then why isn't it simple to understand me?"

She turned about, and there were moments in her embarrassment, now, from which she fairly drew beauty. Her awkwardness was somehow noble; her sense of her predicament was in itself young. "Is it *ever*?" she charmingly threw out.

I felt she must see at this juncture how wonderful I found her, and even that that impression—one's whole consciousness of her personal victory—was a force that, in the last resort, was all on her side. "It was quite worth your while, this sitting up to this hour, to show a fellow how you bloom when other women are fagged. If that was really, with the truth that we're so pulling about laid bare, what you did most want to show, why, then, you've splendidly triumphed, and I congratulate and thank you. No," I quickly went on, "I daresay, to do you justice, the interpretation of my tropes and figures *isn't* 'ever' perfectly simple. You doubtless *have* driven me into a corner with my dangerous explosive, and my only fair course must be therefore to sit on it till you get out of the room. I'm sitting on it now; and I think you'll find you can get out as soon as you've told me *this*. Was the moment your change of view dawned upon you the moment of our exchanging a while ago, in the drawing-room, our few words?"

The light that, under my last assurances, had so considerably revived faded in her a little as she saw me again tackle the theme of her inconstancy; but the prospect of getting rid of me on these terms made my inquiry, none the less, worth trying to face. "That moment?" She showed the effort to think back.

I gave her every assistance. "It was when, after the music, I had been talking to Lady John. You were on a sofa, not far from us, with Gilbert Long; and when, on Lady John's dropping me, I made a slight movement toward you, you most graciously met it by rising and giving me a chance while Mr. Long walked away."

It was as if I had hung the picture before her, so that she had fairly to look at it. But the point that she first, in her effort, took up was not, superficially, the most salient. "Mr. Long walked away?"

"Oh, I don't mean to say that that had anything to do with it."

She continued to think. "To do with what?"

"With the way the situation comes back to me now as possibly marking your crisis."

She wondered. "Was it a 'situation'?"

"That's just what I'm asking you. *Was* it? Was it *the* situation?" But she had quite fallen away again. "I remember the moment you mean—it was when I said I would come to you here. But why should it have struck you as a crisis?"

"It didn't in the least at the time, for I didn't then know you were no longer 'with' me. But in the light of what I've since learned from you I seem to recover an impression which, on the spot, was only vague. The impression," I explained, "of your taking a decision that presented some difficulty, but that was determined by something that had then—and even perhaps a little suddenly—come up for you. That's the point"—I continued to unfold my case—"on which my question bears. *Was* this 'something' your conclusion, then and there, that there's nothing in anything?"

She kept her distance. "'In anything'?"

"And that I could only be, accordingly, out of my mind? Come," I patiently pursued; "such a perception as that had, at some instant or other, to *begin*; and I'm only trying to aid you to recollect when the devil it did!"

"Does it particularly matter?" Mrs. Briss inquired.

I felt my chin. "That depends a little—doesn't it?—on what you mean by 'matter'! It matters for your meeting my curiosity, and that matters, in its turn, as we just arranged, for my releasing you. You may ask of course if my curiosity itself matters; but to that, fortunately, my reply can only be of the clearest. The satisfaction of my curiosity is the pacification of my mind. We've granted, we've accepted, I again press upon you, in respect to that precarious quantity, its topsy-turvy state. Only give me a lead; I don't ask you for more. Let me for an instant see play before me any feeble reflection whatever of the flash of new truth that unsettled you."

I thought for a moment that, in her despair, she would find something that would do. But she only found: "It didn't come in a flash."

I remained all patience. "It came little by little? It began then perhaps earlier in the day than the moment to which I allude? And yet," I continued, "we were pretty well on in the day, I must keep in mind, when I had your last news of your credulity."

"My credulity?"

"Call it then, if you don't like the word, your sympathy."

I had given her time, however, to produce at last something

that, it visibly occurred to her, might pass. "As soon as I was not with you—I mean with you personally—you *never* had my sympathy."

"Is my person then so irresistible?"

Well, she was brave. "It *was*. But it's not, thank God, now!"

"Then there we are again at our mystery! I don't think, you know," I made out for her, "it was my person, really, that gave its charm to my theory; I think it was much more my theory that gave its charm to my person. My person, I flatter myself, has remained through these few hours—hours of tension, but of a tension, you see, purely intellectual—as good as ever; so that if we're not, even in our anomalous situation, in danger from any such source, it's simply that my theory is dead and that the blight of the rest is involved."

My words were indeed many, but she plumped straight through them. "As soon as I was away from you I hated you."

"Hated *me*?"

"Well, hated what you call 'the rest'—hated your theory."

"I see. Yet," I reflected, "you're not at present—though you wish to goodness, no doubt, you *were*—away from me."

"Oh, I don't care now," she said with courage; "since—for you see I believe you—we're away from your delusions."

"You wouldn't, in spite of your belief,"—I smiled at her—"like to be a little further off yet?" But before she could answer, and because also, doubtless, the question had too much the sound of a taunt, I came up, as if for her real convenience, quite in another place. "Perhaps my idea—my timing, that is, of your crisis—is the result, in my mind, of my own association with that particular instant. It comes back to me that what I was most full of while your face signed to me and your voice then so graciously confirmed it, and while too, as I've said, Long walked away—what I was most full of, as a consequence of another go, just ended, at Lady John, was, once more, this same Lady John's want of adjustability to the character you and I, in our associated speculation of the morning, had so candidly tried to fit her with. I was still even then, you see, speculating—all on my own hook, alas!—and it had just rolled over me with renewed force that she was nothing whatever, not the least little bit, to our purpose. The moment, in other words, if you understand, happened to be one of *my* moments;

so that, by the same token, I simply wondered if it mightn't likewise have happened to be one of yours."

"It *was* one of mine," Mrs. Briss replied as promptly as I could reasonably have expected; "in the sense that—as you've only to consider—it was to lead more or less directly to these present words of ours."

If I had only to consider, nothing was more easy; but each time I considered, I was ready to show, the less there seemed left by the act. "Ah, but you had then *already* backed out. *Won't* you understand—for you're a little discouraging—that I want to catch you at the earlier stage?"

"To 'catch' me?" I had indeed expressions!

"Absolutely catch! Focus you under the first shock of the observation that was to make everything fall to pieces for you."

"But I've told you," she stoutly resisted, "that there was no 'first' shock."

"Well, then, the second or the third."

"There was no shock," Mrs. Briss magnificently said, "at all."

It made me somehow break into laughter. "You found it so natural then—and you so rather liked it—to make up your mind of a sudden that you had been steeped in the last intellectual intimacy with a maniac?"

She thought once more, and then, as I myself had just previously done, came up in another place. "I had at the moment you speak of wholly given up any idea of Lady John."

But it was so feeble it made me smile. "Of course you had, you poor innocent! You couldn't otherwise, hours before, have strapped the saddle so tight on another woman."

"I had given up everything," she stubbornly continued.

"It's exactly what, in reference to that juncture, I perfectly embrace."

"Well, even in reference to that juncture," she resumed, "you may catch me as much as you like." With which, suddenly, during some seconds, I saw her hold herself for a leap. "You talk of 'focussing,' but what else, even in those minutes, were you in fact engaged in?"

"Ah, then, you do recognise them," I cried—"those minutes?"

She took her jump, though with something of a flop. "Yes—as, consenting thus to be catechised, I cudgel my brain for your amusement—I do recognise them. I remember what I thought. You focussed—I felt you focus. I saw you wonder whereabouts, in what you call our associated speculation, I would by that time be. I asked myself whether you'd understand if I should try to convey to you simply by my expression such a look as would tell you all. By 'all' I meant the fact that, sorry as I was for you—or perhaps for myself—it had struck me as only fair to let you know as straight as possible that I was nowhere. That was why I stared so, and I of course couldn't explain to you," she lucidly pursued, "to whom my stare had reference."

I hung on her lips. "But you can *now*?"

"Perfectly. To Mr. Long."

I remained suspended. "Ah, but this is lovely! It's what I want."

I saw I should have more of it, and more in fact came. "You were saying just now what you were full of, and I can do the same. I was full of *him*."

I, on my side, was now full of eagerness. "Yes? He had left you full as he walked away?"

She winced a little at this renewed evocation of his retreat, but she took it as she had not done before, and I felt that with another push she would be fairly afloat. "He had reason to walk!"

I wondered. "What had you said to him?"

She pieced it out. "Nothing—or very little. But I had listened."

And to *what*?"

"To what he says. To his platitudes."

"His platitudes?" I stared. "Long's?"

"Why, don't you know he's a prize fool?"

I mused, sceptical but reasonable. "He *was*."

"He *is*!"

Mrs. Briss was superb, but, as I quickly felt I might remind her, there was her possibly weak judgment. "Your confidence is splendid; only mustn't I remember that your sense of the finer kinds of cleverness isn't perhaps absolutely secure? Don't you know?—you also, till just now, thought *me* a prize fool."

If I had hoped, however, here to trip her up, I had reckoned without the impulse, and even perhaps the example, that she properly owed to me. "Oh, no—not anything of that sort, you, at all. Only an intelligent man gone wrong."

I followed, but before I caught up, "Whereas Long's only a stupid man gone right?" I threw out.

It checked her too briefly, and there was indeed something of my own it brought straight back. "I thought that just what you told me, this morning or yesterday, was that you had never known a case of the conversion of an idiot."

I laughed at her readiness. Well, I had wanted to make her fight! "It's true it would have been the only one."

"Ah, you'll have to do without it!" Oh, she was brisk now. "And if you know what I think of him, you know no more than *he* does.

"You mean you told him?"

She hung fire but an instant. "I told him, practically—and it was in fact all I did have to say to him. It was enough, however, and he disgustedly left me on it. Then it was that, as you gave me the chance, I tried to telegraph you—to say to you on the spot and under the sharp impression: 'What on earth do you mean by your nonsense? It doesn't hold water!' It's a pity I didn't succeed!" she continued—for she had become almost voluble. "It would have settled the question, and I should have gone to bed."

I weighed it with the grimace that, I feared, had become almost as fixed as Mrs. Server's. "It would have settled the question perhaps; but I should have lost this impression of you."

"Oh, this impression of me!"

"Ah, but don't undervalue it: it's what I want! What was it then Long had said?"

She had it more and more, but she had it as nothing at all. "Not a word to repeat—you wouldn't believe! He does say nothing at all. One can't remember. It's what I mean. I tried him on purpose, while I thought of you. But he's perfectly stupid. I don't see how we can have fancied——!" I had interrupted her by the movement with which again, uncontrollably tossed on one of my surges of certitude, I turned away. *How* deep they must have been in together for her to have so at last gathered herself up, and in how doubly interesting a light, above all, it seemed to present Long for the future! That was, while I warned myself, what I most read in—literally an implication of the enhancement of this latter side of the prodigy. If his cleverness, under the alarm that, first stirring their consciousness but dimly, had so swiftly developed as to make next of each a mirror for the other, and then to precipitate for them, in some silence deeper than darkness, the exchange of recognitions, admissions and, as they certainly would have phrased it, tips— if his excited acuteness was henceforth to protect itself by dissimulation, what wouldn't perhaps, for one's diversion, be the new spectacle and wonder? I could in a manner already measure this larger play by the amplitude freshly determined in Mrs. Briss, and I was for a moment actually held by the thought of the possible finish our friend would find it in him to give to a represented, a fictive ineptitude. The sharpest jostle to my thought, in this rush, might well have been, I confess, the reflection that as it was I who had arrested, who had spoiled their unconsciousness, so it was natural they should fight against me for a possible life in the state I had given them instead. I had spoiled their unconsciousness, I had destroyed it, and it was consciousness alone that could make them effectively cruel. Therefore, if they were cruel, it was I who had determined it, inasmuch as, consciously, they could only want, they could only intend, to live. Wouldn't that question have been, I managed even now to ask myself, the very basis on which they had inscrutably come together? "It's life, you know," each had said to the other, "and I, accordingly, can only cling to mine. But you, poor dear—shall *you* give up?" "Give up?" the other had replied; "for what do you take me? I shall fight by your side, please, and we can compare and exchange weapons and manœuvres, and you may in every way count upon me."

That was what, with greater vividness, was for the rest of the occasion before me, or behind me; and that I had done it all and had only myself to thank for it was what, from this minute, by the same token, was more and more for me the inner essence of Mrs. Briss's attitude. I know not what heavy admonition of my responsibility had thus suddenly descended on me; but nothing, under it, was indeed more sensible than that practically it paralysed me. And I could only say to myself that this was the price—the price of the secret success, the lonely liberty and the intellectual joy. There were things that for so private and splendid a revel—that of the exclusive king with his Wagner opera—I could only let go, and the special torment of my case was that the condition of light, of the satisfaction of curiosity and of the attestation of triumph, was in this direct way the sacrifice of feeling. There was no point at which my assurance could, by the scientific method, judge itself complete enough not to regard feeling as an interference and, in consequence, as a possible check. If it had to go I knew well who went with it, but I wasn't there to save *them*. I was there to save my priceless pearl of an inquiry and to harden, to that end, my heart. I should need indeed all my hardness, as well as my brightness, moreover, to meet Mrs. Briss on the high level to which I had at last induced her to mount, and, even while I prolonged the movement by which I had momentarily stayed her, the intermission of her speech became itself for me a hint of the peculiar pertinence of caution. It lasted long enough, this drop, to suggest that her attention was the sharper for my having turned away from it, and I should have feared a renewed challenge if she hadn't, by good luck, presently gone on: "There's really nothing in him at all!"

XIV

I HAD faced her again just in time to take it, and I immediately made up my mind how best to do so. "Then I go utterly to pieces!"

"You shouldn't have perched yourself," she laughed—she could by this time almost coarsely laugh—"in such a preposterous place!"

"Ah, that's my affair," I returned, "and if I accept the consequences I don't quite see what you've to say to it. That I do accept them—so far as I make them out as not too intolerable and you as not intending them to be—that I do accept them is what I've been trying to signify to you. Only my fall," I added, "is an inevitable shock. You remarked to me a few minutes since that you didn't recover yourself in a flash. I differ from you, you see, in that *I* do; I take my collapse all at once. Here then I am. I'm smashed. I don't see, as I look about me, a piece I can pick up. I don't attempt to account for my going wrong; I don't attempt to account for yours with me; I don't attempt to account for anything. If Long *is* just what he always was it settles the matter, and the special clincher for us can be but your honest final impression, made precisely more aware of itself by repentance for the levity with which you had originally yielded to my contagion."

She didn't insist on her repentance; she was too taken up with the facts themselves. "Oh, but add to my impression everyone else's impression! Has anyone noticed anything?"

"Ah, I don't know what anyone has noticed. I haven't," I brooded, "ventured—as you know—to ask anyone."

"Well, if you had you'd have seen—seen, I mean, all they don't see. If they had been conscious they'd have talked."

I thought. "To me?"

"Well, I'm not sure to you; people have such a notion of what you embroider on things that they're rather afraid to commit themselves or to lead you on: they're sometimes in, you know," she luminously reminded me, "for more than they bargain for, than they quite know what to do with, or than they care to have on their hands."

I tried to do justice to this account of myself. "You mean I see so much?"

It was a delicate matter, but she risked it. "Don't you sometimes see horrors?"

I wondered. "Well, names are a convenience. People catch me in the act?"

"They certainly think you critical."

"And is criticism the vision of horrors?"

She couldn't quite be sure where I was taking her. "It isn't, perhaps, so much that you see them——"

I started. "As that I perpetrate them?"

She was sure now, however, and wouldn't have it, for she was serious. "Dear no—you don't perpetrate anything. Perhaps it would be better if you did!" she tossed off with an odd laugh. "But—always by people's idea—you like them."

I followed. "Horrors?"

"Well, you don't——"

"Yes——?"

But she wouldn't be hurried now. "You take them too much for what they are. You don't seem to want——"

"To come down on them strong? Oh, but I often do!"

"So much the better then."

"Though I do like—whether for that or not," I hastened to confess, "to look them first well in the face."

Our eyes met, with this, for a minute, but she made nothing of that. "When they *have* no face, then, you can't do it! It isn't at all events now a question," she went on, "of people's keeping anything back, and you're perhaps in any case not the person to whom it would first have come."

I tried to think then who the person would be. "It would have come to Long himself?"

But she was impatient of this. "Oh, one doesn't know what comes—or what doesn't—to Long himself! I'm not sure he's too modest to misrepresent—if he had the intelligence to play a part."

"Which he hasn't!" I concluded.

"Which he hasn't. It's to *me* they might have spoken—or to each other."

"But I thought you exactly held they *had* chattered in accounting for his state by the influence of Lady John."

She got the matter instantly straight. "Not a bit. That chatter was mine only—and produced to meet yours. There had so, by your theory, to be a woman——"

"That, to oblige me, you invented *her*? Precisely. But I thought——"

"You needn't have thought!" Mrs. Briss broke in. "I didn't invent her."

"Then what are you talking about?"

"I didn't invent her," she repeated, looking at me hard.

"She's true." I echoed it in vagueness, though instinctively again in protest; yet I held my breath, for this was really the point at which I felt my companion's forces most to have mustered. Her manner now moreover gave me a great idea of them, and her whole air was of taking immediate advantage of my impression. "Well, see here: since you've wanted it, I'm afraid that, however little you may like it, you'll have to take it. You've pressed me for explanations and driven me much harder than you must have seen I found convenient. If I've seemed to beat about the bush it's because I hadn't only myself to think of. One can be simple for one's self—one can't be, always, for others."

"Ah, to whom do you say it?" I encouragingly sighed; not even yet quite seeing for what issue she was heading.

She continued to make for the spot, whatever it was, with a certain majesty. "I should have preferred to tell you nothing more than what I *have* told you. I should have preferred to close our conversation on the simple announcement of my recovered sense of proportion. But you *have*, I see, got me in too deep."

"O–oh!" I courteously attenuated.

"You've made of me," she lucidly insisted, "too big a talker, too big a thinker, of nonsense."

"Thank you," I laughed, "for intimating that I trifle so agreeably."

"Oh, *you've* appeared not to mind! But let me then at last not fail of the luxury of admitting that *I* mind. Yes, I mind particularly. I may be bad, but I've a grain of gumption."

"'Bad'?" It seemed more closely to concern me.

"Bad I may be. In fact," she pursued at this high pitch and pressure, "there's no doubt whatever I *am*."

"I'm delighted to hear it," I cried, "for it was exactly something strong I wanted of you!"

"It *is* then strong"—and I could see indeed she was ready to satisfy me. "You've worried me for my motive and harassed me for my 'moment,' and I've had to protect others and, at the cost of a decent appearance, to pretend to be myself half an idiot. I've had even, for the same purpose—if you must have it—to depart from the truth; to give you, that is, a false account of the manner of my escape from your tangle. But now the truth shall be told, and others can take care of themselves!" She had so wound herself up with this, reached so the point of fairly heaving with courage and candour, that I for an instant almost miscalculated her direction and believed she was really throwing up her cards. It was as if she had decided, on some still finer lines, just to rub my nose into what I had been spelling out; which would have been an anticipation of my own journey's crown of the most disconcerting sort. I wanted my personal confidence, but I wanted nobody's confession, and without the journey's crown where *was* the personal confidence? Without the personal confidence, moreover, where was the personal honour? That would be really the single thing to which I could attach authority, for a confession might, after all, be itself a lie. Anybody, at all events, could fit the shoe to one. My friend's intention, however, remained but briefly equivocal; my danger passed, and I recognised in its place a still richer assurance. It was not the unnamed, in short, who were to be named. "Lady John *is* the woman."

Yet even this was prodigious. "But I thought your present position was just that she's *not*!"

"Lady John *is* the woman," Mrs. Briss again announced.

"But I thought your present position was just that nobody is!"

"Lady John *is* the woman," she a third time declared.

It naturally left me gaping. "Then there *is* one?" I cried between bewilderment and joy.

"A woman? There's *her*!" Mrs. Briss replied with more force than grammar. "I know," she briskly, almost breezily added, "that I said she wouldn't do (as I had originally said she would do better than anyone), when you a while ago mentioned her. But that was to save her."

"And you don't care now," I smiled, "if she's lost!"

She hesitated. "She *is* lost. But she can take care of herself."

I could but helplessly think of her. "I'm afraid indeed that, with what you've done with her, *I* can't take care of her. But why is she now to the purpose," I articulately wondered, "any more than she was?"

"Why? On the very system you yourself laid down. When we took him for brilliant, she couldn't be. But now that we see him as he is——"

"We can only see her also as *she* is?" Well, I tried, as far as my amusement would permit, so to see her; but still there were difficulties. "Possibly!" I at most conceded. "Do you owe your discovery, however, wholly to my system? My system, where so much made for protection," I explained, "wasn't intended to have the effect of exposure."

"It appears to have been at all events intended," my companion returned, "to have the effect of driving me to the wall; and the consequence of *that* effect is nobody's fault but your own."

She was all logic now, and I could easily see, between my light and my darkness, how she would remain so. Yet I was scarce satisfied. "And it's only on 'that effect'——?"

"That I've made up my mind?" She was positively free at last to enjoy my discomfort. "Wouldn't it be surely, if your ideas were worth anything, enough? But it isn't," she added, "only on that. It's on something else."

I had after an instant extracted from this the single meaning it could appear to yield. "I'm to understand that you *know*?"

"That they're intimate enough for anything?" She faltered, but she brought it out. "I know."

It was the oddest thing in the world for a little, the way this affected me without my at all believing it. It was preposterous, hang though it would with her somersault, and she had quite succeeded in giving it the note of sincerity. It was the mere sound of it that, as I felt even at the time, made it a little of a blow—a blow of the smart of which I was conscious just long enough inwardly to murmur: "What if she *should* be right?" She had for these seconds the advantage of stirring within me the memory of her having indeed, the day previous, at Paddington, "known" as I hadn't. It had been really on what she *then* knew that we originally started, and an element of our start had been that I admired her freedom. The form of it, at least—so beautifully had she recovered herself—was all there now. Well, I at any rate reflected, it wasn't the form that need trouble me, and I quickly enough put her a question that related only to the matter. "Of course if she is—it *is* smash!"

"And haven't you yet got used to its being?"

I kept my eyes on her; I traced the buried figure in the ruins. "She's good enough for a fool; and so"—I made it out—"is he! If he *is* the same ass—yes—they *might* be."

"*And* he is," said Mrs. Briss, "the same ass!"

I continued to look at her. "He would have no need then of her having transformed and inspired him."

"Or of her having *de*formed and idiotised herself," my friend subjoined.

Oh, how it sharpened my look! "No, no—she wouldn't need that."

"The great point is that *he* wouldn't!" Mrs. Briss laughed.

I kept it up. "She would do perfectly."

Mrs. Briss was not behind. "My dear man, she has *got* to do!"

This was brisker still, but I held my way. "Almost anyone would do."

It seemed for a little, between humour and sadness, to strike her. "Almost anyone *would*. Still," she less pensively declared, "we want the right one."

"Surely; the right one"—I could only echo it. "But how," I then proceeded, "has it happily been confirmed to you?"

It pulled her up a trifle. "'Confirmed'——?"

"That he's her lover."

My eyes had been meeting hers without, as it were, hers quite meeting mine. But at this there had to be intercourse. "By my husband."

It pulled *me* up a trifle. "Brissenden knows?"

She hesitated; then, as if at my tone, gave a laugh. "Don't you suppose I've told him?"

I really couldn't but admire her. "Ah—so you *have* talked!"

It didn't confound her. "One's husband isn't talk. You're cruel moreover," she continued, "to my joke. It was Briss, poor dear, who talked—though, I mean, only to me. *He* knows."

I cast about. "Since when?"

But she had it ready. "Since this evening."

Once more I couldn't but smile. "Just in time then! And the *way* he knows——?"

"Oh, the way!"—she had at this a slight drop. But she came up again. "I take his word."

"You haven't then asked him?"

"The beauty of it was—half an hour ago, upstairs—that I *hadn't* to ask. He came out with it himself, and *that*—to give you the whole thing—was, if you like, my moment. He dropped it on me," she continued to explain, "without in the least, sweet innocent, knowing what he was doing; more, at least, that is, than give her away."

"Which," I concurred, "was comparatively nothing!"

But she had no ear for irony, and she made out still more of her story. "He's simple—but he sees."

"And when he sees"—I completed the picture—"he luckily tells."

She quite agreed with me that it was lucky, but without prejudice to his acuteness and to what had been in him moreover a natural revulsion. "He has seen, in short; there comes some chance when one does. His, as luckily as you please, came this evening. If you ask me what it showed him you ask more than *I've* either cared or had time to ask. Do you consider, for that matter"—she put it to me—"that one does ask?" As her high smoothness—such was the wonder of this reascendancy— almost deprived me of my means, she was wise and gentle with me. "Let us leave it alone."

I fairly, while my look at her turned rueful, scratched my head. "Don't you think it a little late for that?"

"Late for everything!" she impatiently said. "But there you are."

I fixed the floor. There indeed I was. But I tried to stay there—just there only—as short a time as possible. Something, moreover, after all, caught me up. "But if Brissenden already knew——?"

"If he knew——?" She still gave me, without prejudice to her ingenuity—and indeed it was a part of this—all the work she could.

"Why, that Long and Lady John were thick?"

"Ah, then," she cried, "you admit they *are*!"

"Am I not admitting everything you tell me? But the more I admit," I explained, "the more I must understand. It's *to* admit, you see, that I inquire. If Briss came down with Lady John yesterday to oblige Mr. Long——"

"He didn't come," she interrupted, "to oblige Mr. Long!"

"Well, then, to oblige Lady John herself——"

"He didn't come to oblige Lady John herself!"

"Well, then, to oblige his clever wife——"

"He didn't come to oblige his clever wife! He came," said Mrs. Briss, "just to amuse himself. He *has* his amusements, and it's odd," she remarkably laughed, "that you should grudge them to him!"

"It would be odd indeed if I did! But put his proceeding," I continued, "on any ground you like; you described to me the purpose of it as a screening of the pair."

"I described to you the purpose of it as nothing of the sort. I didn't describe to you the purpose of it," said Mrs. Briss, "at all. I described to you," she triumphantly set forth, "the *effect* of it—which is a very different thing."

I could only meet her with admiration. "You're of an astuteness——!"

"Of course I'm of an astuteness! I *see* effects. And I saw that one. How much Briss himself had seen it is, as I've told you, another matter; and what he had, at any rate, quite taken the affair for was the sort of flirtation in which, if one is a friend to either party, and one's own feelings are not at stake, one may now and then give people a lift. Haven't I asked you before," she demanded, "if you suppose he would have given one had he had an idea where these people *are*?"

"I scarce know what you have asked me before!" I sighed; "and 'where they are' is just what you haven't told me."

"It's where my husband was so annoyed unmistakably to discover them." And as if she had quite fixed the point she passed to another. "He's peculiar, dear old Briss, but in a way by which, if one uses him—by which, I mean, if one depends on him—at all, one gains, I think, more than one loses. Up to a certain point, in any case that's the least a case for subtlety, he sees nothing at all; but beyond it—when once he does wake up—he'll go through a house. Nothing then escapes him, and what he drags to light is sometimes appalling."

"Rather," I thoughtfully responded—"since witness this occasion!"

"But isn't the interest of this occasion, as I've already suggested," she propounded, "simply that it makes an end, bursts a bubble, rids us of an incubus and permits us to go to bed in peace? I thank God," she moralised, "for dear old Briss to-night."

"So do I," I after a moment returned; "but I shall do so with still greater fervour if you'll have for the space of another question a still greater patience." With which, as a final movement from her seemed to say how much this was to ask, I had on my own side a certain exasperation of soreness for all I had to acknowledge—even were it mere acknowledgment—that she had brought rattling down. "Remember," I pleaded, "that you're costing me a perfect palace of thought!"

I could see too that, held unexpectedly by something in my tone, she really took it in. Couldn't I even almost see that, for an odd instant, she regretted the blighted pleasure of the pursuit of truth with me? I needed, at all events, no better proof either of the sweet or of the bitter in her comprehension than the accent with which she replied: "Oh, those who live in glass houses——"

"Shouldn't—no, I know they shouldn't—throw stones; and that's precisely why I don't." I had taken her immediately up, and I held her by it and by something better still. "You, from your fortress of granite, can chuck them about as you will! All the more reason, however," I quickly added, "that, before my frail, but, as I maintain, quite sublime structure, you honour me, for a few seconds, with an intelligent look at it. I seem myself to see it again, perfect in every part," I pursued, "even while I thus speak to you, and to feel afresh that, weren't the wretched accident of its weak foundation, it wouldn't have the shadow of a flaw. I've spoken of it in my conceivable regret," I conceded, "as already a mere heap of disfigured fragments; but that was the extravagance of my vexation, my despair. It's in point of fact so beautifully fitted that it comes apart piece by piece—which, so far as that goes, you've seen it do in the last quarter of an hour at your own touch, quite handing me the pieces, one by one, yourself and watching me stack them along the ground. They're not even in this state—see!" I wound up—"a pile of ruins!" I wound up, as I say, but only for long enough to have, with the vibration, the exaltation, of my eloquence, my small triumph as against her great one. "I should almost like, piece by piece, to hand them back to you." And this time I completed my figure. "I believe that, for the very charm of it, you'd find yourself placing them by your own sense in their order and rearing once more the splendid pile. Will you take just *one* of them from me again," I insisted, "and let me see if only to have it in your hands doesn't positively start you off? That's what I meant just now by asking you for another answer." She had remained silent, as if really in the presence of the rising magnificence of my metaphor, and it was not too late for the one chance left me. "There was nothing, you know, I had so fitted as your account of poor Mrs. Server when, on our seeing them, from the terrace, together below, you struck off your explanation that old Briss was *her* screen for Long."

"Fitted?"—and there was sincerity in her surprise. "I thought my stupid idea the one for which you had exactly no use!"

"I had no use," I instantly concurred, "for your stupid idea, but I had great use for your stupidly, alas! having it. *That* fitted beautifully," I smiled, "till the piece came out. And even now," I added, "I don't feel it quite accounted for."

"Their being there together?"

"No. Your not liking it that they were."

She stared. "Not liking it?"

I could see how little indeed she minded now, but I also kept the thread of my own intellectual history. "Yes. Your not liking it is what I speak of as the piece. I hold it, you see, up before you. What, artistically, would you do with it?"

But one might take a horse to water——! I held it up before her, but I couldn't make her look at it. "How do you know what I mayn't, or may, have liked?"

It did bring me to. "Because you were conscious of not telling me? Well, even if you didn't——!"

"That made no difference," she inquired with a generous derision, "because you could always imagine? Of course you could always imagine—which is precisely what is the matter with you! But I'm surprised at your coming to me with it once more as evidence of anything."

I stood rebuked, and even more so than I showed her, for she need, obviously, only decline to take one of my counters to deprive it of all value as coin. When she pushed it across I had but to pocket it again. "It *is* the weakness of my case," I feebly and I daresay awkwardly mused at her, "that any particular thing you don't grant me becomes straightway the strength of yours. Of course, however"—and I gave myself a shake—"I'm absolutely rejoicing (am I not?) in the strength of yours. The weakness of my own is what, under your instruction, I'm now going into; but don't you see how much weaker it will show if I draw from you the full expression of your indifference? How *could* you in fact care when what you were at the very moment urging on me so hard was the extravagance of Mrs. Server's conduct? That extravagance then proved her, to your eyes, the woman who had a connection with Long to keep the world off the scent of—though you maintained that in spite of the dust she kicked up by it she was, at a pinch, now and then to be caught with him. That instead of being caught with him she was caught only with Brissenden annoyed you naturally for the moment; but what was that annoyance compared to your appreciation of her showing—by undertaking your husband, of all people!—just the more markedly *as* extravagant?"

She had been sufficiently interested this time to follow me. "What was it indeed?"

I greeted her acquiescence, but I insisted. "And yet if she *is* extravagant—what do you do with it?"

"I thought you wouldn't hear of it!" she exclaimed.

I sought to combine firmness with my mildness. "What do you do with it?"

But she could match me at this. "I thought you wouldn't hear of it!"

"It's not a question of *my* dispositions. It's a question of her having been, or not been, for you 'all over the place,' and of everyone's also being, for you, on the chatter about it. You go by that in respect to Long—by your holding, that is, that nothing has been noticed; therefore mustn't you go by it in respect to *her*—since I understand from you that everything has?"

"Everything always is," Mrs. Briss agreeably replied, "in a place and a party like this; but so little—anything in particular—that, with people moving 'every which' way, it comes to the same as if nothing was. Things are not, also, gouged out to *your* tune, and it depends, still further, on what you mean by 'extravagant.'"

"I mean whatever you yourself meant."

"Well, I myself mean no longer, you know, what I did mean."

"She isn't then——?"

But suddenly she was almost sharp with me. "Isn't what?"

"What the woman we so earnestly looked for would have to be."

"All gone?" She had hesitated, but she went on with decision. "No, she isn't all gone, since there was enough of her left to make up to poor Briss."

"Precisely—and it's just what we saw, and just what, with her other dashes of the same sort, led us to have to face the question of her being—well, what I say. Or rather," I added, "what *you* say. That is," I amended, to keep perfectly straight, "what you say you *don't* say."

I took indeed too many precautions for my friend not to have to look at them. "Extravagant?" The irritation of the word had grown for her, yet I risked repeating it, and with the effect of its giving her another pause. "I tell you she *isn't* that!"

"Exactly; and it's only to ask you what in the world then she *is*."

"She's horrid!" said Mrs. Briss.

"'Horrid'?" I gloomily echoed.

"Horrid. It wasn't," she then developed with decision, "a 'dash,' as you say, 'of the same sort'—though goodness knows of what sort you mean: it wasn't, to be plain, a 'dash' at all." My companion *was* plain. "She settled. She stuck." And finally, as I could but echo her again: "She made love to him."

"But—a—really?"

"Really. That's how I knew."

I was at sea. "'Knew'? But you saw."

"I knew—that is I learnt—more than I saw. I knew she couldn't be gone."

It in fact brought light. "Knew it by *him*?"

"He told me," said Mrs. Briss.

It brought light, but it brought also, I fear, for me, another queer grimace. "Does he then regularly tell?"

"Regularly. But what he tells," she did herself the justice to declare, "is not always so much to the point as the two things I've repeated to you."

Their weight then suggested that I should have them over again. "His revelation, in the first place, of Long and Lady John?"

"And his revelation in the second"—she spoke of it as a broad joke—"of May Server and himself."

There was something in her joke that was a chill to my mind; but I nevertheless played up. "And what does he say that's further interesting about *that*?"

"Why, that she's awfully sharp."

I gasped—she turned it out so. "*She*—Mrs. Server?"

It made her, however, equally stare. "Why, isn't it the very thing you maintained?"

I felt her dreadful logic, but I couldn't—with my exquisite image all contrasted, as in a flash from flint, with this monstrosity—so much as entertain her question. I could only stupidly again sound it. "Awfully sharp?"

"You after all then now don't?" It was she herself whom the words at present described! "Then what on earth *do* you think?" The strange mixture in my face naturally made her ask it, but everything, within a minute, had somehow so given way under the touch of her supreme assurance, the presentation of her own now finished system, that I daresay I couldn't at the moment have in the least trusted myself to tell her. She left me, however, in fact, small time—she only took enough, with her negations arrayed and her insolence recaptured, to judge me afresh, which she did as she gathered herself up into the strength of twenty-five. I didn't after all—it appeared part of my smash—know the weight of her husband's years, but I knew the weight of my own. They might have been a thousand, and nothing but the sense of them would in a moment, I saw, be left me. "My poor dear, you *are* crazy, and I bid you good-night!"

Nothing but the sense of them—on my taking it from her without a sound and watching her, through the lighted rooms, retreat and disappear—*was* at first left me; but after a minute something else came, and I grew conscious that her verdict lingered. She had so had the last word that, to get out of its planted presence, I shook myself, as I had done before, from my thought. When once I had started to my room indeed—and to preparation for a livelier start as soon as the house should stir again—I almost breathlessly hurried. Such a last word—the word that put me altogether nowhere—was too unacceptable not to prescribe afresh that prompt test of escape to other air for which I had earlier in the evening seen so much reason. I *should* certainly never again, on the spot, quite hang together, even though it wasn't really that I hadn't three times her method. What I too fatally lacked was her tone.

THE WINGS OF THE DOVE

PREFACE

"THE WINGS OF THE DOVE," published in 1902, represents to my memory a very old—if I shouldn't perhaps rather say a very young—motive; I can scarce remember the time when the situation on which this long-drawn fiction mainly rests was not vividly present to me. The idea, reduced to its essence, is that of a young person conscious of a great capacity for life, but early stricken and doomed, condemned to die under short respite, while also enamoured of the world; aware moreover of the condemnation and passionately desiring to "put in" before extinction as many of the finer vibrations as possible, and so achieve, however briefly and brokenly, the sense of having lived. Long had I turned it over, standing off from it, yet coming back to it; convinced of what might be done with it, yet seeing the theme as formidable. The image so figured would be, at best, but half the matter; the rest would be all the picture of the struggle involved, the adventure brought about, the gain recorded or the loss incurred, the precious experience somehow compassed. These things, I had from the first felt, would require much working-out; that indeed was the case with most things worth working at all; yet there are subjects and subjects, and this one seemed particularly to bristle. It was formed, I judged, to make the wary adventurer walk round and round it—it had in fact a charm that invited and mystified alike that attention; not being somehow what one thought of as a "frank" subject, after the fashion of some, with its elements well in view and its whole character in its face. It stood there with secrets and compartments, with possible treacheries and traps; it might have a great deal to give, but would probably ask for equal services in return, and would collect this debt to the last shilling. It involved, to begin with, the placing in the strongest light a person infirm and ill—a case sure to prove difficult and to require much handling; though giving perhaps, with other matters, one of those chances for good taste, possibly even for the play of the very best in the world, that are not only always to be invoked and cultivated, but that are absolutely to be jumped at from the moment they make a sign.

Yes then, the case prescribed for its central figure a sick young woman, at the whole course of whose disintegration and the whole ordeal of whose consciousness one would have quite honestly to assist. The expression of her state and that of one's intimate relation to it might therefore well need to be discreet and ingenious; a reflexion that fortunately grew and grew, however, in proportion as I focussed my image—roundabout which, as it persisted, I repeat, the interesting possibilities and the attaching wonderments, not to say the insoluble mysteries, thickened apace. Why had one to look so straight in the face and so closely to cross-question that idea of making one's protagonist "sick"?—as if to be menaced with death or danger hadn't been from time immemorial, for heroine or hero, the very shortest of all cuts to the interesting state. Why should a figure be disqualified for a central position by the particular circumstance that might most quicken, that might crown with a fine intensity, its liability to many accidents, its consciousness of all relations? This circumstance, true enough, might disqualify it for many activities—even though we should have imputed to it the unsurpassable activity of passionate, of inspired resistance. This last fact was the real issue, for the way grew straight from the moment one recognised that the poet essentially *can't* be concerned with the act of dying. Let him deal with the sickest of the sick, it is still by the act of living that they appeal to him, and appeal the more as the conditions plot against them and prescribe the battle. The process of life gives way fighting, and often may so shine out on the lost ground as in no other connexion. One had had moreover, as a various chronicler, one's secondary physical weaklings and failures, one's accessory invalids—introduced with a complacency that made light of criticism. To Ralph Touchett in "The Portrait of a Lady," for instance, his deplorable state of health was not only no drawback; I had clearly been right in counting it, for any happy effect he should produce, a positive good mark, a direct aid to pleasantness and vividness. The reason of this moreover could never in the world have been his fact of sex; since men, among the mortally afflicted, suffer on the whole more overtly and more grossly than women, and resist with a ruder, an inferior strategy. I had thus to take *that* anomaly for what it was worth, and I give it here but as one of the ambigu-

ities amid which my subject ended by making itself at home
and seating itself quite in confidence.

With the clearness I have just noted, accordingly, the last
thing in the world it proposed to itself was to be the record
predominantly of a collapse. I don't mean to say that my
offered victim was not present to my imagination, constantly,
as dragged by a greater force than any she herself could exert;
she had been given me from far back as contesting every inch
of the road, as catching at every object the grasp of which
might make for delay, as clutching these things to the last moment of her strength. Such an attitude and such movements,
the passion they expressed and the success they in fact represented, what were they in truth but the soul of drama?—
which is the portrayal, as we know, of a catastrophe determined in spite of oppositions. My young woman would *herself*
be the opposition—to the catastrophe announced by the associated Fates, powers conspiring to a sinister end and, with
their command of means, finally achieving it, yet in such straits
really to *stifle* the sacred spark that, obviously, a creature so animated, an adversary so subtle, couldn't but be felt worthy,
under whatever weaknesses, of the foreground and the lime-
light. She would meanwhile wish, moreover, all along, to live
for particular things, she would found her struggle on particular human interests, which would inevitably determine, in respect to her, the attitude of other persons, persons affected in
such a manner as to make them part of the action. If her impulse to wrest from her shrinking hour still as much of the
fruit of life as possible, if this longing can take effect only by
the aid of others, their participation (appealed to, entangled
and coerced as they find themselves) becomes their drama
too—that of their promoting her illusion, under her importunity, for reasons, for interests and advantages, from motives
and points of view, of their own. Some of these promptings,
evidently, would be of the highest order—others doubtless
mightn't; but they would make up together, for her, contribu-
tively, her sum of experience, represent to her somehow, in
good faith or in bad, what she should have *known*. Somehow,
too, at such a rate, one would see the persons subject to them
drawn in as by some pool of a Lorelei—see them terrified and
tempted and charmed; bribed away, it may even be, from

more prescribed and natural orbits, inheriting from their connexion with her strange difficulties and still stranger opportunities, confronted with rare questions and called upon for new discriminations. Thus the scheme of her situation would, in a comprehensive way, see itself constituted; the rest of the interest would be in the number and nature of the particulars. Strong among these, naturally, the need that life should, apart from her infirmity, present itself to our young woman as quite dazzlingly liveable, and that if the great pang for her is in what she must give up we shall appreciate it the more from the sight of all she has.

One would see her then as possessed of all things, all but the single most precious assurance; freedom and money and a mobile mind and personal charm, the power to interest and attach; attributes, each one, enhancing the value of a future. From the moment his imagination began to deal with her at close quarters, in fact, nothing could more engage her designer than to work out the detail of her perfect rightness for her part; nothing above all more solicit him than to recognise fifty reasons for her national and social status. She should be the last fine flower—blooming alone, for the fullest attestation of her freedom—of an "old" New York stem; the happy congruities thus preserved for her being matters, however, that I may not now go into, and this even though the fine association that shall yet elsewhere await me is of a sort, at the best, rather to defy than to encourage exact expression. There goes with it, for the heroine of "The Wings of the Dove," a strong and special implication of liberty, liberty of action, of choice, of appreciation, of contact—proceeding from sources that provide better for large independence, I think, than any other conditions in the world—and this would be in particular what we should feel ourselves deeply concerned with. I had from far back mentally projected a certain sort of young American as more the "heir of all the ages" than any other young person whatever (and precisely on those grounds I have just glanced at but to pass them by for the moment); so that here was a chance to confer on some such figure a supremely touching value. To be the heir of all the ages only to know yourself, as that consciousness should deepen, balked of your inheritance, would be to play the part, it struck me, or at least to arrive at the type, in the light on the whole the most becoming. Otherwise, truly, what a perilous part to play *out*—what a suspicion of "swagger" in positively attempting it! So at least I could reason—so I even think I *had* to—to keep my subject to a decent compactness. For already, from an early stage, it had begun richly to people itself: the difficulty was to see whom the situation I had primarily projected might, by this, that or the other turn, *not* draw in. My business was to watch its turns as the fond parent watches a child perched, for its first riding-lesson, in the saddle; yet its interest, I had all the while to recall, was just in its making, on such a scale, for developments.

What one had discerned, at all events, from an early stage, was that a young person so devoted and exposed, a creature with her security hanging so by a hair, couldn't but fall somehow into some abysmal trap—this being, dramatically speaking, what such a situation most naturally implied and imposed. Didn't the truth and a great part of the interest also reside in the appearance that she would constitute for others (given her passionate yearning to live while she might) a complication as great as any they might constitute for herself?—which is what I mean when I speak of such matters as "natural." They would be as natural, these tragic, pathetic, ironic, these indeed for the most part sinister, liabilities, to her living associates, as they could be to herself as prime subject. If her story was to consist, as it could so little help doing, of her being let in, as we say, for this, that and the other irreducible anxiety, how could she not have put a premium on the acquisition, by any close sharer of her life, of a consciousness similarly embarrassed? I have named the Rhine-maiden, but our young friend's existence would create rather, all round her, very much that whirlpool movement of the waters produced by the sinking of a big vessel or the failure of a great business; when we figure to ourselves the strong narrowing eddies, the immense force of suction, the general engulfment that, for any neighbouring object, makes immersion inevitable. I need scarce say, however, that in spite of these communities of doom I saw the main dramatic complication much more prepared *for* my vessel of sensibility than by her—the work of other hands (though with her own imbrued too, after all, in the measure of their never not being, in some direction, generous and extravagant, and thereby provoking).

The great point was, at all events, that if in a predicament she was to be, accordingly, it would be of the essence to create the predicament promptly and build it up solidly, so that it should have for us as much as possible its ominous air of awaiting her. That reflexion I found, betimes, not less inspiring than urgent; one begins so, in such a business, by looking about for one's compositional key, unable as one can only be to move till one has found it. To start without it is to pretend to enter the train and, still more, to remain in one's seat, without a ticket. Well—in the steady light and for the continued charm of these verifications—I had secured my ticket over the tolerably long line laid down for "The Wings of the Dove" from the moment I had noted that there could be no full presentation of Milly Theale as *engaged* with elements amid which she was to draw her breath in such pain, should not the elements have been, with all solicitude, duly prefigured. If one had seen that her stricken state was but half her case, the correlative half being the state of others as affected by her (they too should have a "case," bless them, quite as much as she!) then I was free to choose, as it were, the half with which I should begin. If, as I had fondly noted, the little world determined for her was to "bristle"—I delighted in the term!—with meanings, so, by the same token, could I but make my medal hang free, its obverse and its reverse, its face and its back, would beautifully become optional for the spectator. I somehow wanted them correspondingly embossed, wanted them inscribed and figured with an equal salience; yet it was none the less visibly my "key," as I have said, that though my regenerate young New Yorker, and what might depend on her, should form my centre, my circumference was every whit as treatable. Therefore I must trust myself to know when to proceed from the one and when from the other. Preparatively and, as it were, yearningly—given the whole ground—one began, in the event, with the outer ring, approaching the centre thus by narrowing circumvallations. There, full-blown, accordingly, from one hour to the other, rose one's process—for which there remained all the while so many amusing formulae.

The medal *did* hang free—I felt this perfectly, I remember, from the moment I had comfortably laid the ground provided in my first Book, ground from which Milly is superficially so absent. I scarce remember perhaps a case—I like even with this public grossness to insist on it—in which the curiosity of "beginning far back," as far back as possible, and even of going, to the same tune, far "behind," that is behind the face of the subject, was to assert itself with less scruple. The free hand, in this connexion, was above all agreeable—the hand the freedom of which I owed to the fact that the work had ignominiously failed, in advance, of all power to see itself "serialised." This failure had repeatedly waited, for me, upon shorter fictions; but the considerable production we here discuss was (as "The Golden Bowl" was to be, two or three years later) born, not otherwise than a little bewilderedly, into a world of periodicals and editors, of roaring "successes" in fine, amid which it was well-nigh unnotedly to lose itself. There is fortunately something bracing, ever, in the alpine chill, that of some high icy *arête*, shed by the cold editorial shoulder; sour grapes may at moments fairly intoxicate and the story-teller worth his salt rejoice to feel again how many accommodations he can practise. Those addressed to "conditions of publication" have in a degree their interesting, or at least their provoking, side; but their charm is qualified by the fact that the prescriptions here spring from a soil often wholly alien to the ground of the work itself. They are almost always the fruit of another air altogether and conceived in a light liable to represent *within* the circle of the work itself little else than darkness. Still, when not too blighting, they often operate as a tax on ingenuity—that ingenuity of the expert craftsman which likes to be taxed very much to the same tune to which a well-bred horse likes to be saddled. The best and finest ingenuities, nevertheless, with all respect to that truth, are apt to be, not one's compromises, but one's fullest conformities, and I well remember, in the case before us, the pleasure of feeling my divisions, my proportions and general rhythm, rest all on permanent rather than in any degree on momentary proprieties. It was enough for my alternations, thus, that they were good in themselves; it was in fact so much for them that I really think any further account of the constitution of the book reduces itself to a just notation of the law they followed.

There was the "fun," to begin with, of establishing one's successive centres—of fixing them so exactly that the portions of the subject commanded by them as by happy points of view, and accordingly treated from them, would constitute, so to speak, sufficiently solid *blocks* of wrought material, squared to the sharp edge, as to have weight and mass and carrying power; to make for construction, that is, to conduce to effect and to provide for beauty. Such a block, obviously, is the whole preliminary presentation of Kate Croy, which, from the first, I recall, absolutely declined to enact itself save in terms of amplitude. Terms of amplitude, terms of atmosphere, those terms, and those terms only, in which images assert their fulness and roundness, their power to revolve, so that they have sides and backs, parts in the shade as true as parts in the sun—these were plainly to be my conditions, right and left, and I was so far from overrating the amount of expression the whole thing, as I saw and felt it, would require, that to retrace the way at present is, alas, more than anything else, but to mark the gaps and the lapses, to miss, one by one, the intentions that, with the best will in the world, were not to fructify. I have just said that the process of the general attempt is described from the moment the "blocks" are numbered, and that would be a true enough picture of my plan. Yet one's plan, alas, is one thing and one's result another; so that I am perhaps nearer the point in saying that this last strikes me at present as most characterised by the happy features that *were*, under my first and most blest illusion, to have contributed to it. I meet them all, as I renew acquaintance, I mourn for them all as I remount the stream, the absent values, the palpable voids, the missing links, the mocking shadows, that reflect, taken together, the early bloom of one's good faith. Such cases are of course far from abnormal—so far from it that some acute mind ought surely to have worked out by this time the "law" of the degree in which the artist's energy fairly depends on his fallibility. How much and how often, and in what connexions and with what almost infinite variety, must he be a dupe, that of his prime object, to be at all measurably a master, that of his actual substitute for it—or in other words at all appreciably to exist? He places, after an earnest survey, the piers of his bridge—he has at least sounded deep enough, heaven knows, for their brave position; yet the bridge spans the stream, after the fact, in apparently complete independence of these properties, the principal grace of the original design. *They* were an illusion, for their necessary hour; but the span itself, whether of a single arch or of many, seems by the oddest chance in the world to be a reality; since, actually, the rueful builder, passing under it, sees figures and hears sounds above: he makes out, with his heart in his throat, that it bears and is positively being "used."

The building-up of Kate Croy's consciousness to the capacity for the load little by little to be laid on it was, by way of example, to have been a matter of as many hundred close-packed bricks as there are actually poor dozens. The image of her so compromised and compromising father was all effectively to have pervaded her life, was in a certain particular way to have tampered with her spring; by which I mean that the shame and the irritation and the depression, the general poisonous influence of him, were to have been *shown*, with a truth beyond the compass even of one's most emphasised "word of honour" for it, to do these things. But where do we find him, at this time of day, save in a beggarly scene or two which scarce arrives at the dignity of functional reference? He but "looks in," poor beautiful dazzling, damning apparition that he was to have been; he sees his place so taken, his company so little missed, that, cocking again that fine form of hat which has yielded him for so long his one effective cover, he turns away with a whistle of indifference that nobly misrepresents the deepest disappointment of his life. One's poor word of honour has *had* to pass muster for the show. Every one, in short, was to have enjoyed so much better a chance that, like stars of the theatre condescending to oblige, they have had to take small parts, to content themselves with minor identities, in order to come on at all. I haven't the heart now, I confess, to adduce the detail of so many lapsed importances; the explanation of most of which, after all, I take to have been in the crudity of a truth beating full upon me through these reconsiderations, the odd inveteracy with which picture, at almost any turn, is jealous of drama, and drama (though on the whole with a greater patience, I think) suspicious of picture. Between them, no doubt, they do much for the theme; yet each baffles insidiously the other's ideal and eats round the edges of its position; each is too ready to say "I can take the thing for 'done' only when done in *my* way." The residuum of comfort for the witness of these broils is of course meanwhile in the convenient reflexion, invented for him in the twilight of time and the infancy of art by the Angel, not to say by the Demon, of Compromise, that nothing is so easy to "do" as not to be thankful for almost any stray help in its getting done. It wasn't, after this fashion, by making good one's dream of Lionel Croy that my structure was to stand on its feet—any more than it was by letting him go that I was to be left irretrievably lamenting. The who and the what, the how and the why, the whence and the whither of Merton Densher, these, no less, were quantities and attributes that should have danced about him with the antique grace of nymphs and fauns circling round a bland Hermes and crowning him with flowers. One's main anxiety, for each one's agents, is that the air of each shall be *given*; but what does the whole thing become, after all, as one goes, but a series of sad places at which the hand of generosity has been cautioned and stayed? The young man's situation, personal, professional, social, was to have been so decanted for us that we should get all the taste; we were to have been penetrated with Mrs. Lowder, by the same token, saturated with her presence, her "personality," and felt all her weight in the scale. We were to have revelled in Mrs. Stringham, my heroine's attendant friend, her fairly choral Bostonian, a subject for innumerable touches, and in an extended and above all an *animated* reflexion of Milly Theale's experience of English society; just as the strength and sense of the situation in Venice, for our gathered friends, was to have come to us in a deeper draught out of a larger cup, and just as the pattern of Densher's final position and fullest consciousness there was to have been marked in fine stitches, all silk and gold, all pink and silver, that have had to remain, alas, but entwined upon the reel.

It isn't, no doubt, however—to recover, after all, our critical balance—that the pattern didn't, for each compartment, get itself somehow wrought, and that we mightn't thus, piece by piece, opportunity offering, trace it over and study it. The thing has doubtless, as a whole, the advantage that each piece is true to its pattern, and that while it pretends to make no simple statement it yet never lets go its scheme of clearness. Applications of this scheme are continuous and exemplary enough, though I scarce leave myself room to glance at them. The clearness is obtained in Book First—or otherwise, as I have said, in the first "piece," each Book having its subordinate and con- tributive pattern—through the associated consciousness of my two prime young persons, for whom I early recognised that I should have to consent, under stress, to a practical *fusion* of consciousness. It is into the young woman's "ken" that Mer- ton Densher is represented as swimming; but her mind is not here, rigorously, the one reflector. There are occasions when it plays this part, just as there are others when his plays it, and an intelligible plan consists naturally not a little in fixing such oc- casions and making them, on one side and the other, sufficient to themselves. Do I sometimes in fact forfeit the advantage of that distinctness? Do I ever abandon one centre for another after the former has been postulated? From the moment we proceed by "centres"—and I have never, I confess, embraced the logic of any superior process—they must *be*, each, as a basis, selected and fixed; after which it is that, in the high interest of economy of treatment, they determine and rule. There is no economy of treatment without an adopted, a related point of view, and though I understand, under certain degrees of pres- sure, a represented community of vision between several parties to the action when it makes for concentration, I understand no breaking-up of the register, no sacrifice of the recording con- sistency, that doesn't rather scatter and weaken. In this truth resides the secret of the discriminated occasion—that aspect of the subject which we have our noted choice of treating either as picture or scenically, but which is apt, I think, to show its fullest worth in the Scene. Beautiful exceedingly, for that matter, those occasions or parts of an occasion when the bound- ary line between picture and scene bears a little the weight of the double pressure.

Such would be the case, I can't but surmise, for the long passage that forms here before us the opening of Book Fourth, where all the offered life centres, to intensity, in the disclosure of Milly's single throbbing consciousness, but where, for a due rendering, everything has to be brought to a head. This passage, the view of her introduction to Mrs. Lowder's circle, has its mate, for illustration, later on in the book and at a crisis for which the occasion submits to another rule. My registers or "reflectors," as I so conveniently name them (burnished indeed

as they generally are by the intelligence, the curiosity, the passion, the force of the moment, whatever it be, directing them),
work, as we have seen, in arranged alternation; so that in the
second connexion I here glance at it is Kate Croy who is, "for
all she is worth," turned on. She is turned on largely at Venice,
where the appearances, rich and obscure and portentous (another word I rejoice in) as they have by that time become and
altogether exquisite as they remain, are treated almost wholly
through her vision of them and Densher's (as to the lucid
interplay of which conspiring and conflicting agents there
would be a great deal to say). It is in Kate's consciousness that
at the stage in question the drama is brought to a head, and the
occasion on which, in the splendid saloon of poor Milly's hired
palace, she takes the measure of her friend's festal evening,
squares itself to the same synthetic firmness as the compact
constructional block inserted by the scene at Lancaster Gate.
Milly's situation ceases at a given moment to be "renderable"
in terms closer than those supplied by Kate's intelligence, or,
in a richer degree, by Densher's, or, for one fond hour, by poor
Mrs. Stringham's (since to that sole brief futility is this last par-
ticipant, crowned by my original plan with the quaintest func-
tions, in fact reduced); just as Kate's relation with Densher and
Densher's with Kate have ceased previously, and are then to
cease again, to be projected for us, so far as Milly is concerned
with them, on any more responsible plate than that of the
latter's admirable anxiety. It is as if, for these aspects, the impersonal plate—in other words the poor author's comparatively cold affirmation or thin guarantee—had felt itself a figure
of attestation at once too gross and too bloodless, likely to
affect us as an abuse of privilege when not as an abuse of
knowledge.

Heaven forbid, we say to ourselves during almost the whole
Venetian climax, heaven forbid we should "know" anything
more of our ravaged sister than what Densher darkly pieces
together, or than what Kate Croy pays, heroically, it must be
owned, at the hour of her visit alone to Densher's lodging, for
her superior handling and her dire profanation of. For we
have time, while this passage lasts, to turn round critically;
we have time to recognise intentions and proprieties; we have
time to catch glimpses of an economy of composition, as I put

it, interesting in itself: all in spite of the author's scarce more than half-dissimulated despair at the inveterate displacement of his general centre. "The Wings of the Dove" happens to offer perhaps the most striking example I may cite (though with public penance for it already performed) of my regular failure to keep the appointed halves of my whole equal. Here the makeshift middle—for which the best I can say is that it's always rueful and never impudent—reigns with even more than its customary contrition, though passing itself off perhaps too with more than its usual craft. Nowhere, I seem to recall, had the need of dissimulation been felt so as anguish; nowhere had I condemned a luckless theme to complete its revolution, burdened with the accumulation of its difficulties, the difficulties that grow with a theme's development, in quarters so cramped. Of course, as every novelist knows, it is difficulty that inspires; only, for that perfection of charm, it must have been difficulty inherent and congenital, and not difficulty "caught" by the wrong frequentations. The latter half, that is the false and deformed half, of "The Wings" would verily, I think, form a signal object-lesson for a literary critic bent on improving his occasion to the profit of the budding artist. This whole corner of the picture bristles with "dodges"—such as he should feel himself all committed to recognise and denounce—for disguising the reduced scale of the exhibition, for foreshortening at any cost, for imparting to patches the value of presences, for dressing objects in an *air* as of the dimensions they can't possibly have. Thus he would have his free hand for pointing out what a tangled web we weave when—well, when, through our mislaying or otherwise trifling with our blest pair of compasses, we have to produce the illusion of mass without the illusion of extent. *There* is a job quite to the measure of most of our monitors—and with the interest for them well enhanced by the preliminary cunning quest for the spot where deformity has begun.

I recognise meanwhile, throughout the long earlier reach of the book, not only no deformities but, I think, a positively close and felicitous application of method, the preserved consistencies of which, often illusive, but never really lapsing, it would be of a certain diversion, and might be of some profit, to follow. The author's accepted task at the outset has been to suggest with force the nature of the tie formed between the two young persons first introduced—to give the full impression of its peculiar worried and baffled, yet clinging and confident, ardour. The picture constituted, so far as may be, is that of a pair of natures well-nigh consumed by a sense of their intimate affinity and congruity, the reciprocity of their desire, and thus passionately impatient of barriers and delays, yet with qualities of intelligence and character that they are meanwhile extraordinarily able to draw upon for the enrichment of their relation, the extension of their prospect and the support of their "game." They are far from a common couple, Merton Densher and Kate Croy, as befits the remarkable fashion in which fortune was to waylay and opportunity was to distinguish them—the whole strange truth of their response to which opening involves also, in its order, no vulgar art of exhibition; but what they have most to tell us is that, all unconsciously and with the best faith in the world, all by mere force of the terms of their superior passion combined with their superior diplomacy, they are laying a trap for the great innocence to come. If I like, as I have confessed, the "portentous" look, I was perhaps never to set so high a value on it as for all this prompt provision of forces unwittingly waiting to close round my eager heroine (to the eventual deep chill of her eagerness) as the result of her mere lifting of a latch. Infinitely interesting to have built up the relation of the others to the point at which its aching restlessness, its need to affirm itself otherwise than by an exasperated patience, meets as with instinctive relief and recognition the possibilities shining out of Milly Theale. Infinitely interesting to have prepared and organised, correspondingly, that young woman's precipitations and liabilities, to have constructed, for Drama essentially to take possession, the whole bright house of her exposure.

These references, however, reflect too little of the detail of the treatment imposed; such a detail as I for instance get hold of in the fact of Densher's interview with Mrs. Lowder before he goes to America. It forms, in this preliminary picture, the one patch not strictly seen over Kate Croy's shoulder; though it's notable that immediately after, at the first possible moment, we surrender again to our major convenience, as it happens to be at the time, that of our drawing breath through the

young woman's lungs. Once more, in other words, before we
know it, Densher's direct vision of the scene at Lancaster Gate
is replaced by her apprehension, her contributive assimilation,
of his experience: it melts back into that accumulation, which
we have been, as it were, saving up. Does my apparent deviation here count accordingly as a muddle?—one of the muddles
ever blooming so thick in any soil that fails to grow reasons
and determinants. No, distinctly not; for I had definitely
opened the door, as attention of perusal of the first two Books
will show, to the subjective community of my young pair. (Attention of perusal, I thus confess by the way, is what I at every
point, as well as here, absolutely invoke and take for granted; a
truth I avail myself of this occasion to note once for all—in the
interest of that variety of ideal reigning, I gather, in the connexion. The enjoyment of a work of art, the acceptance of an
irresistible illusion, constituting, to my sense, our highest experience of "luxury," the luxury is not greatest, by my consequent measure, when the work asks for as little attention as
possible. It is greatest, it is delightfully, divinely great, when we
feel the surface, like the thick ice of the skater's pond, bear
without cracking the strongest pressure we throw on it. The
sound of the crack one may recognise, but never surely to call
it a luxury.) That I had scarce availed myself of the privilege of
seeing with Densher's eyes is another matter; the point is that
I had intelligently marked my possible, my occasional need of
it. So, at all events, the constructional "block" of the first two
Books compactly forms itself. A new block, all of the squarest
and not a little of the smoothest, begins with the Third—by
which I mean of course a new mass of interest governed from
a new centre. Here again I make prudent *provision*—to be sure
to keep my centre strong. It dwells mainly, we at once see, in
the depths of Milly Theale's "case," where, close beside it, however, we meet a supplementary reflector, that of the lucid even
though so quivering spirit of her dedicated friend.

The more or less associated consciousness of the two women
deals thus, unequally, with the next presented face of the subject
—deals with it to the exclusion of the dealing of others; and if,
for a highly particular moment, I allot to Mrs. Stringham the
responsibility of the direct appeal to us, it is again, charming to
relate, on behalf of that play of the portentous which I cherish

so as a "value" and am accordingly for ever setting in motion. There is an hour of evening, on the alpine height, at which it becomes of the last importance that our young woman should testify eminently in this direction. But as I was to find it long since of a blest wisdom that no expense should be incurred or met, in any corner of picture of mine, without some concrete image of the account kept of it, that is of its being organically re-economised, so under that dispensation Mrs. Stringham has to register the transaction. Book Fifth is a new block mainly in its provision of a new set of occasions, which readopt, for their order, the previous centre, Milly's now almost full-blown consciousness. At my game, with renewed zest, of driving portents home, I have by this time all the choice of those that are to brush that surface with a dark wing. They are used, to our profit, on an elastic but a definite system; by which I mean that having to sound here and there a little deep, as a test, for my basis of method, I find it everywhere obstinately present. It draws the "occasion" into tune and keeps it so, to repeat my tiresome term; my nearest approach to muddlement is to have sometimes—but not too often—to break my occasions small. Some of them succeed in remaining ample and in really aspiring then to the higher, the sustained lucidity. The whole actual centre of the work, resting on a misplaced pivot and lodged in Book Fifth, pretends to a long reach, or at any rate to the larger foreshortening—though bringing home to me, on re-perusal, what I find striking, charming and curious, the author's instinct everywhere for the *indirect* presentation of his main image. I note how, again and again, I go but a little way with the direct—that is with the straight exhibition of Milly; it resorts for relief, this process, whenever it can, to some kinder, some merciful indirection: all as if to approach her circuitously, deal with her at second hand, as an unspotted princess is ever dealt with; the pressure all round her kept easy for her, the sounds, the movements regulated, the forms and ambiguities made charming. All of which proceeds, obviously, from her painter's tenderness of imagination about her, which reduces him to watching her, as it were, through the successive windows of other people's interest in her. So, if we talk of princesses, do the balconies opposite the palace gates, do the coigns of vantage and respect enjoyed for a fee, rake from afar the mystic figure in the gilded coach as it comes forth into the great *place*. But my use of windows and balconies is doubtless at best an extravagance by itself, and as to what there may be to note, of this and other supersubtleties, other arch-refinements, of tact and taste, of design and instinct, in "The Wings of the Dove," I become conscious of overstepping my space without having brought the full quantity to light. The failure leaves me with a burden of residuary comment of which I yet boldly hope elsewhere to discharge myself.

HENRY JAMES.

The Doctor's Door

I

SHE waited, Kate Croy, for her father to come in, but he kept
her unconscionably, and there were moments at which she
showed herself, in the glass over the mantel, a face positively
pale with the irritation that had brought her to the point of
going away without sight of him. It was at this point, however,
that she remained; changing her place, moving from the
shabby sofa to the armchair upholstered in a glazed cloth that
gave at once—she had tried it—the sense of the slippery and
of the sticky. She had looked at the sallow prints on the walls
and at the lonely magazine, a year old, that combined, with a
small lamp in coloured glass and a knitted white centre-piece
wanting in freshness, to enhance the effect of the purplish cloth
on the principal table; she had above all from time to time taken
a brief stand on the small balcony to which the pair of long
windows gave access. The vulgar little street, in this view,
offered scant relief from the vulgar little room; its main office
was to suggest to her that the narrow black house-fronts, adjusted to a standard that would have been low even for backs,
constituted quite the publicity implied by such privacies. One
felt them in the room exactly as one felt the room—the hundred like it or worse—in the street. Each time she turned in
again, each time, in her impatience, she gave him up, it was to
sound to a deeper depth, while she tasted the faint flat emana-
tion of things, the failure of fortune and of honour. If she continued to wait it was really in a manner that she mightn't add
the shame of fear, of individual, of personal collapse, to all the
other shames. To feel the street, to feel the room, to feel the
table-cloth and the centre-piece and the lamp, gave her a small
salutary sense at least of neither shirking nor lying. This whole
vision was the worst thing yet—as including in particular the
interview to which she had braced herself; and for what had
she come but for the worst? She tried to be sad so as not to be
angry, but it made her angry that she couldn't be sad. And yet

where was misery, misery too beaten for blame and chalk-marked by fate like a "lot" at a common auction, if not in these merciless signs of mere mean stale feelings?

Her father's life, her sister's, her own, that of her two lost brothers—the whole history of their house had the effect of some fine florid voluminous phrase, say even a musical, that dropped first into words and notes without sense and then, hanging unfinished, into no words nor any notes at all. Why should a set of people have been put in motion, on such a scale and with such an air of being equipped for a profitable journey, only to break down without an accident, to stretch themselves in the wayside dust without a reason? The answer to these questions was not in Chirk Street, but the questions themselves bristled there, and the girl's repeated pause before the mirror and the chimney-place might have represented her nearest approach to an escape from them. Wasn't it in fact the partial escape from this "worst" in which she was steeped to be able to make herself out again as agreeable to see? She stared into the tarnished glass too hard indeed to be staring at her beauty alone. She readjusted the poise of her black closely-feathered hat; retouched, beneath it, the thick fall of her dusky hair; kept her eyes aslant no less on her beautiful averted than on her beautiful presented oval. She was dressed altogether in black, which gave an even tone, by contrast, to her clear face and made her hair more harmoniously dark. Outside, on the balcony, her eyes showed as blue; within, at the mirror, they showed almost as black. She was handsome, but the degree of it was not sustained by items and aids; a circumstance moreover playing its part at almost any time in the impression she produced. The impression was one that remained, but as regards the sources of it no sum in addition would have made up the total. She had stature without height, grace without motion, presence without mass. Slender and simple, frequently soundless, she was somehow always in the line of the eye—she counted singularly for its pleasure. More "dressed," often, with fewer accessories, than other women, or less dressed, should occasion require, with more, she probably couldn't have given the key to these felicities. They were mysteries of which her friends were conscious—those friends whose general explanation was to say that she was clever, whether or no it were taken by the world as the cause or as the effect of her charm. If she saw more things than her fine face in the dull glass of her father's lodgings she might have seen that after all she was not herself a fact in the collapse. She didn't hold herself cheap, she didn't make for misery. Personally, no, she wasn't chalk-marked for auction. She hadn't given up yet, and the broken sentence, if she was the last word, *would* end with a sort of meaning. There was a minute during which, though her eyes were fixed, she quite visibly lost herself in the thought of the way she might still pull things round had she only been a man. It was the name, above all, she would take in hand—the precious name she so liked and that, in spite of the harm her wretched father had done it, wasn't yet past praying for. She loved it in fact the more tenderly for that bleeding wound. But what could a penniless girl do with it but let it go?

When her father at last appeared she became, as usual, instantly aware of the futility of any effort to hold him to anything. He had written her he was ill, too ill to leave his room, and that he must see her without delay; and if this had been, as was probable, the sketch of a design he was indifferent even to the moderate finish required for deception. He had clearly wanted, for the perversities he called his reasons, to see her, just as she herself had sharpened for a talk; but she now again felt, in the inevitability of the freedom he used with her, all the old ache, her poor mother's very own, that he couldn't touch you ever so lightly without setting up. No relation with him could be so short or so superficial as not to be somehow to your hurt; and this, in the strangest way in the world, not because he desired it to be—feeling often, as he surely must, the profit for him of its not being—but because there was never a mistake for you that he could leave unmade, nor a conviction of his impossibility in you that he could approach you without strengthening. He might have awaited her on the sofa in his sitting-room, or might have stayed in bed and received her in that situation. She was glad to be spared the sight of such penetralia, but it would have reminded her a little less that there was no truth in him. This was the weariness of every fresh meeting; he dealt out lies as he might the cards from the greasy old pack for the game of diplomacy to which you were to sit down with him. The inconvenience—as always happens in such cases—was not that you minded what was false, but that you missed what was true. He might be ill and it might suit you to know it, but no contact with him, for this, could ever be straight enough. Just so he even might die, but Kate fairly wondered on what evidence of his own she would some day have to believe it.

He had not at present come down from his room, which she knew to be above the one they were in: he had already been out of the house, though he would either, should she challenge him, deny it or present it as a proof of his extremity. She had, however, by this time, quite ceased to challenge him; not only, face to face with him, vain irritation dropped, but he breathed upon the tragic consciousness in such a way that after a moment nothing of it was left. The difficulty was not less that he breathed in the same way upon the comic: she almost believed that with this latter she might still have found a foothold for clinging to him. He had ceased to be amusing— he was really too inhuman. His perfect look, which had floated him so long, was practically perfect still; but one had long since for every occasion taken it for granted. Nothing could have better shown than the actual how right one had been. He looked exactly as much as usual—all pink and silver as to skin and hair, all straightness and starch as to figure and dress; the man in the world least connected with anything unpleasant. He was so particularly the English gentleman and the fortunate settled normal person. Seen at a foreign table d'hôte he suggested but one thing: "In what perfection England produces them!" He had kind safe eyes, and a voice which, for all its clean fulness, told the quiet tale of its having never had once to raise itself. Life had met him so, half-way, and had turned round so to walk with him, placing a hand in his arm and fondly leaving him to choose the pace. Those who knew him a little said "How he does dress!"—those who knew him better said "How *does* he?" The one stray gleam of comedy just now in his daughter's eyes was the absurd feeling he momentarily made her have of being herself "looked up" by him in sordid lodgings. For a minute after he came in it was as if the place were her own and he the visitor with susceptibilities. He gave you absurd feelings, he had indescribable arts, that quite turned the tables: this had been always how he came to see her mother so long as her mother would see him. He came from places they had often not known about, but he patronised Lexham Gardens. Kate's only actual expression of impatience, however, was "I'm glad you're so much better!"

"I'm not so much better, my dear—I'm exceedingly unwell; the proof of which is precisely that I've been out to the chemist's—that beastly fellow at the corner." So Mr. Croy showed he could qualify the humble hand that assuaged him. "I'm taking something he has made up for me. It's just why I've sent for you—that you may see me as I really am."

"Oh papa, it's long since I've ceased to see you otherwise than as you really are! I think we've all arrived by this time at the right word for that: 'You're beautiful—*n'en parlons plus.*' You're as beautiful as ever—you look lovely." He judged meanwhile her own appearance, as she knew she could always trust him to do; recognising, estimating, sometimes disapproving, what she wore, showing her the interest he continued to take in her. He might really take none at all, yet she virtually knew herself the creature in the world to whom he was least indifferent. She had often enough wondered what on earth, at the pass he had reached, could give him pleasure, and had come back on these occasions to that. It gave him pleasure that she was handsome, that she was in her way a tangible value. It was at least as marked, nevertheless, that he derived none from similar conditions, so far as they *were* similar, in his other child. Poor Marian might be handsome, but he certainly didn't care. The hitch here of course was that, with whatever beauty, her sister, widowed and almost in want, with four bouncing children, had no such measure. She asked him the next thing how long he had been in his actual quarters, though aware of how little it mattered, how little any answer he might make would probably have in common with the truth. She failed in fact to notice his answer, truthful or not, already occupied as she was with what she had on her own side to say to him. This was really what had made her wait—what superseded the small remainder of her resentment at his constant practical impertinence; the result of all of which was that within a minute she had brought it out. "Yes—even now I'm willing to go with you. I don't know what you may have wished to say to me, and even if you hadn't written you would within a day or two

have heard from me. Things have happened, and I've only
waited, for seeing you, till I should be quite sure. I *am* quite
sure. I'll go with you."

It produced an effect. "Go with me where?"

"Anywhere. I'll stay with you. Even here." She had taken off
her gloves and, as if she had arrived with her plan, she sat down.

Lionel Croy hung about in his disengaged way—hovered
there as if looking, in consequence of her words, for a pretext
to back out easily: on which she immediately saw she had discounted, as it might be called, what he had himself been
preparing. He wished her not to come to him, still less to settle with him, and had sent for her to give her up with some
style and state; a part of the beauty of which, however, was to
have been his sacrifice to her own detachment. There was no
style, no state, unless she wished to forsake him. His idea had
accordingly been to surrender her to her wish with all nobleness; it had by no means been to have positively to keep her
off. She cared, however, not a straw for his embarrassment—
feeling how little, on her own part, she was moved by charity.
She had seen him, first and last, in so many attitudes that she
could now deprive him quite without compunction of the luxury of a new one. Yet she felt the disconcerted gasp in his tone
as he said: "Oh my child, I can never consent to that!"

"What then are you going to do?"

"I'm turning it over," said Lionel Croy. "You may imagine if
I'm not thinking."

"Haven't you thought then," his daughter asked, "of what I
speak of? I mean of my being ready."

Standing before her with his hands behind him and his legs
a little apart, he swayed slightly to and fro, inclined toward her
as if rising on his toes. It had an effect of conscientious deliberation. "No—I haven't. I couldn't. I wouldn't." It was so re-
spectable a show that she felt afresh, and with the memory of
their old despair, the despair at home, how little his appearance
ever by any chance told about him. His plausibility had been
the heaviest of her mother's crosses; inevitably so much more
present to the world than whatever it was that was horrid—
thank God they didn't really know!—that he had done. He
had positively been, in his way, by the force of his particular

type, a terrible husband not to live with; his type reflecting so invidiously on the woman who had found him distasteful. Had this thereby not kept directly present to Kate herself that it might, on some sides, prove no light thing for her to leave uncompanion'd a parent with such a face and such a manner? Yet if there was much she neither knew nor dreamed of it passed between them at this very moment that he was quite familiar with himself as the subject of such quandaries. If he recognised his younger daughter's happy aspect as a tangible value, he had from the first still more exactly appraised every point of his own. The great wonder was not that in spite of everything these points had helped him; the great wonder was that they hadn't helped him more. However, it was, to its eternal recurrent tune, helping him all the while; her drop into patience with him showed how it was helping him at this moment. She saw the next instant precisely the line he would take. "Do you really ask me to believe you've been making up your mind to that?"

She had to consider her own line. "I don't think I care, papa, what you believe. I never, for that matter, think of you as believing anything; hardly more," she permitted herself to add, "than I ever think of you as yourself believed. I don't know you, father, you see."

"And it's your idea that you may make that up?"

"Oh dear, no; not at all. That's no part of the question. If I haven't understood you by this time I never shall, and it doesn't matter. It has seemed to me you may be lived with, but not that you may be understood. Of course I've not the least idea how you get on."

"I don't get on," Mr. Croy almost gaily replied.

His daughter took the place in again, and it might well have seemed odd that with so little to meet the eye there should be so much to show. What showed was the ugliness—so positive and palpable that it was somehow sustaining. It was a medium, a setting, and to that extent, after all, a dreadful sign of life; so that it fairly gave point to her answer. "Oh I beg your pardon. You flourish."

"Do you throw it up at me again," he pleasantly put to her, "that I've not made away with myself?"

She treated the question as needing no reply; she sat there for real things. "You know how all our anxieties, under mamma's will, have come out. She had still less to leave than she feared. We don't know how we lived. It all makes up about two hundred a year for Marian, and two for me, but I give up a hundred to Marian."

"Oh you weak thing!" her father sighed as from depths of enlightened experience.

"For you and me together," she went on, "the other hundred would do something."

"And what would do the rest?"

"Can you yourself do nothing?"

He gave her a look; then, slipping his hands into his pockets and turning away, stood for a little at the window she had left open. She said nothing more—she had placed him there with that question, and the silence lasted a minute, broken by the call of an appealing costermonger, which came in with the mild March air, with the shabby sunshine, fearfully unbecoming to the room, and with the small homely hum of Chirk Street. Presently he moved nearer, but as if her question had quite dropped. "I don't see what has so suddenly wound you up."

"I should have thought you might perhaps guess. Let me at any rate tell you. Aunt Maud has made me a proposal. But she has also made me a condition. She wants to keep me."

"And what in the world else *could* she possibly want?"

"Oh I don't know—many things. I'm not so precious a capture," the girl a little dryly explained. "No one has ever wanted to keep me before."

Looking always what was proper, her father looked now still more surprised than interested. "You've not had proposals?" He spoke as if that were incredible of Lionel Croy's daughter; as if indeed such an admission scarce consorted, even in filial intimacy, with her high spirit and general form.

"Not from rich relations. She's extremely kind to me, but it's time, she says, that we should understand each other."

Mr. Croy fully assented. "Of course it is—high time; and I can quite imagine what she means by it."

"Are you very sure?"

"Oh perfectly. She means that she'll 'do' for you handsomely if you'll break off all relations with me. You speak of her condition. Her condition's of course that."

"Well then," said Kate, "it's what has wound me up. Here I am."

He showed with a gesture how thoroughly he had taken it in; after which, within a few seconds, he had quite congruously turned the situation about. "Do you really suppose me in a position to justify your throwing yourself upon me?"

She waited a little, but when she spoke it was clear. "Yes."

"Well then, you're of feebler intelligence than I should have ventured to suppose you."

"Why so? You live. You flourish. You bloom."

"Ah how you've all always hated me!" he murmured with a pensive gaze again at the window.

"No one could be less of a mere cherished memory," she declared as if she had not heard him. "You're an actual person, if there ever was one. We agreed just now that you're beautiful. You strike me, you know, as—in your own way—much more firm on your feet than I. Don't put it to me therefore as monstrous that the fact that we're after all parent and child should at present in some manner count for us. My idea has been that it should have some effect for each of us. I don't at all, as I told you just now," she pursued, "make out your life; but whatever it is I hereby offer to accept it. And, on my side, I'll do everything I can for you."

"I see," said Lionel Croy. Then with the sound of extreme relevance: "And what *can* you?" She only, at this, hesitated, and he took up her silence. "You can describe yourself—*to* yourself—as, in a fine flight, giving up your aunt for me; but what good, I should like to know, would your fine flight do me?" As she still said nothing he developed a little. "We're not possessed of so much, at this charming pass, please to remember, as that we can afford not to take hold of any perch held out to us. I like the way you talk, my dear, about 'giving up'! One doesn't give up the use of a spoon because one's reduced to living on broth. And your spoon, that is your aunt, please consider, is partly mine as well." She rose now, as if in sight of the term of her effort, in sight of the futility and the weariness of many things, and moved back to the poor little glass

with which she had communed before. She retouched here
again the poise of her hat, and this brought to her father's lips
another remark—in which impatience, however, had already
been replaced by a free flare of appreciation. "Oh you're all
right! Don't muddle yourself up with *me*!"

His daughter turned round to him. "The condition Aunt
Maud makes is that I shall have absolutely nothing to do with
you; never see you, nor speak nor write to you, never go near
you nor make you a sign, nor hold any sort of communication
with you. What she requires is that you shall simply cease to
exist for me."

He had always seemed—it was one of the marks of what
they called the "unspeakable" in him—to walk a little more
on his toes, as if for jauntiness, under the touch of offence.
Nothing, however, was more wonderful than what he sometimes would take for offence, unless it might be what he
sometimes wouldn't. He walked at any rate on his toes now.
"A very proper requirement of your Aunt Maud, my dear—I
don't hesitate to say it!" Yet as this, much as she had seen, left
her silent at first from what might have been a sense of sickness, he had time to go on: "That's her condition then. But
what are her promises? Just what does she engage to do? You
must work it, you know."

"You mean make her feel," Kate asked after a moment,
"how much I'm attached to you?"

"Well, what a cruel invidious treaty it is for you to sign. I'm
a poor ruin of an old dad to make a stand about giving up—I
quite agree. But I'm not, after all, quite the old ruin not to get
something *for* giving up."

"Oh I think her idea," said Kate almost gaily now, "is that I
shall get a great deal."

He met her with his inimitable amenity. "But does she give
you the items?"

The girl went through the show. "More or less, I think. But
many of them are things I dare say I may take for granted—
things women can do for each other and that you wouldn't
understand."

"There's nothing I understand so well, always, as the things
I needn't! But what I want to do, you see," he went on, "is to

put it to your conscience that you've an admirable opportunity; and that it's moreover one for which, after all, damn you,
you've really to thank *me*."

"I confess I don't see," Kate observed, "what my 'conscience' has to do with it."

"Then, my dear girl, you ought simply to be ashamed of
yourself. Do you know what you're a proof of, all you hard
hollow people together?" He put the question with a charming
air of sudden spiritual heat. "Of the deplorably superficial
morality of the age. The family sentiment, in our vulgarised
brutalised life, has gone utterly to pot. There was a day when a
man like me—by which I mean a parent like me—would have
been for a daughter like you quite a distinct value; what's called
in the business world, I believe, an 'asset.'" He continued sociably to make it out. "I'm not talking only of what you might,
with the right feeling, do *for* me, but of what you might—it's
what I call your opportunity—do *with* me. Unless indeed," he
the next moment imperturbably threw off, "they come a good
deal to the same thing. Your duty as well as your chance, if
you're capable of seeing it, is to use me. Show family feeling by
seeing what I'm good for. If you had it as *I* have it you'd see
I'm still good—well, for a lot of things. There's in fact, my
dear," Mr. Croy wound up, "a coach-and-four to be got out of
me." His lapse, or rather his climax, failed a little of effect indeed through an undue precipitation of memory. Something
his daughter had said came back to him. "You've settled to
give away half your little inheritance?"

Her hesitation broke into laughter. "No—I haven't 'settled'
anything."

"But you mean practically to let Marian collar it?" They
stood there face to face, but she so denied herself to his challenge that he could only go on. "You've a view of three hundred a year for her in addition to what her husband left her
with? Is *that*," the remote progenitor of such wantonness audibly wondered, "your morality?"

Kate found her answer without trouble. "Is it your idea that
I should give you everything?"

The "everything" clearly struck him—to the point even of
determining the tone of his reply. "Far from it. How can you

ask that when I refuse what you tell me you came to offer? Make of my idea what you can; I think I've sufficiently expressed it, and it's at any rate to take or to leave. It's the only one, I may nevertheless add; it's the basket with all my eggs. It's my conception, in short, of your duty."

The girl's tired smile watched the word as if it had taken on a small grotesque visibility. "You're wonderful on such subjects! I think I should leave you in no doubt," she pursued, "that if I were to sign my aunt's agreement I should carry it out, in honour, to the letter."

"Rather, my own love! It's just your honour that I appeal to. The only way to play the game *is* to play it. There's no limit to what your aunt can do for you."

"Do you mean in the way of marrying me?"

"What else should I mean? Marry properly—"

"And then?" Kate asked as he hung fire.

"And then—well, I *will* talk with you. I'll resume relations."

She looked about her and picked up her parasol. "Because you're not so afraid of any one else in the world as you are of *her*? My husband, if I should marry, would be at the worst less of a terror? If that's what you mean there may be something in it. But doesn't it depend a little also on what you mean by my getting a proper one? However," Kate added as she picked out the frill of her little umbrella, "I don't suppose your idea of him is *quite* that he should persuade you to live with us."

"Dear no—not a bit." He spoke as not resenting either the fear or the hope she imputed; met both imputations in fact with a sort of intellectual relief. "I place the case for you wholly in your aunt's hands. I take her view with my eyes shut; I accept in all confidence any man she selects. If he's good enough for *her*—elephantine snob as she is—he's good enough for me; and quite in spite of the fact that she'll be sure to select one who can be trusted to be nasty to me. My only interest is in your doing what she wants. You shan't be so beastly poor, my darling," Mr. Croy declared, "if I can help it."

"Well then good-bye, papa," the girl said after a reflexion on this that had perceptibly ended for her in a renunciation of further debate. "Of course you understand that it may be for long."

Her companion had hereupon one of his finest inspirations. "Why not frankly for ever? You must do me the justice to see that I don't do things, that I've never done them, by halves—that if I offer you to efface myself it's for the final fatal sponge I ask, well saturated and well applied."

She turned her handsome quiet face upon him at such length that it might indeed have been for the last time. "I don't know what you're like."

"No more do I, my dear. I've spent my life in trying in vain to discover. Like nothing—more's the pity. If there had been many of us and we could have found each other out there's no knowing what we mightn't have done. But it doesn't matter now. Good-bye, love." He looked even not sure of what she would wish him to suppose on the subject of a kiss, yet also not embarrassed by his uncertainty.

She forbore in fact for a moment longer to clear it up. "I wish there were some one here who might serve—for any contingency—as a witness that I *have* put it to you that I'm ready to come."

"Would you like me," her father asked, "to call the landlady?"

"You may not believe me," she pursued, "but I came really hoping you might have found some way. I'm very sorry at all events to leave you unwell." He turned away from her on this and, as he had done before, took refuge, by the window, in a stare at the street. "Let me put it—unfortunately without a witness," she added after a moment, "that there's only one word you really need speak."

When he took these words up it was still with his back to her. "If I don't strike you as having already spoken it our time has been singularly wasted."

"I'll engage with you in respect to my aunt exactly to what she wants of me in respect to you. She wants me to choose. Very well, I *will* choose. I'll wash my hands of her for you to just that tune."

He at last brought himself round. "Do you know, dear, you make me sick? I've tried to be clear, and it isn't fair."

But she passed this over; she was too visibly sincere. "Father!"

"I don't quite see what's the matter with you," he said,

"and if you can't pull yourself together I'll—upon my honour —take you in hand. Put you into a cab and deliver you again safe at Lancaster Gate."

She was really absent, distant. "Father."

It was too much, and he met it sharply. "Well?"

"Strange as it may be to you to hear me say it, there's a good you can do me and a help you can render."

"Isn't it then exactly what I've been trying to make you feel?"

"Yes," she answered patiently, "but so in the wrong way. I'm perfectly honest in what I say, and I know what I'm talking about. It isn't that I'll pretend I could have believed a month ago in anything to call aid or support from you. The case is changed—that's what has happened; my difficulty is a new one. But even now it's not a question of anything I should ask you in a way to 'do.' It's simply a question of your not turning me away—taking yourself out of my life. It's simply a question of your saying: 'Yes then, since you will, we'll stand together. We won't worry in advance about how or where; we'll have a faith and find a way.' That's all—*that* would be the good you'd do me. I should *have* you, and it would be for my benefit. Do you see?"

If he didn't it wasn't for want of looking at her hard. "The matter with you is that you're in love, and that your aunt knows and—for reasons, I'm sure, perfect—hates and opposes it. Well she may! It's a matter in which I trust her with my eyes shut. Go, please." Though he spoke not in anger—rather in infinite sadness—he fairly turned her out. Before she took it up he had, as the fullest expression of what he felt, opened the door of the room. He had fairly, in his deep disapproval, a generous compassion to spare. "I'm sorry for her, deluded woman, if she builds on you."

Kate stood a moment in the draught. "She's not the person *I* pity most, for, deluded in many ways though she may be, she's not the person who's most so. I mean," she explained, "if it's a question of what you call building on me."

He took it as if what she meant might be other than her description of it. "You're deceiving *two* persons then, Mrs. Lowder and somebody else?"

She shook her head with detachment. "I've no intention of

that sort with respect to any one now—to Mrs. Lowder least of all. If you fail me"—she seemed to make it out for herself—"that has the merit at least that it simplifies. I shall go my way—as I see my way."

"Your way, you mean then, will be to marry some blackguard without a penny?"

"You demand a great deal of satisfaction," she observed, "for the little you give."

It brought him up again before her as with a sense that she was not to be hustled, and though he glared at her a little this had long been the practical limit to his general power of objection. "If you're base enough to incur your aunt's reprobation you're base enough for my argument. What, if you're not thinking of an utterly improper person, do your speeches to me signify? Who *is* the beggarly sneak?" he went on as her response failed.

Her response, when it came, was cold but distinct. "He has every disposition to make the best of you. He only wants in fact to be kind to you."

"Then he *must* be an ass! And how in the world can you consider it to improve him for me," her father pursued, "that he's also destitute and impossible? There are boobies and boobies even—the right and the wrong—and you appear to have carefully picked out one of the wrong. Your aunt knows *them*, by good fortune; I perfectly trust, as I tell you, her judgement for them; and you may take it from me once for all that I won't hear of any one of whom *she* won't." Which led up to his last word. "If you should really defy us both—!"

"Well, papa?"

"Well, my sweet child, I think that—reduced to insignificance as you may fondly believe me—I should still not be quite without some way of making you regret it."

She had a pause, a grave one, but not, as appeared, that she might measure this danger. "If I shouldn't do it, you know, it wouldn't be because I'm afraid of you."

"Oh if you don't do it," he retorted, "you may be as bold as you like!"

"Then you can do nothing at all for me?"

He showed her, this time unmistakeably—it was before her there on the landing, at the top of the tortuous stairs and in the midst of the strange smell that seemed to cling to them—how vain her appeal remained. "I've never pretended to do more than my duty; I've given you the best and the clearest advice." And then came up the spring that moved him. "If it only displeases you, you can go to Marian to be consoled." What he couldn't forgive was her dividing with Marian her scant share of the provision their mother had been able to leave them. She should have divided it with *him*.

II

SHE had gone to Mrs. Lowder on her mother's death—gone with an effort the strain and pain of which made her at present, as she recalled them, reflect on the long way she had travelled since then. There had been nothing else to do—not a penny in the other house, nothing but unpaid bills that had gathered thick while its mistress lay mortally ill, and the admonition that there was nothing she must attempt to raise money on, since everything belonged to the "estate." How the estate would turn out at best presented itself as a mystery altogether gruesome; it had proved in fact since then a residuum a trifle less scant than, with her sister, she had for some weeks feared; but the girl had had at the beginning rather a wounded sense of its being watched on behalf of Marian and her children. What on earth was it supposed that *she* wanted to do to it? She wanted in truth only to give up—to abandon her own interest, which she doubtless would already have done hadn't the point been subject to Aunt Maud's sharp intervention. Aunt Maud's intervention was all sharp now, and the other point, the great one, was that it was to be, in this light, either all put up with or all declined. Yet at the winter's end, nevertheless, she could scarce have said what stand she conceived she had taken. It wouldn't be the first time she had seen herself obliged to accept with smothered irony other people's interpretation of her conduct. She often ended by giving up to them—it seemed really the way to live—the version that met their convenience.

The tall rich heavy house at Lancaster Gate, on the other side of the Park and the long South Kensington stretches, had figured to her, through childhood, through girlhood, as the remotest limit of her vague young world. It was further off and more occasional than anything else in the comparatively compact circle in which she revolved, and seemed, by a rigour early marked, to be reached through long, straight, discouraging vistas, perfect telescopes of streets, and which kept lengthening and straightening, whereas almost everything else in life was either at the worst roundabout Cromwell Road or at the

furthest in the nearer parts of Kensington Gardens. Mrs. Lowder was her only "real" aunt, not the wife of an uncle, and had
been thereby, both in ancient days and when the greater trouble came, the person, of all persons, properly to make some
sign; in accord with which our young woman's feeling was
founded on the impression, quite cherished for years, that the
signs made across the interval just mentioned had never been
really in the note of the situation. The main office of this relative for the young Croys—apart from giving them their fixed
measure of social greatness—had struck them as being to form
them to a conception of what they were not to expect. When
Kate came to think matters over with wider knowledge, she
failed quite to see how Aunt Maud could have been different
—she had rather perceived by this time how many other things
might have been; yet she also made out that if they had all consciously lived under a liability to the chill breath of *ultima
Thule* they couldn't, either, on the facts, very well have done
less. What in the event appeared established was that if Mrs.
Lowder had disliked them she yet hadn't disliked them so much
as they supposed. It had at any rate been for the purpose of
showing how she struggled with her aversion that she sometimes came to see them, that she at regular periods invited
them to her house and in short, as it now looked, kept them
along on the terms that would best give her sister the perennial
luxury of a grievance. This sister, poor Mrs. Croy, the girl knew,
had always judged her resentfully, and had brought them up,
Marian, the boys and herself, to the idea of a particular attitude, for signs of the practice of which they watched each
other with awe. The attitude was to make plain to Aunt Maud,
with the same regularity as her invitations, that they sufficed—
thanks awfully—to themselves. But the ground of it, Kate lived
to discern, was that this was only because *she* didn't suffice to
them. The little she offered was to be accepted under protest,
yet not really because it was excessive. It wounded them—
there was the rub!—because it fell short.

The number of new things our young lady looked out on
from the high south window that hung over the Park—this
number was so great (though some of the things were only old
ones altered and, as the phrase was of other matters, done up)
that life at present turned to her view from week to week more

and more the face of a striking and distinguished stranger. She
had reached a great age—for it quite seemed to her that at
twenty-five it was late to reconsider, and her most general sense
was a shade of regret that she hadn't known earlier. The world
was different—whether for worse or for better—from her
rudimentary readings, and it gave her the feeling of a wasted
past. If she had only known sooner she might have arranged
herself more to meet it. She made at all events discoveries
every day, some of which were about herself and others about
other persons. Two of these—one under each head—more
particularly engaged, in alternation, her anxiety. She saw as she
had never seen before how material things spoke to her. She
saw, and she blushed to see, that if in contrast with some of its
old aspects life now affected her as a dress successfully "done
up," this was exactly by reason of the trimmings and lace, was
a matter of ribbons and silk and velvet. She had a dire accessi-
bility to pleasure from such sources. She liked the charming
quarters her aunt had assigned her—liked them literally more
than she had in all her other days liked anything; and nothing
could have been more uneasy than her suspicion of her relative's view of this truth. Her relative was prodigious—she had
never done her relative justice. These larger conditions all tasted
of her, from morning till night; but she was a person in respect
to whom the growth of acquaintance could only—strange as it
might seem—keep your heart in your mouth.

The girl's second great discovery was that, so far from having
been for Mrs. Lowder a subject of superficial consideration,
the blighted home in Lexham Gardens had haunted her nights
and her days. Kate had spent, all winter, hours of observation
that were not less pointed for being spent alone; recent events,
which her mourning explained, assured her a measure of isolation, and it was in the isolation above all that her neighbour's influence worked. Sitting far downstairs Aunt Maud
was yet a presence from which a sensitive niece could feel herself extremely under pressure. She knew herself now, the sensitive niece, as having been marked from far back. She knew
more than she could have told you, by the upstairs fire, in a
whole dark December afternoon. She knew so much that her
knowledge was what fairly kept her there, making her at times
circulate more endlessly between the small silk-covered sofa

that stood for her in the firelight and the great grey map of Middlesex spread beneath her lookout. To go down, to forsake her refuge, was to meet some of her discoveries halfway, to have to face them or fly before them; whereas they were at such a height only like the rumble of a far-off siege heard in the provisioned citadel. She had almost liked, in these weeks, what had created her suspense and her stress: the loss of her mother, the submersion of her father, the discomfort of her sister, the confirmation of their shrunken prospects, the certainty, in especial, of her having to recognise that should she behave, as she called it, decently—that is still do something for others—she would be herself wholly without supplies. She held that she had a right to sadness and stillness; she nursed them for their postponing power. What they mainly postponed was the question of a surrender, though she couldn't yet have said exactly of what: a general surrender of everything—that was at moments the way it presented itself—to Aunt Maud's looming "personality." It was by her personality that Aunt Maud was prodigious, and the great mass of it loomed because, in the thick, the foglike air of her arranged existence, there were parts doubtless magnified and parts certainly vague. They represented at all events alike, the dim and the distinct, a strong will and a high hand. It was perfectly present to Kate that she might be devoured, and she compared herself to a trembling kid, kept apart a day or two till her turn should come, but sure sooner or later to be introduced into the cage of the lioness.

The cage was Aunt Maud's own room, her office, her counting-house, her battlefield, her especial scene, in fine, of action, situated on the ground-floor, opening from the main hall and figuring rather to our young woman on exit and entrance as a guard-house or a toll-gate. The lioness waited—the kid had at least that consciousness; was aware of the neighbourhood of a morsel she had reason to suppose tender. She would have been meanwhile a wonderful lioness for a show, an extraordinary figure in a cage or anywhere; majestic, magnificent, high-coloured, all brilliant gloss, perpetual satin, twinkling bugles and flashing gems, with a lustre of agate eyes, a sheen of raven hair, a polish of complexion that was like that of well-kept china and that—as if the skin were too tight—told especially at curves and corners. Her niece had a quiet name for her—she kept it quiet: thinking of her, with a free fancy, as somehow typically insular, she talked to herself of Britannia of the Market Place—Britannia unmistakeable but with a pen on her ear—and felt she should not be happy till she might on some occasion add to the rest of the panoply a helmet, a shield, a trident and a ledger. It wasn't in truth, however, that the forces with which, as Kate felt, she would have to deal were those most suggested by an image simple and broad; she was learning after all each day to know her companion, and what she had already most perceived was the mistake of trusting to easy analogies. There was a whole side of Britannia, the side of her florid philistinism, her plumes and her train, her fantastic furniture and heaving bosom, the false gods of her taste and false notes of her talk, the sole contemplation of which would be dangerously misleading. She was a complex and subtle Britannia, as passionate as she was practical, with a reticule for her prejudices as deep as that other pocket, the pocket full of coins stamped in her image, that the world best knew her by. She carried on in short, behind her aggressive and defensive front, operations determined by her wisdom. It was in fact as a besieger, we have hinted, that our young lady, in the provisioned citadel, had for the present most to think of her, and what made her formidable in this character was that she was unscrupulous and immoral. So at all events in silent sessions and a youthful off-hand way Kate conveniently pictured her: what this sufficiently represented being that her weight was in the scale of certain dangers—those dangers that, by our showing, made the younger woman linger and lurk above, while the elder, below, both militant and diplomatic, covered as much of the ground as possible. Yet what were the dangers, after all, but just the dangers of life and of London? Mrs. Lowder *was* London, *was* life—the roar of the siege and the thick of the fray. There were some things, after all, of which Britannia was afraid; but Aunt Maud was afraid of nothing—not even, it would appear, of arduous thought.

These impressions, none the less, Kate kept so much to herself that she scarce shared them with poor Marian, the ostensible purpose of her frequent visits to whom yet continued to be to talk over everything. One of her reasons for holding off from the last concession to Aunt Maud was that she might be the more free to commit herself to this so much nearer and so much less fortunate relative, with whom Aunt Maud would have almost nothing direct to do. The sharpest pinch of her state, meanwhile, was exactly that all intercourse with her sister had the effect of casting down her courage and tying her hands, adding daily to her sense of the part, not always either up-lifting or sweetening, that the bond of blood might play in one's life. She was face to face with it now, with the bond of blood; the consciousness of it was what she seemed most clearly to have "come into" by the death of her mother, much of that consciousness as her mother had absorbed and carried away. Her haunting harassing father, her menacing uncompromising aunt, her portionless little nephews and nieces, were figures that caused the chord of natural piety superabundantly to vi-brate. Her manner of putting it to herself—but more especially in respect to Marian—was that she saw what you might be brought to by the cultivation of consanguinity. She had taken, in the old days, as she supposed, the measure of this liability; those being the days when, as the second-born, she had thought no one in the world so pretty as Marian, no one so charming, so clever, so assured in advance of happiness and success. The view was different now, but her attitude had been obliged, for many reasons, to show as the same. The subject of this estimate was no longer pretty, as the reason for thinking her clever was no longer plain; yet, bereaved, disappointed, de-moralised, querulous, she was all the more sharply and insis-tently Kate's elder and Kate's own. Kate's most constant feeling about her was that she would make her, Kate, do things; and always, in comfortless Chelsea, at the door of the small house the small rent of which she couldn't help having on her mind, she fatalistically asked herself, before going in, which thing it would probably be this time. She noticed with profundity that disappointment made people selfish; she marvelled at the serenity—it was the poor woman's only one—of what Marian took for granted: her own state of abasement as the second-born, her life reduced to mere inexhaustible sisterhood. She existed in that view wholly for the small house in Chelsea; the moral of which moreover, of course, was that the more you gave yourself the less of you was left. There were always people to snatch at you, and it would never occur to *them* that they were eating you up. They did that without tasting.

There was no such misfortune, or at any rate no such discomfort, she further reasoned, as to be formed at once for being and for seeing. You always saw, in this case something else than what you were, and you got in consequence none of the peace of your condition. However, as she never really let Marian see what she was Marian might well not have been aware that she herself saw. Kate was accordingly to her own vision not a hypocrite of virtue, for she gave herself up; but she was a hypocrite of stupidity, for she kept to herself everything that was not herself. What she most kept was the particular sentiment with which she watched her sister instinctively neglect nothing that would make for her submission to their aunt; a state of the spirit that perhaps marked most sharply how poor you might become when you minded so much the absence of wealth. It was through Kate that Aunt Maud should be worked, and nothing mattered less than what might become of Kate in the process. Kate was to burn her ships in short, so that Marian should profit; and Marian's desire to profit was quite oblivious of a dignity that had after all its reasons—if it had only understood them—for keeping itself a little stiff. Kate, to be properly stiff for both of them, would therefore have had to be selfish, have had to prefer an ideal of behaviour—than which nothing ever was more selfish—to the possibility of stray crumbs for the four small creatures. The tale of Mrs. Lowder's disgust at her elder niece's marriage to Mr. Condrip had lost little of its point; the incredibly fatuous behaviour of Mr. Condrip, the parson of a dull suburban parish, with a saintly profile which was always in evidence, being so distinctly on record to keep criticism consistent. He had presented his profile on system, having, goodness knew, nothing else to present—nothing at all to full-face the world with, no imagination of the propriety of living and minding his business. Criticism had remained on Aunt Maud's part consistent enough; she was not a person to regard such proceedings as less of a mistake for having acquired more of the privilege of pathos. She hadn't been forgiving, and the only approach she made to overlooking them was by overlooking—with the surviving delinquent—the solid little phalanx that now represented them. Of the two sinister ceremonies that she lumped together, the marriage and the interment, she had been present at the former, just as she had sent Marian before it a liberal cheque; but this had not been for her more than the shadow of an admitted link with Mrs. Condrip's course. She disapproved of clamorous children for whom there was no prospect; she disapproved of weeping widows who couldn't make their errors good; and she had thus put within Marian's reach one of the few luxuries left when so much else had gone, an easy pretext for a constant grievance. Kate Croy remembered well what their mother, in a different quarter, had made of it; and it was Marian's marked failure to pluck the fruit of resentment that committed them as sisters to an almost equal fellowship in abjection. If the theory was that, yes, alas, one of the pair had ceased to be noticed, but that the other was noticed enough to make up for it, who would fail to see that Kate couldn't separate herself without a cruel pride? That lesson became sharp for our young lady the day after her interview with her father.

"I can't imagine," Marian on this occasion said to her, "how you can think of anything else in the world but the horrid way we're situated."

"And, pray, how do you know," Kate enquired in reply, "anything about my thoughts? It seems to me I give you sufficient proof of how much I think of *you*. I don't really, my dear, know what else you've to do with!"

Marian's retort on this was a stroke as to which she had supplied herself with several kinds of preparation, but there was none the less something of an unexpected note in its promptitude. She had foreseen her sister's general fear; but here, ominously, was the special one. "Well, your own business is of course your own business, and you may say there's no one less in a position than I to preach to you. But, all the same, if you wash your hands of me for ever in consequence, I won't, for this once, keep back that I don't consider you've a right, as we all stand, to throw yourself away."

It was after the children's dinner, which was also their mother's, but which their aunt mostly contrived to keep from ever becoming her own luncheon; and the two young women were still in the presence of the crumpled table-cloth, the dispersed pinafores, the scraped dishes, the lingering odour of boiled food. Kate had asked with ceremony if she might put up a window a little, and Mrs. Condrip had replied without it that she might do as she liked. She often received such enquiries as if they reflected in a manner on the pure essence of her little ones. The four had retired, with much movement and noise, under imperfect control of the small Irish governess whom their aunt had hunted up for them and whose brooding resolve not to prolong so uncrowned a martyrdom she already more than suspected. Their mother had become for Kate—who took it just for the effect of being their mother—quite a different thing from the mild Marian of the past: Mr. Condrip's widow expansively obscured that image. She was little more than a ragged relic, a plain prosaic result of him—as if she had somehow been pulled through him as through an obstinate funnel, only to be left crumpled and useless and with nothing in her but what he accounted for. She had grown red and almost fat, which were not happy signs of mourning; less and less like any Croy, particularly a Croy in trouble, and sensibly like her husband's two unmarried sisters, who came to see her, in Kate's view, much too often and stayed too long, with the consequence of inroads upon the tea and bread-and-butter—matters as to which Kate, not unconcerned with the tradesmen's books, had feelings. About them moreover Marian *was* touchy, and her nearer relative, who observed and weighed things, noted as an oddity that she would have taken any reflexion on them as a reflexion on herself. If that was what marriage necessarily did to you Kate Croy would have questioned marriage. It was at any rate a grave example of what a man—and such a man!—might make of a woman. She could see how the Condrip pair pressed their brother's widow on the subject of Aunt Maud—who wasn't, after all, *their* aunt; made her, over their interminable cups, chatter and even swagger about Lancaster Gate, made her more vulgar than it had seemed written that any Croy could possibly become on such a subject. They laid it down, they rubbed it in, that Lancaster Gate was to be kept in sight, and that she, Kate, was to keep it; so that, curiously, or at all events sadly, our young woman was sure of being in her own person more permitted to them as an object of comment than they would in turn ever be permitted to herself. The beauty of which too was that Marian didn't love them. But they were Condrips—they had grown near the rose; they were almost like Bertie and Maudie, like Kitty and Guy. They talked of the dead to her, which Kate never did; it being a relation in which Kate could but mutely listen. She couldn't indeed too often say to herself that if that was what marriage did to you—! It may easily be guessed therefore that the ironic light of such reserves fell straight across the field of Marian's warning. "I don't quite see," she answered, "where in particular it strikes you that my danger lies. I'm not conscious, I assure you, of the least disposition to 'throw' myself anywhere. I feel that for the present I've been quite sufficiently thrown."

"You don't feel"—Marian brought it all out—"that you'd like to marry Merton Densher?"

Kate took a moment to meet this enquiry. "Is it your idea that if I should feel so I would be bound to give you notice, so that you might step in and head me off? Is that your idea?" the girl asked. Then as her sister also had a pause, "I don't know what makes you talk of Mr. Densher," she observed.

"I talk of him just because you don't. That you never do, in spite of what I know—that's what makes me think of him. Or rather perhaps it's what makes me think of *you*. If you don't know by this time what I hope for you, what I dream of—my attachment being what it is—it's no use my attempting to tell you." But Marian had in fact warmed to her work, and Kate was sure she had discussed Mr. Densher with the Miss Condrips. "If I name that person I suppose it's because I'm so afraid of him. If you want really to know, he fills me with terror. If you want really to know, in fact, I dislike him as much as I dread him."

"And yet don't think it dangerous to abuse him to me?"

"Yes," Mrs. Condrip confessed, "I do think it dangerous; but how can I speak of him otherwise? I dare say, I admit, that I shouldn't speak of him at all. Only I do want you for once, as I said just now, to know."

"To know what, my dear?"

"That I should regard it," Marian promptly returned, "as far and away the worst thing that has happened to us yet."

"Do you mean because he hasn't money?"

"Yes, for one thing. And because I don't believe in him."

Kate was civil but mechanical. "What do you mean by not believing in him?"

"Well, being sure he'll never get it. And you *must* have it. You *shall* have it."

"To give it to you?"

Marian met her with a readiness that was practically pert. "To *have* it, first. Not at any rate to go on not having it. Then we should see."

"We should indeed!" said Kate Croy. It was talk of a kind she loathed, but if Marian chose to be vulgar what was one to do? It made her think of the Miss Condrips with renewed aversion. "I like the way you arrange things—I like what you take for granted. If it's so easy for us to marry men who want us to scatter gold, I wonder we any of us do anything else. I don't see so many of them about, nor what interest I might ever have for them. You live, my dear," she presently added, "in a world of vain thoughts."

"Not so much as you, Kate; for I see what I see and you can't turn it off that way." The elder sister paused long enough for the younger's face to show, in spite of superiority, an apprehension. "I'm not talking of any man but Aunt Maud's man, nor of any money even, if you like, but Aunt Maud's money. I'm not talking of anything but your doing what *she* wants. You're wrong if you speak of anything that I want of you; I want nothing but what she does. That's good enough for me!" —and Marian's tone struck her companion as of the lowest. "If I don't believe in Merton Densher I do at least in Mrs. Lowder."

"Your ideas are the more striking," Kate returned, "that they're the same as papa's. I had them from him, you'll be interested to know—and with all the brilliancy you may imagine —yesterday."

Marian clearly was interested to know. "He has been to see you?"

"No, I went to him."

"Really?" Marian wondered. "For what purpose?"

"To tell him I'm ready to go to him."

Marian stared. "To leave Aunt Maud—?"

"For my father, yes."

She had fairly flushed, poor Mrs. Condrip, with horror. "You're ready—?"

"So I told him. I couldn't tell him less."

"And pray could you tell him more?" Marian gasped in her distress. "What in the world is he *to* us? You bring out such a thing as that this way?"

They faced each other—the tears were in Marian's eyes. Kate watched them there a moment and then said: "I had thought it well over—over and over. But you needn't feel injured. I'm not going. He won't have me."

Her companion still panted—it took time to subside. "Well, *I* wouldn't have you—wouldn't receive you at all, I can assure you—if he had made you any other answer. I do feel injured—at your having been willing. If you were to go to papa, my dear, you'd have to stop coming to me." Marian put it thus, indefinably, as a picture of privation from which her companion might shrink. Such were the threats she could complacently make, could think herself masterful for making. "But if he won't take you," she continued, "he shows at least his sharpness."

Marian had always her views of sharpness; she was, as her sister privately commented, great on that resource. But Kate had her refuge from irritation. "He won't take me," she simply repeated. "But he believes, like you, in Aunt Maud. He threatens me with his curse if I leave her."

"So you *won't?*" As the girl at first said nothing her companion caught at it. "You won't, of course? I see you won't. But I don't see why, conveniently, I shouldn't insist to you once for all on the plain truth of the whole matter. The truth, my dear, of your duty. Do you ever think about *that?* It's the greatest duty of all."

"There you are again," Kate laughed. "Papa's also immense on my duty."

"Oh I don't pretend to be immense, but I pretend to know more than you do of life; more even perhaps than papa." Marian seemed to see that personage at this moment, nevertheless, in the light of a kinder irony. "Poor old papa!"

She sighed it with as many condonations as her sister's ear had more than once caught in her "Dear old Aunt Maud!" These were things that made Kate turn for the time sharply away, and she gathered herself now to go. They were the note again of the abject; it was hard to say which of the persons in question had most shown how little they liked her. The younger woman proposed at any rate to let discussion rest, and she believed that, for herself, she had done so during the ten minutes elapsing, thanks to her wish not to break off short, before she could gracefully withdraw. It then appeared, however, that Marian had been discussing still, and there was something that at the last Kate had to take up. "Whom do you mean by Aunt Maud's young man?"

"Whom should I mean but Lord Mark?"

"And where do you pick up such vulgar twaddle?" Kate demanded with her clear face. "How does such stuff, in this hole, get to you?"

She had no sooner spoken than she asked herself what had become of the grace to which she had sacrificed. Marian certainly did little to save it, and nothing indeed was so inconsequent as her ground of complaint. She desired her to "work" Lancaster Gate as she believed that scene of abundance could be worked; but she now didn't see why advantage should be taken of the bloated connexion to put an affront on her own poor home. She appeared in fact for the moment to take the position that Kate kept her in her "hole" and then heartlessly reflected on her being in it. Yet she didn't explain how she had picked up the report on which her sister had challenged her—so that it was thus left to her sister to see in it once more a sign of the creeping curiosity of the Miss Condrips. They lived in a deeper hole than Marian, but they kept their ear to the ground, they spent their days in prowling, whereas Marian, in garments and shoes that seemed steadily to grow looser and larger, never prowled. There were times when Kate wondered if the Miss Condrips were offered her by fate as a warning for her own future—to be taken as showing her what she herself might become at forty if she let things too recklessly go. What was expected of her by others—and by so many of them—could, all the same, on occasion, present itself as beyond a joke; and this was just now the aspect it particularly wore. She was not only to quarrel with Merton Densher for the pleasure of her five spectators—with the Miss Condrips there were five; she was to set forth in pursuit of Lord Mark on some preposterous theory of the premium attached to success. Mrs. Lowder's hand had hung out the premium, and it figured at the end of the course as a bell that would ring, break out into public clamour, as soon as touched. Kate reflected sharply enough on the weak points of this fond fiction, with the result at last of a certain chill for her sister's confidence; though Mrs. Condrip still took refuge in the plea—which was after all the great point—that their aunt would be munificent when their aunt should be content. The exact identity of her candidate was a detail; what was of the essence was her conception of the kind of match it was open to her niece to make with her aid. Marian always spoke of marriages as "matches," but that was again a detail. Mrs. Lowder's "aid" meanwhile awaited them—if not to light the way to Lord Mark, then to somebody better. Marian would put up, in fine, with somebody better; she only wouldn't put up with somebody so much worse. Kate had once more to go through all this before a graceful issue was reached. It was reached by her paying with the sacrifice of Mr. Densher for her reduction of Lord Mark to the absurd. So they separated softly enough. She was to be let off hearing about Lord Mark so long as she made it good that she wasn't underhand about any one else. She had denied everything and every one, she reflected as she went away—and that was a relief; but it also made rather a clean sweep of the future. The prospect put on a bareness that already gave her something in common with the Miss Condrips.

BOOK SECOND

I

ERTON DENSHER, who passed the best hours of each
night at the office of his newspaper, had at times, during
the day, to make up for it, a sense, or at least an appearance, of
leisure, in accordance with which he was not infrequently to be
met in different parts of the town at moments when men of
business are hidden from the public eye. More than once
during the present winter's end he had deviated toward three
o'clock, or toward four, into Kensington Gardens, where he
might for a while, on each occasion, have been observed to de-
mean himself as a person with nothing to do. He made his way
indeed, for the most part, with a certain directness over to the
north side; but once that ground was reached his behaviour
was noticeably wanting in point. He moved, seemingly at random, from alley to alley; he stopped for no reason and remained idly agaze; he sat down in a chair and then changed to
a bench; after which he walked about again, only again to repeat both the vagueness and the vivacity. Distinctly he was a
man either with nothing at all to do or with ever so much to
think about; and it was not to be denied that the impression he
might often thus easily make had the effect of causing the burden of proof in certain directions to rest on him. It was a little
the fault of his aspect, his personal marks, which made it almost
impossible to name his profession.

He was a longish, leanish, fairish young Englishman, not
unamenable, on certain sides, to classification—as for instance
by being a gentleman, by being rather specifically one of the
educated, one of the generally sound and generally civil; yet,
though to that degree neither extraordinary nor abnormal, he
would have failed to play straight into an observer's hands. He
was young for the House of Commons, he was loose for the
Army. He was refined, as might have been said, for the City
and, quite apart from the cut of his cloth, sceptical, it might
have been felt, for the Church. On the other hand he was

credulous for diplomacy, or perhaps even for science, while he
was perhaps at the same time too much in his mere senses for
poetry and yet too little in them for art. You would have got
fairly near him by making out in his eyes the potential recognition of ideas; but you would have quite fallen away again on
the question of the ideas themselves. The difficulty with Densher was that he looked vague without looking weak—idle
without looking empty. It was the accident, possibly, of his
long legs, which were apt to stretch themselves; of his straight
hair and his well-shaped head, never, the latter, neatly smooth,
and apt into the bargain, at the time of quite other calls upon
it, to throw itself suddenly back and, supported behind by his
uplifted arms and interlocked hands, place him for uncon-
scionable periods in communion with the ceiling, the tree-tops,
the sky. He was in short visibly absent-minded, irregularly
clever, liable to drop what was near and to take up what was
far; he was more a prompt critic than a prompt follower of custom. He suggested above all, however, that wondrous state of
youth in which the elements, the metals more or less precious,
are so in fusion and fermentation that the question of the final
stamp, the pressure that fixes the value, must wait for comparative coolness. And it was a mark of his interesting mixture
that if he was irritable it was by a law of considerable subtlety
—a law that in intercourse with him it might be of profit,
though not easy, to master. One of the effects of it was that he
had for you surprises of tolerance as well as of temper.

He loitered, on the best of the relenting days, the several occasions we speak of, along the part of the Gardens nearest to
Lancaster Gate, and when, always, in due time, Kate Croy
came out of her aunt's house, crossed the road and arrived by
the nearest entrance, there was a general publicity in the proceeding which made it slightly anomalous. If their meeting
was to be bold and free it might have taken place within-doors;
if it was to be shy or secret it might have taken place almost
anywhere better than under Mrs. Lowder's windows. They
failed indeed to remain attached to that spot; they wandered
and strolled, taking in the course of more than one of these interviews a considerable walk, or else picked out a couple of
chairs under one of the great trees and sat as much apart—
apart from every one else—as possible. But Kate had each

time, at first, the air of wishing to expose herself to pursuit and
capture if those things were in question. She made the point
that she wasn't underhand, any more than she was vulgar; that
the Gardens were charming in themselves and this use of them
a matter of taste; and that, if her aunt chose to glare at her
from the drawing-room or to cause her to be tracked and overtaken, she could at least make it convenient that this should be
easily done. The fact was that the relation between these
young persons abounded in such oddities as were not inaptly
symbolised by assignations that had a good deal more appearance than motive. Of the strength of the tie that held them we
shall sufficiently take the measure; but it was meanwhile almost obvious that if the great possibility had come up for them
it had done so, to an exceptional degree, under the protection
of the famous law of contraries. Any deep harmony that might
eventually govern them would not be the result of their having
much in common—having anything in fact but their affection;
and would really find its explanation in some sense, on the part
of each, of being poor where the other was rich. It is nothing
new indeed that generous young persons often admire most
what nature hasn't given them—from which it would appear,
after all, that our friends were both generous.

Merton Densher had repeatedly said to himself—and from
far back—that he should be a fool not to marry a woman whose
value would be in her differences; and Kate Croy, though
without having quite so philosophised, had quickly recognised
in the young man a precious unlikeness. He represented what
her life had never given her and certainly, without some such
aid as his, never would give her; all the high dim things she
lumped together as of the mind. It was on the side of the mind
that Densher was rich for her and mysterious and strong; and
he had rendered her in especial the sovereign service of making
that element real. She had had all her days to take it terribly on
trust, no creature she had ever encountered having been able
to testify for it directly. Vague rumours of its existence had
made their precarious way to her; but nothing had, on the
whole, struck her as more likely than that she should live and
die without the chance to verify them. The chance had come—
it was an extraordinary one—on the day she first met Densher;
and it was to the girl's lasting honour that she knew on the spot

what she was in presence of. That occasion indeed, for everything that straightway flowered in it, would be worthy of high
commemoration; Densher's perception went out to meet the
young woman's and quite kept pace with her own recognition.
Having so often concluded on the fact of his weakness, as he
called it, for life—his strength merely for thought—life, he
logically opined, was what he must somehow arrange to annex
and possess. This was so much a necessity that thought by itself only went on in the void; it was from the immediate air of
life that it must draw its breath. So the young man, ingenious
but large, critical but ardent too, made out both his case and
Kate Croy's. They had originally met before her mother's
death—an occasion marked for her as the last pleasure permitted by the approach of that event; after which the dark months
had interposed a screen and, for all Kate knew, made the end
one with the beginning.

The beginning—to which she often went back—had been a
scene, for our young woman, of supreme brilliancy; a party
given at a "gallery" hired by a hostess who fished with big nets.
A Spanish dancer, understood to be at that moment the delight of the town, an American reciter, the joy of a kindred
people, an Hungarian fiddler, the wonder of the world at large
—in the name of these and other attractions the company in
which Kate, by a rare privilege, found herself had been freely
convoked. She lived under her mother's roof, as she considered,
obscurely, and was acquainted with few persons who entertained on that scale; but she had had dealings with two or
three connected, as appeared, with such—two or three through
whom the stream of hospitality, filtered or diffused, could thus
now and then spread to outlying receptacles. A good-natured
lady in fine, a friend of her mother and a relative of the lady of
the gallery, had offered to take her to the party in question and
had there fortified her, further, with two or three of those introductions that, at large parties, lead to other things—that
had at any rate on this occasion culminated for her in conversation with a tall fair, a slightly unbrushed and rather awkward,
but on the whole a not dreary, young man. The young man
had affected her as detached, as—it was indeed what he called
himself—awfully at sea, as much more distinct from what surrounded them than any one else appeared to be, and even as

probably quite disposed to be making his escape when pulled up to be placed in relation with her. He gave her his word for it indeed, this same evening, that only their meeting had prevented his flight, but that now he saw how sorry he should have been to miss it. This point they had reached by midnight, and though for the value of such remarks everything was in the tone, by midnight the tone was there too. She had had originally her full apprehension of his coerced, certainly of his vague, condition—full apprehensions often being with her immediate; then she had had her equal consciousness that within five minutes something between them had—well, she couldn't call it anything but *come*. It was nothing to look at or to handle, but was somehow everything to feel and to know; it was that something for each of them had happened.

They had found themselves regarding each other straight, and for a longer time on end than was usual even at parties in galleries; but that in itself after all would have been a small affair for two such handsome persons. It wasn't, in a word, simply that their eyes had met; other conscious organs, faculties, feelers had met as well, and when Kate afterwards imaged to herself the sharp deep fact she saw it, in the oddest way, as a particular performance. She had observed a ladder against a garden-wall and had trusted herself so to climb it as to be able to see over into the probable garden on the other side. On reaching the top she had found herself face to face with a gentleman engaged in a like calculation at the same moment, and the two enquirers had remained confronted on their ladders. The great point was that for the rest of that evening they had been perched—they had not climbed down; and indeed during the time that followed Kate at least had had the perched feeling —it was as if she were there aloft without a retreat. A simpler expression of all this is doubtless but that they had taken each other in with interest; and without a happy hazard six months later the incident would have closed in that account of it. The accident meanwhile had been as natural as anything in London ever is: Kate had one afternoon found herself opposite Mr. Densher on the Underground Railway. She had entered the train at Sloane Square to go to Queen's Road, and the carriage in which she took her place was all but full. Densher was already in it—on the other bench and at the furthest angle; she was sure of him before they had again started. The day and the hour were darkness, there were six other persons and she had been busy seating herself; but her consciousness had gone to him as straight as if they had come together in some bright stretch of a desert. They had on neither part a second's hesitation; they looked across the choked compartment exactly as if she had known he would be there and he had expected her to come in; so that, though in the conditions they could only exchange the greeting of movements, smiles, abstentions, it would have been quite in the key of these passages that they should have alighted for ease at the very next station. Kate was in fact sure the very next station was the young man's true goal —which made it clear he was going on only from the wish to speak to her. He had to go on, for this purpose, to High Street Kensington, as it was not till then that the exit of a passenger gave him his chance.

His chance put him however in quick possession of the seat facing her, the alertness of his capture of which seemed to show her his impatience. It helped them moreover, with strangers on either side, little to talk; though this very restriction perhaps made such a mark for them as nothing else could have done. If the fact that their opportunity had again come round for them could be so intensely expressed without a word, they might very well feel on the spot that it had not come round for nothing. The extraordinary part of the matter was that they were not in the least meeting where they had left off, but ever so much further on, and that these added links added still another between High Street and Notting Hill Gate, and then worked between the latter station and Queen's Road an extension really inordinate. At Notting Hill Gate Kate's right-hand neighbour descended, whereupon Densher popped straight into that seat; only there was not much gained when a lady the next instant popped into Densher's. He could say almost nothing—Kate scarce knew, at least, what he said; she was so occupied with a certainty that one of the persons opposite, a youngish man with a single eye-glass which he kept constantly in position, had made her out from the first as visibly, as strangely affected. If such a person made her out what then did Densher do?—a question in truth sufficiently answered when, on their reaching her station, he instantly followed her out of the train. That had been the real beginning—the beginning of everything else; the other time, the time at the party, had been but the beginning of *that*. Never in life before had she so let herself go; for always before—so far as small adventures could have been in question for her—there had been, by the vulgar measure, more to go upon. He had walked with her to Lancaster Gate, and then she had walked with him away from it—for all the world, she said to herself, like the housemaid giggling to the baker.

This appearance, she was afterwards to feel, had been all in order for a relation that might precisely best be described in the terms of the baker and the housemaid. She could say to herself that from that hour they had kept company: that had come to represent, technically speaking, alike the range and the limit of their tie. He had on the spot, naturally, asked leave to call upon her—which, as a young person who wasn't really young, who didn't pretend to be a sheltered flower, she as rationally gave. That—she was promptly clear about it—was now her only possible basis; she was just the contemporary London female, highly modern, inevitably battered, honourably free. She had of course taken her aunt straight into her confidence —had gone through the form of asking her leave; and she subsequently remembered that though on this occasion she had left the history of her new alliance as scant as the facts themselves, Mrs. Lowder had struck her at the time as surprisingly mild. The occasion had been in every way full of the reminder that her hostess was deep: it was definitely then that she had begun to ask herself what Aunt Maud was, in vulgar parlance, "up to." "You may receive, my dear, whom you like"—that was what Aunt Maud, who in general objected to people's doing as they liked, had replied; and it bore, this unexpectedness, a good deal of looking into. There were many explanations, and they were all amusing—amusing, that is, in the line of the sombre and brooding amusement cultivated by Kate in her actual high retreat. Merton Densher came the very next Sunday; but Mrs. Lowder was so consistently magnanimous as to make it possible to her niece to see him alone. She saw him, however, on the Sunday following, in order to invite him to dinner; and when, after dining, he came again—which he did three times, she found means to treat his visit as preponderantly to herself. Kate's conviction that she didn't like him made that remarkable; it added to the evidence, by this time voluminous, that she was remarkable all round. If she had been, in the way of energy, merely usual she would have kept her dislike direct; whereas it was now as if she were seeking to know him in order to see best where to "have" him. That was one of the reflexions made in our young woman's high retreat; she smiled from her lookout, in the silence that was only the fact of hearing irrelevant sounds, as she caught the truth that you could easily accept people when you wanted them so to be delivered to you. When Aunt Maud wished them dispatched it was not to be done by deputy; it was clearly always a matter reserved for her own hand.

But what made the girl wonder most was the implication of so much diplomacy in respect to her own value. What view might she take of her position in the light of this appearance that her companion feared so as yet to upset her? It was as if Densher were accepted partly under the dread that if he hadn't been she would act in resentment. Hadn't her aunt considered the danger that she would in that case have broken off, have seceded? The danger was exaggerated—she would have done nothing so gross; but that, it would seem, was the way Mrs. Lowder saw her and believed her to be reckoned with. What importance therefore did she really attach to her, what strange interest could she take in their keeping on terms? Her father and her sister had their answer to this—even without knowing how the question struck her: they saw the lady of Lancaster Gate as panting to make her fortune, and the explanation of that appetite was that, on the accident of a nearer view than she had before enjoyed, she had been charmed, been dazzled. They approved, they admired in her one of the belated fancies of rich capricious violent old women—the more marked moreover because the result of no plot; and they piled up the possible fruits for the person concerned. Kate knew what to think of her own power thus to carry by storm; she saw herself as handsome, no doubt, but as hard, and felt herself as clever but as cold; and as so much too imperfectly ambitious, futhermore, that it was a pity, for a quiet life, she couldn't decide to be either finely or stupidly indifferent. Her intelligence sometimes kept her still—too still—but her want of it was restless; so that she got the good, it seemed to her, of neither extreme. She saw herself at present, none the less, in a situation, and even her sad disillusioned mother, dying, but with Aunt Maud interviewing the nurse on the stairs, had not failed to remind her that it was of the essence of situations to be, under Providence, worked. The dear woman had died in the belief that she was actually working the one then recognised.

Kate took one of her walks with Densher just after her visit to Mr. Croy; but most of it went, as usual, to their sitting in talk. They had under the trees by the lake the air of old friends —particular phases of apparent earnestness in which they might have been settling every question in their vast young world; and periods of silence, side by side, perhaps even more, when "A long engagement!" would have been the final reading of the signs on the part of a passer struck with them, as it was so easy to be. They would have presented themselves thus as very old friends rather than as young persons who had met for the first time but a year before and had spent most of the interval without contact. It was indeed for each, already, as if they were older friends; and though the succession of their meetings might, between them, have been straightened out, they only had a confused sense of a good many, very much alike, and a confused intention of a good many more, as little different as possible. The desire to keep them just as they were had perhaps to do with the fact that in spite of the presumed diagnosis of the stranger there had been for them as yet no formal, no final understanding. Densher had at the very first pressed the question, but that, it had been easy to reply, was too soon; so that a singular thing had afterwards happened. They had accepted their acquaintance as too short for an engagement, but they had treated it as long enough for almost anything else, and marriage was somehow before them like a temple without an avenue. They belonged to the temple and they met in the grounds; they were in the stage at which grounds in general offered much scattered refreshment. But Kate had meanwhile had so few confidants that she wondered at the source of her father's suspicions. The diffusion of rumour was of course always remarkable in London, and for Marian not less—as Aunt Maud touched neither directly—the mystery had worked. No doubt she had been seen. Of course she had been seen. She had taken no trouble not to be seen, and it was a thing she was clearly incapable of taking. But she had been seen how?—and what *was* there to see? She was in love—she knew that: but it was wholly her own business, and she had the sense of having conducted herself, of still so doing, with almost violent conformity.

"I've an idea—in fact I feel sure—that Aunt Maud means to write to you; and I think you had better know it." So much as this she said to him as soon as they met, but immediately adding to it: "So as to make up your mind how to take her. I know pretty well what she'll say to you."

"Then will you kindly tell me?"

She thought a little. "I can't do that. I should spoil it. She'll do the best for her own idea."

"Her idea, you mean, that I'm a sort of a scoundrel; or, at the best, not good enough for you?"

They were side by side again in their penny chairs, and Kate had another pause. "Not good enough for *her*."

"Oh I see. And that's necessary."

He put it as a truth rather more than as a question; but there had been plenty of truths between them that each had contradicted. Kate, however, let this one sufficiently pass, only saying the next moment: "She has behaved extraordinarily."

"And so have we," Densher declared. "I think, you know, we've been awfully decent."

"For ourselves, for each other, for people in general, yes. But not for *her*. For her," said Kate, "we've been monstrous. She has been giving us rope. So if she does send for you," the girl repeated, "you must know where you are."

"That I always know. It's where *you* are that concerns me."

"Well," said Kate after an instant, "her idea of that is what you'll have from her." He gave her a long look, and whatever else people who wouldn't let her alone might have wished, for her advancement, his long looks were the thing in the world she could never have enough of. What she felt was that, whatever might happen, she must keep them, must make them most completely her possession; and it was already strange enough that she reasoned, or at all events began to act, as if she might work them in with other and alien things, privately cherish them and yet, as regards the rigour of it, pay no price. She

looked it well in the face, she took it intensely home, that they
were lovers; she rejoiced to herself and, frankly, to him, in their
wearing of the name; but, distinguished creature that, in her
way, she was, she took a view of this character that scarce
squared with the conventional. The character itself she insisted
on as their right, taking that so for granted that it didn't seem
even bold; but Densher, though he agreed with her, found
himself moved to wonder at her simplifications, her values.
Life might prove difficult—was evidently going to; but meanwhile they had each other, and that was everything. This was
her reasoning, but meanwhile, for *him*, each other was what
they didn't have, and it was just the point. Repeatedly, however, it was a point that, in the face of strange and special
things, he judged it rather awkwardly gross to urge. It was impossible to keep Mrs. Lowder out of their scheme. She stood
there too close to it and too solidly; it had to open a gate, at a
given point, do what they would, to take her in. And she came
in, always, while they sat together rather helplessly watching
her, as in a coach-and-four; she drove round their prospect as
the principal lady at the circus drives round the ring, and she
stopped the coach in the middle to alight with majesty. It was
our young man's sense that she was magnificently vulgar, but
yet quite that this wasn't all. It wasn't with her vulgarity that
she felt his want of means, though that might have helped her
richly to embroider it; nor was it with the same infirmity that
she was strong original dangerous.

His want of means—of means sufficient for any one but
himself—was really the great ugliness, and was moreover at no
time more ugly for him than when it rose there, as it did seem
to rise, all shameless, face to face with the elements in Kate's
life colloquially and conveniently classed by both of them as
funny. He sometimes indeed, for that matter, asked himself if
these elements were as funny as the innermost fact, so often
vivid to him, of his own consciousness—his private inability to
believe he should ever be rich. His conviction on this head was
in truth quite positive and a thing by itself; he failed, after
analysis, to understand it, though he had naturally more lights
on it than any one else. He knew how it subsisted in spite of an
equal consciousness of his being neither mentally nor physically quite helpless, neither a dunce nor a cripple; he knew it to

be absolute, though secret, and also, strange to say, about common undertakings, not discouraging, not prohibitive. Only now was he having to think if it were prohibitive in respect to marriage; only now, for the first time, had he to weigh his case in scales. The scales, as he sat with Kate, often dangled in the line of his vision; he saw them, large and black, while he talked or listened, take, in the bright air, singular positions. Sometimes the right was down and sometimes the left; never a happy equipoise—one or the other always kicking the beam. Thus was kept before him the question of whether it were more ignoble to ask a woman to take her chance with you, or to accept it from your conscience that her chance could be at the best but one of the degrees of privation; whether too, otherwise, marrying for money mightn't after all be a smaller cause of shame than the mere dread of marrying without. Through these variations of mood and view, nevertheless, the mark on his forehead stood clear; he saw himself remain without whether he married or not. It was a line on which his fancy could be admirably active; the innumerable ways of making money were beautifully present to him; he could have handled them for his newspaper as easily as he handled everything. He was quite aware how he handled everything; it was another mark on his forehead: the pair of smudges from the thumb of fortune, the brand on the passive fleece, dated from the primal hour and kept each other company. He wrote, as for print, with deplorable ease; since there had been nothing to stop him even at the age of ten, so there was as little at twenty; it was part of his fate in the first place and part of the wretched public's in the second. The innumerable ways of making money were, no doubt, at all events, what his imagination often was busy with after he had tilted his chair and thrown back his head with his hands clasped behind it. What would most have prolonged that attitude, moreover, was the reflexion that the ways were ways only for others. Within the minute now—however this might be—he was aware of a nearer view than he had yet quite had of those circumstances on his companion's part that made least for simplicity of relation. He saw above all how she saw them herself, for she spoke of them at present with the last frankness, telling him of her visit to her father and giving him, in an account of her subsequent scene with her sister, an instance of how she was perpetually reduced to patching-up, in one way or another, that unfortunate woman's hopes.

"The tune," she exclaimed, "to which we're a failure as a family!" With which he had it all again from her—and this time, as it seemed to him, more than all: the dishonour her father had brought them, his folly and cruelty and wickedness; the wounded state of her mother, abandoned despoiled and helpless, yet, for the management of such a home as remained to them, dreadfully unreasonable too; the extinction of her two young brothers—one, at nineteen, the eldest of the house, by typhoid fever contracted at a poisonous little place, as they had afterwards found out, that they had taken for a summer; the other, the flower of the flock, a middy on the *Britannia*, dreadfully drowned, and not even by an accident at sea, but by cramp, unrescued, while bathing, too late in the autumn, in a wretched little river during a holiday visit to the home of a shipmate. Then Marian's unnatural marriage, in itself a kind of spiritless turning of the other cheek to fortune: her actual wretchedness and plaintiveness, her greasy children, her impossible claims, her odious visitors—these things completed the proof of the heaviness, for them all, of the hand of fate. Kate confessedly described them with an excess of impatience; it was much of her charm for Densher that she gave in general that turn to her descriptions, partly as if to amuse him by free and humorous colour, partly—and that charm was the greatest—as if to work off, for her own relief, her constant perception of the incongruity of things. She had seen the general show too early and too sharply, and was so intelligent that she knew it and allowed for that misfortune; therefore when, in talk with him, she was violent and almost unfeminine, it was quite as if they had settled, for intercourse, on the short cut of the fantastic and the happy language of exaggeration. It had come to be definite between them at a primary stage that, if they could have no other straight way, the realm of thought at least was open to them. They could think whatever they liked about whatever they would—in other words they could say it. Saying it for each other, for each other alone, only of course added to the taste. The implication was thereby constant that what they said when not together had no taste for them at all, and nothing could have served more to launch them, at special hours, on their small floating island than such an assumption that they were only making believe everywhere else. Our young man, it must be added, was conscious enough that it was Kate who profited most by this particular play of the fact of intimacy. It always struck him she had more life than he to react from, and when she recounted the dark disasters of her house and glanced at the hard odd offset of her present exaltation—since as exaltation it was apparently to be considered—he felt his own grey domestic annals make little show. It was naturally, in all such reference, the question of her father's character that engaged him most, but her picture of her adventure in Chirk Street gave him a sense of how little as yet that character was clear to him. What was it, to speak plainly, that Mr. Croy had originally done?

"I don't know—and I don't want to. I only know that years and years ago—when I was about fifteen—something or other happened that made him impossible. I mean impossible for the world at large first, and then, little by little, for mother. We of course didn't know it at the time," Kate explained, "but we knew it later; and it was, oddly enough, my sister who first made out that he had done something. I can hear her now—the way, one cold black Sunday morning when, on account of an extraordinary fog, we hadn't gone to church, she broke it to me by the school-room fire. I was reading a history-book by the lamp—when we didn't go to church we had to read history-books—and I suddenly heard her say, out of the fog, which was in the room, and apropos of nothing: 'Papa has done something wicked.' And the curious thing was that I believed it on the spot and have believed it ever since, though she could tell me nothing more—neither what was the wickedness, nor how she knew, nor what would happen to him, nor anything else about it. We had our sense always that all sorts of things *had* happened, were all the while happening, to him; so that when Marian only said she was sure, tremendously sure, that she had made it out for herself, but that that was enough, I took her word for it—it seemed somehow so natural. We were not, however, to ask mother—which made it more natural still, and I said never a word. But mother, strangely enough, spoke of it to me, in time, of her own accord—this was very much later on. He hadn't been with us for ever so long, but we were used to that. She must have had some fear, some conviction that I had an idea, some idea of her own that it was the best thing to do. She came out as abruptly as Marian had done: 'If you hear anything against your father—anything I mean except that he's odious and vile—remember it's perfectly false.' That was the way I knew it was true, though I recall my saying to her then that I of course knew it wasn't. She might have told me it was true, and yet have trusted me to contradict fiercely enough any accusation of him that I should meet—to contradict it much more fiercely and effectively, I think, than she would have done herself. As it happens, however," the girl went on, "I've never had occasion, and I've been conscious of it with a sort of surprise. It has made the world seem at times more decent. No one has so much as breathed to me. That has been a part of the silence, the silence that surrounds him, the silence that, for the world, has washed him out. He doesn't exist for people. And yet I'm as sure as ever. In fact, though I know no more than I did then, I'm more sure. And that," she wound up, "is what I sit here and tell you about my own father. If you don't call it a proof of confidence I don't know what will satisfy you."

"It satisfies me beautifully," Densher returned, "but it doesn't, my dear child, very greatly enlighten me. You don't, you know, really tell me anything. It's so vague that what am I to think but that you may very well be mistaken? What has he done, if no one can name it?"

"He has done everything."

"Oh—everything! Everything's nothing."

"Well then," said Kate, "he has done some particular thing. It's known—only, thank God, not to us. But it has been the end of him. *You* could doubtless find out with a little trouble. You can ask about."

Densher for a moment said nothing; but the next moment he made it up. "I wouldn't find out for the world, and I'd rather lose my tongue than put a question."

"And yet it's a part of me," said Kate.

"A part of you?"

"My father's dishonour." Then she sounded for him, but

more deeply than ever yet, her note of proud still pessimism. "How can such a thing as that not be the great thing in one's life?"

She had to take from him again, on this, one of his long looks, and she took it to its deepest, its headiest dregs. "I shall ask you, for the great thing in your life," he said, "to depend on *me* a little more." After which, just debating, "Doesn't he belong to some club?" he asked.

She had a grave headshake. "He used to—to many."

"But he has dropped them?"

"They've dropped *him*. Of that I'm sure. It ought to do for you. I offered him," the girl immediately continued—"and it was for that I went to him—to come and be with him, make a home for him so far as is possible. But he won't hear of it."

Densher took this in with marked but generous wonder. "You offered him—'impossible' as you describe him to me—to live with him and share his disadvantages?" The young man saw for the moment only the high beauty of it. "You *are* gallant!"

"Because it strikes you as being brave for him?" She wouldn't in the least have this. "It wasn't courage—it was the opposite. I did it to save myself—to escape."

He had his air, so constant at this stage, as of her giving him finer things than any one to think about. "Escape from what?"

"From everything."

"Do you by any chance mean from me?"

"No; I spoke to him of you, told him—or what amounted to it—that I would bring you, if he would allow it, with me."

"But he won't allow it," said Densher.

"Won't hear of it on any terms. He won't help me, won't save me, won't hold out a finger to me," Kate went on. "He simply wriggles away, in his inimitable manner, and throws me back."

"Back then, after all, thank goodness," Densher concurred, "on me."

But she spoke again as with the sole vision of the whole scene she had evoked. "It's a pity, because you'd like him. He's wonderful—he's charming." Her companion gave one of the laughs that showed again how inveterately he felt in her tone something that banished the talk of other women, so far as he knew other women, to the dull desert of the conventional, and she had already continued. "He would make himself delightful to you."

"Even while objecting to me?"

"Well, he likes to please," the girl explained—"personally. I've seen it make him wonderful. He would appreciate you and be clever with you. It's to *me* he objects—that is as to my liking you."

"Heaven be praised then," cried Densher, "that you like me enough for the objection!"

But she met it after an instant with some inconsequence. "I don't. I offered to give you up, if necessary, to go to him. But it made no difference, and that's what I mean," she pursued, "by his declining me on any terms. The point is, you see, that I don't escape."

Densher wondered. "But if you didn't wish to escape *me*?"

"I wished to escape Aunt Maud. But he insists that it's through her and through her only that I may help him; just as Marian insists that it's through her, and through her only, that I can help *her*. That's what I mean," she again explained, "by their turning me back."

The young man thought. "Your sister turns you back too?"

"Oh with a push!"

"But have you offered to live with your sister?"

"I would in a moment if she'd have me. That's all my virtue —a narrow little family feeling. I've a small stupid piety—I don't know what to call it." Kate bravely stuck to that; she made it out. "Sometimes, alone, I've to smother my shrieks when I think of my poor mother. She went through things— they pulled her down; I know what they were now—I didn't then, for I was a pig; and my position, compared with hers, is an insolence of success. That's what Marian keeps before me; that's what papa himself, as I say, so inimitably does. My position's a value, a great value, for them both"—she followed and followed. Lucid and ironic, she knew no merciful muddle. "It's *the* value—the only one they have."

Everything between our young couple moved to-day, in spite of their pauses, their margin, to a quicker measure—the quickness and anxiety playing lightning-like in the sultriness. Densher watched, decidedly, as he had never done before. "And the fact you speak of holds you!"

"Of course it holds me. It's a perpetual sound in my ears. It makes me ask myself if I've any right to personal happiness, any right to anything but to be as rich and overflowing, as smart and shining, as I can be made."

Densher had a pause. "Oh you might by good luck have the personal happiness too."

Her immediate answer to this was a silence like his own; after which she gave him straight in the face, but quite simply and quietly: "Darling!"

It took him another moment; then he was also quiet and simple. "Will you settle it by our being married to-morrow— as we can, with perfect ease, civilly?"

"Let us wait to arrange it," Kate presently replied, "till after you've seen her."

"Do you call that adoring me?" Densher demanded.

They were talking, for the time, with the strangest mixture of deliberation and directness, and nothing could have been more in the tone of it than the way she at last said: "You're afraid of her yourself."

He gave rather a glazed smile. "For young persons of a great distinction and a very high spirit we're a caution!"

"Yes," she took it straight up; "we're hideously intelligent. But there's fun in it too. We must get our fun where we can. I think," she added, and for that matter not without courage, "our relation's quite beautiful. It's not a bit vulgar. I cling to some saving romance in things."

It made him break into a laugh that had more freedom than his smile. "How you must be afraid you'll chuck me!"

"No, no, *that* would be vulgar. But of course," she admitted, "I do see my danger of doing something base."

"Then what can be so base as sacrificing me?"

"I *shan't* sacrifice you. Don't cry out till you're hurt. I shall sacrifice nobody and nothing, and that's just my situation, that I want and that I shall try for everything. That," she wound up, "is how I see myself (and how I see you quite as much) acting for them."

"For 'them'?"—and the young man extravagantly marked his coldness. "Thank you!"

"Don't you care for them?"

"Why should I? What are they to me but a serious nuisance?"

As soon as he had permitted himself this qualification of the unfortunate persons she so perversely cherished he repented of his roughness—and partly because he expected a flash from her. But it was one of her finest sides that she sometimes flashed with a mere mild glow. "I don't see why you don't make out a little more that if we avoid stupidity we may do *all*. We may keep her."

He stared. "Make her pension us?"

"Well, wait at least till we've seen."

He thought. "Seen what can be got out of her?"

Kate for a moment said nothing. "After all I never asked her; never, when our troubles were at the worst, appealed to her nor went near her. She fixed upon me herself, settled on me with her wonderful gilded claws."

"You speak," Densher observed, "as if she were a vulture."

"Call it an eagle—with a gilded beak as well, and with wings for great flights. If she's a thing of the air, in short—say at once a great seamed silk balloon—I never myself got into her car. I was her choice."

It had really, her sketch of the affair, a high colour and a great style; at all of which he gazed a minute as at a picture by a master. "What she must see in you!"

"Wonders!" And, speaking it loud, she stood straight up. "Everything. There it is."

Yes, there it was, and as she remained before him he continued to face it. "So that what you mean is that I'm to do my part in somehow squaring her?"

"See her, see her," Kate said with impatience.

"And grovel to her?"

"Ah do what you like!" And she walked in her impatience away.

II

His eyes had followed her at this time quite long enough, before he overtook her, to make out more than ever in the poise of her head, the pride of her step—he didn't know what best to call it—a part at least of Mrs. Lowder's reasons. He consciously winced while he figured his presenting himself as a reason opposed to these; though at the same moment, with the source of Aunt Maud's inspiration thus before him, he was prepared to conform, by almost any abject attitude or profitable compromise, to his companion's easy injunction. He would do as *she* liked—his own liking might come off as it would. He would help her to the utmost of his power; for, all the rest of this day and the next, her easy injunction, tossed off that way as she turned her beautiful back, was like the crack of a great whip in the blue air, the high element in which Mrs. Lowder hung. He wouldn't grovel perhaps—he wasn't quite ready for that; but he would be patient, ridiculous, reasonable, unreasonable, and above all deeply diplomatic. He would be clever with all his cleverness—which he now shook hard, as he sometimes shook his poor dear shabby old watch, to start it up again. It wasn't, thank goodness, as if there weren't plenty of that "factor" (to use one of his great newspaper-words), and with what they could muster between them it would be little to the credit of their star, however pale, that defeat and surrender—surrender so early, so immediate—should have to ensue. It was not indeed that he thought of that disaster as at the worst a direct sacrifice of their possibilities: he imaged it—which was enough—as some proved vanity, some exposed fatuity in the idea of bringing Mrs. Lowder round. When shortly afterwards, in this lady's vast drawing-room—the apartments at Lancaster Gate had struck him from the first as of prodigious extent—he awaited her, at her request, conveyed in a "reply-paid" telegram, his theory was that of their still clinging to their idea, though with a sense of the difficulty of it really enlarged to the scale of the place.

He had the place for a long time—it seemed to him a quarter of an hour—to himself; and while Aunt Maud kept him and kept him, while observation and reflexion crowded on him, he asked himself what was to be expected of a person who could treat one like that. The visit, the hour were of her own proposing, so that her delay, no doubt, was but part of a general plan of putting him to inconvenience. As he walked to and fro, however, taking in the message of her massive florid furniture, the immense expression of her signs and symbols, he had as little doubt of the inconvenience he was prepared to suffer. He found himself even facing the thought that he had nothing to fall back on, and that that was as great an humiliation in a good cause as a proud man could desire. It hadn't yet been so distinct to him that he made no show—literally not the smallest; so complete a show seemed made there all about him; so almost abnormally affirmative, so aggressively erect, were the huge heavy objects that syllabled his hostess's story. "When all's said and done, you know, she's colossally vulgar"—he had once all but noted that of her to her niece; only just keeping it back at the last, keeping it to himself with all its danger about it. It mattered because it bore so directly, and he at all events quite felt it a thing that Kate herself would some day bring out to him. It bore directly at present, and really all the more that somehow, strangely, it didn't in the least characterise the poor woman as dull or stale. She was vulgar with freshness, almost with beauty, since there was beauty, to a degree, in the play of so big and bold a temperament. She was in fine quite the largest possible quantity to deal with; and he was in the cage of the lioness without his whip—the whip, in a word, of a supply of proper retorts. He had no retort but that he loved the girl— which in such a house as that was painfully cheap. Kate had mentioned to him more than once that her aunt was Passionate, speaking of it as a kind of offset and uttering it as with a capital P, marking it as something that he might, that he in fact ought to, turn about in some way to their advantage. He wondered at this hour to what advantage he could turn it; but the case grew less simple the longer he waited. Decidedly there was something he hadn't enough of.

His slow march to and fro seemed to give him the very measure; as he paced and paced the distance it became the desert of his poverty; at the sight of which expanse moreover he could pretend to himself as little as before that the desert looked

redeemable. Lancaster Gate looked rich—that was all the effect; which it was unthinkable that any state of his own should
ever remotely resemble. He read more vividly, more critically,
as has been hinted, the appearances about him; and they did
nothing so much as make him wonder at his æsthetic reaction.
He hadn't known—and in spite of Kate's repeated reference to
her own rebellions of taste—that he should "mind" so much
how an independent lady might decorate her house. It was the
language of the house itself that spoke to him, writing out for
him with surpassing breadth and freedom the associations and
conceptions, the ideals and possibilities of the mistress. Never,
he felt sure, had he seen so many things so unanimously ugly
—operatively, ominously so cruel. He was glad to have found
this last name for the whole character; "cruel" somehow played
into the subject for an article—an article that his impression
put straight into his mind. He would write about the heavy
horrors that could still flourish, that lifted their undiminished
heads, in an age so proud of its short way with false gods; and
it would be funny if what he should have got from Mrs. Lowder were to prove after all but a small amount of copy. Yet
the great thing, really the dark thing, was that, even while he
thought of the quick column he might add up, he felt it less
easy to laugh at the heavy horrors than to quail before them. He
couldn't describe and dismiss them collectively, call them either
Mid-Victorian or Early—not being certain they were range-
able under one rubric. It was only manifest they were splendid
and were furthermore conclusively British. They constituted
an order and abounded in rare material—precious woods,
metals, stuffs, stones. He had never dreamed of anything so
fringed and scalloped, so buttoned and corded, drawn everywhere so tight and curled everywhere so thick. He had never
dreamed of so much gilt and glass, so much satin and plush, so
much rosewood and marble and malachite. But it was above
all the solid forms, the wasted finish, the misguided cost, the
general attestation of morality and money, a good conscience
and a big balance. These things finally represented for him a
portentous negation of his own world of thought—of which,
for that matter, in presence of them, he became as for the first
time hopelessly aware. They revealed it to him by their merciless difference.

His interview with Aunt Maud, none the less, took by no means the turn he had expected. Passionate though her nature, no doubt, Mrs. Lowder on this occasion neither threatened nor appealed. Her arms of aggression, her weapons of defence, were presumably close at hand, but she left them untouched and unmentioned, and was in fact so bland that he properly perceived only afterwards how adroit she had been. He properly perceived something else as well, which complicated his case; he shouldn't have known what to call it if he hadn't called it her really imprudent good nature. Her blandness, in other words, wasn't mere policy—he wasn't dangerous enough for policy: it was the result, he could see, of her fairly liking him a little. From the moment she did that she herself became more interesting, and who knew what might happen should he take to liking *her*? Well, it was a risk he naturally must face. She fought him at any rate but with one hand, with a few loose grains of stray powder. He recognised at the end of ten minutes, and even without her explaining it, that if she had made him wait it hadn't been to wound him; they had by that time almost directly met on the fact of her intention. She had wanted him to think for himself of what she proposed to say to him—not having otherwise announced it; wanted to let it come home to him on the spot, as she had shrewdly believed it would. Her first question, on appearing, had practically been as to whether he hadn't taken her hint, and this enquiry assumed so many things that it immediately made discussion frank and large. He knew, with the question put, that the hint was just what he *had* taken; knew that she had made him quickly forgive her the display of her power; knew that if he didn't take care he should understand her, and the strength of her purpose, to say nothing of that of her imagination, nothing of the length of her purse, only too well. Yet he pulled himself up with the thought too that he wasn't going to be afraid of understanding her; he was just going to understand and understand without detriment to the feeblest, even, of his passions. The play of one's mind gave one away, at the best, dreadfully, in action, in the need for action, where simplicity was all; but when one couldn't prevent it the thing was to make it complete. There would never be mistakes but for the original fun of mistakes. What he must *use* his fatal intelligence for was to

resist. Mrs. Lowder meanwhile might use it for whatever she
liked.

It was after she had begun her statement of her own idea
about Kate that he began on his side to reflect that—with her
manner of offering it as really sufficient if he would take the
trouble to embrace it—she couldn't half hate him. That was
all, positively, she seemed to show herself for the time as attempting; clearly, if she did her intention justice she would
have nothing more disagreeable to do. "If I hadn't been ready
to go very much further, you understand, I wouldn't have gone
so far. I don't care what you repeat to her—the more you repeat to her perhaps the better; and at any rate there's nothing
she doesn't already know. I don't say it for her; I say it for you
—when I want to reach my niece I know how to do it straight."
So Aunt Maud delivered herself—as with homely benevolence,
in the simplest but the clearest terms; virtually conveying
that, though a word to the wise was doubtless, in spite of the
adage, *not* always enough, a word to the good could never fail
to be. The sense our young man read into her words was that
she liked him because he was good—was really by her measure
good enough: good enough that is to give up her niece for her
and go his way in peace. But *was* he good enough—by his own
measure? He fairly wondered, while she more fully expressed
herself, if it might be his doom to prove so. "She's the finest
possible creature—of course you flatter yourself you know it.
But I know it quite as well as you possibly can—by which I
mean a good deal better yet; and the tune to which I'm ready
to prove my faith compares favourably enough, I think, with
anything you can do. I don't say it because she's my niece—
that's nothing to me: I might have had fifty nieces, and I
wouldn't have brought one of them to this place if I hadn't
found her to my taste. I don't say I wouldn't have done something else, but I wouldn't have put up with her presence.
Kate's presence, by good fortune, I marked early. Kate's presence—unluckily for *you*—is everything I could possibly wish.
Kate's presence is, in short, as fine as you know, and I've been
keeping it for the comfort of my declining years. I've watched
it long; I've been saving it up and letting it, as you say of in-
vestments, appreciate; and you may judge whether, now it has
begun to pay so, I'm likely to consent to treat for it with any

but a high bidder. I can do the best with her, and I've my idea of the best."

"Oh I quite conceive," said Densher, "that your idea of the best isn't me."

It was an oddity of Mrs. Lowder's that her face in speech was like a lighted window at night, but that silence immediately drew the curtain. The occasion for reply allowed by her silence was never easy to take, yet she was still less easy to interrupt. The great glaze of her surface, at all events, gave her visitor no present help. "I didn't ask you to come to hear what it isn't—I asked you to come to hear what it *is.*"

"Of course," Densher laughed, "that's very great indeed."

His hostess went on as if his contribution to the subject were barely relevant. "I want to see her high, high up—high up and in the light."

"Ah you naturally want to marry her to a duke and are eager to smooth away any hitch."

She gave him so, on this, the mere effect of the drawn blind that it quite forced him at first into the sense, possibly just, of his having shown for flippant, perhaps even for low. He had been looked at so, in blighted moments of presumptuous youth, by big cold public men, but never, so far as he could recall, by any private lady. More than anything yet it gave him the measure of his companion's subtlety, and thereby of Kate's possible career. "Don't be *too* impossible!"—he feared from his friend, for a moment, some such answer as that; and then felt, as she spoke otherwise, as if she were letting him off easily. "I want her to marry a great man." That was all; but, more and more, it was enough; and if it hadn't been her next words would have made it so. "And I think of her what I think. There you are."

They sat for a little face to face upon it, and he was conscious of something deeper still, of something she wished him to understand if he only would. To that extent she did appeal —appealed to the intelligence she desired to show she believed him to possess. He was meanwhile, at all events, not the man wholly to fail of comprehension. "Of course I'm aware how little I can answer to any fond proud dream. You've a view—a grand one; into which I perfectly enter. I thoroughly understand what I'm not, and I'm much obliged to you for not

reminding me of it in any rougher way." She said nothing—
she kept that up; it might even have been to let him go further,
if he was capable of it, in the way of poorness of spirit. It was
one of those cases in which a man couldn't show, if he showed
at all, save for poor; unless indeed he preferred to show for asi-
nine. It was the plain truth: he *was*—on Mrs. Lowder's basis,
the only one in question—a very small quantity, and he did
know, damnably, what made quantities large. He desired to be
perfectly simple, yet in the midst of that effort a deeper apprehension throbbed. Aunt Maud clearly conveyed it, though he
couldn't later on have said how. "You don't really matter, I believe, so much as you think, and I'm not going to make you a
martyr by banishing you. Your performances with Kate in the
Park are ridiculous so far as they're meant as consideration for
me; and I had much rather see you myself—since you're, in
your way, my dear young man, delightful—and arrange with
you, count with you, as I easily, as I perfectly should. Do you
suppose me so stupid as to quarrel with you if it's not really
necessary? It won't—it would be too absurd!—*be* necessary. I
can bite your head off any day, any day I really open my
mouth; and I'm dealing with you now, see—and successfully
judge—without opening it. I do things handsomely all round
—I place you in the presence of the plan with which, from the
moment it's a case of taking you seriously, you're incompati-
ble. Come then as near it as you like, walk all round it—don't
be afraid you'll hurt it!—and live on with it before you."

He afterwards felt that if she hadn't absolutely phrased all
this it was because she so soon made him out as going with her
far enough. He was so pleasantly affected by her asking no
promise of him, her not proposing he should pay for her indulgence by his word of honour not to interfere, that he gave
her a kind of general assurance of esteem. Immediately afterwards then he was to speak of these things to Kate, and what
by that time came back to him first of all was the way he had
said to her—he mentioned it to the girl—very much as one of
a pair of lovers says in a rupture by mutual consent: "I hope
immensely of course that you'll always regard me as a friend."
This had perhaps been going far—he submitted it all to Kate;
but really there had been so much in it that it was to be looked
at, as they might say, wholly in its own light. Other things than

those we have presented had come up before the close of his scene with Aunt Maud, but this matter of her not treating him as a peril of the first order easily predominated. There was moreover plenty to talk about on the occasion of his subsequent passage with our young woman, it having been put to him abruptly, the night before, that he might give himself a lift and do his newspaper a service—so flatteringly was the case expressed—by going for fifteen or twenty weeks to America. The idea of a series of letters from the United States from the strictly social point of view had for some time been nursed in the inner sanctuary at whose door he sat, and the moment was now deemed happy for letting it loose. The imprisoned thought had, in a word, on the opening of the door, flown straight out into Densher's face, or perched at least on his shoulder, making him look up in surprise from his mere inky office-table. His account of the matter to Kate was that he couldn't refuse—not being in a position as yet to refuse anything; but that his being chosen for such an errand confounded his sense of proportion. He was definite as to his scarce knowing how to measure the honour, which struck him as equivocal; he hadn't quite supposed himself the man for the class of job. This confused consciousness, he intimated, he had promptly enough betrayed to his manager; with the effect, however, of seeing the question surprisingly clear up. What it came to was that the sort of twaddle that wasn't in his chords was, unexpectedly, just what they happened this time not to want. They wanted his letters, for queer reasons, about as good as he could let them come; he was to play his own little tune and not be afraid: that was the whole point.

It would have been the whole, that is, had there not been a sharper one still in the circumstance that he was to start at once. His mission, as they called it at the office, would probably be over by the end of June, which was desirable; but to bring that about he must now not lose a week; his enquiries, he understood, were to cover the whole ground, and there were reasons of state—reasons operating at the seat of empire in Fleet Street—why the nail should be struck on the head. Densher made no secret to Kate of his having asked for a day to decide; and his account of that matter was that he felt he owed it to her to speak to her first. She assured him on this that nothing so much as that scruple had yet shown her how they were bound together: she was clearly proud of his letting a thing of such importance depend on her, but she was clearer still as to his instant duty. She rejoiced in his prospect and urged him to his task; she should miss him too dreadfully—of course she should miss him; but she made so little of it that she spoke with jubilation of what he would see and would do. She made so much of this last quantity that he laughed at her innocence, though also with scarce the heart to give her the real size of his drop in the daily bucket. He was struck at the same time with her happy grasp of what had really occurred in Fleet Street—all the more that it was his own final reading. He was to pull the subject up—that was just what they wanted; and it would take more than all the United States together, visit them each as he might, to let *him* down. It was just because he didn't nose about and babble, because he wasn't the usual gossipmonger, that they had picked him out. It was a branch of their correspondence with which they evidently wished a new tone associated, such a tone as, from now on, it would have always to take from his example.

"How you ought indeed, when you understand so well, to be a journalist's wife!" Densher exclaimed in admiration even while she struck him as fairly hurrying him off.

But she was almost impatient of the praise. "What do you expect one *not* to understand when one cares for you?"

"Ah then I'll put it otherwise and say 'How much you care for me!'"

"Yes," she assented; "it fairly redeems my stupidity. I *shall*, with a chance to show it," she added, "have some imagination for you."

She spoke of the future this time as so little contingent that he felt a queerness of conscience in making her the report that he presently arrived at on what had passed for him with the real arbiter of their destiny. The way for that had been blocked a little by his news from Fleet Street; but in the crucible of their happy discussion this element soon melted into the other, and in the mixture that ensued the parts were not to be distinguished. The young man moreover, before taking his leave, was to see why Kate had spoken with a wisdom indifferent to that, and was to come to the vision by a devious way that

deepened the final cheer. Their faces were turned to the illumined quarter as soon as he had answered her question on the
score of their being to appearance able to play patience, a
prodigious game of patience, with success. It was for the possibility of the appearance that she had a few days before so
earnestly pressed him to see her aunt; and if after his hour with
that lady it had not struck Densher that he had seen her to the
happiest purpose the poor facts flushed with a better meaning
as Kate, one by one, took them up.

"If she consents to your coming why isn't that everything?"

"It is everything; everything *she* thinks it. It's the probability
—I mean as Mrs. Lowder measures probability—that I may be
prevented from becoming a complication for her by some
arrangement, *any* arrangement, through which you shall see
me often and easily. She's sure of my want of money, and that
gives her time. She believes in my having a certain amount of
delicacy, in my wishing to better my state before I put the pis-
tol to your head in respect to sharing it. The time this will take
figures for her as the time that will help her if she doesn't spoil
her chance by treating me badly. She doesn't at all wish moreover," Densher went on, "to treat me badly, for I believe, upon
my honour, odd as it may sound to you, that she personally
rather likes me and that if you weren't in question I might
almost become her pet young man. She doesn't disparage intellect and culture—quite the contrary; she wants them to
adorn her board and be associated with her name; and I'm
sure it has sometimes cost her a real pang that I should be so
desirable, at once, and so impossible." He paused a moment,
and his companion then saw how strange a smile was in his
face—a smile as strange even as the adjunct in her own of this
informing vision. "I quite suspect her of believing that, if the
truth were known, she likes me literally better than—deep
down—you yourself do: wherefore she does me the honour to
think I may be safely left to kill my own cause. There, as I say,
comes in her margin. I'm not the sort of stuff of romance that
wears, that washes, that survives use, that resists familiarity.
Once in any degree admit that, and your pride and prejudice
will take care of the rest!—the pride fed full, meanwhile, by the
system she means to practise with you, and the prejudice excited by the comparisons she'll enable you to make, from which

I shall come off badly. She likes me, but she'll never like me so much as when she has succeeded a little better in making me look wretched. For then *you'll* like me less."

Kate showed for this evocation a due interest, but no alarm; and it was a little as if to pay his tender cynicism back in kind that she after an instant replied: "I see, I see—what an immense affair she must think me! One was aware, but you deepen the impression."

"I think you'll make no mistake," said Densher, "in letting it go as deep as it will."

He had given her indeed, she made no scruple of showing, plenty to amuse herself with. "Her facing the music, her making you boldly as welcome as you say—that's an awfully big theory, you know, and worthy of all the other big things that in one's acquaintance with people give her a place so apart."

"Oh she's grand," the young man allowed; "she's on the scale altogether of the car of Juggernaut—which was a kind of image that came to me yesterday while I waited for her at Lancaster Gate. The things in your drawing-room there were like the forms of the strange idols, the mystic excrescences, with which one may suppose the front of the car to bristle."

"Yes, aren't they?" the girl returned; and they had, over all that aspect of their wonderful lady, one of those deep and free interchanges that made everything but confidence a false note for them. There were complications, there were questions; but they were so much more together than they were anything else. Kate uttered for a while no word of refutation of Aunt Maud's "big" diplomacy, and they left it there, as they would have left any other fine product, for a monument to her powers. But, Densher related further, he had had in other respects too the car of Juggernaut to face; he omitted nothing from his account of his visit, least of all the way Aunt Maud had frankly at last—though indeed only under artful pressure—fallen foul of his very type, his want of the right marks, his foreign accidents, his queer antecedents. She had told him he was but half a Briton, which, he granted Kate, would have been dreadful if he hadn't so let himself in for it.

"I was really curious, you see," he explained, "to find out from her what sort of queer creature, what sort of social anomaly, in the light of such conventions as hers, such an education as mine makes one pass for."

Kate said nothing for a little; but then, "Why should you care?" she asked.

"Oh," he laughed, "I like her so much; and then, for a man of my trade, her views, her spirit, are essentially a thing to get hold of: they belong to the great public mind that we meet at every turn and that we must keep setting up 'codes' with. Besides," he added, "I want to please her personally."

"Ah yes, we must please her personally!" his companion echoed; and the words may represent all their definite recognition, at the time, of Densher's politic gain. They had in fact between this and his start for New York many matters to handle, and the question he now touched upon came up for Kate above all. She looked at him as if he had really told her aunt more of his immediate personal story than he had ever told herself. This, if it had been so, was an accident, and it perched him there with her for half an hour, like a cicerone and his victim on a tower-top, before as much of the bird's-eye view of his early years abroad, his migratory parents, his Swiss schools, his German university, as she had easy attention for. A man, he intimated, a man of their world, would have spotted him straight as to many of these points; a man of their world, so far as they had a world, would have been through the English mill. But it was none the less charming to make his confession to a woman; women had in fact for such differences blessedly more imagination and blessedly more sympathy. Kate showed at present as much of both as his case could require; when she had had it from beginning to end she declared that she now made out more than ever yet what she loved him for. She had herself, as a child, lived with some continuity in the world across the Channel, coming home again still a child; and had participated after that, in her teens, in her mother's brief but repeated retreats to Dresden, to Florence, to Biarritz, weak and expensive attempts at economy from which there stuck to her—though in general coldly expressed, through the instinctive avoidance of cheap raptures—the religion of foreign things. When it was revealed to her how many more foreign things were in Merton Densher than he had hitherto taken the

trouble to catalogue, she almost faced him as if he were a map
of the continent or a handsome present of a delightful new
"Murray." He hadn't meant to swagger, he had rather meant
to plead, though with Mrs. Lowder he had meant also a little
to explain. His father had been, in strange countries, in twenty
settlements of the English, British chaplain, resident or occasional, and had had for years the unusual luck of never wanting
a billet. His career abroad had therefore been unbroken, and
as his stipend had never been great he had educated his children, at the smallest cost, in the schools nearest; which was
also a saving of railway-fares. Densher's mother, it further appeared, had practised on her side a distinguished industry, to
the success of which—so far as success ever crowned it—this
period of exile had much contributed: she copied, patient lady,
famous pictures in great museums, having begun with a happy
natural gift and taking in betimes the scale of her opportunity.
Copyists abroad of course swarmed, but Mrs. Densher had had
a sense and a hand of her own, had arrived at a perfection that
persuaded, that even deceived, and that made the "placing" of
her work blissfully usual. Her son, who had lost her, held her
image sacred, and the effect of his telling Kate all about her, as
well as about other matters until then mixed and dim, was to
render his history rich, his sources full, his outline anything but
common. He had come round, he had come back, he insisted
abundantly, to being a Briton: his Cambridge years, his happy
connexion, as it had proved, with his father's college, amply
certified to that, to say nothing of his subsequent plunge
into London, which filled up the measure. But brave enough
though his descent to English earth, he had passed, by the way,
through zones of air that had left their ruffle on his wings—he
had been exposed to initiations indelible. Something had happened to him that could never be undone.

When Kate Croy said to him as much he besought her not
to insist, declaring that this indeed was what was gravely the
matter with him, that he had been but too probably spoiled for
native, for insular use. On which, not unnaturally, she insisted
the more, assuring him, without mitigation, that if he was various and complicated, complicated by wit and taste, she
wouldn't for the world have had him more helpless; so that he
was driven in the end to accuse her of putting the dreadful

truth to him in the hollow guise of flattery. She was making him out as all abnormal in order that she might eventually find him impossible, and since she could make it out but with his aid she had to bribe him by feigned delight to help her. If her last word for him in the connexion was that the way he saw himself was just a precious proof the more of his having tasted of the tree and being thereby prepared to assist her to eat, this gives the happy tone of their whole talk, the measure of the flight of time in the near presence of his settled departure. Kate showed, however, that she was to be more literally taken when she spoke of the relief Aunt Maud would draw from the prospect of his absence.

"Yet one can scarcely see why," he replied, "when she fears me so little."

His friend weighed his objection. "Your idea is that she likes you so much that she'll even go so far as to regret losing you?"

Well, he saw it in their constant comprehensive way. "Since what she builds on is the gradual process of your alienation, she may take the view that the process constantly requires me. Mustn't I be there to keep it going? It's in my exile that it may languish."

He went on with that fantasy, but at this point Kate ceased to attend. He saw after a little that she had been following some thought of her own, and he had been feeling the growth of something determinant even through the extravagance of much of the pleasantry, the warm transparent irony, into which their livelier intimacy kept plunging like a confident swimmer. Suddenly she said to him with extraordinary beauty: "I engage myself to you for ever."

The beauty was in everything, and he could have separated nothing—couldn't have thought of her face as distinct from the whole joy. Yet her face had a new light. "And I pledge you —I call God to witness!—every spark of my faith; I give you every drop of my life." That was all, for the moment, but it was enough, and it was almost as quiet as if it were nothing. They were in the open air, in an alley of the Gardens; the great space, which seemed to arch just then higher and spread wider for them, threw them back into deep concentration. They moved by a common instinct to a spot, within sight, that struck them as fairly sequestered, and there, before their time together

was spent, they had extorted from concentration every advance
it could make them. They had exchanged vows and tokens,
sealed their rich compact, solemnised, so far as breathed words
and murmured sounds and lighted eyes and clasped hands
could do it, their agreement to belong only, and to belong
tremendously, to each other. They were to leave the place accordingly an affianced couple, but before they left it other
things still had passed. Densher had declared his horror of
bringing to a premature end her happy relation with her aunt;
and they had worked round together to a high level of discretion. Kate's free profession was that she wished not to deprive
him of Mrs. Lowder's countenance, which in the long run she
was convinced he would continue to enjoy; and as by a blest
turn Aunt Maud had demanded of him no promise that would
tie his hands they should be able to propitiate their star in their
own way and yet remain loyal. One difficulty alone stood out,
which Densher named.

"Of course it will never do—we must remember that—from
the moment you allow her to found hopes of you for any one
else in particular. So long as her view is content to remain as
general as at present appears I don't see that we deceive her. At
a given hour, you see, she must be undeceived: the only thing
therefore is to be ready for the hour and to face it. Only, after
all, in that case," the young man observed, "one doesn't quite
make out what we shall have got from her."

"What she'll have got from *us?*" Kate put it with a smile.
"What she'll have got from us," the girl went on, "is her own affair—it's for *her* to measure. I asked her for nothing," she
added; "I never put myself upon her. She must take her risks,
and she surely understands them. What we shall have got from
her is what we've already spoken of," Kate further explained;
"it's that we shall have gained time. And so, for that matter, will
she."

Densher gazed a little at all this clearness; his gaze was not at
the present hour into romantic obscurity. "Yes; no doubt, in
our particular situation, time's everything. And then there's
the joy of it."

She hesitated. "Of our secret?"

"Not so much perhaps of our secret in itself, but of what's

represented and, as we must somehow feel, secured to us and made deeper and closer by it." And his fine face, relaxed into happiness, covered her with all his meaning. "Our being as we are."

It was as if for a moment she let the meaning sink into her. "So gone?"

"So gone. So extremely gone. However," he smiled, "we shall go a good deal further." Her answer to which was only the softness of her silence—a silence that looked out for them both at the far reach of their prospect. This was immense, and they thus took final possession of it. They were practically united and splendidly strong; but there were other things— things they were precisely strong enough to be able successfully to count with and safely to allow for; in consequence of which they would for the present, subject to some better reason, keep their understanding to themselves. It was not indeed however till after one more observation of Densher's that they felt the question completely straightened out. "The only thing of course is that she may any day absolutely put it to you."

Kate considered. "Ask me where, on my honour, we are? She may, naturally; but I doubt if in fact she will. While you're away she'll make the most of that drop of the tension. She'll leave me alone."

"But there'll be my letters."

The girl faced his letters. "Very, very many?"

"Very, very, very many—more than ever; and you know what that is! And then," Densher added, "there'll be yours."

"Oh I shan't leave mine on the hall-table. I shall post them myself."

He looked at her a moment. "Do you think then I had best address you elsewhere?" After which, before she could quite answer, he added with some emphasis: "I'd rather not, you know. It's straighter."

She might again have just waited. "Of course it's straighter. Don't be afraid I shan't be straight. Address me," she continued, "where you like. I shall be proud enough of its being known you write to me."

He turned it over for the last clearness. "Even at the risk of its really bringing down the inquisition?"

Well, the last clearness now filled her. "I'm not afraid of the inquisition. If she asks if there's anything definite between us I know perfectly what I shall say."

"That I *am* of course 'gone' for you?"

"That I love you as I shall never in my life love any one else, and that she can make what she likes of that." She said it out so splendidly that it was like a new profession of faith, the fulness of a tide breaking through; and the effect of that in turn was to make her companion meet her with such eyes that she had time again before he could otherwise speak. "Besides, she's just as likely to ask *you*."

"Not while I'm away."

"Then when you come back."

"Well then," said Densher, "we shall have had our particular joy. But what I feel is," he candidly added, "that, by an idea of her own, her superior policy, she *won't* ask me. She'll let me off. I shan't have to lie to her."

"It will be left all to me?" asked Kate.

"All to you!" he tenderly laughed.

But it was oddly, the very next moment, as if he had perhaps been a shade too candid. His discrimination seemed to mark a possible, a natural reality, a reality not wholly disallowed by the account the girl had just given of her own intention. There *was* a difference in the air—even if none other than the supposedly usual difference in truth between man and woman; and it was almost as if the sense of this provoked her. She seemed to cast about an instant, and then she went back a little resentfully to something she had suffered to pass a minute before. She appeared to take up rather more seriously than she need the joke about her freedom to deceive. Yet she did this too in a beautiful way. "Men are too stupid—even you. You didn't understand just now why, if I post my letters myself, it won't be for anything so vulgar as to hide them."

"Oh you named it—for the pleasure."

"Yes; but you didn't, you don't, understand what the pleasure may be. There are refinements—!" she more patiently dropped. "I mean of consciousness, of sensation, of appreciation," she went on. "No," she sadly insisted—"men *don't* know. They know in such matters almost nothing but what women show them."

This was one of the speeches, frequent in her, that, liberally, joyfully, intensely adopted and, in itself, as might be, embraced, drew him again as close to her, and held him as long, as their conditions permitted. "Then that's exactly why we've such an abysmal need of you!"

BOOK THIRD

I

THE two ladies who, in advance of the Swiss season, had been warned that their design was unconsidered, that the passes wouldn't be clear, nor the air mild, nor the inns open— the two ladies who, characteristically, had braved a good deal of possibly interested remonstrance were finding themselves, as their adventure turned out, wonderfully sustained. It was the judgement of the head-waiters and other functionaries on the Italian lakes that approved itself now as interested; they themselves had been conscious of impatiences, of bolder dreams—at least the younger had; so that one of the things they made out together—making out as they did an endless variety—was that in those operatic palaces of the Villa d'Este, of Cadenabbia, of Pallanza and Stresa, lone women, however re-enforced by a travelling-library of instructive volumes, were apt to be beguiled and undone. Their flights of fancy more-over had been modest; they had for instance risked nothing vital in hoping to make their way by the Brünig. They were making it in fact happily enough as we meet them, and were only wishing that, for the wondrous beauty of the early high-climbing spring, it might have been longer and the places to pause and rest more numerous.

Such at least had been the intimated attitude of Mrs. String-ham, the elder of the companions, who had her own view of the impatiences of the younger, to which, however, she offered an opposition but of the most circuitous. She moved, the admirable Mrs. Stringham, in a fine cloud of observation and suspicion; she was in the position, as she believed, of knowing much more about Milly Theale than Milly herself knew, and yet of having to darken her knowledge as well as make it active. The woman in the world least formed by nature, as she was quite aware, for duplicities and labyrinths, she found herself dedicated to personal subtlety by a new set of circumstances, above all by a new personal relation; had now in fact to recognise that an education in the occult—she could scarce say what to call it—had begun for her the day she left New York with Mildred. She had come on from Boston for that purpose; had seen little of the girl—or rather had seen her but briefly, for Mrs. Stringham, when she saw anything at all, saw much, saw everything —before accepting her proposal; and had accordingly placed herself, by her act, in a boat that she more and more estimated as, humanly speaking, of the biggest, though likewise, no doubt, in many ways, by reason of its size, of the safest. In Boston, the winter before, the young lady in whom we are interested had, on the spot, deeply, yet almost tacitly, appealed to her, dropped into her mind the shy conceit of some assistance, some devotion to render. Mrs. Stringham's little life had often been visited by shy conceits—secret dreams that had fluttered their hour between its narrow walls without, for any great part, so much as mustering courage to look out of its rather dim windows. But this imagination—the fancy of a possible link with the remarkable young thing from New York— *had* mustered courage: had perched, on the instant, at the clearest lookout it could find, and might be said to have remained there till, only a few months later, it had caught, in surprise and joy, the unmistakeable flash of a signal.

Milly Theale had Boston friends, such as they were, and of recent making; and it was understood that her visit to them— a visit that was not to be meagre—had been undertaken, after a series of bereavements, in the interest of the particular peace that New York couldn't give. It was recognised, liberally enough, that there were many things—perhaps even too many—New York *could* give; but this was felt to make no difference in the important truth that what you had most to do, under the discipline of life, or of death, was really to feel your situation as grave. Boston could help you to that as nothing else could, and it had extended to Milly, by every presumption, some such measure of assistance. Mrs. Stringham was never to forget—for the moment had not faded, nor the infinitely fine vibration it set up in any degree ceased—her own first sight of the striking apparition, then unheralded and unexplained: the slim, constantly pale, delicately haggard, anomalously, agreeably angular young person, of not more than two-and-twenty summers, in spite of her marks, whose hair was somehow exceptionally red even for the real thing, which it innocently confessed to being, and whose clothes were remarkably black even for robes of mourning, which was the meaning they expressed. It was New York mourning, it was New York hair, it was a New York history, confused as yet, but multitudinous, of the loss of parents, brothers, sisters, almost every human appendage, all on a scale and with a sweep that had required the greater stage; it was a New York legend of affecting, of romantic isolation, and, beyond everything, it was by most accounts, in respect to the mass of money so piled on the girl's back, a set of New York possibilities. She was alone, she was stricken, she was rich, and in particular was strange—a combination in itself of a nature to engage Mrs. Stringham's attention. But it was the strangeness that most determined our good lady's sympathy, convinced as she had to be that it was greater than any one else—any one but the sole Susan Stringham—supposed. Susan privately settled it that Boston was not in the least seeing her, was only occupied with her seeing Boston, and that any assumed affinity between the two characters was delusive and vain. *She* was seeing her, and she had quite the finest moment of her life in now obeying the instinct to conceal the vision. She couldn't explain it—no one would understand. They would say clever Boston things—Mrs. Stringham was from Burlington, Vermont, which she boldly upheld as the real heart of New England, Boston being "too far south"—but they would only darken counsel.

There could be no better proof (than this quick intellectual split) of the impression made on our friend, who shone herself, she was well aware, with but the reflected light of the admirable city. She too had had her discipline, but it had not made her striking; it had been prosaically usual, though doubtless a decent dose; and had only made her usual to match it—usual, that is, as Boston went. She had lost first her husband and then her mother, with whom, on her husband's death, she had lived again; so that now, childless, she was but more sharply single than before. Yet she sat rather coldly light, having, as she called it, enough to live on—so far, that is, as she lived by bread alone: how little indeed she was regularly content with that diet appeared from the name she had made—Susan Shepherd Stringham—as a contributor to the best magazines. She wrote short stories, and she fondly believed she had her "note," the art of showing New England without showing it wholly in the kitchen. She had not herself been brought up in the kitchen; she knew others who had not; and to speak for them had thus become with her a literary mission. To *be* in truth literary had ever been her dearest thought, the thought that kept her bright little nippers perpetually in position. There were masters, models, celebrities, mainly foreign, whom she finally accounted so and in whose light she ingeniously laboured; there were others whom, however chattered about, she ranked with the inane, for she bristled with discriminations; but all categories failed her—they ceased at least to signify—as soon as she found herself in presence of the real thing, the romantic life itself. That was what she saw in Mildred—what positively made her hand a while tremble too much for the pen. She had had, it seemed to her, a revelation—such as even New England refined and grammatical couldn't give; and, all made up as she was of small neat memories and ingenuities, little industries and ambitions, mixed with something moral, personal, that was still more intensely responsive, she felt her new friend would have done her an ill turn if their friendship shouldn't develop, and yet that nothing would be left of anything else if it should. It was for the surrender of everything else that she was, however, quite prepared, and while she went about her usual Boston business with her usual Boston probity she was really all the while holding herself. She wore her "handsome" felt hat, so Tyrolese, yet somehow, though feathered from the eagle's wing, so truly domestic, with the same straightness and security; she attached her fur boa with the same honest precautions; she preserved her balance on the ice-slopes with the same practised skill; she opened, each evening, her *Transcript* with the same interfusion of suspense and resignation; she attended her almost daily concert with the same expenditure of patience and the same economy of passion; she flitted in and out of the Public Library with the air of conscientiously returning or bravely carrying off in her pocket the key of knowledge itself; and finally—it was what she most did—she watched the thin trickle of a fictive "love-interest" through that somewhat serpentine channel, in the magazines, which she mainly managed to keep clear for it. But the real thing all the while was elsewhere; the real thing had gone back to New York, leaving behind it the two unsolved questions, quite distinct, of why it *was* real, and whether she should ever be so near it again.

For the figure to which these questions attached themselves she had found a convenient description—she thought of it for herself always as that of a girl with a background. The great reality was in the fact that, very soon, after but two or three meetings, the girl with the background, the girl with the crown of old gold and the mourning that was not as the mourning of Boston, but at once more rebellious in its gloom and more frivolous in its frills, had told her she had never seen any one like her. They had met thus as opposed curiosities, and that simple remark of Milly's—if simple it was—became the most important thing that had ever happened to her; it deprived the love-interest, for the time, of actuality and even of pertinence; it moved her first, in short, in a high degree, to gratitude, and then to no small compassion. Yet in respect to this relation at least it was what did prove the key of knowledge; it lighted up as nothing else could do the poor young woman's history. That the potential heiress of all the ages should never have seen any one like a mere typical subscriber, after all, to the *Transcript* was a truth that—in especial as announced with modesty, with humility, with regret—described a situation. It laid upon the elder woman, as to the void to be filled, a weight of responsibility; but in particular it led her to ask whom poor Mildred *had* then seen, and what range of contacts it had taken to produce such queer surprises. That was really the enquiry that had ended by clearing the air: the key of knowledge was felt to click in the lock from the moment it flashed upon Mrs. Stringham that her friend had been starved for culture. Culture was what she herself represented for her, and it was living up to that principle that would surely prove the great business. She knew, the clever lady, what the principle itself represented, and the limits of her own store; and a certain alarm would have grown upon her if something else hadn't grown faster. This was, fortunately for her—and we give it in her own words— the sense of a harrowing pathos. That, primarily, was what appealed to her, what seemed to open the door of romance for her still wider than any, than a still more reckless, connexion with the "picture-papers." For such was essentially the point: it was rich, romantic, abysmal, to have, as was evident, thousands and thousands a year, to have youth and intelligence and, if not beauty, at least in equal measure a high dim charming ambiguous oddity, which was even better, and then on top of all to enjoy boundless freedom, the freedom of the wind in the desert—it was unspeakably touching to be so equipped and yet to have been reduced by fortune to little humble-minded mistakes.

It brought our friend's imagination back again to New York, where aberrations were so possible in the intellectual sphere, and it in fact caused a visit she presently paid there to overflow with interest. As Milly had beautifully invited her, so she would hold out if she could against the strain of so much confidence in her mind; and the remarkable thing was that even at the end of three weeks she *had* held out. But by this time her mind had grown comparatively bold and free; it was dealing with new quantities, a different proportion altogether—and that had made for refreshment: she had accordingly gone home in convenient possession of her subject. New York was vast, New York was startling, with strange histories, with wild cosmopolite backward generations that accounted for anything; and to have got nearer the luxuriant tribe of which the rare creature was the final flower, the immense extravagant unregulated cluster, with free-living ancestors, handsome dead cousins, lurid uncles, beautiful vanished aunts, persons all busts and curls, preserved, though so exposed, in the marble of famous French chisels—all this, to say nothing of the effect of closer growths of the stem, was to have had one's small worldspace both crowded and enlarged. Our couple had at all events effected an exchange; the elder friend had been as consciously intellectual as possible, and the younger, abounding in personal revelation, had been as unconsciously distinguished. This was poetry—it was also history—Mrs. Stringham thought, to a finer tune even than Maeterlinck and Pater, than Marbot and Gregorovius. She appointed occasions for the reading of these authors with her hostess, rather perhaps than actually achieved great spans; but what they managed and what they missed speedily sank for her into the dim depths of the merely relative, so quickly, so strongly had she clutched her central clue. All her scruples and hesitations, all her anxious enthusiasms, had reduced themselves to a single alarm—the fear that she really might act on her companion clumsily and coarsely. She was positively afraid of what she might do to her, and to avoid that, to avoid it with piety and passion, to do, rather, nothing at all, to leave her untouched because no touch one could apply, however light, however just, however earnest and anxious, would be half good enough, would be anything but an ugly smutch upon perfection—this now imposed itself as a consistent, an inspiring thought.

Less than a month after the event that had so determined Mrs. Stringham's attitude—close upon the heels, that is, of her return from New York—she was reached by a proposal that brought up for her the kind of question her delicacy might have to contend with. Would she start for Europe with her young friend at the earliest possible date, and should she be willing to do so without making conditions? The enquiry was launched by wire; explanations, in sufficiency, were promised; extreme urgency was suggested and a general surrender invited. It was to the honour of her sincerity that she made the surrender on the spot, though it was not perhaps altogether to that of her logic. She had wanted, very consciously, from the first, to give something up for her new acquaintance, but she had now no doubt that she was practically giving up all. What settled this was the fulness of a particular impression, the impression that had throughout more and more supported her and which she would have uttered so far as she might by saying that the charm of the creature was positively in the creature's greatness. She would have been content so to leave it; unless indeed she had said, more familiarly, that Mildred was the biggest impression of her life. That was at all events the biggest account of her, and none but a big clearly would do. Her situation, as such things were called, was on the grand scale; but it still was not that. It was her nature, once for all—a nature that reminded Mrs. Stringham of the term always used in the newspapers about the great new steamers, the inordinate number of "feet of water" they drew; so that if, in your little boat, you had chosen to hover and approach, you had but yourself to thank, when once motion was started, for the way the draught pulled you. Milly drew the feet of water, and odd though it might seem that a lonely girl, who was not robust and who hated sound and show, should stir the stream like a leviathan, her companion floated off with the sense of rocking violently at her side. More than prepared, however, for that excitement, Mrs. Stringham mainly failed of ease in respect to her own consistency. To attach herself for an indefinite time seemed a roundabout way of holding her hands off. If she wished to be sure of neither touching nor smutching, the straighter plan would doubtless have been not to keep her friend within reach. This in fact she fully recognised, and with it the degree to which she desired that the girl should lead her life, a life certain to be so much finer than that of anybody else. The difficulty, however, by good fortune, cleared away as soon as she had further recognised, as she was speedily able to do, that she Susan Shepherd—the name with which Milly for the most part amused herself—was *not* anybody else. She had renounced that character; she had now no life to lead; and she honestly believed that she was thus supremely equipped for leading Milly's own. No other person whatever, she was sure, had to an equal degree this qualification, and it was really to assert it that she fondly embarked.

Many things, though not in many weeks, had come and gone since then, and one of the best of them doubtless had been the voyage itself, by the happy southern course, to the succession of Mediterranean ports, with the dazzled wind-up at Naples. Two or three others had preceded this; incidents, indeed rather lively marks, of their last fortnight at home, and one of which had determined on Mrs. Stringham's part a rush to New York, forty-eight breathless hours there, previous to her final rally. But the great sustained sea-light had drunk up the rest of the picture, so that for many days other questions and other possibilities sounded with as little effect as a trio of penny whistles might sound in a Wagner overture. It was the Wagner overture that practically prevailed, up through Italy, where Milly had already been, still further up and across the Alps, which were also partly known to Mrs. Stringham; only perhaps "taken" to a time not wholly congruous, hurried in fact on account of the girl's high restlessness. She had been expected, she had frankly promised, to be restless—that was partly why she was "great" —or was a consequence, at any rate, if not a cause; yet she had not perhaps altogether announced herself as straining so hard at the cord. It was familiar, it was beautiful to Mrs. Stringham that she had arrears to make up, the chances that had lapsed for her through the wanton ways of forefathers fond of Paris, but not of its higher sides, and fond almost of nothing else; but the vagueness, the openness, the eagerness without point and the interest without pause—all a part of the charm of her oddity as at first presented—had become more striking in proportion as they triumphed over movement and change. She had arts and idiosyncrasies of which no great account could have been given, but which were a daily grace if you lived with them; such as the art of being almost tragically impatient and yet making it as light as air; of being inexplicably sad and yet making it as clear as noon; of being unmistakeably gay and yet making it as soft as dusk. Mrs. Stringham by this time understood everything, was more than ever confirmed in wonder and admiration, in her view that it was life enough simply to feel her companion's feelings; but there were special keys she had not yet added to her bunch, impressions that of a sudden were apt to affect her as new.

This particular day on the great Swiss road had been, for some reason, full of them, and they referred themselves, provisionally, to some deeper depth than she had touched—though into two or three such depths, it must be added, she had peeped long enough to find herself suddenly draw back. It was not Milly's unpacified state, in short, that now troubled her—though certainly, as Europe was the great American sedative, the failure was to some extent to be noted: it was the suspected presence of something behind the state—which, however, could scarcely have taken its place there since their departure. What a fresh motive of unrest could suddenly have sprung from was in short not to be divined. It was but half an explanation to say that excitement, for each of them, had naturally dropped, and that what they had left behind, or tried to—the great serious facts of life, as Mrs. Stringham liked to call them—was once more coming into sight as objects loom through smoke when smoke begins to clear; for these were general appearances from which the girl's own aspect, her really larger vagueness, seemed rather to disconnect itself. The nearest approach to a personal anxiety indulged in as yet by the elder lady was on her taking occasion to wonder if what she had more than

anything else got hold of mightn't be one of the finer, one of
the finest, one of the rarest—as she called it so that she might
call it nothing worse—cases of American intensity. She had just
had a moment of alarm—asked herself if her young friend were
merely going to treat her to some complicated drama of
nerves. At the end of a week, however, with their further
progress, her young friend had effectively answered the question and given her the impression, indistinct indeed as yet, of
something that had a reality compared with which the nervous
explanation would have been coarse. Mrs. Stringham found
herself from that hour, in other words, in presence of an explanation that remained a muffled and intangible form, but that
assuredly, should it take on sharpness, would explain everything and more than everything, would become instantly the
light in which Milly was to be read.

Such a matter as this may at all events speak of the style in
which our young woman could affect those who were near
her, may testify to the sort of interest she could inspire. She
worked—and seemingly quite without design—upon the sympathy, the curiosity, the fancy of her associates, and we shall
really ourselves scarce otherwise come closer to her than by
feeling their impression and sharing, if need be, their confusion. She reduced them, Mrs. Stringham would have said, to a
consenting bewilderment; which was precisely, for that good
lady, on a last analysis, what was most in harmony with her
greatness. She exceeded, escaped measure, was surprising only
because *they* were so far from great. Thus it was that on this
wondrous day by the Brünig the spell of watching her had
grown more than ever irresistible; a proof of what—or of a
part of what—Mrs. Stringham had, with all the rest, been reduced to. She had almost the sense of tracking her young friend
as if at a given moment to pounce. She knew she shouldn't
pounce, she hadn't come out to pounce; yet she felt her attention secretive, all the same, and her observation scientific. She
struck herself as hovering like a spy, applying tests, laying traps,
concealing signs. This would last, however, only till she should
fairly know what was the matter; and to watch was after all,
meanwhile, a way of clinging to the girl, not less than an occupation, a satisfaction in itself. The pleasure of watching
moreover, if a reason were needed, came from a sense of her

beauty. Her beauty hadn't at all originally seemed a part of the situation, and Mrs. Stringham had even in the first flush of friendship not named it grossly to any one; having seen early that for stupid people—and who, she sometimes secretly asked herself, wasn't stupid?—it would take a great deal of explaining. She had learned not to mention it till it was mentioned first—which occasionally happened, but not too often; and then she was there in force. Then she both warmed to the perception that met her own perception, and disputed it, suspiciously, as to special items; while, in general, she had learned to refine even to the point of herself employing the word that most people employed. She employed it to pretend she was also stupid and so have done with the matter; spoke of her friend as plain, as ugly even, in a case of especially dense insistence; but as, in appearance, so "awfully full of things." This was her own way of describing a face that, thanks doubtless to rather too much forehead, too much nose and too much mouth, together with too little mere conventional colour and conventional line, was expressive, irregular, exquisite, both for speech and for silence. When Milly smiled it was a public event—when she didn't it was a chapter of history. They had stopped on the Brünig for luncheon, and there had come up for them under the charm of the place the question of a longer stay.

Mrs. Stringham was now on the ground of thrilled recognitions, small sharp echoes of a past which she kept in a well-thumbed case, but which, on pressure of a spring and exposure to the air, still showed itself ticking as hard as an honest old watch. The embalmed "Europe" of her younger time had partly stood for three years of Switzerland, a term of continuous school at Vevey, with rewards of merit in the form of silver medals tied by blue ribbons and mild mountain-passes attacked with alpenstocks. It was the good girls who, in the holidays, were taken highest, and our friend could now judge, from what she supposed her familiarity with the minor peaks, that she had been one of the best. These reminiscences, sacred today because prepared in the hushed chambers of the past, had been part of the general train laid for the pair of sisters, daughters early fatherless, by their brave Vermont mother, who struck her at present as having apparently, almost like Columbus, worked out, all unassisted, a conception of the other side of the globe. She had focussed Vevey, by the light of nature and with extraordinary completeness, at Burlington; after which she had embarked, sailed, landed, explored and, above all, made good her presence. She had given her daughters the five years in Switzerland and Germany that were to leave them ever afterwards a standard of comparison for all cycles of Cathay, and to stamp the younger in especial—Susan was the younger—with a character, that, as Mrs. Stringham had often had occasion, through life, to say to herself, made all the difference. It made all the difference for Mrs. Stringham, over and over again and in the most remote connexions, that, thanks to her parent's lonely thrifty hardy faith, she was a woman of the world. There were plenty of women who were all sorts of things that she wasn't, but who, on the other hand, were not that, and who didn't know *she* was (which she liked—it relegated them still further) and didn't know either how it enabled her to judge them. She had never seen herself so much in this light as during the actual phase of her associated, if slightly undirected, pilgrimage; and the consciousness gave perhaps to her plea for a pause more intensity than she knew. The irrecoverable days had come back to her from far off; they were part of the sense of the cool upper air and of everything else that hung like an indestructible scent to the torn garment of youth—the taste of honey and the luxury of milk, the sound of cattle-bells and the rush of streams, the fragrance of trodden balms and the dizziness of deep gorges.

Milly clearly felt these things too, but they affected her companion at moments—that was quite the way Mrs. Stringham would have expressed it—as the princess in a conventional tragedy might have affected the confidant if a personal emotion had ever been permitted to the latter. That a princess could only be a princess was a truth with which, essentially, a confidant, however responsive, had to live. Mrs. Stringham was a woman of the world, but Milly Theale was a princess, the only one she had yet had to deal with, and this, in its way too, made all the difference. It was a perfectly definite doom for the wearer—it was for every one else an office nobly filled. It might have represented possibly, with its involved loneliness and other mysteries, the weight under which she fancied her companion's admirable head occasionally, and ever so submissively,

bowed. Milly had quite assented at luncheon to their staying
over, and had left her to look at rooms, settle questions,
arrange about their keeping on their carriage and horses; cares
that had now moreover fallen to Mrs. Stringham as a matter of
course and that yet for some reason, on this occasion particularly, brought home to her—all agreeably, richly, almost grandly
—what it was to live with the great. Her young friend had in a
sublime degree a sense closed to the general question of difficulty, which she got rid of furthermore not in the least as one
had seen many charming persons do, by merely passing it on
to others. She kept it completely at a distance: it never entered
the circle; the most plaintive confidant couldn't have dragged
it in; and to tread the path of a confidant was accordingly to
live exempt. Service was in other words so easy to render that
the whole thing was like court life without the hardships. It
came back of course to the question of money, and our obser-
vant lady had by this time repeatedly reflected that if one were
talking of the "difference," it was just this, this incomparably
and nothing else, that when all was said and done most made
it. A less vulgarly, a less obviously purchasing or parading person she couldn't have imagined; but it prevailed even as the
truth of truths that the girl couldn't get away from her wealth.
She might leave her conscientious companion as freely alone
with it as possible and never ask a question, scarce even tolerate a reference; but it was in the fine folds of the helplessly expensive little black frock that she drew over the grass as she
now strolled vaguely off; it was in the curious and splendid
coils of hair, "done" with no eye whatever to the *mode du
jour*, that peeped from under the corresponding indifference
of her hat, the merely personal tradition that suggested a sort
of noble inelegance; it lurked between the leaves of the uncut
but antiquated Tauchnitz volume of which, before going out,
she had mechanically possessed herself. She couldn't dress it
away, nor walk it away, nor read it away, nor think it away; she
could neither smile it away in any dreamy absence nor blow it
away in any softened sigh. She couldn't have lost it if she had
tried—that was what it was to be really rich. It had to be *the*
thing you were. When at the end of an hour she hadn't returned
to the house Mrs. Stringham, though the bright afternoon was
yet young, took, with precautions, the same direction, went to

join her in case of her caring for a walk. But the purpose of joining her was in truth less distinct than that of a due regard for a possibly preferred detachment: so that, once more, the good lady proceeded with a quietness that made her slightly "underhand" even in her own eyes. She couldn't help that, however, and she didn't care, sure as she was that what she really wanted wasn't to overstep but to stop in time. It was to be able to stop in time that she went softly, but she had on this occasion further to go than ever yet, for she followed in vain, and at last with some anxiety, the footpath she believed Milly to have taken. It wound up a hillside and into the higher Alpine meadows in which, all these last days, they had so often wanted, as they passed above or below, to stray; and then it obscured itself in a wood, but always going up, up, and with a small cluster of brown old high-perched châlets evidently for its goal. Mrs. Stringham reached in due course the châlets, and there received from a bewildered old woman, a very fearful person to behold, an indication that sufficiently guided her. The young lady had been seen not long before passing further on, over a crest and to a place where the way would drop again, as our unappeased enquirer found it in fact, a quarter of an hour later, markedly and almost alarmingly to do. It led somewhere, yet apparently quite into space, for the great side of the mountain appeared, from where she pulled up, to fall away altogether, though probably but to some issue below and out of sight. Her uncertainty moreover was brief, for she next became aware of the presence on a fragment of rock, twenty yards off, of the Tauchnitz volume the girl had brought out and that therefore pointed to her shortly previous passage. She had rid herself of the book, which was an encumbrance, and meant of course to pick it up on her return; but as she hadn't yet picked it up what on earth had become of her? Mrs. Stringham, I hasten to add, was within a few moments to see; but it was quite an accident that she hadn't, before they were over, betrayed by her deeper agitation the fact of her own nearness.

The whole place, with the descent of the path and as a sequel to a sharp turn that was masked by rocks and shrubs, appeared to fall precipitously and to become a "view" pure and simple, a view of great extent and beauty, but thrown forward and vertiginous. Milly, with the promise of it from just above, had gone straight down to it, not stopping till it was all before her; and here, on what struck her friend as the dizzy edge of it, she was seated at her ease. The path somehow took care of itself and its final business, but the girl's seat was a slab of rock at the end of a short promontory or excrescence that merely pointed off to the right at gulfs of air and that was so placed by good fortune, if not by the worst, as to be at last completely visible. For Mrs. Stringham stifled a cry on taking in what she believed to be the danger of such a perch for a mere maiden; her liability to slip, to slide, to leap, to be precipitated by a single false movement, by a turn of the head—how could one tell?—into whatever was beneath. A thousand thoughts, for the minute, roared in the poor lady's ears, but without reaching, as happened, Milly's. It was a commotion that left our observer intensely still and holding her breath. What had first been offered her was the possibility of a latent intention—however wild the idea—in such a posture; of some betrayed accordance of Milly's caprice with a horrible hidden obsession. But since Mrs. Stringham stood as motionless as if a sound, a syllable, must have produced the start that would be fatal, so even the lapse of a few seconds had partly a reassuring effect. It gave her time to receive the impression which, when she some minutes later softly retraced her steps, was to be the sharpest she carried away. This was the impression that if the girl was deeply and recklessly meditating there she wasn't meditating a jump; she was on the contrary, as she sat, much more in a state of uplifted and unlimited possession that had nothing to gain from violence. She was looking down on the kingdoms of the earth, and though indeed that of itself might well go to the brain, it wouldn't be with a view of renouncing them. Was she choosing among them or did she want them all? This question, before Mrs. Stringham had decided what to do, made others vain; in accordance with which she saw, or believed she did, that if it might be dangerous to call out, to sound in any way a surprise, it would probably be safe enough to withdraw as she had come. She watched a while longer, she held her breath, and she never knew afterwards what time had elapsed.

Not many minutes probably, yet they hadn't seemed few, and they had given her so much to think of, not only while creeping home, but while waiting afterwards at the inn, that she was still busy with them when, late in the afternoon, Milly reappeared. She had stopped at the point of the path where the Tauchnitz lay, had taken it up and, with the pencil attached to her watch-guard, had scrawled a word—*à bientôt!*—across the cover; after which, even under the girl's continued delay, she had measured time without a return of alarm. For she now saw that the great thing she had brought away was precisely a conviction that the future wasn't to exist for her princess in the form of any sharp or simple release from the human predicament. It wouldn't be for her a question of a flying leap and thereby of a quick escape. It would be a question of taking full in the face the whole assault of life, to the general muster of which indeed her face might have been directly presented as she sat there on her rock. Mrs. Stringham was thus able to say to herself during still another wait of some length that if her young friend still continued absent it wouldn't be because—whatever the opportunity—she had cut short the thread. She wouldn't have committed suicide; she knew herself unmistakeably reserved for some more complicated passage; this was the very vision in which she had, with no little awe, been discovered. The image that thus remained with the elder lady kept the character of a revelation. During the breathless minutes of her watch she had seen her companion afresh; the latter's type, aspect, marks, her history, her state, her beauty, her mystery, all unconsciously betrayed themselves to the Alpine air, and all had been gathered in again to feed Mrs. Stringham's flame. They are things that will more distinctly appear for us, and they are meanwhile briefly represented by the enthusiasm that was stronger on our friend's part than any doubt. It was a consciousness she was scarce yet used to carrying, but she had as beneath her feet a mine of something precious. She seemed to herself to stand near the mouth, not yet quite cleared. The mine but needed working and would certainly yield a treasure. She wasn't thinking, either, of Milly's gold.

II

T HE girl said nothing, when they met, about the words scrawled on the Tauchnitz, and Mrs. Stringham then noticed that she hadn't the book with her. She had left it lying and probably would never remember it at all. Her comrade's decision was therefore quickly made not to speak of having followed her; and within five minutes of her return, wonderfully enough, the preoccupation denoted by her forgetfulness further declared itself. "Should you think me quite abominable if I were to say that after all—?"

Mrs. Stringham had already thought, with the first sound of the question, everything she was capable of thinking, and had immediately made such a sign that Milly's words gave place to visible relief at her assent. "You don't care for our stop here— you'd rather go straight on? We'll start then with the peep of to-morrow's dawn—or as early as you like; it's only rather late now to take the road again." And she smiled to show how she meant it for a joke that an instant onward rush was what the girl would have wished. "I bullied you into stopping," she added; "so it serves me right."

Milly made in general the most of her good friend's jokes; but she humoured this one a little absently. "Oh yes, you do bully me." And it was thus arranged between them, with no discussion at all, that they would resume their journey in the morning. The younger tourist's interest in the detail of the matter—in spite of a declaration from the elder that she would consent to be dragged anywhere—appeared almost immediately afterwards quite to lose itself; she promised, however, to think till supper of where, with the world all before them, they might go—supper having been ordered for such time as permitted of lighted candles. It had been agreed between them that lighted candles at wayside inns, in strange countries, amid mountain scenery, gave the evening meal a peculiar poetry— such being the mild adventures, the refinements of impression, that they, as they would have said, went in for. It was now as if, before this repast, Milly had designed to "lie down"; but at the end of three minutes more she wasn't lying down, she was saying instead, abruptly, with a transition that was like a jump of four thousand miles: "What was it that, in New York, on the ninth, when you saw him alone, Doctor Finch said to you?"

It was not till later that Mrs. Stringham fully knew why the question had startled her still more than its suddenness explained; though the effect of it even at the moment was almost to frighten her into a false answer. She had to think, to remember the occasion, the "ninth," in New York, the time she had seen Doctor Finch alone, and to recall the words he had then uttered; and when everything had come back it was quite, at first, for a moment, as if he had said something that immensely mattered. He hadn't, however, in fact; it was only as if he might perhaps after all have been going to. It was on the sixth—within ten days of their sailing—that she had hurried from Boston under the alarm, a small but a sufficient shock, of hearing that Mildred had suddenly been taken ill, had had, from some obscure cause, such an upset as threatened to stay their journey. The bearing of the accident had happily soon presented itself as slight, and there had been in the event but a few hours of anxiety; the journey had been pronounced again not only possible, but, as representing "change," highly advisable; and if the zealous guest had had five minutes by herself with the Doctor this was clearly no more at his instance than at her own. Almost nothing had passed between them but an easy exchange of enthusiasms in respect to the remedial properties of "Europe"; and due assurance, as the facts came back to her, she was now able to give. "Nothing whatever, on my word of honour, that you mayn't know or mightn't then have known. I've no secret with him about you. What makes you suspect it? I don't quite make out how you know I did see him alone."

"No—you never told me," said Milly. "And I don't mean," she went on, "during the twenty-four hours while I was bad, when your putting your heads together was natural enough. I mean after I was better—the last thing before you went home."

Mrs. Stringham continued to wonder. "Who told you I saw him then?"

"*He* didn't himself—nor did you write me it afterwards. We speak of it now for the first time. That's exactly why!" Milly declared—with something in her face and voice that, the next moment, betrayed for her companion that she had really known nothing, had only conjectured and, chancing her charge, made a hit. Yet why had her mind been busy with the question? "But if you're not, as you now assure me, in his confidence," she smiled, "it's no matter."

"I'm not in his confidence—he had nothing to confide. But are you feeling unwell?"

The elder woman was earnest for the truth, though the possibility she named was not at all the one that seemed to fit— witness the long climb Milly had just indulged in. The girl showed her constant white face, but this her friends had all learned to discount, and it was often brightest when superficially not bravest. She continued for a little mysteriously to smile. "I don't know—haven't really the least idea. But it might be well to find out."

Mrs. Stringham at this flared into sympathy. "Are you in trouble—in pain?"

"Not the least little bit. But I sometimes wonder—!"

"Yes"—she pressed: "wonder what?"

"Well, if I shall have much of it."

Mrs. Stringham stared. "Much of what? Not of pain?"

"Of everything. Of everything I have."

Anxiously again, tenderly, our friend cast about. "You 'have' everything; so that when you say 'much' of it—"

"I only mean," the girl broke in, "shall I have it for long? That is if I *have* got it."

She had at present the effect, a little, of confounding, or at least of perplexing her comrade, who was touched, who was always touched, by something helpless in her grace and abrupt in her turns, and yet actually half made out in her a sort of mocking light. "If you've got an ailment?"

"If I've got everything," Milly laughed.

"Ah *that*—like almost nobody else."

"Then for how long?"

Mrs. Stringham's eyes entreated her; she had gone close to her, half-enclosed her with urgent arms. "Do you want to see some one?" And then as the girl only met it with a slow headshake, though looking perhaps a shade more conscious: "We'll go straight to the best near doctor." This too, however, produced but a gaze of qualified assent and a silence, sweet and vague, that left everything open. Our friend decidedly lost herself. "Tell me, for God's sake, if you're in distress."

"I don't think I've really *everything*," Milly said as if to explain—and as if also to put it pleasantly.

"But what on earth can I do for you?"

The girl debated, then seemed on the point of being able to say; but suddenly changed and expressed herself otherwise. "Dear, dear thing—I'm only too happy!"

It brought them closer, but it rather confirmed Mrs. Stringham's doubt. "Then what's the matter?"

"That's the matter—that I can scarcely bear it."

"But what is it you think you haven't got?"

Milly waited another moment; then she found it, and found for it a dim show of joy. "The power to resist the bliss of what I *have*!"

Mrs. Stringham took it in—her sense of being "put off" with it, the possible, probable irony of it—and her tenderness renewed itself in the positive grimness of a long murmur. "Whom will you see?"—for it was as if they looked down from their height at a continent of doctors. "Where will you first go?"

Milly had for the third time her air of consideration; but she came back with it to her plea of some minutes before. "I'll tell you at supper—good-bye till then." And she left the room with a lightness that testified for her companion to something that again particularly pleased her in the renewed promise of motion. The odd passage just concluded, Mrs. Stringham mused as she once more sat alone with a hooked needle and a ball of silk, the "fine" work with which she was always provided —this mystifying mood had simply been precipitated, no doubt, by their prolonged halt, with which the girl hadn't really been in sympathy. One had only to admit that her complaint was in fact but the excess of the joy of life, and everything *did* then fit. She couldn't stop for the joy, but she could go on for it, and with the pulse of her going on she floated again, was restored to her great spaces. There was no evasion of any truth—so at least Susan Shepherd hoped—in one's sitting there while the twilight deepened and feeling still more finely that the position of this young lady was magnificent. The evening at that height had naturally turned to cold, and the travellers had bespoken a fire with their meal; the great Alpine road asserted its brave presence through the small panes of the low clean windows, with incidents at the inn-door, the yellow diligence, the great waggons, the hurrying hooded private conveyances, reminders, for our fanciful friend, of old stories, old pictures, historic flights, escapes, pursuits, things that had happened, things indeed that by a sort of strange congruity helped her to read the meanings of the greatest interest into the relation in which she was now so deeply involved. It was natural that this record of the magnificence of her companion's position should strike her as after all the best meaning she could extract; for she herself was seated in the magnificence as in a court-carriage—she came back to that, and such a method of progression, such a view from crimson cushions, would evidently have a great deal more to give. By the time the candles were lighted for supper and the short white curtains drawn Milly had reappeared, and the little scenic room had then all its romance. That charm moreover was far from broken by the words in which she, without further loss of time, satisfied her patient mate. "I want to go straight to London."

It was unexpected, corresponding with no view positively taken at their departure; when England had appeared, on the contrary, rather relegated and postponed—seen for the moment, as who should say, at the end of an avenue of preparations and introductions. London, in short, might have been supposed to be the crown, and to be achieved, like a siege, by gradual approaches. Milly's actual fine stride was therefore the more exciting, as any simplification almost always was to Mrs. Stringham; who, besides, was afterwards to recall as a piece of that very "exposition" dear to the dramatist the terms in which, between their smoky candles, the girl had put her preference and in which still other things had come up, come while the clank of waggon-chains in the sharp air reached their ears, with the stamp of hoofs, the rattle of buckets and the foreign questions, foreign answers, that were all alike a part of the cheery converse of the road. The girl brought it out in truth as she might have brought a huge confession, something she admitted herself shy about and that would seem to show her as frivolous; it had rolled over her that what she wanted of Europe was "people," so far as they were to be had, and that, if her friend really wished to know, the vision of this same equivocal quantity was what had haunted her during their previous days, in museums and churches, and what was again spoiling for her the pure taste of scenery. She was all for scenery—yes; but she wanted it human and personal, and all she could say was that there would be in London—wouldn't there?—more of that kind than anywhere else. She came back to her idea that if it wasn't for long—if nothing should happen to be so for *her*— why the particular thing she spoke of would probably have most to give her in the time, would probably be less than anything else a waste of her remainder. She produced this last consideration indeed with such gaiety that Mrs. Stringham was not again disconcerted by it, was in fact quite ready—if talk of early dying was in order—to match it from her own future. Good, then; they would eat and drink because of what might happen to-morrow; and they would direct their course from that moment with a view to such eating and drinking. They ate and drank that night, in truth, as in the spirit of this decision; whereby the air, before they separated, felt itself the clearer.

It had cleared perhaps to a view only too extensive—extensive, that is, in proportion to the signs of life presented. The idea of "people" was not so entertained on Milly's part as to connect itself with particular persons, and the fact remained for each of the ladies that they would, completely unknown, disembark at Dover amid the completely unknowing. They had no relation already formed; this plea Mrs. Stringham put forward to see what it would produce. It produced nothing at first but the observation on the girl's side that what she had in mind was no thought of society nor of scraping acquaintance; nothing was further from her than to desire the opportunities represented for the compatriot in general by a trunkful of "letters." It wasn't a question, in short, of the people the compatriot was after; it was the human, the English picture itself, as they might see it in their own way—the concrete world inferred so fondly from what one had read and dreamed. Mrs. Stringham did every justice to this concrete world, but when later on an occasion chanced to present itself she made a point of not omitting to remark that it might be a comfort to know in advance one or two of the human particles of its concretion. This still, however, failed, in vulgar parlance, to "fetch" Milly, so that she had presently to go all the way. "Haven't I understood from you, for that matter, that you gave Mr. Densher something of a promise?"

There was a moment, on this, when Milly's look had to be taken as representing one of two things—either that she was completely vague about the promise or that Mr. Densher's name itself started no train. But she really couldn't be so vague about the promise, the partner of these hours quickly saw, without attaching it to something; it had to be a promise to somebody in particular to be so repudiated. In the event, accordingly, she acknowledged Mr. Merton Densher, the so unusually "bright" young Englishman who had made his appearance in New York on some special literary business— wasn't it?—shortly before their departure, and who had been three or four times in her house during the brief period between her visit to Boston and her companion's subsequent stay with her; but she required much reminding before it came back to her that she had mentioned to this companion just afterwards the confidence expressed by the personage in question in her never doing so dire a thing as to come to London without, as the phrase was, looking a fellow up. She had left him the enjoyment of his confidence, the form of which might have appeared a trifle free—this she now reasserted; she had done nothing either to impair or to enhance it; but she had also left Mrs. Stringham, in the connexion and at the time, rather sorry to have missed Mr. Densher. She had thought of him again after that, the elder woman; she had likewise gone so far as to notice that Milly appeared not to have done so—which the girl might easily have betrayed; and, interested as she was in everything that concerned her, she had made out for herself, for herself only and rather idly, that, but for interruptions, the young Englishman might have become a better acquaintance. His being an acquaintance at all was one of the signs that in the first days had helped to place Milly, as a young person with the world before her, for sympathy and wonder. Isolated, un-mothered, unguarded, but with her other strong marks, her big house, her big fortune, her big freedom, she had lately be-gun to "receive," for all her few years, as an older woman might have done—as was done, precisely, by princesses who had public considerations to observe and who came of age very early. If it was thus distinct to Mrs. Stringham then that

Mr. Densher had gone off somewhere else in connexion with his errand before her visit to New York, it had been also not undiscoverable that he had come back for a day or two later on, that is after her own second excursion—that he had in fine reappeared on a single occasion on his way to the West: his way from Washington as she believed, though he was out of sight at the time of her joining her friend for their departure. It hadn't occurred to her before to exaggerate—it had not occurred to her that she could; but she seemed to become aware to-night that there had been just enough in this relation to meet, to provoke, the free conception of a little more.

She presently put it that, at any rate, promise or no promise, Milly would at a pinch be able, in London, to act on his permission to make him a sign; to which Milly replied with readiness that her ability, though evident, would be none the less quite wasted, inasmuch as the gentleman would to a certainty be still in America. He had a great deal to do there—which he would scarce have begun; and in fact she might very well not have thought of London at all if she hadn't been sure he wasn't yet near coming back. It was perceptible to her companion that the moment our young woman had so far committed herself she had a sense of having overstepped; which was not quite patched up by her saying the next minute, possibly with a certain failure of presence of mind, that the last thing she desired was the air of running after him. Mrs. Stringham wondered privately what question there could be of any such appearance—the danger of which thus suddenly came up; but she said for the time nothing of it—she only said other things: one of which was, for instance, that if Mr. Densher was away he was away, and this the end of it: also that of course they must be discreet at any price. But what was the measure of discretion, and how was one to be sure? So it was that, as they sat there, she produced her own case: *she* had a possible tie with London, which she desired as little to disown as she might wish to risk presuming on it. She treated her companion, in short, for their evening's end, to the story of Maud Manningham, the odd but interesting English girl who had formed her special affinity in the old days at the Vevey school; whom she had written to, after their separation, with a regularity that had at first faltered and then altogether failed, yet that had been for the time quite a fine case of crude constancy; so that it had in fact flickered up again of itself on the occasion of the marriage of each. They had then once more fondly, scrupulously written—Mrs. Lowder first; and even another letter or two had afterwards passed. This, however, had been the end— though with no rupture, only a gentle drop: Maud Manningham had made, she believed, a great marriage, while she herself had made a small; on top of which, moreover, distance, difference, diminished community and impossible reunion had done the rest of the work. It was but after all these years that reunion had begun to show as possible—if the other party to it, that is, should be still in existence. That was exactly what it now appeared to our friend interesting to ascertain, as, with one aid and another, she believed she might. It was an experiment she would at all events now make if Milly didn't object.

Milly in general objected to nothing, and though she asked a question or two she raised no present plea. Her questions— or at least her own answers to them—kindled on Mrs. Stringham's part a backward train: she hadn't known till to-night how much she remembered, or how fine it might be to see what had become of large high-coloured Maud, florid, alien, exotic—which had been just the spell—even to the perceptions of youth. There was the danger—she frankly touched it— that such a temperament mightn't have matured, with the years, all in the sense of fineness: it was the sort of danger that, in renewing relations after long breaks, one had always to look in the face. To gather in strayed threads was to take a risk—for which, however, she was prepared if Milly was. The possible "fun," she confessed, was by itself rather tempting; and she fairly sounded, with this—wound up a little as she was—the note of fun as the harmless final right of fifty years of mere New England virtue. Among the things she was afterwards to recall was the indescribable look dropped on her, at that, by her companion; she was still seated there between the candles and before the finished supper, while Milly moved about, and the look was long to figure for her as an inscrutable comment on *her* notion of freedom. Challenged, at any rate, as for the last wise word, Milly showed perhaps, musingly, charmingly, that, though her attention had been mainly soundless, her friend's story—produced as a resource unsuspected, a card from up the sleeve—half-surprised, half-beguiled her. Since the matter, such as it was, depended on that, she brought out before she went to bed an easy, a light "Risk everything!"

This quality in it seemed possibly a little to deny weight to Maud Lowder's evoked presence—as Susan Stringham, still sitting up, became, in excited reflexion, a trifle more conscious. Something determinant, when the girl had left her, took place in her—nameless but, as soon as she had given way, coercive. It was as if she knew again, in this fulness of time, that she had been, after Maud's marriage, just sensibly outlived or, as people nowadays said, shunted. Mrs. Lowder had left her behind, and on the occasion, subsequently, of the corresponding date in her own life—not the second, the sad one, with its dignity of sadness, but the first, with the meagreness of its supposed felicity—she had been, in the same spirit, almost patronisingly pitied. If that suspicion, even when it had ceased to matter, had never quite died out for her, there was doubtless some oddity in its now offering itself as a link, rather than as another break, in the chain; and indeed there might well have been for her a mood in which the notion of the development of patronage in her quondam schoolmate would have settled her question in another sense. It was actually settled—if the case be worth our analysis—by the happy consummation, the poetic justice, the generous revenge, of her having at last something to show. Maud, on their parting company, had appeared to have so much, and would now—for wasn't it also in general quite the rich law of English life?—have, with accretions, promotions, expansions, ever so much more. Very good; such things might be; she rose to the sense of being ready for them. Whatever Mrs. Lowder might have to show—and one hoped one did the presumptions all justice—she would have nothing like Milly Theale, who constituted the trophy producible by poor Susan. Poor Susan lingered late—till the candles were low, and as soon as the table was cleared she opened her neat portfolio. She hadn't lost the old clue; there were connexions she remembered, addresses she could try; so the thing was to begin. She wrote on the spot.

BOOK FOURTH

I

IT HAD all gone so fast after this that Milly uttered but the truth nearest to hand in saying to the gentleman on her right —who was, by the same token, the gentleman on her hostess's left—that she scarce even then knew where she was: the words marking her first full sense of a situation really romantic. They were already dining, she and her friend, at Lancaster Gate, and surrounded, as it seemed to her, with every English accessory; though her consciousness of Mrs. Lowder's existence, and still more of her remarkable identity, had been of so recent and so sudden a birth. Susie, as she was apt to call her companion for a lighter change, had only had to wave a neat little wand for the fairy-tale to begin at once; in consequence of which Susie now glittered—for, with Mrs. Stringham's new sense of success, it came to that—in the character of a fairy godmother. Milly had almost insisted on dressing her, for the present occasion, as one; and it was no fault of the girl's if the good lady hadn't now appeared in a peaked hat, a short petticoat and diamond shoe-buckles, brandishing the magic crutch. The good lady bore herself in truth not less contentedly than if these insignia had marked her work; and Milly's observation to Lord Mark had doubtless just been the result of such a light exchange of looks with her as even the great length of the table couldn't baffle. There were twenty persons between them, but this sustained passage was the sharpest sequel yet to that other comparison of views during the pause on the Swiss pass. It almost appeared to Milly that their fortune had been unduly precipitated—as if properly they were in the position of having ventured on a small joke and found the answer out of proportion grave. She couldn't at this moment for instance have said whether, with her quickened perceptions, she were more enlivened or oppressed; and the case might in fact have been serious hadn't she, by good fortune, from the moment the picture loomed, quickly made up her mind that what finally most concerned her was neither to seek nor to shirk, wasn't even to wonder too much, but was to let things come as they would, since there was little enough doubt of how they would go.

Lord Mark had been brought to her before dinner—not by Mrs. Lowder, but by the handsome girl, that lady's niece, who was now at the other end and on the same side as Susie; he had taken her in, and she meant presently to ask him about Miss Croy, the handsome girl, actually offered to her sight—though now in a splendid way—but for the second time. The first time had been the occasion—only three days before—of her calling at their hotel with her aunt and then making, for our other two heroines, a great impression of beauty and eminence. This impression had remained so with Milly that at present, and although her attention was aware at the same time of everything else, her eyes were mainly engaged with Kate Croy when not engaged with Susie. That wonderful creature's eyes moreover readily met them—she ranked now as a wonderful creature; and it seemed part of the swift prosperity of the American visitors that, so little in the original reckoning, she should yet appear conscious, charmingly, frankly conscious, of possibilities of friendship for them. Milly had easily and, as a guest, gracefully generalised: English girls had a special strong beauty which particularly showed in evening dress—above all when, as was strikingly the case with this one, the dress itself was what it should be. That observation she had all ready for Lord Mark when they should, after a little, get round to it. She seemed even now to see that there might be a good deal they would get round to; the indication being that, taken up once for all with her other neighbour, their hostess would leave them much to themselves. Mrs. Lowder's other neighbour was the Bishop of Murrum—a real bishop, such as Milly had never seen, with a complicated costume, a voice like an old-fashioned wind instrument, and a face all the portrait of a prelate; while the gentleman on our young lady's left, a gentleman thick-necked, large and literal, who looked straight before him and as if he were not to be diverted by vain words from that pursuit, clearly counted as an offset to the possession of Lord Mark. As Milly made out these things—with a shade of exhilaration at the way she already fell in—she saw how she was justified of her plea for people and her love of life. It wasn't then, as the prospect seemed to show, so difficult to get into the current, or to stand at any rate on the bank. It was easy to get near—if they *were* near; and yet the elements were different enough from any of her old elements, and positively rich and strange.

She asked herself if her right-hand neighbour would understand what she meant by such a description of them should she throw it off; but another of the things to which precisely her sense was awakened was that no, decidedly, he wouldn't. It was nevertheless by this time open to her that his line would be to be clever; and indeed, evidently, no little of the interest was going to be in the fresh reference and fresh effect both of people's cleverness and of their simplicity. She thrilled, she consciously flushed, and all to turn pale again, with the certitude —it had never been so present—that she should find herself completely involved: the very air of the place, the pitch of the occasion, had for her both so sharp a ring and so deep an undertone. The smallest things, the faces, the hands, the jewels of the women, the sound of words, especially of names, across the table, the shape of the forks, the arrangement of the flowers, the attitude of the servants, the walls of the room, were all touches in a picture and denotements in a play; and they marked for her moreover her alertness of vision. She had never, she might well believe, been in such a state of vibration; her sensibility was almost too sharp for her comfort: there were for example more indications than she could reduce to order in the manner of the friendly niece, who struck her as distinguished and interesting, as in fact surprisingly genial. This young woman's type had, visibly, other possibilities; yet here, of its own free movement, it had already sketched a relation. Were they, Miss Croy and she, to take up the tale where their two elders had left it off so many years before?—were they to find they liked each other and to try for themselves whether a scheme of constancy on more modern lines could be worked? She had doubted, as they came to England, of Maud Manningham, had believed her a broken reed and a vague resource, had seen their dependence on her as a state of mind that would have been shamefully silly—so far as it *was* dependence—had they wished to do anything so inane as "get into society." To have made their pilgrimage all for the sake of such society as Mrs. Lowder might have in reserve for them—that didn't bear thinking of at all, and she herself had quite chosen her course for curiosity about other matters. She would have described this curiosity as a desire to see the places she had read about, and *that* description of her motive she was prepared to give her neighbour—even though, as a consequence of it, he should find how little she had read. It was almost at present as if her poor prevision had been rebuked by the majesty—she could scarcely call it less—of the event, or at all events by the commanding character of the two figures (she could scarcely call *that* less either) mainly presented. Mrs. Lowder and her niece, however dissimilar, had at least in common that each was a great reality. That was true, primarily, of the aunt—so true that Milly wondered how her own companion had arrived in other years at so odd an alliance; yet she none the less felt Mrs. Lowder as a person of whom the mind might in two or three days roughly make the circuit. She would sit there massive at least while one attempted it; whereas Miss Croy, the handsome girl, would indulge in incalculable movements that might interfere with one's tour. She was the amusing resisting ominous fact, none the less, and each other person and thing was just such a fact; and it served them right, no doubt, the pair of them, for having rushed into their adventure.

Lord Mark's intelligence meanwhile, however, had met her own quite sufficiently to enable him to tell her how little he could clear up her situation. He explained, for that matter—or at least he hinted—that there was no such thing to-day in London as saying where any one was. Every one was everywhere—nobody was anywhere. He should be put to it—yes, frankly—to give a name of any sort or kind to their hostess's "set." *Was* it a set at all, or wasn't it, and were there not really no such things as sets in the place any more?—was there anything but the groping and pawing, that of the vague billows of some great greasy sea in mid-Channel, of masses of bewildered people trying to "get" they didn't know what or where? He threw out the question, which seemed large; Milly felt that at the end of five minutes he had thrown out a great many, though he followed none more than a step or two; perhaps he would prove suggestive, but he helped her as yet to no discriminations: he spoke as if he had given them up from too much knowledge. He was thus at the opposite extreme from herself, but, as a consequence of it, also wandering and lost; and he was furthermore, for all his temporary incoherence, to which she guessed there would be some key, as packed a concretion as either Mrs. Lowder or Kate. The only light in which he placed the former of these ladies was that of an extraordinary woman—a most extraordinary woman, and "the more extraordinary the more one knows her," while of the latter he said nothing for the moment but that she was tremendously, yes, quite tremendously, good-looking. It was some time, she thought, before his talk showed his cleverness, and yet each minute she believed in that mystery more, quite apart from what her hostess had told her on first naming him. Perhaps he was one of the cases she had heard of at home—those characteristic cases of people in England who concealed their play of mind so much more than they advertised it. Even Mr. Densher a little did that. And what made Lord Mark, at any rate, so real either, when this was a trick he had apparently so mastered? His type somehow, as by a life, a need, an intention of its own, took all care for vividness off his hands; that was enough. It was difficult to guess his age—whether he were a young man who looked old or an old man who looked young; it seemed to prove nothing, as against other things, that he was bald and, as might have been said, slightly stale, or, more delicately perhaps, dry: there was such a fine little fidget of preoccupied life in him, and his eyes, at moments—though it was an appearance they could suddenly lose—were as candid and clear as those of a pleasant boy. Very neat, very light, and so fair that there was little other indication of his moustache than his constantly feeling it—which was again boyish—he would have affected her as the most intellectual person present if he had not affected her as the most frivolous. The latter quality was rather in his look than in anything else, though he constantly wore his double eye-glass, which was, much more, Bostonian and thoughtful.

The idea of his frivolity had, no doubt, to do with his personal designation, which represented—as yet, for our young woman, a little confusedly—a connexion with an historic patriciate, a class that in turn, also confusedly, represented an affinity with a social element she had never heard otherwise described than as "fashion." The supreme social element in New York had never known itself but as reduced to that category, and though Milly was aware that, as applied to a territorial and political aristocracy, the label was probably too simple, she had for the time none other at hand. She presently, it is true, enriched her idea with the perception that her interlocutor was indifferent; yet this, indifferent as aristocracies notoriously were, saw her but little further, inasmuch as she felt that, in the first place, he would much rather get on with her than not, and in the second was only thinking of too many matters of his own. If he kept her in view on the one hand and kept so much else on the other—the way he crumbed up his bread was a proof—why did he hover before her as a potentially insolent noble? She couldn't have answered the question, and it was precisely one of those that swarmed. They were complicated, she might fairly have said, by his visibly knowing, having known from afar off, that she was a stranger and an American, and by his none the less making no more of it than if she and her like were the chief of his diet. He took her, kindly enough, but imperturbably, irreclaimably, for granted, and it wouldn't in the least help that she herself knew him, as quickly, for having been in her country and threshed it out. There would be nothing for her to explain or attenuate or brag about; she could neither escape nor prevail by her strangeness; he would have, for that matter, on such a subject, more to tell her than to learn from her. She might learn from *him* why she was so different from the handsome girl—which she didn't know, being merely able to feel it; or at any rate might learn from him why the handsome girl was so different from her.

On these lines, however, they would move later; the lines immediately laid down were, in spite of his vagueness for his own convenience, definite enough. She was already, he observed to her, thinking what she should say on her other side —which was what Americans were always doing. She needn't in conscience say anything at all; but Americans never knew that, nor ever, poor creatures, yes (*she* had interposed the "poor creatures!") what not to do. The burdens they took on—the things, positively, they made an affair of! This easy and after all friendly jibe at her race was really for her, on her new friend's part, the note of personal recognition so far as she required it; and she gave him a prompt and conscious example of morbid anxiety by insisting that her desire to be, herself, "lovely" all round was justly founded on the lovely way Mrs. Lowder had met her. He was directly interested in that, and it was not till afterwards she fully knew how much more information about their friend he had taken than given. Here again for instance was a characteristic note: she had, on the spot, with her first plunge into the obscure depths of a society constituted from far back, encountered the interesting phenomenon of complicated, of possibly sinister motive. However, Maud Manningham (her name, even in her presence, somehow still fed the fancy) *had*, all the same, been lovely, and one was going to meet her now quite as far on as one had one's self been met. She had been with them at their hotel—they were a pair—before even they had supposed she could have got their letter. Of course indeed they had written in advance, but they had followed that up very fast. She had thus engaged them to dine but two days later, and on the morrow again, without waiting for a return visit, without waiting for anything, she had called with her niece. It was as if she really cared for them, and it was magnificent fidelity—fidelity to Mrs. Stringham, her own companion and Mrs. Lowder's former schoolmate, the lady with the charming face and the rather high dress down there at the end.

Lord Mark took in through his nippers these balanced attributes of Susie. "But isn't Mrs. Stringham's fidelity then equally magnificent?"

"Well, it's a beautiful sentiment; but it isn't as if she had anything to *give*."

"Hasn't she got you?" Lord Mark asked without excessive delay.

"Me—to give Mrs. Lowder?" Milly had clearly not yet seen herself in the light of such an offering. "Oh I'm rather a poor present; and I don't feel as if, even at that, I had as yet quite been given."

"You've been shown, and if our friend has jumped at you it comes to the same thing." He made his jokes, Lord Mark, without amusement for himself; yet it wasn't that he was grim.

"To be seen, you must recognise, *is*, for you, to be jumped at; and, if it's a question of being shown, here you are again. Only it has now been taken out of your friend's hands; it's Mrs. Lowder already who's getting the benefit. Look round the table, and you'll make out, I think, that you're being, from top to bottom, jumped at."

"Well then," said Milly, "I seem also to feel that I like it better than being made fun of."

It was one of the things she afterwards saw—Milly was for ever seeing things afterwards—that her companion had here had some way of his own, quite unlike any one's else, of assuring her of his consideration. She wondered how he had done it, for he had neither apologised nor protested. She said to herself at any rate that he had led her on; and what was most odd was the question by which he had done so. "Does she know much about you?"

"No, she just likes us."

Even for this his travelled lordship, seasoned and saturated, had no laugh. "I mean *you* particularly. Has that lady with the charming face, which *is* charming, told her?"

Milly cast about. "Told her what?"

"Everything."

This, with the way he dropped it, again considerably moved her—made her feel for a moment that as a matter of course she was a subject for disclosures. But she quickly found her answer. "Oh as for that you must ask *her*."

"Your clever companion?"

"Mrs. Lowder."

He replied to this that their hostess was a person with whom there were certain liberties one never took, but that he was none the less fairly upheld, inasmuch as she was for the most part kind to him and as, should he be very good for a while, she would probably herself tell him. "And I shall have at any rate in the meantime the interest of seeing what she does with you. That will teach me more or less, you see, how much she knows."

Milly followed this—it was lucid, but it suggested something apart. "How much does she know about *you*?"

"Nothing," said Lord Mark serenely. "But that doesn't

matter—for what she does with me." And then as to anticipate
Milly's question about the nature of such doing: "This for instance—turning me straight on for *you*."

The girl thought. "And you mean she wouldn't if she did
know—?"

He met it as if it were really a point. "No. I believe, to do
her justice, she still would. So you can be easy."

Milly had the next instant then acted on the permission.
"Because you're even at the worst the best thing she has?"

With this he was at last amused. "I was till you came. You're
the best now."

It was strange his words should have given her the sense of
his knowing, but it was positive that they did so, and to the extent of making her believe them, though still with wonder.
That really from this first of their meetings was what was most
to abide with her: she accepted almost helplessly—she surrendered so to the inevitable in it—being the sort of thing, as he
might have said, that he at least thoroughly believed he had, in
going about, seen enough of for all practical purposes. Her
submission was naturally moreover not to be impaired by her
learning later on that he had paid at short intervals, though at
a time apparently just previous to her own emergence from the
obscurity of extreme youth, three separate visits to New York,
where his nameable friends and his contrasted contacts had
been numerous. His impression, his recollection of the whole
mixed quantity, was still visibly rich. It had helped him to place
her, and she was more and more sharply conscious of having—
as with the door sharply slammed upon her and the guard's
hand raised in signal to the train—been popped into the compartment in which she was to travel for him. It was a use of her
that many a girl would have been doubtless quick to resent;
and the kind of mind that thus, in our young lady, made all for
mere seeing and taking is precisely one of the charms of our
subject. Milly had practically just learned from him, had made
out, as it were, from her rumbling compartment, that he gave
her the highest place among their friend's actual properties.
She was a success, that was what it came to, he presently assured her, and this was what it was to be a success; it always
happened before one could know it. One's ignorance was in
fact often the greatest part of it. "You haven't had time yet,"

he said; "this is nothing. But you'll see. You'll see everything. You *can*, you know—everything you dream of."

He made her more and more wonder; she almost felt as if he were showing her visions while he spoke; and strangely enough, though it was visions that had drawn her on, she hadn't had them in connexion—that is in such preliminary and necessary connexion—with such a face as Lord Mark's, such eyes and such a voice, such a tone and such a manner. He had for an instant the effect of making her ask herself if she were after all going to be afraid; so distinct was it for fifty seconds that a fear passed over her. There they were again—yes, certainly: Susie's overture to Mrs. Lowder had been their joke, but they had pressed in that gaiety an electric bell that continued to sound. Positively while she sat there she had the loud rattle in her ears, and she wondered during these moments why the others didn't hear it. They didn't stare, they didn't smile, and the fear in her that I speak of was but her own desire to stop it. That dropped, however, as if the alarm itself had ceased; she seemed to have seen in a quick though tempered glare that there were two courses for her, one to leave London again the first thing in the morning, the other to do nothing at all. Well, she would do nothing at all; she was already doing it; more than that, she had already done it, and her chance was gone. She gave herself up—she had the strangest sense, on the spot, of so deciding; for she had turned a corner before she went on again with Lord Mark. Inexpressive but intensely significant, he met as no one else could have done the very question she had suddenly put to Mrs. Stringham on the Brünig. Should she have it, whatever she did have, that question had been, for long? "Ah so possibly not," her neighbour appeared to reply; "therefore, don't you see? *I'm* the way." It was vivid that he might be, in spite of his absence of flourish; the way being doubtless just *in* that absence. The handsome girl, whom she didn't lose sight of and who, she felt, kept her also in view—Mrs. Lowder's striking niece would perhaps be the way as well, for in her too was the absence of flourish, though she had little else, so far as one could tell, in common with Lord Mark. Yet how indeed *could* one tell, what did one understand, and of what was one, for that matter, provisionally conscious but of their being somehow together in what they represented? Kate Croy, fine but friendly, looked over at her as really with a guess at Lord Mark's effect on her. If she could guess this effect what then did she know about it and in what degree had she felt it her-self? Did that represent, as between them, anything particular, and should she have to count with them as duplicating, as in-tensifying by a mutual intelligence, the relation into which she was sinking? Nothing was so odd as that she should have to recognise so quickly in each of these glimpses of an instant the various signs of a relation; and this anomaly itself, had she had more time to give to it, might well, might almost terribly have suggested to her that her doom was to live fast. It was queerly a question of the short run and the consciousness proportion-ately crowded.

These were immense excursions for the spirit of a young person at Mrs. Lowder's mere dinner-party; but what was so significant and so admonitory as the fact of their being possi-ble? What could they have been but just a part, already, of the crowded consciousness? And it was just a part likewise that while plates were changed and dishes presented and periods in the banquet marked; while appearances insisted and phenom-ena multiplied and words reached her from here and there like plashes of a slow thick tide; while Mrs. Lowder grew somehow more stout and more instituted and Susie, at her distance and in comparison, more thinly improvised and more different— different, that is, from every one and every thing: it was just a part that while this process went forward our young lady alighted, came back, taking up her destiny again as if she had been able by a wave or two of her wings to place herself briefly in sight of an alternative to it. Whatever it was it had showed in this brief interval as better than the alternative; and it now pre-sented itself altogether in the image and in the place in which she had left it. The image was that of her being, as Lord Mark had declared, a success. This depended more or less of course on his idea of the thing—into which at present, however, she wouldn't go. But, renewing soon, she had asked him what he meant then that Mrs. Lowder would do with her, and he had replied that this might safely be left. "She'll get back," he pleasantly said, "her money." He could say it too—which was singular—without affecting her either as vulgar or as "nasty";

and he had soon explained himself by adding: "Nobody here, you know, does anything for nothing."

"Ah if you mean that we shall reward her as hard as ever we can, nothing is more certain. But she's an idealist," Milly continued, "and idealists, in the long run, I think, *don't* feel that they lose."

Lord Mark seemed, within the limits of his enthusiasm, to find this charming. "Ah she strikes you as an idealist?"

"She idealises *us*, my friend and me, absolutely. She sees us in a light," said Milly. "That's all I've got to hold on by. So don't deprive me of it."

"I wouldn't think of such a thing for the world. But do you suppose," he continued as if it were suddenly important for him—"do you suppose she sees *me* in a light?"

She neglected his question for a little, partly because her attention attached itself more and more to the handsome girl, partly because, placed so near their hostess, she wished not to show as discussing her too freely. Mrs. Lowder, it was true, steering in the other quarter a course in which she called at subjects as if they were islets in an archipelago, continued to allow them their ease, and Kate Croy at the same time steadily revealed herself as interesting. Milly in fact found of a sudden her ease—found it all as she bethought herself that what Mrs. Lowder was really arranging for was a report on her quality and, as perhaps might be said her value, from Lord Mark. She wished him, the wonderful lady, to have no pretext for not knowing what he thought of Miss Theale. Why his judgement so mattered remained to be seen; but it was this divination that in any case now determined Milly's rejoinder. "No. She knows you. She has probably reason to. And you all here know each other—I see that—so far as you know anything. You know what you're used to, and it's your being used to it—that, and that only—that makes you. But there are things you don't know."

He took it in as if it might fairly, to do him justice, be a point. "Things that *I* don't—with all the pains I take and the way I've run about the world to leave nothing unlearned?"

Milly thought, and it was perhaps the very truth of his claim —its not being negligible—that sharpened her impatience and

thereby her wit. "You're *blasé*, but you're not enlightened.
You're familiar with everything, but conscious really of
nothing. What I mean is that you've no imagination."

Lord Mark at this threw back his head, ranging with his eyes
the opposite side of the room and showing himself at last so
much more flagrantly diverted that it fairly attracted their
hostess's notice. Mrs. Lowder, however, only smiled on Milly
for a sign that something racy was what she had expected, and
resumed, with a splash of her screw, her cruise among the
islands. "Oh I've heard that," the young man replied, "before!"

"There it is then. You've heard everything before. You've
heard *me* of course before, in my country, often enough."

"Oh never too often," he protested. "I'm sure I hope I shall
still hear you again and again."

"But what good then has it done you?" the girl went on as if
now frankly to amuse him.

"Oh you'll see when you know me."

"But most assuredly I shall never know you."

"Then that will be exactly," he laughed, "the good!"

If it established thus that they couldn't or wouldn't mix,
why did Milly none the less feel through it a perverse quick-
ening of the relation to which she had been in spite of herself
appointed? What queerer consequence of their not mixing than
their talking—for it was what they had arrived at—almost intimately? She wished to get away from him, or indeed, much
rather, away from herself so far as she was present to him. She
saw already—wonderful creature, after all, herself too—that
there would be a good deal more of him to come for her, and
that the special sign of their intercourse would be to keep herself out of the question. Everything else might come in—only
never that; and with such an arrangement they would perhaps
even go far. This in fact might quite have begun, on the spot,
with her returning again to the topic of the handsome girl. If
she was to keep herself out she could naturally best do so by
putting in somebody else. She accordingly put in Kate Croy,
being ready to that extent—as she was not at all afraid for her
—to sacrifice her if necessary. Lord Mark himself, for that
matter, had made it easy by saying a little while before that no
one among them did anything for nothing. "What then"—she
was aware of being abrupt—"does Miss Croy, if she's so inter-

ested, do it for? What has she to gain by *her* lovely welcome? Look at her *now*!" Milly broke out with characteristic freedom of praise, though pulling herself up also with a compunctious "Oh!" as the direction thus given to their eyes happened to coincide with a turn of Kate's face to them. All she had meant to do was to insist that this face was fine; but what she had in fact done was to renew again her effect of showing herself to its possessor as conjoined with Lord Mark for some interested view of it. He had, however, promptly met her question.

"To gain? Why your acquaintance."

"Well, what's my acquaintance to *her*? She can care for me— she must feel that—only by being sorry for me; and that's why she's lovely: to be already willing to take the trouble to be. It's the height of the disinterested."

There were more things in this than one that Lord Mark might have taken up; but in a minute he had made his choice. "Ah then I'm nowhere, for I'm afraid *I'm* not sorry for you in the least. What do you make then," he asked, "of your success?"

"Why just the great reason of all. It's just because our friend there sees it that she pities me. She understands," Milly said; "she's better than any of you. She's beautiful."

He appeared struck with this at last—with the point the girl made of it; to which she came back even after a diversion created by a dish presented between them. "Beautiful in character, I see. *Is* she so? You must tell me about her."

Milly wondered. "But haven't you known her longer than I? Haven't you seen her for yourself?"

"No—I've failed with her. It's no use. I don't make her out. And I assure you I really should like to." His assurance had in fact for his companion a positive suggestion of sincerity; he affected her as now saying something he did feel; and she was the more struck with it as she was still conscious of the failure even of curiosity he had just shown in respect to herself. She had meant something—though indeed for herself almost only—in speaking of their friend's natural pity; it had doubtless been a note of questionable taste, but it had quavered out in spite of her and he hadn't so much as cared to enquire "Why 'natural'?" Not that it wasn't really much better for her that he shouldn't: explanations would in truth have taken her much too far. Only she now perceived that, in comparison, her word about this other person really "drew" him; and there were things in that probably, many things, as to which she would learn more and which glimmered there already as part and parcel of that larger "real" with which, in her new situation, she was to be beguiled. It was in fact at the very moment, this element, not absent from what Lord Mark was further saying. "So you're wrong, you see, as to our knowing all about each other. There are cases where we break down. I at any rate give *her* up—up, that is, to you. You must do her for me—tell me, I mean, when you know more. You'll notice," he pleasantly wound up, "that I've confidence in you."

"Why shouldn't you have?" Milly asked, observing in this, as she thought, a fine, though for such a man a surprisingly artless, fatuity. It was as if there might have been a question of her falsifying for the sake of her own show—that is of the failure of her honesty to be proof against her desire to keep well with him herself. She didn't, none the less, otherwise protest against his remark; there was something else she was occupied in seeing. It was the handsome girl alone, one of his own species and his own society, who had made him feel uncertain; of his certainties about a mere little American, a cheap exotic, imported almost wholesale and whose habitat, with its conditions of climate, growth and cultivation, its immense profusion but its few varieties and thin development, he was perfectly satisfied. The marvel was too that Milly understood his satisfaction —feeling she expressed the truth in presently saying: "Of course; I make out that she must be difficult; just as I see that I myself must be easy." And that was what, for all the rest of this occasion, remained with her—as the most interesting thing that *could* remain. She was more and more content herself to be easy; she would have been resigned, even had it been brought straighter home to her, to passing for a cheap exotic. Provisionally, at any rate, that protected her wish to keep herself, with Lord Mark, in abeyance. They *had* all affected her as inevitably knowing each other, and if the handsome girl's place among them was something even their initiation couldn't deal with—why then she would indeed be a quantity.

II

Tʜᴀᴛ sense of quantities, separate or mixed, was really, no doubt, what most prevailed at first for our slightly gasping American pair; it found utterance for them in their frequent remark to each other that they had no one but themselves to thank. It dropped from Milly more than once that if she had ever known it was so easy—! though her exclamation mostly ended without completing her idea. This, however, was a trifle to Mrs. Stringham, who cared little whether she meant that in this case she would have come sooner. She couldn't have come sooner, and she perhaps on the contrary meant—for it would have been like her—that she wouldn't have come at all; why it was so easy being at any rate a matter as to which her companion had begun quickly to pick up views. Susie kept some of these lights for the present to herself, since, freely communicated, they might have been a little disturbing; with which, moreover, the quantities that we speak of as surrounding the two ladies were in many cases quantities of things—and of other things—to talk about. Their immediate lesson accordingly was that they just had been caught up by the incalculable strength of a wave that was actually holding them aloft and that would naturally dash them wherever it liked. They meanwhile, we hasten to add, made the best of their precarious position, and if Milly had had no other help for it she would have found not a little in the sight of Susan Shepherd's state. The girl had had nothing to say to her, for three days, about the "success" announced by Lord Mark—which they saw, besides, otherwise established; she was too taken up, too touched, by Susie's own exaltation. Susie glowed in the light of her justified faith; everything had happened that she had been acute enough to think least probable; she had appealed to a possible delicacy in Maud Manningham—a delicacy, mind you, but *barely* possible—and her appeal had been met in a way that was an honour to human nature. This proved sensibility of the lady of Lancaster Gate performed verily for both our friends during these first days the office of a fine floating gold-dust, something that threw over the prospect a harmonising blur. The forms, the colours behind it were strong and deep—we have seen how they already stood out for Milly; but nothing, comparatively, had had so much of the dignity of truth as the fact of Maud's fidelity to a sentiment. That was what Susie was proud of, much more than of her great place in the world, which she was moreover conscious of not as yet wholly measuring. That was what was more vivid even than her being—in senses more worldly and in fact almost in the degree of a revelation—English and distinct and positive, with almost no inward but with the finest outward resonance.

Susan Shepherd's word for her, again and again, was that she was "large"; yet it was not exactly a case, as to the soul, of echoing chambers: she might have been likened rather to a capacious receptacle, originally perhaps loose, but now drawn as tightly as possible over its accumulated contents—a packed mass, for her American admirer, of curious detail. When the latter good lady, at home, had handsomely figured her friends as not small—which was the way she mostly figured them—there was a certain implication that they were spacious because they were empty. Mrs. Lowder, by a different law, was spacious because she was full, because she had something in common, even in repose, with a projectile, of great size, loaded and ready for use. That indeed, to Susie's romantic mind, announced itself as half the charm of their renewal—a charm as of sitting in springtime, during a long peace, on the daisied grassy bank of some great slumbering fortress. True to her psychological instincts, certainly, Mrs. Stringham had noted that the "sentiment" she rejoiced in on her old schoolmate's part was all a matter of action and movement, was not, save for the interweaving of a more frequent plump "dearest" than she would herself perhaps have used, a matter of much other embroidery. She brooded with interest on this further mark of race, feeling in her own spirit a different economy. The joy, for her, was to know *why* she acted—the reason was half the business; whereas with Mrs. Lowder there might have been no reason: "why" was the trivial seasoning-substance, the vanilla or the nutmeg, omittable from the nutritive pudding without spoiling it. Mrs. Lowder's desire was clearly sharp that their young companions should also prosper together; and Mrs. Stringham's account of it all to Milly, during the first days, was that when, at Lancaster

Gate, she was not occupied in telling, as it were, about her, she was occupied in hearing much of the history of her hostess's brilliant niece.

They had plenty, on these lines, the two elder women, to give and to take, and it was even not quite clear to the pilgrim from Boston that what she should mainly have arranged for in London was not a series of thrills for herself. She had a bad conscience, indeed almost a sense of immorality, in having to recognise that she was, as she said, carried away. She laughed to Milly when she also said that she didn't know where it would end; and the principle of her uneasiness was that Mrs. Lowder's life bristled for her with elements that she was really having to look at for the first time. They represented, she believed, the world, the world that, as a consequence of the cold shoulder turned to it by the Pilgrim Fathers, had never yet boldly crossed to Boston—it would surely have sunk the stoutest Cunarder—and she couldn't pretend that she faced the prospect simply because Milly had had a caprice. She was in the act herself of having one, directed precisely to their present spectacle. She could but seek strength in the thought that she had never had one—or had never yielded to one, which came to the same thing—before. The sustaining sense of it all moreover as literary material—that quite dropped from her. She must wait, at any rate, she should see: it struck her, so far as she had got, as vast, obscure, lurid. She reflected in the watches of the night that she was probably just going to love it for itself—that is for itself and Milly. The odd thing was that she could think of Milly's loving it without dread—or with dread at least not on the score of conscience, only on the score of peace. It was a mercy at all events, for the hour, that their two spirits jumped together.

While, for this first week that followed their dinner, she drank deep at Lancaster Gate, her companion was no less happily, appeared to be indeed on the whole quite as romantically, provided for. The handsome English girl from the heavy English house had been as a figure in a picture stepping by magic out of its frame: it was a case in truth for which Mrs. Stringham presently found the perfect image. She had lost none of her grasp, but quite the contrary, of that other conceit in virtue of which Milly was the wandering princess: so what could be more in harmony now than to see the princess waited upon at the city gate by the worthiest maiden, the chosen daughter of the burgesses? It was the real again, evidently, the amusement of the meeting for the princess too; princesses living for the most part, in such an appeased way, on the plane of mere elegant representation. That was why they pounced, at city gates, on deputed flower-strewing damsels; that was why, after effigies, processions and other stately games, frank human company was pleasant to them. Kate Croy really presented herself to Milly—the latter abounded for Mrs. Stringham in accounts of it—as the wondrous London girl in person (by what she had conceived, from far back, of the London girl; conceived from the tales of travellers and the anecdotes of New York, from old porings over *Punch* and a liberal acquaintance with the fiction of the day). The only thing was that she was nicer, since the creature in question had rather been, to our young woman, an image of dread. She had thought of her, at her best, as handsome just as Kate was, with turns of head and tones of voice, felicities of stature and attitude, things "put on" and, for that matter, put off, all the marks of the product of a packed society who should be at the same time the heroine of a strong story. She placed this striking young person from the first in a story, saw her, by a necessity of the imagination, for a heroine, felt it the only character in which she wouldn't be wasted; and this in spite of the heroine's pleasant abruptness, her forbearance from gush, her umbrellas and jackets and shoes—as these things sketched themselves to Milly—and something rather of a breezy boy in the carriage of her arms and the occasional freedom of her slang.

When Milly had settled that the extent of her good will itself made her shy, she had found for the moment quite a sufficient key, and they were by that time thoroughly afloat together. This might well have been the happiest hour they were to know, attacking in friendly independence their great London —the London of shops and streets and suburbs oddly interesting to Milly, as well as of museums, monuments, "sights" oddly unfamiliar to Kate, while their elders pursued a separate course; these two rejoicing not less in their intimacy and each thinking the other's young woman a great acquisition for her own. Milly expressed to Susan Shepherd more than once that

Kate had some secret, some smothered trouble, besides all the rest of her history; and that if she had so good-naturedly helped Mrs. Lowder to meet them this was exactly to create a diversion, to give herself something else to think about. But on the case thus postulated our young American had as yet had no light: she only felt that when the light should come it would greatly deepen the colour; and she liked to think she was prepared for anything. What she already knew moreover was full, to her vision, of English, of eccentric, of Thackerayan character—Kate Croy having gradually become not a little explicit on the subject of her situation, her past, her present, her general predicament, her small success, up to the present hour, in contenting at the same time her father, her sister, her aunt and herself. It was Milly's subtle guess, imparted to her Susie, that the girl had somebody else as well, as yet unnamed, to content—it being manifest that such a creature couldn't help having; a creature not perhaps, if one would, exactly formed to inspire passions, since that always implied a certain silliness, but essentially seen, by the admiring eye of friendship, under the clear shadow of some probably eminent male interest. The clear shadow, from whatever source projected, hung at any rate over Milly's companion the whole week, and Kate Croy's handsome face smiled out of it, under bland skylights, in the presence alike of old masters passive in their glory and of thoroughly new ones, the newest, who bristled restlessly with pins and brandished snipping shears.

It was meanwhile a pretty part of the intercourse of these young ladies that each thought the other more remarkable than herself—that each thought herself, or assured the other she did, a comparatively dusty object and the other a favourite of nature and of fortune and covered thereby with the freshness of the morning. Kate was amused, amazed, at the way her friend insisted on "taking" her, and Milly wondered if Kate were sincere in finding her the most extraordinary—quite apart from her being the most charming—person she had come across. They had talked, in long drives, and quantities of history had not been wanting—in the light of which Mrs. Lowder's niece might superficially seem to have had the best of the argument. Her visitor's American references, with their bewildering immensities, their confounding moneyed New

York, their excitements of high pressure, their opportunities of
wild freedom, their record of used-up relatives, parents, clever
eager fair slim brothers—these the most loved—all engaged, as
well as successive superseded guardians, in a high extravagance
of speculation and dissipation that had left this exquisite being
her black dress, her white face and her vivid hair as the mere
last broken link: such a picture quite threw into the shade the
brief biography, however sketchily amplified, of a mere middle-
class nobody in Bayswater. And though that indeed might be
but a Bayswater way of putting it, in addition to which Milly
was in the stage of interest in Bayswater ways, this critic so far
prevailed that, like Mrs. Stringham herself, she fairly got her
companion to accept from her that she was quite the nearest
approach to a practical princess Bayswater could hope ever to
know. It was a fact—it became one at the end of three days—
that Milly actually began to borrow from the handsome girl a
sort of view of her state; the handsome girl's impression of it
was clearly so sincere. This impression was a tribute, a tribute
positively to power, power the source of which was the last
thing Kate treated as a mystery. There were passages, under all
their skylights, the succession of their shops being large, in
which the latter's easy yet the least bit dry manner sufficiently
gave out that if *she* had had so deep a pocket—!

It was not moreover by any means with not having the
imagination of expenditure that she appeared to charge her
friend, but with not having the imagination of terror, of thrift,
the imagination or in any degree the habit of a conscious dependence on others. Such moments, when all Wigmore Street,
for instance, seemed to rustle about and the pale girl herself to
be facing the different rustlers, usually so undiscriminated, as
individual Britons too, Britons personal, parties to a relation
and perhaps even intrinsically remarkable—such moments in
especial determined for Kate a perception of the high happiness of her companion's liberty. Milly's range was thus immense; she had to ask nobody for anything, to refer nothing to
any one; her freedom, her fortune and her fancy were her law;
an obsequious world surrounded her, she could sniff up at
every step its fumes. And Kate, these days, was altogether in
the phase of forgiving her so much bliss; in the phase more-

over of believing that, should they continue to go on together, she would abide in that generosity. She had at such a point as this no suspicion of a rift within the lute—by which we mean not only none of anything's coming between them, but none of any definite flaw in so much clearness of quality. Yet, all the same, if Milly, at Mrs. Lowder's banquet, had described herself to Lord Mark as kindly used by the young woman on the other side because of some faintly-felt special propriety in it, so there really did match with this, privately, on the young woman's part, a feeling not analysed but divided, a latent impression that Mildred Theale was not, after all, a person to change places, to change even chances with. Kate, verily, would perhaps not quite have known what she meant by this discrimination, and she came near naming it only when she said to herself that, rich as Milly was, one probably wouldn't—which was singular—ever hate her for it. The handsome girl had, with herself, these felicities and crudities: it wasn't obscure to her that, without some very particular reason to help, it might have proved a test of one's philosophy not to be irritated by a mistress of millions, or whatever they were, who, as a girl, so easily might have been, like herself, only vague and cruelly female. She was by no means sure of liking Aunt Maud as much as *she* deserved, and Aunt Maud's command of funds was obviously inferior to Milly's. There was thus clearly, as pleading for the latter, some influence that would later on become distinct; and meanwhile, decidedly, it was enough that she was as charming as she was queer and as queer as she was charming—all of which was a rare amusement; as well, for that matter, as further sufficient that there were objects of value she had already pressed on Kate's acceptance. A week of her society in these conditions—conditions that Milly chose to sum up as ministering immensely, for a blind vague pilgrim, to aid and comfort—announced itself from an early hour as likely to become a week of presents, acknowledgements, mementoes, pledges of gratitude and admiration, that were all on one side. Kate as promptly embraced the propriety of making it clear that she must forswear shops till she should receive some guarantee that the contents of each one she entered as a humble companion shouldn't be placed at her feet; yet that was in truth not before she had found herself in possession, under whatever protests, of several precious ornaments and other minor conveniences.

Great was the absurdity too that there should have come a day, by the end of the week, when it appeared that all Milly would have asked in definite "return," as might be said, was to be told a little about Lord Mark and to be promised the privilege of a visit to Mrs. Condrip. Far other amusements had been offered her, but her eagerness was shamelessly human, and she seemed really to count more on the revelation of the anxious lady at Chelsea than on the best nights of the opera. Kate admired, and showed it, such an absence of fear: to the fear of being bored in such a connexion she would have been so obviously entitled. Milly's answer to this was the plea of her curiosities—which left her friend wondering as to their odd direction. Some among them, no doubt, were rather more intelligible, and Kate had heard without wonder that she was blank about Lord Mark. This young lady's account of him, at the same time, professed itself frankly imperfect; for what they best knew him by at Lancaster Gate was a thing difficult to explain. One knew people in general by something they had to show, something that, either for them or against, could be touched or named or proved; and she could think of no other case of a value taken as so great and yet flourishing untested. His value was his future, which had somehow got itself as accepted by Aunt Maud as if it had been his good cook or his steam-launch. She, Kate, didn't mean she thought him a humbug; he might do great things—but they were as yet, so to speak, all he had done. On the other hand it was of course something of an achievement, and not open to every one, to have got one's self taken so seriously by Aunt Maud. The best thing about him doubtless, on the whole, was that Aunt Maud believed in him. She was often fantastic, but she knew a humbug, and—no, Lord Mark wasn't that. He had been a short time in the House, on the Tory side, but had lost his seat on the first opportunity, and this was all he had to point to. However, he pointed to nothing; which was very possibly just a sign of his real cleverness, one of those that the really clever had in common with the really void. Even Aunt Maud frequently admitted that there was a good deal, for her view of him, to bring up the rear. And he wasn't meanwhile himself indifferent—indifferent to himself—for he was working Lancaster Gate for all it was worth: just as it was, no doubt, working *him*, and just as the working and the worked were in London, as one might explain, the parties to every relation.

Kate did explain, for her listening friend; every one who had anything to give—it was true they were the fewest—made the sharpest possible bargain for it, got at least its value in return. The strangest thing furthermore was that this might be in cases a happy understanding. The worker in one connexion was the worked in another; it was as broad as it was long—with the wheels of the system, as might be seen, wonderfully oiled. People could quite like each other in the midst of it, as Aunt Maud, by every appearance, quite liked Lord Mark, and as Lord Mark, it was to be hoped, liked Mrs. Lowder, since if he didn't he was a greater brute than one could believe. She, Kate, hadn't yet, it was true, made out what he was doing for her—besides which the dear woman needed him, even at the most he could do, much less than she imagined; so far as all of which went, moreover, there were plenty of things on every side she hadn't yet made out. She believed, on the whole, in any one Aunt Maud took up; and she gave it to Milly as worth thinking of that, whatever wonderful people this young lady might meet in the land, she would meet no more extraordinary woman. There were greater celebrities by the million, and of course greater swells, but a bigger *person*, by Kate's view, and a larger natural handful every way, would really be far to seek. When Milly enquired with interest if Kate's belief in *her* was primarily on the lines of what Mrs. Lowder "took up," her interlocutress could handsomely say yes, since by the same principle she believed in herself. Whom but Aunt Maud's niece, pre-eminently, had Aunt Maud taken up, and who was thus more in the current, with her, of working and of being worked? "You may ask," Kate said, "what in the world *I* have to give; and that indeed is just what I'm trying to learn. There must be something, for her to think she can get it out of me. She *will* get it—trust her; and then I shall see what it is; which I beg you to believe I should never have found out for myself." She declined to treat any question of Milly's own "paying" power as discussable; that Milly would pay a hundred per cent

—and even to the end, doubtless, through the nose—was just the beautiful basis on which they found themselves.

These were fine facilities, pleasantries, ironies, all these luxuries of gossip and philosophies of London and of life, and they became quickly, between the pair, the common form of talk, Milly professing herself delighted to know that something was to be done with her. If the most remarkable woman in England was to do it, so much the better, and if the most remarkable woman in England had them both in hand together why what could be jollier for each? When she reflected indeed a little on the oddity of her wanting two at once Kate had the natural reply that it was exactly what showed her sincerity. She invariably gave way to feeling, and feeling had distinctly popped up in her on the advent of her girlhood's friend. The way the cat would jump was always, in presence of anything that moved her, interesting to see; visibly enough, moreover, it hadn't for a long time jumped anything like so far. This in fact, as we already know, remained the marvel for Milly Theale, who, on sight of Mrs. Lowder, had found fifty links in respect to Susie absent from the chain of association. She knew so herself what she thought of Susie that she would have expected the lady of Lancaster Gate to think something quite different; the failure of which endlessly mystified her. But her mystification was the cause for her of another fine impression, inasmuch as when she went so far as to observe to Kate that Susan Shepherd—and especially Susan Shepherd emerging so uninvited from an irrelevant past—ought by all the proprieties simply to have bored Aunt Maud, her confidant agreed to this without a protest and abounded in the sense of her wonder. Susan Shepherd at least bored the niece—that was plain; this young woman saw nothing in her—nothing to account for anything, not even for Milly's own indulgence: which little fact became in turn to the latter's mind a fact of significance. It was a light on the handsome girl—representing more than merely showed—that poor Susie was simply as nought to her. This was in a manner too a general admonition to poor Susie's companion, who seemed to see marked by it the direction in which she had best most look out. It just faintly rankled in her that a person who was good enough and to spare for Milly Theale shouldn't be good enough for another girl; though,

oddly enough, she could easily have forgiven Mrs. Lowder
herself the impatience. Mrs. Lowder didn't feel it, and Kate
Croy felt it with ease; yet in the end, be it added, she grasped
the reason, and the reason enriched her mind. Wasn't it sufficiently the reason that the handsome girl was, with twenty
other splendid qualities, the least bit brutal too, and didn't she
suggest, as no one yet had done for her new friend, that
there might be a wild beauty in that, and even a strange grace?
Kate wasn't brutally brutal—which Milly had hitherto benightedly supposed the only way; she wasn't even aggressively
so, but rather indifferently, defensively and, as might be said,
by the habit of anticipation. She simplified in advance, was
beforehand with her doubts, and knew with singular quickness
what she wasn't, as they said in New York, going to like. In
that way at least people were clearly quicker in England than at
home; and Milly could quite see after a little how such instincts might become usual in a world in which dangers
abounded. There were clearly more dangers roundabout Lancaster Gate than one suspected in New York or could dream of
in Boston. At all events, with more sense of them, there were
more precautions, and it was a remarkable world altogether in
which there could be precautions, on whatever ground,
against Susie.

III

SHE certainly made up with Susie directly, however, for any allowance she might have had privately to extend to tepid appreciation; since the late and long talks of these two embraced not only everything offered and suggested by the hours they spent apart, but a good deal more besides. She might be as detached as the occasion required at four o'clock in the afternoon, but she used no such freedom to any one about anything as she habitually used about everything to Susan Shepherd at midnight. All the same, it should with much less delay than this have been mentioned, she hadn't yet—hadn't, that is, at the end of six days—produced any news for her comrade to compare with an announcement made her by the latter as a result of a drive with Mrs. Lowder, for a change, in the remarkable Battersea Park. The elder friends had sociably revolved there while the younger ones followed bolder fancies in the admirable equipage appointed to Milly at the hotel—a heavier, more emblazoned, more amusing chariot than she had ever, with "stables" notoriously mismanaged, known at home; whereby, in the course of the circuit, more than once repeated, it had "come out," as Mrs. Stringham said, that the couple at Lancaster Gate were, of all people, acquainted with Mildred's other English friend, the gentleman, the one connected with the English newspaper (Susie hung fire a little over his name) who had been with her in New York so shortly previous to present adventures. He had been named of course in Battersea Park—else he couldn't have been identified; and Susie had naturally, before she could produce her own share in the matter as a kind of confession, to make it plain that her allusion was to Mr. Merton Densher. This was because Milly had at first a little air of not knowing whom she meant; and the girl really kept, as well, a certain control of herself while she remarked that the case was surprising, the chance one in a thousand. They knew him, both Maud and Miss Croy knew him, she gathered too, rather well, though indeed it wasn't on any show of intimacy that he had happened to be mentioned. It hadn't been—Susie made the point—she herself who brought him in: he had in fact not been brought in at all, but only referred to as a young journalist known to Mrs. Lowder and who had lately gone to their wonderful country—Mrs. Lowder always said "your wonderful country"—on behalf of his journal. But Mrs. Stringham had taken it up—with the tips of her fingers indeed; and that was the confession: she had, without meaning any harm, recognised Mr. Densher as an acquaintance of Milly's, though she had also pulled herself up before getting in too far. Mrs. Lowder had been struck, clearly—it wasn't too much to say; then she also, it had rather seemed, had pulled herself up; and there had been a little moment during which each might have been keeping something from the other. "Only," said Milly's informant, "I luckily remembered in time that I had nothing whatever to keep—which was much simpler and nicer. I don't know what Maud has, but there it is. She was interested, distinctly, in your knowing him—in his having met you over there with so little loss of time. But I ventured to tell her it hadn't been so long as to make you as yet great friends. I don't know if I was right."

Whatever time this explanation might have taken, there had been moments enough in the matter now—before the elder woman's conscience had done itself justice—to enable Milly to reply that although the fact in question doubtless had its importance she imagined they wouldn't find the importance overwhelming. It *was* odd that their one Englishman should so instantly fit; it wasn't, however, miraculous—they surely all had often seen how extraordinarily "small," as every one said, was the world. Undoubtedly also Susie had done just the plain thing in not letting his name pass. Why in the world should there be a mystery?—and what an immense one they would appear to have made if he should come back and find they had concealed their knowledge of him! "I don't know, Susie dear," the girl observed, "what you think I have to conceal."

"It doesn't matter, at a given moment," Mrs. Stringham returned, "what you know or don't know as to what I think; for you always find out the very next minute, and when you do find out, dearest, you never *really* care. Only," she presently asked, "have you heard of him from Miss Croy?"

"Heard of Mr. Densher? Never a word. We haven't mentioned him. Why should we?"

"That *you* haven't I understand; but that your friend hasn't," Susie opined, "may mean something."

"May mean what?"

"Well," Mrs. Stringham presently brought out, "I tell you all when I tell you that Maud asks me to suggest to you that it may perhaps be better for the present not to speak of him: not to speak of him to her niece, that is, unless she herself speaks to you first. But Maud thinks she won't."

Milly was ready to engage for anything; but in respect to the facts—as they so far possessed them—it all sounded a little complicated. "Is it because there's anything between them?"

"No—I gather not; but Maud's state of mind is precautionary. She's afraid of something. Or perhaps it would be more correct to say she's afraid of everything."

"She's afraid, you mean," Milly asked, "of their—a—liking each other?"

Susie had an intense thought and then an effusion. "My dear child, we move in a labyrinth."

"Of course we do. That's just the fun of it!" said Milly with a strange gaiety. Then she added: "Don't tell me that—in this for instance—there are not abysses. I want abysses."

Her friend looked at her—it was not unfrequently the case—a little harder than the surface of the occasion seemed to require; and another person present at such times might have wondered to what inner thought of her own the good lady was trying to fit the speech. It was too much her disposition, no doubt, to treat her young companion's words as symptoms of an imputed malady. It was none the less, however, her highest law to be light when the girl was light. She knew how to be quaint with the new quaintness—the great Boston gift; it had been happily her note in the magazines; and Maud Lowder, to whom it was new indeed and who had never heard anything remotely like it, quite cherished her, as a social resource, by reason of it. It shouldn't therefore fail her now; with it in fact one might face most things. "Ah then let us hope we shall sound the depths—I'm prepared for the worst—of sorrow and sin! But she would like her niece—we're not ignorant of that, are we?—to marry Lord Mark. Hasn't she told you so?"

"Hasn't Mrs. Lowder told me?"

"No; hasn't Kate? It isn't, you know, that she doesn't know it."

Milly had, under her comrade's eyes, a minute of mute detachment. She had lived with Kate Croy for several days in a state of intimacy as deep as it had been sudden, and they had clearly, in talk, in many directions, proceeded to various extremities. Yet it now came over her as in a clear cold wave that there was a possible account of their relations in which the quantity her new friend had told her might have figured as small, as smallest, beside the quantity she hadn't. She couldn't say at any rate whether or no Kate had made the point that her aunt designed her for Lord Mark: it had only sufficiently come out—which had been, moreover, eminently guessable—that she was involved in her aunt's designs. Somehow, for Milly, brush it over nervously as she might and with whatever simplifying hand, this abrupt extrusion of Mr. Densher altered all proportions, had an effect on all values. It was fantastic of her to let it make a difference that she couldn't in the least have defined—and she was at least, even during these instants, rather proud of being able to hide, on the spot, the difference it did make. Yet all the same the effect for her was, almost violently, of that gentleman's having been there—having been where she had stood till now in her simplicity—before her. It would have taken but another free moment to make her see abysses—since abysses were what she wanted—in the mere circumstance of his own silence, in New York, about his English friends. There had really been in New York little time for anything; but, had she liked, Milly could have made it out for herself that he had avoided the subject of Miss Croy and that Miss Croy was yet a subject it could never be natural to avoid. It was to be added at the same time that even if his silence had been a labyrinth—which was absurd in view of all the other things too he couldn't possibly have spoken of—this was exactly what must suit her, since it fell under the head of the plea she had just uttered to Susie. These things, however, came and went, and it set itself up between the companions, for the occasion, in the oddest way, both that their happening all to know Mr. Densher—except indeed that Susie didn't, but probably would —was a fact attached, in a world of rushing about, to one of the common orders of chance; and yet further that it was amusing—oh awfully amusing!—to be able fondly to hope that there was "something *in*" its having been left to crop up with such suddenness. There seemed somehow a possibility that the ground or, as it were, the air might in a manner have undergone some pleasing preparation; though the question of this possibility would probably, after all, have taken some threshing out. The truth, moreover—and there they were, already, our pair, talking about it, the "truth"!—hadn't in fact quite cropped out. This, obviously, in view of Mrs. Lowder's request to her old friend.

It was accordingly on Mrs. Lowder's recommendation that nothing should be said to Kate—it was on all this might cover in Aunt Maud that the idea of an interesting complication could best hope to perch; and when in fact, after the colloquy we have reported, Milly saw Kate again without mentioning any name, her silence succeeded in passing muster with her as the beginning of a new sort of fun. The sort was all the newer by its containing measurably a small element of anxiety: when she had gone in for fun before it had been with her hands a little more free. Yet it *was*, none the less, rather exciting to be conscious of a still sharper reason for interest in the handsome girl, as Kate continued even now pre-eminently to remain for her; and a reason—this was the great point—of which the young woman herself could have no suspicion. Twice over thus, for two or three hours together, Milly found herself seeing Kate, quite fixing her, in the light of the knowledge that it was a face on which Mr. Densher's eyes had more or less familiarly rested and which, by the same token, had looked, rather *more* beautifully than less, into his own. She pulled herself up indeed with the thought that it had inevitably looked, as beautifully as one would, into thousands of faces in which one might one's self never trace it; but just the odd result of the thought was to intensify for the girl that side of her friend which she had doubtless already been more prepared than she quite knew to think of as the "other," the not wholly calculable. It was fantastic, and Milly was aware of this; but the other side was what had, of a sudden, been turned straight toward her by the show of Mr. Densher's propinquity. She hadn't the excuse of knowing it for Kate's own, since nothing whatever as yet proved it particularly to be such. Never mind; it was with this other side now fully presented that Kate came and went, kissed her for greeting and for parting, talked, as usual, of everything but—as it had so abruptly become for Milly—*the* thing. Our young woman, it is true, would doubtless not have tasted so sharply a difference in this pair of occasions hadn't she been tasting so peculiarly her own possible betrayals. What happened was that afterwards, on separation, she wondered if the matter hadn't mainly been that she herself was so "other," so taken up with the unspoken; the strangest thing of all being, still subsequently, that when she asked herself how Kate could have failed to feel it she became conscious of being here on the edge of a great darkness. She should never know how Kate truly felt about anything such a one as Milly Theale should give her to feel. Kate would never—and not from ill will nor from duplicity, but from a sort of failure of common terms— reduce it to such a one's comprehension or put it within her convenience.

It was as such a one, therefore, that, for three or four days more, Milly watched Kate as just such another; and it was presently as such a one that she threw herself into their promised visit, at last achieved, to Chelsea, the quarter of the famous Carlyle, the field of exercise of his ghost, his votaries, and the residence of "poor Marian," so often referred to and actually a somewhat incongruous spirit there. With our young woman's first view of poor Marian everything gave way but the sense of how in England, apparently, the social situation of sisters could be opposed, how common ground for a place in the world could quite fail them: a state of things sagely perceived to be involved in an hierarchical, an aristocratic order. Just whereabouts in the order Mrs. Lowder had established her niece was a question not wholly void as yet, no doubt, of ambiguity— though Milly was withal sure Lord Mark could exactly have fixed the point if he would, fixing it at the same time for Aunt Maud herself; but it was clear Mrs. Condrip was, as might have been said, in quite another geography. She wouldn't have been to be found on the same social map, and it was as if her visitors had turned over page after page together before the final relief of their benevolent "Here!" The interval was bridged of course, but the bridge verily was needed, and the impression left Milly to wonder if, in the general connexion, it were of bridges or of intervals that the spirit not locally disciplined would find itself most conscious. It was as if at home, by contrast, there were neither—neither the difference itself, from position to position, nor, on either side, and particularly on one, the awfully good manner, the conscious sinking of a consciousness, that made up for it. The conscious sinking, at all events, and the awfully good manner, the difference, the bridge, the interval, the skipped leaves of the social atlas—these, it was to be confessed, had a little, for our young lady, in default of stouter stuff, to work themselves into the light literary legend—a mixed wandering echo of Trollope, of Thackeray, perhaps mostly of Dickens—under favour of which her pilgrimage had so much appealed. She could relate to Susie later on, late the same evening, that the legend, before she had done with it, had run clear, that the adored author of "The Newcomes," in fine, had been on the whole the note: the picture lacking thus more than she had hoped, or rather perhaps showing less than she had feared, a certain possibility of Pickwickian outline. She explained how she meant by this that Mrs. Condrip hadn't altogether proved another Mrs. Nickleby, nor even—for she might have proved almost anything, from the way poor worried Kate had spoken—a widowed and aggravated Mrs. Micawber.

Mrs. Stringham, in the midnight conference, intimated rather yearningly that, however the event might have turned, the side of English life such experiences opened to Milly were just those she herself seemed "booked"—as they were all, roundabout her now, always saying—to miss: she had begun to have a little, for her fellow observer, these moments of fanciful reaction (reaction in which she was once more all Susan Shepherd) against the high sphere of colder conventions into which her overwhelming connexion with Maud Manningham had rapt her. Milly never lost sight for long of the Susan Shepherd side of her, and was always there to meet it when it came up and vaguely, tenderly, impatiently to pat it, abounding in the assurance that they would still provide for it. They had, however, to-night another matter in hand; which proved to be presently, on the girl's part, in respect to her hour of Chelsea, the revelation that Mrs. Condrip, taking a few minutes when Kate was away with one of the children, in bed upstairs for some small complaint, had suddenly (without its being in the least "led up to") broken ground on the subject of Mr. Densher, mentioned him with impatience as a person in love with her sister. "She wished me, if I cared for Kate, to know," Milly said—"for it would be quite too dreadful, and one might do something."

Susie wondered. "Prevent anything coming of it? That's easily said. Do what?"

Milly had a dim smile. "I think that what she would like is that I should come a good deal to see *her* about it."

"And doesn't she suppose you've anything else to do?"

The girl had by this time clearly made it out. "Nothing but to admire and make much of her sister—whom she doesn't, however, herself in the least understand—and give up one's time, and everything else, to it." It struck the elder friend that she spoke with an almost unprecedented approach to sharpness; as if Mrs. Condrip had been rather indescribably disconcerting. Never yet so much as just of late had Mrs. Stringham seen her companion exalted, and by the very play of something within, into a vague golden air that left irritation below. That was the great thing with Milly—it was her characteristic poetry, or at least it was Susan Shepherd's. "But she made a point," the former continued, "of my keeping what she says from Kate. I'm not to mention that she has spoken."

"And why," Mrs. Stringham presently asked, "is Mr. Densher so dreadful?"

Milly had, she thought, a delay to answer—something that suggested a fuller talk with Mrs. Condrip than she inclined perhaps to report. "It isn't so much he himself." Then the girl spoke a little as for the romance of it; one could never tell, with her, where romance would come in. "It's the state of his fortunes."

"And is that very bad?"

"He has no 'private means,' and no prospect of any. He has no income, and no ability, according to Mrs. Condrip, to make one. He's as poor, she calls it, as 'poverty,' and she says she knows what that is."

Again Mrs. Stringham considered, and it presently produced something. "But isn't he brilliantly clever?"

Milly had also then an instant that was not quite fruitless. "I haven't the least idea."

To which, for the time, Susie only replied "Oh!"—though by the end of a minute she had followed it with a slightly musing "I see"; and that in turn with: "It's quite what Maud Lowder thinks."

"That he'll never do anything?"

"No—quite the contrary: that he's exceptionally able."

"Oh yes; I know"—Milly had again, in reference to what her friend had already told her of this, her little tone of a moment before. "But Mrs. Condrip's own great point is that Aunt Maud herself won't hear of any such person. Mr. Densher, she holds—that's the way, at any rate, it was explained to me—won't ever be either a public man or a rich man. If he were public she'd be willing, as I understand, to help him; if he were rich—without being anything else—she'd do her best to swallow him. As it is she taboos him."

"In short," said Mrs. Stringham as with a private purpose, "she told you, the sister, all about it. But Mrs. Lowder likes him," she added.

"Mrs. Condrip didn't tell me that."

"Well, she does, all the same, my dear, extremely."

"Then there it is!" On which, with a drop and one of those sudden slightly sighing surrenders to a vague reflux and a general fatigue that had recently more than once marked themselves for her companion, Milly turned away. Yet the matter wasn't left so, that night, between them, albeit neither perhaps could afterwards have said which had first come back to it. Milly's own nearest approach at least, for a little, to doing so, was to remark that they appeared all—every one they saw—to think tremendously of money. This prompted in Susie a laugh, not untender, the innocent meaning of which was that it came, as a subject for indifference, money did, easier to some people than to others: she made the point in fairness, however, that you couldn't have told, by any too crude transparency of air, what place it held for Maud Manningham. She did her worldliness with grand proper silences—if it mightn't better be put perhaps that she did her detachment with grand occasional pushes. However Susie put it, in truth, she was really, in justice to herself, thinking of the difference, as favourites of fortune, between her old friend and her new. Aunt Maud sat somehow in the midst of her money, founded on it and surrounded by it, even if with a masterful high manner about it, her manner of looking, hard and bright, as if it weren't there. Milly, about hers, had no manner at all—which was possibly, from a point of view, a fault: she was at any rate far away on the edge of it, and you hadn't, as might be said, in order to get at her nature, to traverse, by whatever avenue, any piece of her property. It was clear, on the other hand, that Mrs. Lowder was keeping her wealth as for purposes, imaginations, ambitions, that would figure as large, as honourably unselfish, on the day they should take effect. She would impose her will, but her will would be only that a person or two shouldn't lose a benefit by not sub-mitting if they could be made to submit. To Milly, as so much younger, such far views couldn't be imputed: there was no-body she was supposable as interested for. It was too soon, since she wasn't interested for herself. Even the richest woman, at her age, lacked motive, and Milly's motive doubtless had plenty of time to arrive. She was meanwhile beautiful, simple, sublime without it—whether missing it and vaguely reaching out for it or not; and with it, for that matter, in the event, would really be these things just as much. Only then she might very well have, like Aunt Maud, a manner. Such were the con-nexions, at all events, in which the colloquy of our two ladies freshly flickered up—in which it came round that the elder asked the younger if she had herself, in the afternoon, named Mr. Densher as an acquaintance.

"Oh no—I said nothing of having seen him. I remem-bered," the girl explained, "Mrs. Lowder's wish."

"But that," her friend observed after a moment, "was for si-lence to Kate."

"Yes—but Mrs. Condrip would immediately have told Kate."

"Why so?—since she must dislike to talk about him."

"Mrs. Condrip must?" Milly thought. "What she would like most is that her sister should be brought to think ill of him; and if anything she can tell her will help that—" But the girl dropped suddenly here, as if her companion would see.

Her companion's interest, however, was all for what she

herself saw. "You mean she'll immediately speak?" Mrs. String-ham gathered that this was what Milly meant, but it left still a question. "How will it be against him that you know him?"

"Oh how can I say? It won't be so much one's knowing him as one's having kept it out of sight."

"Ah," said Mrs. Stringham as for comfort, "*you* haven't kept it out of sight. Isn't it much rather Miss Croy herself who has?"

"It isn't my acquaintance with him," Milly smiled, "that she has dissimulated."

"She has dissimulated only her own? Well then the responsibility's hers."

"Ah but," said the girl, not perhaps with marked consequence, "she has a right to do as she likes."

"Then so, my dear, have you!" smiled Susan Shepherd.

Milly looked at her as if she were almost venerably simple, but also as if this were what one loved her for. "We're not quarrelling about it, Kate and I, *yet*."

"I only meant," Mrs. Stringham explained, "that I don't see what Mrs. Condrip would gain."

"By her being able to tell Kate?" Milly thought. "I only meant that I don't see what I myself should gain."

"But it will have to come out—that he knows you both—some time."

Milly scarce assented. "Do you mean when he comes back?"

"He'll find you both here, and he can hardly be looked to, I take it, to 'cut' either of you for the sake of the other."

This placed the question at last on a basis more distinctly cheerful. "I might get at him somehow beforehand," the girl suggested; "I might give him what they call here the 'tip'—that he's not to know me when we meet. Or, better still, I mightn't be here at all."

"Do you want to run away from him?"

It was, oddly enough, an idea Milly seemed half to accept. "I don't know *what* I want to run away from!"

It dispelled, on the spot—something, to the elder woman's ear, in the sad, sweet sound of it—any ghost of any need of explaining. The sense was constant for her that their relation might have been afloat, like some island of the south, in a great warm sea that represented, for every conceivable chance, a margin, an outer sphere, of general emotion; and the effect of the occurrence of anything in particular was to make the sea submerge the island, the margin flood the text. The great wave now for a moment swept over. "I'll go anywhere else in the world you like."

But Milly came up through it. "Dear old Susie—how I do work you!"

"Oh this is nothing yet."

"No indeed—to what it will be."

"You're not—and it's vain to pretend," said dear old Susie, who had been taking her in, "as sound and strong as I insist on having you."

"Insist, insist—the more the better. But the day I *look* as sound and strong as that, you know," Milly went on—"on that day I shall be just sound and strong enough to take leave of you sweetly for ever. That's where one is," she continued thus agreeably to embroider, "when even one's *most* 'beaux moments' aren't such as to qualify, so far as appearance goes, for anything gayer than a handsome cemetery. Since I've lived all these years as if I were dead, I shall die, no doubt, as if I were alive—which will happen to be as you want me. So, you see," she wound up, "you'll never really know where I am. Except indeed when I'm gone; and then you'll only know where I'm not."

"I'd die *for* you," said Susan Shepherd after a moment.

"'Thanks awfully'! Then stay here for me."

"But we can't be in London for August, nor for many of all these next weeks."

"Then we'll go back."

Susie blenched. "Back to America?"

"No, abroad—to Switzerland, Italy, anywhere. I mean by your staying 'here' for me," Milly pursued, "your staying with me wherever I may be, even though we may neither of us know at the time where it is. No," she insisted, "I *don't* know where I am, and you never will, and it doesn't matter—and I dare say it's quite true," she broke off, "that everything will have to come out." Her friend would have felt of her that she joked about it now, hadn't her scale from grave to gay been a thing of such unnameable shades that her contrasts were never sharp. She made up for failures of gravity by failures of mirth; if she hadn't, that is, been at times as earnest as might have been liked, so she was certain not to be at other times as easy as she would like herself. "I must face the music. It isn't at any rate its 'coming out,'" she added; "it's that Mrs. Condrip would put the fact before her to his injury."

Her companion wondered. "But how to *his?*"

"Why if he pretends to love her—!"

"And does he only 'pretend'?"

"I mean if, trusted by her in strange countries, he forgets her so far as to make up to other people."

The amendment, however, brought Susie in, as with gaiety, for a comfortable end. "Did he make up, the false creature, to *you?*"

"No—but the question isn't of that. It's of what Kate might be made to believe."

"That, given the fact of his having evidently more or less followed up his acquaintance with you, to say nothing of your obvious weird charm, he must have been all ready if you had a little bit led him on?"

Milly neither accepted nor qualified this; she only said after a moment and as with a conscious excess of the pensive: "No, I don't think she'd quite wish to suggest that I made up to *him;* for that I should have had to do so would only bring out his constancy. All I mean is," she added—and now at last, as with a supreme impatience—"that her being able to make him out a little a person who could give cause for jealousy would evidently help her, since she's afraid of him, to do him in her sister's mind a useful ill turn."

Susan Shepherd perceived in this explanation such signs of an appetite for motive as would have sat gracefully even on one of her own New England heroines. It was seeing round several corners; but that was what New England heroines did, and it was moreover interesting for the moment to make out how many her young friend had actually undertaken to see round. Finally, too, weren't they braving the deeps? They got their amusement where they could. "Isn't it only," she asked, "rather probable she'd see that Kate's knowing him as (what's the pretty old word?) *volage*—?"

"Well?" She hadn't filled out her idea, but neither, it seemed, could Milly.

"Well, might but do what that often does—by all *our* blessed

little laws and arrangements at least: excite Kate's own sentiment instead of depressing it."

The idea was bright, yet the girl but beautifully stared.
"Kate's own sentiment? Oh she didn't speak of that. I don't
think," she added as if she had been unconsciously giving a
wrong impression, "I don't think Mrs. Condrip imagines *she's*
in love."

It made Mrs. Stringham stare in turn. "Then what's her
fear?"

"Well, only the fact of Mr. Densher's possibly himself
keeping it up—the fear of some final result from *that*."

"Oh," said Susie, intellectually a little disconcerted—"she
looks far ahead!"

At this, however, Milly threw off another of her sudden
vague "sports." "No—it's only we who do."

"Well, don't let us be more interested for them than they
are for themselves!"

"Certainly not"—the girl promptly assented. A certain interest nevertheless remained; she appeared to wish to be clear.
"It wasn't of anything on Kate's own part she spoke."

"You mean she thinks her sister distinctly doesn't care for
him?"

It was still as if, for an instant, Milly had to be sure of what
she meant; but there it presently was. "If she did care Mrs.
Condrip would have told me."

What Susan Shepherd seemed hereupon for a little to wonder was why then they had been talking so. "But did you ask
her?"

"Ah no!"

"Oh!" said Susan Shepherd.

Milly, however, easily explained that she wouldn't have
asked her for the world.

BOOK FIFTH

I

LORD MARK looked at her to-day in particular as if to wring from her a confession that she had originally done him injustice; and he was entitled to whatever there might be in it of advantage or merit that his intention really in a manner took effect: he cared about something, after all, sufficiently to make her feel absurdly as if she *were* confessing—all the while it was quite the case that neither justice nor injustice was what had been in question between them. He had presented himself at the hotel, had found her and had found Susan Shepherd at home, had been "civil" to Susan—it was just that shade, and Susan's fancy had fondly caught it; and then had come again and missed them, and then had come and found them once more: besides letting them easily see that if it hadn't by this time been the end of everything—which they could feel in the exhausted air, that of the season at its last gasp—the places they might have liked to go to were such as they would have had only to mention. Their feeling was—or at any rate their modest general plea—that there was no place they would have liked to go to; there was only the sense of finding they liked, wherever they were, the place to which they had been brought. Such was highly the case as to their current consciousness—which could be indeed, in an equally eminent degree, but a matter of course; impressions this afternoon having by a happy turn of their wheel been gathered for them into a splendid cluster, an offering like an armful of the rarest flowers. They were in presence of the offering—they had been led up to it; and if it had been still their habit to look at each other across distances for increase of unanimity his hand would have been silently named between them as the hand applied to the wheel. He had administered the touch that, under light analysis, made the difference—the difference of their not having lost, as Susie on the spot and at the hour phrased it again and again, both for herself and for such others as the question might concern, so beautiful and interesting an experience; the difference also, in fact, of Mrs. Lowder's not having lost it either, though it was superficially with Mrs. Lowder they had come, and though it was further with that lady that our young woman was directly engaged during the half-hour or so of her most agreeably inward response to the scene.

The great historic house had, for Milly, beyond terrace and garden, as the centre of an almost extravagantly grand Watteau-composition, a tone as of old gold kept "down" by the quality of the air, summer full-flushed but attuned to the general perfect taste. Much, by her measure, for the previous hour, appeared, in connexion with this revelation of it, to have happened to her—a quantity expressed in introductions of charming new people, in walks through halls of armour, of pictures, of cabinets, of tapestry, of tea-tables, in an assault of reminders that this largeness of style was the sign of *appointed* felicity. The largeness of style was the great containing vessel, while everything else, the pleasant personal affluence, the easy murmurous welcome, the honoured age of illustrious host and hostess, all at once so distinguished and so plain, so public and so shy, became but this or that element of the infusion. The elements melted together and seasoned the draught, the essence of which might have struck the girl as distilled into the small cup of iced coffee she had vaguely accepted from somebody, while a fuller flood somehow kept bearing her up— all the freshness of response of her young life, the freshness of the first and only prime. What had perhaps brought on just now a kind of climax was the fact of her appearing to make out, through Aunt Maud, what was really the matter. It couldn't be less than a climax for a poor shaky maiden to find it put to her of a sudden that she herself was the matter—for that was positively what, on Mrs. Lowder's part, it came to. Everything was great, of course, in great pictures, and it was doubtless precisely a part of the brilliant life—since the brilliant life, as one had faintly figured it, just *was* humanly led—that all impressions within its area partook of its brilliancy; still, letting that pass, it fairly stamped an hour as with the official seal for one to be able to take in so comfortably one's companion's broad blandness. "You must stay among us—you must stay; anything else is impossible and ridiculous; you don't know yet, no doubt—you can't; but you will soon enough: you can stay in *any* position." It had been as the murmurous consecration to follow the murmurous welcome; and even if it were but part of Aunt Maud's own spiritual ebriety—for the dear woman, one could see, was spiritually "keeping" the day—it served to Milly, then and afterwards, as a high-water mark of the imagination.

It was to be the end of the short parenthesis which had begun but the other day at Lancaster Gate with Lord Mark's informing her that she was a "success"—the key thus again struck; and though no distinct, no numbered revelations had crowded in, there had, as we have seen, been plenty of incident for the space and the time. There had been thrice as much, and all gratuitous and genial—if, in portions, not exactly hitherto *the* revelation—as three unprepared weeks could have been expected to produce. Mrs. Lowder had improvised a "rush" for them, but out of elements, as Milly was now a little more freely aware, somewhat roughly combined. Therefore if at this very instant she had her reasons for thinking of the parenthesis as about to close—reasons completely personal—she had on behalf of her companion a divination almost as deep. The parenthesis would close with this admirable picture, but the admirable picture still would show Aunt Maud as not absolutely sure either if she herself were destined to remain in it. What she was doing, Milly might even not have escaped seeming to see, was to talk herself into a sublimer serenity while she ostensibly talked Milly. It was fine, the girl fully felt, the way she did talk *her*, little as, at bottom, our young woman needed it or found other persuasions at fault. It was in particular during the minutes of her grateful absorption of iced coffee—qualified by a sharp doubt of her wisdom—that she most had in view Lord Mark's relation to her being there, or at least to the question of her being amused at it. It wouldn't have taken much by the end of five minutes quite to make her feel that this relation was charming. It might, once more, simply have been that everything, anything, was charming when one was so justly and completely charmed; but, frankly, she hadn't supposed anything so serenely sociable could settle itself between them as the friendly understanding that was at present somehow in the air. They were, many of them together, near the marquee that had been erected on a stretch of sward as a

temple of refreshment and that happened to have the property
—which was all to the good—of making Milly think of a "dur-
bar"; her iced coffee had been a consequence of this connexion, through which, further, the bright company scattered
about fell thoroughly into place. Certain of its members might
have represented the contingent of "native princes"—familiar,
but scarce the less grandly gregarious term!—and Lord Mark
would have done for one of these even though for choice he
but presented himself as a supervisory friend of the family. The
Lancaster Gate family, he clearly intended, in which he included its American recruits, and included above all Kate Croy
—a young person blessedly easy to take care of. She knew people, and people knew her, and she was the handsomest thing
there—this last a declaration made by Milly, in a sort of soft
midsummer madness, a straight skylark-flight of charity, to
Aunt Maud.

Kate had for her new friend's eyes the extraordinary and attaching property of appearing at a given moment to show as a
beautiful stranger, to cut her connexions and lose her identity,
letting the imagination for the time make what it would of
them—make her merely a person striking from afar, more and
more pleasing as one watched, but who was above all a subject
for curiosity. Nothing could have given her, as a party to a relation, a greater freshness than this sense, which sprang up at
its own hours, of one's being as curious about her as if one
hadn't known her. It had sprung up, we have gathered, as
soon as Milly had seen her after hearing from Mrs. Stringham
of her knowledge of Merton Densher; she had *looked* then
other and, as Milly knew the real critical mind would call it,
more objective; and our young woman had foreseen it of her
on the spot that she would often look so again. It was exactly
what she was doing this afternoon; and Milly, who had amusements of thought that were like the secrecies of a little girl
playing with dolls when conventionally "too big," could almost
settle to the game of what one would suppose her, how one
would place her, if one didn't know her. She became thus, intermittently, a figure conditioned only by the great facts of aspect, a figure to be waited for, named and fitted. This was
doubtless but a way of feeling that it was of her essence to be
peculiarly what the occasion, whatever it might be, demanded

when its demand was highest. There were probably ways enough, on these lines, for such a consciousness; another of them would be for instance to say that she was made for great social uses. Milly wasn't wholly sure she herself knew what great social uses might be—unless, as a good example, to exert just that sort of glamour in just that sort of frame were one of them: she would have fallen back on knowing sufficiently that they existed at all events for her friend. It imputed a primness, all round, to be reduced but to saying, by way of a translation of one's amusement, that she was always so *right*—since that, too often, was what the *insupportables* themselves were; yet it was, in overflow to Aunt Maud, what she had to content herself withal—save for the lame enhancement of saying she was lovely. It served, despite everything, the purpose, strengthened the bond that for the time held the two ladies together, distilled in short its drop of rose-colour for Mrs. Lowder's own view. That was really the view Milly had, for most of the rest of the occasion, to give herself to immediately taking in; but it didn't prevent the continued play of those swift cross-lights, odd beguilements of the mind, at which we have already glanced.

Mrs. Lowder herself found it enough simply to reply, in respect to Kate, that she was indeed a luxury to take about the world: she expressed no more surprise than that at her "rightness" to-day. Didn't it by this time sufficiently shine out that it was precisely *as* the very luxury she was proving that she had, from far back, been appraised and waited for? Crude elation, however, might be kept at bay, and the circumstance none the less made clear that they were all swimming together in the blue. It came back to Lord Mark again, as he seemed slowly to pass and repass and conveniently to linger before them; he was personally the note of the blue—like a suspended skein of silk within reach of the broiderer's hand. Aunt Maud's free-moving shuttle took a length of him at rhythmic intervals; and one of the accessory truths that flickered across to Milly was that he ever so consentingly knew he was being worked in. This was almost like an understanding with her at Mrs. Lowder's expense, which she would have none of; she wouldn't for the world have had him make any such point as that he wouldn't have launched them at Matcham—or whatever it was he *had* done—only for Aunt Maud's *beaux yeux*. What he had done, it would have been guessable, was something he had for some time been desired in vain to do; and what they were all now profiting by was a change comparatively sudden, the cessation of hope delayed. What had caused the cessation easily showed itself as none of Milly's business; and she was luckily, for that matter, in no real danger of hearing from him directly that her individual weight had been felt in the scale. Why then indeed was it an effect of his diffused but subdued participation that he might absolutely have been saying to her "Yes, let the dear woman take her own tone"? "Since she's here she may stay," he might have been adding—"for whatever she can make of it. But you and I are different." Milly knew *she* was different in truth—his own difference was his own affair; but also she knew that after all, even at their distinctest, Lord Mark's "tips" in this line would be tacit. He practically placed her—it came round again to that—under no obligation whatever. It was a matter of equal ease, moreover, her letting Mrs. Lowder take a tone. She might have taken twenty—they would have spoiled nothing.

"You must stay on with us; you *can*, you know, in any position you like; any, any, *any*, my dear child"—and her emphasis went deep. "You must make your home with us; and it's really open to you to make the most beautiful one in the world. You mustn't be under a mistake—under any of any sort; and you must let us all think for you a little, take care of you and watch over you. Above all you must help me with Kate, and you must stay a little *for* her; nothing for a long time has happened to me so good as that you and she should have become friends. It's beautiful; it's great; it's everything. What makes it perfect is that it should have come about through our dear delightful Susie, restored to me, after so many years, by such a miracle. No—that's more charming to me than even your hitting it off with Kate. God has been good to one—positively; for I couldn't, at my age, have made a new friend—undertaken, I mean, out of whole cloth, the real thing. It's like changing one's bankers—after fifty: one doesn't do that. That's why Susie has been kept for me, as you seem to keep people in your wonderful country, in lavender and pink paper—coming back at last as straight as out of a fairy-tale and with you as an attendant

fairy." Milly hereupon replied appreciatively that such a description of herself made her feel as if pink paper were her dress
and lavender its trimming; but Aunt Maud wasn't to be deterred by a weak joke from keeping it up. The young person
under her protection could feel besides that she kept it up in
perfect sincerity. She was somehow at this hour a very happy
woman, and a part of her happiness might precisely have been
that her affections and her views were moving as never before
in concert. Unquestionably she loved Susie; but she also loved
Kate and loved Lord Mark, loved their funny old host and
hostess, loved every one within range, down to the very servant who came to receive Milly's empty ice-plate—down, for
that matter, to Milly herself, who was, while she talked, really
conscious of the enveloping flap of a protective mantle, a shelter with the weight of an Eastern carpet. An Eastern carpet, for
wishing-purposes of one's own, was a thing to be on rather
than under; still, however, if the girl should fail of breath it
wouldn't be, she could feel, by Mrs. Lowder's fault. One of
the last things she was afterwards to recall of this was Aunt
Maud's going on to say that she and Kate must stand together
because together they could do anything. It was for Kate of
course she was essentially planning; but the plan, enlarged and
uplifted now, somehow required Milly's prosperity too for its
full operation, just as Milly's prosperity at the same time involved Kate's. It was nebulous yet, it was slightly confused, but
it was comprehensive and genial, and it made our young
woman understand things Kate had said of her aunt's possibilities, as well as characterisations that had fallen from Susan
Shepherd. One of the most frequent on the lips of the latter
had been that dear Maud was a grand natural force.

II

A PRIME reason, we must add, why sundry impressions were not to be fully present to the girl till later on was that they yielded at this stage, with an effect of sharp supersession, to a detached quarter of an hour—her only one—with Lord Mark. "Have you seen the picture in the house, the beautiful one that's so like you?"—he was asking that as he stood before her; having come up at last with his smooth intimation that any wire he had pulled and yet wanted not to remind her of wasn't quite a reason for his having no joy at all.

"I've been through rooms and I've seen pictures. But if I'm 'like' anything so beautiful as most of them seemed to me—!" It needed in short for Milly some evidence which he only wanted to supply. She was the image of the wonderful Bronzino, which she must have a look at on every ground. He had thus called her off and led her away; the more easily that the house within was above all what had already drawn round her its mystic circle. Their progress meanwhile was not of the straightest; it was an advance, without haste, through innumerable natural pauses and soft concussions, determined for the most part by the appearance before them of ladies and gentlemen, singly, in couples, in clusters, who brought them to a stand with an inveterate "I say, Mark." What they said she never quite made out; it was their all so domestically knowing him, and his knowing them, that mainly struck her, while her impression, for the rest, was but of fellow strollers more vaguely afloat than themselves, supernumeraries mostly a little battered, whether as jaunty males or as ostensibly elegant women. They might have been moving a good deal by a momentum that had begun far back, but they were still brave and personable, still warranted for continuance as long again, and they gave her, in especial collectively, a sense of pleasant voices, pleasanter than those of actors, of friendly empty words and kind lingering eyes that took somehow pardonable liberties. The lingering eyes looked her over, the lingering eyes were what went, in almost confessed simplicity, with the pointless "I say, Mark"; and what was really most flagrant of all was that, as a pleasant matter of course, if she didn't mind, he seemed to suggest their letting people, poor dear things, have the benefit of her.

The odd part was that he made her herself believe, for amusement, in the benefit, measured by him in mere manner—for wonderful, of a truth, was, as a means of expression, his slightness of emphasis—that her present good nature conferred. It was, as she could easily see, a mild common carnival of good nature—a mass of London people together, of sorts and sorts, but who mainly knew each other and who, in their way, did, no doubt, confess to curiosity. It had gone round that she was there; questions about her would be passing; the easiest thing was to run the gauntlet with *him*—just as the easiest thing was in fact to trust him generally. Couldn't she know for herself, passively, how little harm they meant her?—to that extent that it made no difference whether or not he introduced them. The strangest thing of all for Milly was perhaps the uplifted assurance and indifference with which she could simply give back the particular bland stare that appeared in such cases to mark civilisation at its highest. It was so little her fault, this oddity of what had "gone round" about her, that to accept it without question might be as good a way as another of feeling life. It was inevitable to supply the probable description—that of the awfully rich young American who was so queer to behold, but nice, by all accounts, to know; and she had really but one instant of speculation as to fables or fantasies perchance originally launched. She asked herself once only if Susie could, inconceivably, have been blatant about her; for the question, on the spot, was really blown away for ever. She knew in fact on the spot and with sharpness just why she had "elected" Susan Shepherd: she had had from the first hour the conviction of her being precisely the person in the world least possibly a trumpeter. So it wasn't their fault, it wasn't their fault, and anything might happen that would, and everything now again melted together, and kind eyes were always kind eyes—if it were never to be worse than that! She got with her companion into the house; they brushed, beneficently, past all their accidents. The Bronzino was, it appeared, deep within, and the long afternoon light lingered for them on patches of old colour and waylaid them, as they went, in nooks and opening vistas.

It was all the while for Milly as if Lord Mark had really had something other than this spoken pretext in view; as if there were something he wanted to say to her and were only—consciously yet not awkwardly, just delicately—hanging fire. At the same time it was as if the thing had practically been said by the moment they came in sight of the picture; since what it appeared to amount to was "Do let a fellow who isn't a fool take care of you a little." The thing somehow, with the aid of the Bronzino, was done; it hadn't seemed to matter to her before if he were a fool or no; but now, just where they were, she liked his not being; and it was all moreover none the worse for coming back to something of the same sound as Mrs. Lowder's so recent reminder. She too wished to take care of her—and wasn't it, *à peu près*, what all the people with the kind eyes were wishing? Once more things melted together— the beauty and the history and the facility and the splendid midsummer glow: it was a sort of magnificent maximum, the pink dawn of an apotheosis coming so curiously soon. What in fact befell was that, as she afterwards made out, it was Lord Mark who said nothing in particular—it was she herself who said all. She couldn't help that—it came; and the reason it came was that she found herself, for the first moment, looking at the mysterious portrait through tears. Perhaps it was her tears that made it just then so strange and fair—as wonderful as he had said: the face of a young woman, all splendidly drawn, down to the hands, and splendidly dressed; a face almost livid in hue, yet handsome in sadness and crowned with a mass of hair, rolled back and high, that must, before fading with time, have had a family resemblance to her own. The lady in question, at all events, with her slightly Michael-angelesque squareness, her eyes of other days, her full lips, her long neck, her recorded jewels, her brocaded and wasted reds, was a very great personage—only unaccompanied by a joy. And she was dead, dead, dead. Milly recognised her exactly in words that had nothing to do with her. "I shall never be better than this."

He smiled for her at the portrait. "Than she? You'd scarce need to be better, for surely that's well enough. But you *are*, one feels, as it happens, better; because, splendid as she is, one doubts if she was good."

He hadn't understood. She was before the picture, but she

had turned to him, and she didn't care if for the minute he noticed her tears. It was probably as good a moment as she should ever have with him. It was perhaps as good a moment as she should have with any one, or have in any connexion whatever. "I mean that everything this afternoon has been too beautiful, and that perhaps everything together will never be so right again. I'm very glad therefore you've been a part of it."

Though he still didn't understand her he was as nice as if he had; he didn't ask for insistence, and that was just a part of his looking after her. He simply protected her now from herself, and there was a world of practice in it. "Oh we must talk about these things!"

Ah they had already done that, she knew, as much as she ever would; and she was shaking her head at her pale sister the next moment with a world, on her side, of slowness. "I wish I could see the resemblance. Of course her complexion's green," she laughed; "but mine's several shades greener."

"It's down to the very hands," said Lord Mark.

"Her hands are large," Milly went on, "but mine are larger. Mine are huge."

"Oh you go her, all round, 'one better'—which is just what I said. But you're a pair. You must surely catch it," he added as if it were important to his character as a serious man not to appear to have invented his plea.

"I don't know—one never knows one's self. It's a funny fancy, and I don't imagine it would have occurred—"

"I see it *has* occurred"—he had already taken her up. She had her back, as she faced the picture, to one of the doors of the room, which was open, and on her turning as he spoke she saw that they were in the presence of three other persons, also, as appeared, interested enquirers. Kate Croy was one of these; Lord Mark had just become aware of her, and she, all arrested, had immediately seen, and made the best of it, that she was far from being first in the field. She had brought a lady and a gentleman to whom she wished to show what Lord Mark was showing Milly, and he took her straightway as a reenforcement. Kate herself had spoken, however, before he had had time to tell her so.

"*You* had noticed too?"—she smiled at him without looking at Milly. "Then I'm not original—which one always hopes one has been. But the likeness is so great." And now she looked at Milly—for whom again it was, all round indeed, kind, kind eyes. "Yes, there you are, my dear, if you want to know. And you're superb." She took now but a glance at the picture, though it was enough to make her question to her friends not too straight. "Isn't she superb?"

"I brought Miss Theale," Lord Mark explained to the latter, "quite off my own bat."

"I wanted Lady Aldershaw," Kate continued to Milly, "to see for herself."

"Les grands esprits se rencontrent!" laughed her attendant gentleman, a high but slightly stooping, shambling and wavering person who represented urbanity by the liberal aid of certain prominent front teeth and whom Milly vaguely took for some sort of great man.

Lady Aldershaw meanwhile looked at Milly quite as if Milly had been the Bronzino and the Bronzino only Milly. "Superb, superb. Of course I had noticed you. It *is* wonderful," she went on with her back to the picture, but with some other eagerness which Milly felt gathering, felt directing her motions now. It was enough—they were introduced, and she was saying "I wonder if you could give us the pleasure of coming—" She wasn't fresh, for she wasn't young, even though she denied at every pore that she was old; but she was vivid and much bejewelled for the midsummer daylight; and she was all in the palest pinks and blues. She didn't think, at this pass, that she could "come" anywhere—Milly didn't; and she already knew that somehow Lord Mark was saving her from the question. He had interposed, taking the words out of the lady's mouth and not caring at all if the lady minded. That was clearly the right way to treat her—at least for him; as she had only dropped, smiling, and then turned away with him. She had been dealt with—it would have done an enemy good. The gentleman still stood, a little helpless, addressing himself to the intention of urbanity as if it were a large loud whistle; he had been sighing sympathy, in his way, while the lady made her overture; and Milly had in this light soon arrived at their identity. They were Lord and Lady Aldershaw, and the wife was the clever one. A minute or two later the situation had changed, and she knew it afterwards to have been by the subtle operation of Kate. She was herself saying that she was afraid she must go now if Susie could be found; but she was sitting down on the nearest seat to say it. The prospect, through opened doors, stretched before her into other rooms, down the vista of which Lord Mark was strolling with Lady Aldershaw, who, close to him and much intent, seemed to show from behind as peculiarly expert. Lord Aldershaw, for his part, had been left in the middle of the room, while Kate, with her back to him, was standing before her with much sweetness of manner. The sweetness was all for *her*; she had the sense of the poor gentleman's having somehow been handled as Lord Mark had handled his wife. He dangled there, he shambled a little; then he bethought himself of the Bronzino, before which, with his eye-glass, he hovered. It drew from him an odd vague sound, not wholly distinct from a grunt, and a "Humph—most remarkable!" which lighted Kate's face with amusement. The next moment he had creaked away over polished floors after the others and Milly was feeling as if *she* had been rude. But Lord Aldershaw was in every way a detail and Kate was saying to her that she hoped she wasn't ill.

Thus it was that, aloft there in the great gilded historic chamber and the presence of the pale personage on the wall, whose eyes all the while seemed engaged with her own, she found herself suddenly sunk in something quite intimate and humble and to which these grandeurs were strange enough witnesses. It had come up, in the form in which she had had to accept it, all suddenly, and nothing about it, at the same time, was more marked than that she had in a manner plunged into it to escape from something else. Something else, from her first vision of her friend's appearance three minutes before, had been present to her even through the call made by the others on her attention; something that was perversely *there*, she was more and more uncomfortably finding, at least for the first moments and by some spring of its own, with every renewal of their meeting. "Is it the way she looks to *him*?" she asked herself—the perversity being how she kept in remembrance that Kate was known to him. It wasn't a fault in Kate—nor in him assuredly; and she had a horror, being generous and tender, of treating either of them as if it had been. To Densher himself she couldn't make it up—he was too far away; but her secondary impulse was to make it up to Kate. She did so now with a strange soft energy—the impulse immediately acting. "Will you render me to-morrow a great service?"

"Any service, dear child, in the world."

"But it's a secret one—nobody must know. I must be wicked and false about it."

"Then I'm your woman," Kate smiled, "for that's the kind of thing I love. *Do* let us do something bad. You're impossibly without sin, you know."

Milly's eyes, on this, remained a little with their companion's. "Ah I shan't perhaps come up to your idea. It's only to deceive Susan Shepherd."

"Oh!" said Kate as if this were indeed mild.

"But thoroughly—as thoroughly as I can."

"And for cheating," Kate asked, "my powers will contribute? Well, I'll do my best for you." In accordance with which it was presently settled between them that Milly should have the aid and comfort of her presence for a visit to Sir Luke Strett. Kate had needed a minute for enlightenment, and it was quite grand for her comrade that this name should have said nothing to her. To Milly herself it had for some days been secretly saying much. The personage in question was, as she explained, the greatest of medical lights—if she had got hold, as she believed (and she had used to this end the wisdom of the serpent) of the right, the special man. She had written to him three days before, and he had named her an hour, eleven-twenty; only it had come to her on the eve that she couldn't go alone. Her maid on the other hand wasn't good enough, and Susie was too good. Kate had listened above all with high indulgence. "And I'm betwixt and between, happy thought! Too good for what?"

Milly thought. "Why to be worried if it's nothing. And to be still more worried—I mean before she need be—if it isn't."

Kate fixed her with deep eyes. "What in the world is the matter with you?" It had inevitably a sound of impatience, as if it had been a challenge really to produce something; so that Milly felt her for the moment only as a much older person, standing above her a little, doubting the imagined ailments, suspecting the easy complaints, of ignorant youth. It somewhat checked her, further, that the matter with her was what exactly as yet she wanted knowledge about; and she immediately declared, for conciliation, that if she were merely fanciful Kate would see her put to shame. Kate vividly uttered, in return, the hope that, since she could come out and be so charming, could so universally dazzle and interest, she wasn't all the while in distress or in anxiety—didn't believe herself to be in any degree seriously menaced. "Well, I want to make out—to make out!" was all that this consistently produced. To which Kate made clear answer: "Ah then let us by all means!"

"I thought," Milly said, "you'd like to help me. But I must ask you, please, for the promise of absolute silence."

"And how, if you *are* ill, can your friends remain in ignorance?"

"Well, if I am it must of course finally come out. But I can go for a long time." Milly spoke with her eyes again on her painted sister's—almost as if under their suggestion. She still sat there before Kate, yet not without a light in her face. "That will be one of my advantages. I think I could die without its being noticed."

"You're an extraordinary young woman," her friend, visibly held by her, declared at last. "What a remarkable time to talk of such things!"

"Well, we won't talk, precisely"—Milly got herself together again. "I only wanted to make sure of you."

"Here in the midst of—!" But Kate could only sigh for wonder—almost visibly too for pity.

It made a moment during which her companion waited on her word; partly as if from a yearning, shy but deep, to have her case put to her just as Kate was struck by it; partly as if the hint of pity were already giving a sense to her whimsical "shot," with Lord Mark, at Mrs. Lowder's first dinner. Exactly this—the handsome girl's compassionate manner, her friendly descent from her own strength—was what she had then foretold. She took Kate up as if positively for the deeper taste of it. "Here in the midst of what?"

"Of everything. There's nothing you can't have. There's nothing you can't do."

"So Mrs. Lowder tells me."

It just kept Kate's eyes fixed as possibly for more of that; then, however, without waiting, she went on. "We all adore you."

"You're wonderful—you dear things!" Milly laughed.

"No, it's *you*." And Kate seemed struck with the real interest of it. "In three weeks!"

Milly kept it up. "Never were people on such terms! All the more reason," she added, "that I shouldn't needlessly torment you."

"But me? what becomes of *me*?" said Kate.

"Well, you"—Milly thought—"if there's anything to bear you'll bear it."

"But I *won't* bear it!" said Kate Croy.

"Oh yes you will: all the same! You'll pity me awfully, but you'll help me very much. And I absolutely trust you. So there we are." There they were then, since Kate had so to take it; but there, Milly felt, she herself in particular was; for it was just the point at which she had wished to arrive. She had wanted to prove to herself that she didn't horribly blame her friend for any reserve; and what better proof could there be than this quite special confidence? If she desired to show Kate that she really believed Kate liked her, how could she show it more than by asking her help?

III

WHAT it really came to, on the morrow, this first time—the time Kate went with her—was that the great man had, a little, to excuse himself; had, by a rare accident—for he kept his consulting-hours in general rigorously free—but ten minutes to give her; ten mere minutes which he yet placed at her service in a manner that she admired still more than she could meet it: so crystal-clean the great empty cup of attention that he set between them on the table. He was presently to jump into his carriage, but he promptly made the point that he must see her again, see her within a day or two; and he named for her at once another hour—easing her off beautifully too even then in respect to her possibly failing of justice to her errand. The minutes affected her in fact as ebbing more swiftly than her little army of items could muster, and they would probably have gone without her doing much more than secure another hearing, hadn't it been for her sense, at the last, that she had gained above all an impression. The impression—all the sharp growth of the final few moments—was neither more nor less than that she might make, of a sudden, in quite another world, another straight friend, and a friend who would moreover be, wonderfully, the most appointed, the most thoroughly adjusted of the whole collection, inasmuch as he would somehow wear the character scientifically, ponderably, proveably—not just loosely and sociably. Literally, furthermore, it wouldn't really depend on herself, Sir Luke Strett's friendship, in the least: perhaps what made her most stammer and pant was its thus queerly coming over her that she might find she had interested him even beyond her intention, find she was in fact launched in some current that would lose itself in the sea of science. At the same time that she struggled, however, she also surrendered; there was a moment at which she almost dropped the form of stating, of explaining, and threw herself, without violence, only with a supreme pointless quaver that had turned the next instant to an intensity of interrogative stillness, upon his general goodwill. His large settled face, though firm, was not, as she had thought at first, hard; he looked, in the oddest manner, to her fancy, half like a general and half like a bishop, and she was soon sure that, within some such handsome range, what it would show her would be what was good, what was best for her. She had established, in other words, in this time-saving way, a relation with it; and the relation was the special trophy that, for the hour, she bore off. It was like an absolute possession, a new resource altogether, something done up in the softest silk and tucked away under the arm of memory. She hadn't had it when she went in, and she had it when she came out; she had it there under her cloak, but dissimulated, invisibly carried, when smiling, smiling, she again faced Kate Croy. That young lady had of course awaited her in another room, where, as the great man was to absent himself, no one else was in attendance; and she rose for her with such a face of sympathy as might have graced the vestibule of a dentist. "Is it out?" she seemed to ask as if it had been a question of a tooth; and Milly indeed kept her in no suspense at all.

"He's a dear. I'm to come again."

"But what does he say?"

Milly was almost gay. "That I'm not to worry about anything in the world, and that if I'll be a good girl and do exactly what he tells me he'll take care of me for ever and ever."

Kate wondered as if things scarce fitted. "But does he allow then that you're ill?"

"I don't know what he allows, and I don't care. I *shall* know, and whatever it is it will be enough. He knows all about me, and I like it. I don't hate it a bit."

Still, however, Kate stared. "But could he, in so few minutes, ask you enough—?"

"He asked me scarcely anything—he doesn't need to do anything so stupid," Milly said. "He can tell. He knows," she repeated; "and when I go back—for he'll have thought me over a little—it will be all right."

Kate after a moment made the best of this. "Then when are we to come?"

It just pulled her friend up, for even while they talked—at least it was one of the reasons—she stood there suddenly, irrelevantly, in the light of her *other* identity, the identity she would have for Mr. Densher. This was always, from one instant to another, an incalculable light, which, though it might go off faster than it came on, necessarily disturbed. It sprang, with a perversity all its own, from the fact that, with the lapse of hours and days, the chances themselves that made for his being named continued so oddly to fail. There were twenty, there were fifty, but none of them turned up. This in particular was of course not a juncture at which the least of them would naturally be present; but it would make, none the less, Milly saw, another day practically all stamped with avoidance. She saw in a quick glimmer, and with it all Kate's unconsciousness; and then she shook off the obsession. But it had lasted long enough to qualify her response. No, she had shown Kate how she trusted her; and that, for loyalty, would somehow do. "Oh, dear thing, now that the ice is broken I shan't trouble *you* again."

"You'll come alone?"

"Without a scruple. Only I shall ask you, please, for your absolute discretion still."

Outside, at a distance from the door, on the wide pavement of the great contiguous square, they had to wait again while their carriage, which Milly had kept, completed a further turn of exercise, engaged in by the coachman for reasons of his own. The footman was there and had indicated that he was making the circuit; so Kate went on while they stood. "But don't you ask a good deal, darling, in proportion to what you give?"

This pulled Milly up still shorter—so short in fact that she yielded as soon as she had taken it in. But she continued to smile. "I see. Then you *can* tell."

"I don't want to 'tell,'" said Kate. "I'll be as silent as the tomb if I can only have the truth from you. All I want is that you shouldn't keep from me how you find out that you really are."

"Well then I won't ever. But you see for yourself," Milly went on, "how I really am. I'm satisfied. I'm happy."

Kate looked at her long. "I believe you like it. The way things turn out for you—!"

Milly met her look now without a thought of anything but the spoken. She had ceased to be Mr. Densher's image; she stood for nothing but herself, and she was none the less fine. Still, still, what had passed was a fair bargain and it would do. "Of course I like it. I feel—I can't otherwise describe it—as if

I had been on my knees to the priest. I've confessed and I've been absolved. It has been lifted off."

Kate's eyes never quitted her. "He must have liked *you*."

"Oh—doctors!" Milly said. "But I hope," she added, "he didn't like me too much." Then as if to escape a little from her friend's deeper sounding, or as impatient for the carriage, not yet in sight, her eyes, turning away, took in the great stale square. As its staleness, however, was but that of London fairly fatigued, the late hot London with its dance all danced and its story all told, the air seemed a thing of blurred pictures and mixed echoes, and an impression met the sense—an impression that broke the next moment through the girl's tightened lips. "Oh it's a beautiful big world, and every one, yes, every one—!" It presently brought her back to Kate, and she hoped she didn't actually look as much as if she were crying as she must have looked to Lord Mark among the portraits at Matcham.

Kate at all events understood. "Every one wants to be so nice?"

"So nice," said the grateful Milly.

"Oh," Kate laughed, "we'll pull you through! And won't you now bring Mrs. Stringham?"

But Milly after an instant was again clear about that. "Not till I've seen him once more."

She was to have found this preference, two days later, abundantly justified; and yet when, in prompt accordance with what had passed between them, she reappeared before her distinguished friend—that character having for him in the interval built itself up still higher—the first thing he asked her was whether she had been accompanied. She told him, on this, straightway, everything; completely free at present from her first embarrassment, disposed even—as she felt she might become—to undue volubility, and conscious moreover of no alarm from his thus perhaps wishing she had not come alone. It was exactly as if, in the forty-eight hours that had passed, her acquaintance with him had somehow increased and his own knowledge in particular received mysterious additions. They had been together, before, scarce ten minutes; but the relation, the one the ten minutes had so beautifully created, was there to take straight up: and this not, on his own part, from mere professional heartiness, mere bedside manner, which she

would have disliked—much rather from a quiet pleasant air in
him of having positively asked about her, asked here and asked
there and found out. Of course he couldn't in the least have
asked, or have wanted to; there was no source of information
to his hand, and he had really needed none: he had found out
simply by his genius—and found out, she meant, literally
everything. Now she knew not only that she didn't dislike this
—the state of being found out about; but that on the contrary
it was truly what she had come for, and that for the time at
least it would give her something firm to stand on. She struck
herself as aware, aware as she had never been, of really not
having had from the beginning anything firm. It would be
strange for the firmness to come, after all, from her learning in
these agreeable conditions that she was in some way doomed;
but above all it would prove how little she had hitherto had to
hold her up. If she was now to be held up by the mere process
—since that was perhaps on the cards—of being let down, this
would only testify in turn to her queer little history. *That* sense
of loosely rattling had been no process at all; and it was ridiculously true that her thus sitting there to see her life put into the
scales represented her first approach to the taste of orderly
living. Such was Milly's romantic version—that her life, especially by the fact of this second interview, *was* put into the
scales; and just the best part of the relation established might
have been, for that matter, that the great grave charming man
knew, had known at once, that it was romantic, and in that
measure allowed for it. Her only doubt, her only fear, was
whether he perhaps wouldn't even take advantage of her being
a little romantic to treat her as romantic altogether. This doubtless was her danger with him; but she should see, and dangers
in general meanwhile dropped and dropped.

The very place, at the end of a few minutes, the commodi-
ous "handsome" room, far back in the fine old house, soundless from position, somewhat sallow with years of celebrity,
somewhat sombre even at midsummer—the very place put on
for her a look of custom and use, squared itself solidly round
her as with promises and certainties. She had come forth to see
the world, and this then was to be the world's light, the rich
dusk of a London "back," these the world's walls, those the
world's curtains and carpet. She should be intimate with the

great bronze clock and mantel-ornaments, conspicuously presented in gratitude and long ago; she should be as one of the
circle of eminent contemporaries, photographed, engraved,
signatured, and in particular framed and glazed, who made up
the rest of the decoration, and made up as well so much of the
human comfort; and while she thought of all the clean truths,
unfringed, unfingered, that the listening stillness, strained into
pauses and waits, would again and again, for years, have kept
distinct, she also wondered what *she* would eventually decide
upon to present in gratitude. She would give something better
at least than the brawny Victorian bronzes. This was precisely
an instance of what she felt he knew of her before he had done
with her: that she was secretly romancing at that rate, in the
midst of so much else that was more urgent, all over the place.
So much for her secrets with him, none of which really required
to be phrased. It would have been thoroughly a secret for her
from any one else that without a dear lady she had picked up
just before coming over she wouldn't have a decently near
connexion of any sort, for such an appeal as she was making, to
put forward: no one in the least, as it were, to produce for re-
spectability. But *his* seeing it she didn't mind a scrap, and not a
scrap either his knowing how she had left the dear lady in the
dark. She had come alone, putting her friend off with a fraud:
giving a pretext of shops, of a whim, of she didn't know what
—the amusement of being for once in the streets by herself.
The streets by herself were new to her—she had always had in
them a companion or a maid; and he was never to believe
moreover that she couldn't take full in the face anything he
might have to say. He was softly amused at her account of her
courage; though he yet showed it somehow without soothing
her too grossly. Still, he did want to know whom she had.
Hadn't there been a lady with her on Wednesday?

"Yes—a different one. Not the one who's travelling with
me. I've told *her*."

Distinctly he was amused, and it added to his air—the greatest charm of all—of giving her lots of time. "You've told her
what?"

"Well," said Milly, "that I visit you in secret."

"And how many persons will she tell?"

"Oh she's devoted. Not one."

"Well, if she's devoted doesn't that make another friend for you?"

It didn't take much computation, but she nevertheless had to think a moment, conscious as she was that he distinctly *would* want to fill out his notion of her—even a little, as it were, to warm the air for her. That however—and better early than late—he must accept as of no use; and she herself felt for an instant quite a competent certainty on the subject of any such warming. The air, for Milly Theale, was, from the very nature of the case, destined never to rid itself of a considerable chill. This she could tell him with authority, if she could tell him nothing else; and she seemed to see now, in short, that it would importantly simplify. "Yes, it makes another; but they all together wouldn't make—well, I don't know what to call it but the difference. I mean when one *is*—really alone. I've never seen anything like the kindness." She pulled up a minute while he waited—waited again as if with his reasons for letting her, for almost making her, talk. What she herself wanted was not, for the third time, to cry, as it were, in public. She *had* never seen anything like the kindness, and she wished to do it justice; but she knew what she was about, and justice was not wronged by her being able presently to stick to her point. "Only one's situation is what it is. It's *me* it concerns. The rest is delightful and useless. Nobody can really help. That's why I'm by myself to-day. I *want* to be—in spite of Miss Croy, who came with me last. If you can help, so much the better—and also of course if one can a little one's self. Except for that—you and me doing our best—I like you to see me just as I am. Yes, I like it—and I don't exaggerate. Shouldn't one, at the start, show the worst —so that anything after that may be better? It wouldn't make any real difference—it *won't* make any, anything that may happen won't—to any one. Therefore I feel myself, this way, with you, just as I am; and—if you do in the least care to know—it quite positively bears me up."

She put it as to his caring to know, because his manner seemed to give her all her chance, and the impression was there for her to take. It was strange and deep for her, this impression, and she did accordingly take it straight home. It showed him—showed him in spite of himself—as allowing, somewhere far within, things comparatively remote, things in

fact quite, as she would have said, outside, delicately to weigh
with him; showed him as interested on her behalf in other
questions beside the question of what was the matter with her.
She accepted such an interest as regular in the highest type of
scientific mind—his own *being* the highest, magnificently—because otherwise obviously it wouldn't be there; but she could
at the same time take it as a direct source of light upon herself,
even though that might present her a little as pretending to
equal him. Wanting to know more about a patient than how a
patient was constructed or deranged couldn't be, even on the
part of the greatest of doctors, anything but some form or
other of the desire to let the patient down easily. When that
was the case the reason, in turn, could only be, too manifestly,
pity; and when pity held up its telltale face like a head on a
pike, in a French revolution, bobbing before a window, what
was the inference but that the patient was bad? He might say
what he would now—she would always have seen the head at
the window; and in fact from this moment she only wanted
him to say what he would. He might say it too with the greater
ease to himself as there wasn't one of her divinations that—*as*
her own—he would in any way put himself out for. Finally, if
he was making her talk she *was* talking, and what it could at any
rate come to for him was that she wasn't afraid. If he wanted
to do the dearest thing in the world for her he would show her
he believed she wasn't; which undertaking of hers—not to have
misled him—was what she counted at the moment as her presumptuous little hint to him that she was as good as himself. It
put forward the bold idea that he could really *be* misled; and
there actually passed between them for some seconds a sign, a
sign of the eyes only, that they knew together where they were.
This made, in their brown old temple of truth, its momentary
flicker; then what followed it was that he had her, all the same,
in his pocket; and the whole thing wound up for that consummation with his kind dim smile. Such kindness was wonderful
with such dimness; but brightness—that even of sharp steel—
was of course for the other side of the business, and it would
all come in for her to one tune or another. "Do you mean," he
asked, "that you've no relations at all?—not a parent, not a sister, not even a cousin nor an aunt?"

She shook her head as with the easy habit of an interviewed

heroine or a freak of nature at a show. "Nobody whatever"—
but the last thing she had come for was to be dreary about it.
"I'm a survivor—a survivor of a general wreck. You see," she
added, "how that's to be taken into account—that every one
else *has* gone. When I was ten years old there were, with my
father and my mother, six of us. I'm all that's left. But they
died," she went on, to be fair all round, "of different things.
Still, there it is. And, as I told you before, I'm American. Not
that I mean that makes me worse. However, you'll probably
know what it makes me."

"Yes"—he even showed amusement for it. "I know perfectly
what it makes you. It makes you, to begin with, a capital case."

She sighed, though gratefully, as if again before the social
scene. "Ah there you are!"

"Oh no; there 'we' aren't at all! There I am only—but as
much as you like. I've no end of American friends: there *they*
are, if you please, and it's a fact that you couldn't very well be
in a better place than in their company. It puts you with plenty
of others—and that isn't pure solitude." Then he pursued:
"I'm sure you've an excellent spirit; but don't try to bear more
things than you need." Which after an instant he further explained. "Hard things have come to you in youth, but you
mustn't think life will be for you all hard things. You've the
right to be happy. You must make up your mind to it. You
must accept any form in which happiness may come."

"Oh I'll accept any whatever!" she almost gaily returned.
"And it seems to me, for that matter, that I'm accepting a new
one every day. Now *this*!" she smiled.

"This is very well so far as it goes. You can depend on me,"
the great man said, "for unlimited interest. But I'm only, after
all, one element in fifty. We must gather in plenty of others.
Don't mind who knows. Knows, I mean, that you and I are
friends."

"Ah you do want to see some one!" she broke out. "You want
to get at some one who cares for me." With which, however,
as he simply met this spontaneity in a manner to show that he
had often had it from young persons of her race, and that he was
familiar even with the possibilities of *their* familiarity, she felt
her freedom rendered vain by his silence, and she immediately

tried to think of the most reasonable thing she could say. This would be, precisely, on the subject of that freedom, which she now quickly spoke of as complete. "That's of course by itself a great boon; so please don't think I don't know it. I can do exactly what I like—anything in all the wide world. I haven't a creature to ask—there's not a finger to stop me. I can shake about till I'm black and blue. That perhaps isn't *all* joy; but lots of people, I know, would like to try it." He had appeared about to put a question, but then had let her go on, which she promptly did, for she understood him the next moment as having thus taken it from her that her means were as great as might be. She had simply given it to him so, and this was all that would ever pass between them on the odious head. Yet she couldn't help also knowing that an important effect, for his judgement, or at least for his amusement—which was his feeling, since, marvellously, he did have feeling—was produced by it. All her little pieces had now then fallen together for him like the morsels of coloured glass that used to make combinations, under the hand, in the depths of one of the polygonal peepshows of childhood. "So that if it's a question of my doing anything under the sun that will help—!"

"You'll *do* anything under the sun? Good." He took that beautifully, ever so pleasantly, for what it was worth; but time was needed—the minutes or so were needed on the spot—to deal even provisionally with the substantive question. It was convenient, in its degree, that there was nothing she wouldn't do; but it seemed also highly and agreeably vague that she should have to do anything. They thus appeared to be taking her, together, for the moment, and almost for sociability, as prepared to proceed to gratuitous extremities; the upshot of which was in turn that after much interrogation, auscultation, exploration, much noting of his own sequences and neglecting of hers, had duly kept up the vagueness, they might have struck themselves, or may at least strike us, as coming back from an undeterred but useless voyage to the North Pole. Milly was ready, under orders, for the North Pole; which fact was doubtless what made a blinding anticlimax of her friend's actual abstention from orders. "No," she heard him again distinctly repeat it, "I don't want you for the present to do anything at all; anything, that is, but obey a small prescription or two that will be made clear to you, and let me within a few days come to see you at home."

It was at first heavenly. "Then you'll see Mrs. Stringham." But she didn't mind a bit now.

"Well, I shan't be afraid of Mrs. Stringham." And he said it once more as she asked once more: "Absolutely not; I 'send' you nowhere. England's all right—anywhere that's pleasant, convenient, decent, will be all right. You say you can do exactly as you like. Oblige me therefore by being so good as to do it. There's only one thing: you ought of course, now, as soon as I've seen you again, to get out of London."

Milly thought. "May I then go back to the Continent?"

"By all means back to the Continent. Do go back to the Continent."

"Then how will you keep seeing me? But perhaps," she quickly added, "you won't want to keep seeing me."

He had it all ready; he had really everything all ready. "I shall follow you up; though if you mean that I don't want you to keep seeing *me*—"

"Well?" she asked.

It was only just here that he struck her the least bit as stumbling. "Well, see all you can. That's what it comes to. Worry about nothing. You *have* at least no worries. It's a great rare chance."

She had got up, for she had had from him both that he would send her something and would advise her promptly of the date of his coming to her, by which she was virtually dismissed. Yet for herself one or two things kept her. "May I come back to England too?"

"Rather! Whenever you like. But always, when you do come, immediately let me know."

"Ah," said Milly, "it won't be a great going to and fro."

"Then if you'll stay with us so much the better."

It touched her, the way he controlled his impatience of her; and the fact itself affected her as so precious that she yielded to the wish to get more from it. "So you don't think I'm out of my mind?"

"Perhaps that *is*," he smiled, "all that's the matter."

She looked at him longer. "No, that's too good. Shall I at any rate suffer?"

"Not a bit."

"And yet then live?"

"My dear young lady," said her distinguished friend, "isn't to 'live' exactly what I'm trying to persuade you to take the trouble to do?"

IV

S HE had gone out with these last words so in her ears that
when once she was well away—back this time in the great
square alone—it was as if some instant application of them had
opened out there before her. It was positively, that effect, an
excitement that carried her on; she went forward into space
under the sense of an impulse received—an impulse simple and
direct, easy above all to act upon. She was borne up for the
hour, and now she knew why she had wanted to come by herself. No one in the world could have sufficiently entered into
her state; no tie would have been close enough to enable a
companion to walk beside her without some disparity. She literally felt, in this first flush, that her only company must be the
human race at large, present all round her, but inspiringly impersonal, and that her only field must be, then and there, the
grey immensity of London. Grey immensity had somehow of a
sudden become her element; grey immensity was what her distinguished friend had, for the moment, furnished her world
with and what the question of "living," as he put it to her,
living by option, by volition, inevitably took on for its immediate face. She went straight before her, without weakness, altogether with strength; and still as she went she was more glad to
be alone, for nobody—not Kate Croy, not Susan Shepherd
either—would have wished to rush with her as she rushed. She
had asked him at the last whether, being on foot, she might go
home so, or elsewhere, and he had replied as if almost amused
again at her extravagance: "You're active, luckily, by nature—
it's beautiful: therefore rejoice in it. *Be* active, without folly—
for you're not foolish: be as active as you can and as you like."
That had been in fact the final push, as well as the touch that
most made a mixture of her consciousness—a strange mixture
that tasted at one and the same time of what she had lost and
what had been given her. It was wonderful to her, while she
took her random course, that these quantities felt so equal: she
had been treated—hadn't she?—as if it were in her power to
live; and yet one wasn't treated so—was one?—unless it had
come up, quite as much, that one might die. The beauty of the

bloom had gone from the small old sense of safety—that was distinct: she had left it behind her there for ever. But the beauty of the idea of a great adventure, a big dim experiment or struggle in which she might more responsibly than ever before take a hand, had been offered her instead. It was as if she had had to pluck off her breast, to throw away, some friendly ornament, a familiar flower, a little old jewel, that was part of her daily dress; and to take up and shoulder as a substitute some queer defensive weapon, a musket, a spear, a battle-axe —conducive possibly in a higher degree to a striking appearance, but demanding all the effort of the military posture.

She felt this instrument, for that matter, already on her back, so that she proceeded now in very truth after the fashion of a soldier on a march—proceeded as if, for her initiation, the first charge had been sounded. She passed along unknown streets, over dusty littery ways, between long rows of fronts not enhanced by the August light; she felt good for miles and only wanted to get lost; there were moments at corners, where she stopped and chose her direction, in which she quite lived up to his injunction to rejoice that she was active. It was like a new pleasure to have so new a reason; she would affirm without delay her option, her volition; taking this personal possession of what surrounded her was a fair affirmation to start with; and she really didn't care if she made it at the cost of alarms for Susie. Susie would wonder in due course "whatever," as they said at the hotel, had become of her; yet this would be nothing either, probably, to wonderments still in store. Wonderments in truth, Milly felt, even now attended her steps: it was quite as if she saw in people's eyes the reflexion of her appearance and pace. She found herself moving at times in regions visibly not haunted by odd-looking girls from New York, duskily draped, sable-plumed, all but incongruously shod and gazing about them with extravagance; she might, from the curiosity she clearly excited in by-ways, in side-streets peopled with grimy children and costermongers' carts, which she hoped were slums, literally have had her musket on her shoulder, have announced herself as freshly on the war-path. But for the fear of overdoing the character she would here and there have begun conversation, have asked her way; in spite of the fact that, as this would help the requirements of adventure, her way was exactly what she wanted not to know. The difficulty was that she at last accidentally found it; she had come out, she presently saw, at the Regent's Park, round which on two or three occasions with Kate Croy her public chariot had solemnly rolled. But she went into it further now; this was the real thing; the real thing was to be quite away from the pompous roads, well within the centre and on the stretches of shabby grass. Here were benches and smutty sheep; here were idle lads at games of ball, with their cries mild in the thick air; here were wanderers anxious and tired like herself; here doubtless were hundreds of others just in the same box. Their box, their great common anxiety, what was it, in this grim breathing-space, but the practical question of life? They could live if they would; that is, like herself, they had been told so: she saw them all about her, on seats, digesting the information, recognising it again as something in a slightly different shape familiar enough, the blessed old truth that they would live if they could. All she thus shared with them made her wish to sit in their company; which she so far did that she looked for a bench that was empty, eschewing a still emptier chair that she saw hard by and for which she would have paid, with superiority, a fee.

The last scrap of superiority had soon enough left her, if only because she before long knew herself for more tired than she had proposed. This and the charm, after a fashion, of the situation in itself made her linger and rest; there was an accepted spell in the sense that nobody in the world knew where she was. It was the first time in her life that this had happened; somebody, everybody appeared to have known before, at every instant of it, where she was; so that she was now suddenly able to put it to herself that that hadn't been a life. This present kind of thing therefore might be—which was where precisely her distinguished friend seemed to be wishing her to come out. He wished her also, it was true, not to make, as she was perhaps doing now, too much of her isolation; at the same time, however, as he clearly desired to deny her no decent source of interest. He was interested—she arrived at that—in her appealing to as many sources as possible; and it fairly filtered into her, as she sat and sat, that he was essentially propping her up. Had she been doing it herself she would have called it bolstering—the bolstering that was simply for the weak; and she thought and thought as she put together the proofs that it was as one of the weak he was treating her. It was of course as one of the weak that she had gone to him—but oh with how sneaking a hope that he might pronounce her, as to all indispensables, a veritable young lioness! What indeed she was really confronted with was the consciousness that he hadn't after all pronounced her anything: she nursed herself into the sense that he had beautifully got out of it. Did he think, however, she wondered, that he could keep out of it to the end?—though as she weighed the question she yet felt it a little unjust. Milly weighed, in this extraordinary hour, questions numerous and strange; but she had happily, before she moved, worked round to a simplification. Stranger than anything for instance was the effect of its rolling over her that, when one considered it, he might perhaps have "got out" by one door but to come in with a beautiful beneficent dishonesty by another. It kept her more intensely motionless there that what he might fundamentally be "up to" was some disguised intention of standing by her as a friend. Wasn't that what women always said they wanted to do when they deprecated the addresses of gentlemen they couldn't more intimately go on with? It was what they, no doubt, sincerely fancied they could make of men of whom they couldn't make husbands. And she didn't even reason that it was by a similar law the expedient of doctors in general for the invalids of whom they couldn't make patients: she was somehow so sufficiently aware that *her* doctor was—however fatuous it might sound—exceptionally moved. This was the damning little fact—if she could talk of damnation: that she could believe herself to have caught him in the act of irrelevantly liking her. She hadn't gone to him to be liked, she had gone to him to be judged; and he was quite a great enough man to be in the habit, as a rule, of observing the difference. She could like *him*, as she distinctly did—that was another matter; all the more that her doing so was now, so obviously for herself, compatible with judgement. Yet it would have been all portentously mixed had not, as we say, a final and merciful wave, chilling rather, but washing clear, come to her assistance.

It came of a sudden when all other thought was spent. She had been asking herself why, if her case was grave—and she knew what she meant by that—he should have talked to her at all about what she might with futility "do"; or why on the other hand, if it were light, he should attach an importance to the office of friendship. She had him, with her little lonely acuteness—as acuteness went during the dog-days in the Regent's Park—in a cleft stick: she either mattered, and then she was ill; or she didn't matter, and then she was well enough. Now he was "acting," as they said at home, as if she did matter —until he should prove the contrary. It was too evident that a person at his high pressure must keep his inconsistencies, which were probably his highest amusements, only for the very greatest occasions. Her prevision, in fine, of just where she should catch him furnished the light of that judgement in which we describe her as daring to indulge. And the judgement it was that made her sensation simple. He *had* distinguished her— that was the chill. He hadn't known—how could he?—that she was devilishly subtle, subtle exactly in the manner of the suspected, the suspicious, the condemned. He in fact confessed to it, in his way, as to an interest in her combinations, her funny race, her funny losses, her funny gains, her funny freedom, and, no doubt, above all, her funny manners—funny, like those of Americans at their best, without being vulgar, legitimating amiability and helping to pass it off. In his appreciation of these redundancies he dressed out for her the compassion he so signally permitted himself to waste; but its operation for herself was as directly divesting, denuding, exposing. It reduced her to her ultimate state, which was that of a poor girl— with her rent to pay for example—staring before her in a great city. Milly had her rent to pay, her rent for her future; everything else but how to meet it fell away from her in pieces, in tatters. This was the sensation the great man had doubtless not purposed. Well, she must go home, like the poor girl, and see. There might after all be ways; the poor girl too would be thinking. It came back for that matter perhaps to views already presented. She looked about her again, on her feet, at her scattered melancholy comrades—some of them so melancholy as to be down on their stomachs in the grass, turned away, ignoring, burrowing; she saw once more, with them, those two faces of the question between which there was so little to choose for inspiration. It was perhaps superficially more striking that one could live if one would; but it was more appealing, insinuating, irresistible in short, that one would live if one could.

She found after this, for the day or two, more amusement than she had ventured to count on in the fact, if it were not a mere fancy, of deceiving Susie; and she presently felt that what made the difference was the mere fancy—as this *was* one—of a countermove to her great man. His taking on himself—should he do so—to get at her companion made her suddenly, she held, irresponsible, made any notion of her own all right for her; though indeed at the very moment she invited herself to enjoy this impunity she became aware of new matter for surprise, or at least for speculation. Her idea would rather have been that Mrs. Stringham would have looked at her hard—her sketch of the grounds of her independent long excursion showing, she could feel, as almost cynically superficial. Yet the dear woman so failed, in the event, to avail herself of any right of criticism that it was sensibly tempting to wonder for an hour if Kate Croy had been playing perfectly fair. Hadn't she possibly, from motives of the highest benevolence, promptings of the finest anxiety, just given poor Susie what she would have called the straight tip? It must immediately be mentioned, however, that, quite apart from a remembrance of the distinctness of Kate's promise, Milly, the next thing, found her explanation in a truth that had the merit of being general. If Susie at this crisis suspiciously spared her, it was really that Susie was always suspiciously sparing her—yet occasionally too with portentous and exceptional mercies. The girl was conscious of how she dropped at times into inscrutable impenetrable deferences— attitudes that, though without at all intending it, made a difference for familiarity, for the ease of intimacy. It was as if she recalled herself to manners, to the law of court-etiquette— which last note above all helped our young woman to a just appreciation. It was definite for her, even if not quite solid, that to treat her as a princess was a positive need of her companion's mind; wherefore she couldn't help it if this lady had her transcendent view of the way the class in question were treated. Susan had read history, had read Gibbon and Froude and Saint-Simon; she had high lights as to the special allowances made for the class, and, since she saw them, when young,

as effete and overtutored, inevitably ironic and infinitely refined, one must take it for amusing if she inclined to an indulgence verily Byzantine. If one *could* only be Byzantine!—wasn't
that what she insidiously led one on to sigh? Milly tried to
oblige her—for it really placed Susan herself so handsomely to
be Byzantine now. The great ladies of that race—it would be
somewhere in Gibbon—were apparently not questioned about
their mysteries. But oh poor Milly and hers! Susan at all events
proved scarce more inquisitive than if she had been a mosaic at
Ravenna. Susan was a porcelain monument to the odd moral
that consideration might, like cynicism, have abysses. Besides,
the Puritan finally disencumbered—! What starved generations
wasn't Mrs. Stringham, in fancy, going to make up for?

Kate Croy came straight to the hotel—came that evening
shortly before dinner; specifically and publicly moreover, in a
hansom that, driven apparently very fast, pulled up beneath
their windows almost with the clatter of an accident, a "smash."
Milly, alone, as happened, in the great garnished void of their
sitting-room, where, a little, really, like a caged Byzantine, she
had been pacing through the queer long-drawn almost sinister
delay of night, an effect she yet liked—Milly, at the sound, one
of the French windows standing open, passed out to the balcony that overhung, with pretensions, the general entrance,
and so was in time for the look that Kate, alighting, paying her
cabman, happened to send up to the front. The visitor moreover had a shilling back to wait for, during which Milly, from
the balcony, looked down at her, and a mute exchange, but
with smiles and nods, took place between them on what had
occurred in the morning. It was what Kate had called for, and
the tone was thus almost by accident determined for Milly
before her friend came up. What was also, however, determined
for her was, again, yet irrepressibly again, that the image presented to her, the splendid young woman who looked so particularly handsome in impatience, with the fine freedom of her
signal, was the peculiar property of somebody else's vision,
that this fine freedom in short was the fine freedom she showed
Mr. Densher. Just so was how she looked to him, and just so
was how Milly was held by her—held as by the strange sense of
seeing through that distant person's eyes. It lasted, as usual,

the strange sense, but fifty seconds; yet in so lasting it produced an effect. It produced in fact more than one, and we
take them in their order. The first was that it struck our young
woman as absurd to say that a girl's looking so to a man could
possibly be without connexions; and the second was that by
the time Kate had got into the room Milly was in mental possession of the main connexion it must have for herself.

She produced this commodity on the spot—produced it in
straight response to Kate's frank "Well, what?" The enquiry
bore of course, with Kate's eagerness, on the issue of the
morning's scene, the great man's latest wisdom, and it doubtless affected Milly a little as the cheerful demand for news is
apt to affect troubled spirits when news is not, in one of the
neater forms, prepared for delivery. She couldn't have said
what it was exactly that on the instant determined her; the
nearest description of it would perhaps have been as the more
vivid impression of all her friend took for granted. The contrast between this free quantity and the maze of possibilities
through which, for hours, she had herself been picking her
way, put on, in short, for the moment, a grossness that even
friendly forms scarce lightened: it helped forward in fact the
revelation to herself that she absolutely had nothing to tell.
Besides which, certainly, there was something else—an influence at the particular juncture still more obscure. Kate had
lost, on the way upstairs, the look—*the* look—that made her
young hostess so subtly think and one of the signs of which
was that she never kept it for many moments at once; yet she
stood there, none the less, so in her bloom and in her strength,
so completely again the "handsome girl" beyond all others, the
"handsome girl" for whom Milly had at first gratefully taken
her, that to meet her now with the note of the plaintive would
amount somehow to a surrender, to a confession. *She* would
never in her life be ill; the greatest doctor would keep her, at
the worst, the fewest minutes; and it was as if she had asked
just *with* all this practical impeccability for all that was most
mortal in her friend. These things, for Milly, inwardly danced
their dance; but the vibration produced and the dust kicked up
had lasted less than our account of them. Almost before she
knew it she was answering, and answering beautifully, with no

consciousness of fraud, only as with a sudden flare of the famous "will-power" she had heard about, read about, and which was what her medical adviser had mainly thrown her back on. "Oh it's all right. He's lovely."

Kate was splendid, and it would have been clear for Milly now, had the further presumption been needed, that she had said no word to Mrs. Stringham. "You mean you've been absurd?"

"Absurd." It was a simple word to say, but the consequence of it, for our young woman, was that she felt it, as soon as spoken, to have done something for her safety.

And Kate really hung on her lips. "There's nothing at all the matter?"

"Nothing to worry about. I shall need a little watching, but I shan't have to do anything dreadful, or even in the least inconvenient. I can do in fact as I like." It was wonderful for Milly how just to put it so made all its pieces fall at present quite properly into their places.

Yet even before the full effect came Kate had seized, kissed, blessed her. "My love, you're too sweet! It's too dear! But it's as I was sure." Then she grasped the full beauty. "You can do as you like?"

"Quite. Isn't it charming?"

"Ah but catch you," Kate triumphed with gaiety, "*not* doing—! And what *shall* you do?"

"For the moment simply enjoy it. Enjoy"—Milly was completely luminous—"having got out of my scrape."

"Learning, you mean, so easily, that you *are* well?"

It was as if Kate had but too conveniently put the words into her mouth. "Learning, I mean, so easily, that I *am* well."

"Only no one's of course well enough to stay in London now. He can't," Kate went on, "want this of you."

"Mercy no—I'm to knock about. I'm to go to places."

"But not beastly 'climates'—Engadines, Rivieras, boredoms?"

"No; just, as I say, where I prefer. I'm to go in for pleasure."

"Oh the duck!"—Kate, with her own shades of familiarity, abounded. "But what kind of pleasure?"

"The highest," Milly smiled.

Her friend met it as nobly. "Which *is* the highest?"

"Well, it's just our chance to find out. You must help me."

"What have I wanted to do but help you," Kate asked, "from the moment I first laid eyes on you?" Yet with this too Kate had her wonder. "I like your talking, though, about that. What help, with your luck all round, do you need?"

V

MILLY indeed at last couldn't say; so that she had really for the time brought it along to the point so oddly marked for her by her visitor's arrival, the truth that she was enviably strong. She carried this out, from that evening, for each hour still left her, and the more easily perhaps that the hours were now narrowly numbered. All she actually waited for was Sir Luke Strett's promised visit; as to her proceeding on which, however, her mind was quite made up. Since he wanted to get at Susie he should have the freest access, and then perhaps he would see how he liked it. What was between *them* they might settle as between them, and any pressure it should lift from her own spirit they were at liberty to convert to their use. If the dear man wished to fire Susan Shepherd with a still higher ideal, he would only after all, at the worst, have Susan on his hands. If devotion, in a word, was what it would come up for the interested pair to organise, she was herself ready to consume it as the dressed and served dish. He had talked to her of her "appetite," her account of which, she felt, must have been vague. But for devotion, she could now see, this appetite would be of the best. Gross, greedy, ravenous—these were doubtless the proper names for her: she was at all events resigned in advance to the machinations of sympathy. The day that followed her lonely excursion was to be the last but two or three of their stay in London; and the evening of that day practically ranked for them as, in the matter of outside relations, the last of all. People were by this time quite scattered, and many of those who had so liberally manifested in calls, in cards, in evident sincerity about visits, later on, over the land, had positively passed in music out of sight; whether as members, these latter, more especially, of Mrs. Lowder's immediate circle or as members of Lord Mark's—our friends being by this time able to make the distinction. The general pitch had thus decidedly dropped, and the occasions still to be dealt with were special and few. One of these, for Milly, announced itself as the doctor's call already mentioned, as to which she had now had a note from him: the single other, of importance, was their ap-

388

pointed leave-taking—for the shortest separation—in respect
to Mrs. Lowder and Kate. The aunt and the niece were to dine
with them alone, intimately and easily—as easily as should be
consistent with the question of their afterwards going on together to some absurdly belated party, at which they had had it
from Aunt Maud that they would do well to show. Sir Luke
was to make his appearance on the morrow of this, and in respect to that complication Milly had already her plan.

The night was at all events hot and stale, and it was late
enough by the time the four ladies had been gathered in, for
their small session, at the hotel, where the windows were still
open to the high balconies and the flames of the candles, behind the pink shades—disposed as for the vigil of watchers—
were motionless in the air in which the season lay dead. What
was presently settled among them was that Milly, who betrayed on this occasion a preference more marked than usual,
shouldn't hold herself obliged to climb that evening the social
stair, however it might stretch to meet her, and that, Mrs.
Lowder and Mrs. Stringham facing the ordeal together, Kate
Croy should remain with her and await their return. It was a
pleasure to Milly, ever, to send Susan Shepherd forth; she saw
her go with complacency, liked, as it were, to put people off
with her, and noted with satisfaction, when she so moved to
the carriage, the further denudation—a markedly ebbing tide
—of her little benevolent back. If it wasn't quite Aunt Maud's
ideal, moreover, to take out the new American girl's funny
friend instead of the new American girl herself, nothing could
better indicate the range of that lady's merit than the spirit in
which—as at the present hour for instance—she made the best
of the minor advantage. And she did this with a broad cheerful
absence of illusion; she did it—confessing even as much to poor
Susie—because, frankly, she *was* good-natured. When Mrs.
Stringham observed that her own light was too abjectly borrowed and that it was as a link alone, fortunately not missing,
that she was valued, Aunt Maud concurred to the extent of the
remark: "Well, my dear, you're better than nothing." To-night
furthermore it came up for Milly that Aunt Maud had something particular in mind. Mrs. Stringham, before adjourning
with her, had gone off for some shawl or other accessory, and
Kate, as if a little impatient for their withdrawal, had wandered

out to the balcony, where she hovered for the time unseen, though with scarce more to look at than the dim London stars and the cruder glow, up the street, on a corner, of a small public-house in front of which a fagged cab-horse was thrown into relief. Mrs. Lowder made use of the moment: Milly felt as soon as she had spoken that what she was doing was somehow for use.

"Dear Susan tells me that you saw in America Mr. Densher —whom I've never till now, as you may have noticed, asked you about. But do you mind at last, in connexion with him, doing something for me?" She had lowered her fine voice to a depth, though speaking with all her rich glibness; and Milly, after a small sharpness of surprise, was already guessing the sense of her appeal. "Will you name him, in any way you like, to *her*"—and Aunt Maud gave a nod at the window; "so that you may perhaps find out whether he's back?"

Ever so many things, for Milly, fell into line at this; it was a wonder, she afterwards thought, that she could be conscious of so many at once. She smiled hard, however, for them all. "But I don't know that it's important to me to 'find out.'" The array of things was further swollen, however, even as she said this, by its striking her as too much to say. She therefore tried as quickly to say less. "Except you mean of course that it's important to *you*." She fancied Aunt Maud was looking at her almost as hard as she was herself smiling, and that gave her another impulse. "You know I never *have* yet named him to her; so that if I should break out now—"

"Well?"—Mrs. Lowder waited.

"Why she may wonder what I've been making a mystery of. She hasn't mentioned him, you know," Milly went on, "herself."

"No"—her friend a little heavily weighed it—"she wouldn't. So it's she, you see then, who has made the mystery."

Yes, Milly but wanted to see; only there was so much. "There has been of course no particular reason." Yet that indeed was neither here nor there. "Do you think," she asked, "he *is* back?"

"It will be about his time, I gather, and rather a comfort to me definitely to know."

"Then can't you ask her yourself?"

"Ah we never speak of him!"

It helped Milly for the moment to the convenience of a puzzled pause. "Do you mean he's an acquaintance of whom you
disapprove for her?"

Aunt Maud, as well, just hung fire. "I disapprove of *her* for
the poor young man. She doesn't care for him."

"And *he* cares so much—?"

"Too much, too much. And my fear is," said Mrs. Lowder,
"that he privately besets her. She keeps it to herself, but I don't
want her worried. Neither, in truth," she both generously and
confidentially concluded, "do I want *him*."

Milly showed all her own effort to meet the case. "But what
can *I* do?"

"You can find out where they are. If I myself try," Mrs. Lowder explained, "I shall appear to treat them as if I supposed
them deceiving me."

"And you don't. You don't," Milly mused for her, "suppose
them deceiving you."

"Well," said Aunt Maud, whose fine onyx eyes failed to
blink even though Milly's questions might have been taken as
drawing her rather further than she had originally meant to
go—"well, Kate's thoroughly aware of my views for her, and
that I take her being with me at present, in the way she *is* with
me, if you know what I mean, for a loyal assent to them. Therefore as my views don't happen to provide a place at all for Mr.
Densher, much, in a manner, as I like him"—therefore in short
she had been prompted to this step, though she completed her
sense, but sketchily, with the rattle of her large fan.

It assisted them for the moment perhaps, however, that
Milly was able to pick out of her sense what might serve as the
clearest part of it. "You do like him then?"

"Oh dear yes. Don't you?"

Milly waited, for the question was somehow as the sudden
point of something sharp on a nerve that winced. She just
caught her breath, but she had ground for joy afterwards, she
felt, in not really having failed to choose with quickness sufficient, out of fifteen possible answers, the one that would best
serve her. She was then almost proud, as well, that she had
cheerfully smiled. "I did—three times—in New York." So came
and went, in these simple words, the speech that was to figure

for her, later on, that night, as the one she had ever uttered that cost her most. She was to lie awake for the gladness of not having taken any line so really inferior as the denial of a happy impression.

For Mrs. Lowder also moreover her simple words were the right ones; they were at any rate, that lady's laugh showed, in the natural note of the racy. "You dear American thing! But people may be very good and yet not good for what one wants."

"Yes," the girl assented, "even I suppose when what one wants is something very good."

"Oh my child, it would take too long just now to tell you all *I* want! I want everything at once and together—and ever so much for you too, you know. But you've seen us," Aunt Maud continued; "you'll have made out."

"Ah," said Milly, "I *don't* make out;" for again—it came that way in rushes—she felt an obscurity in things. "Why, if our friend here doesn't like him—"

"Should I conceive her interested in keeping things from me?" Mrs. Lowder did justice to the question. "My dear, how can you ask? Put yourself in her place. She meets me, but on *her* terms. Proud young women are proud young women. And proud old ones are—well, what *I* am. Fond of you as we both are, you can help us."

Milly tried to be inspired. "Does it come back then to my asking her straight?"

At this, however, finally, Aunt Maud threw her up. "Oh if you've so many reasons not—!"

"I've not so many," Milly smiled—"but I've one. If I break out so suddenly on my knowing him, what will she make of my not having spoken before?"

Mrs. Lowder looked blank at it. "Why should you care what she makes? You may have only been decently discreet."

"Ah I *have* been," the girl made haste to say.

"Besides," her friend went on, "I suggested to you, through Susan, your line."

"Yes, that reason's a reason for *me*."

"And for *me*," Mrs. Lowder insisted. "She's not therefore so stupid as not to do justice to grounds so marked. You can tell her perfectly that I had asked you to say nothing."

"And may I tell her that you've asked me now to speak?"

Mrs. Lowder might well have thought, yet, oddly, this pulled her up. "You can't do it without—?"

Milly was almost ashamed to be raising so many difficulties. "I'll do what I can if you'll kindly tell me one thing more." She faltered a little—it was so prying; but she brought it out. "Will he have been writing to her?"

"It's exactly, my dear, what I should like to know!" Mrs. Lowder was at last impatient. "Push in for yourself and I dare say she'll tell you."

Even now, all the same, Milly had not quite fallen back. "It will be pushing in," she continued to smile, "for *you*." She allowed her companion, however, no time to take this up. "The point will be that if he *has* been writing she may have answered."

"But what point, you subtle thing, is that?"

"It isn't subtle, it seems to me, but quite simple," Milly said, "that if she has answered she has very possibly spoken of me."

"Very certainly indeed. But what difference will it make?"

The girl had a moment, at this, of thinking it natural Mrs. Lowder herself should so fail of subtlety. "It will make the difference that he'll have written her in reply that he knows me. And that, in turn," our young woman explained, "will give an oddity to my own silence."

"How so, if she's perfectly aware of having given you no opening? The only oddity," Aunt Maud lucidly professed, "is for yourself. It's in *her* not having spoken."

"Ah there we are!" said Milly.

And she had uttered it, evidently, in a tone that struck her friend. "Then it *has* troubled you?"

But the enquiry had only to be made to bring the rare colour with fine inconsequence to her face. "Not really the least little bit!" And, quickly feeling the need to abound in this sense, she was on the point, to cut short, of declaring that she cared, after all, no scrap how much she obliged. Only she felt at this instant too the intervention of still other things. Mrs. Lowder was in the first place already beforehand, already affected as by the sudden vision of her having herself pushed too far. Milly could never judge from her face of her uppermost motive—it was so little, in its hard smooth sheen, that kind of human countenance. She looked hard when she spoke fair; the only thing was that when she spoke hard she didn't likewise look soft. Something, none the less, had arisen in her now—a full appreciable tide, entering by the rupture of some bar. She announced that if what she had asked was to prove in the least a bore her young friend was not to dream of it; making her young friend at the same time, by the change in her tone, dream on the spot more profusely. She spoke, with a belated light, Milly could apprehend—she could always apprehend—from pity; and the result of that perception, for the girl, was singular: it proved to her as quickly that Kate, keeping her secret, had been straight with her. From Kate distinctly then, as to why she was to be pitied, Aunt Maud knew nothing, and was thereby simply putting in evidence the fine side of her own character. This fine side was that she could almost at any hour, by a kindled preference or a diverted energy, glow for another interest than her own. She exclaimed as well, at this moment, that Milly must have been thinking round the case much more than she had supposed; and this remark could affect the girl as quickly and as sharply as any other form of the charge of weakness. It was what every one, if she didn't look out, would soon be saying—"There's something the matter with you!" What one was therefore one's self concerned immediately to establish was that there was nothing at all. "I shall like to help you; I shall like, so far as that goes, to help Kate herself," she made such haste as she could to declare; her eyes wandering meanwhile across the width of the room to that dusk of the balcony in which their companion perhaps a little unaccountably lingered. She suggested hereby her impatience to begin; she almost overtly wondered at the length of the opportunity this friend was giving them—referring it, however, so far as words went, to the other friend and breaking off with an amused: "How tremendously Susie must be beautifying!"

It only marked Aunt Maud, none the less, as too preoccupied for her allusion. The onyx eyes were fixed upon her with a polished pressure that must signify some enriched benevolence. "Let it go, my dear. We shall after all soon enough see."

"If he *has* come back we shall certainly see," Milly after a moment replied; "for he'll probably feel that he can't quite civilly not come to see me. Then *there*," she remarked, "we

shall be. It wouldn't then, you see, come through Kate at all—
it would come through him. Except," she wound up with a
smile, "that he won't find me."

She had the most extraordinary sense of interesting her
guest, in spite of herself, more than she wanted; it was as if her
doom so floated her on that she couldn't stop—by very much
the same trick it had played her with her doctor. "Shall you
run away from him?"

She neglected the question, wanting only now to get off.
"Then," she went on, "you'll deal with Kate directly."

"Shall you run away from *her*?" Mrs. Lowder profoundly
enquired, while they became aware of Susie's return through
the room, opening out behind them, in which they had dined.

This affected Milly as giving her but an instant; and suddenly, with it, everything she felt in the connexion rose to her
lips for a question that, even as she put it, she knew she was
failing to keep colourless. "Is it your own belief that he *is* with
her?"

Aunt Maud took it in—took in, that is, everything of the
tone that she just wanted her not to; and the result for some
seconds was but to make their eyes meet in silence. Mrs.
Stringham had rejoined them and was asking if Kate had gone
—an enquiry at once answered by this young lady's reappearance. They saw her again in the open window, where, looking
at them, she had paused—producing thus on Aunt Maud's part
almost too impressive a "Hush!" Mrs. Lowder indeed without
loss of time smothered any danger in a sweeping retreat with
Susie; but Milly's words to her, just uttered, about dealing
with her niece directly, struck our young woman as already re-
coiling on herself. Directness, however evaded, would be, fully,
for *her*; nothing in fact would ever have been for her so direct
as the evasion. Kate had remained in the window, very handsome and upright, the outer dark framing in a highly favourable way her summery simplicities and lightnesses of dress.
Milly had, given the relation of space, no real fear she had
heard their talk; only she hovered there as with conscious eyes
and some added advantage. Then indeed, with small delay, her
friend sufficiently saw. The conscious eyes, the added advantage were but those she had now always at command—those
proper to the person Milly knew as known to Merton Densher.

It was for several seconds again as if the *total* of her identity had been that of the person known to him—a determination having for result another sharpness of its own. Kate had positively but to be there just as she was to tell her he had come back. It seemed to pass between them in fine without a word that he was in London, that he was perhaps only round the corner; and surely therefore no dealing of Milly's with her would yet have been so direct.

VI

IT WAS doubtless because this queer form of directness had in itself, for the hour, seemed so sufficient that Milly was afterwards aware of having really, all the while—during the strange indescribable session before the return of their companions—done nothing to intensify it. If she was most aware only afterwards, under the long and discurtained ordeal of the morrow's dawn, that was because she had really, till their evening's end came, ceased after a little to miss anything from their ostensible comfort. What was behind showed but in gleams and glimpses; what was in front never at all confessed to not holding the stage. Three minutes hadn't passed before Milly quite knew she should have done nothing Aunt Maud had just asked her. She knew it moreover by much the same light that had acted for her with that lady and with Sir Luke Strett. It pressed upon her then and there that she was still in a current determined, through her indifference, timidity, bravery, generosity—she scarce could say which—by others; that not she but the current acted, and that somebody else always was the keeper of the lock or the dam. Kate for example had but to open the flood-gate: the current moved in its mass—the current, as it had been, of her doing as Kate wanted. What, somehow, in the most extraordinary way in the world, *had* Kate wanted but to be, of a sudden, more interesting than she had ever been? Milly, for their evening then, quite held her breath with the appreciation of it. If she hadn't been sure her companion would have had nothing, from her moments with Mrs. Lowder, to go by, she would almost have seen the admirable creature "cutting in" to anticipate a danger. This fantasy indeed, while they sat together, dropped after a little; even if only because other fantasies multiplied and clustered, making fairly, for our young woman, the buoyant medium in which her friend talked and moved. They sat together, I say, but Kate moved as much as she talked; she figured there, restless and charming, just perhaps a shade perfunctory, repeatedly quitting her place, taking slowly, to and fro, in the trailing folds of her light dress, the length of the room—almost avowedly performing for the pleasure of her hostess.

Mrs. Lowder had said to Milly at Matcham that she and her niece, as allies, could practically conquer the world; but though it was a speech about which there had even then been a vague grand glamour the girl read into it at present more of an approach to a meaning. Kate, for that matter, by herself, could conquer anything, and *she*, Milly Theale, was probably concerned with the "world" only as the small scrap of it that most impinged on her and that was therefore first to be dealt with. On this basis of being dealt with she would doubtless herself do her share of the conquering: she would have something to supply, Kate something to take—each of them thus, to that tune, something for squaring with Aunt Maud's ideal. This in short was what it came to now—that the occasion, in the quiet late lamplight, had the quality of a rough rehearsal of the possible big drama. Milly knew herself dealt with—handsomely, completely: she surrendered to the knowledge, for so it was, she felt, that she supplied her helpful force. And what Kate had to take Kate took as freely and to all appearance as gratefully; accepting afresh, with each of her long, slow walks, the relation between them so established and consecrating her companion's surrender simply by the interest she gave it. The interest to Milly herself we naturally mean; the interest to Kate Milly felt as probably inferior. It easily and largely came for their present talk, for the quick flight of the hour before the breach of the spell—it all came, when considered, from the circumstance, not in the least abnormal, that the handsome girl was in extraordinary "form." Milly remembered her having said that she was at her best late at night; remembered it by its having, with its fine assurance, made her wonder when *she* was at her best and how happy people must be who had such a fixed time. She had no time at all; she was never at her best—unless indeed it were exactly, as now, in listening, watching, admiring, collapsing. If Kate moreover, quite mercilessly, had never been so good, the beauty and the marvel of it was that she had never really been so frank: being a person of such a calibre, as Milly would have said, that, even while "dealing" with you and thereby, as it were, picking her steps, she could let

herself go, could, in irony, in confidence, in extravagance, tell
you things she had never told before. That was the impression—that she was telling things, and quite conceivably for her
own relief as well; almost as if the errors of vision, the mistakes
of proportion, the residuary innocence of spirit still to be
remedied on the part of her auditor, had their moments of
proving too much for her nerves. She went at them just now,
these sources of irritation, with an amused energy that it would
have been open to Milly to regard as cynical and that was nevertheless called for—as to this the other was distinct—by the way
that in certain connexions the American mind broke down. It
seemed at least—the American mind as sitting there thrilled
and dazzled in Milly—not to understand English society without a separate confrontation with *all* the cases. It couldn't proceed by—there was some technical term she lacked until Milly
suggested both analogy and induction, and then, differently,
instinct, none of which were right: it had to be led up and introduced to each aspect of the monster, enabled to walk all
round it, whether for the consequent exaggerated ecstasy or
for the still more (as appeared to this critic) disproportionate
shock. It might, the monster, Kate conceded, loom large for
those born amid forms less developed and therefore no doubt
less amusing; it might on some sides be a strange and dreadful
monster, calculated to devour the unwary, to abase the proud,
to scandalise the good; but if one had to live with it one must,
not to be for ever sitting up, learn how: which was virtually in
short to-night what the handsome girl showed herself as
teaching.

She gave away publicly, in this process, Lancaster Gate and
everything it contained; she gave away, hand over hand, Milly's
thrill continued to note, Aunt Maud and Aunt Maud's glories
and Aunt Maud's complacencies; she gave herself away most
of all, and it was naturally what most contributed to her candour. She didn't speak to her friend once more, in Aunt Maud's
strain, of how they could scale the skies; she spoke, by her
bright perverse preference on this occasion, of the need, in the
first place, of being neither stupid nor vulgar. It might have
been a lesson, for our young American, in the art of seeing
things as they were—a lesson so various and so sustained that

the pupil had, as we have shown, but receptively to gape. The odd thing furthermore was that it could serve its purpose while explicitly disavowing every personal bias. It wasn't that she disliked Aunt Maud, who was everything she had on other occasions declared; but the dear woman, ineffaceably stamped by inscrutable nature and a dreadful art, wasn't—how *could* she be?—what she wasn't. She wasn't any one. She wasn't anything. She wasn't anywhere. Milly mustn't think it—one couldn't, as a good friend, let her. Those hours at Matcham were *inespérées*, were pure manna from heaven; or if not wholly that perhaps, with humbugging old Lord Mark as a backer, were vain as a ground for hopes and calculations. Lord Mark was very well, but he wasn't *the* cleverest creature in England, and even if he had been he still wouldn't have been the most obliging. He weighed it out in ounces, and indeed each of the pair was really waiting for what the other would put down.

"She has put down *you*," said Milly, attached to the subject still; "and I think what you mean is that, on the counter, she still keeps hold of you."

"Lest"—Kate took it up—"he should suddenly grab me and run? Oh as he isn't ready to run he's much less ready, naturally, to grab. I *am*—you're so far right as that—on the counter, when I'm not in the shop-window; in and out of which I'm thus conveniently, commercially whisked: the essence, all of it, of my position, and the price, as properly, of my aunt's protection." Lord Mark was substantially what she had begun with as soon as they were alone; the impression was even yet with Milly of her having sounded his name, having imposed it, as a topic, in direct opposition to the other name that Mrs. Lowder had left in the air and that all her own look, as we have seen, kept there at first for her companion. The immediate strange effect had been that of her consciously needing, as it were, an *alibi*—which, successfully, she so found. She had worked it to the end, ridden it to and fro across the course marked for Milly by Aunt Maud, and now she had quite, so to speak, broken it in. "The bore is that if she wants him so much—wants him, heaven forgive her! for *me*—he has put us all out, since your arrival, by wanting somebody else. I don't mean somebody else than you."

Milly threw off the charm sufficiently to shake her head.

"Then I haven't made out who it is. If I'm any part of his alternative he had better stop where he is."

"Truly, truly?—always, always?"

Milly tried to insist with an equal gaiety. "Would you like me to swear?"

Kate appeared for a moment—though that was doubtless but gaiety too—to think. "Haven't we been swearing enough?"

"You have perhaps, but I haven't, and I ought to give you the equivalent. At any rate there it is. 'Truly, truly' as you say— 'always, always.' So I'm not in the way."

"Thanks," said Kate—"but that doesn't help me."

"Oh it's as simplifying for *him* that I speak of it."

"The difficulty really is that he's a person with so many ideas that it's particularly hard to simplify for him. That's exactly of course what Aunt Maud has been trying. He won't," Kate firmly continued, "make up his mind about me."

"Well," Milly smiled, "give him time."

Her friend met it in perfection. "One's *doing* that—one *is*. But one remains all the same but one of his ideas."

"There's no harm in that," Milly returned, "if you come out in the end as the best of them. What's a man," she pursued, "especially an ambitious one, without a variety of ideas?"

"No doubt. The more the merrier." And Kate looked at her grandly. "One can but hope to come out, and do nothing to prevent it."

All of which made for the impression, fantastic or not, of the *alibi*. The splendour, the grandeur were for Milly the bold ironic spirit behind it, so interesting too in itself. What, further, was not less interesting was the fact, as our young woman noted it, that Kate confined her point to the difficulties, so far as *she* was concerned, raised only by Lord Mark. She referred now to none that her own taste might present; which circumstance again played its little part. She was doing what she liked in respect to another person, but she was in no way committed to the other person, and her moreover talking of Lord Mark as not young and not true were only the signs of her clear self-consciousness, were all in the line of her slightly hard but scarce the less graceful extravagance. She didn't wish to show too much her consent to be arranged for, but that was a different thing from not wishing sufficiently to give it. There was something on it all, as well, that Milly still found occasion to say. "If your aunt has been, as you tell me, put out by me, I feel she has remained remarkably kind."

"Oh but she has—whatever might have happened in that respect—plenty of use for you! You put her in, my dear, more than you put her out. You don't half see it, but she has clutched your petticoat. You can do anything—you can do, I mean, lots that *we* can't. You're an outsider, independent and standing by yourself; you're not hideously relative to tiers and tiers of others." And Kate, facing in that direction, went further and further; wound up, while Milly gaped, with extraordinary words. "We're of no use to you—it's decent to tell you. You'd be of use to us, but that's a different matter. My honest advice to you would be—" she went indeed all lengths—"to drop us while you can. It would be funny if you didn't soon see how awfully better you can do. We've not really done for you the least thing worth speaking of—nothing you mightn't easily have had in some other way. Therefore you're under no obligation. You won't want us next year; we shall only continue to want *you.* But that's no reason for you, and you mustn't pay too dreadfully for poor Mrs. Stringham's having let you in. She has the best conscience in the world; she's enchanted with what she has done; but you shouldn't take your people from *her.* It has been quite awful to see you do it."

Milly tried to be amused, so as not—it was too absurd—to be fairly frightened. Strange enough indeed—if not natural enough—that, late at night thus, in a mere mercenary house, with Susie away, a want of confidence should possess her. She recalled, with all the rest of it, the next day, piecing things together in the dawn, that she had felt herself alone with a creature who paced like a panther. That was a violent image, but it made her a little less ashamed of having been scared. For all her scare, none the less, she had now the sense to find words. "And yet without Susie I shouldn't have had *you.*"

It had been at this point, however, that Kate flickered highest. "Oh you may very well loathe me yet!"

Really at last, thus, it had been too much; as, with her own least feeble flare, after a wondering watch, Milly had shown. She hadn't cared; she had too much wanted to know; and, though a small solemnity of remonstrance, a sombre strain, had broken into her tone, it was to figure as her nearest approach to serving Mrs. Lowder. "Why do you say such things to me?"

This unexpectedly had acted, by a sudden turn of Kate's attitude, as a happy speech. She had risen as she spoke, and Kate had stopped before her, shining at her instantly with a softer brightness. Poor Milly hereby enjoyed one of her views of how people, wincing oddly, were often touched by her. "Because you're a dove." With which she felt herself ever so delicately, so considerately, embraced; not with familiarity or as a liberty taken, but almost ceremonially and in the manner of an *accolade*; partly as if, though a dove who could perch on a finger, one were also a princess with whom forms were to be observed. It even came to her, through the touch of her companion's lips, that this form, this cool pressure, fairly sealed the sense of what Kate had just said. It was moreover, for the girl, like an inspiration: she found herself accepting as the right one, while she caught her breath with relief, the name so given her. She met it on the instant as she would have met revealed truth; it lighted up the strange dusk in which she lately had walked. *That* was what was the matter with her. She was a dove. Oh *wasn't* she?—it echoed within her as she became aware of the sound, outside, of the return of their friends. There was, the next thing, little enough doubt about it after Aunt Maud had been two minutes in the room. She had come up, Mrs. Lowder, with Susan—which she needn't have done, at that hour, instead of letting Kate come down to her; so that Milly could be quite sure it was to catch hold, in some way, of the loose end they had left. Well, the way she did catch was simply to make the point that it didn't now in the least matter. She had mounted the stairs for this, and she had her moment again with her younger hostess while Kate, on the spot, as the latter at the time noted, gave Susan Shepherd unwonted opportunities. Kate was in other words, as Aunt Maud engaged her friend, listening with the handsomest response to Mrs. Stringham's impression of the scene they had just quitted. It was in the tone of the fondest indulgence—almost, really, that of dove cooing to dove—that Mrs. Lowder expressed to Milly the hope that it had all gone beautifully. Her "all" had an ample benevolence; it soothed and simplified; she spoke as if it were the two young women, not she and her comrade, who had been facing the town together. But Milly's answer had prepared itself while Aunt Maud was on the stair; she had felt in a rush all the reasons that would make it the most dovelike; and she gave it, while she was about it, as earnest, as candid. "I don't *think*, dear lady, he's here."

It gave her straightway the measure of the success she could have as a dove: that was recorded in the long look of deep criticism, a look without a word, that Mrs. Lowder poured forth. And the word, presently, bettered it still. "Oh you exquisite thing!" The luscious innuendo of it, almost startling, lingered in the room, after the visitors had gone, like an oversweet fragrance. But left alone with Mrs. Stringham Milly continued to breathe it: she studied again the dovelike and so set her companion to mere rich reporting that she averted all enquiry into her own case.

That, with the new day, was once more her law—though she saw before her, of course, as something of a complication, her need, each time, to decide. She should have to be clear as to how a dove *would* act. She settled it, she thought, well enough this morning by quite readopting her plan in respect to Sir Luke Strett. That, she was pleased to reflect, had originally been pitched in the key of a merely iridescent drab; and although Mrs. Stringham, after breakfast, began by staring at it as if it had been a priceless Persian carpet suddenly unrolled at her feet, she had no scruple, at the end of five minutes, in leaving her to make the best of it. "Sir Luke Strett comes, by appointment, to see me at eleven, but I'm going out on purpose. He's to be told, please, deceptively, that I'm at home, and you, as my representative, when he comes up, are to see him instead. He'll like that, this time, better. So do be nice to him." It had taken, naturally, more explanation, and the mention, above all, of the fact that the visitor was the greatest of doctors; yet when once the key had been offered Susie slipped it on her bunch, and her young friend could again feel her lovely imagination operate. It operated in truth very much as Mrs. Lowder's, at the last, had done the night before: it made the air heavy once more with the extravagance of assent. It might, afresh, almost have frightened our young woman to see how people rushed to meet her: *had* she then so little time to

live that the road must always be spared her? It was as if they
were helping her to take it out on the spot. Susie—she couldn't
deny, and didn't pretend to—might, of a truth, on *her* side,
have treated such news as a flash merely lurid; as to which, to
do Susie justice, the pain of it was all there. But, none the less,
the margin always allowed her young friend was all there as
well; and the proposal now made her—what was it in short but
Byzantine? The vision of Milly's perception of the propriety of
the matter had, at any rate, quickly engulfed, so far as her attitude was concerned, any surprise and any shock; so that she
only desired, the next thing, perfectly to possess the facts.
Milly could easily speak, on this, as if there were only one: she
made nothing of such another as that she had felt herself menaced. The great fact, in fine, was that she *knew* him to desire
just now, more than anything else, to meet, quite apart, some
one interested in her. Who therefore so interested as her faithful Susan? The only other circumstance that, by the time she
had quitted her friend, she had treated as worth mentioning
was the circumstance of her having at first intended to keep
quiet. She had originally best seen herself as sweetly secretive.
As to that she had changed, and her present request was the
result. She didn't say why she had changed, but she trusted her
faithful Susan. Their visitor would trust her not less, and she
herself would adore their visitor. Moreover he wouldn't—the
girl felt sure—tell her anything dreadful. The worst would be
that he was in love and that he needed a confidant to work it.
And now she was going to the National Gallery.

VII

THE idea of the National Gallery had been with her from the moment of her hearing from Sir Luke Strett about his hour of coming. It had been in her mind as a place so meagrely visited, as one of the places that had seemed at home one of the attractions of Europe and one of its highest aids to culture, but that—the old story—the typical frivolous always ended by sacrificing to vulgar pleasures. She had had perfectly, at those whimsical moments on the Brünig, the half-shamed sense of turning her back on such opportunities for real improvement as had figured to her, from of old, in connexion with the continental tour, under the general head of "pictures and things"; and at last she knew for what she had done so. The plea had been explicit—she had done so for life as opposed to learning; the upshot of which had been that life was now beautifully provided for. In spite of those few dips and dashes into the many-coloured stream of history for which of late Kate Croy had helped her to find time, there were possible great chances she had neglected, possible great moments she should, save for to-day, have all but missed. She might still, she had felt, overtake one or two of them among the Titians and the Turners; she had been honestly nursing the hour, and, once she was in the benignant halls, her faith knew itself justified. It was the air she wanted and the world she would now exclusively choose; the quiet chambers, nobly overwhelming, rich but slightly veiled, opened out round her and made her presently say "If I could lose myself *here*!" There were people, people in plenty, but, admirably, no personal question. It was immense, outside, the personal question; but she had blissfully left it outside, and the nearest it came, for a quarter of an hour, to glimmering again into view was when she watched for a little one of the more earnest of the lady-copyists. Two or three in particular, spectacled, aproned, absorbed, engaged her sympathy to an absurd extent, seemed to show her for the time the right way to live. She should have been a lady-copyist—it met so the case. The case was the case of escape, of living under water, of

being at once impersonal and firm. There it was before one—
one had only to stick and stick.

Milly yielded to this charm till she was almost ashamed; she
watched the lady-copyists till she found herself wondering
what would be thought by others of a young woman, of ade-
quate aspect, who should appear to regard them as the pride of
the place. She would have liked to talk to them, to get, as it
figured to her, into their lives, and was deterred but by the fact
that she didn't quite see herself as purchasing imitations and
yet feared she might excite the expectation of purchase. She
really knew before long that what held her was the mere refuge,
that something within her was after all too weak for the Turners
and Titians. They joined hands about her in a circle too vast,
though a circle that a year before she would only have desired
to trace. They were truly for the larger, not for the smaller life,
the life of which the actual pitch, for example, was an interest, the interest of compassion, in misguided efforts. She marked
absurdly her little stations, blinking, in her shrinkage of curiosity, at the glorious walls, yet keeping an eye on vistas and approaches, so that she shouldn't be flagrantly caught. The vistas
and approaches drew her in this way from room to room, and
she had been through many parts of the show, as she supposed, when she sat down to rest. There were chairs in scant
clusters, places from which one could gaze. Milly indeed at
present fixed her eyes more than elsewhere on the appearance,
first, that she couldn't quite, after all, have accounted to an ex-
aminer for the order of her "schools," and then on that of her
being more tired than she had meant, in spite of her having
been so much less intelligent. They found, her eyes, it should
be added, other occupation as well, which she let them freely
follow: they rested largely, in her vagueness, on the vagueness
of other visitors; they attached themselves in especial, with
mixed results, to the surprising stream of her compatriots. She
was struck with the circumstance that the great museum, early
in August, was haunted with these pilgrims, as also with that of
her knowing them from afar, marking them easily, each and all,
and recognising not less promptly that they had ever new
lights for her—new lights on their own darkness. She gave herself up at last, and it was a consummation like another: what

she should have come to the National Gallery for to-day
would be to watch the copyists and reckon the Baedekers. That
perhaps was the moral of a menaced state of health—that one
would sit in public places and count the Americans. It passed
the time in a manner; but it seemed already the second line of
defence, and this notwithstanding the pattern, so unmistakeable, of her country-folk. They were cut out as by scissors,
coloured, labelled, mounted; but their relation to her failed to
act—they somehow did nothing for her. Partly, no doubt, they
didn't so much as notice or know her, didn't even recognise
their community of collapse with her, the sign on her, as she
sat there, that for her too Europe was "tough." It came to her
idly thus—for her humour could still play—that she didn't
seem then the same success with them as with the inhabitants
of London, who had taken her up on scarce more of an acquaintance. She could wonder if they would be different
should she go back with this glamour attached; and she could
also wonder, if it came to that, whether she should ever go
back. Her friends straggled past, at any rate, in all the vividness
of their absent criticism, and she had even at last the sense of
taking a mean advantage.

There was a finer instant, however, at which three ladies,
clearly a mother and daughters, had paused before her under
compulsion of a comment apparently just uttered by one of
them and referring to some object on the other side of the
room. Milly had her back to the object, but her face very much
to her young compatriot, the one who had spoken and in whose
look she perceived a certain gloom of recognition. Recognition, for that matter, sat confessedly in her own eyes: she *knew*
the three, generically, as easily as a school-boy with a crib in his
lap would know the answer in class; she felt, like the school-
boy, guilty enough—questioned, as honour went, as to her
right so to possess, to dispossess, people who hadn't consciously provoked her. She would have been able to say where
they lived, and also how, had the place and the way been but
amenable to the positive; she bent tenderly, in imagination,
over marital, paternal Mr. Whatever-he-was, at home, eternally
named, with all the honours and placidities, but eternally un-
seen and existing only as some one who could be financially
heard from. The mother, the puffed and composed whiteness

of whose hair had no relation to her apparent age, showed a countenance almost chemically clean and dry; her companions wore an air of vague resentment humanised by fatigue; and the three were equally adorned with short cloaks of coloured cloth surmounted by little tartan hoods. The tartans were doubtless conceivable as different, but the cloaks, curiously, only thinkable as one. "Handsome? Well, if you choose to say so." It was the mother who had spoken, who herself added, after a pause during which Milly took the reference as to a picture: "In the English style." The three pair of eyes had converged, and their possessors had for an instant rested, with the effect of a drop of the subject, on this last characterisation—with that, too, of a gloom not less mute in one of the daughters than murmured in the other. Milly's heart went out to them while they turned their backs; she said to herself that they ought to have known her, that there was something between them they might have beautifully put together. But she had lost *them* also—they were cold; they left her in her weak wonder as to what they had been looking at. The "handsome" disposed her to turn—all the more that the "English style" would be the English school, which she liked; only she saw, before moving, by the array on the side facing her, that she was in fact among small Dutch pictures. The action of this was again appreciable—the dim surmise that it wouldn't then be by a picture that the spring in the three ladies had been pressed. It was at all events time she should go, and she turned as she got on her feet. She had had behind her one of the entrances and various visitors who had come in while she sat, visitors single and in pairs—by one of the former of whom she felt her eyes suddenly held.

This was a gentleman in the middle of the place, a gentleman who had removed his hat and was for a moment, while he glanced, absently, as she could see, at the top tier of the collection, tapping his forehead with his pocket-handkerchief. The occupation held him long enough to give Milly time to take for granted—and a few seconds sufficed—that his face was the object just observed by her friends. This could only have been because she concurred in their tribute, even qualified; and indeed "the English style" of the gentleman—perhaps by instant contrast to the American—was what had had the arresting power. This arresting power, at the same time—and that was the marvel—had already sharpened almost to pain, for in the very act of judging the bared head with detachment she felt herself shaken by a knowledge of it. It was Merton Densher's own, and he was standing there, standing long enough unconscious for her to fix him and then hesitate. These successions were swift, so that she could still ask herself in freedom if she had best let him see her. She could still reply to this that she shouldn't like him to catch her in the effort to prevent it; and she might further have decided that he was too preoccupied to see anything had not a perception intervened that surpassed the first in violence. She was unable to think afterwards how long she had looked at him before knowing herself as otherwise looked at; all she was coherently to put together was that she had had a second recognition without his having noticed her. The source of this latter shock was nobody less than Kate Croy—Kate Croy who was suddenly also in the line of vision and whose eyes met her eyes at their next movement. Kate was but two yards off—Mr. Densher wasn't alone. Kate's face specifically said so, for after a stare as blank at first as Milly's it broke into a far smile. That was what, wonderfully—in addition to the marvel of their meeting—passed from her for Milly; the instant reduction to easy terms of the fact of their being there, the two young women, together. It was perhaps only afterwards that the girl fully felt the connexion between this touch and her already established conviction that Kate was a prodigious person; yet on the spot she none the less, in a degree, knew herself handled and again, as she had been the night before, dealt with—absolutely even dealt with for her greater pleasure. A minute in fine hadn't elapsed before Kate had somehow made her provisionally take everything as natural. The provisional was just the charm—acquiring that character from one moment to the other; it represented happily so much that Kate would explain on the very first chance. This left moreover—and that was the greatest wonder—all due margin for amusement at the way things happened, the monstrous oddity of their turning up in such a place on the very heels of their having separated without allusion to it. The handsome girl was thus literally in control of the scene by the time Merton Densher was ready to exclaim with a high flush or a vivid blush—

one didn't distinguish the embarrassment from the joy—"Why
Miss Theale: fancy!" and "Why Miss Theale: what luck!"

Miss Theale had meanwhile the sense that for him too, on
Kate's part, something wonderful and unspoken was determinant; and this although, distinctly, his companion had no more
looked at him with a hint than he had looked at her with a
question. He had looked and was looking only at Milly herself,
ever so pleasantly and considerately—she scarce knew what to
call it; but without prejudice to her consciousness, all the
same, that women got out of predicaments better than men.
The predicament of course wasn't definite nor phraseable—
and the way they let all phrasing pass was presently to recur to
our young woman as a characteristic triumph of the civilised
state; but she took it for granted, insistently, with a small private flare of passion, because the one thing she could think of
to do for him was to show him how she eased him off. She
would really, tired and nervous, have been much disconcerted
if the opportunity in question hadn't saved her. It was what
had saved her most, what had made her, after the first few seconds, almost as brave for Kate as Kate was for her, had made
her only ask herself what their friend would like of her. That he
was at the end of three minutes, without the least complicated
reference, so smoothly "their" friend was just the effect of their
all being sublimely civilised. The flash in which he saw this was,
for Milly, fairly inspiring—to that degree in fact that she was
even now, on such a plane, yearning to be supreme. It took, no
doubt, a big dose of inspiration to treat as not funny—or at
least as not unpleasant—the anomaly, for Kate, that *she* knew
their gentleman, and for herself, that Kate was spending the
morning with him; but everything continued to make for this
after Milly had tasted of her draught. She was to wonder in
subsequent reflexion what in the world they had actually said,
since they had made such a success of what they didn't say;
the sweetness of the draught for the time, at any rate, was to
feel success assured. What depended on this for Mr. Densher
was all obscurity to her, and she perhaps but invented the
image of his need as a short cut to accommodation. Whatever
the facts, their perfect manners, all round, saw them through.
The finest part of Milly's own inspiration, it may further be

mentioned, was the quick perception that what would be of most service was, so to speak, her own native wood-note. She had long been conscious with shame for her thin blood, or at least for her poor economy, of her unused margin as an American girl—closely indeed as in English air the text might appear to cover the page. She still had reserves of spontaneity, if not of comicality; so that all this cash in hand could now find employment. She became as spontaneous as possible and as American as it might conveniently appeal to Mr. Densher, after his travels, to find her. She said things in the air, and yet flattered herself that she struck him as saying them not in the tone of agitation but in the tone of New York. In the tone of New York agitation was beautifully discounted, and she had now a sufficient view of how much it might accordingly help her.

The help was fairly rendered before they left the place; when her friends presently accepted her invitation to adjourn with her to luncheon at her hotel it was in Fifth Avenue that the meal might have waited. Kate had never been there so straight, but Milly was at present taking her; and if Mr. Densher had been he had at least never had to come so fast. She proposed it as the natural thing—proposed it as the American girl; and she saw herself quickly justified by the pace at which she was followed. The beauty of the case was that to do it all she had only to appear to take Kate's hint. This had said in its fine first smile "Oh yes, our look's queer—but give me time"; and the American girl could give time as nobody else could. What Milly thus gave she therefore made them take—even if, as they might surmise, it was rather more than they wanted. In the porch of the museum she expressed her preference for a four-wheeler; they would take their course in that guise precisely to multiply the minutes. She was more than ever justified by the positive charm that her spirit imparted even to their use of this conveyance; and she touched her highest point—that is certainly for herself—as she ushered her companions into the presence of Susie. Susie was there with luncheon as well as with her return in prospect; and nothing could now have filled her own consciousness more to the brim than to see this good friend take in how little she was abjectly anxious. The cup itself actually offered to this good friend might in truth well be startling, for it was composed beyond question of ingredients oddly mixed. She caught Susie fairly looking at her as if to know whether she had brought in guests to hear Sir Luke Strett's report. Well, it was better her companion should have too much than too little to wonder about; she had come out "anyway," as they said at home, for the interest of the thing; and interest truly sat in her eyes. Milly was none the less, at the sharpest crisis, a little sorry for her; she could of necessity extract from the odd scene so comparatively little of a soothing secret. She saw Mr. Densher suddenly popping up, but she saw nothing else that had happened. She saw in the same way her young friend indifferent to her young friend's doom, and she lacked what would explain it. The only thing to keep her in patience was the way, after luncheon, Kate almost, as might be said, made up to her. This was actually perhaps as well what most kept Milly herself in patience. It had in fact for our young woman a positive beauty—was so marked as a deviation from the handsome girl's previous courses. Susie had been a bore to the handsome girl, and the change was now suggestive. The two sat together, after they had risen from table, in the apartment in which they had lunched, making it thus easy for the other guest and his entertainer to sit in the room adjacent. This, for the latter personage, was the beauty; it was almost, on Kate's part, like a prayer to be relieved. If she honestly liked better to be "thrown with" Susan Shepherd than with their other friend, why that said practically everything. It didn't perhaps altogether say why she had gone out with him for the morning, but it said, as one thought, about as much as she could say to his face.

Little by little indeed, under the vividness of Kate's behaviour, the probabilities fell back into their order. Merton Densher was in love and Kate couldn't help it—could only be sorry and kind: wouldn't that, without wild flurries, cover everything? Milly at all events tried it as a cover, tried it hard, for the time; pulled it over her, in the front, the larger room, drew it up to her chin with energy. If it didn't, so treated, do everything for her, it did so much that she could herself supply the rest. She made that up by the interest of her great question, the question of whether, seeing him once more, with all that, as she called it to herself, had come and gone, her impression of him would be different from the impression received in

New York. That had held her from the moment of their leaving
the museum; it kept her company through their drive and
during luncheon; and now that she was a quarter of an hour
alone with him it became acute. She was to feel at this crisis
that no clear, no common answer, no direct satisfaction on this
point, was to reach her; she was to see her question itself simply go to pieces. She couldn't tell if he were different or not,
and she didn't know nor care if *she* were: these things had
ceased to matter in the light of the only thing she did know.
This was that she liked him, as she put it to herself, as much as
ever; and if that were to amount to liking a new person the
amusement would be but the greater. She had thought him at
first very quiet, in spite of his recovery from his original confusion; though even the shade of bewilderment, she yet perceived, had not been due to such vagueness on the subject of
her reintensified identity as the probable sight, over there, of
many thousands of her kind would sufficiently have justified.
No, he was quiet, inevitably, for the first half of the time, because Milly's own lively line—the line of spontaneity—made
everything else relative; and because too, so far as Kate was
spontaneous, it was ever so finely in the air among them that
the normal pitch must be kept. Afterwards, when they had got
a little more used, as it were, to each other's separate felicity,
he had begun to talk more, clearly bethinking himself at a
given moment of what *his* natural lively line would be. It would
be to take for granted she must wish to hear of the States, and
to give her in its order everything he had seen and done there.
He abounded, of a sudden—he almost insisted; he returned,
after breaks, to the charge; and the effect was perhaps the more
odd as he gave no clue whatever to what he had admired, as he
went, or to what he hadn't. He simply drenched her with his
sociable story—especially during the time they were away from
the others. She had stopped then being American—all to let
him be English; a permission of which he took, she could feel,
both immense and unconscious advantage. She had really
never cared less for the States than at this moment; but that
had nothing to do with the matter. It would have been the occasion of her life to learn about them, for nothing could put
him off, and he ventured on no reference to what had happened for herself. It might have been almost as if he had

known that the greatest of all these adventures was her doing just what she did then.

It was at this point that she saw the smash of her great question complete, saw that all she had to do with was the sense of being there with him. And there was no chill for this in what she also presently saw—that, however he had begun, he was now acting from a particular desire, determined either by new facts or new fancies, to be like every one else, simplifyingly "kind" to her. He had caught on already as to manner—fallen into line with every one else; and if his spirits verily *had* gone up it might well be that he had thus felt himself lighting on the remedy for all awkwardness. Whatever he did or he didn't Milly knew she should still like him—there was no alternative to that; but her heart could none the less sink a little on feeling how much his view of her was destined to have in common with —as she now sighed over it—*the* view. She could have dreamed of his not having *the* view, of his having something or other, if need be quite viewless, of his own; but he might have what he could with least trouble, and *the* view wouldn't be after all a positive bar to her seeing him. The defect of it in general—if she might so ungraciously criticise—was that, by its sweet universality, it made relations rather prosaically a matter of course. It anticipated and superseded the—likewise sweet—operation of real affinities. It was this that was doubtless marked in her power to keep him now—this and her glassy lustre of attention to his pleasantness about the scenery in the Rockies. She was in truth a little measuring her success in detaining him by Kate's success in "standing" Susan. It wouldn't be, if she could help it, Mr. Densher who should first break down. Such at least was one of the forms of the girl's inward tension; but beneath even this deep reason was a motive still finer. What she had left at home on going out to give it a chance was meanwhile still, was more sharply and actively, there. What had been at the top of her mind about it and then been violently pushed down—this quantity was again working up. As soon as their friends should go Susie would break out, and what she would break out upon wouldn't be—interested in that gentleman as she had more than once shown herself—the personal fact of Mr. Densher. Milly had found in her face at luncheon a feverish glitter, and it told what she was full of. She didn't care now for Mr. Densher's personal fact. Mr. Densher had risen before her only to find his proper place in her imagination already of a sudden occupied. His personal fact failed, so far as she was concerned, to *be* personal, and her companion noticed the failure. This could only mean that she was full to the brim of Sir Luke Strett and of what she had had from him. What *had* she had from him? It was indeed now working upward again that Milly would do well to know, though knowledge looked stiff in the light of Susie's glitter. It was therefore on the whole because Densher's young hostess was divided from it by so thin a partition that she continued to cling to the Rockies.

BOOK SIXTH

I

I SAY, you know, Kate—you *did* stay!" had been Merton Densher's punctual remark on their adventure after they had, as it were, got out of it; an observation which she not less promptly, on her side, let him see that she forgave in him only because he was a man. She had to recognise, with whatever disappointment, that it was doubtless the most helpful he could make in this character. The fact of the adventure was flagrant between them; they had looked at each other, on gaining the street, as people look who have just rounded together a dangerous corner, and there was therefore already enough unanimity sketched out to have lighted, for her companion, anything equivocal in her action. But the amount of light men *did* need!—Kate could have been eloquent at this moment about that. What, however, on his seeing more, struck him as most distinct in her was her sense that, reunited after his absence and having been now half the morning together, it behooved them to face without delay the question of handling their immediate future. That it would require some handling, that they should still have to deal, deal in a crafty manner, with difficulties and delays, was the great matter he had come back to, greater than any but the refreshed consciousness of their personal need of each other. This need had had twenty minutes, the afternoon before, to find out where it stood, and the time was fully accounted for by the charm of the demonstration. He had arrived at Euston at five, having wired her from Liverpool the moment he landed, and she had quickly decided to meet him at the station, whatever publicity might attend such an act. When he had praised her for it on alighting from his train she had answered frankly enough that such things should be taken at a jump. She didn't care to-day who saw her, and she profited by it for her joy. To-morrow, inevitably, she should have time to think and then, as inevitably, would become a baser creature, a creature of alarms and precautions. It was none the less for to-morrow at an early hour that she had appointed their next meeting, keeping in mind for the present a particular obligation to show at Lancaster Gate by six o'clock. She had given, with imprecations, her reason—people to tea, eternally, and a promise to Aunt Maud; but she had been liberal enough on the spot and had suggested the National Gallery for the morning quite as with an idea that had ripened in expectancy. They might be seen there too, but nobody would know them; just as, for that matter, now, in the refreshment-room to which they had adjourned, they would incur the notice but, at the worst, of the unacquainted. They would "have something" there for the facility it would give. Thus had it already come up for them again that they had no place of convenience.

He found himself on English soil with all sorts of feelings, but he hadn't quite faced having to reckon with a certain ruefulness in regard to that subject as one of the strongest. He was aware later on that there were questions his impatience had shirked; whereby it actually rather smote him, for want of preparation and assurance, that he had nowhere to "take" his love. He had taken it thus, at Euston—and on Kate's own suggestion—into the place where people had beer and buns, and had ordered tea at a small table in the corner; which, no doubt, as they were lost in the crowd, did well enough for a stop-gap. It perhaps did as well as her simply driving with him to the door of his lodging, which had had to figure as the sole device of his own wit. That wit, the truth was, had broken down a little at the sharp prevision that once at his door they would have to hang back. She would have to stop there, wouldn't come in with him, couldn't possibly; and he shouldn't be able to ask her, would feel he couldn't without betraying a deficiency of what would be called, even at their advanced stage, respect for her: that again was all that was clear except the further fact that it was maddening. Compressed and concentrated, confined to a single sharp pang or two, but none the less in wait for him there on the Euston platform and lifting its head as that of a snake in the garden, was the disconcerting sense that "respect," in their game, seemed somehow—he scarce knew what to call it—a fifth wheel to the coach. It was properly an inside thing, not an outside, a thing to make love

greater, not to make happiness less. They had met again for
happiness, and he distinctly felt, during his most lucid moment
or two, how he must keep watch on anything that really menaced that boon. If Kate had consented to drive away with him
and alight at his house there would probably enough have occurred for them, at the foot of his steps, one of those strange
instants between man and woman that blow upon the red
spark, the spark of conflict, ever latent in the depths of passion.
She would have shaken her head—oh sadly, divinely—on the
question of coming in; and he, though doing all justice to her
refusal, would have yet felt his eyes reach further into her own
than a possible word at such a time could reach. This would
have meant the suspicion, the dread of the shadow, of an ad-
verse will. Lucky therefore in the actual case that the scant
minutes took another turn and that by the half-hour she did in
spite of everything contrive to spend with him Kate showed so
well how she could deal with things that maddened. She
seemed to ask him, to beseech him, and all for his better comfort, to leave her, now and henceforth, to treat them in her
own way.

She had still met it in naming so promptly, for their early
convenience, one of the great museums; and indeed with such
happy art that his fully seeing where she had placed him hadn't
been till after he left her. His absence from her for so many
weeks had had such an effect upon him that his demands, his
desires had grown; and only the night before, as his ship
steamed, beneath summer stars, in sight of the Irish coast, he
had felt all the force of his particular necessity. He hadn't in
other words at any point doubted he was on his way to say to
her that really their mistake must end. Their mistake was to
have believed that they *could* hold out—hold out, that is, not
against Aunt Maud, but against an impatience that, prolonged
and exasperated, made a man ill. He had known more than
ever, on their separating in the court of the station, how ill a
man, and even a woman, could feel from such a cause; but he
struck himself as also knowing that he had already suffered
Kate to begin finely to apply antidotes and remedies and subtle
sedatives. It had a vulgar sound—as throughout, in love, the
names of things, the verbal terms of intercourse, were, compared with love itself, horribly vulgar; but it was as if, after all,

he might have come back to find himself "put off," though it would take him of course a day or two to see. His letters from the States had pleased whom it concerned, though not so much as he had meant they should; and he should be paid according to agreement and would now take up his money. It wasn't in truth very much to take up, so that he hadn't in the least come back flourishing a chequebook; that new motive for bringing his mistress to terms he couldn't therefore pretend to produce. The ideal certainty would have been to be able to present a change of prospect as a warrant for the change of philosophy, and without it he should have to make shift but with the pretext of the lapse of time. The lapse of time—not so many weeks after all, she might always of course say—couldn't at any rate have failed to do something for him; and that consideration it was that had just now tided him over, all the more that he had his vision of what it had done personally for Kate. This had come out for him with a splendour that almost scared him even in their small corner of the room at Euston—almost scared him because it just seemed to blaze at him that waiting was the game of dupes. Not yet had she been so the creature he had originally seen; not yet had he felt so soundly safely sure. It was all there for him, playing on his pride of possession as a hidden master in a great dim church might play on the grandest organ. His final sense was that a woman couldn't be like that and then ask of one the impossible.

She had been like that afresh on the morrow; and so for the hour they had been able to float in the mere joy of contact—such contact as their situation in pictured public halls permitted. This poor makeshift for closeness confessed itself in truth, by twenty small signs of unrest even on Kate's part, inadequate; so little could a decent interest in the interesting place presume to remind them of its claims. They had met there in order not to meet in the streets and not again, with an equal want of invention and of style, at a railway-station; not again, either, in Kensington Gardens, which, they could easily and tacitly agree, would have had too much of the taste of their old frustrations. The present taste, the taste that morning in the pictured halls, had been a variation; yet Densher had at the end of a quarter of an hour fully known what to conclude from it. This fairly consoled him for their awkwardness, as if he had been watching it affect her. She might be as nobly charming as she liked, and he had seen nothing to touch her in the States; she couldn't pretend that in such conditions as those she herself *believed* it enough to appease him. She couldn't pretend she believed he would believe it enough to render her a like service. It wasn't enough for that purpose—she as good as showed him it wasn't. That was what he could be glad, by demonstration, to have brought her to. He would have said to her had he put it crudely and on the spot: "*Now* am I to understand you that you consider this sort of thing can go on?" It would have been open to her, no doubt, to reply that to have him with her again, to have him all kept and treasured, so still, under her grasping hand, as she had held him in their yearning interval, was a sort of thing that he must allow her to have no quarrel about; but that would be a mere gesture of her grace, a mere sport of her subtlety. She knew as well as he what they wanted; in spite of which indeed he scarce could have said how beautifully he mightn't once more have named it and urged it if she hadn't, at a given moment, blurred, as it were, the accord. They had soon seated themselves for better talk, and so they had remained a while, intimate and superficial. The immediate things to say had been many, for they hadn't exhausted them at Euston. They drew upon them freely now, and Kate appeared quite to forget—which was prodigiously becoming to her—to look about for surprises. He was to try afterwards, and try in vain, to remember what speech or what silence of his own, what natural sign of the eyes or accidental touch of the hand, had precipitated for her, in the midst of this, a sudden different impulse. She had got up, with inconsequence, as if to break the charm, though he wasn't aware of what he had done at the moment to make the charm a danger. She had patched it up agreeably enough the next minute by some odd remark about some picture, to which he hadn't so much as replied; it being quite independently of this that he had himself exclaimed on the dreadful closeness of the rooms. He had observed that they must go out again to breathe; and it was as if their common consciousness, while they passed into another part, was that of persons who, infinitely engaged together, had been startled and were trying to look natural. It was probably while they were so occupied—as the young man

subsequently reconceived—that they had stumbled upon his
little New York friend. He thought of her for some reason as
little, though she was of about Kate's height, to which, any
more than to any other felicity in his mistress, he had never applied the diminutive.

What was to be in the retrospect more distinct to him was
the process by which he had become aware that Kate's acquaintance with her was greater than he had gathered. She had
written of it in due course as a new and amusing one, and he
had written back that he had met over there, and that he much
liked, the young person; whereupon she had answered that he
must find out about her at home. Kate, in the event, however,
had not returned to that, and he had of course, with so many
things to find out about, been otherwise taken up. Little Miss
Theale's individual history was not stuff for his newspaper; besides which, moreover, he was seeing but too many little Miss
Theales. They even went so far as to impose themselves as one
of the groups of social phenomena that fell into the scheme of
his public letters. For this group in especial perhaps—the irrepressible, the supereminent young persons—his best pen was
ready. Thus it was that there could come back to him in London, an hour or two after their luncheon with the American
pair, the sense of a situation for which Kate hadn't wholly prepared him. Possibly indeed as marked as this was his recovered
perception that preparations, of more than one kind, had been
exactly what, both yesterday and to-day, he felt her as having
in hand. That appearance in fact, if he dwelt on it, so ministered to apprehension as to require some brushing away. He
shook off the suspicion to some extent, on their separating
first from their hostesses and then from each other, by the aid
of a long and rather aimless walk. He was to go to the office
later, but he had the next two or three hours, and he gave himself as a pretext that he had eaten much too much. After Kate
had asked him to put her into a cab—which, as an announced,
a resumed policy on her part, he found himself deprecating—
he stood a while by a corner and looked vaguely forth at his
London. There was always doubtless a moment for the absen-
tee recaptured—*the* moment, that of the reflux of the first
emotion—at which it was beyond disproof that one was back.
His full parenthesis was closed, and he was once more but a

sentence, of a sort, in the general text, the text that, from his momentary street-corner, showed as a great grey page of print that somehow managed to be crowded without being "fine." The grey, however, was more or less the blur of a point of view not yet quite seized again; and there would be colour enough to come out. He was back, flatly enough, but back to possibilities and prospects, and the ground he now somewhat sightlessly covered was the act of renewed possession.

He walked northward without a plan, without suspicion, quite in the direction his little New York friend, in her restless ramble, had taken a day or two before. He reached, like Milly, the Regent's Park; and though he moved further and faster he finally sat down, like Milly, from the force of thought. For him too in this position, be it added—and he might positively have occupied the same bench—various troubled fancies folded their wings. He had no more yet said what he really wanted than Kate herself had found time. She should hear enough of that in a couple of days. He had practically not pressed her as to what most concerned them; it had seemed so to concern them during these first hours but to hold each other, spiritually speaking, close. This at any rate was palpable, that there were at present more things rather than fewer between them. The explanation about the two ladies would be part of the lot, yet could wait with all the rest. They were not meanwhile certainly what most made him roam—the missing explanations weren't. That was what she had so often said before, and always with the effect of suddenly breaking off: "Now please call me a good cab." Their previous encounters, the times when they had reached in their stroll the south side of the park, had had a way of winding up with this special irrelevance. It was effectively what most divided them, for he would generally, but for her reasons, have been able to jump in with her. What did she think he wished to do to her?—it was a question he had had occasion to put. A small matter, however, doubtless—since, when it came to that, they didn't depend on cabs good or bad for the sense of union: its importance was less from the particular loss than as a kind of irritating mark of her expertness. This expertness, under providence, had been great from the first, so far as joining him was concerned; and he was critical only because it had been still greater, even from the first too, in respect to leaving him. He had put the question to her again that afternoon, on the repetition of her appeal—had asked her once more what she supposed he wished to do. He recalled, on his bench in the Regent's Park, the freedom of fancy, funny and pretty, with which she had answered; recalled the moment itself, while the usual hansom charged them, during which he felt himself, disappointed as he was, grimacing back at the superiority of her very "humour," in its added grace of gaiety, to the celebrated solemn American. Their fresh appointment had been at all events by that time made, and he should see what her choice in respect to it—a surprise as well as a relief—would do toward really simplifying. It meant either new help or new hindrance, though it took them at least out of the streets. And her naming this privilege had naturally made him ask if Mrs. Lowder knew of his return.

"Not from me," Kate had replied. "But I shall speak to her now." And she had argued, as with rather a quick fresh view, that it would now be quite easy. "We've behaved for months so properly that I've margin surely for my mention of you. You'll come to see *her*, and she'll leave you with me; she'll show her good nature, and her lack of betrayed fear, in that. With her, you know, you've never broken, quite the contrary, and she likes you as much as ever. We're leaving town; it will be the end; just now therefore it's nothing to ask. I'll ask tonight," Kate had wound up, "and if you'll leave it to me—my cleverness, I assure you, has grown infernal—I'll make it all right."

He had of course thus left it to her and he was wondering more about it now than he had wondered there in Brook Street. He repeated to himself that if it wasn't in the line of triumph it was in the line of muddle. This indeed, no doubt, was as a part of his wonder for still other questions. Kate had really got off without meeting his little challenge about the terms of their intercourse with her dear Milly. Her dear Milly, it was sensible, *was* somehow in the picture. Her dear Milly, popping up in his absence, occupied—he couldn't have said quite why he felt it—more of the foreground than one would have expected her in advance to find clear. She took up room, and it was almost as if room had been made for her. Kate had appeared to take for granted he would know why it had been made; but that was just the point. It was a foreground in which he himself, in which his connexion with Kate, scarce enjoyed a space to turn round. But Miss Theale was perhaps at the present juncture a possibility of the same sort as the softened, if not the squared, Aunt Maud. It might be true of her also that if she weren't a bore she'd be a convenience. It rolled over him of a sudden, after he had resumed his walk, that this might easily be what Kate had meant. The charming girl adored her—Densher had for himself made out that—and would protect, would lend a hand, to their interviews. These might take place, in other words, on her premises, which would remove them still better from the streets. *That* was an explanation which did hang together. It was impaired a little, of a truth, by this fact that their next encounter was rather markedly not to depend upon her. Yet this fact in turn would be accounted for by the need of more preliminaries. One of the things he conceivably should gain on Thursday at Lancaster Gate would be a further view of that propriety.

II

IT WAS extraordinary enough that he should actually be finding himself, when Thursday arrived, none so wide of the mark. Kate hadn't come all the way to this for him, but she had come to a good deal by the end of a quarter of an hour. What she had begun with was her surprise at her appearing to have left him on Tuesday anything more to understand. The parts, as he now saw, under her hand, did fall more or less together, and it wasn't even as if she had spent the interval in twisting and fitting them. She was bright and handsome, not fagged and worn, with the general clearness; for it certainly stuck out enough that if the American ladies themselves weren't to be squared, which was absurd, they fairly imposed the necessity of trying Aunt Maud again. One couldn't say to them, kind as she had been to them: "We'll meet, please, whenever you'll let us, at your house; but we count on you to help us to keep it secret." They must in other terms inevitably speak to Aunt Maud—it would be of the last awkwardness to ask them not to: Kate had embraced all this in her choice of speaking first. What Kate embraced altogether was indeed wonderful to-day for Densher, though he perhaps struck himself rather as getting it out of her piece by piece than as receiving it in a steady light. He had always felt, however, that the more he asked of her the more he found her prepared, as he imaged it, to hand out. He had said to her more than once even before his absence: "You keep the key of the cupboard, and I foresee that when we're married you'll dole me out my sugar by lumps." She had replied that she rejoiced in his assumption that sugar would be his diet, and the domestic arrangement so prefigured might have seemed already to prevail. The supply from the cupboard at this hour was doubtless, of a truth, not altogether cloyingly sweet; but it met in a manner his immediate requirements. If her explanations at any rate prompted questions the questions no more exhausted them than they exhausted her patience. And they were naturally, of the series, the simpler; as for instance in his taking it from her that Miss Theale then could do nothing for them. He frankly brought out what he had ventured to think possible. "If we can't meet here and we've really exhausted the charms of the open air and the crowd, some such little raft in the wreck, some occasional opportunity like that of Tuesday, has been present to me these two days as better than nothing. But if our friends are so accountable to this house of course there's no more to be said. And it's one more nail, thank God, in the coffin of our odious delay." He was but too glad without more ado to point the moral. "Now I hope you see we can't work it anyhow."

If she laughed for this—and her spirits seemed really high— it was because of the opportunity that, at the hotel, he had most shown himself as enjoying. "Your idea's beautiful when one remembers that you hadn't a word except for Milly." But she was as beautifully good-humoured. "You might of course get used to her—you *will*. You're quite right—so long as they're with us or near us." And she put it, lucidly, that the dear things couldn't *help*, simply as charming friends, giving them a lift. "They'll speak to Aunt Maud, but they won't shut their doors to us: that would be another matter. A friend always helps—and she's a friend." She had left Mrs. Stringham by this time out of the question; she had reduced it to Milly. "Besides, she particularly likes us. She particularly likes *you*. I say, old boy, make something of that." He felt her dodging the ultimatum he had just made sharp, his definite reminder of how little, at the best, they could work it; but there were certain of his remarks—those mostly of the sharper penetration— that it had been quite her practice from the first not formally, not reverently to notice. She showed the effect of them in ways less trite. This was what happened now: he didn't think in truth that she wasn't really minding. She took him up, none the less, on a minor question. "You say we can't meet here, but you see it's just what we do. What could be more lovely than this?"

It wasn't to torment him—that again he didn't believe; but he had to come to the house in some discomfort, so that he frowned a little at her calling it thus a luxury. Wasn't there an element in it of coming back into bondage? The bondage might be veiled and varnished, but he knew in his bones how little the very highest privileges of Lancaster Gate could ever be a sign of their freedom. They were upstairs, in one of the smaller apartments of state, a room arranged as a boudoir, but visibly unused—it defied familiarity—and furnished in the ugliest of blues. He had immediately looked with interest at the closed doors, and Kate had met his interest with the assurance that it was all right, that Aunt Maud did them justice—so far, that was, as this particular time was concerned; that they should be alone and have nothing to fear. But the fresh allusion to this that he had drawn from her acted on him now more directly, brought him closer still to the question. They *were* alone—it *was* all right: he took in anew the shut doors and the permitted privacy, the solid stillness of the great house. They connected themselves on the spot with something made doubly vivid in him by the whole present play of her charming strong will. What it amounted to was that he couldn't have her—hanged if he could!—evasive. He couldn't and he wouldn't—wouldn't have her inconvenient and elusive. He didn't want her deeper than himself, fine as it might be as wit or as character; he wanted to keep her where their communications would be straight and easy and their intercourse independent. The effect of this was to make him say in a moment: "Will you take me just as I am?"

She turned a little pale for the tone of truth in it—which qualified to his sense delightfully the strength of her will; and the pleasure he found in this was not the less for her breaking out after an instant into a strain that stirred him more than any she had ever used with him. "Ah do let me try myself! I assure you I see my way—so don't spoil it: wait for me and give me time. Dear man," Kate said, "only believe in me, and it will be beautiful."

He hadn't come back to hear her talk of his believing in her as if he didn't; but he had come back—and it all was upon him now—to seize her with a sudden intensity that her manner of pleading with him had made, as happily appeared, irresistible. He laid strong hands upon her to say, almost in anger, "Do you love me, love me, love me?" and she closed her eyes as with the sense that he might strike her but that she could gratefully take it. Her surrender was her response, her response her surrender; and, though scarce hearing what she said, he so profited by these things that it could for the time be ever so intimately appreciable to him that he was keeping her. The long embrace in which they held each other was the rout of evasion, and he took from it the certitude that what she had from him was real to her. It was stronger than an uttered vow, and the name he was to give it in afterthought was that she had been sublimely sincere. *That* was all he asked—sincerity making a basis that would bear almost anything. This settled so much, and settled it so thoroughly, that there was nothing left to ask her to swear to. Oaths and vows apart, now they could talk. It seemed in fact only now that their questions were put on the table. He had taken up more expressly at the end of five minutes her plea for her own plan, and it was marked that the difference made by the passage just enacted was a difference in favour of her choice of means. Means had somehow suddenly become a detail—her province and her care; it had grown more consistently vivid that her intelligence was one with her passion. "I certainly don't want," he said—and he could say it with a smile of indulgence—"to be all the while bringing it up that I don't trust you."

"I should hope not! What do you think I want to do?"

He had really at this to make out a little what he thought, and the first thing that put itself in evidence was of course the oddity, after all, of their game, to which he could but frankly allude. "We're doing, at the best, in trying to temporise in so special a way, a thing most people would call us fools for." But his visit passed, all the same, without his again attempting to make "just as he was" serve. He had no more money just as he was than he had had just as he had been, or than he should have, probably, when it came to that, just as he always would be; whereas she, on her side, in comparison with her state of some months before, had measureably more to relinquish. He easily saw how their meeting at Lancaster Gate gave more of an accent to that quantity than their meeting at stations or in parks; and yet on the other hand he couldn't urge this against it. If Mrs. Lowder was indifferent her indifference added in a manner to what Kate's taking him as he was would call on her to sacrifice. Such in fine was her art with him that she seemed to put the question of their still waiting into quite other terms than the terms of ugly blue, of florid Sèvres, of complicated brass, in which their boudoir expressed it. She said almost all in fact by saying, on this article of Aunt Maud, after he had once more pressed her, that when he should see her, as must inevitably soon happen, he would understand. "Do you mean," he asked at this, "that there's any *definite* sign of her coming round? I'm not talking," he explained, "of mere hypocrisies in her, or mere brave duplicities. Remember, after all, that supremely clever as we are, and as strong a team, I admit, as there is going—remember that she can play with us quite as much as we play with her."

"She doesn't want to play with *me*, my dear," Kate lucidly replied; "she doesn't want to make me suffer a bit more than she need. She cares for me too much, and everything she does or doesn't do has a value. *This* has a value—her being as she has been about us to-day. I believe she's in her room, where she's keeping strictly to herself while you're here with me. But that isn't 'playing'—not a bit."

"What is it then," the young man returned—"from the moment it isn't her blessing and a cheque?"

Kate was complete. "It's simply her absence of smallness. There *is* something in her above trifles. She *generally* trusts us; she doesn't propose to hunt us into corners; and if we frankly ask for a thing—why," said Kate, "she shrugs, but she lets it go. She has really but one fault—she's indifferent, on such ground as she has taken about us, to details. However," the girl cheerfully went on, "it isn't in detail we fight her."

"It seems to me," Densher brought out after a moment's thought of this, "that it's in detail we deceive her"—a speech that, as soon as he had uttered it, applied itself for him, as also visibly for his companion, to the afterglow of their recent embrace.

Any confusion attaching to this adventure, however, dropped from Kate, whom, as he could see with sacred joy, it must take more than that to make compunctious. "I don't say we can do it again. I mean," she explained, "meet here."

Densher indeed had been wondering where they could do it again. If Lancaster Gate was so limited that issue reappeared. "I mayn't come back at all?"

"Certainly—to see her. It's she, really," his companion smiled, "who's in love with you."

But it made him—a trifle more grave—look at her a moment. "Don't make out, you know, that every one's in love with me."

She hesitated. "I don't say every one."

"You said just now Miss Theale."

"I said she liked you—yes."

"Well, it comes to the same thing." With which, however, he pursued: "Of course I ought to thank Mrs. Lowder in person. I mean for *this*—as from myself."

"Ah but, you know, not too much!" She had an ironic gaiety for the implications of his "this," besides wishing to insist on a general prudence. "She'll wonder what you're thanking her for!"

Densher did justice to both considerations. "Yes, I can't very well tell her all."

It was perhaps because he said it so gravely that Kate was again in a manner amused. Yet she gave out light. "You can't very well 'tell' her anything, and that doesn't matter. Only be nice to her. Please her; make her see how clever you are—only without letting her see that you're trying. If you're charming to her you've nothing else to do."

But she oversimplified too. "I can be 'charming' to her, so far as I see, only by letting her suppose I give you up—which I'll be hanged if I do! It *is*," he said with feeling, "a game."

"Of course it's a game. But she'll never suppose you give me up—or I give *you*—if you keep reminding her how you enjoy our interviews."

"Then if she has to see us as obstinate and constant," Densher asked, "what good does it do?"

Kate was for a moment checked. "What good does what—?"

"Does my pleasing her—does anything. I *can't*," he impatiently declared, "please her."

Kate looked at him hard again, disappointed at his want of consistency; but it appeared to determine in her something better than a mere complaint. "Then *I* can! Leave it to me." With which she came to him under the compulsion, again, that had united them shortly before, and took hold of him in her urgency to the same tender purpose. It was her form of entreaty renewed and repeated, which made after all, as he met it, their great fact clear. And it somehow clarified *all* things so to possess each other. The effect of it was that, once more, on these terms, he could only be generous. He had so on the spot then left everything to her that she reverted in the course of a few moments to one of her previous—and as positively seemed —her most precious ideas. "You accused me just now of saying that Milly's in love with you. Well, if you come to that, I do say it. So there you are. That's the good she'll do us. It makes a basis for her seeing you—so that she'll help us to go on."

Densher stared—she was wondrous all round. "And what sort of a basis does it make for my seeing *her*?"

"Oh I don't mind!" Kate smiled.

"Don't mind my leading her on?"

She put it differently. "Don't mind her leading *you*."

"Well, she won't—so it's nothing not to mind. But how can that 'help,'" he pursued, "with what she knows?"

"What she knows? That needn't prevent."

He wondered. "Prevent her loving us?"

"Prevent her helping you. She's *like* that," Kate Croy explained.

It took indeed some understanding. "Making nothing of the fact that I love another?"

"Making everything," said Kate. "To console you."

"But for what?"

"For not getting your other."

He continued to stare. "But how does she know—?"

"That you *won't* get her? She doesn't; but on the other hand she doesn't know you will. Meanwhile she sees you baffled, for she knows of Aunt Maud's stand. *That*"—Kate was lucid—"gives her the chance to be nice to you."

"And what does it give *me*," the young man none the less rationally asked, "the chance to be? A brute of a humbug to her?"

Kate so possessed her facts, as it were, that she smiled at his violence. "You'll extraordinarily like her. She's exquisite. And there are reasons. I mean others."

"What others?"

"Well, I'll tell you another time. Those I give you," the girl added, "are enough to go on with."

"To go on to what?"

"Why, to seeing her again—say as soon as you can: which, moreover, on all grounds, is no more than decent of you."

He of course took in her reference, and he had fully in mind what had passed between them in New York. It had been no great quantity, but it had made distinctly at the time for his pleasure; so that anything in the nature of an appeal in the name of it could have a slight kindling consequence. "Oh I shall naturally call again without delay. Yes," said Densher, "her being in love with me is nonsense; but I must, quite independently of that, make every acknowledgement of favours received."

It appeared practically all Kate asked. "Then you see. I shall meet you there."

"I don't quite see," he presently returned, "why she should wish to receive *you* for it."

"She receives me for myself—that is for *her* self. She thinks no end of me. That I should have to drum it into you!"

Yet still he didn't take it. "Then I confess she's beyond me."

Well, Kate could but leave it as she saw it. "She regards me as already—in these few weeks—her dearest friend. It's quite separate. We're in, she and I, ever so deep." And it was to confirm this that, as if it had flashed upon her that he was somewhere at sea, she threw out at last her own real light. "She doesn't of course know I care for *you*. She thinks I care so little that it's not worth speaking of." That he *had* been somewhere at sea these remarks made quickly clear, and Kate hailed the effect with surprise. "Have you been supposing that she does know—?"

"About our situation? Certainly, if you're such friends as you show me—and if you haven't otherwise represented it to her." She uttered at this such a sound of impatience that he stood artlessly vague. "You *have* denied it to her?"

She threw up her arms at his being so backward. "'Denied it'? My dear man, we've never spoken of you."

"Never, never?"

"Strange as it may appear to your glory—never."

He couldn't piece it together. "But won't Mrs. Lowder have spoken?"

"Very probably. But of *you*. Not of me."

This struck him as obscure. "How does she know me but as part and parcel of you?"

"How?" Kate triumphantly asked. "Why exactly to make nothing of it, to have nothing to do with it, to stick consistently to her line about it. Aunt Maud's line is to keep all reality out of our relation—that is out of my being in danger from you—by not having so much as suspected or heard of it. She'll get rid of it, as she believes, by ignoring it and sinking it—if she only does so hard enough. Therefore *she*, in her manner, 'denies' it if you will. That's how she knows you otherwise than as part and parcel of me. She won't for a moment have allowed either to Mrs. Stringham or to Milly that I've in any way, as they say, distinguished you."

"And you don't suppose," said Densher, "that they must have made it out for themselves?"

"No, my dear, I don't; not even," Kate declared, "after Milly's so funnily bumping against us on Tuesday."

"She doesn't see from *that*—?"

"That you're, so to speak, mad about me. Yes, she sees, no doubt, that you regard me with a complacent eye—for you show it, I think, always too much and too crudely. But nothing beyond that. *I* don't show it too much; I don't perhaps—to please you completely where others are concerned— show it enough."

"Can you show it or not as you like?" Densher demanded.

It pulled her up a little, but she came out resplendent. "Not where *you* are concerned. Beyond seeing that you're rather gone," she went on, "Milly only sees that I'm decently good to you."

"Very good indeed she must think it!"

"Very good indeed then. She easily sees me," Kate smiled, "as very good indeed."

The young man brooded. "But in a sense to take some explaining."

"Then I explain." She was really fine; it came back to her essential plea for her freedom of action and his beauty of trust. "I mean," she added, "I *will* explain."

"And what will *I* do?"

"Recognise the difference it must make if she thinks." But

here in truth Kate faltered. It was his silence alone that, for the moment, took up her apparent meaning; and before he again spoke she had returned to remembrance and prudence. They were now not to forget that, Aunt Maud's liberality having put them on their honour, they mustn't spoil their case by abusing it. He must leave her in time; they should probably find it would help them. But she came back to Milly too. "Mind you go to see her."

Densher still, however, took up nothing of this. "Then I may come again?"

"For Aunt Maud—as much as you like. But we can't again," said Kate, "play her *this* trick. I can't see you here alone."

"Then where?"

"Go to see Milly," she for all satisfaction repeated.

"And what good will that do me?"

"Try it and you'll see."

"You mean you'll manage to be there?" Densher asked. "Say you are, how will that give us privacy?"

"Try it—you'll see," the girl once more returned. "We must manage as we can."

"That's precisely what *I* feel. It strikes me we might manage better." His idea of this was a thing that made him an instant hesitate; yet he brought it out with conviction. "Why won't you come to *me*?"

It was a question her troubled eyes seemed to tell him he was scarce generous in expecting her definitely to answer, and by looking to him to wait at least she appealed to something that she presently made him feel as his pity. It was on that special shade of tenderness that he thus found himself thrown back; and while he asked of his spirit and of his flesh just what concession they could arrange she pressed him yet again on the subject of her singular remedy for their embarrassment. It might have been irritating had she ever struck him as having in her mind a stupid corner. "You'll see," she said, "the difference it will make."

Well, since she wasn't stupid she was intelligent; it was he who was stupid—the proof of which was that he would do what she liked. But he made a last effort to understand, her allusion to the "difference" bringing him round to it. He indeed caught at something subtle but strong even as he spoke. "Is what you meant a moment ago that the difference will be in her being made to believe you hate me?"

Kate, however, had simply, for this gross way of putting it, one of her more marked shows of impatience; with which in fact she sharply closed their discussion. He opened the door on a sign from her, and she accompanied him to the top of the stairs with an air of having so put their possibilities before him that questions were idle and doubts perverse. "I verily believe I *shall* hate you if you spoil for me the beauty of what I see!"

III

H E WAS really, notwithstanding, to hear more from her of
what she saw; and the very next occasion had for him
still other surprises than that. He received from Mrs. Lowder
on the morning after his visit to Kate the telegraphic expression of a hope that he might be free to dine with them that
evening; and his freedom affected him as fortunate even though
in some degree qualified by her missive. "Expecting American
friends whom I'm so glad to find you know!" His knowledge
of American friends was clearly an accident of which he was to
taste the fruit to the last bitterness. This apprehension, however, we hasten to add, enjoyed for him, in the immediate
event, a certain merciful shrinkage; the immediate event being
that, at Lancaster Gate, five minutes after his due arrival, prescribed him for eight-thirty, Mrs. Stringham came in alone.
The long daylight, the postponed lamps, the habit of the hour,
made dinners late and guests still later; so that, punctual as he
was, he had found Mrs. Lowder alone, with Kate herself not
yet in the field. He had thus had with her several bewildering
moments—bewildering by reason, fairly, of their tacit invitation to him to be supernaturally simple. This was exactly, goodness knew, what he wanted to be; but he had never had it so
largely and freely—*so* supernaturally simply, for that matter—
imputed to him as of easy achievement. It was a particular in
which Aunt Maud appeared to offer herself as an example, appeared to say quite agreeably: "What I want of you, don't you
see? is to be just exactly as *I* am." The quantity of the article
required was what might especially have caused him to stagger
—he liked so, in general, the quantities in which Mrs. Lowder
dealt. He would have liked as well to ask her how feasible she
supposed it for a poor young man to resemble her at any
point; but he had after all soon enough perceived that he was
doing as she wished by letting his wonder show just a little as
silly. He was conscious moreover of a small strange dread of
the results of discussion with her—strange, truly, because it
was her good nature, not her asperity, that he feared. Asperity
might have made him angry—in which there was always a

comfort; good nature, in his conditions, had a tendency to make him ashamed—which Aunt Maud indeed, wonderfully, liking him for himself, quite struck him as having guessed. To spare him therefore she also avoided discussion; she kept him down by refusing to quarrel with him. This was what she now proposed to him to enjoy, and his secret discomfort was his sense that on the whole it was what would best suit him. Being kept down was a bore, but his great dread, verily, was of being ashamed, which was a thing distinct; and it mattered but little that he was ashamed of that too.

It was of the essence of his position that in such a house as this the tables could always be turned on him. "What do you offer, what do you offer?"—the place, however muffled in convenience and decorum, constantly hummed for him with that thick irony. The irony was a renewed reference to obvious bribes, and he had already seen how little aid came to him from denouncing the bribes as ugly in form. That was what the precious metals—they alone—could afford to be; it was vain enough for him accordingly to try to impart a gloss to his own comparative brummagem. The humiliation of this impotence was precisely what Aunt Maud sought to mitigate for him by keeping him down; and as her effort to that end had doubtless never yet been so visible he had probably never felt so definitely placed in the world as while he waited with her for her half-dozen other guests. She welcomed him genially back from the States, as to his view of which her few questions, though not coherent, were comprehensive, and he had the amusement of seeing in her, as through a clear glass, the outbreak of a plan and the sudden consciousness of a curiosity. She became aware of America, under his eyes, as a possible scene for social operations; the idea of a visit to the wonderful country had clearly but just occurred to her, yet she was talking of it, at the end of a minute, as her favourite dream. He didn't believe in it, but he pretended to; this helped her as well as anything else to treat him as harmless and blameless. She was so engaged, with the further aid of a complete absence of allusions, when the highest effect was given her method by the beautiful entrance of Kate. The method therefore received support all round, for no young man could have been less formidable than the person to the relief of whose shyness her niece ostensibly came.

The ostensible, in Kate, struck him altogether, on this occasion, as prodigious; while scarcely less prodigious, for that matter, was his own reading, on the spot, of the relation between his companions—a relation lighted for him by the straight look, not exactly loving nor lingering, yet searching and soft, that, on the part of their hostess, the girl had to reckon with as she advanced. It took her in from head to foot, and in doing so it told a story that made poor Densher again the least bit sick: it marked so something with which Kate habitually and consummately reckoned.

That was the story—that she was always, for her beneficent dragon, under arms; living up, every hour, but especially at festal hours, to the "value" Mrs. Lowder had attached to her. High and fixed, this estimate ruled on each occasion at Lancaster Gate the social scene; so that he now recognised in it something like the artistic idea, the plastic substance, imposed by tradition, by genius, by criticism, in respect to a given character, on a distinguished actress. As such a person was to dress the part, to walk, to look, to speak, in every way to express, the part, so all this was what Kate was to do for the character she had undertaken, under her aunt's roof, to represent. It was made up, the character, of definite elements and touches—things all perfectly ponderable to criticism; and the way for her to meet criticism was evidently at the start to be sure her make-up had had the last touch and that she looked at least no worse than usual. Aunt Maud's appreciation of that to-night was indeed managerial, and the performer's own contribution fairly that of the faultless soldier on parade. Densher saw himself for the moment as in his purchased stall at the play; the watchful manager was in the depths of a box and the poor actress in the glare of the footlights. But she *passed*, the poor performer—he could see how she always passed; her wig, her paint, her jewels, every mark of her expression impeccable, and her entrance accordingly greeted with the proper round of applause. Such impressions as we thus note for Densher come and go, it must be granted, in very much less time than notation demands; but we may none the less make the point that there was, still further, time among them for him to feel almost too scared to take part in the ovation. He struck himself as having lost, for the minute, his presence of mind—so that in

any case he only stared in silence at the older woman's technical challenge and at the younger one's disciplined face. It was as
if the drama—it thus came to him, for the fact of a drama there
was no blinking—was between *them*, them quite preponderantly; with Merton Densher relegated to mere spectatorship, a
paying place in front, and one of the most expensive. This was
why his appreciation had turned for the instant to fear—had
just turned, as we have said, to sickness; and in spite of the fact
that the disciplined face did offer him over the footlights, as he
believed, the small gleam, fine faint but exquisite, of a special
intelligence. So might a practised performer, even when raked
by double-barrelled glasses, seem to be all in her part and yet
convey a sign to the person in the house she loved best.

The drama, at all events, as Densher saw it, meanwhile went
on—amplified soon enough by the advent of two other guests,
stray gentlemen both, stragglers in the rout of the season, who
visibly presented themselves to Kate during the next moments
as subjects for a like impersonal treatment and sharers in a like
usual mercy. At opposite ends of the social course, they dis-
played, in respect to the "figure" that each, in his way, made,
one the expansive, the other the contractile effect of the perfect
white waistcoat. A scratch company of two innocuous youths
and a pacified veteran was therefore what now offered itself to
Mrs. Stringham, who rustled in a little breathless and full of
the compunction of having had to come alone. Her companion, at the last moment, had been indisposed—positively not
well enough, and so had packed her off, insistently, with excuses, with wild regrets. This circumstance of their charming
friend's illness was the first thing Kate took up with Densher
on their being able after dinner, without bravado, to have ten
minutes "naturally," as she called it—which wasn't what *he* did
—together; but it was already as if the young man had, by an
odd impression, throughout the meal, not been wholly deprived of Miss Theale's participation. Mrs. Lowder had made
dear Milly the topic, and it proved, on the spot, a topic as familiar to the enthusiastic younger as to the sagacious older
man. Any knowledge they might lack Mrs. Lowder's niece was
moreover alert to supply, while Densher himself was freely appealed to as the most privileged, after all, of the group. Wasn't

it he who had in a manner invented the wonderful creature—through having seen her first, caught her in her native jungle? Hadn't he more or less paved the way for her by his prompt recognition of her rarity, by preceding her, in a friendly spirit—as he had the "ear" of society—with a sharp flashlight or two?

He met, poor Densher, these enquiries as he could, listening with interest, yet with discomfort; wincing in particular, dry journalist as he was, to find it seemingly supposed of him that he had put his pen—oh his "pen!"—at the service of private distinction. The ear of society?—they were talking, or almost, as if he had publicly paragraphed a modest young lady. They dreamt dreams, in truth, he appeared to perceive, that fairly waked *him* up, and he settled himself in his place both to resist his embarrassment and to catch the full revelation. His embarrassment came naturally from the fact that if he could claim no credit for Miss Theale's success, so neither could he gracefully insist on his not having been concerned with her. What touched him most nearly was that the occasion took on somehow the air of a commemorative banquet, a feast to celebrate a brilliant if brief career. There was of course more said about the heroine than if she hadn't been absent, and he found himself rather stupefied at the range of Milly's triumph. Mrs. Lowder had wonders to tell of it; the two wearers of the waistcoat, either with sincerity or with hypocrisy, professed in the matter an equal expertness; and Densher at last seemed to know himself in presence of a social "case." It was Mrs. Stringham, obviously, whose testimony would have been most invoked hadn't she been, as her friend's representative, rather confined to the function of inhaling the incense; so that Kate, who treated her beautifully, smiling at her, cheering and consoling her across the table, appeared benevolently both to speak and to interpret for her. Kate spoke as if she wouldn't perhaps understand *their* way of appreciating Milly, but would let them none the less, in justice to their good will, express it in their coarser fashion. Densher himself wasn't unconscious in respect to this of a certain broad brotherhood with Mrs. Stringham; wondering indeed, while he followed the talk, how it might move American nerves. He had only heard of them before, but in his recent tour he had caught them in the remarkable fact, and there was now a moment or two when it came to him that he had perhaps—and not in the way of an escape—taken a lesson from them.

They quivered, clearly, they hummed and drummed, they leaped and bounded in Mrs. Stringham's typical organism—this lady striking him as before all things excited, as, in the native phrase, keyed-up, to a perception of more elements in the occasion than he was himself able to count. She was accessible to sides of it, he imagined, that were as yet obscure to him; for, though she unmistakeably rejoiced and soared, he none the less saw her at moments as even more agitated than pleasure required. It was a state of emotion in her that could scarce represent simply an impatience to report at home. Her little dry New England brightness—he had "sampled" all the shades of the American complexity, if complexity it were—had its actual reasons for finding relief most in silence; so that before the subject was changed he perceived (with surprise at the others) that they had given her enough of it. He had quite had enough of it himself by the time he was asked if it were true that their friend had really not made in her own country the mark she had chalked so large in London. It was Mrs. Lowder herself who addressed him that enquiry; while he scarce knew if he were the more impressed with her launching it under Mrs. Stringham's nose or with her hope that he would allow to London the honour of discovery. The less expansive of the white waistcoats propounded the theory that they saw in London—for all that was said—much further than in the States: it wouldn't be the first time, he urged, that they had taught the Americans to appreciate (especially when it was funny) some native product. He didn't mean that Miss Theale was funny—though she was weird, and this was precisely her magic; but it might very well be that New York, in having her to show, hadn't been aware of its luck. There *were* plenty of people who were nothing over there and yet were awfully taken up in England; just as—to make the balance right, thank goodness—they sometimes sent out beauties and celebrities who left the Briton cold. The Briton's temperature in truth wasn't to be calculated—a formulation of the matter that was not reached, however, without producing in Mrs. Stringham a final feverish sally. She announced that if the point of view for a proper admiration of her young friend *had* seemed to fail a little in New York, there was no manner of doubt of her having carried Boston by storm. It pointed the moral that Boston, for the finer taste, left New York nowhere; and the good lady, as the exponent of this doctrine—which she set forth at a certain length—made, obviously, to Densher's mind, her nearest approach to supplying the weirdness in which Milly's absence had left them deficient. She made it indeed effective for him by suddenly addressing him. "You know nothing, sir—but not the least little bit—about my friend."

He hadn't pretended he did, but there was a purity of reproach in Mrs. Stringham's face and tone, a purity charged apparently with solemn meanings; so that for a little, small as had been his claim, he couldn't but feel that she exaggerated. He wondered what she did mean, but while doing so he defended himself. "I certainly don't know enormously much—beyond her having been most kind to me, in New York, as a poor bewildered and newly landed alien, and my having tremendously appreciated it." To which he added, he scarce knew why, what had an immediate success. "Remember, Mrs. Stringham, that you weren't then present."

"Ah there you are!" said Kate with much gay expression, though what it expressed he failed at the time to make out.

"You weren't present *then*, dearest," Mrs. Lowder richly concurred. "You don't know," she continued with mellow gaiety, "how far things may have gone."

It made the little woman, he could see, really lose her head. She had more things in that head than any of them in any other; unless perhaps it were Kate, whom he felt as indirectly watching him during this foolish passage, though it pleased him—and because of the foolishness—not to meet her eyes. He met Mrs. Stringham's, which affected him: with her he could on occasion clear it up—a sense produced by the mute communion between them and really the beginning, as the event was to show, of something extraordinary. It was even already a little the effect of this communion that Mrs. Stringham perceptibly faltered in her retort to Mrs. Lowder's joke. "Oh it's precisely my point that Mr. Densher *can't* have had vast opportunities." And then she smiled at him. "I wasn't away, you know, long."

It made everything, in the oddest way in the world, immediately right for him. "And I wasn't *there* long, either." He positively saw with it that nothing for him, so far as she was concerned, would again be wrong. "She's beautiful, but I don't say she's easy to know."

"Ah she's a thousand and one things!" replied the good lady, as if now to keep well with him.

He asked nothing better. "She was off with you to these parts before I knew it. I myself was off too—away off to wonderful parts, where I had endlessly more to see."

"But you didn't forget her!" Aunt Maud interposed with almost menacing archness.

"No, of course I didn't forget her. One doesn't forget such charming impressions. But I never," he lucidly maintained, "chattered to others about her."

"She'll thank you for that, sir," said Mrs. Stringham with a flushed firmness.

"Yet doesn't silence in such a case," Aunt Maud blandly enquired, "very often quite prove the depth of the impression?"

He would have been amused, hadn't he been slightly displeased, at all they seemed desirous to fasten on him. "Well, the impression was as deep as you like. But I really want Miss Theale to know," he pursued for Mrs. Stringham, "that I don't figure by any consent of my own as an authority about her."

Kate came to his assistance—if assistance it was—before their friend had had time to meet this charge. "You're right about her not being easy to know. One *sees* her with intensity —sees her more than one sees almost any one; but then one discovers that that isn't knowing her and that one may know better a person whom one doesn't 'see,' as I say, half so much."

The discrimination was interesting, but it brought them back to the fact of her success; and it was at that comparatively gross circumstance, now so fully placed before them, that Milly's anxious companion sat and looked—looked very much as some spectator in an old-time circus might have watched the oddity of a Christian maiden, in the arena, mildly, caressingly, martyred. It was the nosing and fumbling not of lions and tigers but of domestic animals let loose as for the joke. Even the joke made Mrs. Stringham uneasy, and her mute communion with Densher, to which we have alluded, was more and more determined by it. He wondered afterwards if Kate had made this out; though it was not indeed till much later on that he found himself, in thought, dividing the things she might have been conscious of from the things she must have missed. If she actually missed, at any rate, Mrs. Stringham's discomfort, that but showed how her own idea held her. Her own idea was, by insisting on the fact of the girl's prominence as a feature of the season's end, to keep Densher in relation, for the rest of them, both to present and to past. "It's everything that has happened *since* that makes you naturally a little shy about her. You don't know what has happened since, but we do; we've seen it and followed it; we've a little been *of* it." The great thing for him, at this, as Kate gave it, *was* in fact quite irresistibly that the case was a real one—the kind of thing that, when one's patience was shorter than one's curiosity, one had vaguely taken for possible in London, but in which one had never been even to this small extent concerned. The little American's sudden social adventure, her happy and, no doubt, harmless flourish, had probably been favoured by several accidents, but it had been favoured above all by the simple springboard of the scene, by one of those common caprices of the numberless foolish flock, gregarious movements as inscrutable as ocean-currents. The huddled herd had drifted to her blindly —it might as blindly have drifted away. There had been of course a signal, but the great reason was probably the absence at the moment of a larger lion. The bigger beast would come and the smaller would then incontinently vanish. It was at all events characteristic, and what was of the essence of it was grist to his scribbling mill, matter for his journalising hand. That hand already, in intention, played over it, the "motive," as a sign of the season, a feature of the time, of the purely expeditious and rough-and-tumble nature of the social boom. The boom as in *itself* required—that would be the note; the subject of the process a comparatively minor question. Anything was boomable enough when nothing else was more so: the author of the "rotten" book, the beauty who was no beauty, the heiress who was only that, the stranger who was for the most part saved from being inconveniently strange but by being inconveniently familiar, the American whose Americanism had been long desperately discounted, the creature in fine as to whom spangles or spots of any sufficiently marked and exhibited sort could be loudly enough predicated.

So he judged at least, within his limits, and the idea that what he had thus caught in the fact was the trick of fashion and the tone of society went so far as to make him take up again his sense of independence. He had supposed himself civilised; but if this was civilisation—! One could smoke one's pipe outside when twaddle was within. He had rather avoided, as we have remarked, Kate's eyes, but there came a moment when he would fairly have liked to put it, across the table, to her: "I say, light of my life, is *this* the great world?" There came another, it must be added—and doubtless as a result of something that, over the cloth, did hang between them—when she struck him as having quite answered: "Dear no—for what do you take me? Not the least little bit: only a poor silly, though quite harmless, imitation." What she might have passed for saying, however, was practically merged in what she did say, for she came overtly to his aid, very much as if guessing some of his thoughts. She enunciated, to relieve his bewilderment, the obvious truth that you couldn't leave London for three months at that time of the year and come back to find your friends just where they were. As they had *of course* been jigging away they might well be so red in the face that you wouldn't know them. She reconciled in fine his disclaimer about Milly with that honour of having discovered her which it was vain for him modestly to shirk. He *had* unearthed her, but it was they, all of them together, who had developed her. She was always a charmer, one of the greatest ever seen, but she wasn't the person he had "backed."

Densher was to feel sure afterwards that Kate had had in these pleasantries no conscious, above all no insolent purpose of making light of poor Susan Shepherd's property in their young friend—which property, by such remarks, was very much pushed to the wall; but he was also to know that Mrs. Stringham had secretly resented them, Mrs. Stringham holding the opinion, of which he was ultimately to have a glimpse, that all the Kate Croys in Christendom were but dust for the feet of her Milly. That, it was true, would be what she must reveal only when driven to her last entrenchments and well cornered in her passion—the rare passion of friendship, the sole passion of her little life save the one other, more imperturbably cerebral, that she entertained for the art of Guy de Maupassant. She slipped in the observation that her Milly was incapable of change, was just exactly, on the contrary, the same Milly; but this made little difference in the drift of Kate's contention. She was perfectly kind to Susie: it was as if she positively knew her as handicapped for any disagreement by feeling that she, Kate, had "type," and by being committed to admiration of type. Kate had occasion subsequently—she found it somehow—to mention to our young man Milly's having spoken to her of this view on the good lady's part. She would like—Milly had had it from her—to put Kate Croy in a book and see what she could so do with her. "Chop me up fine or serve me whole"— it was a way of being got at that Kate professed she dreaded. It would be Mrs. Stringham's, however, she understood, because Mrs. Stringham, oddly, felt that with such stuff as the strange English girl was made of, stuff that (in spite of Maud Manningham, who was full of sentiment) she had never known, there was none other to be employed. These things were of later evidence, yet Densher might even then have felt them in the air. They were practically in it already when Kate, waiving the question of her friend's chemical change, wound up with the comparatively unobjectionable proposition that he must now, having missed so much, take them all up, on trust, further on. He met it peacefully, a little perhaps as an example to Mrs. Stringham—"Oh as far on as you like!" This even had its effect: Mrs. Stringham appropriated as much of it as might be meant for herself. The nice thing about her was that she could measure how much; so that by the time dinner was over they had really covered ground.

IV

THE younger of the other men, it afterwards appeared, was
most in his element at the piano; so that they had coffee
and comic songs upstairs—the gentlemen, temporarily relin-
quished, submitting easily in this interest to Mrs. Lowder's
parting injunction not to sit too tight. Our especial young
man sat tighter when restored to the drawing-room; he made
it out perfectly with Kate that they might, off and on, foregather without offence. He had perhaps stronger needs in this
general respect than she; but she had better names for the
scant risks to which she consented. It was the blessing of a big
house that intervals were large and, of an August night, that
windows were open; whereby, at a given moment, on the wide
balcony, with the songs sufficiently sung, Aunt Maud could
hold her little court more freshly. Densher and Kate, during
these moments, occupied side by side a small sofa—a luxury
formulated by the latter as the proof, under criticism, of their
remarkably good conscience. "To seem not to know each
other—once you're here—would be," the girl said, "to overdo
it"; and she arranged it charmingly that they *must* have some
passage to put Aunt Maud off the scent. She would be wondering otherwise what in the world they found their account
in. For Densher, none the less, the profit of snatched moments, snatched contacts, was partial and poor; there were in
particular at present more things in his mind than he could
bring out while watching the windows. It was true, on the
other hand, that she suddenly met most of them—and more
than he could see on the spot—by coming out for him with a
reference to Milly that was not in the key of those made at dinner. "She's not a bit right, you know. I mean in health. Just see
her to-night. I mean it looks grave. For you she would have
come, you know, if it had been at all possible."

He took this in such patience as he could muster. "What in
the world's the matter with her?"

But Kate continued without saying. "Unless indeed your
being here has been just a reason for her funking it."

"What in the world's the matter with her?" Densher asked again.

"Why just what I've told you—that she likes you so much."

"Then why should she deny herself the joy of meeting me?"

Kate cast about—it would take so long to explain. "And perhaps it's true that she *is* bad. She easily may be."

"Quite easily, I should say, judging by Mrs. Stringham, who's visibly preoccupied and worried."

"Visibly enough. Yet it mayn't," said Kate, "be only for that."

"For what then?"

But this question too, on thinking, she neglected. "Why, if it's anything real, doesn't that poor lady go home? She'd be anxious, and she has done all she need to be civil."

"I think," Densher remarked, "she has been quite beautifully civil."

It made Kate, he fancied, look at him the least bit harder; but she was already, in a manner, explaining. "Her preoccupation is probably on two different heads. One of them would make her hurry back, but the other makes her stay. She's commissioned to tell Milly all about you."

"Well then," said the young man between a laugh and a sigh, "I'm glad I felt, downstairs, a kind of 'drawing' to her. Wasn't I rather decent to her?"

"Awfully nice. You've instincts, you fiend. It's all," Kate declared, "as it should be."

"Except perhaps," he after a moment cynically suggested, "that she isn't getting much good of me now. Will she report to Milly on *this*?" And then as Kate seemed to wonder what "this" might be: "On our present disregard for appearances."

"Ah leave appearances to me!" She spoke in her high way. "I'll make them all right. Aunt Maud, moreover," she added, "has her so engaged that she won't notice." Densher felt, with this, that his companion had indeed perceptive flights he couldn't hope to match—had for instance another when she still subjoined: "And Mrs. Stringham's appearing to respond just in order to make that impression."

"Well," Densher dropped with some humour, "life's very interesting! I hope it's really as much so for you as you make it for others; I mean judging by what you make it for me. You seem to me to represent it as thrilling for *ces dames*, and in a different way for each: Aunt Maud, Susan Shepherd, Milly. But what *is*," he wound up, "the matter? Do you mean she's as ill as she looks?"

Kate's face struck him as replying at first that his derisive speech deserved no satisfaction; then she appeared to yield to a need of her own—the need to make the point that "as ill as she looked" was what Milly scarce could be. If she had been as ill as she looked she could scarce be a question with them, for her end would in that case be near. She believed herself nevertheless—and Kate couldn't help believing her too—seriously menaced. There was always the fact that they had been on the point of leaving town, the two ladies, and had suddenly been pulled up. "We bade them good-bye—or all but—Aunt Maud and I, the night before Milly, popping so very oddly into the National Gallery for a farewell look, found you and me together. They were then to get off a day or two later. But they've not got off—they're not getting off. When I see them—and I saw them this morning—they have showy reasons. They do mean to go, but they've postponed it." With which the girl brought out: "They've postponed it for *you*." He protested so far as a man might without fatuity, since a protest was itself credulous; but Kate, as ever, understood herself. "You've made Milly change her mind. She wants not to miss you—though she wants also not to show she wants you; which is why, as I hinted a moment ago, she may consciously have hung back to-night. She doesn't know when she may see you again—she doesn't know she ever may. She doesn't see the future. It has opened out before her in these last weeks as a dark confused thing."

Densher wondered. "After the tremendous time you've all been telling me she has had?"

"That's it. There's a shadow across it."

"The shadow, you consider, of some physical break-up?"

"Some physical break-down. Nothing less. She's scared. She has so much to lose. And she wants more."

"Ah well," said Densher with a sudden strange sense of discomfort, "couldn't one say to her that she can't have everything?"

"No—for one wouldn't want to. She really," Kate went on,

"has been somebody here. Ask Aunt Maud—you may think me prejudiced," the girl oddly smiled. "Aunt Maud will tell you—the world's before her. It has all come since you saw her, and it's a pity you've missed it, for it certainly would have amused you. She has really been a perfect success—I mean of course so far as possible in the scrap of time—and she has taken it like a perfect angel. If you can imagine an angel with a thumping bank-account you'll have the simplest expression of the kind of thing. Her fortune's absolutely huge; Aunt Maud has had all the facts, or enough of them, in the last confidence, from 'Susie,' and Susie speaks by book. Take them then, in the last confidence, from *me*. There she is." Kate expressed above all what it most came to. "It's open to her to make, you see, the very greatest marriage. I assure you we're not vulgar about her. Her possibilities are quite plain."

Densher showed he neither disbelieved nor grudged them. "But what good then on earth can I do her?"

Well, she had it ready. "You can console her."

"And for what?"

"For all that, if she's stricken, she must see swept away. I shouldn't care for her if she hadn't so much," Kate very simply said. And then as it made him laugh not quite happily: "I shouldn't trouble about her if there were one thing she did have." The girl spoke indeed with a noble compassion. "She has nothing."

"Not all the young dukes?"

"Well we must see—see if anything can come of them. She at any rate does love life. To have met a person like you," Kate further explained, "is to have felt you become, with all the other fine things, a part of life. Oh she has you arranged!"

"*You* have, it strikes me, my dear"—and he looked both detached and rueful. "Pray what am I to do with the dukes?"

"Oh the dukes will be disappointed!"

"Then why shan't I be?"

"You'll have expected less," Kate wonderfully smiled. "Besides, you *will* be. You'll have expected enough for that."

"Yet it's what you want to let me in for?"

"I want," said the girl, "to make things pleasant for her. I use, for the purpose, what I have. You're what I have of most precious, and you're therefore what I use most."

He looked at her long. "I wish I could use *you* a little more."
After which, as she continued to smile at him, "Is it a bad case
of lungs?" he asked.

Kate showed for a little as if she wished it might be. "Not
lungs, I think. Isn't consumption, taken in time, now curable?"

"People are, no doubt, patched up." But he wondered. "Do
you mean she has something that's past patching?" And before
she could answer: "It's really as if her appearance put her outside of such things—being, in spite of her youth, that of a person who has been through all it's conceivable she should be
exposed to. She affects one, I should say, as a creature saved
from a shipwreck. Such a creature may surely, in these days, on
the doctrine of chances, go to sea again with confidence. She
has *had* her wreck—she has met her adventure."

"Oh I grant you her wreck!"—Kate was all response so far.
"But do let her have still her adventure. There are wrecks that
are not adventures."

"Well—if there be also adventures that are not wrecks!"
Densher in short was willing, but he came back to his point.
"What I mean is that she has none of the effect—on one's
nerves or whatever—of an invalid."

Kate on her side did this justice. "No—that's the beauty of
her."

"The beauty—?"

"Yes, she's so wonderful. She won't show for that, any more
than your watch, when it's about to stop for want of being
wound up, gives you convenient notice or shows as different
from usual. She won't die, she won't live, by inches. She won't
smell, as it were, of drugs. She won't taste, as it were, of medicine. No one will know."

"Then what," he demanded, frankly mystified now, "are we
talking about? In what extraordinary state *is* she?"

Kate went on as if, at this, making it out in a fashion for herself. "I believe that if she's ill at all she's very ill. I believe that
if she's bad she's not a *little* bad. I can't tell you why, but that's
how I see her. She'll really live or she'll really not. She'll have it
all or she'll miss it all. Now I don't think she'll have it all."

Densher had followed this with his eyes upon her, her own
having thoughtfully wandered, and as if it were more impres-

sive than lucid. "You 'think' and you 'don't think,' and yet you remain all the while without an inkling of her complaint?"

"No, not without an inkling; but it's a matter in which I don't want knowledge. She moreover herself doesn't want one to want it: she has, as to what may be preying upon her, a kind of ferocity of modesty, a kind of—I don't know what to call it—intensity of pride. And then and then—" But with this she faltered.

"And then what?"

"I'm a brute about illness. I hate it. It's well for you, my dear," Kate continued, "that you're as sound as a bell."

"Thank you!" Densher laughed. "It's rather good then for yourself too that you're as strong as the sea."

She looked at him now a moment as for the selfish gladness of their young immunities. It was all they had together, but they had it at least without a flaw—each had the beauty, the physical felicity, the personal virtue, love and desire of the other. Yet it was as if that very consciousness threw them back the next moment into pity for the poor girl who had everything else in the world, the great genial good they, alas, didn't have, but failed on the other hand of this. "How we're talking about her!" Kate compunctiously sighed. But there were the facts. "From illness I keep away."

"But you don't—since here you are, in spite of all you say, in the midst of it."

"Ah I'm only watching—!"

"And putting me forward in your place? Thank you!"

"Oh," said Kate, "I'm breaking you in. Let it give you the measure of what I shall expect of you. One can't begin too soon."

She drew away, as from the impression of a stir on the balcony, the hand of which he had a minute before possessed himself; and the warning brought him back to attention. "You haven't even an idea if it's a case for surgery?"

"I dare say it may be; that is that if it comes to anything it may come to that. Of course she's in the highest hands."

"The doctors are after her then?"

"She's after *them*—it's the same thing. I think I'm free to say it now—she sees Sir Luke Strett."

It made him quickly wince. "Ah fifty thousand knives!" Then after an instant: "One seems to guess."

Yes, but she waved it away. "Don't guess. Only do as I tell you."

For a moment now, in silence, he took it all in, might have had it before him. "What you want of me then is to make up to a sick girl."

"Ah but you admit yourself that she doesn't affect you as sick. You understand moreover just how much—and just how little."

"It's amazing," he presently answered, "what you think I understand."

"Well, if you've brought me to it, my dear," she returned, "that has been your way of breaking *me* in. Besides which, so far as making up to her goes, plenty of others will."

Densher for a little, under this suggestion, might have been seeing their young friend on a pile of cushions and in a perpetual tea-gown, amid flowers and with drawn blinds, surrounded by the higher nobility. "Others can follow their tastes. Besides, others are free."

"But so are you, my dear!"

She had spoken with impatience, and her suddenly quitting him had sharpened it; in spite of which he kept his place, only looking up at her. "You're prodigious!"

"Of course I'm prodigious!"—and, as immediately happened, she gave a further sign of it that he fairly sat watching. The door from the lobby had, as she spoke, been thrown open for a gentleman who, immediately finding her within his view, advanced to greet her before the announcement of his name could reach her companion. Densher none the less felt himself brought quickly into relation; Kate's welcome to the visitor became almost precipitately an appeal to her friend, who slowly rose to meet it. "I don't know whether you know Lord Mark." And then for the other party: "Mr. Merton Densher—who has just come back from America."

"Oh!" said the other party while Densher said nothing—occupied as he mainly was on the spot with weighing the sound in question. He recognised it in a moment as less imponderable than it might have appeared, as having indeed positive claims. It wasn't, that is, he knew, the "Oh!" of the idiot, however great the superficial resemblance: it was that of the clever, the accomplished man; it was the very specialty of the speaker, and a deal of expensive training and experience had gone to producing it. Densher felt somehow that, as a thing of value accidentally picked up, it would retain an interest of curiosity. The three stood for a little together in an awkwardness to which he was conscious of contributing his share; Kate failing to ask Lord Mark to be seated, but letting him know that he would find Mrs. Lowder, with some others, on the balcony.

"Oh and Miss Theale I suppose?—as I seemed to hear outside, from below, Mrs. Stringham's unmistakeable voice."

"Yes, but Mrs. Stringham's alone. Milly's unwell," the girl explained, "and was compelled to disappoint us."

"Ah 'disappoint'—rather!" And, lingering a little, he kept his eyes on Densher. "She isn't really bad, I trust?"

Densher, after all he had heard, easily supposed him interested in Milly; but he could imagine him also interested in the young man with whom he had found Kate engaged and whom he yet considered without visible intelligence. That young man concluded in a moment that he was doing what he wanted, satisfying himself as to each. To this he was aided by Kate, who produced a prompt: "Oh dear no; I think not. I've just been reassuring Mr. Densher," she added—"who's as concerned as the rest of us. I've been calming his fears."

"Oh!" said Lord Mark again—and again it was just as good. That was for Densher, the latter could see, or think he saw. And then for the others: "*My* fears would want calming. We must take great care of her. This way?"

She went with him a few steps, and while Densher, hanging about, gave them frank attention, presently paused again for some further colloquy. What passed between them their observer lost, but she was presently with him again, Lord Mark joining the rest. Densher was by this time quite ready for her. "It's *he* who's your aunt's man?"

"Oh immensely."

"I mean for *you*."

"That's what I mean too," Kate smiled. "There he is. Now you can judge."

"Judge of what?"

"Judge of him."

"Why should I judge of him?" Densher asked. "I've nothing to do with him."

"Then why do you ask about him?"

"To judge of you—which is different."

Kate seemed for a little to look at the difference. "To take the measure, do you mean, of my danger?"

He hesitated; then he said: "I'm thinking, I dare say, of Miss Theale's. How does your aunt reconcile his interest in her—?"

"With his interest in me?"

"With her own interest in you," Densher said while she reflected. "If that interest—Mrs. Lowder's—takes the form of Lord Mark, hasn't he rather to look out for the forms *he* takes?"

Kate seemed interested in the question, but "Oh he takes them easily," she answered. "The beauty is that she doesn't trust him."

"That Milly doesn't?"

"Yes—Milly either. But I mean Aunt Maud. Not really."

Densher gave it his wonder. "Takes him to her heart and yet thinks he cheats?"

"Yes," said Kate—"that's the way people are. What they think of their enemies, goodness knows, is bad enough; but I'm still more struck with what they think of their friends. Milly's own state of mind, however," she went on, "is lucky. That's Aunt Maud's security, though she doesn't yet fully recognise it—besides being Milly's own."

"You conceive it a real escape then not to care for him?"

She shook her head in beautiful grave deprecation. "You oughtn't to make me say too much. But I'm glad I don't."

"Don't say too much?"

"Don't care for Lord Mark."

"Oh!" Densher answered with a sound like his lordship's own. To which he added: "You absolutely hold that that poor girl doesn't?"

"Ah you know what I hold about that poor girl!" It had made her again impatient.

Yet he stuck a minute to the subject. "You scarcely call him, I suppose, one of the dukes."

"Mercy, no—far from it. He's not, compared with other possibilities, 'in' it. Milly, it's true," she said, to be exact, "has no natural sense of social values, doesn't in the least understand our differences or know who's who or what's what."

"I see. That," Densher laughed, "is her reason for liking *me*."

"Precisely. She doesn't resemble me," said Kate, "who at least know what I lose."

Well, it had all risen for Densher to a considerable interest. "And Aunt Maud—why shouldn't *she* know? I mean that your friend there isn't really anything. Does she suppose him of ducal value?"

"Scarcely; save in the sense of being uncle to a duke. That's undeniably something. He's the best moreover we can get."

"Oh, oh!" said Densher; and his doubt was not all derisive.

"It isn't Lord Mark's grandeur," she went on without heeding this; "because perhaps in the line of that alone—as he has no money—more could be done. But she's not a bit sordid; she only counts with the sordidness of others. Besides, he's grand enough, with a duke in his family and at the other end of the string. *The* thing's his genius."

"And do you believe in that?"

"In Lord Mark's genius?" Kate, as if for a more final opinion than had yet been asked of her, took a moment to think. She balanced indeed so that one would scarce have known what to expect; but she came out in time with a very sufficient "Yes!"

"Political?"

"Universal. I don't know at least," she said, "what else to call it when a man's able to make himself without effort, without violence, without machinery of any sort, so intensely felt. He has somehow an effect without his being in any traceable way a cause."

"Ah but if the effect," said Densher with conscious superficiality, "isn't agreeable—?"

"Oh but it is!"

"Not surely for every one."

"If you mean not for you," Kate returned, "you may have reasons—and men don't count. Women don't know if it's agreeable or not."

"Then there you are!"

"Yes, precisely—that takes, on his part, genius."

Densher stood before her as if he wondered what everything she thus promptly, easily and above all amusingly met him with, would have been found, should it have come to an analysis, to "take." Something suddenly, as if under a last determinant touch, welled up in him and overflowed—the sense of his good fortune and her variety, of the future she promised, the interest she supplied. "All women but you are stupid. How can I look at another? You're different and different—and then you're different again. No marvel Aunt Maud builds on you—except that you're so much too good for what she builds *for*. Even 'society' won't know how good for it you are; it's too stupid, and you're beyond it. You'd have to pull it uphill—it's you yourself who are at the top. The women one meets—what are they but books one has already read? You're a whole library of the unknown, the uncut." He almost moaned, he ached, from the depth of his content. "Upon my word I've a subscription!"

She took it from him with her face again giving out all it had in answer, and they remained once more confronted and united in their essential wealth of life. "It's you who draw me out. I exist in you. Not in others."

It had been, however, as if the thrill of their association itself pressed in him, as great felicities do, the sharp spring of fear. "See here, you know: don't, *don't*—!"

"Don't what?"

"Don't fail me. It would kill me."

She looked at him a minute with no response but her eyes. "So you think you'll kill *me* in time to prevent it?" She smiled, but he saw her the next instant as smiling through tears; and the instant after this she had got, in respect to the particular point, quite off. She had come back to another, which was one of her own; her own were so closely connected that Densher's were at best but parenthetic. Still she had a distance to go. "You do then see your way?" She put it to him before they joined—as was high time—the others. And she made him understand she meant his way with Milly.

He had dropped a little in presence of the explanation; then she had brought him up to a sort of recognition. He could make out by this light something of what he saw, but a dimness also there was, undispelled since his return. "There's something you must definitely tell me. If our friend knows that all the while—?"

She came straight to his aid, formulating for him his anxiety, though quite to smooth it down. "All the while she and I here were growing intimate, you and I were in unmentioned relation? If she knows that, yes, she knows our relation must have involved your writing to me."

"Then how could she suppose you weren't answering?"

"She doesn't suppose it."

"How then can she imagine you never named her?"

"She doesn't. She knows now I did name her. I've told her everything. She's in possession of reasons that will perfectly do."

Still he just brooded. "She takes things from you exactly as I take them?"

"Exactly as you take them."

"She's just such another victim?"

"Just such another. You're a pair."

"Then if anything happens," said Densher, "we can console each other?"

"Ah something *may* indeed happen," she returned, "if you'll only go straight!"

He watched the others an instant through the window. "What do you mean by going straight?"

"Not worrying. Doing as you like. Try, as I've told you before, and you'll see. You'll have me perfectly, always, to refer to."

"Oh rather, I hope! But if she's going away?"

It pulled Kate up but a moment. "I'll bring her back. There you are. You won't be able to say I haven't made it smooth for you."

He faced it all, and certainly it was queer. But it wasn't the queerness that after another minute was uppermost. He was in a wondrous silken web, and it *was* amusing. "You spoil me!"

He wasn't sure if Mrs. Lowder, who at this juncture reappeared, had caught his word as it dropped from him; probably not, he thought, her attention being given to Mrs. Stringham, with whom she came through and who was now, none too soon, taking leave of her. They were followed by Lord Mark and by the other men, but two or three things happened before any dispersal of the company began. One of these was that Kate found time to say to him with furtive emphasis: "You must go now!" Another was that she next addressed herself in all frankness to Lord Mark, drew near to him with an almost reproachful "Come and talk to *me*!"—a challenge resulting after a minute for Densher in a consciousness of their installation together in an out-of-the-way corner, though not the same he himself had just occupied with her. Still another was that Mrs. Stringham, in the random intensity of her farewells, affected him as looking at him with a small grave intimation, something into which he afterwards read the meaning that if he had happened to desire a few words with her after dinner he would have found her ready. This impression was naturally light, but it just left him with the sense of something by his own act overlooked, unappreciated. It gathered perhaps a slightly sharper shade from the mild formality of her "Good-night, sir!" as she passed him; a matter as to which there was now nothing more to be done, thanks to the alertness of the young man he by this time had appraised as even more harmless than himself. This personage had forestalled him in opening the door for her and was evidently—with a view, Densher might have judged, to ulterior designs on Milly—proposing to attend her to her carriage. What further occurred was that Aunt Maud, having released her, immediately had a word for himself. It was an imperative "Wait a minute," by which she both detained and dismissed him; she was particular about her minute, but he hadn't yet given her, as happened, a sign of withdrawal.

"Return to our little friend. You'll find her really interesting."

"If you mean Miss Theale," he said, "I shall certainly not forget her. But you must remember that, so far as her 'interest' is concerned, I myself discovered, I—as was said at dinner—invented her."

"Well, one seemed rather to gather that you hadn't taken out the patent. Don't, I only mean, in the press of other things, too much neglect her."

Affected, surprised by the coincidence of her appeal with Kate's, he asked himself quickly if it mightn't help him with her. He at any rate could but try. "You're all looking after my manners. That's exactly, you know, what Miss Croy has been saying to me. *She* keeps me up—she has had so much to say about them."

He found pleasure in being able to give his hostess an account of his passage with Kate that, while quite veracious, might be reassuring to herself. But Aunt Maud, wonderfully and facing him straight, took it as if her confidence were supplied with other props. If she saw his intention in it she yet blinked neither with doubt nor with acceptance; she only said imperturbably: "Yes, she'll herself do anything for her friend; so that she but preaches what she practises."

Densher really quite wondered if Aunt Maud knew how far Kate's devotion went. He was moreover a little puzzled by this special harmony; in face of which he quickly asked himself if Mrs. Lowder had bethought herself of the American girl as a distraction for him, and if Kate's mastery of the subject were therefore but an appearance addressed to her aunt. What might really *become* in all this of the American girl was therefore a question that, on the latter contingency, would lose none of its sharpness. However, questions could wait, and it was easy, so far as he understood, to meet Mrs. Lowder. "It isn't a bit, all the same, you know, that I resist. I find Miss Theale charming."

Well, it was all she wanted. "Then don't miss a chance."

"The only thing is," he went on, "that she's—naturally now —leaving town and, as I take it, going abroad."

Aunt Maud looked indeed an instant as if she herself had been dealing with this difficulty. "She won't go," she smiled in spite of it, "till she has seen you. Moreover, when she does go—" She paused, leaving him uncertain. But the next minute he was still more at sea. "We shall go too."

He gave a smile that he himself took for slightly strange. "And what good will that do *me*?"

"We shall be near them somewhere, and you'll come out to us."

"Oh!" he said a little awkwardly.

"I'll see that you do. I mean I'll write to you."

"Ah thank you, thank you!" Merton Densher laughed. She was indeed putting him on his honour, and his honour winced a little at the use he rather helplessly saw himself suffering her to believe she could make of it. "There are all sorts of things," he vaguely remarked, "to consider."

"No doubt. But there's above all the great thing."

"And pray what's that?"

"Why the importance of your not losing the occasion of your life. I'm treating you handsomely, I'm looking after it for you. I *can*—I can smooth your path. She's charming, she's clever and she's good. And her fortune's a real fortune."

Ah there she was, Aunt Maud! The pieces fell together for him as he felt her thus buying him off, and buying him—it would have been funny if it hadn't been so grave—with Miss Theale's money. He ventured, derisive, fairly to treat it as extravagant. "I'm much obliged to you for the handsome offer—"

"Of what doesn't belong to me?" She wasn't abashed. "I don't say it does—but there's no reason it shouldn't to *you*. Mind you, moreover"—she kept it up—"I'm not one who talks in the air. And you owe me something—if you want to know why."

Distinct he felt her pressure; he felt, given her basis, her consistency; he even felt, to a degree that was immediately to receive an odd confirmation, her truth. Her truth, for that matter, was that she believed him bribeable: a belief that for his own mind as well, while they stood there, lighted up the impossible. What then in this light did Kate believe him? But that wasn't what he asked aloud. "Of course I know I owe you thanks for a deal of kind treatment. Your inviting me for instance to-night—!"

"Yes, my inviting you to-night's a part of it. But you don't know," she added, "how far I've gone for you."

He felt himself red and as if his honour were colouring up; but he laughed again as he could. "I see how far you're going."

"I'm the most honest woman in the world, but I've nevertheless done for you what was necessary." And then as her now quite sombre gravity only made him stare: "To start you it *was* necessary. From *me* it has the weight." He but continued to stare, and she met his blankness with surprise. "Don't you understand me? I've told the proper lie for you." Still he only showed her his flushed strained smile; in spite of which, speaking with force and as if he must with a minute's reflexion see what she meant, she turned away from him. "I depend upon you now to make me right!"

The minute's reflexion he was of course more free to take after he had left the house. He walked up the Bayswater Road, but he stopped short, under the murky stars, before the modern church, in the middle of the square that, going eastward, opened out on his left. He had had his brief stupidity, but now he understood. She had guaranteed to Milly Theale through Mrs. Stringham that Kate didn't care for him. She had affirmed through the same source that the attachment was only his. He made it out, he made it out, and he could see what she meant by its starting him. She had described Kate as merely compassionate, so that Milly might be compassionate too. "Proper" indeed it was, her lie—the very properest possible and the most deeply, richly diplomatic. So Milly was successfully deceived.

V

To SEE her alone, the poor girl, he none the less promptly felt, was to see her after all very much on the old basis, the basis of his three visits in New York; the new element, when once he was again face to face with her, not really amounting to much more than a recognition, with a little surprise, of the positive extent of the old basis. Everything but that, everything embarrassing fell away after he had been present five minutes: it was in fact wonderful that their excellent, their pleasant, their permitted and proper and harmless American relation—the legitimacy of which he could thus scarce express in names enough—should seem so unperturbed by other matters. They had both since then had great adventures—such an adventure for him was his mental annexation of her country; and it was now, for the moment, as if the greatest of them all were this acquired consciousness of reasons other than those that had already served. Densher had asked for her, at her hotel, the day after Aunt Maud's dinner, with a rich, that is with a highly troubled, preconception of the part likely to be played for him at present, in any contact with her, by Kate's and Mrs. Lowder's so oddly conjoined and so really superfluous attempts to make her interesting. She had been interesting enough without them—that appeared to-day to come back to him; and, admirable and beautiful as was the charitable zeal of the two ladies, it might easily have nipped in the bud the germs of a friendship inevitably limited but still perfectly open to him. What had happily averted the need of his breaking off, what would as happily continue to avert it, was his own good sense and good humour, a certain spring of mind in him which ministered, imagination aiding, to understandings and allowances and which he had positively never felt such ground as just now to rejoice in the possession of. Many men—he practically made the reflexion—wouldn't have taken the matter that way, would have lost patience, finding the appeal in question irrational, exorbitant; and, thereby making short work with it, would have let it render any further acquaintance with Miss Theale impossible. He had talked with Kate of this young woman's being "sacrificed," and that would have been one way, so far as he was concerned, to sacrifice her. Such, however, had not been the tune to which his at first bewildered view had, since the night before, cleared itself up. It wasn't so much that he failed of being the kind of man who "chucked," for he knew himself as the kind of man wise enough to mark the case in which chucking might be the minor evil and the least cruelty. It was that he liked too much every one concerned willingly to show himself merely impracticable. He liked Kate, goodness knew, and he also clearly enough liked Mrs. Lowder. He liked in particular Milly herself; and hadn't it come up for him the evening before that he quite liked even Susan Shepherd? He had never known himself so generally merciful. It was a footing, at all events, whatever accounted for it, on which he should surely be rather a muff not to manage by one turn or another to escape disobliging. Should he find he couldn't work it there would still be time enough. The idea of working it crystallised before him in such guise as not only to promise much interest—fairly, in case of success, much enthusiasm; but positively to impart to failure an appearance of barbarity.

Arriving thus in Brook Street both with the best intentions and with a margin consciously left for some primary awkwardness, he found his burden, to his great relief, unexpectedly light. The awkwardness involved in the responsibility so newly and so ingeniously traced for him turned round on the spot to present him another face. This was simply the face of his old impression, which he now fully recovered—the impression that American girls, when, rare case, they had the attraction of Milly, were clearly the easiest people in the world. Had what had happened been that this specimen of the class was from the first so committed to ease that nothing subsequent *could* ever make her difficult? That affected him now as still more probable than on the occasion of the hour or two lately passed with her in Kate's society. Milly Theale had recognised no complication, to Densher's view, while bringing him, with his companion, from the National Gallery and entertaining them at luncheon; it was therefore scarce supposable that complications had become so soon too much for her. His pretext for presenting himself was fortunately of the best and simplest; the least he could decently do, given their happy acquaintance, was to call with an enquiry after learning that she had been prevented by illness from meeting him at dinner. And then there was the beautiful accident of her other demonstration; he must at any rate have given a sign as a sequel to the hospitality he had shared with Kate. Well, he was giving one now—such as it was; he was finding her, to begin with, accessible, and very naturally and prettily glad to see him. He had come, after luncheon, early, though not so early but that she might already be out if she were well enough; and she was well enough and yet was still at home. He had an inner glimpse, with this, of the comment Kate would have made on it; it wasn't absent from his thought that Milly would have been at home by *her* account because expecting, after a talk with Mrs. Stringham, that a certain person might turn up. He even—so pleasantly did things go—enjoyed freedom of mind to welcome, on that supposition, a fresh sign of the beautiful hypocrisy of women. He went so far as to enjoy believing the girl *might* have stayed in for him; it helped him to enjoy her behaving as if she hadn't. She expressed, that is, exactly the right degree of surprise; she didn't a bit overdo it: the lesson of which was, perceptibly, that, so far as his late lights had opened the door to any want of the natural in their meetings, he might trust her to take care of it for him as well as for herself.

She had begun this, admirably, on his entrance, with her turning away from the table at which she had apparently been engaged in letter-writing; it was the very possibility of his betraying a concern for her as one of the afflicted that she had within the first minute conjured away. She was never, never—did he understand?—to be one of the afflicted for him; and the manner in which he understood it, something of the answering pleasure that he couldn't help knowing he showed, constituted, he was very soon after to acknowledge, something like a start for intimacy. When things like that could pass people had in truth to be equally conscious of a relation. It soon made one, at all events, when it didn't find one made. She had let him ask—there had been time for that, his allusion to her friend's explanatory arrival at Lancaster Gate without her being inevitable; but she had blown away, and quite as much with the look in her eyes as with the smile on her lips, every ground for anxiety and every chance for insistence. How was she?—

why she was as he thus saw her and as she had reasons of her own, nobody else's business, for desiring to appear. Kate's account of her as too proud for pity, as fiercely shy about so personal a secret, came back to him; so that he rejoiced he could take a hint, especially when he wanted to. The question the girl had quickly disposed of—"Oh it was nothing: I'm all right, thank you!"—was one he was glad enough to be able to banish. It wasn't at all, in spite of the appeal Kate had made to him on it, his affair; for his interest had been invoked in the name of compassion, and the name of compassion was exactly what he felt himself at the end of two minutes forbidden so much as to whisper. He had been sent to see her in order to be sorry for her, and how sorry he might be, quite privately, he was yet to make out. Didn't that signify, however, almost not at all?—inasmuch as, whatever his upshot, he was never to give her a glimpse of it. Thus the ground was unexpectedly cleared; though it was not till a slightly longer time had passed that he read clear, at first with amusement and then with a strange shade of respect, what had most operated. Extraordinarily, quite amazingly, he began to see that if his pity hadn't had to yield to still other things it would have had to yield quite definitely to her own. That was the way the case had turned round: he had made his visit to be sorry for her, but he would repeat it—if he did repeat it—in order that she might be sorry for him. His situation made him, she judged—when once one liked him—a subject for that degree of tenderness: he felt this judgement in her, and felt it as something he should really, in decency, in dignity, in common honesty, have very soon to reckon with.

Odd enough was it certainly that the question originally before him, the question placed there by Kate, should so of a sudden find itself quite dislodged by another. This other, it was easy to see, came straight up with the fact of her beautiful delusion and her wasted charity; the whole thing preparing for him as pretty a case of conscience as he could have desired, and one at the prospect of which he was already wincing. If he was interesting it was because he was unhappy; and if he was unhappy it was because his passion for Kate had spent itself in vain; and if Kate was indifferent, inexorable, it was because she had left Milly in no doubt of it. That above all was what came up for him—how clear an impression of this attitude, how definite an account of his own failure, Kate must have given her friend. His immediate quarter of an hour there with the girl lighted up for him almost luridly such an inference; it was almost as if the other party to their remarkable understanding had been with them as they talked, had been hovering about, had dropped in to look after her work. The value of the work affected him as different from the moment he saw it so expressed in poor Milly. Since it was false that he wasn't loved, so his right was quite quenched to figure on that ground as important; and if he didn't look out he should find himself appreciating in a way quite at odds with straightness the good faith of Milly's benevolence. *There* was the place for scruples; there the need absolutely to mind what he was about. If it wasn't proper for him to enjoy consideration on a perfectly false footing, where was the guarantee that, if he kept on, he mightn't soon himself pretend to the grievance in order not to miss the sweet? Consideration—from a charming girl—was soothing on whatever theory; and it didn't take him far to remember that he had himself as yet done nothing deceptive. It was Kate's description of him, his defeated state, it was none of his own; his responsibility would begin, as he might say, only with acting it out. The sharp point was, however, in the difference between acting and not acting: this difference in fact it was that made the case of conscience. He saw it with a certain alarm rise before him that everything was acting that was not speaking the particular word. "If you like me because you think *she* doesn't, it isn't a bit true: she *does* like me awfully!"—that would have been the particular word; which there were at the same time but too palpably such difficulties about his uttering. Wouldn't it be virtually as indelicate to challenge her as to leave her deluded?—and this quite apart from the exposure, so to speak, of Kate, as to whom it would constitute a kind of betrayal. Kate's design was something so extraordinarily special to Kate that he felt himself shrink from the complications involved in judging it. Not to give away the woman one loved, but to back her up in her mistakes—once they had gone a certain length—that was perhaps chief among the inevitabilities of the abjection of love. Loyalty was of course supremely pre-

scribed in presence of any design on her part, however roundabout, to do one nothing but good.

Densher had quite to steady himself not to be awestruck at
the immensity of the good his own friend must on all this evidence have wanted to do him. Of one thing indeed meanwhile
he was sure: Milly Theale wouldn't herself precipitate his necessity of intervention. She would absolutely never say to him:
"*Is* it so impossible she shall ever care for you seriously?"—
without which nothing could well be less delicate than for him
aggressively to set her right. Kate would be free to do that if
Kate, in some prudence, some contrition, for some better reason in fine, should revise her plan; but he asked himself what,
failing this, *he* could do that wouldn't be after all more gross
than doing nothing. This brought him round again to the acceptance of the fact that the poor girl liked him. She put it, for
reasons of her own, on a simple, a beautiful ground, a ground
that already supplied her with the pretext she required. The
ground was there, that is, in the impression she had received,
retained, cherished; the pretext, over and above it, was the
pretext for acting on it. That she now believed as she did made
her sure at last that she might act; so that what Densher therefore would have struck at would be the root, in her soul, of a
pure pleasure. It positively lifted its head and flowered, this
pure pleasure, while the young man now sat with her, and
there were things she seemed to say that took the words out of
his mouth. These were not all the things she did say; they were
rather what such things meant in the light of what he knew.
Her warning him for instance off the question of how she was,
the quick brave little art with which she did that, represented
to his fancy a truth she didn't utter. "I'm well for *you*—that's
all you have to do with or need trouble about: I shall never be
anything so horrid as ill for you. So there you are; worry about
me, spare me, please, as little as you can. Don't be afraid, in
short, to ignore my 'interesting' side. It isn't, you see, even
now while you sit here, that there aren't lots of others. Only
do *them* justice and we shall get on beautifully." This was what
was folded finely up in her talk—all quite ostensibly about her
impressions and her intentions. She tried to put Densher again
on his American doings, but he wouldn't have that to-day. As

he thought of the way in which, the other afternoon, before Kate, he had sat complacently "jawing," he accused himself of excess, of having overdone it, having made—at least apparently—more of a "set" at their entertainer than he was at all events then intending. He turned the tables, drawing her out about London, about her vision of life there, and only too glad to treat her as a person with whom he could easily have other topics than her aches and pains. He spoke to her above all of the evidence offered him at Lancaster Gate that she had come but to conquer; and when she had met this with full and gay assent—"How could I help being the feature of the season, the what-do-you-call-it, the theme of every tongue?"—they fraternised freely over all that had come and gone for each since their interrupted encounter in New York.

At the same time, while many things in quick succession came up for them, came up in particular for Densher, nothing perhaps was just so sharp as the odd influence of their present conditions on their view of their past ones. It was as if they hadn't known how "thick" they had originally become, as if, in a manner, they had really fallen to remembrance of more passages of intimacy than there had in fact at the time quite been room for. They were in a relation now so complicated, whether by what they said or by what they didn't say, that it might have been seeking to justify its speedy growth by reaching back to one of those fabulous periods in which prosperous states place their beginnings. He recalled what had been said at Mrs. Lowder's about the steps and stages, in people's careers, that absence caused one to miss, and about the resulting frequent sense of meeting them further on; which, with some other matters also recalled, he took occasion to communicate to Milly. The matters he couldn't mention mingled themselves with those he did; so that it would doubtless have been hard to say which of the two groups now played most of a part. He was kept face to face with this young lady by a force absolutely resident in their situation and operating, for his nerves, with the swiftness of the forces commonly regarded by sensitive persons as beyond their control. The current thus determined had positively become for him, by the time he had been ten minutes in the room, something that, but for the absurdity of comparing the very small with the very great, he would freely have likened to the rapids of Niagara. An uncriticised acquaintance between a clever young man and a responsive young woman could do nothing more, at the most, than go, and his actual experiment went and went and went. Nothing probably so conduced to make it go as the marked circumstance that they had spoken all the while not a word about Kate; and this in spite of the fact that, if it were a question for them of what had occurred in the past weeks, nothing had occurred comparable to Kate's predominance. Densher had but the night before appealed to her for instruction as to what he must do about her, but he fairly winced to find how little this came to. She had foretold him of course how little; but it was a truth that looked different when shown him by Milly. It proved to him that the latter had in fact been dealt with, but it produced in him the thought that Kate might perhaps again conveniently be questioned. He would have liked to speak to her before going further—to make sure she really meant him to succeed quite so much. With all the difference that, as we say, came up for him, it came up afresh, naturally, that he might make his visit brief and never renew it; yet the strangest thing of all was that the argument against that issue would have sprung precisely from the beautiful little eloquence involved in Milly's avoidances.

Precipitate these well might be, since they emphasised the fact that she was proceeding in the sense of the assurances she had taken. Over the latter she had visibly not hesitated, for hadn't they had the merit of giving her a chance? Densher quite saw her, felt her take it; the chance, neither more nor less, of help rendered him according to her freedom. It was what Kate had left her with: "Listen to him, I? Never! So do as you like." What Milly "liked" was to do, it thus appeared, as she was doing: our young man's glimpse of which was just what would have been for him not less a glimpse of the peculiar brutality of shaking her off. The choice exhaled its shy fragrance of heroism, for it was not aided by any question of parting with Kate. She would be charming to Kate as well as to Kate's adorer; she would incur whatever pain could dwell for her in the sight—should she continue to be exposed to the sight—of the adorer thrown with the adored. It wouldn't really have taken much more to make him wonder if he hadn't before him one of those rare cases of exaltation—food for fiction, food for poetry—in which a man's fortune with the woman who doesn't care for him is positively promoted by the woman who does. It was as if Milly had said to herself: "Well, he can at least meet her in my society, if that's anything to him; so that my line can only be to make my society attractive." She certainly couldn't have made a different impression if she *had* so reasoned. All of which, none the less, didn't prevent his soon enough saying to her, quite as if she were to be whirled into space: "And now, then, what becomes of you? Do you begin to rush about on visits to country-houses?"

She disowned the idea with a headshake that, put on what face she would, couldn't help betraying to him something of her suppressed view of the possibility—ever, ever perhaps—of any such proceedings. They weren't at any rate for her now. "Dear no. We go abroad for a few weeks somewhere of high air. That has been before us for many days; we've only been kept on by last necessities here. However, everything's done and the wind's in our sails."

"May you scud then happily before it! But when," he asked, "do you come back?"

She looked ever so vague; then as if to correct it: "Oh when the wind turns. And what do you do with your summer?"

"Ah I spend it in sordid toil. I drench it with mercenary ink. My work in your country counts for play as well. You see what's thought of the pleasure your country can give. My holiday's over."

"I'm sorry you had to take it," said Milly, "at such a different time from ours. If you could but have worked while we've been working—"

"I might be playing while you play? Oh the distinction isn't so great with me. There's a little of each for me, of work and of play, in either. But you and Mrs. Stringham, with Miss Croy and Mrs. Lowder—you all," he went on, "have been given up, like navvies or niggers, to real physical toil. Your rest is something you've earned and you need. My labour's comparatively light."

"Very true," she smiled; "but all the same I like mine."

"It doesn't leave you 'done'?"

"Not a bit. I don't get tired when I'm interested. Oh I could go far."

He bethought himself. "Then why don't you?—since you've got here, as I learn, the whole place in your pocket."

"Well, it's a kind of economy—I'm saving things up. I've enjoyed so what you speak of—though your account of it's fantastic—that I'm watching over its future, that I can't help being anxious and careful. I want—in the interest itself of what I've had and may still have—not to make stupid mistakes. The way not to make them is to get off again to a distance and see the situation from there. I shall keep it fresh," she wound up as if herself rather pleased with the ingenuity of her statement— "I shall keep it fresh, by that prudence, for my return."

"Ah then you *will* return? Can you promise one that?"

Her face fairly lighted at his asking for a promise; but she made as if bargaining a little. "Isn't London rather awful in winter?"

He had been going to ask her if she meant for the invalid; but he checked the infelicity of this and took the enquiry as referring to social life. "No—I like it, with one thing and another; it's less of a mob than later on; and it would have for *us* the merit—should you come here then—that we should probably see more of you. So do reappear for us—if it isn't a question of climate."

She looked at that a little graver. "If what isn't a question—?"

"Why the determination of your movements. You spoke just now of going somewhere for that."

"For better air?"—she remembered. "Oh yes, one certainly wants to get out of London in August."

"Rather, of course!"—he fully understood. "Though I'm glad you've hung on long enough for me to catch you. Try us at any rate," he continued, "once more."

"Whom do you mean by 'us'?" she presently asked.

It pulled him up an instant—representing, as he saw it might have seemed, an allusion to himself as conjoined with Kate, whom he was proposing not to mention any more than his hostess did. But the issue was easy. "I mean all of us together, every one you'll find ready to surround you with sympathy."

It made her, none the less, in her odd charming way, challenge him afresh. "Why do you say sympathy?"

"Well, it's doubtless a pale word. What we *shall* feel for you will be much nearer worship."

"As near then as you like!" With which at last Kate's name was sounded. "The people I'd most come back for are the people you know. I'd do it for Mrs. Lowder, who has been beautifully kind to me."

"So she has to *me*," said Densher. "I feel," he added as she at first answered nothing, "that, quite contrary to anything I originally expected, I've made a good friend of her."

"*I* didn't expect it either—its turning out as it has. But I did," said Milly, "with Kate. I shall come back for her too. I'd do anything"—she kept it up—"for Kate."

Looking at him as with conscious clearness while she spoke, she might for the moment have effectively laid a trap for whatever remains of the ideal straightness in him were still able to pull themselves together and operate. He was afterwards to say to himself that something had at that moment hung for him by a hair. "Oh I know what one would do for Kate!"—it had hung for him by a hair to break out with that, which he felt he had really been kept from by an element in his consciousness stronger still. The proof of the truth in question was precisely in his silence; resisting the impulse to break out was what he *was* doing for Kate. This at the time moreover came and went quickly enough; he was trying the next minute but to make Milly's allusion easy for herself. "Of course I know what friends you are—and of course I understand," he permitted himself to add, "any amount of devotion to a person so charming. That's the good turn then she'll do us all—I mean her working for your return."

"Oh you don't know," said Milly, "how much I'm really on her hands."

He could but accept the appearance of wondering how much he might show he knew. "Ah she's very masterful."

"She's great. Yet I don't say she bullies me."

"No—that's not the way. At any rate it isn't hers," he smiled. He remembered, however, then that an undue acquaintance with Kate's ways was just what he mustn't show; and he pursued the subject no further than to remark with a good intention that had the further merit of representing a truth: "I don't feel as if I knew her—really to call know."

"Well, if you come to that, I don't either!" she laughed. The words gave him, as soon as they were uttered, a sense of responsibility for his own; though during a silence that ensued for a minute he had time to recognise that his own contained after all no element of falsity. Strange enough therefore was it that he could go too far—if it *was* too far—without being false. His observation was one he would perfectly have made to Kate herself. And before he again spoke, and before Milly did, he took time for more still—for feeling how just here it was that he must break short off if his mind was really made up not to go further. It was as if he had been at a corner—and fairly put there by his last speech; so that it depended on him whether or no to turn it. The silence, if prolonged but an instant, might even have given him a sense of her waiting to see what he would do. It was filled for them the next thing by the sound, rather voluminous for the August afternoon, of the approach, in the street below them, of heavy carriage-wheels and of horses trained to "step." A rumble, a great shake, a considerable effective clatter, had been apparently succeeded by a pause at the door of the hotel, which was in turn accompanied by a due display of diminished prancing and stamping. "You've a visitor," Densher laughed, "and it must be at least an ambassador."

"It's only my own carriage; it does that—isn't it wonderful? —every day. But we find it, Mrs. Stringham and I, in the innocence of our hearts, very amusing." She had got up, as she spoke, to assure herself of what she said; and at the end of a few steps they were together on the balcony and looking down at her waiting chariot, which made indeed a brave show. "Is it very awful?"

It was to Densher's eyes—save for its absurd heaviness— only pleasantly pompous. "It seems to me delightfully rococo. But how do I know? You're mistress of these things, in contact with the highest wisdom. You occupy a position, moreover, thanks to which your carriage—well, by this time, in the eye of London, also occupies one." But she was going out, and he mustn't stand in her way. What had happened the next minute was first that she had denied she was going out, so that he might prolong his stay; and second that she had said she would go out with pleasure if he would like to drive—that in fact there were always things to do, that there had been a question for her to-day of several in particular, and that this in short was why the carriage had been ordered so early. They perceived, as she said these things, that an enquirer had presented himself, and, coming back, they found Milly's servant announcing the carriage and prepared to accompany her. This appeared to have for her the effect of settling the matter—on the basis, that is, of Densher's happy response. Densher's happy response, however, had as yet hung fire, the process we have described in him operating by this time with extreme intensity. The system of not pulling up, not breaking off, had already brought him headlong, he seemed to feel, to where they actually stood; and just now it was, with a vengeance, that he must do either one thing or the other. He had been waiting for some moments, which probably seemed to him longer than they were; this was because he was anxiously watching himself wait. He couldn't keep that up for ever; and since one thing or the other was what he must do, it was for the other that he presently became conscious of having decided. If he had been drifting it settled itself in the manner of a bump, of considerable violence, against a firm object in the stream. "Oh yes; I'll go with you with pleasure. It's a charming idea."

She gave no look to thank him—she rather looked away; she only said at once to her servant, "In ten minutes"; and then to her visitor, as the man went out, "We'll go somewhere—I shall like that. But I must ask of you time—as little as possible—to get ready." She looked over the room to provide for him, keep him there. "There are books and things—plenty; and I dress very quickly." He caught her eyes only as she went, on which he thought them pretty and touching.

Why especially touching at that instant he could certainly scarce have said; it was involved, it was lost in the sense of her wishing to oblige him. Clearly what had occurred was her having wished it so that she had made him simply wish, in civil acknowledgement, to oblige *her*; which he had now fully done by turning his corner. He was quite round it, his corner, by the time the door had closed upon her and he stood there alone. Alone he remained for three minutes more—remained with several very living little matters to think about. One of these was the phenomenon—typical, highly American, he would have said—of Milly's extreme spontaneity. It was perhaps rather as if he had sought refuge—refuge from another question—in the almost exclusive contemplation of this. Yet this, in its way, led him nowhere; not even to a sound generalisation about American girls. It was spontaneous for his young friend to have asked him to drive with her alone—since she hadn't mentioned her companion; but she struck him after all as no more advanced in doing it than Kate, for instance, who wasn't an American girl, might have struck him in not doing it. Besides, Kate *would* have done it, though Kate wasn't at all, in the same sense as Milly, spontaneous. And then in addition Kate *had* done it—or things very like it. Furthermore he was engaged to Kate—even if his ostensibly not being put her public freedom on other grounds. On all grounds, at any rate, the relation between Kate and freedom, between freedom and Kate, was a different one from any he could associate or cultivate, as to anything, with the girl who had just left him to prepare to give herself up to him. It had never struck him before, and he moved about the room while he thought of it, touching none of the books placed at his disposal. Milly was forward, as might be said, but not advanced; whereas Kate was backward—backward still, comparatively, as an English girl—and yet advanced in a high degree. However—though this didn't straighten it out—Kate was of course two or three years older; which at their time of life considerably counted.

Thus ingeniously discriminating, Densher continued slowly to wander; yet without keeping at bay for long the sense of having rounded his corner. He had so rounded it that he felt himself lose even the option of taking advantage of Milly's absence to retrace his steps. If he might have turned tail, vulgarly speaking, five minutes before, he couldn't turn tail now; he must simply wait there with his consciousness charged to the brim. Quickly enough moreover that issue was closed from without; in the course of three minutes more Miss Theale's servant had returned. He preceded a visitor whom he had met, obviously, at the foot of the stairs and whom, throwing open the door, he loudly announced as Miss Croy. Kate, on following him in, stopped short at sight of Densher—only, after an instant, as the young man saw with free amusement, not from surprise and still less from discomfiture. Densher immediately gave his explanation—Miss Theale had gone to prepare to drive—on receipt of which the servant effaced himself.

"And you're going with her?" Kate asked.

"Yes—with your approval; which I've taken, as you see, for granted."

"Oh," she laughed, "my approval's complete!" She was thoroughly consistent and handsome about it.

"What I mean is of course," he went on—for he was sensibly affected by her gaiety—"at your so lively instigation."

She had looked about the room—she might have been vaguely looking for signs of the duration, of the character of his visit, a momentary aid in taking a decision. "Well, instigation then, as much as you like." She treated it as pleasant, the success of her plea with him; she made a fresh joke of this direct impression of it. "So much so as that? Do you know I think I won't wait?"

"Not to see her—after coming?"

"Well, with you in the field—! I came for news of her, but she must be all right. If she *is*—"

But he took her straight up. "Ah how do I know?" He was moved to say more. "It's not *I* who am responsible for her, my dear. It seems to me it's you." She struck him as making light of a matter that had been costing him sundry qualms; so that they couldn't both be quite just. Either she was too easy or he had been too anxious. He didn't want at all events to feel a fool for that. "I'm doing nothing—and shall not, I assure you, do anything but what I'm told."

Their eyes met with some intensity over the emphasis he had given his words; and he had taken it from her the next moment that he really needn't get into a state. What in the world was the matter? She asked it, with interest, for all answer. "Isn't she better—if she's able to see you?"

"She assures me she's in perfect health."

Kate's interest grew. "I knew she would." On which she added: "It won't have been really for illness that she stayed away last night."

"For what then?"

"Well—for nervousness."

"Nervousness about what?"

"Oh you know!" She spoke with a hint of impatience, smiling however the next moment. "I've told you that."

He looked at her to recover in her face what she had told

him; then it was as if what he saw there prompted him to say: "What have you told *her*?"

She gave him her controlled smile, and it was all as if they remembered where they were, liable to surprise, talking with softened voices, even stretching their opportunity, by such talk, beyond a quite right feeling. Milly's room would be close at hand, and yet they were saying things—! For a moment, none the less, they kept it up. "Ask *her*, if you like; you're free— she'll tell you. Act as you think best; don't trouble about what you think I may or mayn't have told. I'm all right with her," said Kate. "So there you are."

"If you mean *here* I am," he answered, "it's unmistakeable. If you also mean that her believing in you is all I have to do with you're so far right as that she certainly does believe in you."

"Well then take example by her."

"She's really doing it for you," Densher continued. "She's driving me out for you."

"In that case," said Kate with her soft tranquillity, "you can do it a little for *her*. I'm not afraid," she smiled.

He stood before her a moment, taking in again the face she put on it and affected again, as he had already so often been, by more things in this face and in her whole person and presence than he was, to his relief, obliged to find words for. It wasn't, under such impressions, a question of words. "I do nothing for any one in the world but you. But for you I'll do anything."

"Good, good," said Kate. "That's how I like you."

He waited again an instant. "Then you swear to it?"

"To 'it'? To what?"

"Why that you do 'like' me. Since it's all for that, you know, that I'm letting you do—well, God knows what with me."

She gave at this, with a stare, a disheartened gesture—the sense of which she immediately further expressed. "If you don't believe in me then, after all, hadn't you better break off before you've gone further?"

"Break off with you?"

"Break off with Milly. You might go now," she said, "and I'll stay and explain to her why it is."

He wondered—as if it struck him. "What would you say?"

"Why that you find you can't stand her, and that there's nothing for me but to bear with you as I best may."

He considered of this. "How much do you abuse me to her?"

"Exactly enough. As much as you see by her attitude."

Again he thought. "It doesn't seem to me I ought to mind her attitude."

"Well then, just as you like. I'll stay and do my best for you."

He saw she was sincere, was really giving him a chance; and that of itself made things clearer. The feeling of how far he had gone came back to him not in repentance, but in this very vision of an escape; and it was not of what he had done, but of what Kate offered, that he now weighed the consequence. "Won't it make her—her not finding me here—be rather more sure there's something between us?"

Kate thought. "Oh I don't know. It will of course greatly upset her. But you needn't trouble about that. She won't die of it."

"Do you mean she *will*?" Densher presently asked.

"Don't put me questions when you don't believe what I say. You make too many conditions."

She spoke now with a shade of rational weariness that made the want of pliancy, the failure to oblige her, look poor and ugly; so that what it suddenly came back to for him was his deficiency in the things a man of any taste, so engaged, so enlisted, would have liked to make sure of being able to show—imagination, tact, positively even humour. The circumstance is doubtless odd, but the truth is none the less that the speculation uppermost with him at this juncture was: "What if I should begin to bore this creature?" And that, within a few seconds, had translated itself. "If you'll swear again you love me—!"

She looked about, at door and window, as if he were asking for more than he said. "Here? There's nothing between us here," Kate smiled.

"Oh *isn't* there?" Her smile itself, with this, had so settled something for him that he had come to her pleadingly and holding out his hands, which she immediately seized with her own as if both to check him and to keep him. It was by keeping him thus for a minute that she did check him; she held him long enough, while, with their eyes deeply meeting, they waited in silence for him to recover himself and renew his discretion. He coloured as with a return of the sense of where they were, and that gave her precisely one of her usual victories, which immediately took further form. By the time he had dropped her hands he had again taken hold, as it were, of Milly's. It was not at any rate with Milly he had broken. "I'll do all you wish," he declared as if to acknowledge the acceptance of his condition that he had practically, after all, drawn from her—a declaration on which she then, recurring to her first idea, promptly acted.

"If you *are* as good as that I go. You'll tell her that, finding you with her, I wouldn't wait. Say that, you know, from yourself. She'll understand."

She had reached the door with it—she was full of decision; but he had before she left him one more doubt. "I don't see how she can understand enough, you know, without understanding too much."

"You don't need to see."

He required then a last injunction. "I must simply go it blind?"

"You must simply be kind to her."

"And leave the rest to you?"

"Leave the rest to *her*," said Kate disappearing.

It came back then afresh to that, as it had come before. Milly, three minutes after Kate had gone, returned in her array—her big black hat, so little superstitiously in the fashion, her fine black garments throughout, the swathing of her throat, which Densher vaguely took for an infinite number of yards of priceless lace, and which, its folded fabric kept in place by heavy rows of pearls, hung down to her feet like the stole of a priestess. He spoke to her at once of their friend's visit and flight. "She hadn't known she'd find me," he said—and said at present without difficulty. He had so rounded his corner that it wasn't a question of a word more or less.

She took this account of the matter as quite sufficient; she glossed over whatever might be awkward. "I'm sorry—but I of course often see *her*." He felt the discrimination in his favour and how it justified Kate. This was Milly's tone when the matter was left to her. Well, it should now be wholly left.

I

WHEN Kate and Densher abandoned her to Mrs. String-ham on the day of her meeting them together and bringing them to luncheon, Milly, face to face with that companion, had had one of those moments in which the warned, the anxious fighter of the battle of life, as if once again feeling for the sword at his side, carries his hand straight to the quarter of his courage. She laid hers firmly on her heart, and the two women stood there showing each other a strange front. Susan Shepherd had received their great doctor's visit, which had been clearly no small affair for her; but Milly had since then, with insistence, kept in place, against communication and betrayal, as she now practically confessed, the barrier of their invited guests. "You've been too dear. With what I see you're full of you treated them beautifully. *Isn't* Kate charming when she wants to be?"

Poor Susie's expression, contending at first, as in a high fine spasm, with different dangers, had now quite let itself go. She had to make an effort to reach a point in space already so remote. "Miss Croy? Oh she was pleasant and clever. She knew," Mrs. Stringham added. "She knew."

Milly braced herself—but conscious above all, at the moment, of a high compassion for her mate. She made her out as struggling—struggling in all her nature against the betrayal of pity, which in itself, given her nature, could only be a torment. Milly gathered from the struggle how much there was of the pity, and how therefore it was both in her tenderness and in her conscience that Mrs. Stringham suffered. Wonderful and beautiful it was that this impression instantly steadied the girl. Ruefully asking herself on what basis of ease, with the drop of their barrier, they were to find themselves together, she felt the question met with a relief that was almost joy. The basis, the inevitable basis, was that she was going to be sorry for Susie, who, to all appearance, had been condemned in so much more uncomfortable a manner to be sorry for *her*. Mrs. Stringham's sorrow would hurt Mrs. Stringham, but how could her own ever hurt? She had, the poor girl, at all events, on the spot, five minutes of exaltation in which she turned the tables on her friend with a pass of the hand, a gesture of an energy that made a wind in the air. "Kate knew," she asked, "that you were full of Sir Luke Strett?"

"She spoke of nothing, but she was gentle and nice; she seemed to want to help me through." Which the good lady had no sooner said, however, than she almost tragically gasped at herself. She glared at Milly with a pretended pluck. "What I mean is that she saw one had been taken up with something. When I say she knows I should say she's a person who guesses." And her grimace was also, on its side, heroic. "But *she* doesn't matter, Milly."

The girl felt she by this time could face anything. "Nobody matters, Susie. Nobody." Which her next words, however, rather contradicted. "Did he take it ill that I wasn't here to see him? Wasn't it really just what he wanted—to have it out, so much more simply, with *you?*"

"We didn't have anything 'out,' Milly," Mrs. Stringham delicately quavered.

"Didn't he awfully like you," Milly went on, "and didn't he think you the most charming person I could possibly have referred him to for an account of me? Didn't you hit it off tremendously together and in fact fall quite in love, so that it will really be a great advantage for you to have me as a common ground? You're going to make, I can see, no end of a good thing of me."

"My own child, my own child!" Mrs. Stringham pleadingly murmured; yet showing as she did so that she feared the effect even of deprecation.

"Isn't he beautiful and good too himself?—altogether, whatever he may say, a lovely acquaintance to have made? You're just the right people for me—I see it now; and do you know what, between you, you must do?" Then as Susie still but stared, wonderstruck and holding herself: "You must simply see me through. Any way you choose. Make it out together. I, on my side, will be beautiful too, and we'll be—the three of us, with whatever others, oh as many as the case requires, any one you like!—a sight for the gods. I'll be as easy for you as carrying a feather." Susie took it for a moment in such silence that her young friend almost saw her—and scarcely withheld the observation—as taking it for "a part of the disease." This accordingly helped Milly to be, as she judged, definite and wise. "He's at any rate awfully interesting, isn't he?—which is so much to the good. We haven't at least—as we might have, with the way we tumbled into it—got hold of one of the dreary."

"Interesting, dearest?"—Mrs. Stringham felt her feet firmer. "I don't know if he's interesting or not; but I do know, my own," she continued to quaver, "that he's just as much interested as you could possibly desire."

"Certainly—that's it. Like all the world."

"No, my precious, not like all the world. Very much more deeply and intelligently."

"Ah there you are!" Milly laughed. "That's the way, Susie, I want you. So 'buck' up, my dear. We'll have beautiful times with him. Don't worry."

"I'm not worrying, Milly." And poor Susie's face registered the sublimity of her lie.

It was at this that, too sharply penetrated, her companion went to her, met by her with an embrace in which things were said that exceeded speech. Each held and clasped the other as if to console her for this unnamed woe, the woe for Mrs. Stringham of learning the torment of helplessness, the woe for Milly of having *her*, at such a time, to think of. Milly's assumption was immense, and the difficulty for her friend was that of not being able to gainsay it without bringing it more to the proof than tenderness and vagueness could permit. Nothing in fact came to the proof between them but that they could thus cling together—except indeed that, as we have indicated, the pledge of protection and support was all the younger woman's own. "I don't ask you," she presently said, "what he told you for yourself, nor what he told you to tell me, nor how he took it, really, that I had left him to you, nor what passed between you about me in any way. It wasn't to get that out of you that I took my means to make sure of your meeting freely—for there are things I don't want to know. I shall see him again and again and shall know more than enough. All I do want is that you shall see me through on *his* basis, whatever it is; which it's enough—for the purpose—that you yourself should know: that is with him to show you how. I'll make it charming for you—that's what I mean; I'll keep you up to it in such a way that half the time you won't know you're doing it. And for that you're to rest upon me. There. It's understood. We keep each other going, and you may absolutely feel of me that I shan't break down. So, with the way you haven't so much as a dig of the elbow to fear, how could you be safer?"

"He told me I *can* help you—of course he told me that," Susie, on her side, eagerly contended. "Why shouldn't he, and for what else have I come out with you? But he told me nothing dreadful—nothing, nothing, nothing," the poor lady passionately protested. "Only that you must do as you like and as he tells you—which *is* just simply to do as you like."

"I must keep in sight of him. I must from time to time go to him. But that's of course doing as I like. It's lucky," Milly smiled, "that I like going to him."

Mrs. Stringham was here in agreement; she gave a clutch at the account of their situation that most showed it as workable. "That's what *will* be charming for me, and what I'm sure he really wants of me—to help you to do as you like."

"And also a little, won't it be," Milly laughed, "to save me from the consequences? Of course," she added, "there must first *be* things I like."

"Oh I think you'll find some," Mrs. Stringham more bravely said. "I think there *are* some—as for instance just this one. I mean," she explained, "really having us so."

Milly thought. "Just as if I wanted you comfortable about *him*, and him the same about you? Yes—I shall get the good of it."

Susan Shepherd appeared to wander from this into a slight confusion. "Which of them are you talking of?"

Milly wondered an instant—then had a light. "I'm not talking of Mr. Densher." With which moreover she showed amusement. "Though if you can be comfortable about Mr. Densher too so much the better."

"Oh you meant Sir Luke Strett? Certainly he's a fine type. Do you know," Susie continued, "whom he reminds me of? Of *our* great man—Dr. Buttrick of Boston."

Milly recognised Dr. Buttrick of Boston, but she dropped

him after a tributary pause. "What do you think, now that you've seen him, of Mr. Densher?"

It was not till after consideration, with her eyes fixed on her friend's, that Susie produced her answer. "I think he's very handsome."

Milly remained smiling at her, though putting on a little the manner of a teacher with a pupil. "Well, that will do for the first time. I *have* done," she went on, "what I wanted."

"Then that's all *we* want. You see there are plenty of things."

Milly shook her head for the "plenty." "The best is not to know—that includes them all. I don't—I don't know. Nothing about anything—except that you're *with* me. Remember that, please. There won't be anything that, on my side, for you, I shall forget. So it's all right."

The effect of it by this time was fairly, as intended, to sustain Susie, who dropped in spite of herself into the reassuring. "Most certainly it's all right. I think you ought to understand that he sees no reason—"

"Why I shouldn't have a grand long life?" Milly had taken it straight up, as to understand it and for a moment consider it. But she disposed of it otherwise. "Oh of course I know *that*." She spoke as if her friend's point were small.

Mrs. Stringham tried to enlarge it. "Well, what I mean is that he didn't say to me anything that he hasn't said to yourself."

"Really?—I would in his place!" She might have been disappointed, but she had her good humour. "He tells me to *live*"—and she oddly limited the word.

It left Susie a little at sea. "Then what do you want more?"

"My dear," the girl presently said, "I don't 'want,' as I assure you, anything. Still," she added, "I *am* living. Oh yes, I'm living."

It put them again face to face, but it had wound Mrs. Stringham up. "So am I then, you'll see!"—she spoke with the note of her recovery. Yet it was her wisdom now—meaning by it as much as she did—not to say more than that. She had risen by Milly's aid to a certain command of what was before them; the ten minutes of their talk had in fact made her more distinctly aware of the presence in her mind of a new idea. It was really perhaps an old idea with a new value; it had at all events begun during the last hour, though at first but feebly, to shine with a special light. That was because in the morning darkness had so suddenly descended—a sufficient shade of night to bring out the power of a star. The dusk might be thick yet, but the sky had comparatively cleared; and Susan Shepherd's star from this time on continued to twinkle for her. It was for the moment, after her passage with Milly, the one spark left in the heavens. She recognised, as she continued to watch it, that it had really been set there by Sir Luke Strett's visit and that the impressions immediately following had done no more than fix it. Milly's reappearance with Mr. Densher at her heels—or, so oddly perhaps, at Miss Croy's heels, Miss Croy being at Milly's —had contributed to this effect, though it was only with the lapse of the greater obscurity that Susie made that out. The obscurity had reigned during the hour of their friends' visit, faintly clearing indeed while, in one of the rooms, Kate Croy's remarkable advance to her intensified the fact that Milly and the young man were conjoined in the other. If it hadn't acquired on the spot all the intensity of which it was capable, this was be-cause the poor lady still sat in her primary gloom, the gloom the great benignant doctor had practically left behind him.

The intensity the circumstance in question *might* wear to the informed imagination would have been sufficiently re-vealed for us, no doubt—and with other things to our pur-pose—in two or three of those confidential passages with Mrs. Lowder that she now permitted herself. She hadn't yet been so glad that she believed in her old friend; for if she hadn't had, at such a pass, somebody or other to believe in she should cer-tainly have stumbled by the way. Discretion had ceased to con-sist of silence; silence was gross and thick, whereas wisdom should taper, however tremulously, to a point. She betook herself to Lancaster Gate the morning after the colloquy just noted; and there, in Maud Manningham's own sanctum, she gradually found relief in giving an account of herself. An ac-count of herself was one of the things that she had long been in the habit of expecting herself regularly to give—the regular-ity depending of course much on such tests of merit as might, by laws beyond her control, rise in her path. She never spared herself in short a proper sharpness of conception of how she had behaved, and it was a statement that she for the most part found herself able to make. What had happened at present was that nothing, as she felt, was left of her to report to; she was all too sunk in the inevitable and the abysmal. To give an account of herself she must give it to somebody else, and her first instalment of it to her hostess was that she must please let her cry. She couldn't cry, with Milly in observation, at the hotel, which she had accordingly left for that purpose; and the power happily came to her with the good opportunity. She cried and cried at first—she confined herself to that; it was for the time the best statement of her business. Mrs. Lowder moreover intelligently took it as such, though knocking off a note or two more, as she said, while Susie sat near her table. She could resist the contagion of tears, but her patience did justice to her visitor's most vivid plea for it. "I shall never be able, you know, to cry again—at least not ever with *her*; so I must take it out when I can. Even if she does herself it won't be for me to give away; for what would that be but a confession of despair? I'm not with her for that—I'm with her to be regularly sublime. Besides, Milly won't cry herself."

"I'm sure I hope," said Mrs. Lowder, "that she won't have occasion to."

"She won't even if she does have occasion. She won't shed a tear. There's something that will prevent her."

"Oh!" said Mrs. Lowder.

"Yes, her pride," Mrs. Stringham explained in spite of her friend's doubt, and it was with this that her communication took consistent form. It had never been pride, Maud Manningham had hinted, that kept *her* from crying when other things made for it; it had only been that these same things, at such times, made still more for business, arrangements, correspondence, the ringing of bells, the marshalling of servants, the taking of decisions. "I might be crying now," she said, "if I weren't writing letters"—and this quite without harshness for her anxious companion, to whom she allowed just the administrative margin for difference. She had interrupted her no more than she would have interrupted the piano-tuner. It gave poor Susie time; and when Mrs. Lowder, to save appearances and catch the post, had, with her addressed and stamped notes, met at the door of the room the footman summoned by the pressure of a knob, the facts of the case were sufficiently ready for her. It took but two or three, however, given their

importance, to lay the ground for the great one—Mrs. Stringham's interview of the day before with Sir Luke, who had
wished to see her about Milly.

"He had wished it himself?"

"I think he was glad of it. Clearly indeed he was. He stayed
a quarter of an hour. I could see that for *him* it was long. He's
interested," said Mrs. Stringham.

"Do you mean in her case?"

"He says it *isn't* a case."

"What then is it?"

"It isn't, at least," Mrs. Stringham explained, "the case she
believed it to be—thought it at any rate *might* be—when,
without my knowledge, she went to see him. She went because
there was something she was afraid of, and he examined her
thoroughly—he has made sure. She's wrong—she hasn't what
she thought."

"And what did she think?" Mrs. Lowder demanded.

"He didn't tell me."

"And you didn't ask?"

"I asked nothing," said poor Susie—"I only took what he
gave me. He gave me no more than he had to—he was beautiful," she went on. "He *is*, thank God, interested."

"He must have been interested in *you*, dear," Maud Manningham observed with kindness.

Her visitor met it with candour. "Yes, love, I think he *is*. I
mean that he sees what he can do with me."

Mrs. Lowder took it rightly. "For *her*."

"For her. Anything in the world he will or he must. He can
use me to the last bone, and he likes at least that. He says the
great thing for her is to be happy."

"It's surely the great thing for every one. Why, therefore,"
Mrs. Lowder handsomely asked, "should we cry so hard about
it?"

"Only," poor Susie wailed, "that it's so strange, so beyond
us. I mean if she can't be."

"She must be." Mrs. Lowder knew no impossibles. "She
shall be."

"Well—if you'll help. He thinks, you know, we *can* help."

Mrs. Lowder faced a moment, in her massive way, what Sir
Luke Strett thought. She sat back there, her knees apart, not

unlike a picturesque ear-ringed matron at a market-stall; while her friend, before her, dropped their items, tossed the separate truths of the matter one by one, into her capacious apron. "But is that all he came to you for—to tell you she must be happy?"

"That she must be *made* so—that's the point. It seemed enough, as he told me," Mrs. Stringham went on; "he makes it somehow such a grand possible affair."

"Ah well, if he makes it possible!"

"I mean especially he makes it grand. He gave it to me, that is, as *my* part. The rest's his own."

"And what's the rest?" Mrs. Lowder asked.

"I don't know. *His* business. He means to keep hold of her."

"Then why do you say it isn't a 'case'? It must be very much of one."

Everything in Mrs. Stringham confessed to the extent of it. "It's only that it isn't *the* case she herself supposed."

"It's another?"

"It's another."

"Examining her for what she supposed he finds something else?"

"Something else."

"And what does he find?"

"Ah," Mrs. Stringham cried, "God keep me from knowing!"

"He didn't tell you that?"

But poor Susie had recovered herself. "What I mean is that if it's there I shall know in time. He's considering, but I can trust him for it—because he does, I feel, trust me. He's considering," she repeated.

"He's in other words not sure?"

"Well, he's watching. I think that's what he means. She's to get away now, but to come back to him in three months."

"Then I think," said Maud Lowder, "that he oughtn't meanwhile to scare us."

It roused Susie a little, Susie being already enrolled in the great doctor's cause. This came out at least in her glimmer of reproach. "Does it scare us to enlist us for her happiness?"

Mrs. Lowder was rather stiff for it. "Yes; it scares *me*. I'm always scared—I may call it so—till I understand. What happiness is he talking about?"

Mrs. Stringham at this came straight. "Oh you know!"

She had really said it so that her friend had to take it; which the latter in fact after a moment showed herself as having done. A strange light humour in the matter even perhaps suddenly aiding, she met it with a certain accommodation. "Well, say one seems to see. The point is—!" But, fairly too full now of her question, she dropped.

"The point is will it *cure*?"

"Precisely. Is it absolutely a remedy—*the* specific?"

"Well, I should think we might know!" Mrs. Stringham delicately declared.

"Ah but we haven't the complaint."

"Have you never, dearest, been in love?" Susan Shepherd enquired.

"Yes, my child; but not by the doctor's direction."

Maud Manningham had spoken perforce with a break into momentary mirth, which operated—and happily too—as a challenge to her visitor's spirit. "Oh of course we don't ask his leave to fall. But it's something to know he thinks it good for us."

"My dear woman," Mrs. Lowder cried, "it strikes me we know it without him. So that when *that's* all he has to tell us—!"

"Ah," Mrs. Stringham interposed, "it isn't 'all.' I feel Sir Luke will have more; he won't have put me off with anything inadequate. I'm to see him again; he as good as told me that he'll wish it. So it won't be for nothing."

"Then what will it be for? Do you mean he has somebody of his own to propose? Do you mean you told him nothing?"

Mrs. Stringham dealt with these questions. "I showed him I understood him. That was all I could do. I didn't feel at liberty to be explicit; but I felt, even though his visit so upset me, the comfort of what I had from you night before last."

"What I spoke to you of in the carriage when we had left her with Kate?"

"You had *seen*, apparently, in three minutes. And now that he's here, now that I've met him and had my impression of him, I feel," said Mrs. Stringham, "that you've been magnificent."

"Of course I've been magnificent. When," asked Maud Manningham, "was I anything else? But Milly won't be, you know, if she marries Merton Densher."

"Oh it's always magnificent to marry the man one loves. But we're going fast!" Mrs. Stringham woefully smiled.

"The thing *is* to go fast if I see the case right. What had I after all but my instinct of that on coming back with you, night before last, to pick up Kate? I felt what I felt—I knew in my bones the man had returned."

"That's just where, as I say, you're magnificent. But wait," said Mrs. Stringham, "till you've seen him."

"I shall see him immediately"—Mrs. Lowder took it up with decision. "What *is* then," she asked, "your impression?"

Mrs. Stringham's impression seemed lost in her doubts. "How can he ever care for her?"

Her companion, in her companion's heavy manner, sat on it. "By being put in the way of it."

"For God's sake then," Mrs. Stringham wailed, "*put* him in the way! You have him, one feels, in your hand."

Maud Lowder's eyes at this rested on her friend's. "Is that your impression of him?"

"It's my impression, dearest, of you. You handle every one."

Mrs. Lowder's eyes still rested, and Susan Shepherd now felt, for a wonder, not less sincere by seeing that she pleased her. But there was a great limitation. "I don't handle Kate."

It suggested something that her visitor hadn't yet had from her—something the sense of which made Mrs. Stringham gasp. "Do you mean Kate cares for *him*?"

That fact the lady of Lancaster Gate had up to this moment, as we know, enshrouded, and her friend's quick question had produced a change in her face. She blinked—then looked at the question hard; after which, whether she had inadvertently betrayed herself or had only reached a decision and then been affected by the quality of Mrs. Stringham's surprise, she accepted all results. What took place in her for Susan Shepherd was not simply that she made the best of them, but that she suddenly saw more in them to her purpose than she could have imagined. A certain impatience in fact marked in her this transition: she had been keeping back, very hard, an important truth, and wouldn't have liked to hear that she hadn't concealed it cleverly. Susie nevertheless felt herself pass as not a little of a fool with her for not having thought of it. What Susie indeed, however, most thought of at present, in the quick, new light of it, was the wonder of Kate's dissimulation. She had time for that view while she waited for an answer to her cry. "Kate thinks she cares. But she's mistaken. And no one knows it." These things, distinct and responsible, were Mrs. Lowder's retort. Yet they weren't all of it. "*You* don't know it—that must be your line. Or rather your line must be that you deny it utterly."

"Deny that she cares for him?"

"Deny that she so much as thinks that she does. Positively and absolutely. Deny that you've so much as heard of it."

Susie faced this new duty. "To Milly, you mean—if she asks?"

"To Milly, naturally. No one else *will* ask."

"Well," said Mrs. Stringham after a moment, "Milly won't." Mrs. Lowder wondered. "Are you sure?"

"Yes, the more I think of it. And luckily for *me*. I lie badly."

"*I* lie well, thank God," Mrs. Lowder almost snorted, "when, as sometimes will happen, there's nothing else so good. One must always do the best. But without lies then," she went on, "perhaps we can work it out." Her interest had risen; her friend saw her, as within some minutes, more enrolled and in-flamed—presently felt in her what had made the difference. Mrs. Stringham, it was true, descried this at the time but dimly; she only made out at first that Maud had found a reason for helping her. The reason was that, strangely, she might help Maud too, for which she now desired to profess herself ready even to lying. What really perhaps most came out for her was that her hostess was a little disappointed at her doubt of the social solidity of this appliance; and that in turn was to become a steadier light. The truth about Kate's delusion, as her aunt presented it, the delusion about the state of her affections, which might be removed—this was apparently the ground on which they now might more intimately meet. Mrs. Stringham saw herself recruited for the removal of Kate's delusion—by arts, however, in truth, that she as yet quite failed to compass. Or was it perhaps to be only for the removal of Mr. Densher's? —success in which indeed might entail other successes. Before that job, unfortunately, her heart had already failed. She felt that she believed in her bones what Milly believed, and what would now make working for Milly such a dreadful upward tug. All this within her was confusedly present—a cloud of questions out of which Maud Manningham's large seated self loomed, however, as a mass more and more definite, taking in fact for the consultative relation something of the form of an oracle. From the oracle the sound did come—or at any rate the sense did, a sense all accordant with the insufflation she had just seen working. "Yes," the sense was, "I'll help you for Milly, because if that comes off I shall be helped, by its doing so, for Kate"—a view into which Mrs. Stringham could now sufficiently enter. She found herself of a sudden, strange to say, quite willing to operate to Kate's harm, or at least to Kate's good as Mrs. Lowder with a noble anxiety measured it. She found herself in short not caring what became of Kate—only convinced at bottom of the predominance of Kate's star. Kate wasn't in danger, Kate wasn't pathetic; Kate Croy, whatever happened, would take care of Kate Croy. She saw moreover by this time that her friend was travelling even beyond her own speed. Mrs. Lowder had already, in mind, drafted a rough plan of action, a plan vividly enough thrown off as she said: "You must stay on a few days, and you must immediately, both of you, meet him at dinner." In addition to which Maud claimed the merit of having by an instinct of pity, of prescient wisdom, done much, two nights before, to prepare that ground. "The poor child, when I was with her there while you were getting your shawl, quite gave herself away to me."

"Oh I remember how you afterwards put it to me. Though it was nothing more," Susie did herself the justice to observe, "than what I too had quite felt."

But Mrs. Lowder fronted her so on this that she wondered what she had said. "I suppose I ought to be edified at what you can so beautifully give up."

"Give up?" Mrs. Stringham echoed. "Why, I give up nothing —I cling."

Her hostess showed impatience, turning again with some stiffness to her great brass-bound cylinder-desk and giving a push to an object or two disposed there. "*I* give up then. You know how little such a person as Mr. Densher was to be my idea for her. You know what I've been thinking perfectly possible."

"Oh you've been great"—Susie was perfectly fair. "A duke,

a duchess, a princess, a palace: you've made me believe in them too. But where we break down is that *she* doesn't believe in them. Luckily for her—as it seems to be turning out—she doesn't want them. So what's one to do? I assure you I've had many dreams. But I've only one dream now."

Mrs. Stringham's tone in these last words gave so fully her meaning that Mrs. Lowder could but show herself as taking it in. They sat a moment longer confronted on it. "Her having what she does want?"

"If it *will* do anything for her."

Mrs. Lowder seemed to think what it might do; but she spoke for the instant of something else. "It does provoke me a bit, you know—for of course I'm a brute. And I had thought of all sorts of things. Yet it doesn't prevent the fact that we must be decent."

"We must take her"—Mrs. Stringham carried that out—"as she is."

"And we must take Mr. Densher as *he* is." With which Mrs. Lowder gave a sombre laugh. "It's a pity he isn't better!"

"Well, if he were better," her friend rejoined, "you'd have liked him for your niece; and in that case Milly would interfere. I mean," Susie added, "interfere with *you*."

"She interferes with me as it is—not that it matters now. But I saw Kate and her—really as soon as you came to me—set up side by side. I saw your girl—I don't mind telling you—helping my girl; and when I say that," Mrs. Lowder continued, "you'll probably put in for yourself that it was part of the reason of my welcome to you. So you see what I give up. I do give it up. But when I take that line," she further set forth, "I take it handsomely. So good-bye to it all. Good-day to Mrs. Densher! Heavens!" she growled.

Susie held herself a minute. "Even as Mrs. Densher my girl will be somebody."

"Yes, she won't be nobody. Besides," said Mrs. Lowder, "we're talking in the air."

Her companion sadly assented. "We're leaving everything out."

"It's nevertheless interesting." And Mrs. Lowder had another thought. "*He's* not quite nobody either." It brought her back to the question she had already put and which her friend hadn't at the time dealt with. "What in fact do you make of him?"

Susan Shepherd, at this, for reasons not clear even to herself, was moved a little to caution. So she remained general. "He's charming."

She had met Mrs. Lowder's eyes with that extreme pointedness in her own to which people resort when they are not quite candid—a circumstance that had its effect. "Yes; he's charming."

The effect of the words, however, was equally marked; they almost determined in Mrs. Stringham a return of amusement. "I thought you didn't like him!"

"I don't like him for Kate."

"But you don't like him for Milly either."

Mrs. Stringham rose as she spoke, and her friend also got up. "I like him, my dear, for myself."

"Then that's the best way of all."

"Well, it's one way. He's not good enough for my niece, and he's not good enough for you. One's an aunt, one's a wretch and one's a fool."

"Oh *I'm* not—not either," Susie declared.

But her companion kept on. "One lives for others. *You* do that. If I were living for myself I shouldn't at all mind him."

But Mrs. Stringham was sturdier. "Ah if I find him charming it's however I'm living."

Well, it broke Mrs. Lowder down. She hung fire but an instant, giving herself away with a laugh. "Of course he's all right in himself."

"That's all I contend," Susie said with more reserve; and the note in question—what Merton Densher was "in himself"—closed practically, with some inconsequence, this first of their councils.

II

IT HAD at least made the difference for them, they could feel, of an informed state in respect to the great doctor, whom they were now to take as watching, waiting, studying, or at any rate as proposing to himself some such process before he should make up his mind. Mrs. Stringham understood him as considering the matter meanwhile in a spirit that, on this same occasion, at Lancaster Gate, she had come back to a rough notation of before retiring. She followed the course of his reckoning. If what they had talked of *could* happen—if Milly, that is, could have her thoughts taken off herself—it wouldn't do any harm and might conceivably do much good. If it couldn't happen—if, anxiously, though tactfully working, they themselves, conjoined, could do nothing to contribute to it—they would be in no worse a box than before. Only in this latter case the girl would have had her free range for the summer, for the autumn; she would have done her best in the sense enjoined on her, and, coming back at the end to her eminent man, would —besides having more to show him—find him more ready to go on with her. It was visible further to Susan Shepherd—as well as being ground for a second report to her old friend— that Milly did her part for a working view of the general case, inasmuch as she mentioned frankly and promptly that she meant to go and say good-bye to Sir Luke Strett and thank him. She even specified what she was to thank him for, his having been so easy about her behaviour.

"You see I didn't know that—for the liberty I took—I shouldn't afterwards get a stiff note from him."

So much Milly had said to her, and it had made her a trifle rash. "Oh you'll never get a stiff note from him in your life."

She felt her rashness, the next moment, at her young friend's question. "Why not, as well as any one else who has played him a trick?"

"Well, because he doesn't regard it as a trick. He could understand your action. It's all right, you see."

"Yes—I do see. It *is* all right. He's easier with me than with any one else, because that's the way to let me down. He's only making believe, and I'm not worth hauling up."

Rueful at having provoked again this ominous flare, poor Susie grasped at her only advantage. "Do you really accuse a man like Sir Luke Strett of trifling with you?"

She couldn't blind herself to the look her companion gave her—a strange half-amused perception of what she made of it. "Well, so far as it's trifling with me to pity me so much."

"He doesn't pity you," Susie earnestly reasoned. "He just—the same as any one else—likes you."

"He has no business then to like me. He's not the same as any one else."

"Why not, if he wants to work for you?"

Milly gave her another look, but this time a wonderful smile. "Ah there you are!" Mrs. Stringham coloured, for there indeed she was again. But Milly let her off. "Work for me, all the same—work for me! It's of course what I want." Then as usual she embraced her friend. "I'm not going to be as nasty as this to *him*."

"I'm sure I hope not!"—and Mrs. Stringham laughed for the kiss. "I've no doubt, however, he'd take it from you! It's *you*, my dear, who are not the same as any one else."

Milly's assent to which, after an instant, gave her the last word. "No, so that people can take anything from me." And what Mrs. Stringham did indeed resignedly take after this was the absence on her part of any account of the visit then paid. It was the beginning in fact between them of an odd independence—an independence positively of action and custom—on the subject of Milly's future. They went their separate ways with the girl's intense assent; this being really nothing but what she had so wonderfully put in her plea for after Mrs. Stringham's first encounter with Sir Luke. She fairly favoured the idea that Susie had or was to have other encounters—private pointed personal; she favoured every idea, but most of all the idea that she herself was to go on as if nothing were the matter. Since she was to be worked for that would be her way; and though her companion learned from herself nothing of it this was in the event her way with her medical adviser. She put her visit to him on the simplest ground; she had come just to tell him how touched she had been by his good nature. That required little explaining, for, as Mrs. Stringham had said, he quite understood he could but reply that it was all right.

"I had a charming quarter of an hour with that clever lady. You've got good friends."

"So each one of them thinks of all the others. But so I also think," Milly went on, "of all of them together. You're excellent for each other. And it's in that way, I dare say, that you're best for me."

There came to her on this occasion one of the strangest of her impressions, which was at the same time one of the finest of her alarms—the glimmer of a vision that if she should go, as it were, too far, she might perhaps deprive their relation of facility if not of value. Going too far was failing to try at least to remain simple. He would be quite ready to hate her if she did, by heading him off at every point, embarrass his exercise of a kindness that, no doubt, rather constituted for him a high method. Susie wouldn't hate her, since Susie positively wanted to suffer for her; Susie had a noble idea that she might somehow so do her good. Such, however, was not the way in which the greatest of London doctors was to be expected to wish to do it. He wouldn't have time even should he wish; whereby, in a word, Milly felt herself intimately warned. Face to face there with her smooth strong director, she enjoyed at a given moment quite such another lift of feeling as she had known in her crucial talk with Susie. It came round to the same thing; him too she would help to help her if that could possibly be; but if it couldn't possibly be she would assist also to make this right. It wouldn't have taken many minutes more, on the basis in question, almost to reverse for her their characters of patient and physician. What *was* he in fact but patient, what was she but physician, from the moment she embraced once for all the necessity, adopted once for all the policy, of saving him alarms about her subtlety? She would leave the subtlety to him: he would enjoy his use of it, and she herself, no doubt, would in time enjoy his enjoyment. She went so far as to imagine that the inward success of these reflexions flushed her for the minute, to his eyes, with a certain bloom, a comparative appearance of health; and what verily next occurred was that he

gave colour to the presumption. "Every little helps, no doubt!"
—he noticed good-humouredly her harmless sally. "But, help
or no help, you're looking, you know, remarkably well."

"Oh I thought I was," she answered; and it was as if already
she saw his line. Only she wondered what he would have
guessed. If he had guessed anything at all it would be rather
remarkable of him. As for what there *was* to guess, he couldn't
—if this was present to him—have arrived at it save by his own
acuteness. That acuteness was therefore immense; and if it supplied the subtlety she thought of leaving him to, his portion
would be none so bad. Neither, for that matter, would hers be
—which she was even actually enjoying. She wondered if really
then there mightn't be something for her. She hadn't been sure
in coming to him that she was "better," and he hadn't used, he
would be awfully careful not to use, that compromising term
about her; in spite of all of which she would have been ready to
say, for the amiable sympathy of it, "Yes, I *must* be," for he had
this unaided sense of something that had happened to her. It
was a sense unaided, because who could have told him of anything? Susie, she was certain, hadn't yet seen him again, and
there were things it was impossible she could have told him
the first time. Since such was his penetration, therefore, why
shouldn't she gracefully, in recognition of it, accept the new circumstance, the one he was clearly wanting to congratulate her
on, as a sufficient cause? If one nursed a cause tenderly enough
it might produce an effect; and this, to begin with, would be a
way of nursing. "You gave me the other day," she went on,
"plenty to think over, and I've been doing that—thinking it
over—quite as you'll have probably wished me. I think I must
be pretty easy to treat," she smiled, "since you've already done
me so much good."

The only obstacle to reciprocity with him was that he looked
in advance so closely related to all one's possibilities that one
missed the pleasure of really improving it. "Oh no, you're extremely difficult to treat. I've need with you, I assure you, of
all my wit."

"Well, I mean I do come up." She hadn't meanwhile a bit
believed in his answer, convinced as she was that if she *had*
been difficult it would be the last thing he would have told her.
"I'm doing," she said, "as I like."

"Then it's as *I* like. But you must really, though we're having such a decent month, get straight away." In pursuance of which, when she had replied with promptitude that her departure—for the Tyrol and then for Venice—was quite fixed for the fourteenth, he took her up with alacrity. "For Venice? That's perfect, for we shall meet there. I've a dream of it for October, when I'm hoping for three weeks off; three weeks during which, if I can get them clear, my niece, a young person who has quite the whip hand of me, is to take me where she prefers. I heard from her only yesterday that she expects to prefer Venice."

"That's lovely then. I shall expect you there. And anything that, in advance or in any way, I can do for you—!"

"Oh thank you. My niece, I seem to feel, does for me. But it will be capital to find you there."

"I think it ought to make you feel," she said after a moment, "that I *am* easy to treat."

But he shook his head again; he wouldn't have it. "You've not come to that *yet*."

"One has to be so bad for it?"

"Well, I don't think I've ever come to it—to 'ease' of treatment. I doubt if it's possible. I've not, if it is, found any one bad enough. The ease, you see, is for *you*."

"I see—I see."

They had an odd friendly, but perhaps the least bit awkward pause on it; after which Sir Luke asked: "And that clever lady —she goes with you?"

"Mrs. Stringham? Oh dear, yes. She'll stay with me, I hope, to the end."

He had a cheerful blankness. "To the end of what?"

"Well—of everything."

"Ah then," he laughed, "you're in luck. The end of everything is far off. This, you know, I'm hoping," said Sir Luke, "is only the beginning." And the next question he risked might have been a part of his hope. "Just you and she together?"

"No, two other friends; two ladies of whom we've seen more here than of any one and who are just the right people for us."

He thought a moment. "You'll be four women together then?"

"Ah," said Milly, "we're widows and orphans. But I think,"

she added as if to say what she saw would reassure him, "that we shall not be unattractive, as we move, to gentlemen. When you talk of 'life' I suppose you mean mainly gentlemen."

"When I talk of 'life,'" he made answer after a moment during which he might have been appreciating her raciness—"when I talk of life I think I mean more than anything else the beautiful show of it, in its freshness, made by young persons of your age. So go on as you are. I see more and more *how* you are. You can't," he went so far as to say for pleasantness, "better it."

She took it from him with a great show of peace. "One of our companions will be Miss Croy, who came with me here first. It's in *her* that life is splendid; and a part of that is even that she's devoted to me. But she's above all magnificent in herself. So that if you'd like," she freely threw out, "to see *her*—"

"Oh I shall like to see any one who's devoted to you, for clearly it will be jolly to be 'in' it. So that if she's to be at Venice I *shall* see her?"

"We must arrange it—I shan't fail. She moreover has a friend who may also be there"—Milly found herself going on to this. "He's likely to come, I believe, for he always follows her."

Sir Luke wondered. "You mean they're lovers?"

"*He* is," Milly smiled; "but not she. She doesn't care for him."

Sir Luke took an interest. "What's the matter with him?"

"Nothing but that she doesn't like him."

Sir Luke kept it up. "Is he all right?"

"Oh he's very nice. Indeed he's remarkably so."

"And he's to be in Venice?"

"So she tells me she fears. For if he is there he'll be constantly about with her."

"And she'll be constantly about with you?"

"As we're great friends—yes."

"Well then," said Sir Luke, "you won't be four women alone."

"Oh no; I quite recognise the chance of gentlemen. But he won't," Milly pursued in the same wondrous way, "have come, you see, for *me*."

"No—I see. But can't you help him?"

"Can't *you*?" Milly after a moment quaintly asked. Then for the joke of it she explained. "I'm putting you, you see, in relation with my entourage."

It might have been for the joke of it too, by this time, that her eminent friend fell in. "But if this gentleman *isn't* of your 'entourage'? I mean if he's of—what do you call her?—Miss Croy's. Unless indeed you also take an interest in him."

"Oh certainly I take an interest in him!"

"You think there may be then some chance for him?"

"I like him," said Milly, "enough to hope so."

"Then that's all right. But what, pray," Sir Luke next asked, "have I to do with him?"

"Nothing," said Milly, "except that if you're to be there, so may he be. And also that we shan't in that case be simply four dreary women."

He considered her as if at this point she a little tried his patience. "*You're* the least 'dreary' woman I've ever, ever seen. Ever, do you know? There's no reason why you shouldn't have a really splendid life."

"So every one tells me," she promptly returned.

"The conviction—strong already when I had seen you once —is strengthened in me by having seen your friend. There's no doubt about it. The world's before you."

"What did my friend tell you?" Milly asked.

"Nothing that wouldn't have given you pleasure. We talked about you—and freely. I don't deny that. But it shows me I don't require of you the impossible."

She was now on her feet. "I think I know what you require of me."

"Nothing, for you," he went on, "*is* impossible. So go on." He repeated it again—wanting her so to feel that to-day he saw it. "You're all right."

"Well," she smiled—"keep me so."

"Oh you'll get away from me."

"Keep me, keep me," she simply continued with her gentle eyes on him.

She had given him her hand for good-bye, and he thus for a moment did keep her. Something then, while he seemed to think if there were anything more, came back to him; though something of which there wasn't too much to be made. "Of course if there's anything I *can* do for your friend: I mean the gentleman you speak of—?" He gave out in short that he was ready.

"Oh Mr. Densher?" It was as if she had forgotten.

"Mr. Densher—is that his name?"

"Yes—but his case isn't so dreadful." She had within a minute got away from that.

"No doubt—if *you* take an interest." She had got away, but it was as if he made out in her eyes—though they also had rather got away—a reason for calling her back. "Still, if there's anything one can do—?"

She looked at him while she thought, while she smiled. "I'm afraid there's really nothing one can do."

III

NOT yet so much as this morning had she felt herself sink into possession; gratefully glad that the warmth of the Southern summer was still in the high florid rooms, palatial chambers where hard cool pavements took reflexions in their lifelong polish, and where the sun on the stirred sea-water, flickering up through open windows, played over the painted "subjects" in the splendid ceilings—medallions of purple and brown, of brave old melancholy colour, medals as of old reddened gold, embossed and beribboned, all toned with time and all flourished and scolloped and gilded about, set in their great moulded and figured concavity (a nest of white cherubs, friendly creatures of the air) and appreciated by the aid of that second tier of smaller lights, straight openings to the front, which did everything, even with the Baedekers and photographs of Milly's party dreadfully meeting the eye, to make of the place an apartment of state. This at last only, though she had enjoyed the palace for three weeks, seemed to count as effective occupation; perhaps because it was the first time she had been alone—really to call alone—since she had left London, it ministered to her first full and unembarrassed sense of what the great Eugenio had done for her. The great Eugenio, recommended by granddukes and Americans, had entered her service during the last hours of all—had crossed from Paris, after multiplied *pourparlers* with Mrs. Stringham, to whom she had allowed more than ever a free hand, on purpose to escort her to the Continent and encompass her there, and had dedicated to her, from the moment of their meeting, all the treasures of his experience. She had judged him in advance—polyglot and universal, very dear and very deep—as probably but a swindler finished to the finger-tips; for he was for ever carrying one well-kept Italian hand to his heart and plunging the other straight into her pocket, which, as she had instantly observed him to recognise, fitted it like a glove. The remarkable thing was that these elements of their common consciousness had rapidly gathered into an indestructible link, formed the ground of a happy relation; being by this time, strangely, grotesquely, delightfully, what most kept up confidence between them and what most expressed it.

She had seen quickly enough what was happening—the usual thing again, yet once again. Eugenio had, in an interview of five minutes, understood her, had got hold, like all the world, of the idea not so much of the care with which she must be taken up as of the care with which she must be let down. All the world understood her, all the world had got hold; but for nobody yet, she felt, would the idea have been so close a tie or won from herself so patient a surrender. Gracefully, respectfully, consummately enough—always with hands in position and the look, in his thick neat white hair, smooth fat face and black professional, almost theatrical eyes, as of some famous tenor grown too old to make love, but with an art still to make money—did he on occasion convey to her that she was, of all the clients of his glorious career, the one in whom his interest was most personal and paternal. The others had come in the way of business, but for her his sentiment was special. Confidence rested thus on her completely believing that: there was nothing of which she felt more sure. It passed between them every time they conversed; he was abysmal, but this intimacy lived on the surface. He had taken his place already for her among those who were to see her through, and meditation ranked him, in the constant perspective, for the final function, side by side with poor Susie—whom she was now pitying more than ever for having to be herself so sorry and to say so little about it. Eugenio had the general tact of a residuary legatee—which was a character that could be definitely worn; whereas she could see Susie, in the event of her death, in no character at all, Susie being insistently, exclusively concerned in her mere makeshift duration. This principle, for that matter, Milly at present, with a renewed flare of fancy, felt she should herself have liked to believe in. Eugenio had really done for her more than he probably knew—he didn't after all know everything—in having, for the wind-up of the autumn, on a weak word from her, so admirably, so perfectly established her. Her weak word, as a general hint, had been: "At Venice, please, if possible, no dreadful, no vulgar hotel; but, if it can be at all managed—you know what I mean—some fine old rooms, wholly independent, for a series of months. Plenty of them too, and the

more interesting the better: part of a palace, historic and picturesque, but strictly inodorous, where we shall be to ourselves,
with a cook, don't you know?—with servants, frescoes, tapes-
tries, antiquities, the thorough make-believe of a settlement."

The proof of how he better and better understood her was
in all the place; as to his masterly acquisition of which she had
from the first asked no questions. She had shown him enough
what she thought of it, and her forbearance pleased him; with
the part of the transaction that mainly concerned her she
would soon enough become acquainted, and his connexion
with such values as she would then find noted could scarce help
growing, as it were, still more residuary. Charming people,
conscious Venice-lovers, evidently, had given up their house to
her, and had fled to a distance, to other countries, to hide their
blushes alike over what they had, however briefly, alienated,
and over what they had, however durably, gained. They had
preserved and consecrated, and she now—her part of it was
shameless—appropriated and enjoyed. Palazzo Leporelli held
its history still in its great lap, even like a painted idol, a solemn
puppet hung about with decorations. Hung about with pictures and relics, the rich Venetian past, the ineffaceable character, was here the presence revered and served: which brings us
back to our truth of a moment ago—the fact that, more than
ever, this October morning, awkward novice though she might
be, Milly moved slowly to and fro as the priestess of the worship. Certainly it came from the sweet taste of solitude, caught
again and cherished for the hour; always a need of her nature,
moreover, when things spoke to her with penetration. It was
mostly in stillness they spoke to her best; amid voices she lost
the sense. Voices had surrounded her for weeks, and she had
tried to listen, had cultivated them and had answered back;
these had been weeks in which there were other things they
might well prevent her from hearing. More than the prospect
had at first promised or threatened she had felt herself going
on in a crowd and with a multiplied escort; the four ladies pictured by her to Sir Luke Strett as a phalanx comparatively
closed and detached had in fact proved a rolling snowball, condemned from day to day to cover more ground. Susan Shepherd had compared this portion of the girl's excursion to the
Empress Catherine's famous progress across the steppes of

Russia; improvised settlements appeared at each turn of the
road, villagers waiting with addresses drawn up in the language
of London. Old friends in fine were in ambush, Mrs. Lowder's,
Kate Croy's, her own; when the addresses weren't in the language of London they were in the more insistent idioms of
American centres. The current was swollen even by Susie's social connexions; so that there were days, at hotels, at Dolomite
picnics, on lake steamers, when she could almost repay to Aunt
Maud and Kate with interest the debt contracted by the London "success" to which they had opened the door.

Mrs. Lowder's success and Kate's, amid the shock of Milly's
and Mrs. Stringham's compatriots, failed but little, really, of
the concert-pitch; it had gone almost as fast as the boom, over
the sea, of the last great native novel. Those ladies were "so
different"—different, observably enough, from the ladies so
appraising them; it being throughout a case mainly of ladies,
of a dozen at once sometimes, in Milly's apartment, pointing,
also at once, that moral and many others. Milly's companions
were acclaimed not only as perfectly fascinating in themselves,
the nicest people yet known to the acclaimers, but as obvious
helping hands, socially speaking, for the eccentric young
woman, evident initiators and smoothers of her path, possible
subduers of her eccentricity. Short intervals, to her own sense,
stood now for great differences, and this renewed inhalation of
her native air had somehow left her to feel that she already, that
she mainly, struck the compatriot as queer and dissociated. She
moved such a critic, it would appear, as to rather an odd suspicion, a benevolence induced by a want of complete trust: all of
which showed her in the light of a person too plain and too ill-
clothed for a thorough good time, and yet too rich and too
befriended—an intuitive cunning within her managing this
last—for a thorough bad one. The compatriots, in short, by
what she made out, approved her friends for their expert wisdom with her; in spite of which judicial sagacity it was the compatriots who recorded themselves as the innocent parties. She
saw things in these days that she had never seen before, and
she couldn't have said why save on a principle too terrible to
name; whereby she saw that neither Lancaster Gate was what
New York took it for, nor New York what Lancaster Gate fondly
fancied it in coquetting with the plan of a series of American

The Venetian Palace

visits. The plan might have been, humorously, on Mrs. Lowder's part, for the improvement of her social position—and it
had verily in that direction lights that were perhaps but half a
century too prompt; at all of which Kate Croy assisted with the
cool controlled facility that went so well, as the others said,
with her particular kind of good looks, the kind that led you to
expect the person enjoying them *would* dispose of disputa-
tions, speculations, aspirations, in a few very neatly and brightly
uttered words, so simplified in sense, however, that they
sounded, even when guiltless, like rather aggravated slang. It
wasn't that Kate hadn't pretended too that *she* should like to
go to America; it was only that with this young woman Milly
had constantly proceeded, and more than ever of late, on the
theory of intimate confessions, private frank ironies that made
up for their public grimaces and amid which, face to face, they
wearily put off the mask.

These puttings-off of the mask had finally quite become the
form taken by their moments together, moments indeed not
increasingly frequent and not prolonged, thanks to the consciousness of fatigue on Milly's side whenever, as she herself expressed it, she got out of harness. They flourished their masks,
the independent pair, as they might have flourished Spanish
fans; they smiled and sighed on removing them; but the gesture, the smiles, the sighs, strangely enough, might have been
suspected the greatest reality in the business. Strangely enough,
we say, for the volume of effusion in general would have been
found by either on measurement to be scarce proportional to
the paraphernalia of relief. It was when they called each other's
attention to their ceasing to pretend, it was then that what
they were keeping back was most in the air. There was a difference, no doubt, and mainly to Kate's advantage: Milly didn't
quite see what her friend could keep back, was possessed of, in
fine, that would be so subject to retention; whereas it was comparatively plain sailing for Kate that poor Milly had a treasure
to hide. This was not the treasure of a shy, an abject affection
—concealment, on that head, belonging to quite another
phase of such states; it was much rather a principle of pride rel-
atively bold and hard, a principle that played up like a fine steel
spring at the lightest pressure of too near a footfall. Thus insu-
perably guarded was the truth about the girl's own conception

of her validity; thus was a wondering pitying sister condemned wistfully to look at her from the far side of the moat she had dug round her tower. Certain aspects of the connexion of these young women show for us, such is the twilight that gathers about them, in the likeness of some dim scene in a Maeterlinck play; we have positively the image, in the delicate dusk, of the figures so associated and yet so opposed, so mutually watchful: that of the angular pale princess, ostrich-plumed, black-robed, hung about with amulets, reminders, relics, mainly seated, mainly still, and that of the upright restless slow-circling lady of her court who exchanges with her, across the black water streaked with evening gleams, fitful questions and answers. The upright lady, with thick dark braids down her back, drawing over the grass a more embroidered train, makes the whole circuit, and makes it again, and the broken talk, brief and sparingly allusive, seems more to cover than to free their sense. This is because, when it fairly comes to not having others to consider, they meet in an air that appears rather anxiously to wait for their words. Such an impression as that was in fact grave, and might be tragic; so that, plainly enough, systematically at last, they settled to a care of what they said.

There could be no gross phrasing to Milly, in particular, of the probability that if she wasn't so proud she might be pitied with more comfort—more to the person pitying; there could be no spoken proof, no sharper demonstration than the consistently considerate attitude, that this marvellous mixture of her weakness and of her strength, her peril, if such it were, and her option, made her, kept her, irresistibly interesting. Kate's predicament in the matter was, after all, very much Mrs. Stringham's own, and Susan Shepherd herself indeed, in our Maeterlinck picture, might well have hovered in the gloaming by the moat. It may be declared for Kate, at all events, that her sincerity about her friend, through this time, was deep, her compassionate imagination strong; and that these things gave her a virtue, a good conscience, a credibility for herself, so to speak, that were later to be precious to her. She grasped with her keen intelligence the logic of their common duplicity, went unassisted through the same ordeal as Milly's other hushed follower, easily saw that for the girl to be explicit was to betray divinations, gratitudes, glimpses of the felt contrast between

her fortune and her fear—all of which would have contradicted her systematic bravado. That was it, Kate wonderingly
saw: to recognise was to bring down the avalanche—the avalanche Milly lived so in watch for and that might be started by
the lightest of breaths; though less possibly the breath of her
own stifled plaint than that of the vain sympathy, the mere
helpless gaping inference of others. With so many suppressions
as these, therefore, between them, their withdrawal together
to unmask had to fall back, as we have hinted, on a nominal
motive—which was decently represented by a joy at the drop
of chatter. Chatter had in truth all along attended their steps,
but they took the despairing view of it on purpose to have
ready, when face to face, some view or other of something.
The relief of getting out of harness—that was the moral of their
meetings; but the moral of this, in turn, was that they couldn't
so much as ask each other why harness need be worn. Milly
wore it as a general armour.

She was out of it at present, for some reason, as she hadn't
been for weeks; she was always out of it, that is, when alone, and
her companions had never yet so much as just now affected her
as dispersed and suppressed. It was as if still again, still more
tacitly and wonderfully, Eugenio had understood her, taking it
from her without a word and just bravely and brilliantly in the
name, for instance, of the beautiful day: "Yes, get me an hour
alone; take them off—I don't care where; absorb, amuse, detain them; drown them, kill them if you will: so that I may just
a little, all by myself, see where I am." She was conscious of the
dire impatience of it, for she gave up Susie as well as the others
to him—Susie who would have drowned her very self for her;
gave her up to a mercenary monster through whom she thus
purchased respites. Strange were the turns of life and the
moods of weakness; strange the flickers of fancy and the cheats
of hope; yet lawful, all the same—weren't they?—those exper-
iments tried with the truth that consisted, at the worst, but in
practising on one's self. She was now playing with the thought
that Eugenio might *inclusively* assist her: he had brought home
to her, and always by remarks that were really quite soundless,
the conception, hitherto ungrasped, of some complete use of
her wealth itself, some use of it as a counter-move to fate. It
had passed between them as preposterous that with so much

money she should just stupidly and awkwardly *want*—any more want a life, a career, a consciousness, than want a house, a carriage or a cook. It was as if she had had from him a kind of expert professional measure of what he was in a position, at a stretch, to undertake for her; the thoroughness of which, for that matter, she could closely compare with a looseness on Sir Luke Strett's part that—at least in Palazzo Leporelli when mornings were fine—showed as almost amateurish. Sir Luke hadn't said to her "Pay enough money and leave the rest to *me*"—which was distinctly what Eugenio did say. Sir Luke had appeared indeed to speak of purchase and payment, but in reference to a different sort of cash. Those were amounts not to be named nor reckoned, and such moreover as she wasn't sure of having at her command. Eugenio—this was the difference —could name, could reckon, and prices of *his* kind were things she had never suffered to scare her. She had been willing, goodness knew, to pay enough for anything, for everything, and here was simply a new view of the sufficient quantity. She amused herself—for it came to that, since Eugenio was there to sign the receipt—with possibilities of meeting the bill. She was more prepared than ever to pay enough, and quite as much as ever to pay too much. What else—if such were points at which your most trusted servant failed—was the use of being, as the dear Susies of earth called you, a princess in a palace?

She made now, alone, the full circuit of the place, noble and peaceful while the summer sea, stirring here and there a curtain or an outer blind, breathed into its veiled spaces. She had a vision of clinging to it; that perhaps Eugenio could manage. She was *in* it, as in the ark of her deluge, and filled with such a tenderness for it that why shouldn't this, in common mercy, be warrant enough? She would never, never leave it—she would engage to that; would ask nothing more than to sit tight in it and float on and on. The beauty and intensity, the real momentary relief of this conceit, reached their climax in the positive purpose to put the question to Eugenio on his return as she had not yet put it; though the design, it must be added, dropped a little when, coming back to the great saloon from which she had started on her pensive progress, she found Lord Mark, of whose arrival in Venice she had been unaware, and who had now—while a servant was following her through empty rooms—been asked, in her absence, to wait. He had waited then, Lord Mark, he was waiting—oh unmistakeably; never before had he so much struck her as the man to do that on occasion with patience, to do it indeed almost as with gratitude for the chance, though at the same time with a sort of notifying firmness. The odd thing, as she was afterwards to recall, was that her wonder for what had brought him was not immediate, but had come at the end of five minutes; and also, quite incoherently, that she felt almost as glad to see him, and almost as forgiving of his interruption of her solitude, as if he had already been in her thought or acting at her suggestion. He was somehow, at the best, the end of a respite; one might like him very much and yet feel that his presence tempered precious solitude more than any other known to one: in spite of all of which, as he was neither dear Susie, nor dear Kate, nor dear Aunt Maud, nor even, for the least, dear Eugenio in person, the sight of him did no damage to her sense of the dispersal of her friends. She hadn't been so thoroughly alone with him since those moments of his showing her the great portrait at Matcham, the moments that had exactly made the high-water-mark of her security, the moments during which her tears themselves, those she had been ashamed of, were the sign of her consciously rounding her protective promontory, quitting the blue gulf of comparative ignorance and reaching her view of the troubled sea. His presence now referred itself to his presence then, reminding her how kind he had been, altogether, at Matcham, and telling her, unexpectedly, at a time when she could particularly feel it, that, for such kindness and for the beauty of what they remembered together, she hadn't lost him—quite the contrary. To receive him handsomely, to receive him there, to see him interested and charmed, as well, clearly, as delighted to have found her without some other person to spoil it—these things were so pleasant for the first minutes that they might have represented on her part some happy foreknowledge.

She gave an account of her companions while he on his side failed to press her about them, even though describing his appearance, so unheralded, as the result of an impulse obeyed on

the spot. He had been shivering at Carlsbad, belated there and
blue, when taken by it; so that, knowing where they all were,
he had simply caught the first train. He explained how he had
known where they were; he had heard—what more natural?—
from their friends, Milly's and his. He mentioned this betimes,
but it was with his mention, singularly, that the girl became
conscious of her inner question about his reason. She noticed
his plural, which added to Mrs. Lowder or added to Kate; but
she presently noticed also that it didn't affect her as explaining.
Aunt Maud had written to him, Kate apparently—and this was
interesting—had written to him; but their design presumably
hadn't been that he should come and sit there as if rather relieved, so far as *they* were concerned, at postponements. He
only said "Oh!" and again "Oh!" when she sketched their
probable morning for him, under Eugenio's care and Mrs.
Stringham's—sounding it quite as if any suggestion that he
should overtake them at the Rialto or the Bridge of Sighs would
leave him temporarily cold. This precisely it was that, after a
little, operated for Milly as an obscure but still fairly direct
check to confidence. He had known where they all were from
the others, but it was not for the others that, in his actual dispositions, he had come. That, strange to say, was a pity; for,
stranger still to say, she could have shown him more confidence
if he himself had had less intention. His intention so chilled
her, from the moment she found herself divining it, that, just
for the pleasure of going on with him fairly, just for the pleasure of their remembrance together of Matcham and the
Bronzino, the climax of her fortune, she could have fallen to
pleading with him and to reasoning, to undeceiving him in
time. There had been, for ten minutes, with the directness of
her welcome to him and the way this clearly pleased him, something of the grace of amends made, even though he couldn't
know it—amends for her not having been originally sure, for
instance at that first dinner of Aunt Maud's, that he was adequately human. That first dinner of Aunt Maud's added itself
to the hour at Matcham, added itself to other things, to con-
solidate, for her present benevolence, the ease of their relation,
making it suddenly delightful that he had thus turned up. He
exclaimed, as he looked about, on the charm of the place:
"What a temple to taste and an expression of the pride of life,

yet, with all that, what a jolly *home*!"—so that, for his entertainment, she could offer to walk him about though she mentioned that she had just been, for her own purposes, in a
general prowl, taking everything in more susceptibly than
before. He embraced her offer without a scruple and seemed
to rejoice that he was to find her susceptible.

IV

SHE couldn't have said what it was, in the conditions, that renewed the whole solemnity, but by the end of twenty minutes a kind of wistful hush had fallen upon them, as before something poignant in which her visitor also participated. That was nothing verily but the perfection of the charm—or nothing rather but their excluded disinherited state in the presence of it. The charm turned on them a face that was cold in its beauty, that was full of a poetry never to be theirs, that spoke with an ironic smile of a possible but forbidden life. It all rolled afresh over Milly: "Oh the impossible romance—!" The romance for her, yet once more, would be to sit there for ever, through all her time, as in a fortress; and the idea became an image of never going down, of remaining aloft in the divine dustless air, where she would hear but the plash of the water against stone. The great floor on which they moved was at an altitude, and this prompted the rueful fancy. "Ah not to go down—never, never to go down!" she strangely sighed to her friend.

"But why shouldn't you," he asked, "with that tremendous old staircase in your court? There ought of course always to be people at top and bottom, in Veronese costumes, to watch you do it."

She shook her head both lightly and mournfully enough at his not understanding. "Not even for people in Veronese costumes. I mean that the positive beauty is that one needn't go down. I don't move in fact," she added—"now. I've not been out, you know. I stay up. That's how you happily found me."

Lord Mark wondered—he was, oh yes, adequately human. "You don't go about?"

She looked over the place, the storey above the apartments in which she had received him, the sala corresponding to the sala below and fronting the great canal with its gothic arches. The casements between the arches were open, the ledge of the balcony broad, the sweep of the canal, so overhung, admirable, and the flutter toward them of the loose white curtain an invitation to she scarce could have said what. But there was no mystery after a moment; she had never felt so invited to anything as to make that, and that only, just where she was, her adventure. It would be—to this it kept coming back—the adventure of not stirring. "I go about just here."

"Do you mean," Lord Mark presently asked, "that you're really not well?"

They were at the window, pausing, lingering, with the fine old faded palaces opposite and the slow Adriatic tide beneath; but after a minute, and before she answered, she had closed her eyes to what she saw and unresistingly dropped her face into her arms, which rested on the coping. She had fallen to her knees on the cushion of the window-place, and she leaned there, in a long silence, with her forehead down. She knew that her silence was itself too straight an answer, but it was beyond her now to say that she saw her way. She would have made the question itself impossible to others—impossible for example to such a man as Merton Densher; and she could wonder even on the spot what it was a sign of in her feeling for Lord Mark that from his lips it almost tempted her to break down. This was doubtless really because she cared for him so little; to let herself go with him thus, suffer his touch to make her cup overflow, would be the relief—since it was actually, for her nerves, a question of relief—that would cost her least. If he had come to her moreover with the intention she believed, or even if this intention had but been determined in him by the spell of their situation, he mustn't be mistaken about her value—for what value did she now have? It throbbed within her as she knelt there that she had none at all; though, holding herself, not yet speaking, she tried, even in the act, to recover what might be possible of it. With that there came to her a light: wouldn't her value, for the man who should marry her, be precisely in the ravage of her disease? *She* mightn't last, but her money would. For a man in whom the vision of her money should be intense, in whom it should be most of the ground for "making up" to her, any prospective failure on her part to be long for this world might easily count as a positive attraction. Such a man, proposing to please, persuade, secure her, appropriate her for such a time, shorter or longer, as nature and the doctors should allow, would make the best of her, ill, damaged, disagreeable though she might be, for the sake of eventual benefits: she being clearly a person of the sort esteemed likely to do the handsome thing by a stricken and sorrowing husband.

She had said to herself betimes, in a general way, that whatever habits her youth might form, that of seeing an interested suitor in every bush should certainly never grow to be one of them—an attitude she had early judged as ignoble, as poisonous. She had had accordingly in fact as little to do with it as possible and she scarce knew why at the present moment she should have had to catch herself in the act of imputing an ugly motive. It didn't sit, the ugly motive, in Lord Mark's cool English eyes; the darker side of it at any rate showed, to her imagination, but briefly. Suspicion moreover, with this, simplified itself: there was a beautiful reason—indeed there were two— why her companion's motive shouldn't matter. One was that even should he desire her without a penny she wouldn't marry him for the world; the other was that she felt him, after all, perceptively, kindly, very pleasantly and humanly, concerned for her. They were also two things, his wishing to be well, to be very well, with her, and his beginning to feel her as threatened, haunted, blighted; but they were melting together for him, making him, by their combination, only the more sure that, as he probably called it to himself, he liked her. That was presently what remained with her—his really doing it; and with the natural and proper incident of being conciliated by her weakness. Would she really have had him—she could ask herself that—disconcerted or disgusted by it? If he could only be touched enough to do what she preferred, not to raise, not to press any question, he might render her a much better service than by merely enabling her to refuse him. Again, again it was strange, but he figured to her for the moment as the one safe sympathiser. It would have made her worse to talk to others, but she wasn't afraid with him of how he might wince and look pale. She would keep him, that is, her one easy relation— in the sense of easy for himself. Their actual outlook had meanwhile such charm, what surrounded them within and without did so much toward making appreciative stillness as natural as at the opera, that she could consider she hadn't made him hang on her lips when at last, instead of saying if she were well or ill, she repeated: "I go about here. I don't get tired of it. I never should—it suits me so. I adore the place," she went on, "and I don't want in the least to give it up."

"Neither should I if I had your luck. Still, with that luck, for one's *all*—! Should you positively like to live here?"

"I think I should like," said poor Milly after an instant, "to die here."

Which made him, precisely, laugh. That was what she wanted —when a person did care: it was the pleasant human way, without depths of darkness. "Oh it's not good enough for *that*! That requires picking. But can't you keep it? It is, you know, the sort of place to see you in; you carry out the note, fill it, people it, quite by yourself, and you might do much worse—I mean for your friends—than show yourself here a while, three or four months, every year. But it's not my notion for the rest of the time. One has quite other uses for you."

"What sort of a use for me is it," she smilingly enquired, "to kill me?"

"Do you mean we should kill you in England?"

"Well, I've seen you and I'm afraid. You're too much for me—too many. England bristles with questions. This is more, as you say there, my form."

"Oho, oho!"—he laughed again as if to humour her. "Can't you then buy it—for a price? Depend upon it they'll treat for money. That is for money enough."

"I've exactly," she said, "been wondering if they won't. I think I shall try. But if I get it I shall cling to it." They were talking sincerely. "It will be my life—paid for as that. It will become my great gilded shell; so that those who wish to find me must come and hunt me up."

"Ah then you *will* be alive," said Lord Mark.

"Well, not quite extinct perhaps, but shrunken, wasted, wizened; rattling about here like the dried kernel of a nut."

"Oh," Lord Mark returned, "we, much as you mistrust us, can do better for you than that."

"In the sense that you'll feel it better for me really to have it over?"

He let her see now that she worried him, and after a look at her, of some duration, without his glasses—which always altered the expression of his eyes—he re-settled the nippers on his nose and went back to the view. But the view, in turn, soon enough released him. "Do you remember something I said to you that day at Matcham—or at least fully meant to?"

"Oh yes, I remember everything at Matcham. It's another life."

"Certainly it will be—I mean the kind of thing: what I then wanted it to represent for you. Matcham, you know," he continued, "is symbolic. I think I tried to rub that into you a little."

She met him with the full memory of what he had tried—not an inch, not an ounce of which was lost to her. "What I meant is that it seems a hundred years ago."

"Oh for me it comes in better. Perhaps a part of what makes me remember it," he pursued, "is that I was quite aware of what might have been said about what I was doing. I wanted you to take it from me that I should perhaps be able to look after you—well, rather better. Rather better, of course, than certain other persons in particular."

"Precisely—than Mrs. Lowder, than Miss Croy, even than Mrs. Stringham."

"Oh Mrs. Stringham's all right!" Lord Mark promptly amended.

It amused her even with what she had else to think of; and she could show him at all events how little, in spite of the hundred years, she had lost what he alluded to. The way he was with her at this moment made in fact the other moment so vivid as almost to start again the tears it had started at the time. "You could do so much for me, yes. I perfectly understood you."

"I wanted, you see," he despite this explained, "to *fix* your confidence. I mean, you know, in the right place."

"Well, Lord Mark, you did—it's just exactly now, my confidence, where you put it then. The only difference," said Milly, "is that I seem now to have no use for it. Besides," she then went on, "I do seem to feel you disposed to act in a way that would undermine it a little."

He took no more notice of these last words than if she hadn't said them, only watching her at present as with a gradual new light. "Are you *really* in any trouble?"

To this, on her side, she gave no heed. Making out his light was a little a light for herself. "Don't say, don't try to say, anything that's impossible. There are much better things you can do."

He looked straight at it and then straight over it. "It's too monstrous that one can't ask you as a friend what one wants so to know."

"What is it you want to know?" She spoke, as by a sudden turn, with a slight hardness. "Do you want to know if I'm badly ill?"

The sound of it in truth, though from no raising of her voice, invested the idea with a kind of terror, but a terror all for others. Lord Mark winced and flushed—clearly couldn't help it; but he kept his attitude together and spoke even with unwonted vivacity. "Do you imagine I can see you suffer and not say a word?"

"You won't see me suffer—don't be afraid. I shan't be a public nuisance. That's why I should have liked *this*: it's so beautiful in itself and yet it's out of the gangway. You won't know anything about anything," she added; and then as if to make with decision an end: "And you *don't*! No, not even you." He faced her through it with the remains of his expression, and she saw him as clearly—for *him*—bewildered; which made her wish to be sure not to have been unkind. She would be kind once for all; that would be the end. "I'm very badly ill."

"And you don't do anything?"

"I do everything. Everything's *this*," she smiled. "I'm doing it now. One can't do more than live."

"Ah than live in the right way, no. But is *that* what you do? Why haven't you advice?"

He had looked about at the rococo elegance as if there were fifty things it didn't give her, so that he suggested with urgency the most absent. But she met his remedy with a smile. "I've the best advice in the world. I'm acting under it now. I act upon it in receiving you, in talking with you thus. One can't, as I tell you, do more than live."

"Oh live!" Lord Mark ejaculated.

"Well, it's immense for *me*." She finally spoke as if for amusement; now that she had uttered her truth, that he had learnt it from herself as no one had yet done, her emotion had, by the fact, dried up. There she was; but it was as if she would never speak again. "I shan't," she added, "have missed everything."

"Why should you have missed *anything*?" She felt, as he sounded this, to what, within the minute, he had made up his mind. "You're the person in the world for whom that's least necessary; for whom one would call it in fact most impossible; for whom 'missing' at all will surely require an extraordinary amount of misplaced good will. Since you believe in advice, for God's sake take *mine*. I know what you want."

Oh she knew he would know it. But she had brought it on herself—or almost. Yet she spoke with kindness. "I think I want not to be too much worried."

"You want to be adored." It came at last straight. "Nothing would worry you less. I mean as I shall do it. It *is* so"—he firmly kept it up. "You're not loved enough."

"Enough for what, Lord Mark?"

"Why to get the full good of it."

Well, she didn't after all mock at him. "I see what you mean. That full good of it which consists in finding one's self forced to love in return." She had grasped it, but she hesitated. "Your idea is that I might find myself forced to love *you*?"

"Oh 'forced'—!" He was so fine and so expert, so awake to anything the least ridiculous, and of a type with which the preaching of passion somehow so ill consorted—he was so much all these things that he had absolutely to take account of them himself. And he did so, in a single intonation, beautifully. Milly liked him again, liked him for such shades as that, liked him so that it was woeful to see him spoiling it, and still more woeful to have to rank him among those minor charms of existence that she gasped at moments to remember she must give up. "Is it inconceivable to you that you might try?"

"To be so favourably affected by you—?"

"To believe in me. To believe in me," Lord Mark repeated.

Again she hesitated. "To 'try' in return for your trying?"

"Oh I shouldn't have to!" he quickly declared. The prompt neat accent, however, his manner of disposing of her question, failed of real expression, as he himself the next moment intelligently, helplessly, almost comically saw—a failure pointed moreover by the laugh into which Milly was immediately startled. As a suggestion to her of a healing and uplifting passion it *was* in truth deficient; it wouldn't do as the communication of a force that should sweep them both away. And the beauty of him was that he too, even in the act of persuasion, of self-persuasion, could understand that, and could thereby show but the better as fitting into the pleasant commerce of prosperity. The way she let him see that she looked at him was a thing to shut him out, of itself, from services of danger, a thing that made a discrimination against him never yet made—made at least to any consciousness of his own. Born to float in a sustaining air, this would be his first encounter with a judgement formed in the sinister light of tragedy. The gathering dusk of *her* personal world presented itself to him, in her eyes, as an element in which it was vain for him to pretend he could find himself at home, since it was charged with depressions and with dooms, with the chill of the losing game. Almost without her needing to speak, and simply by the fact that there could be, in such a case, no decent substitute for a felt intensity, he had to take it from her that practically he was afraid—whether afraid to protest falsely enough, or only afraid of what might be eventually disagreeable in a compromised alliance, being a minor question. She believed she made out besides, wonderful girl, that he had never quite expected to have to protest about anything beyond his natural convenience—more, in fine, than his disposition and habits, his education as well, his personal *moyens*, in short, permitted. His predicament was therefore one he couldn't like, and also one she willingly would have spared him hadn't he brought it on himself. No man, she was quite aware, could enjoy thus having it from her that he wasn't good for what she would have called her reality. It wouldn't have taken much more to enable her positively to make out in him that he was virtually capable of hinting—had his innermost feeling spoken—at the propriety rather, in his interest, of some cutting down, some dressing up, of the offensive real. He would meet that halfway, but the real must also meet *him*. Milly's sense of it for herself, which was so conspicuously, so financially supported, couldn't, or wouldn't, so accommodate him, and the perception of that fairly showed in his face after a moment like the smart of a blow. It had marked the one minute during which he could again be touching to her. By the time he had tried once more, after all, to insist, he had quite ceased to be so.

By this time she had turned from their window to make a

diversion, had walked him through other rooms, appealing again to the inner charm of the place, going even so far for that purpose as to point afresh her independent moral, to repeat that if one only had such a house for one's own and loved it and cherished it enough, it would pay one back in kind, would close one in from harm. He quite grasped for the quarter of an hour the perch she held out to him—grasped it with one hand, that is, while she felt him attached to his own clue with the other; he was by no means either so sore or so stupid, to do him all justice, as not to be able to behave more or less as if nothing had happened. It was one of his merits, to which she did justice too, that both his native and his acquired notion of behaviour rested on the general assumption that nothing—nothing to make a deadly difference for him—ever *could* happen. It was, socially, a working view like another, and it saw them easily enough through the greater part of the rest of their adventure. Downstairs again, however, with the limit of his stay in sight, the sign of his smarting, when all was said, reappeared for her—breaking out moreover, with an effect of strangeness, in another quite possibly sincere allusion to her state of health. He might for that matter have been seeing what he could do in the way of making it a grievance that she should snub him for a charity, on his own part, exquisitely roused. "It's true, you know, all the same, and I don't care a straw for your trying to freeze one up." He seemed to show her, poor man, bravely, how little he cared. "Everybody knows affection often makes things out when indifference doesn't notice. And that's why I know that *I* notice."

"Are you sure you've got it right?" the girl smiled. "I thought rather that affection was supposed to be blind."

"Blind to faults, not to beauties," Lord Mark promptly returned.

"And are my extremely private worries, my entirely domestic complications, which I'm ashamed to have given you a glimpse of—are they beauties?"

"Yes, for those who care for you—as every one does. Everything about you is a beauty. Besides which I don't believe," he declared, "in the seriousness of what you tell me. It's too absurd you should have *any* trouble about which something can't be done. If you can't get the right thing, who *can*, in all the world, I should like to know? You're the first young woman of your time. I mean what I say." He looked, to do him justice, quite as if he did; not ardent, but clear—simply so competent, in such a position, to compare, that his quiet assertion had the force not so much perhaps of a tribute as of a warrant. "We're all in love with you. I'll put it that way, dropping any claim of my own, if you can bear it better. I speak as one of the lot. You weren't born simply to torment us—you were born to make us happy. Therefore you must listen to us."

She shook her head with her slowness, but this time with all her mildness. "No, I mustn't listen to you—that's just what I mustn't do. The reason is, please, that it simply kills me. I must be as attached to you as you will, since you give that lovely account of yourselves. I give you in return the fullest possible belief of what it would be—" And she pulled up a little. "I give and give and give—there you are; stick to me as close as you like and see if I don't. Only I can't listen or receive or accept— I can't *agree*. I can't make a bargain. I can't really. You must believe that from me. It's all I've wanted to say to you, and why should it spoil anything?"

He let her question fall—though clearly, it might have seemed, because, for reasons or for none, there was so much that *was* spoiled. "You want somebody of your own." He came back, whether in good faith or in bad, to that; and it made her repeat her headshake. He kept it up as if his faith were of the best. "You want somebody, you want somebody."

She was to wonder afterwards if she hadn't been at this juncture on the point of saying something emphatic and vulgar— "Well, I don't at all events want *you*!" What somehow happened, nevertheless, the pity of it being greater than the irritation—the sadness, to her vivid sense, of his being so painfully astray, wandering in a desert in which there was nothing to nourish him—was that his error amounted to positive wrongdoing. She was moreover so acquainted with quite another sphere of usefulness for him that her having suffered him to insist almost convicted her of indelicacy. Why hadn't she stopped him off with her first impression of his purpose? She could do so now only by the allusion she had been wishing not to make. "Do you know I don't think you're doing very right?—and as a thing quite apart, I mean, from my listening to you. That's not right either—except that I'm *not* listening. You oughtn't to have come to Venice to see *me*—and in fact you've not come, and you mustn't behave as if you had. You've much older friends than I, and ever so much better. Really, if you've come at all, you can only have come—properly, and if I may say so honourably—for the best friend, as I believe her to be, that you have in the world."

When once she had said it he took it, oddly enough, as if he had been more or less expecting it. Still, he looked at her very hard, and they had a moment of this during which neither pronounced a name, each apparently determined that the other should. It was Milly's fine coercion, in the event, that was the stronger. "Miss Croy?" Lord Mark asked.

It might have been difficult to make out that she smiled. "Mrs. Lowder." He did make out something, and then fairly coloured for its attestation of his comparative simplicity. "I call *her* on the whole the best. I can't imagine a man's having a better."

Still with his eyes on her he turned it over. "Do you want me to marry Mrs. Lowder?"

At which it seemed to her that it was he who was almost vulgar! But she wouldn't in any way have that. "You know, Lord Mark, what I mean. One isn't in the least turning you out into the cold world. There's no cold world for you at all, I think," she went on; "nothing but a very warm and watchful and expectant world that's waiting for you at any moment you choose to take it up."

He never budged, but they were standing on the polished concrete and he had within a few minutes possessed himself again of his hat. "Do you want me to marry Kate Croy?"

"Mrs. Lowder wants it—I do no wrong, I think, in saying that; and she understands moreover that you know she does."

Well, he showed how beautifully he could take it; and it wasn't obscure to her, on her side, that it was a comfort to deal with a gentleman. "It's ever so kind of you to see such opportunities for me. But what's the use of my tackling Miss Croy?"

Milly rejoiced on the spot to be so able to point out. "Because she's the handsomest and cleverest and most charming creature I ever saw, and because if I were a man I should simply adore her. In fact I do as it is." It was a luxury of response.

"Oh, my dear lady, plenty of people adore her. But that can't further the case of *all*."

"Ah," she went on, "I know about 'people.' If the case of one's bad, the case of another's good. I don't see what you have to fear from any one else," she said, "save through your being foolish, this way, about *me*."

So she said, but she was aware the next moment of what he was making of what she didn't see. "Is it your idea—since we're talking of these things in these ways—that the young lady you describe in such superlative terms is to be had for the asking?"

"Well, Lord Mark, try. She *is* a great person. But don't be humble." She was almost gay.

It was this apparently, at last, that was too much for him. "But don't you really *know*?"

As a challenge, practically, to the commonest intelligence she could pretend to, it made her of course wish to be fair. "I 'know,' yes, that a particular person's very much in love with her."

"Then you must know by the same token that she's very much in love with a particular person."

"Ah I beg your pardon!"—and Milly quite flushed at having so crude a blunder imputed to her. "You're wholly mistaken."

"It's not true?"

"It's not true."

His stare became a smile. "Are you very, very sure?"

"As sure as one can be"—and Milly's manner could match it—"when one has every assurance. I speak on the best authority."

He hesitated. "Mrs. Lowder's?"

"No. I don't call Mrs. Lowder's the best."

"Oh I thought you were just now saying," he laughed, "that everything about her's so good."

"Good for you"—she was perfectly clear. "For you," she went on, "let her authority be the best. She doesn't believe what you mention, and you must know yourself how little she makes of it. So you can take it from her. *I* take it—" But Milly, with the positive tremor of her emphasis, pulled up.

"You take it from Kate?"

"From Kate herself."

"That she's thinking of no one at all?"

"Of no one at all." Then, with her intensity, she went on. "She has given me her word for it."

"Oh!" said Lord Mark. To which he next added: "And what do you call her word?"

It made Milly, on her side, stare—though perhaps partly but with the instinct of gaining time for the consciousness that she was already a little further "in" than she had designed. "Why, Lord Mark, what should *you* call her word?"

"Ah I'm not obliged to say. I've not asked her. You apparently have."

Well, it threw her on her defence—a defence that she felt, however, especially as of Kate. "We're very intimate," she said in a moment; "so that, without prying into each other's affairs, she naturally tells me things."

Lord Mark smiled as at a lame conclusion. "You mean then she made you of her own movement the declaration you quote?"

Milly thought again, though with hindrance rather than help in her sense of the way their eyes now met—met as for their each seeing in the other more than either said. What she most felt that she herself saw was the strange disposition on her companion's part to disparage Kate's veracity. She could be only concerned to "stand up" for that.

"I mean what I say: that when she spoke of her having no private interest—"

"She took her oath to you?" Lord Mark interrupted.

Milly didn't quite see why he should so catechise her; but she met it again for Kate. "She left me in no doubt whatever of her being free."

At this Lord Mark did look at her, though he continued to smile. "And thereby in no doubt of *your* being too?" It was as if as soon as he had said it, however, he felt it as something of a mistake, and she couldn't herself have told by what queer glare at him she had instantly signified that. He at any rate gave her glare no time to act further; he fell back on the spot, and with a light enough movement, within his rights. "That's all very well, but why in the world, dear lady, should she be swearing to you?"

She had to take this "dear lady" as applying to herself; which disconcerted her when he might now so gracefully have used it for the aspersed Kate. Once more it came to her that she must claim her own part of the aspersion. "Because, as I've told you, we're such tremendous friends."

"Oh," said Lord Mark, who for the moment looked as if that might have stood rather for an absence of such rigours. He was going, however, as if he had in a manner, at the last, got more or less what he wanted. Milly felt, while he addressed his next few words to leave-taking, that she had given rather more than she intended or than she should be able, when once more getting herself into hand, theoretically to defend. Strange enough in fact that he had had from her, about herself—and, under the searching spell of the place, infinitely straight—what no one else had had: neither Kate, nor Aunt Maud, nor Merton Densher, nor Susan Shepherd. He had made her within a minute, in particular, she was aware, lose her presence of mind, and she now wished he would take himself off, so that she might either recover it or bear the loss better in solitude. If he paused, however, she almost at the same time saw, it was because of his watching the approach, from the end of the sala, of one of the gondoliers, who, whatever excursions were appointed for the party with the attendance of the others, always, as the most decorative, most sashed and starched, remained at the palace on the theory that she might whimsically want him —which she never, in her caged freedom, had yet done. Brown Pasquale, slipping in white shoes over the marble and suggesting to her perpetually charmed vision she could scarce say what, either a mild Hindoo, too noiseless almost for her nerves, or simply a barefooted seaman on the deck of a ship—Pasquale offered to sight a small salver, which he obsequiously held out to her with its burden of a visiting-card. Lord Mark—and as if also for admiration of him—delayed his departure to let her receive it; on which she read it with the instant effect of another blow to her presence of mind. This precarious quantity was indeed now so gone that even for dealing with Pasquale she had to do her best to conceal its disappearance. The effort was made, none the less, by the time she had asked if the gentleman were below and had taken in the fact that he had come up. He had followed the gondolier and was waiting at the top of the staircase.

"I'll see him with pleasure." To which she added for her companion, while Pasquale went off: "Mr. Merton Densher."

"Oh!" said Lord Mark—in a manner that, making it resound through the great cool hall, might have carried it even to Densher's ear as a judgement of his identity heard and noted once before.

I

DENSHER became aware, afresh, that he disliked his hotel —and all the more promptly that he had had occasion of old to make the same discrimination. The establishment, choked at that season with the polyglot herd, cockneys of all climes, mainly German, mainly American, mainly English, it appeared as the corresponding sensitive nerve was touched, sounded loud and not sweet, sounded anything and everything but Italian, but Venetian. The Venetian was all a dialect, he knew; yet it was pure Attic beside some of the dialects at the bustling inn. It made, "abroad," both for his pleasure and his pain that he had to feel at almost any point how he had been through everything before. He had been three or four times, in Venice, during other visits, through this pleasant irritation of paddling away—away from the concert of false notes in the vulgarised hall, away from the amiable American families and overfed German porters. He had in each case made terms for a lodging more private and not more costly, and he recalled with tenderness these shabby but friendly asylums, the windows of which he should easily know again in passing on canal or through campo. The shabbiest now failed of an appeal to him, but he found himself at the end of forty-eight hours forming views in respect to a small independent *quartiere*, far down the Grand Canal, which he had once occupied for a month with a sense of pomp and circumstance and yet also with a growth of initiation into the homelier Venetian mysteries. The humour of those days came back to him for an hour, and what further befell in this interval, to be brief, was that, emerging on a traghetto in sight of the recognised house, he made out on the green shutters of his old, of his young windows the strips of white pasted paper that figure in Venice as an invitation to tenants. This was in the course of his very first walk apart, a walk replete with impressions to which he responded with force. He had been almost without cessation, since his arrival, at Palazzo

Leporelli, where, as happened, a turn of bad weather on the second day had kept the whole party continuously at home. The episode had passed for him like a series of hours in a museum, though without the fatigue of that; and it had also resembled something that he was still, with a stirred imagination, to find a name for. He might have been looking for the name while he gave himself up, subsequently, to the ramble—he saw that even after years he couldn't lose his way—crowned with his stare across the water at the little white papers.

He was to dine at the palace in an hour or two, and he had lunched there, at an early luncheon, that morning. He had then been out with the three ladies, the three being Mrs. Lowder, Mrs. Stringham and Kate, and had kept afloat with them, under a sufficient Venetian spell, until Aunt Maud had directed him to leave them and return to Miss Theale. Of two circumstances connected with this disposition of his person he was even now not unmindful; the first being that the lady of Lancaster Gate had addressed him with high publicity and as if expressing equally the sense of her companions, who had not spoken, but who might have been taken—yes, Susan Shepherd quite equally with Kate—for inscrutable parties to her plan. What he could as little contrive to forget was that he had, before the two others, as it struck him—that was to say especially before Kate—done exactly as he was bidden; gathered himself up without a protest and retraced his way to the palace. Present with him still was the question of whether he looked a fool for it, of whether the awkwardness he felt as the gondola rocked with the business of his leaving it—they could but make, in submission, for a landing-place that was none of the best— had furnished his friends with such entertainment as was to cause them, behind his back, to exchange intelligent smiles. He had found Milly Theale twenty minutes later alone, and he had sat with her till the others returned to tea. The strange part of this was that it had been very easy, extraordinarily easy. He knew it for strange only when he was away from her, because when he was away from her he was in contact with particular things that made it so. At the time, in her presence, it was as simple as sitting with his sister might have been, and not, if the point were urged, very much more thrilling. He continued to see her as he had first seen her—that remained ineffaceably behind. Mrs. Lowder, Susan Shepherd, his own Kate, might, each in proportion, see her as a princess, as an angel, as a star, but for himself, luckily, she hadn't as yet complications to any point of discomfort: the princess, the angel, the star, were muffled over, ever so lightly and brightly, with the little American girl who had been kind to him in New York and to whom certainly—though without making too much of it for either of them—he was perfectly willing to be kind in return. She appreciated his coming in on purpose, but there was nothing in that—from the moment she was always at home—that they couldn't easily keep up. The only note the least bit high that had even yet sounded between them was this admission on her part that she found it best to remain within. She wouldn't let him call it keeping quiet, for she insisted that her palace—with all its romance and art and history—had set up round her a whirlwind of suggestion that never dropped for an hour. It wasn't therefore, within such walls, confinement, it was the freedom of all the centuries: in respect to which Densher granted good-humouredly that they were then blown together, she and he, as much as she liked, through space.

Kate had found on the present occasion a moment to say to him that he suggested a clever cousin calling on a cousin afflicted, and bored for his pains; and though he denied on the spot the "bored" he could so far see it as an impression he might make that he wondered if the same image wouldn't have occurred to Milly. As soon as Kate appeared again the difference came up—the oddity, as he then instantly felt it, of his having sunk so deep. It was sinking because it was all doing what Kate had conceived for him; it wasn't in the least doing—and that had been his notion of his life—anything he himself had conceived. The difference, accordingly, renewed, sharp, sore, was the irritant under which he had quitted the palace and under which he was to make the best of the business of again dining there. He said to himself that he must make the best of everything; that was in his mind, at the traghetto, even while, with his preoccupation about changing quarters, he studied, across the canal, the look of his former abode. It had done for the past, would it do for the present? would it play in any manner into the general necessity of which he was conscious? That necessity of making the best was the instinct—as he indeed himself

knew—of a man somehow aware that if he let go at one place
he should let go everywhere. If he took off his hand, the hand
that at least helped to hold it together, the whole queer fabric
that built him in would fall away in a minute and admit the
light. It was really a matter of nerves; it was exactly because he
was nervous that he *could* go straight; yet if that condition
should increase he must surely go wild. He was walking in
short on a high ridge, steep down on either side, where the
proprieties—once he could face at all remaining there—
reduced themselves to his keeping his head. It was Kate who
had so perched him, and there came up for him at moments, as
he found himself planting one foot exactly before another, a
sensible sharpness of irony as to her management of him. It
wasn't that she had put him in danger—to be in real danger
with her would have had another quality. There glowed for
him in fact a kind of rage at what he wasn't having; an exasperation, a resentment, begotten truly by the very impatience of
desire, in respect to his postponed and relegated, his so extremely manipulated state. It was beautifully done of her, but
what was the real meaning of it unless that he was perpetually
bent to her will? His idea from the first, from the very first of
his knowing her, had been to be, as the French called it, *bon
prince* with her, mindful of the good humour and generosity,
the contempt, in the matter of confidence, for small outlays
and small savings, that belonged to the man who wasn't generally afraid. There were things enough, goodness knew—for
it was the moral of his plight—that he couldn't afford; but what
had had a charm for him if not the notion of living handsomely,
to make up for it, in another way? of not at all events reading
the romance of his existence in a cheap edition. All he had originally felt in her came back to him, was indeed actually as present as ever—how he had admired and envied what he called to
himself her pure talent for life, as distinguished from his own,
a poor weak thing of the occasion, amateurishly patched up;
only it irritated him the more that this was exactly what was
now, ever so characteristically, standing out in her.

It was thanks to her pure talent for life, verily, that he was
just where he was and that he was above all just *how* he was. The
proof of a decent reaction in him against so much passivity
was, with no great richness, that he at least knew—knew, that

is, how he was, and how little he liked it as a thing accepted in mere helplessness. He was, for the moment, wistful—that above all described it; that was so large a part of the force that, as the autumn afternoon closed in, kept him, on his traghetto, positively throbbing with his question. His question connected itself, even while he stood, with his special smothered soreness, his sense almost of shame; and the soreness and the shame were less as he let himself, with the help of the conditions about him, regard it as serious. It was born, for that matter, partly of the conditions, those conditions that Kate had so almost insolently braved, had been willing, without a pang, to see him ridiculously—ridiculously so far as just complacently —exposed to. How little it *could* be complacently he was to feel with the last thoroughness before he had moved from his point of vantage. His question, as we have called it, was the interesting question of whether he had really no will left. How could he know—that was the point—without putting the matter to the test? It had been right to be *bon prince*, and the joy, something of the pride, of having lived, in spirit, handsomely, was even now compatible with the impulse to look into their account; but he held his breath a little as it came home to him with supreme sharpness that, whereas he had done absolutely everything that Kate had wanted, she had done nothing whatever that he had. So it was in fine that his idea of the test by which he must try that possibility kept referring itself, in the warm early dusk, the approach of the Southern night— "conditions" these, such as we just spoke of—to the glimmer, more and more ghostly as the light failed, of the little white papers on his old green shutters. By the time he looked at his watch he had been for a quarter of an hour at this post of observation and reflexion; but by the time he walked away again he had found his answer to the idea that had grown so importunate. Since a proof of his will was wanted it was indeed very exactly in wait for him—it lurked there on the other side of the Canal. A ferryman at the little pier had from time to time accosted him; but it was a part of the play of his nervousness to turn his back on that facility. He would go over, but he walked, very quickly, round and round, crossing finally by the Rialto. The rooms, in the event, were unoccupied; the ancient padrona was there with her smile all a radiance but her recognition all a fable; the ancient rickety objects too, refined in their shabbiness, amiable in their decay, as to which, on his side, demonstrations were tenderly veracious; so that before he took his way again he had arranged to come in on the morrow.

He was amusing about it that evening at dinner—in spite of an odd first impulse, which at the palace quite melted away, to treat it merely as matter for his own satisfaction. This need, this propriety, he had taken for granted even up to the moment of suddenly perceiving, in the course of talk, that the incident would minister to innocent gaiety. Such was quite its effect, with the aid of his picture—an evocation of the quaint, of the humblest rococo, of a Venetian interior in the true old note. He made the point for his hostess that her own high chambers, though they were a thousand grand things, weren't really this; made it in fact with such success that she presently declared it his plain duty to invite her on some near day to tea. She had expressed as yet—he could feel it as felt among them all—no such clear wish to go anywhere, not even to make an effort for a parish feast, or an autumn sunset, nor to descend her staircase for Titian or Gianbellini. It was constantly Densher's view that, as between himself and Kate, things were understood without saying, so that he could catch in her, as she but too freely could in him, innumerable signs of it, the whole soft breath of consciousness meeting and promoting consciousness. This view was so far justified to-night as that Milly's offer to him of her company was to his sense taken up by Kate in spite of her doing nothing to show it. It fell in so perfectly with what she had desired and foretold that she was—and this was what most struck him—sufficiently gratified and blinded by it not to know, from the false quality of his response, from his tone and his very look, which for an instant instinctively sought her own, that he had answered inevitably, almost shamelessly, in a mere time-gaining sense. It gave him on the spot, her failure of perception, almost a beginning of the advantage he had been planning for—that is at least if she too were not darkly dishonest. She might, he was not unaware, have made out, from some deep part of her, the bearing, in respect to herself, of the little fact he had announced; for she was after all capable of that, capable of guessing and yet of simultaneously hiding her guess. It wound him up a turn or two further, none the less, to impute to her now a weakness of vision by which he could himself feel the stronger. Whatever apprehension of his motive in shifting his abode might have brushed her with its wings, she at all events certainly didn't guess that he was giving their friend a hollow promise. That was what she had herself imposed on him; there had been in the prospect from the first a definite particular point at which hollowness, to call it by its least compromising name, would have to begin. Therefore its hour had now charmingly sounded.

Whatever in life he had recovered his old rooms for, he had not recovered them to receive Milly Theale: which made no more difference in his expression of happy readiness than if he had been—just what he was trying not to be—fully hardened and fully base. So rapid in fact was the rhythm of his inward drama that the quick vision of impossibility produced in him by his hostess's direct and unexpected appeal had the effect, slightly sinister, of positively scaring him. It gave him a measure of the intensity, the reality of his now mature motive. It prompted in him certainly no quarrel with these things, but it made them as vivid as if they already flushed with success. It was before the flush of success that his heart beat almost to dread. The dread was but the dread of the happiness to be compassed; only that was in itself a symptom. That a visit from Milly should, in this projection of necessities, strike him as of the last incongruity, quite as a hateful idea, and above all as spoiling, should one put it grossly, his game—the adoption of such a view might of course have an identity with one of those numerous ways of being a fool that seemed so to abound for him. It would remain none the less the way to which he should be in advance most reconciled. His mature motive, as to which he allowed himself no grain of illusion, had thus in an hour taken imaginative possession of the place: that precisely was how he saw it seated there, already unpacked and settled, for Milly's innocence, for Milly's beauty, no matter how short a time, to be housed with. There were things she would never recognise, never feel, never catch in the air; but this made no difference in the fact that her brushing against them would do nobody any good. The discrimination and the scruple were for *him*. So he felt all the parts of the case together, while Kate showed admirably as feeling none of them. Of course, however—when hadn't it to be his last word?—Kate was always sublime.

That came up in all connexions during the rest of these first days; came up in especial under pressure of the fact that each time our plighted pair snatched, in its passage, at the good fortune of half an hour together, they were doomed—though Densher felt it as all by *his* act—to spend a part of the rare occasion in wonder at their luck and in study of its queer character. This was the case after he might be supposed to have got, in a manner, used to it; it was the case after the girl—ready always, as we say, with the last word—had given him the benefit of her righting of every wrong appearance, a support familiar to him now in reference to other phases. It was still the case after he possibly might, with a little imagination, as she freely insisted, have made out, by the visible working of the crisis, what idea on Mrs. Lowder's part had determined it. Such as the idea was—and that it suited Kate's own book she openly professed—he had only to see how things were turning out to feel it strikingly justified. Densher's reply to all this vividness was that of course Aunt Maud's intervention hadn't been occult, even for *his* vividness, from the moment she had written him, with characteristic concentration, that if he should see his way to come to Venice for a fortnight she should engage he would find it no blunder. It took Aunt Maud really to do such things in such ways; just as it took him, he was ready to confess, to do such others as he must now strike them all—didn't he?—as committed to. Mrs. Lowder's admonition had been of course a direct reference to what she had said to him at Lancaster Gate before his departure the night Milly had failed them through illness; only it had at least matched that remarkable outbreak in respect to the quantity of good nature it attributed to him. The young man's discussions of his situation —which were confined to Kate; he had none with Aunt Maud herself—suffered a little, it may be divined, by the sense that he couldn't put everything off, as he privately expressed it, on other people. His ears, in solitude, were apt to burn with the reflexion that Mrs. Lowder had simply tested him, seen him as he was and made out what could be done with him. She had had but to whistle for him and he had come. If she had taken for granted his good nature she was as justified as Kate declared. This awkwardness of his conscience, both in respect to his general plasticity, the fruit of his feeling plasticity, within limits, to be a mode of life like another—certainly better than some, and particularly in respect to such confusion as might reign about what he had really come for—this inward ache was not wholly dispelled by the style, charming as that was, of Kate's poetic versions. Even the high wonder and delight of Kate couldn't set him right with himself when there was something quite distinct from these things that kept him wrong.

In default of being right with himself he had meanwhile, for one thing, the interest of seeing—and quite for the first time in his life—whether, on a given occasion, that might be quite so necessary to happiness as was commonly assumed and as he had up to this moment never doubted. He was engaged distinctly in an adventure—he who had never thought himself cut out for them, and it fairly helped him that he was able at moments to say to himself that he mustn't fall below it. At his hotel, alone, by night, or in the course of the few late strolls he was finding time to take through dusky labyrinthine alleys and empty *campi*, overhung with mouldering palaces, where he paused in disgust at his want of ease and where the sound of a rare footstep on the enclosed pavement was like that of a re-tarded dancer in a banquet-hall deserted—during these inter-ludes he entertained cold views, even to the point, at moments, on the principle that the shortest follies are the best, of thinking of immediate departure as not only possible but as indicated. He had however only to cross again the threshold of Palazzo Leporelli to see all the elements of the business com-pose, as painters called it, differently. It began to strike him then that departure wouldn't curtail, but would signally coarsen his folly, and that above all, as he hadn't really "begun" anything, had only submitted, consented, but too generously indulged and condoned the beginnings of others, he had no call to treat himself with superstitious rigour. The single thing that was clear in complications was that, whatever happened, one was to behave as a gentleman—to which was added indeed the per-haps slightly less shining truth that complications might some-times have their tedium beguiled by a study of the question of how a gentleman would behave. This question, I hasten to add, was not in the last resort Densher's greatest worry. Three women were looking to him at once, and, though such a predicament could never be, from the point of view of facility, quite the ideal, it yet had, thank goodness, its immediate workable law. The law was not to be a brute—in return for amiabilities. He hadn't come all the way out from England to be a brute. He hadn't thought of what it might give him to have a fortnight, however handicapped, with Kate in Venice, to be a brute. He hadn't treated Mrs. Lowder as if in responding to her suggestion he had understood her—he hadn't done that either to be a brute. And what he had prepared least of all for such an anti-climax was the prompt and inevitable, the achieved surrender—*as* a gentleman, oh that indubitably!—to the unexpected impression made by poor pale exquisite Milly as the mistress of a grand old palace and the dispenser of an hospitality more irresistible, thanks to all the conditions, than any ever known to him.

This spectacle had for him an eloquence, an authority, a felicity—he scarce knew by what strange name to call it—for which he said to himself that he had not consciously bargained. Her welcome, her frankness, sweetness, sadness, brightness, her disconcerting poetry, as he made shift at moments to call it, helped as it was by the beauty of her whole setting and by the perception at the same time, on the observer's part, that this element gained from her, in a manner, for effect and harmony, as much as it gave—her whole attitude had, to his imagination, meanings that hung about it, waiting upon her, hovering, dropping and quavering forth again, like vague faint snatches, mere ghosts of sound, of old-fashioned melancholy music. It was positively well for him, he had his times of reflecting, that he couldn't put it off on Kate and Mrs. Lowder, as a gentleman so conspicuously wouldn't, that—well, that he had been rather taken in by not having known in advance! There had been now five days of it all without his risking even to Kate alone any hint of what he ought to have known and of what in particular therefore had taken him in. The truth was doubtless that really, when it came to any free handling and naming of things, they were living together, the five of them, in an air in which an ugly effect of "blurting out" might easily be produced. He came back with his friend on each occasion to the blest miracle of renewed propinquity, which had a double

virtue in that favouring air. He breathed on it as if he could
scarcely believe it, yet the time had passed, in spite of this privilege, without his quite committing himself, for her ear, to any
such comment on Milly's high style and state as would have
corresponded with the amount of recognition it had produced
in him. Behind everything for him was his renewed remembrance, which had fairly become a habit, that he had been the
first to know her. This was what they had all insisted on, in her
absence, that day at Mrs. Lowder's; and this was in especial
what had made him feel its influence on his immediately paying
her a second visit. Its influence had been all there, been in the
high-hung, rumbling carriage with them, from the moment
she took him to drive, covering them in together as if it had
been a rug of softest silk. It had worked as a clear connexion
with something lodged in the past, something already their
own. He had more than once recalled how he had said to himself even at that moment, at some point in the drive, that he
was not *there*, not just as he was in so doing it, through Kate and
Kate's idea, but through Milly and Milly's own, and through
himself and *his* own, unmistakeably—as well as through the
little facts, whatever they had amounted to, of his time in
New York.

II

THERE was at last, with everything that made for it, an occasion when he got from Kate, on what she now spoke of as his eternal refrain, an answer of which he was to measure afterwards the precipitating effect. His eternal refrain was the way he came back to the riddle of Mrs. Lowder's view of her profit—a view so hard to reconcile with the chances she gave them to meet. Impatiently, at this, the girl denied the chances, wanting to know from him, with a fine irony that smote him rather straight, whether he felt their opportunities as anything so grand. He looked at her deep in the eyes when she had sounded this note; it was the least he could let her off with for having made him visibly flush. For some reason then, with it, the sharpness dropped out of her tone, which became sweet and sincere. "'Meet,' my dear man," she expressively echoed; "does it strike you that we get, after all, so very much out of our meetings?"

"On the contrary—they're starvation diet. All I mean is— and it's all I've meant from the day I came—that we at least get more than Aunt Maud."

"Ah but you see," Kate replied, "you don't understand what Aunt Maud gets."

"Exactly so—and it's what I don't understand that keeps me so fascinated with the question. *She* gives me no light; she's prodigious. She takes everything as of a natural—!"

"She takes it as 'of a natural' that at this rate I shall be making my reflexions about you. There's every appearance for her," Kate went on, "that what she had made her mind up to as possible *is* possible; that what she had thought more likely than not to happen *is* happening. The very essence of her, as you surely by this time have made out for yourself, is that when she adopts a view she—well, to her own sense, really brings the thing about, fairly terrorises with her view any other, any opposite view, and those, not less, who represent that. I've often thought success comes to her"—Kate continued to study the phenomenon—"by the spirit in her that dares and defies her idea not to prove the right one. One has seen it so again and again, in the face of everything, *become* the right one."

Densher had for this, as he listened, a smile of the largest response. "Ah my dear child, if you can explain I of course needn't not 'understand.' I'm condemned to that," he on his side presently explained, "only when understanding fails." He took a moment; then he pursued: "Does she think she terrorises *us*?" To which he added while, without immediate speech, Kate but looked over the place: "Does she believe anything so stiff as that you've really changed about me?" He knew now that he was probing the girl deep—something told him so; but that was a reason the more. "Has she got it into her head that you dislike me?"

To this, of a sudden, Kate's answer was strong. "You could yourself easily put it there!"

He wondered. "By telling her so?"

"No," said Kate as with amusement at his simplicity; "I don't ask that of you."

"Oh my dear," Densher laughed, "when you ask, you know, so little—!"

There was a full irony in this, on his own part, that he saw her resist the impulse to take up. "I'm perfectly justified in what I've asked," she quietly returned. "It's doing beautifully for you." Their eyes again intimately met, and the effect was to make her proceed. "You're not a bit unhappy."

"Oh ain't I?" he brought out very roundly.

"It doesn't practically show—which is enough for Aunt Maud. You're wonderful, you're beautiful," Kate said; "and if you really want to know whether I believe you're doing it you may take from me perfectly that I see it coming." With which, by a quick transition, as if she had settled the case, she asked him the hour.

"Oh only twelve-ten"—he had looked at his watch. "We've taken but thirteen minutes; we've time yet."

"Then we must walk. We must go toward them."

Densher, from where they had been standing, measured the long reach of the Square. "They're still in their shop. They're safe for half an hour."

"That shows then, that shows!" said Kate.

This colloquy had taken place in the middle of Piazza San
Marco, always, as a great social saloon, a smooth-floored, blue-
roofed chamber of amenity, favourable to talk; or rather, to be
exact, not in the middle, but at the point where our pair had
paused by a common impulse after leaving the great mosque-
like church. It rose now, domed and pinnacled, but a little way
behind them, and they had in front the vast empty space, enclosed by its arcades, to which at that hour movement and traf-
fic were mostly confined. Venice was at breakfast, the Venice of
the visitor and the possible acquaintance, and, except for the
parties of importunate pigeons picking up the crumbs of perpetual feasts, their prospect was clear and they could see their
companions hadn't yet been, and weren't for a while longer
likely to be, disgorged by the lace-shop, in one of the *loggie*,
where, shortly before, they had left them for a look-in—the
expression was artfully Densher's—at Saint Mark's. Their
morning had happened to take such a turn as brought this
chance to the surface; yet his allusion, just made to Kate, hadn't
been an overstatement of their general opportunity. The worst
that could be said of their general opportunity was that it was
essentially in presence—in presence of every one; every one
consisting at this juncture, in a peopled world, of Susan Shepherd, Aunt Maud and Milly. But the proof how, even in presence, the opportunity could become special was furnished
precisely by this view of the compatibility of their comfort with
a certain amount of lingering. The others had assented to their
not waiting in the shop; it was of course the least the others
could do. What had really helped them this morning was the
fact that, on his turning up, as he always called it, at the palace,
Milly had not, as before, been able to present herself. Custom
and use had hitherto seemed fairly established; on his coming
round, day after day—eight days had been now so conveniently
marked—their friends, Milly's and his, conveniently dispersed
and left him to sit with her till luncheon. Such was the perfect
operation of the scheme on which he had been, as he phrased
it to himself, had out; so that certainly there was that amount
of justification for Kate's vision of success. He *had*, for Mrs.
Lowder—he couldn't help it while sitting there—the air, which
was the thing to be desired, of no absorption in Kate sufficiently
deep to be alarming. He had failed their young hostess each

morning as little as she had failed him; it was only to-day that she hadn't been well enough to see him.

That had made a mark, all round; the mark was in the way in which, gathered in the room of state, with the place, from the right time, all bright and cool and beflowered, as always, to receive her descent, they—the rest of them—simply looked at each other. It was lurid—lurid, in all probability, for each of them privately—that they had uttered no common regrets. It was strange for our young man above all that, if the poor girl was indisposed to *that* degree, the hush of gravity, of apprehension, of significance of some sort, should be the most the case—that of the guests—could permit itself. The hush, for that matter, continued after the party of four had gone down to the gondola and taken their places in it. Milly had sent them word that she hoped they would go out and enjoy themselves, and this indeed had produced a second remarkable look, a look as of their knowing, one quite as well as the other, what such a message meant as provision for the alternative beguilement of Densher. She wished not to have spoiled his morning, and he had therefore, in civility, to take it as pleasantly patched up. Mrs. Stringham had helped the affair out, Mrs. Stringham who, when it came to that, knew their friend better than any of them. She knew her so well that she knew herself as acting in exquisite compliance with conditions comparatively obscure, approximately awful to them, by not thinking it necessary to stay at home. She had corrected that element of the perfunctory which was the slight fault, for all of them, of the occasion; she had invented a preference for Mrs. Lowder and herself; she had remembered the fond dreams of the visitation of lace that had hitherto always been brushed away by accidents, and it had come up as well for her that Kate had, the day before, spoken of the part played by fatality in her own failure of real acquaintance with the inside of Saint Mark's. Densher's sense of Susan Shepherd's conscious intervention had by this time a corner of his mind all to itself; something that had begun for them at Lancaster Gate was now a sentiment clothed in a shape; her action, ineffably discreet, had at all events a way of affecting him as for the most part subtly, even when not superficially, in his own interest. They were not, as a pair, as a "team," really united; there were too many persons, at least three, and too many things, between them; but meanwhile something was preparing that would draw them closer. He scarce knew what: probably nothing but his finding, at some hour when it would be a service to do so, that she had all the while understood him. He even had a presentiment of a juncture at which the understanding of every one else would fail and this deep little person's alone survive.

Such was to-day, in its freshness, the moral air, as we may say, that hung about our young friends; these had been the small accidents and quiet forces to which they owed the advantage we have seen them in some sort enjoying. It seemed in fact fairly to deepen for them as they stayed their course again; the splendid Square, which had so notoriously, in all the years, witnessed more of the joy of life than any equal area in Europe, furnished them, in their remoteness from earshot, with solitude and security. It was as if, being in possession, they could say what they liked; and it was also as if, in consequence of that, each had an apprehension of what the other wanted to say. It was most of all for them, moreover, as if this very quantity, seated on their lips in the bright historic air, where the only sign for their ears was the flutter of the doves, begot in the heart of each a fear. There might have been a betrayal of that in the way Densher broke the silence resting on her last words. "What did you mean just now that I can do to make Mrs. Lowder believe? For myself, stupidly, if you will, I don't see, from the moment I can't lie to her, what else there *is* but lying."

Well, she could tell him. "You can say something both handsome and sincere to her about Milly—whom you honestly like so much. That wouldn't be lying; and, coming from you, it would have an effect. You don't, you know, say much about her." And Kate put before him the fruit of observation. "You don't, you know, speak of her at all."

"And has Aunt Maud," Densher asked, "told you so?" Then as the girl, for answer, only seemed to bethink herself, "You must have extraordinary conversations!" he exclaimed.

Yes, she had bethought herself. "We have extraordinary conversations."

His look, while their eyes met, marked him as disposed to hear more about them; but there was something in her own, apparently, that defeated the opportunity. He questioned her in a moment on a different matter, which had been in his mind a week, yet in respect to which he had had no chance so good as this. "Do you happen to know then, as such wonderful things pass between you, what she makes of the incident, the other day, of Lord Mark's so very superficial visit?—his having spent here, as I gather, but the two or three hours necessary for seeing our friend and yet taken no time at all, since he went off by the same night's train, for seeing any one else. What can she make of his not having waited to see *you*, or to see herself—with all he owes her?"

"Oh of course," said Kate, "she understands. He came to make Milly his offer of marriage—he came for nothing but that. As Milly wholly declined it his business was for the time at an end. He couldn't quite on the spot turn round to make up to *us*."

Kate had looked surprised that, as a matter of taste on such an adventurer's part, Densher shouldn't see it. But Densher was lost in another thought. "Do you mean that when, turning up myself, I found him leaving her, that was what had been taking place between them?"

"Didn't you make it out, my dear?" Kate enquired.

"What sort of a blundering weathercock then *is* he?" the young man went on in his wonder.

"Oh don't make too little of him!" Kate smiled. "Do you pretend that Milly didn't tell you?"

"How great an ass he had made of himself?"

Kate continued to smile. "You *are* in love with her, you know."

He gave her another long look. "Why, since she has refused him, should my opinion of Lord Mark show it? I'm not obliged, however, to think well of him for such treatment of the other persons I've mentioned, and I feel I don't understand from you why Mrs. Lowder should."

"She doesn't—but she doesn't care," Kate explained. "You know perfectly the terms on which lots of London people live together even when they're supposed to live very well. He's not committed to us—he was having his try. Mayn't an unsatisfied man," she asked, "always have his try?"

"And come back afterwards, with confidence in a welcome, to the victim of his inconstancy?"

Kate consented, as for argument, to be thought of as a victim. "Oh but he has *had* his try at *me*. So it's all right."

"Through your also having, you mean, refused him?"

She balanced an instant during which Densher might have just wondered if pure historic truth were to suffer a slight strain. But she dropped on the right side. "I haven't let it come to that. I've been too discouraging. Aunt Maud," she went on—now as lucid as ever—"considers, no doubt, that she has a pledge from him in respect to me; a pledge that would have been broken if Milly had accepted him. As the case stands that makes no difference."

Densher laughed out. "It isn't *his* merit that he has failed."

"It's still his merit, my dear, that he's Lord Mark. He's just what he was, and what he knew he was. It's not for me either to reflect on him after I've so treated him."

"Oh," said Densher impatiently, "you've treated him beautifully."

"I'm glad," she smiled, "that you can still be jealous." But before he could take it up she had more to say. "I don't see why it need puzzle you that Milly's so marked line gratifies Aunt Maud more than anything else can displease her. What does she see but that Milly herself recognises her situation with you as too precious to be spoiled? Such a recognition as that can't but seem to her to involve in some degree your own recognition. Out of which she therefore gets it that the more you have for Milly the less you have for me."

There were moments again—we know that from the first they had been numerous—when he felt with a strange mixed passion the mastery of her mere way of putting things. There was something in it that bent him at once to conviction and to reaction. And this effect, however it be named, now broke into his tone. "Oh if she began to know what I have for you—!"

It wasn't ambiguous, but Kate stood up to it. "Luckily for us we may really consider she doesn't. So successful have we been."

"Well," he presently said, "I take from you what you give me, and I suppose that, to be consistent—to stand on my feet where I do stand at all—I ought to thank you. Only, you know, what you give me seems to me, more than anything else, the larger and larger size of my job. It seems to me more than anything else what you expect of me. It never seems to me somehow what I may expect of *you*. There's so much you *don't* give me."

She appeared to wonder. "And pray what is it I don't—?"

"I give you proof," said Densher. "You give me none."

"What then do you call proof?" she after a moment ventured to ask.

"Your doing something for me."

She considered with surprise. "Am I not doing *this* for you? Do you call this nothing?"

"Nothing at all."

"Ah I risk, my dear, everything for it."

They had strolled slowly further, but he was brought up short. "I thought you exactly contend that, with your aunt so bamboozled, you risk nothing!"

It was the first time since the launching of her wonderful idea that he had seen her at a loss. He judged the next instant moreover that she didn't like it—either the being so or the being seen, for she soon spoke with an impatience that showed her as wounded; an appearance that produced in himself, he no less quickly felt, a sharp pang of indulgence. "What then do you wish me to risk?"

The appeal from danger touched him, but all to make him, as he would have said, worse. "What I wish is to be loved. How can I feel at this rate that I *am*?" Oh she understood him, for all she might so bravely disguise it, and that made him feel straighter than if she hadn't. Deep, always, was his sense of life with her—deep as it had been from the moment of those signs of life that in the dusky London of two winters ago they had originally exchanged. He had never taken her for unguarded, ignorant, weak; and if he put to her a claim for some intenser faith between them this was because he believed it could reach her and she could meet it. "I can go on perhaps," he said, "with help. But I can't go on without."

She looked away from him now, and it showed him how she understood. "We ought to be there—I mean when they come out."

"They *won't* come out—not yet. And I don't care if they do." To which he straightway added, as if to deal with the charge of selfishness that his words, sounding for himself, struck him as enabling her to make: "Why not have done with it all and face the music as we are?" It broke from him in perfect sincerity. "Good God, if you'd only *take* me!"

It brought her eyes round to him again, and he could see how, after all, somewhere deep within, she felt his rebellion more sweet than bitter. Its effect on her spirit and her sense was visibly to hold her an instant. "We've gone too far," she none the less pulled herself together to reply. "Do you want to kill her?"

He had an hesitation that wasn't all candid. "Kill, you mean, Aunt Maud?"

"You know whom I mean. We've told too many lies."

Oh at this his head went up. "I, my dear, have told none!"

He had brought it out with a sharpness that did him good, but he had naturally, none the less, to take the look it made her give him. "Thank you very much."

Her expression, however, failed to check the words that had already risen to his lips. "Rather than lay myself open to the least appearance of it I'll go this very night."

"Then go," said Kate Croy.

He knew after a little, while they walked on again together, that what was in the air for him, and disconcertingly, was not the violence, but much rather the cold quietness, of the way this had come from her. They walked on together, and it was for a minute as if their difference had become of a sudden, in all truth, a split—as if the basis of his departure had been settled. Then, incoherently and still more suddenly, recklessly moreover, since they now might easily, from under the arcades, be observed, he passed his hand into her arm with a force that produced for them another pause. "I'll tell any lie you want, any your idea requires, if you'll only come to me."

"Come to you?"

"Come to me."

"How? Where?"

She spoke low, but there was somehow, for his uncertainty, a wonder in her being so equal to him. "To my rooms, which are perfectly possible, and in taking which, the other day, I had you, as you must have felt, in view. We can arrange it—with two grains of courage. People in our case always arrange it." She listened as for the good information, and there was sup-

port for him—since it was a question of his going step by step
—in the way she took no refuge in showing herself shocked.
He had in truth not expected of her that particular vulgarity,
but the absence of it only added the thrill of a deeper reason to
his sense of possibilities. For the knowledge of what she was he
had absolutely to *see* her now, incapable of refuge, stand there
for him in all the light of the day and of his admirable merciless
meaning. Her mere listening in fact made him even understand himself as he hadn't yet done. Idea for idea, his own was
thus already, and in the germ, beautiful. "There's nothing for
me possible but to feel that I'm not a fool. It's all I have to say,
but you must know what it means. *With* you I can do it—I'll
go as far as you demand or as you will yourself. Without you—
I'll be hanged! And I must be sure."

She listened so well that she was really listening after he had
ceased to speak. He had kept his grasp of her, drawing her close,
and though they had again, for the time, stopped walking, his
talk—for others at a distance—might have been, in the match-
less place, that of any impressed tourist to any slightly more
detached companion. On possessing himself of her arm he had
made her turn, so that they faced afresh to Saint Mark's, over
the great presence of which his eyes moved while she twiddled
her parasol. She now, however, made a motion that confronted
them finally with the opposite end. Then only she spoke—
"Please take your hand out of my arm." He understood at once:
she had made out in the shade of the gallery the issue of the
others from their place of purchase. So they went to them side
by side, and it was all right. The others had seen them as well
and waited for them, complacent enough, under one of the
arches. They themselves too—he argued that Kate would argue
—looked perfectly ready, decently patient, properly accommodating. They themselves suggested nothing worse—always by
Kate's system—than a pair of the children of a supercivilised
age making the best of an awkwardness. They didn't nevertheless hurry—that would overdo it; so he had time to feel, as it
were, what he felt. He felt, ever so distinctly—it was with this
he faced Mrs. Lowder—that he was already in a sense possessed of what he wanted. There was more to come—everything; he had by no means, with his companion, had it all out.
Yet what he was possessed of was real—the fact that she hadn't

thrown over his lucidity the horrid shadow of cheap reprobation. Of this he had had so sore a fear that its being dispelled
was in itself of the nature of bliss. The danger had dropped—it
was behind him there in the great sunny space. So far she was
good for what he wanted.

III

S HE was good enough, as it proved, for him to put to her that evening, and with further ground for it, the next sharpest question that had been on his lips in the morning—which his other preoccupation had then, to his consciousness, crowded out. His opportunity was again made, as befell, by his learning from Mrs. Stringham, on arriving, as usual, with the close of day, at the palace, that Milly must fail them again at dinner, but would to all appearance be able to come down later. He had found Susan Shepherd alone in the great saloon, where even more candles than their friend's large common allowance—she grew daily more splendid; they were all struck with it and chaffed her about it—lighted up the pervasive mystery of Style. He had thus five minutes with the good lady before Mrs. Lowder and Kate appeared—minutes illumined indeed to a longer reach than by the number of Milly's candles.

"*May* she come down—ought she if she isn't really up to it?"

He had asked that in the wonderment always stirred in him by glimpses—rare as were these—of the inner truth about the girl. There was of course a question of health—it was in the air, it was in the ground he trod, in the food he tasted, in the sounds he heard, it was everywhere. But it was everywhere with the effect of a request to him—to his very delicacy, to the common discretion of others as well as his own—that no allusion to it should be made. There had practically been none, that morning, on her explained non-appearance—the absence of it, as we know, quite monstrous and awkward; and this passage with Mrs. Stringham offered him his first licence to open his eyes. He had gladly enough held them closed; all the more that his doing so performed for his own spirit a useful function. If he positively wanted not to be brought up with his nose against Milly's facts, what better proof could he have that his conduct was marked by straightness? It was perhaps pathetic for her, and for himself was perhaps even ridiculous; but he hadn't even the amount of curiosity that he would have had about an ordinary friend. He might have shaken himself at moments to try, for a sort of dry decency, to have it; but that too,

it appeared, wouldn't come. In what therefore was the duplicity? He was at least sure about his feelings—it being so
established that he had none at all. They were all for Kate, without a feather's weight to spare. He was acting for Kate—not,
by the deviation of an inch, for her friend. He was accordingly
not interested, for had he been interested he would have cared,
and had he cared he would have wanted to know. Had he
wanted to know he wouldn't have been purely passive, and it
was his pure passivity that had to represent his dignity and his
honour. His dignity and his honour, at the same time, let us
add, fortunately fell short to-night of spoiling his little talk
with Susan Shepherd. One glimpse—it was as if she had wished
to give him that; and it was as if, for himself, on current terms,
he could oblige her by accepting it. She not only permitted,
she fairly invited him to open his eyes. "I'm so glad you're
here." It was no answer to his question, but it had for the moment to serve. And the rest was fully to come.

He smiled at her and presently found himself, as a kind of
consequence of communion with her, talking her own language. "It's a very wonderful experience."

"Well"—and her raised face shone up at him—"that's all I
want you to feel about it. If I weren't afraid," she added, "there
are things I should like to say to you."

"And what are you afraid of, please?" he encouragingly
asked.

"Of other things that I may possibly spoil. Besides, I don't,
you know, seem to have the chance. You're always, you know,
with her."

He was strangely supported, it struck him, in his fixed smile;
which was the more fixed as he felt in these last words an exact
description of his course. It was an odd thing to have come to,
but he *was* always with her. "Ah," he none the less smiled,
"I'm not with her now."

"No—and I'm so glad, since I get this from it. She's ever so
much better."

"Better? Then she *has* been worse?"

Mrs. Stringham waited. "She has been marvellous—that's
what she has been. She *is* marvellous. But she's really better."

"Oh then if she's really better—!" But he checked himself,
wanting only to be easy about it and above all not to appear

engaged to the point of mystification. "We shall miss her the more at dinner."

Susan Shepherd, however, was all there for him. "She's keeping herself. You'll see. You'll not really need to miss anything. There's to be a little party."

"Ah I do see—by this aggravated grandeur."

"Well, it *is* lovely, isn't it? I want the whole thing. She's lodged for the first time as she ought, from her type, to be; and doing it—I mean bringing out all the glory of the place—makes her really happy. It's a Veronese picture, as near as can be—with me as the inevitable dwarf, the small blackamoor, put into a corner of the foreground for effect. If I only had a hawk or a hound or something of that sort I should do the scene more honour. The old housekeeper, the woman in charge here, has a big red cockatoo that I might borrow and perch on my thumb for the evening." These explanations and sundry others Mrs. Stringham gave, though not all with the result of making him feel that the picture closed him in. What part was there for *him*, with his attitude that lacked the highest style, in a composition in which everything else would have it? "They won't, however, be at dinner, the few people she expects—they come round afterwards from their respective hotels; and Sir Luke Strett and his niece, the principal ones, will have arrived from London but an hour or two ago. It's for *him* she has wanted to do something—to let it begin at once. We shall see more of him, because she likes him; and I'm so glad—she'll be glad too —that *you're* to see him." The good lady, in connexion with it, was urgent, was almost unnaturally bright. "So I greatly hope—!" But her hope fairly lost itself in the wide light of her cheer.

He considered a little this appearance, while she let him, he thought, into still more knowledge than she uttered. "What is it you hope?"

"Well, that you'll stay on."

"Do you mean after dinner?" She meant, he seemed to feel, so much that he could scarce tell where it ended or began.

"Oh that, of course. Why we're to have music—beautiful instruments and songs; and not Tasso declaimed as in the guide-books either. She has arranged it—or at least I have. That is Eugenio has. Besides, you're in the picture."

"Oh—I!" said Densher almost with the gravity of a real protest.

"You'll be the grand young man who surpasses the others and holds up his head and the wine-cup. What we hope," Mrs. Stringham pursued, "is that you'll be faithful to us—that you've not come for a mere foolish few days."

Densher's more private and particular shabby realities turned, without comfort, he was conscious, at this touch, in the artificial repose he had in his anxiety about them but half-managed to induce. The way smooth ladies, travelling for their pleasure and housed in Veronese pictures, talked to plain embarrassed working-men, engaged in an unprecedented sacrifice of time and of the opportunity for modest acquisition! The things they took for granted and the general misery of explaining! He couldn't tell them how he had tried to work, how it was partly what he had moved into rooms for, only to find himself, almost for the first time in his life, stricken and sterile; because that would give them a false view of the source of his restlessness, if not of the degree of it. It would operate, indirectly perhaps, but infallibly, to add to that weight as of expected performance which these very moments with Mrs. Stringham caused more and more to settle on his heart. He had incurred it, the expectation of performance; the thing was done, and there was no use talking; again, again the cold breath of it was in the air. So there he was. And at best he floundered. "I'm afraid you won't understand when I say I've very tiresome things to consider. Botherations, necessities at home. The pinch, the pressure in London."

But she understood in perfection; she rose to the pinch and the pressure and showed how they had been her own very element. "Oh the daily task and the daily wage, the golden guerdon or reward? No one knows better than I how they haunt one in the flight of the precious deceiving days. Aren't they just what I myself have given up? I've given up all to follow *her*. I wish you could feel as I do. And can't you," she asked, "write about Venice?"

He very nearly wished, for the minute, that he could feel as she did; and he smiled for her kindly. "Do *you* write about Venice?"

"No; but I would—oh wouldn't I?—if I hadn't so completely

given up. She's, you know, my princess, and to one's princess—"

"One makes the whole sacrifice?"

"Precisely. There you are!"

It pressed on him with this that never had a man been in so
many places at once. "I quite understand that she's yours.
Only you see she's not mine." He felt he could somehow, for
honesty, risk that, as he had the moral certainty she wouldn't
repeat it and least of all to Mrs. Lowder, who would find in it
a disturbing implication. This was part of what he liked in the
good lady, that she didn't repeat, and also that she gave him a
delicate sense of her shyly wishing him to know it. That was in
itself a hint of possibilities between them, of a relation, beneficent and elastic for him, which wouldn't engage him further
than he could see. Yet even as he afresh made this out he felt
how strange it all was. She wanted, Susan Shepherd then, as
appeared, the same thing Kate wanted, only wanted it, as still
further appeared, in so different a way and from a motive so
different, even though scarce less deep. Then Mrs. Lowder
wanted, by so odd an evolution of her exuberance, exactly what
each of the others did; and he was between them all, he was in
the midst. Such perceptions made occasions—well, occasions
for fairly wondering if it mightn't be best just to consent, lux-
uriously, to *be* the ass the whole thing involved. Trying not to
be and yet keeping in it was of the two things the more asi-
nine. He was glad there was no male witness; it was a circle of
petticoats; he shouldn't have liked a man to see him. He only
had for a moment a sharp thought of Sir Luke Strett, the great
master of the knife whom Kate in London had spoken of Milly
as in commerce with, and whose renewed intervention at such
a distance, just announced to him, required some accounting
for. He had a vision of great London surgeons—if this one was
a surgeon—as incisive all round; so that he should perhaps after
all not wholly escape the ironic attention of his own sex. The
most he might be able to do was not to care; while he was
trying not to he could take that in. It was a train, however, that
brought up the vision of Lord Mark as well. Lord Mark had
caught him twice in the fact—the fact of his absurd posture;
and that made a second male. But it was comparatively easy
not to mind Lord Mark.

His companion had before this taken him up, and in a tone to confirm her discretion, on the matter of Milly's not being his princess. "Of course she's not. You must do something first."

Densher gave it his thought. "Wouldn't it be rather *she* who must?"

It had more than he intended the effect of bringing her to a stand. "I see. No doubt, if one takes it so." Her cheer was for the time in eclipse, and she looked over the place, avoiding his eyes, as in the wonder of what Milly could do. "And yet she has wanted to be kind."

It made him on the spot feel a brute. "Of course she has. No one could be more charming. She has treated me as if *I* were somebody. Call her my hostess as I've never had nor imagined a hostess, and I'm with you altogether. Of course," he added in the right spirit for her, "I do see that it's quite court life."

She promptly showed how this was almost all she wanted of him. "That's all I mean, if you understand it of such a court as never was: one of the courts of heaven, the court of a reigning seraph, a sort of a vice-queen of an angel. That will do perfectly."

"Oh well then I grant it. Only court life as a general thing, you know," he observed, "isn't supposed to pay."

"Yes, one has read; but this is beyond any book. That's just the beauty here; it's why she's the great and only princess. With her, at her court," said Mrs. Stringham, "it does pay." Then as if she had quite settled it for him: "You'll see for yourself."

He waited a moment, but said nothing to discourage her. "I think you were right just now. One must do something first."

"Well, you've done something."

"No—I don't see that. I can do more."

Oh well, she seemed to say, if he would have it so! "You can do everything, you know."

"Everything" was rather too much for him to take up gravely, and he modestly let it alone, speaking the next moment, to avert fatuity, of a different but a related matter. "Why has she sent for Sir Luke Strett if, as you tell me, she's so much better?"

"She hasn't sent. He has come of himself," Mrs. Stringham explained. "He has wanted to come."

"Isn't that rather worse then—if it means he mayn't be easy?"

"He was coming, from the first, for his holiday. She has known that these several weeks." After which Mrs. Stringham added: "You can *make* him easy."

"*I* can?" he candidly wondered. It was truly the circle of petticoats. "What have I to do with it for a man like that?"

"How do you know," said his friend, "what he's like? He's not like any one you've ever seen. He's a great beneficent being."

"Ah then he can do without me. I've no call, as an outsider, to meddle."

"Tell him, all the same," Mrs. Stringham urged, "what you think."

"What I think of Miss Theale?" Densher stared. It was, as they said, a large order. But he found the right note. "It's none of his business."

It did seem a moment for Mrs. Stringham too the right note. She fixed him at least with an expression still bright, but searching, that showed almost to excess what she saw in it; though what this might be he was not to make out till afterwards. "Say *that* to him then. Anything will do for him as a means of getting at you."

"And why should he get at me?"

"Give him a chance to. Let him talk to you. Then you'll see."

All of which, on Mrs. Stringham's part, sharpened his sense of immersion in an element rather more strangely than agreeably warm—a sense that was moreover, during the next two or three hours, to be fed to satiety by several other impressions. Milly came down after dinner, half a dozen friends—objects of interest mainly, it appeared, to the ladies of Lancaster Gate—having by that time arrived; and with this call on her attention, the further call of her musicians ushered by Eugenio, but personally and separately welcomed, and the supreme opportunity offered in the arrival of the great doctor, who came last of all, he felt her diffuse in wide warm waves the spell of a general, a beatific mildness. There was a deeper depth of it, doubtless, for some than for others; what he in particular knew of it was that he seemed to stand in it up to his neck. He moved about in it and it made no plash; he floated, he noiselessly swam in it, and they were all together, for that matter, like fishes in a crystal pool. The effect of the place, the beauty of the scene, had probably much to do with it; the golden grace of the high rooms, chambers of art in themselves, took care, as an influence, of the general manner, and made people bland without making them solemn. They were only people, as Mrs. Stringham had said, staying for the week or two at the inns, people who during the day had fingered their Baedekers, gaped at their frescoes and differed, over fractions of francs, with their gondoliers. But Milly, let loose among them in a wonderful white dress, brought them somehow into relation with something that made them more finely genial; so that if the Veronese picture of which he had talked with Mrs. Stringham was not quite constituted, the comparative prose of the previous hours, the traces of insensibility qualified by "beating down," were at last almost nobly disowned. There was perhaps something for him in the accident of his seeing her for the first time in white, but she hadn't yet had occasion—circulating with a clearness intensified—to strike him as so happily pervasive. She was different, younger, fairer, with the colour of her braided hair more than ever a not altogether lucky challenge to attention; yet he was loth wholly to explain it by her having quitted this once, for some obscure yet doubtless charming reason, her almost monastic, her hitherto inveterate black. Much as the change did for the value of her presence, she had never yet, when all was said, made it for *him*; and he was not to fail of the further amusement of judging her determined in the matter by Sir Luke Strett's visit. If he could in this connexion have felt jealous of Sir Luke Strett, whose strong face and type, less assimilated by the scene perhaps than any others, he was anon to study from the other side of the saloon, that would doubtless have been most amusing of all. But he couldn't be invidious, even to profit by so high a tide; he felt himself too much "in" it, as he might have said: a moment's reflexion put him more in than any one. The way Milly neglected him for other cares while Kate and Mrs. Lowder, without so much as the attenuation of a joke, introduced him to English ladies—that was itself a proof; for nothing really of so close a communion had up to this time passed between them as the single bright look and the three gay words (all ostensibly of the last lightness) with which her confessed consciousness brushed by him.

She was acquitting herself to-night as hostess, he could see,

under some supreme idea, an inspiration which was half her
nerves and half an inevitable harmony; but what he especially
recognised was the character that had already several times
broken out in her and that she so oddly appeared able, by
choice or by instinctive affinity, to keep down or to display. She
was the American girl as he had originally found her—found
her at certain moments, it was true, in New York, more than at
certain others; she was the American girl as, still more than
then, he had seen her on the day of her meeting him in London and in Kate's company. It affected him as a large though
queer social resource in her—such as a man, for instance, to his
diminution, would never in the world be able to command;
and he wouldn't have known whether to see it in an extension
or a contraction of "personality," taking it as he did most directly for a confounding extension of surface. Clearly too it
was the right thing this evening all round: that came out for
him in a word from Kate as she approached him to wreak on
him a second introduction. He had under cover of the music
melted away from the lady toward whom she had first pushed
him; and there was something in her to affect him as telling
evasively a tale of their talk in the Piazza. To what did she want
to coerce him as a form of penalty for what he had done to her
there? It was thus in contact uppermost for him that he had
done something; not only caused her perfect intelligence to
act in his interest, but left her unable to get away, by any mere
private effort, from his inattackable logic. With him thus in
presence, and near him—and it had been as unmistakeable
through dinner—there was no getting away for her at all, there
was less of it than ever: so she could only either deal with the
question straight, either frankly yield or ineffectually struggle or
insincerely argue, or else merely express herself by following
up the advantage she did possess. It was part of that advantage
for the hour—a brief fallacious makeweight to his pressure—
that there were plenty of things left in which he must feel her
will. They only told him, these indications, how much she was,
in such close quarters, feeling his; and it was enough for him
again that her very aspect, as great a variation in its way as
Milly's own, gave him back the sense of his action. It had never
yet in life been granted him to know, almost materially to taste,
as he could do in these minutes, the state of what was vulgarly

called conquest. He had lived long enough to have been on
occasion "liked," but it had never begun to be allowed him to
be liked to any such tune in any such quarter. It was a liking
greater than Milly's—or it would be: he felt it in him to answer
for that. So at all events he read the case while he noted that
Kate was somehow—for Kate—wanting in lustre. As a striking
young presence she was practically superseded; of the mildness
that Milly diffused she had assimilated all her share; she might
fairly have been dressed to-night in the little black frock,
superficially indistinguishable, that Milly had laid aside. This
represented, he perceived, the opposite pole from such an effect as that of her wonderful entrance, under her aunt's eyes—
he had never forgotten it—the day of their younger friend's
failure at Lancaster Gate. She was, in her accepted efface-
ment—it was actually her acceptance that made the beauty and
repaired the damage—under her aunt's eyes now; but whose
eyes were not effectually preoccupied? It struck him none the
less certainly that almost the first thing she said to him showed
an exquisite attempt to appear if not unconvinced at least self-
possessed.

"Don't you think her good enough *now?*"

Almost heedless of the danger of overt freedoms, she eyed
Milly from where they stood, noted her in renewed talk, over
her further wishes, with the members of her little orchestra,
who had approached her with demonstrations of deference
enlivened by native humours—things quite in the line of old
Venetian comedy. The girl's idea of music had been happy—a
real solvent of shyness, yet not drastic; thanks to the intermissions, discretions, a general habit of mercy to gathered bar-
barians, that reflected the good manners of its interpreters,
representatives though these might be but of the order in which
taste was natural and melody rank. It was easy at all events to
answer Kate. "Ah my dear, you know how good I think her!"

"But she's *too* nice," Kate returned with appreciation.
"Everything suits her so—especially her pearls. They go so
with her old lace. I'll trouble you really to look at them." Densher, though aware he had seen them before, had perhaps not
"really" looked at them, and had thus not done justice to the
embodied poetry—his mind, for Milly's aspects, kept coming
back to that—which owed them part of its style. Kate's face, as

she considered them, struck him: the long, priceless chain, wound twice round the neck, hung, heavy and pure, down the front of the wearer's breast—so far down that Milly's trick, evidently unconscious, of holding and vaguely fingering and entwining a part of it, conduced presumably to convenience. "She's a dove," Kate went on, "and one somehow doesn't think of doves as bejewelled. Yet they suit her down to the ground."

"Yes—down to the ground is the word." Densher saw now how they suited her, but was perhaps still more aware of something intense in his companion's feeling about them. Milly was indeed a dove; this was the figure, though it most applied to her spirit. Yet he knew in a moment that Kate was just now, for reasons hidden from him, exceptionally under the impression of that element of wealth in her which was a power, which was a great power, and which was dove-like only so far as one remembered that doves have wings and wondrous flights, have them as well as tender tints and soft sounds. It even came to him dimly that such wings could in a given case—*had*, truly, in the case with which he was concerned—spread themselves for protection. Hadn't they, for that matter, lately taken an inordinate reach, and weren't Kate and Mrs. Lowder, weren't Susan Shepherd and he, wasn't *he* in particular, nestling under them to a great increase of immediate ease? All this was a brighter blur in the general light, out of which he heard Kate presently going on.

"Pearls have such a magic that they suit every one."

"They would uncommonly suit you," he frankly returned.

"Oh yes, I see myself!"

As she saw herself, suddenly, he saw her—she would have been splendid; and with it he felt more what she was thinking of. Milly's royal ornament had—under pressure now not wholly occult—taken on the character of a symbol of differences, differences of which the vision was actually in Kate's face. It might have been in her face too that, well as she certainly would look in pearls, pearls were exactly what Merton Densher would never be able to give her. Wasn't *that* the great difference that Milly to-night symbolised? She unconsciously represented to Kate, and Kate took it in at every pore, that there was nobody with whom she had less in common than a remarkably handsome girl married to a man unable to make her on any such lines as that the least little present. Of these absurdities, however, it was not till afterwards that Densher thought. He could think now, to any purpose, only of what Mrs. Stringham had said to him before dinner. He could but come back to his friend's question of a minute ago. "She's certainly good enough, as you call it, in the sense that I'm assured she's better. Mrs. Stringham, an hour or two since, was in great feather to me about it. She evidently believes her better."

"Well, if they choose to call it so—!"

"And what do *you* call it—as against them?"

"I don't call it anything to any one but you. I'm not 'against' them!" Kate added as with just a fresh breath of impatience for all he had to be taught.

"That's what I'm talking about," he said. "What do you call it to me?"

It made her wait a little. "She isn't better. She's worse. But that has nothing to do with it."

"Nothing to do?" He wondered.

But she was clear. "Nothing to do with *us*. Except of course that we're doing our best for her. We're making her want to live." And Kate again watched her. "To-night she does want to live." She spoke with a kindness that had the strange property of striking him as inconsequent—so much, and doubtless so unjustly, had all her clearness been an implication of the hard. "It's wonderful. It's beautiful."

"It's beautiful indeed."

He hated somehow the helplessness of his own note; but she had given it no heed. "She's doing it for *him*"—and she nodded in the direction of Milly's medical visitor. "She wants to be for him at her best. But she can't deceive him."

Densher had been looking too; which made him say in a moment: "And do you think *you* can? I mean, if he's to be with us here, about your sentiments. If Aunt Maud's so thick with him—!"

Aunt Maud now occupied in fact a place at his side and was visibly doing her best to entertain him, though this failed to prevent such a direction of his own eyes—determined, in the way such things happen, precisely by the attention of the others —as Densher became aware of and as Kate promptly marked. "He's looking at *you*. He wants to speak to you."

"So Mrs. Stringham," the young man laughed, "advised me he would."

"Then let him. Be right with him. I don't need," Kate went on in answer to the previous question, "to deceive him. Aunt Maud, if it's necessary, will do that. I mean that, knowing nothing about me, he can see me only as she sees me. She sees me now so well. He has nothing to do with me."

"Except to reprobate you," Densher suggested.

"For not caring for *you*? Perfectly. As a brilliant young man driven by it into your relation with Milly—as all *that* I leave you to him."

"Well," said Densher sincerely enough, "I think I can thank you for leaving me to some one easier perhaps with me than yourself."

She had been looking about again meanwhile, the lady having changed her place, for the friend of Mrs. Lowder's to whom she had spoken of introducing him. "All the more reason why I should commit you then to Lady Wells."

"Oh but wait." It was not only that he distinguished Lady Wells from afar, that she inspired him with no eagerness, and that, somewhere at the back of his head, he was fairly aware of the question, in germ, of whether this was the kind of person he should be involved with when they were married. It was furthermore that the consciousness of something he had not got from Kate in the morning, and that logically much concerned him, had been made more keen by these very moments —to say nothing of the consciousness that, with their general smallness of opportunity, he must squeeze each stray instant hard. If Aunt Maud, over there with Sir Luke, noted him as a little "attentive," that might pass for a futile demonstration on the part of a gentleman who had to confess to having, not very gracefully, changed his mind. Besides, just now, he didn't care for Aunt Maud except in so far as he was immediately to show. "How can Mrs. Lowder think me disposed of with any finality, if I'm disposed of only to a girl who's dying? If you're right about that, about the state of the case, you're wrong about Mrs. Lowder's being squared. If Milly, as you say," he lucidly pursued, "can't deceive a great surgeon, or whatever, the great surgeon won't deceive other people—not those, that is, who are closely concerned. He won't at any rate deceive Mrs.

Stringham, who's Milly's greatest friend; and it will be very odd if Mrs. Stringham deceives Aunt Maud, who's her own."

Kate showed him at this the cold glow of an idea that really was worth his having kept her for. "Why will it be odd? I marvel at your seeing your way so little."

Mere curiosity even, about his companion, had now for him its quick, its slightly quaking intensities. He had compared her once, we know, to a "new book," an uncut volume of the highest, the rarest quality; and his emotion (to justify that) was again and again like the thrill of turning the page. "Well, you know how deeply I marvel at the way *you* see it!"

"It doesn't in the least follow," Kate went on, "that anything in the nature of what you call deception on Mrs. Stringham's part will be what you call odd. Why shouldn't she hide the truth?"

"From Mrs. Lowder?" Densher stared. "Why should she?"

"To please you."

"And how in the world can it please me?"

Kate turned her head away as if really at last almost tired of his density. But she looked at him again as she spoke. "Well then to please Milly." And before he could question: "Don't you feel by this time that there's nothing Susan Shepherd won't do for you?"

He had verily after an instant to take it in, so sharply it corresponded with the good lady's recent reception of him. It was queerer than anything again, the way they all came together round him. But that was an old story, and Kate's multiplied lights led him on and on. It was with a reserve, however, that he confessed this. "She's ever so kind. Only her view of the right thing may not be the same as yours."

"How can it be anything different if it's the view of serving you?"

Densher for an instant, but only for an instant, hung fire. "Oh the difficulty is that I don't, upon my honour, even yet quite make out how yours does serve me."

"It helps you—put it then," said Kate very simply—"to serve *me*. It gains you time."

"Time for what?"

"For everything!" She spoke at first, once more, with impatience; then as usual she qualified. "For anything that may happen."

Densher had a smile, but he felt it himself as strained. "You're cryptic, love!"

It made her keep her eyes on him, and he could thus see that, by one of those incalculable motions in her without which she wouldn't have been a quarter so interesting, they half-filled with tears from some source he had too roughly touched. "I'm taking a trouble for you I never dreamed I should take for any human creature."

Oh it went home, making him flush for it; yet he soon enough felt his reply on his lips. "Well, isn't my whole insistence to you now that I can conjure trouble away?" And he let it, his insistence, come out again; it had so constantly had, all the week, but its step or two to make. "There *need* be none whatever between us. There need be nothing but our sense of each other."

It had only the effect at first that her eyes grew dry while she took up again one of the so numerous links in her close chain. "You can tell her anything you like, anything whatever."

"Mrs. Stringham? I *have* nothing to tell her."

"You can tell her about *us.* I mean," she wonderfully pursued, "that you do still like me."

It was indeed so wonderful that it amused him. "Only not that you still like me."

She let his amusement pass. "I'm absolutely certain she wouldn't repeat it."

"I see. To Aunt Maud."

"You don't quite see. Neither to Aunt Maud nor to any one else." Kate then, he saw, was always seeing Milly much more, after all, than he was; and she showed it again as she went on. "*There*, accordingly, is your time."

She did at last make him think, and it was fairly as if light broke, though not quite all at once. "You must let me say I *do* see. Time for something in particular that I understand you regard as possible. Time too that, I further understand, is time for you as well."

"Time indeed for me as well." And encouraged visibly by his glow of concentration, she looked at him as through the air she had painfully made clear. Yet she was still on her guard. "Don't think, however, I'll do *all* the work for you. If you want things named you must name them."

He had quite, within the minute, been turning names over; and there was only one, which at last stared at him there dreadful, that properly fitted. "Since she's to die I'm to marry her?"

It struck him even at the moment as fine in her that she met it with no wincing nor mincing. She might for the grace of silence, for favour to their conditions, have only answered him with her eyes. But her lips bravely moved. "To marry her."

"So that when her death has taken place I shall in the natural course have money?"

It was before him enough now, and he had nothing more to ask; he had only to turn, on the spot, considerably cold with the thought that all along—to his stupidity, his timidity—it had been, it had been only, what she meant. Now that he was in possession moreover she couldn't forbear, strangely enough, to pronounce the words she hadn't pronounced: they broke through her controlled and colourless voice as if she should be ashamed, to the very end, to have flinched. "You'll in the natural course have money. We shall in the natural course be free."

"Oh, oh, oh!" Densher softly murmured.

"Yes, yes, yes." But she broke off. "Come to Lady Wells."

He never budged—there was too much else. "I'm to propose it then—marriage—on the spot?"

There was no ironic sound he needed to give it; the more simply he spoke the more he seemed ironic. But she remained consummately proof. "Oh I can't go into that with you, and from the moment you don't wash your hands of me I don't think you ought to ask me. You must act as you like and as you can."

He thought again. "I'm far—as I sufficiently showed you this morning—from washing my hands of you."

"Then," said Kate, "it's all right."

"All right?" His eagerness flamed. "You'll come?"

But he had had to see in a moment that it wasn't what she meant. "You'll have a free hand, a clear field, a chance—well, quite ideal."

"Your descriptions"—her "ideal" was such a touch!—"are

prodigious. And what I don't make out is how, caring for me, you can like it."

"I don't like it, but I'm a person, thank goodness, who can do what I don't like."

It wasn't till afterwards that, going back to it, he was to read into this speech a kind of heroic ring, a note of character that belittled his own incapacity for action. Yet he saw indeed even at the time the greatness of knowing so well what one wanted. At the time too, moreover, he next reflected that he after all knew what *he* did. But something else on his lips was uppermost. "What I don't make out then is how you can even bear it."

"Well, when you know me better you'll find out how much I can bear." And she went on before he could take up, as it were, her too many implications. That it was left to him to know her, spiritually, "better" after his long sacrifice to knowledge—this for instance was a truth he hadn't been ready to receive so full in the face. She had mystified him enough, heaven knew, but that was rather by his own generosity than by hers. And what, with it, did she seem to suggest she might incur at his hands? In spite of these questions she was carrying him on. "All you'll have to do will be to stay."

"And proceed to my business under your eyes?"

"Oh dear no—we shall go."

" 'Go?' " he wondered. "Go when, go where?"

"In a day or two—straight home. Aunt Maud wishes it now."

It gave him all he could take in to think of. "Then what becomes of Miss Theale?"

"What I tell you. She stays on, and you stay with her."

He stared. "All alone?"

She had a smile that was apparently for his tone. "You're old enough—with plenty of Mrs. Stringham."

Nothing might have been so odd for him now, could he have measured it, as his being able to feel, quite while he drew from her these successive cues, that he was essentially "seeing what she would say"—an instinct compatible for him therefore with that absence of a need to know her better to which she had a moment before done injustice. If it hadn't been appearing to him in gleams that she would somewhere break down, he probably couldn't have gone on. Still, as she wasn't breaking down there was nothing for him but to continue. "Is your going Mrs. Lowder's idea?"

"Very much indeed. Of course again you see what it does for us. And I don't," she added, "refer only to our going, but to Aunt Maud's view of the general propriety of it."

"I see again, as you say," Densher said after a moment. "It makes everything fit."

"Everything."

The word, for a little, held the air, and he might have seemed the while to be looking, by no means dimly now, at all it stood for. But he had in fact been looking at something else. "You leave her here then to die?"

"Ah she believes she won't die. Not if you stay. I mean," Kate explained, "Aunt Maud believes."

"And that's all that's necessary?"

Still indeed she didn't break down. "Didn't we long ago agree that what she believes is the principal thing for us?"

He recalled it, under her eyes, but it came as from long ago. "Oh yes. I can't deny it." Then he added: "So that if I stay—"

"It won't"—she was prompt—"be our fault."

"If Mrs. Lowder still, you mean, suspects us?"

"If she still suspects us. But she won't."

Kate gave it an emphasis that might have appeared to leave him nothing more; and he might in fact well have found nothing if he hadn't presently found: "But what if she doesn't accept me?"

It produced in her a look of weariness that made the patience of her tone the next moment touch him. "You can but try."

"Naturally I can but try. Only, you see, one has to try a little hard to propose to a dying girl."

"She isn't for you as if she's dying." It had determined in Kate the flash of *justesse* he could perhaps most, on consideration, have admired, since her retort touched the truth. There before him was the fact of how Milly to-night impressed him, and his companion, with her eyes in his own and pursuing his impression to the depths of them, literally now perched on the fact in triumph. She turned her head to where their friend was again in range, and it made him turn his, so that they watched a minute in concert. Milly, from the other side, happened at the moment to notice them, and she sent across toward them in response all the candour of her smile, the lustre of her pearls, the value of her life, the essence of her wealth. It brought them together again with faces made fairly grave by the reality she put into their plan. Kate herself grew a little pale for it, and they had for a time only a silence. The music, however, gay and vociferous, had broken out afresh and protected more than interrupted them. When Densher at last spoke it was under cover.

"I might stay, you know, without trying."

"Oh to stay *is* to try."

"To have for herself, you mean, the appearance of it?"

"I don't see how you can have the appearance more."

Densher waited. "You think it then possible she may *offer* marriage?"

"I can't think—if you really want to know—what she may *not* offer!"

"In the manner of princesses, who do such things?"

"In any manner you like. So be prepared."

Well, he looked as if he almost were. "It will be for me then to accept. But that's the way it must come."

Kate's silence, so far, let it pass; but she presently said: "You'll, on your honour, stay then?"

His answer made her wait, but when it came it was distinct. "Without you, you mean?"

"Without us."

"And you yourselves go at latest—?"

"Not later than Thursday."

It made three days. "Well," he said, "I'll stay, on my honour, if you'll come to me. On *your* honour."

Again, as before, this made her momentarily rigid, with a rigour out of which, at a loss, she vaguely cast about her. Her rigour was more to him, nevertheless, than all her readiness; for her readiness was the woman herself, and this other thing a mask, a stop-gap and a "dodge." She cast about, however, as happened, and not for the instant in vain. Her eyes, turned over the room, caught at a pretext. "Lady Wells is tired of waiting: she's coming—see—to *us.*"

Densher saw in fact, but there was a distance for their visitor to cross, and he still had time. "If you decline to understand me I wholly decline to understand you. I'll do nothing."

"Nothing?" It was as if she tried for the minute to plead.

"I'll do nothing. I'll go off before you. I'll go to-morrow."

He was to have afterwards the sense of her having then, as the phrase was—and for vulgar triumphs too—seen he meant it. She looked again at Lady Wells, who was nearer, but she quickly came back. "And if I do understand?"

"I'll do everything."

She found anew a pretext in her approaching friend: he was fairly playing with her pride. He had never, he then knew, tasted, in all his relation with her, of anything so sharp—too sharp for mere sweetness—as the vividness with which he saw himself master in the conflict. "Well, I understand."

"On your honour?"

"On my honour."

"You'll come?"

"I'll come."

I

I T WAS after they had gone that he truly felt the difference, which was most to be felt moreover in his faded old rooms. He had recovered from the first a part of his attachment to this scene of contemplation, within sight, as it was, of the Rialto bridge, on the hither side of that arch of associations and the left going up the Canal; he had seen it in a particular light, to which, more and more, his mind and his hands adjusted it; but the interest the place now wore for him had risen at a bound, becoming a force that, on the spot, completely engaged and absorbed him, and relief from which—if relief was the name— he could find only by getting away and out of reach. What had come to pass within his walls lingered there as an obsession importunate to all his senses; it lived again, as a cluster of pleasant memories, at every hour and in every object; it made every- thing but itself irrelevant and tasteless. It remained, in a word, a conscious watchful presence, active on its own side, for ever to be reckoned with, in face of which the effort at detachment was scarcely less futile than frivolous. Kate had come to him; it was only once—and this not from any failure of their need, but from such impossibilities, for bravery alike and for subtlety, as there was at the last no blinking; yet she had come, that once, to stay, as people called it; and what survived of her, what re- minded and insisted, was something he couldn't have banished if he had wished. Luckily he didn't wish, even though there might be for a man almost a shade of the awful in so unquali- fied a consequence of his act. It had simply *worked*, his idea, the idea he had made her accept; and all erect before him, really covering the ground as far as he could see, was the fact of the gained success that this represented. It was, otherwise, but the fact of the idea as directly applied, as converted from a lumi- nous conception into an historic truth. He had known it before but as desired and urged, as convincingly insisted on for the help it would render; so that at present, *with* the help rendered, it seemed to acknowledge its office and to set up, for memory and faith, an insistence of its own. He had in fine judged his friend's pledge in advance as an inestimable value, and what he must now know his case for was that of a possession of the value to the full. Wasn't it perhaps even rather the value that possessed *him*, kept him thinking of it and waiting on it, turning round and round it and making sure of it again from this side and that?

It played for him—certainly in this prime afterglow—the part of a treasure kept at home in safety and sanctity, something he was sure of finding in its place when, with each return, he worked his heavy old key in the lock. The door had but to open for him to be with it again and for it to be all there; so intensely there that, as we say, no other act was possible to him than the renewed act, almost the hallucination, of intimacy. Wherever he looked or sat or stood, to whatever aspect he gave for the instant the advantage, it was in view as nothing of the moment, nothing begotten of time or of chance could be, or ever would; it was in view as, when the curtain has risen, the play on the stage is in view, night after night, for the fiddlers. He remained thus, in his own theatre, in his single person, perpetual orchestra to the ordered drama, the confirmed "run"; playing low and slow, moreover, in the regular way, for the situations of most importance. No other visitor was to come to him; he met, he bumped occasionally, in the Piazza or in his walks, against claimants to acquaintance, remembered or forgotten, at present mostly effusive, sometimes even inquisitive; but he gave no address and encouraged no approach; he couldn't for his life, he felt, have opened his door to a third person. Such a person would have interrupted him, would have profaned his secret or perhaps have guessed it; would at any rate have broken the spell of what he conceived himself—in the absence of anything "to show"—to be inwardly doing. He was giving himself up—that was quite enough—to the general feeling of his renewed engagement to fidelity. The force of the engagement, the quantity of the article to be supplied, the special solidity of the contract, the way, above all, as a service for which the price named by him had been magnificently paid, his equivalent office was to take effect—such items might well fill his consciousness when there was nothing from outside to interfere. Never was a consciousness more rounded and fastened down over what filled it; which is precisely what we have spoken of as, in its degree, the oppression of success, the somewhat chilled state—tending to the solitary—of supreme recognition. If it was slightly awful to feel so justified, this was by the loss of the warmth of the element of mystery. The lucid reigned instead of it, and it was into the lucid that he sat and stared. He shook himself out of it a dozen times a day, tried to break by his own act his constant still communion. It wasn't still communion she had meant to bequeath him; it was the very different business of that kind of fidelity of which the other name was careful action.

Nothing, he perfectly knew, was less like careful action than the immersion he enjoyed at home. The actual grand queerness was that to be faithful to Kate he had positively to take his eyes, his arms, his lips straight off her—he had to let her alone. He had to remember it was time to go to the palace—which in truth was a mercy, since the check was not less effectual than imperative. What it came to, fortunately, as yet, was that when he closed the door behind him for an absence he always shut her in. Shut her out—it came to that rather, when once he had got a little away; and before he reached the palace, much more after hearing at his heels the bang of the greater *portone*, he felt free enough not to know his position as oppressively false. As Kate was *all* in his poor rooms, and not a ghost of her left for the grander, it was only on reflexion that the falseness came out; so long as he left it to the mercy of beneficent chance it offered him no face and made of him no claim that he couldn't meet without aggravation of his inward sense. This aggravation had been his original horror; yet what—in Milly's presence, each day—was horror doing with him but virtually letting him off? He shouldn't perhaps get off to the end; there was time enough still for the possibility of shame to pounce. Still, however, he did constantly a little more what he liked best, and that kept him for the time more safe. What he liked best was, in any case, to know *why* things were as he felt them; and he knew it pretty well, in this case, ten days after the retreat of his other friends. He then fairly perceived that—even putting their purity of motive at its highest—it was neither Kate nor he who made his strange relation to Milly, who made her own, so far as it might be, innocent; it was neither of them who practically purged it—if practically purged it was. Milly herself did everything—so far at least as he was concerned— Milly herself, and Milly's house, and Milly's hospitality, and Milly's manner, and Milly's character, and, perhaps still more than anything else, Milly's imagination, Mrs. Stringham and Sir Luke indeed a little aiding: whereby he knew the blessing of a fair pretext to ask himself what more he had to do. Something incalculable wrought for them—for him and Kate; something outside, beyond, above themselves, and doubtless ever so much better than they: which wasn't a reason, however—its being so much better—for them not to profit by it. Not to profit by it, so far as profit could be reckoned, would have been to go directly against it; and the spirit of generosity at present engendered in Densher could have felt no greater pang than by his having to go directly against Milly.

To go *with* her was the thing, so far as she could herself go; which, from the moment her tenure of her loved palace stretched on, was possible but by his remaining near her. This remaining was of course on the face of it the most "marked" of demonstrations—which was exactly why Kate had required it; it was so marked that on the very evening of the day it had taken effect Milly herself hadn't been able not to reach out to him, with an exquisite awkwardness, for some account of it. It was as if she had wanted from him some name that, now they were to be almost alone together, they could, for their further ease, know it and call it by—it being, after all, almost rudimentary that his presence, of which the absence of the others made quite a different thing, couldn't but have for himself some definite basis. She only wondered about the basis it would have for himself, and how he would describe it; that would quite do for her—it even would have done for her, he could see, had he produced some reason merely trivial, had he said he was waiting for money or clothes, for letters or for orders from Fleet Street, without which, as she might have heard, newspaper men never took a step. He hadn't in the event quite sunk to that; but he had none the less had there with her, that night, on Mrs. Stringham's leaving them alone—Mrs. Stringham proved really prodigious—his acquaintance with a shade of awkwardness darker than any Milly could know. He had supposed himself beforehand, on the question of what he was doing or pretending, in possession of some tone that would serve; but there were three minutes of his feeling incapable of promptness quite in the same degree in which a gentleman whose pocket has been picked feels incapable of purchase. It even didn't help him, oddly, that he was sure Kate would in some way have spoken for him—or rather not so much in some way as in one very particular way. He hadn't asked her, at the last, what she might, in the connexion, have said; nothing would have induced him to put such a question after she had been to see him: his lips were so sealed by that passage, his spirit in fact so hushed, in respect to any charge upon her freedom. There was something he could only therefore read back into the probabilities, and when he left the palace an hour afterwards it was with a sense of having breathed there, in the very air, the truth he had been guessing.

Just this perception it was, however, that had made him for the time ugly to himself in his awkwardness. It was horrible, with this creature, to *be* awkward; it was odious to be seeking excuses for the relation that involved it. Any relation that involved it was by the very fact as much discredited as a dish would be at dinner if one had to take medicine as a sauce. What Kate would have said in one of the young women's last talks was that—if Milly absolutely must have the truth about it— Mr. Densher was staying because she had really seen no way but to require it of him. If he stayed he didn't follow her—or didn't appear to her aunt to be doing so; and when she kept him from following her Mrs. Lowder couldn't pretend, in scenes, the renewal of which at this time of day was painful, that she after all didn't snub him as she might. She did nothing in fact *but* snub him—wouldn't that have been part of the story?—only Aunt Maud's suspicions were of the sort that had repeatedly to be dealt with. He had been, by the same token, reasonable enough—as he now, for that matter, well might; he had consented to oblige them, aunt and niece, by giving the plainest sign possible that he could exist away from London. To exist away from London was to exist away from Kate Croy —which was a gain, much appreciated, to the latter's comfort. There was a minute, at this hour, out of Densher's three, during which he knew the terror of Milly's uttering some such allusion to their friend's explanation as he must meet with words that wouldn't destroy it. To destroy it was to destroy everything, to destroy probably Kate herself, to destroy in particular by a breach of faith still uglier than anything else the beauty of their own last passage. He had given her his word of honour that if she would come to him he would act absolutely in her sense, and he had done so with a full enough vision of what her sense implied. What it implied for one thing was that to-night in the great saloon, noble in its half-lighted beauty, and straight in the white face of his young hostess, divine in her trust, or at any rate inscrutable in her mercy—what it implied was that he should lie with his lips. The single thing, of all things, that could save him from it would be Milly's letting him off after having thus scared him. What made her mercy inscrutable was that if she had already more than once saved him it was yet apparently without knowing how nearly he was lost.

These were transcendent motions, not the less blest for being obscure; whereby yet once more he was to feel the pressure lighten. He was kept on his feet in short by the felicity of her not presenting him with Kate's version as a version to adopt. He couldn't stand up to lie—he felt as if he should have to go down on his knees. As it was he just sat there shaking a little for nervousness the leg he had crossed over the other. She was sorry for his suffered snub, but he had nothing more to subscribe to, to perjure himself about, than the three or four inanities he had, on his own side, feebly prepared for the crisis. He scrambled a little higher than the reference to money and clothes, letters and directions from his manager; but he brought out the beauty of the chance for him—there before him like a temptress painted by Titian—to do a little quiet writing. He was vivid for a moment on the difficulty of writing quietly in London; and he was precipitate, almost explosive, on his idea, long cherished, of a book.

The explosion lighted her face. "You'll do your book here?"

"I hope to begin it."

"It's something you haven't begun?"

"Well, only just."

"And since you came?"

She was so full of interest that he shouldn't perhaps after all be too easily let off. "I tried to think a few days ago that I had broken ground."

Scarcely anything, it was indeed clear, could have let him in deeper. "I'm afraid we've made an awful mess of your time."

"Of course you have. But what I'm hanging on for now is precisely to repair that ravage."

"Then you mustn't mind me, you know."

"You'll see," he tried to say with ease, "how little I shall mind anything."

"You'll want"—Milly had thrown herself into it—"the best part of your days."

He thought a moment: he did what he could to wreathe it in smiles. "Oh I shall make shift with the worst part. The best will be for *you*." And he wished Kate could hear him. It didn't help him moreover that he visibly, even pathetically, imaged to her by such touches his quest for comfort against discipline. He was to bury Kate's so signal snub, and also the hard law she had now laid on him, under a high intellectual effort. This at least was his crucifixion—that Milly was so interested. She was so interested that she presently asked him if he found his rooms propitious, while he felt that in just decently answering her he put on a brazen mask. He should need it quite particularly were she to express again her imagination of coming to tea with him—an extremity that he saw he was not to be spared. "We depend on you, Susie and I, you know, not to forget we're coming"—the extremity was but to face that remainder, yet it demanded all his tact. Facing their visit itself—to that, no matter what he might have to do, he would never consent, as we know, to be pushed; and this even though it might be exactly such a demonstration as would figure for him at the top of Kate's list of his proprieties. He could wonder freely enough, deep within, if Kate's view of that especial propriety had not been modified by a subsequent occurrence; but his deciding that it was quite likely not to have been had no effect on his own preference for tact. It pleased him to think of "tact" as his present prop in doubt; that glossed his predicament over, for it was of application among the sensitive and the kind. He wasn't inhuman, in fine, so long as it would serve. It had to serve now, accordingly, to help him not to sweeten Milly's hopes. He didn't want to be rude to them, but he still less wanted them to flower again in the particular connexion; so that, casting about him in his anxiety for a middle way to meet her, he put his foot, with unhappy effect, just in the wrong place. "Will it be safe for you to break into your custom of not leaving the house?"

"'Safe'—?" She had for twenty seconds an exquisite pale glare. Oh but he didn't need it, by that time, to wince; he had winced for himself as soon as he had made his mistake. He had done what, so unforgettably, she had asked him in London not to do; he had touched, all alone with her here, the supersensitive nerve of which she had warned him. He had not, since the occasion in London, touched it again till now; but he saw himself freshly warned that it was able to bear still less. So for the moment he knew as little what to do as he had ever known it in his life. He couldn't emphasise that he thought of her as dying, yet he couldn't pretend he thought of her as indifferent to precautions. Meanwhile too she had narrowed his choice. "You suppose me so awfully bad?"

He turned, in his pain, within himself; but by the time the colour had mounted to the roots of his hair he had found what he wanted. "I'll believe whatever you tell me."

"Well then, I'm splendid."

"Oh I don't need you to tell me that."

"I mean I'm capable of life."

"I've never doubted it."

"I mean," she went on, "that I want so to live—!"

"Well?" he asked while she paused with the intensity of it.

"Well, that I know I *can.*"

"Whatever you do?" He shrank from solemnity about it.

"Whatever I do. If I want to."

"If you want to do it?"

"If I want to live. I *can,*" Milly repeated.

He had clumsily brought it on himself, but he hesitated with all the pity of it. "Ah then *that* I believe."

"I will, I will," she declared; yet with the weight of it somehow turned for him to mere light and sound.

He felt himself smiling through a mist. "You simply must!"

It brought her straight again to the fact. "Well then, if you say it, why mayn't we pay you our visit?"

"Will it help you to live?"

"Every little helps," she laughed; "and it's very little for me, in general, to stay at home. Only I shan't want to miss it—!"

"Yes?"—she had dropped again.

"Well, on the day you give us a chance."

It was amazing what so brief an exchange had at this point done with him. His great scruple suddenly broke, giving way to something inordinately strange, something of a nature to become clear to him only when he had left her. "You can come," he said, "when you like."

What had taken place for him, however—the drop, almost with violence, of everything but a sense of her own reality—apparently showed in his face or his manner, and even so vividly that she could take it for something else. "I see how you feel—that I'm an awful bore about it and that, sooner than have any such upset, you'll go. So it's no matter."

"No matter? Oh!"—he quite protested now.

"If it drives you away to escape us. We want you not to go."

It was beautiful how she spoke for Mrs. Stringham. Whatever it was, at any rate, he shook his head. "I won't go."

"Then *I* won't go!" she brightly declared.

"You mean you won't come to me?"

"No—never now. It's over. But it's all right. I mean, apart from that," she went on, "that I won't do anything I oughtn't or that I'm not forced to."

"Oh who can ever force you?" he asked with his hand-to-mouth way, at all times, of speaking for her encouragement. "You're the least coercible of creatures."

"Because, you think, I'm so free?"

"The freest person probably now in the world. You've got everything."

"Well," she smiled, "call it so. I don't complain."

On which again, in spite of himself, it let him in. "No I know you don't complain."

As soon as he had said it he had himself heard the pity in it. His telling her she had "everything" was extravagant kind humour, whereas his knowing so tenderly that she didn't complain was terrible kind gravity. Milly felt, he could see, the difference; he might as well have praised her outright for looking death in the face. This was the way she just looked *him* again, and it was of no attenuation that she took him up more gently than ever. "It isn't a merit—when one sees one's way."

"To peace and plenty? Well, I dare say not."

"I mean to keeping what one has."

"Oh that's success. If what one has is good," Densher said at random, "it's enough to try for."

"Well, it's my limit. I'm not trying for more." To which then she added with a change: "And now about your book."

"My book—?" He had got in a moment so far from it.

"The one you're now to understand that nothing will induce either Susie or me to run the risk of spoiling."

He cast about, but he made up his mind. "I'm not doing a book."

"Not what you said?" she asked in a wonder. "You're not writing?"

He already felt relieved. "I don't know, upon my honour, what I'm doing."

It made her visibly grave; so that, disconcerted in another way, he was afraid of what she would see in it. She saw in fact exactly what he feared, but again his honour, as he called it, was saved even while she didn't know she had threatened it. Taking his words for a betrayal of the sense that he, on his side, *might* complain, what she clearly wanted was to urge on him some such patience as he should be perhaps able to arrive at with her indirect help. Still more clearly, however, she wanted to be sure of how far she might venture; and he could see her make out in a moment that she had a sort of test.

"Then if it's not for your book—?"

"What *am* I staying for?"

"I mean with your London work—with all you have to do. Isn't it rather empty for you?"

"Empty for me?" He remembered how Kate had held that she might propose marriage, and he wondered if this were the way she would naturally begin it. It would leave him, such an incident, he already felt, at a loss, and the note of his finest anxiety might have been in the vagueness of his reply. "Oh well—!"

"I ask too many questions?" She settled it for herself before he could protest. "You stay because you've got to."

He grasped at it. "I stay because I've got to." And he

couldn't have said when he had uttered it if it were loyal to
Kate or disloyal. It gave her, in a manner, away; it showed the
tip of the ear of her plan. Yet Milly took it, he perceived, but as
a plain statement of his truth. He was waiting for what Kate
would have told her of—the permission from Lancaster Gate
to come any nearer. To remain friends with either niece or
aunt he mustn't stir without it. All this Densher read in the
girl's sense of the spirit of his reply; so that it made him feel he
was lying, and he had to think of something to correct that.
What he thought of was, in an instant, "Isn't it enough, whatever may be one's other complications, to stay after all for
you?"

"Oh you must judge."

He was by this time on his feet to take leave, and was also at
last too restless. The speech in question at least wasn't disloyal
to Kate; that was the very tone of their bargain. So was it, by
being loyal, another kind of lie, the lie of the uncandid profession of a motive. He was staying so little "for" Milly that he
was staying positively against her. He didn't, none the less,
know, and at last, thank goodness, didn't care. The only thing
he could say might make it either better or worse. "Well then,
so long as I don't go, you must think of me all *as* judging!"

II

HE didn't go home, on leaving her—he didn't want to; he walked instead, through his narrow ways and his *campi* with gothic arches, to a small and comparatively sequestered café where he had already more than once found refreshment and comparative repose, together with solutions that consisted mainly and pleasantly of further indecisions. It was a literal fact that those awaiting him there to-night, while he leaned back on his velvet bench with his head against a florid mirror and his eyes not looking further than the fumes of his tobacco, might have been regarded by him as a little less limp than usual. This wasn't because, before getting to his feet again, there was a step he had seen his way to; it was simply because the acceptance of his position took sharper effect from his sense of what he had just had to deal with. When half an hour before, at the palace, he had turned about to Milly on the question of the impossibility so inwardly felt, turned about on the spot and under her eyes, he had acted, by the sudden force of his seeing much further, seeing how little, how not at all, impossibilities mattered. It wasn't a case for pedantry; when people were at *her* pass everything was allowed. And her pass was now, as by the sharp click of a spring, just completely his own—to the extent, as he felt, of her deep dependence on him. Anything he should do or shouldn't would have close reference to her life, which was thus absolutely in his hands—and ought never to have reference to anything else. It was on the cards for him that he might kill her—that was the way he read the cards as he sat in his customary corner. The fear in this thought made him let everything go, kept him there actually, all motionless, for three hours on end. He renewed his consumption and smoked more cigarettes than he had ever done in the time. What had come out for him had come out, with this first intensity, as a terror; so that action itself, of any sort, the right as well as the wrong—if the difference even survived—had heard in it a vivid "Hush!" the injunction to keep from that moment intensely still. He thought in fact while his vigil lasted of several different ways for his doing so, and the hour might have served him as a lesson in going on tiptoe.

What he finally took home, when he ventured to leave the place, was the perceived truth that he might on any other system go straight to destruction. Destruction was represented for him by the idea of his really bringing to a point, on Milly's side, anything whatever. Nothing so "brought," he easily argued, but *must* be in one way or another a catastrophe. He was mixed up in her fate, or her fate, if that should be better, was mixed up in *him*, so that a single false motion might either way snap the coil. They helped him, it was true, these considerations, to a degree of eventual peace, for what they luminously amounted to was that he was to do nothing, and that fell in after all with the burden laid on him by Kate. He was only not to budge without the girl's leave—not, oddly enough at the last, to move without it, whether further or nearer, any more than without Kate's. It was to this his wisdom reduced itself—to the need again simply to be kind. That was the same as being still—as studying to create the minimum of vibration. He felt himself as he smoked shut up to a room on the wall of which something precious was too precariously hung. A false step would bring it down, and it must hang as long as possible. He was aware when he walked away again that even Fleet Street wouldn't at this juncture successfully touch him. His manager might wire that he was wanted, but he could easily be deaf to his manager. His money for the idle life might be none too much; happily, however, Venice was cheap, and it was moreover the queer fact that Milly in a manner supported him. The greatest of his expenses really was to walk to the palace to dinner. He didn't want, in short, to give that up, and he should probably be able, he felt, to stay his breath and his hand. He should be able to be still enough through everything.

He tried that for three weeks, with the sense after a little of not having failed. There had to be a delicate art in it, for he wasn't trying—quite the contrary—to be either distant or dull. That would not have been being "nice," which in its own form was the real law. That too might just have produced the vibration he desired to avert; so that he best kept everything in place by not hesitating or fearing, as it were, to let himself go—go in the direction, that is to say, of staying. It depended on where he went; which was what he meant by taking care. When one went on tiptoe one could turn off for retreat without betraying the manœuvre. Perfect tact—the necessity for which he had from the first, as we know, happily recognised— was to keep all intercourse in the key of the absolutely settled. It was settled thus for instance that they were indissoluble good friends, and settled as well that her being the American girl was, just in time and for the relation they found themselves concerned in, a boon inappreciable. If, at least, as the days went on, she was to fall short of her prerogative of the great national, the great maidenly ease, if she didn't diviningly and responsively desire and labour to record herself as possessed of it, this wouldn't have been for want of Densher's keeping her, with his idea, well up to it—wouldn't have been in fine for want of his encouragement and reminder. He didn't perhaps in so many words speak to her of the quantity itself as of the thing she was least to intermit; but he talked of it, freely, in what he flattered himself was an impersonal way, and this held it there before her—since he was careful also to talk pleasantly. It was at once their idea, when all was said, and the most marked of their conveniences. The type was so elastic that it could be stretched to almost anything; and yet, not stretched, it kept down, remained normal, remained properly within bounds. And he *had* meanwhile, thank goodness, without being too much disconcerted, the sense, for the girl's part of the business, of the queerest conscious compliance, of her doing very much what he wanted, even though without her quite seeing why. She fairly touched this once in saying: "Oh yes, you like us to be as we are because it's a kind of facilitation to you that we don't quite measure: I think one would have to be English to measure it!"—and that too, strangely enough, without prejudice to her good nature. She might have been conceived as doing—that is of being—what he liked in order perhaps only to judge where it would take them. They really as it went on *saw* each other at the game; she knowing he tried to keep her in tune with his conception, and he knowing she thus knew it. Add that he again knew she knew, and yet that nothing was spoiled by it, and we get a fair impression of the line they found most completely workable. The strangest fact of all for us must be that the success he himself thus promoted was precisely what figured to his gratitude as the something above and beyond him, above and beyond Kate, that made for daily decency. There would scarce have been felicity—certainly too little of the right lubricant—had not the national character so invoked been, not less inscrutably than entirely, in Milly's chords. It made up her unity and was the one thing he could unlimitedly take for granted.

He did so then, daily, for twenty days, without deepened fear of the undue vibration that was keeping him watchful. He knew in his nervousness that he was living at best from day to day and from hand to mouth; yet he had succeeded, he believed, in avoiding a mistake. All women had alternatives, and Milly's would doubtless be shaky too; but the national character was firm in her, whether as all of her, practically, by this time, or but as a part; the national character that, in a woman still so young, made of the air breathed a virtual non-conductor. It wasn't till a certain occasion when the twenty days had passed that, going to the palace at tea-time, he was met by the information that the signorina padrona was not "receiving." The announcement met him, in the court, on the lips of one of the gondoliers, met him, he thought, with such a conscious eye as the knowledge of his freedoms of access, hitherto conspicuously shown, could scarce fail to beget. Densher had not been at Palazzo Leporelli among the mere receivable, but had taken his place once for all among the involved and included, so that on being so flagrantly braved he recognised after a moment the propriety of a further appeal. Neither of the two ladies, it appeared, received, and yet Pasquale was not prepared to say that either was *poco bene.* He was yet not prepared to say that either was anything, and he would have been blank, Densher mentally noted, if the term could ever apply to members of a race in whom vacancy was but a nest of darknesses—not a vain surface, but a place of withdrawal in which something obscure, something always ominous, indistinguishably lived. He felt afresh indeed at this hour the force of the veto laid within the palace on any mention, any cognition, of the liabilities of its mistress. The state of her health was never confessed to there as a reason. How much it might deeply be taken for one was another matter; of which he grew fully aware on carrying his question further. This appeal was to his friend Eugenio, whom he immediately sent for, with whom, for three rich minutes, protected from the weather, he was confronted in the gallery that led from the water-steps to the court, and whom he always called, in meditation, his friend; seeing it was so elegantly presumable he would have put an end to him if he could. That produced a relation which required a name of its own, an intimacy of consciousness in truth for each—an intimacy of eye, of ear, of general sensibility, of everything but tongue. It had been, in other words, for the five weeks, far from occult to our young man that Eugenio took a view of him not less finely formal than essentially vulgar, but which at the same time he couldn't himself raise an eyebrow to prevent. It was all in the air now again; it was as much between them as ever while Eugenio waited on him in the court.

The weather, from early morning, had turned to storm, the first sea-storm of the autumn, and Densher had almost invidiously brought him down the outer staircase—the massive ascent, the great feature of the court, to Milly's *piano nobile*. This was to pay him—it was the one chance—for all imputations; the imputation in particular that, clever, *tanto bello* and not rich, the young man from London was—by the obvious way— pressing Miss Theale's fortune hard. It was to pay him for the further ineffable intimation that a gentleman must take the young lady's most devoted servant (interested scarcely less in the high attraction) for a strangely casual appendage if he counted in such a connexion on impunity and prosperity. These interpretations were odious to Densher for the simple reason that they might have been so true of the attitude of an inferior man, and three things alone, accordingly, had kept him from righting himself. One of these was that his critic sought expression only in an impersonality, a positive inhumanity, of politeness; the second was that refinements of expression in a friend's servant were not a thing a visitor could take action on; and the third was the fact that the particular attribution of motive did him after all no wrong. It was his own fault if the vulgar view, the view that might have been taken of an inferior man, happened so incorrigibly to fit him. He apparently wasn't so different from inferior men as that came to. If therefore, in fine, Eugenio figured to him as "my friend" because he was conscious of his seeing so much of him, what he made him see on the same lines in the course of their present interview was ever so much more. Densher felt that he marked himself, no doubt, as insisting, by dissatisfaction with the gondolier's an-swer, on the pursuit taken for granted in him; and yet felt it only in the augmented, the exalted distance that was by this time es-tablished between them. Eugenio had of course reflected that a word to Miss Theale from such a pair of lips would cost him his place; but he could also bethink himself that, so long as the word never came—and it was, on the basis he had arranged, impossible—he enjoyed the imagination of mounting guard. He had never so mounted guard, Densher could see, as during these minutes in the damp *loggia* where the storm-gusts were strong; and there came in fact for our young man, as a result of his presence, a sudden sharp sense that everything had turned to the dismal. Something had happened—he didn't know what; and it wasn't Eugenio who would tell him. What Eugenio told him was that he thought the ladies—as if their liability had been equal—were a "leetle" fatigued, just a "leetle leetle," and without any cause named for it. It was one of the signs of what Densher felt in him that, by a profundity, a true deviltry of re-source, he always met the latter's Italian with English and his English with Italian. He now, as usual, slightly smiled at him in the process—but ever so slightly this time, his manner also being attuned, our young man made out, to the thing, what-ever it was, that constituted the rupture of peace.

This manner, while they stood a long minute facing each other over all they didn't say, played a part as well in the sud-den jar to Densher's protected state. It was a Venice all of evil that had broken out for them alike, so that they were together in their anxiety, if they really could have met on it; a Venice of cold lashing rain from a low black sky, of wicked wind raging through narrow passes, of general arrest and interruption, with the people engaged in all the water-life huddled, stranded and wageless, bored and cynical, under archways and bridges. Our young man's mute exchange with his friend contained meanwhile such a depth of reference that, had the pressure been but slightly prolonged, they might have reached a point at which they were equally weak. Each had verily something in mind that would have made a hash of mutual suspicion and in presence of which, as a possibility, they were more united than disjoined. But it was to have been a moment for Densher that nothing could ease off—not even the formal propriety with which his interlocutor finally attended him to the *portone* and bowed upon his retreat. Nothing had passed about his coming back, and the air had made itself felt as a non-conductor of messages. Densher knew of course, as he took his way again, that Eugenio's invitation to return was not what he missed; yet he knew at the same time that what had happened to him was part of his punishment. Out in the square beyond the *fonda-menta* that gave access to the landgate of the palace, out where the wind was higher, he fairly, with the thought of it, pulled his umbrella closer down. It couldn't be, his consciousness, un-seen enough by others—the base predicament of having, by a concatenation, just to *take* such things: such things as the fact that one very acute person in the world, whom he couldn't dispose of as an interested scoundrel, enjoyed an opinion of him that there was no attacking, no disproving, no (what was worst of all) even noticing. One had come to a queer pass when a servant's opinion so mattered. Eugenio's would have mattered even if, as founded on a low vision of appearances, it had been quite wrong. It was the more disagreeable accordingly that the vision of appearances was quite right, and yet was scarcely less low.

Such as it was, at any rate, Densher shook it off with the more impatience that he was independently restless. He had to walk in spite of weather, and he took his course, through crooked ways, to the Piazza, where he should have the shelter of the galleries. Here, in the high arcade, half Venice was crowded close, while, on the Molo, at the limit of the expanse, the old columns of the Saint Theodore and of the Lion were the frame of a door wide open to the storm. It was odd for him, as he moved, that it should have made such a difference—if the dif-ference wasn't only that the palace had for the first time failed of a welcome. There was more, but it came from that; that gave the harsh note and broke the spell. The wet and the cold were now to reckon with, and it was to Densher precisely as if he had seen the obliteration, at a stroke, of the margin on a faith in which they were all living. The margin had been his name for it—for the thing that, though it had held out, could bear no shock. The shock, in some form, had come, and he wondered about it while, threading his way among loungers as vague as himself, he dropped his eyes sightlessly on the rubbish in shops. There were stretches of the gallery paved with squares of red marble, greasy now with the salt spray; and the whole place, in its huge elegance, the grace of its conception and the beauty of its detail, was more than ever like a great drawing-room, the drawing-room of Europe, profaned and bewildered by some reverse of fortune. He brushed shoulders with brown men whose hats askew, and the loose sleeves of whose pendent jackets, made them resemble melancholy maskers. The tables and chairs that overflowed from the cafés were gathered, still with a pretence of service, into the arcade, and here and there a spectacled German, with his coat-collar up, partook publicly of food and philosophy. These were impressions for Densher too, but he had made the whole circuit thrice before he stopped short, in front of Florian's, with the force of his sharpest. His eye had caught a face within the café—he had spotted an acquaintance behind the glass. The person he had thus paused long enough to look at twice was seated, well within range, at a small table on which a tumbler, half-emptied and evidently neglected, still remained; and though he had on his knee, as he leaned back, a copy of a French newspaper—the heading of the *Figaro* was visible—he stared straight before him at the little opposite rococo wall. Densher had him for a minute in profile, had him for a time during which his identity produced, however quickly, all the effect of establishing connexions—connexions startling and direct; and then, as if it were the one thing more needed, seized the look, determined by a turn of the head, that might have been a prompt result of the sense of being noticed. This wider view showed him *all* Lord Mark—Lord Mark as encountered, several weeks before, the day of the first visit of each to Palazzo Leporelli. For it had been all Lord Mark that was going out, on that occasion, as he came in—he had felt it, in the hall, at the time; and he was accordingly the less at a loss to recognise in a few seconds, as renewed meeting brought it to the surface, the same potential quantity.

It was a matter, the whole passage—it could only be—but of a few seconds; for as he might neither stand there to stare nor on the other hand make any advance from it, he had presently

resumed his walk, this time to another pace. It had been for all
the world, during his pause, as if he had caught his answer to
the riddle of the day. Lord Mark had simply faced him—as he
had faced *him*, not placed by him, not at first—as one of the
damp shuffling crowd. Recognition, though hanging fire, had
then clearly come; yet no light of salutation had been struck
from these certainties. Acquaintance between them was scant
enough for neither to take it up. That neither had done so was
not, however, what now mattered, but that the gentleman at
Florian's should be in the place at all. He couldn't have been in
it long; Densher, as inevitably a haunter of the great meeting-
ground, would in that case have seen him before. He paid
short visits; he was on the wing; the question for him even as
he sat there was of his train or of his boat. He had come back
for something—as a sequel to his earlier visit; and whatever he
had come back for it had had time to be done. He might have
arrived but last night or that morning; he had already made
the difference. It was a great thing for Densher to get this answer. He held it close, he hugged it, quite leaned on it as he
continued to circulate. It kept him going and going—it made
him no less restless. But it explained—and that was much, for
with explanations he might somehow deal. The vice in the air,
otherwise, was too much like the breath of fate. The weather
had changed, the rain was ugly, the wind wicked, the sea impossible, *because* of Lord Mark. It was because of him, *a for-
tiori*, that the palace was closed. Densher went round again
twice; he found the visitor each time as he had found him first.
Once, that is, he was staring before him; the next time he was
looking over his *Figaro*, which he had opened out. Densher
didn't again stop, but left him apparently unconscious of his
passage—on another repetition of which Lord Mark had disappeared. He had spent but the day; he would be off that night;
he had now gone to his hotel for arrangements. These things
were as plain to Densher as if he had had them in words. The
obscure had cleared for him—if cleared it was; there was something he didn't see, the great thing; but he saw so round it
and so close to it that this was almost as good. He had been
looking at a man who had done what he had come for, and for
whom, as done, it temporarily sufficed. The man had come
again to see Milly, and Milly had received him. His visit would

have taken place just before or just after luncheon, and it was
the reason why he himself had found her door shut.

He said to himself that evening, he still said even on the
morrow, that he only wanted a reason, and that with this perception of one he could now mind, as he called it, his business.
His business, he had settled, as we know, was to keep thoroughly still; and he asked himself why it should prevent this
that he could feel, in connexion with the crisis, so remarkably
blameless. He gave the appearances before him all the benefit
of being critical, so that if blame were to accrue he shouldn't
feel he had dodged it. But it wasn't a bit he who, that day, had
touched her, and if she was upset it wasn't a bit his act. The
ability so to think about it amounted for Densher during several hours to a kind of exhilaration. The exhilaration was
heightened fairly, besides, by the visible conditions—sharp,
striking, ugly to him—of Lord Mark's return. His constant
view of it, for all the next hours, of which there were many,
was as a demonstration on the face of it sinister even to his own
actual ignorance. He didn't need, for seeing it as evil, seeing it
as, to a certainty, in a high degree "nasty," to know more about
it than he had so easily and so wonderfully picked up. You
couldn't drop on the poor girl that way without, by the fact,
being brutal. Such a visit was a descent, an invasion, an aggression, constituting precisely one or other of the stupid shocks
he himself had so decently sought to spare her. Densher had
indeed drifted by the next morning to the reflexion—which he
positively, with occasion, might have brought straight out—
that the only delicate and honourable way of treating a person
in such a state was to treat her as *he*, Merton Densher, did.
With time, actually—for the impression but deepened—this
sense of the contrast, to the advantage of Merton Densher, became a sense of relief, and that in turn a sense of escape. It was
for all the world—and he drew a long breath on it—as if a special danger for him had passed. Lord Mark had, without in the
least intending such a service, got it straight out of the way. It
was *he*, the brute, who had stumbled into just the wrong inspiration and who had therefore produced, for the very person he
had wished to hurt, an impunity that was comparative innocence, that was almost like purification. The person he had
wished to hurt could only be the person so unaccountably

hanging about. To keep still meanwhile was, for this person, more comprehensively, to keep it all up; and to keep it all up was, if that seemed on consideration best, not, for the day or two, to go back to the palace.

The day or two passed—stretched to three days; and with the effect, extraordinarily, that Densher felt himself in the course of them washed but the more clean. Some sign would come if his return should have the better effect; and he was at all events, in absence, without the particular scruple. It wouldn't have been meant for him by either of the women that he was to come back but to face Eugenio. That was impossible—the being again denied; for it made him practically answerable, and answerable was what he wasn't. There was no neglect either in absence, inasmuch as, from the moment he didn't get in, the one message he could send up would be some hope on the score of health. Since accordingly that sort of expression was definitely forbidden him he had only to wait—which he was actually helped to do by his feeling with the lapse of each day more and more wound up to it. The days in themselves were anything but sweet; the wind and the weather lasted, the fireless cold hinted at worse; the broken charm of the world about was broken into smaller pieces. He walked up and down his rooms and listened to the wind—listened also to tinkles of bells and watched for some servant of the palace. He might get a note, but the note never came; there were hours when he stayed at home not to miss it. When he wasn't at home he was in circulation again as he had been at the hour of his seeing Lord Mark. He strolled about the Square with the herd of refugees; he raked the approaches and the cafés on the chance the brute, as he now regularly imaged him, *might* be still there. He could only be there, he knew, to be received afresh; and that—one had but to think of it—would be indeed stiff. He had gone, however—it was proved; though Densher's care for the question either way only added to what was most acrid in the taste of his present ordeal. It all came round to what he was doing for Milly—spending days that neither relief nor escape could purge of a smack of the abject. What was it but abject for a man of his parts to be reduced to such pastimes? What was it but sordid for him, shuffling about in the rain, to have to peep into shops and to consider possible meetings? What was it but odious to find himself wondering what, as between him and another man, a possible meeting would produce? There recurred moments when in spite of everything he felt no straighter than another man. And yet even on the third day, when still nothing had come, he more than ever knew that he wouldn't have budged for the world.

He thought of the two women, in their silence, at last—he at all events thought of Milly—as probably, for her reasons, now intensely wishing him to go. The cold breath of her reasons was, with everything else, in the air; but he didn't care for them any more than for her wish itself, and he would stay in spite of her, stay in spite of odium, stay in spite perhaps of some final experience that would be, for the pain of it, all but unbearable. That would be his one way, purified though he was, to mark his virtue beyond any mistake. It would be accepting the disagreeable, and the disagreeable would be a proof; a proof of his not having stayed for the thing—the agreeable, as it were—that Kate had named. The thing Kate had named was not to have been the odium of staying in spite of hints. It was part of the odium as actual too that Kate was, for her comfort, just now well aloof. These were the first hours since her flight in which his sense of what she had done for him on the eve of that event was to incur a qualification. It was strange, it was perhaps base, to be thinking such things so soon; but one of the intimations of his solitude was that she had provided for herself. She was out of it all, by her act, as much as he was in it; and this difference grew, positively, as his own intensity increased. She had said in their last sharp snatch of talk—sharp though thickly muffled, and with every word in it final and deep, unlike even the deepest words they had ever yet spoken: "Letters? Never—*now*. Think of it. Impossible." So that as he had sufficiently caught her sense—into which he read, all the same, a strange inconsequence—they had practically wrapped their understanding in the breach of their correspondence. He had moreover, on losing her, done justice to her law of silence; for there was doubtless a finer delicacy in his not writing to her than in his writing as he must have written had he spoken of themselves. That would have been a turbid strain, and her idea had been to be noble; which, in a degree, was a manner. Only it left her, for the pinch, comparatively at ease. And it left *him*, in the conditions, peculiarly alone. He was alone, that is, till, on the afternoon of his third day, in gathering dusk and renewed rain, with his shabby rooms looking doubtless, in their confirmed dreariness, for the mere eyes of others, at their worst, the grinning padrona threw open the door and introduced Mrs. Stringham. That made at a bound a difference, especially when he saw that his visitor was weighted. It appeared part of her weight that she was in a wet waterproof, that she allowed her umbrella to be taken from her by the good woman without consciousness or care, and that her face, under her veil, richly rosy with the driving wind, was—and the veil too—as splashed as if the rain were her tears.

III

THEY came to it almost immediately; he was to wonder afterwards at the fewness of their steps. "She has turned her face to the wall."

"You mean she's worse?"

The poor lady stood there as she had stopped; Densher had, in the instant flare of his eagerness, his curiosity, all responsive at sight of her, waved away, on the spot, the padrona, who had offered to relieve her of her mackintosh. She looked vaguely about through her wet veil, intensely alive now to the step she had taken and wishing it not to have been in the dark, but clearly, as yet, seeing nothing. "I don't know *how* she is—and it's why I've come to you."

"I'm glad enough you've come," he said, "and it's quite—you make me feel—as if I had been wretchedly waiting for you."

She showed him again her blurred eyes—she had caught at his word. "Have you been wretched?"

Now, however, on his lips, the word expired. It would have sounded for him like a complaint, and before something he already made out in his visitor he knew his own trouble as small. Hers, under her damp draperies, which shamed his lack of a fire, was great, and he felt she had brought it all with her. He answered that he had been patient and above all that he had been still. "As still as a mouse—you'll have seen it for yourself. Stiller, for three days together, than I've ever been in my life. It has seemed to me the only thing."

This qualification of it as a policy or a remedy was straightway for his friend, he saw, a light that her own light could answer. "It has been best. I've wondered for you. But it has been best," she said again.

"Yet it has done no good?"

"I don't know. I've been afraid you were gone." Then as he gave a headshake which, though slow, was deeply mature: "You *won't* go?"

"Is to 'go,'" he asked, "to be still?"

"Oh I mean if you'll stay for me."

"I'll do anything for you. Isn't it for you alone now I can?"

She thought of it, and he could see even more of the relief she was taking from him. His presence, his face, his voice, the old rooms themselves, so meagre yet so charged, where Kate had admirably been to him—these things counted for her, now she had them, as the help she had been wanting: so that she still only stood there taking them all in. With it however popped up characteristically a throb of her conscience. What she thus tasted was almost a personal joy. It told Densher of the three days she on her side had spent. "Well, anything you do for me—*is* for her too. Only, only—!"

"Only nothing now matters?"

She looked at him a minute as if he were the fact itself that he expressed. "Then you know?"

"Is she dying?" he asked for all answer.

Mrs. Stringham waited—her face seemed to sound him. Then her own reply was strange. "She hasn't so much as named you. We haven't spoken."

"Not for three days?"

"No more," she simply went on, "than if it were all over. Not even by the faintest allusion."

"Oh," said Densher with more light, "you mean you haven't spoken about *me*?"

"About what else? No more than if you were dead."

"Well," he answered after a moment, "I *am* dead."

"Then *I* am," said Susan Shepherd with a drop of her arms on her waterproof.

It was a tone that, for the minute, imposed itself in its dry despair; it represented, in the bleak place, which had no life of its own, none but the life Kate had left—the sense of which, for that matter, by mystic channels, might fairly be reaching the visitor—the very impotence of their extinction. And Densher had nothing to oppose it withal, nothing but again: "Is she dying?"

It made her, however, as if these were crudities, almost material pangs, only say as before: "Then you know?"

"Yes," he at last returned, "I know. But the marvel to me is that *you* do. I've no right in fact to imagine or to assume that you do."

"You may," said Susan Shepherd, "all the same. I know."

"Everything?"

Her eyes, through her veil, kept pressing him. "No—not everything. That's why I've come."

"That I shall really tell you?" With which, as she hesitated and it affected him, he brought out in a groan a doubting "Oh, oh!" It turned him from her to the place itself, which was a part of what was in him, was the abode, the worn shrine more than ever, of the fact in possession, the fact, now a thick association, for which he had hired it. *That* was not for telling, but Susan Shepherd was, none the less, so decidedly wonderful that the sense of it might really have begun, by an effect already operating, to be a part of her knowledge. He saw, and it stirred him, that she hadn't come to judge him; had come rather, so far as she might dare, to pity. This showed him her own abasement—that, at any rate, of grief; and made him feel with a rush of friendliness that he liked to be with her. The rush had quickened when she met his groan with an attenuation.

"We shall at all events—if that's anything—be together."

It was his own good impulse in herself. "It's what I've ventured to feel. It's much." She replied in effect, silently, that it was whatever he liked; on which, so far as he had been afraid for anything, he knew his fear had dropped. The comfort was huge, for it gave back to him something precious, over which, in the effort of recovery, his own hand had too imperfectly closed. Kate, he remembered, had said to him, with her sole and single boldness—and also on grounds he hadn't then measured—that Mrs. Stringham was a person who *wouldn't*, at a pinch, in a stretch of confidence, wince. It was but another of the cases in which Kate was always showing. "You don't think then very horridly of me?"

And her answer was the more valuable that it came without nervous effusion—quite as if she understood what he might conceivably have believed. She turned over in fact what she thought, and that was what helped him. "Oh you've been extraordinary!"

It made him aware the next moment of how they had been planted there. She took off her cloak with his aid, though when she had also, accepting a seat, removed her veil, he recognised in her personal ravage that the words she had just uttered to him were the one flower she had to throw. They were all her consolation for him, and the consolation even still depended on the event. She sat with him at any rate in the grey clearance, as sad as a winter dawn, made by their meeting. The image she again evoked for him loomed in it but the larger. "She has turned her face to the wall."

He saw with the last vividness, and it was as if, in their silences, they were simply so leaving what he saw. "She doesn't speak at all? I don't mean not of me."

"Of nothing—of no one." And she went on, Susan Shepherd, giving it out as she had had to take it. "She doesn't *want* to die. Think of her age. Think of her goodness. Think of her beauty. Think of all she is. Think of all she *has*. She lies there stiffening herself and clinging to it all. So I thank God—!" the poor lady wound up with a wan inconsequence.

He wondered. "You thank God—?"

"That she's so quiet."

He continued to wonder. "*Is* she so quiet?"

"She's more than quiet. She's grim. It's what she has never been. So you see—all these days. I can't tell you—but it's better so. It would kill me if she *were* to tell me."

"To tell you?" He was still at a loss.

"How she feels. How she clings. How she doesn't want it."

"How she doesn't want to die? Of course she doesn't want it." He had a long pause, and they might have been thinking together of what they could even now do to prevent it. This, however, was not what he brought out. Milly's "grimness" and the great hushed palace were present to him; present with the little woman before him as she must have been waiting there and listening. "Only, what harm have *you* done her?"

Mrs. Stringham looked about in her darkness. "I don't know. I come and talk of her here with you."

It made him again hesitate. "Does she utterly hate me?"

"I don't know. How *can* I? No one ever will."

"She'll never tell?"

"She'll never tell."

Once more he thought. "She must be magnificent."

"She *is* magnificent."

His friend, after all, helped him, and he turned it, so far as he could, all over. "Would she see me again?"

It made his companion stare. "Should you like to see her?"

"You mean as you describe her?" He felt her surprise, and it took him some time. "No."

"Ah then!" Mrs. Stringham sighed.

"But if she could bear it I'd do anything."

She had for the moment her vision of this, but it collapsed. "I don't see what you can do."

"I don't either. But *she* might."

Mrs. Stringham continued to think. "It's too late."

"Too late for her to see—?"

"Too late."

The very decision of her despair—it was after all so lucid—kindled in him a heat. "But the doctor, all the while—?"

"Tacchini? Oh he's kind. He comes. He's proud of having been approved and coached by a great London man. He hardly in fact goes away; so that I scarce know what becomes of his other patients. He thinks her, justly enough, a great personage; he treats her like royalty; he's waiting on events. But she has barely consented to see him, and, though she has told him, generously—for she *thinks* of me, dear creature—that he may come, that he may stay, for my sake, he spends most of his time only hovering at her door, prowling through the rooms, trying to entertain me, in that ghastly saloon, with the gossip of Venice, and meeting me, in doorways, in the sala, on the staircase, with an agreeable intolerable smile. We don't," said Susan Shepherd, "talk of her."

"By her request?"

"Absolutely. I don't do what she doesn't wish. We talk of the price of provisions."

"By her request too?"

"Absolutely. She named it to me as a subject when she said, the first time, that if it would be any comfort to me he might stay as much as we liked."

Densher took it all in. "But he isn't any comfort to you!"

"None whatever. That, however," she added, "isn't his fault. Nothing's any comfort."

"Certainly," Densher observed, "as I but too horribly feel, *I'm* not."

"No. But I didn't come for that."

"You came for *me*."

"Well then call it that." But she looked at him a moment

with eyes filled full, and something came up in her the next instant from deeper still. "I came at bottom of course—"

"You came at bottom of course for our friend herself. But if
it's, as you say, too late for me to do anything?"

She continued to look at him, and with an irritation, which
he saw grow in her, from the truth itself. "So I did say. But, with
you here"—and she turned her vision again strangely about
her—"with you here, and with everything, I feel we mustn't
abandon her."

"God forbid we should abandon her."

"Then you *won't*?" His tone had made her flush again.

"How do you mean I 'won't,' if she abandons *me*? What can
I do if she won't see me?"

"But you said just now you wouldn't like it."

"I said I shouldn't like it in the light of what you tell me. I
shouldn't like it only to see her as you make me. I should like
it if I could help her. But even then," Densher pursued without faith, "she would have to want it first herself. And there,"
he continued to make out, "is the devil of it. She *won't* want it
herself. She *can't*!"

He had got up in his impatience of it, and she watched him
while he helplessly moved. "There's one thing you can do.
There's only that, and even for that there are difficulties. But
there *is* that." He stood before her with his hands in his pockets, and he had soon enough, from her eyes, seen what was
coming. She paused as if waiting for his leave to utter it, and as
he only let her wait they heard in the silence, on the Canal, the
renewed downpour of rain. She had at last to speak, but, as if
still with her fear, she only half-spoke. "I think you really know
yourself what it is."

He did know what it was, and with it even, as she said—
rather!—there were difficulties. He turned away on them, on
everything, for a moment; he moved to the other window and
looked at the sheeted channel, wider, like a river, where the
houses opposite, blurred and belittled, stood at twice their distance. Mrs. Stringham said nothing, was as mute in fact, for the
minute, as if she had "had" him, and he was the first again to
speak. When he did so, however, it was not in straight answer to
her last remark—he only started from that. He said, as he came
back to her, "Let me, you know, *see*—one must understand,"

almost as if he had for the time accepted it. And what he wished to understand was where, on the essence of the question, was the voice of Sir Luke Strett. If they talked of not giving her up shouldn't *he* be the one least of all to do it? "Aren't we, at the worst, in the dark without him?"

"Oh," said Mrs. Stringham, "it's he who has kept me going. I wired the first night, and he answered like an angel. He'll come like one. Only he can't arrive, at the nearest, till Thursday afternoon."

"Well then that's something."

She considered. "Something—yes. She likes him."

"Rather! I can see it still, the face with which, when he was here in October—that night when she was in white, when she had people there and those musicians—she committed him to my care. It was beautiful for both of us—she put us in relation. She asked me, for the time, to take him about; I did so, and we quite hit it off. That proved," Densher said with a quick sad smile, "that she liked him."

"He liked *you*," Susan Shepherd presently risked.

"Ah I know nothing about that."

"You ought to then. He went with you to galleries and churches; you saved his time for him, showed him the choicest things, and you perhaps will remember telling me myself that if he hadn't been a great surgeon he might really have been a great judge. I mean of the beautiful."

"Well," the young man admitted, "that's what he is—in having judged *her*. He hasn't," he went on, "judged her for nothing. His interest in her—which we must make the most of—can only be supremely beneficent."

He still roamed, while he spoke, with his hands in his pockets, and she saw him, on this, as her eyes sufficiently betrayed, trying to keep his distance from the recognition he had a few moments before partly confessed to. "I'm glad," she dropped, "you like him!"

There was something for him in the sound of it. "Well, I do no more, dear lady, than you do yourself. Surely *you* like him. Surely, when he was here, we all liked him."

"Yes, but I seem to feel I know what he thinks. And I should think, with all the time you spent with him, you'd know it," she said, "yourself."

Densher stopped short, though at first without a word. "We never spoke of her. Neither of us mentioned her, even to sound her name, and nothing whatever in connexion with her passed between us."

Mrs. Stringham stared up at him, surprised at this picture. But she had plainly an idea that after an instant resisted it. "That was his professional propriety."

"Precisely. But it was also my sense of that virtue in him, and it was something more besides." And he spoke with sudden intensity. "I couldn't *talk* to him about her!"

"Oh!" said Susan Shepherd.

"I can't talk to any one about her."

"Except to *me*," his friend continued.

"Except to you." The ghost of her smile, a gleam of significance, had waited on her words, and it kept him, for honesty, looking at her. For honesty too—that is for his own words—he had quickly coloured: he was sinking so, at a stroke, the burden of his discourse with Kate. His visitor, for the minute, while their eyes met, might have been watching him hold it down. And he *had* to hold it down—the effort of which, precisely, made him red. He couldn't let it come up; at least not yet. She might make what she would of it. He attempted to repeat his statement, but he really modified it. "Sir Luke, at all events, had nothing to tell me, and I had nothing to tell him. Make-believe talk was impossible for us, and—"

"And *real*"—she had taken him right up with a huge emphasis—"was more impossible still." No doubt—he didn't deny it; and she had straightway drawn her conclusion. "Then that proves what I say—that there were immensities between you. Otherwise you'd have chattered."

"I dare say," Densher granted, "we were both thinking of her."

"You were neither of you thinking of any one else. That's why you kept together."

Well, that too, if she desired, he took from her; but he came straight back to what he had originally said. "I haven't a notion, all the same, of what he thinks." She faced him, visibly, with the question into which he had already observed that her special shade of earnestness was perpetually flowering, right and left—"Are you *very* sure?"—and he could only note her apparent difference from himself. "You, I judge, believe that he thinks she's gone."

She took it, but she bore up. "It doesn't matter what I believe."

"Well, we shall see"—and he felt almost basely superficial. More and more, for the last five minutes, had he known she had brought something with her, and never in respect to anything had he had such a wish to postpone. He would have liked to put everything off till Thursday; he was sorry it was now Tuesday; he wondered if he were afraid. Yet it wasn't of Sir Luke, who was coming; nor of Milly, who was dying; nor of Mrs. Stringham, who was sitting there. It wasn't, strange to say, of Kate either, for Kate's presence affected him suddenly as having swooned or trembled away. Susan Shepherd's, thus prolonged, had cast on it some influence under which it had ceased to act. She was as absent to his sensibility as she had constantly been, since her departure, absent, as an echo or a reference, from the palace; and it was the first time, among the objects now surrounding him, that his sensibility so noted her. He knew soon enough that it was of himself he was afraid, and that even, if he didn't take care, he should infallibly be more so. "Meanwhile," he added for his companion, "it has been everything for me to see you."

She slowly rose at the words, which might almost have conveyed to her the hint of his taking care. She stood there as if she had in fact seen him abruptly moved to dismiss her. But the abruptness would have been in this case so marked as fairly to offer ground for insistence to her imagination of his state. It would take her moreover, she clearly showed him she was thinking, but a minute or two to insist. Besides, she had already said it. "Will you do it if *he* asks you? I mean if Sir Luke himself puts it to you. And will you give him"—oh she was earnest now!—"the opportunity to put it to you?"

"The opportunity to put what?"

"That if you deny it to her, that may still do something."

Densher felt himself—as had already once befallen him in the quarter of an hour—turn red to the top of his forehead. Turning red had, however, for him, as a sign of shame, been, so to speak, discounted: his consciousness of it at the present moment was rather as a sign of his fear. It showed him sharply enough of what he was afraid. "If I deny what to her?"

Hesitation, on the demand, revived in her, for hadn't he all along been letting her see that he knew? "Why, what Lord Mark told her."

"And what did Lord Mark tell her?"

Mrs. Stringham had a look of bewilderment—of seeing him as suddenly perverse. "I've been judging that you yourself know." And it was she who now blushed deep.

It quickened his pity for her, but he was beset too by other things. "Then *you* know—"

"Of his dreadful visit?" She stared. "Why it's what has done it."

"Yes—I understand that. But you also know—"

He had faltered again, but all she knew she now wanted to say. "I'm speaking," she said soothingly, "of what he told her. It's *that* that I've taken you as knowing."

"Oh!" he sounded in spite of himself.

It appeared to have for her, he saw the next moment, the quality of relief, as if he had supposed her thinking of something else. Thereupon, straightway, that lightened it. "Oh you thought I've known it for *true*!"

Her light had heightened her flush, and he saw that he had betrayed himself. Not, however, that it mattered, as he immediately saw still better. There it was now, all of it at last, and this at least there was no postponing. They were left with her idea—the one she was wishing to make him recognise. He had expressed ten minutes before his need to understand, and she was acting after all but on that. Only what he was to understand was no small matter; it might be larger even than as yet appeared.

He took again one of his turns, not meeting what she had last said; he mooned a minute, as he would have called it, at a window; and of course she could see that she had driven him to the wall. She did clearly, without delay, see it; on which her sense of having "caught" him became as promptly a scruple, which she spoke as if not to press. "What I mean is that he told her you've been all the while engaged to Miss Croy."

He gave a jerk round; it was almost—to hear it—the touch

of a lash; and he said—idiotically, as he afterwards knew—the first thing that came into his head. "All *what* while?"

"Oh it's not I who say it." She spoke in gentleness. "I only repeat to you what he told her."

Densher, from whom an impatience had escaped, had already caught himself up. "Pardon my brutality. Of course I know what you're talking about. I saw him, toward the evening," he further explained, "in the Piazza; only just saw him—through the glass at Florian's—without any words. In fact I scarcely know him—there wouldn't have been occasion. It was but once, moreover—he must have gone that night. But I knew he wouldn't have come for nothing, and I turned it over—what he would have come for."

Oh so had Mrs. Stringham. "He came for exasperation."

Densher approved. "He came to let her know that he knows better than she for whom it was she had a couple of months before, in her fool's paradise, refused him."

"How you *do* know!"—and Mrs. Stringham almost smiled.

"I know that—but I don't know the good it does him."

"The good, he thinks, if he has patience—not too much— may be to come. He doesn't know what he has done to her. Only *we*, you see, do that."

He saw, but he wondered. "She kept from him—what she felt?"

"She was able—I'm sure of it—not to show anything. He dealt her his blow, and she took it without a sign." Mrs. Stringham, it was plain, spoke by book, and it brought into play again her appreciation of what she related. "She's magnificent."

Densher again gravely assented. "Magnificent!"

"And *he*," she went on, "is an idiot of idiots."

"An idiot of idiots." For a moment, on it all, on the stupid doom in it, they looked at each other. "Yet he's thought so awfully clever."

"So awfully—it's Maud Lowder's own view. And he was nice, in London," said Mrs. Stringham, "to *me*. One could almost pity him—he has had such a good conscience."

"That's exactly the inevitable ass."

"Yes, but it wasn't—I could see from the only few things she first told me—that he meant *her* the least harm. He intended none whatever."

"That's always the ass at his worst," Densher returned. "He only of course meant harm to me."

"And good to himself—he thought that would come. He had been unable to swallow," Mrs. Stringham pursued, "what had happened on his other visit. He had been then too sharply humiliated."

"Oh I saw that."

"Yes, and he also saw you. He saw you received, as it were, while he was turned away."

"Perfectly," Densher said—"I've filled it out. And also that he has known meanwhile for *what* I was then received. For a stay of all these weeks. He had had it to think of."

"Precisely—it was more than he could bear. But he has it," said Mrs. Stringham, "to think of still."

"Only, after all," asked Densher, who himself somehow, at this point, was having more to think of even than he had yet had—"only, after all, how has he happened to know? That is, to know enough."

"What do you call enough?" Mrs. Stringham enquired.

"He can only have acted—it would have been his sole safety —from full knowledge."

He had gone on without heeding her question; but, face to face as they were, something had none the less passed between them. It was this that, after an instant, made her again interrogative. "What do you mean by full knowledge?"

Densher met it indirectly. "Where has he been since October?"

"I think he has been back to England. He came in fact, I've reason to believe, straight from there."

"Straight to do this job? All the way for his half-hour?"

"Well, to try again—with the help perhaps of a new fact. To make himself possibly right with her—a different attempt from the other. He had at any rate something to tell her, and he didn't know his opportunity would reduce itself to half an hour. Or perhaps indeed half an hour would be just what was most effective. It *has* been!" said Susan Shepherd.

Her companion took it in, understanding but too well; yet as she lighted the matter for him more, really, than his own courage had quite dared—putting the absent dots on several i's—he saw new questions swarm. They had been till now in a bunch, entangled and confused; and they fell apart, each showing for itself. The first he put to her was at any rate abrupt. "Have you heard of late from Mrs. Lowder."

"Oh yes, two or three times. She depends naturally upon news of Milly."

He hesitated. "And does she depend, naturally, upon news of *me*?"

His friend matched for an instant his deliberation.

"I've given her none that hasn't been decently good. This will have been the first."

"'This'?" Densher was thinking.

"Lord Mark's having been here, and her being as she is."

He thought a moment longer. "What has Mrs. Lowder written about him? Has she written that he has been with them?"

"She has mentioned him but once—it was in her letter before the last. Then she said something."

"And what did she say?"

Mrs. Stringham produced it with an effort. "Well it was in reference to Miss Croy. That she thought Kate was thinking of him. Or perhaps I should say rather that he was thinking of *her* —only it seemed this time to have struck Maud that he was seeing the way more open to him."

Densher listened with his eyes on the ground, but he presently raised them to speak, and there was that in his face which proved him aware of a queerness in his question. "Does she mean he has been encouraged to *propose* to her niece?"

"I don't know what she means."

"Of course not"—he recovered himself; "and I oughtn't to seem to trouble you to piece together what I can't piece myself. Only I 'guess,'" he added, "I *can* piece it."

She spoke a little timidly, but she risked it. "I dare say I can piece it too."

It was one of the things in her—and his conscious face took it from her as such—that from the moment of her coming in had seemed to mark for him, as to what concerned him, the long jump of her perception. They had parted four days earlier with many things, between them, deep down. But these things were now on their troubled surface, and it wasn't he who had brought them so quickly up. Women were wonderful—at least this one was. But so, not less, was Milly, was Aunt Maud; so,

most of all, was his very Kate. Well, he already knew what he
had been feeling about the circle of petticoats. They were all
such petticoats! It was just the fineness of his tangle. The sense
of that, in its turn, for us too, might have been not uncon-
nected with his putting to his visitor a question that quite
passed over her remark. "Has Miss Croy meanwhile written to
our friend?"

"Oh," Mrs. Stringham amended, "*her* friend also. But not a
single word that I know of."

He had taken it for certain she hadn't—the thing being after
all but a shade more strange than his having himself, with
Milly, never for six weeks mentioned the young lady in question. It was for that matter but a shade more strange than
Milly's not having mentioned her. In spite of which, and however inconsequently, he blushed anew for Kate's silence. He
got away from it in fact as quickly as possible, and the furthest
he could get was by reverting for a minute to the man they had
been judging. "How did he manage to get *at* her? She had
only—with what had passed between them before—to say she
couldn't see him."

"Oh she was disposed to kindness. She was easier," the good
lady explained with a slight embarrassment, "than at the other
time."

"Easier?"

"She was off her guard. There was a difference."

"Yes. But exactly not *the* difference."

"Exactly not the difference of her having to be harsh. Perfectly. She could afford to be the opposite." With which, as he
said nothing, she just impatiently completed her sense. "She
had had *you* here for six weeks."

"Oh!" Densher softly groaned.

"Besides, I think he must have written her first—written I
mean in a tone to smooth his way. That it would be a kindness
to himself. Then on the spot—"

"On the spot," Densher broke in, "he unmasked? The horrid little beast!"

It made Susan Shepherd turn slightly pale, though quick-
ening, as for hope, the intensity of her look at him. "Oh he
went off without an alarm."

"And he must have gone off also without a hope."

"Ah that, certainly."

"Then it *was* mere base revenge. Hasn't he known her, into the bargain," the young man asked—"didn't he, weeks before, see her, judge her, feel her, as having for such a suit as his not more perhaps than a few months to live?"

Mrs. Stringham at first, for reply, but looked at him in silence; and it gave more force to what she then remarkably added. "He has doubtless been aware of what you speak of, just as you have yourself been aware."

"He has wanted her, you mean, just *because*—?"

"Just because," said Susan Shepherd:

"The hound!" Merton Densher brought out. He moved off, however, with a hot face, as soon as he had spoken, conscious again of an intention in his visitor's reserve. Dusk was now deeper, and after he had once more taken counsel of the dreariness without he turned to his companion. "Shall we have lights—a lamp or the candles?"

"Not for me."

"Nothing?"

"Not for me."

He waited at the window another moment and then faced his friend with a thought. "He *will* have proposed to Miss Croy. That's what has happened."

Her reserve continued. "It's you who must judge."

"Well, I do judge. Mrs. Lowder will have done so too—only *she*, poor lady, wrong. Miss Croy's refusal of him will have struck him"—Densher continued to make it out—"as a phenomenon requiring a reason."

"And you've been clear to him *as* the reason?"

"Not too clear—since I'm sticking here and since that has been a fact to make his descent on Miss Theale relevant. But clear enough. He has believed," said Densher bravely, "that I may have been a reason at Lancaster Gate, and yet at the same time have been up to something in Venice."

Mrs. Stringham took her courage from his own. "'Up to' something? Up to what?"

"God knows. To some 'game,' as they say. To some deviltry. To some duplicity."

"Which of course," Mrs. Stringham observed, "is a monstrous supposition." Her companion, after a stiff minute—sensibly long for each—fell away from her again, and then added to it another minute, which he spent once more looking out with his hands in his pockets. This was no answer, he perfectly knew, to what she had dropped, and it even seemed to state for his own ears that no answer was possible. She left him to himself, and he was glad she had declined, for their further colloquy, the advantage of lights. These would have been an advantage mainly to herself. Yet she got her benefit too even from the absence of them. It came out in her very tone when at last she addressed him—so differently, for confidence—in words she had already used. "If Sir Luke himself asks it of you as something you can do for *him*, will you deny to Milly herself what she has been made so dreadfully to believe?"

Oh how he knew he hung back! But at last he said: "You're absolutely certain then that she does believe it?"

"Certain?" She appealed to their whole situation. "Judge!"

He took his time again to judge. "Do *you* believe it?"

He was conscious that his own appeal pressed her hard; it eased him a little that her answer must be a pain to her discretion. She answered none the less, and he was truly the harder pressed. "What I believe will inevitably depend more or less on your action. You can perfectly settle it—if you care. I promise to believe you down to the ground if, to save her life, you consent to a denial."

"But a denial, when it comes to that—confound the whole thing, don't you see!—of exactly what?"

It was as if he were hoping she would narrow; but in fact she enlarged. "Of everything."

Everything had never even yet seemed to him so incalculably much. "Oh!" he simply moaned into the gloom.

IV

T HE near Thursday, coming nearer and bringing Sir Luke Strett, brought also blessedly an abatement of other rigours. The weather changed, the stubborn storm yielded, and the autumn sunshine, baffled for many days, but now hot and almost vindictive, came into its own again and, with an almost audible pæan, a suffusion of bright sound that was one with the bright colour, took large possession. Venice glowed and plashed and called and chimed again; the air was like a clap of hands, and the scattered pinks, yellows, blues, sea-greens, were like a hanging-out of vivid stuffs, a laying-down of fine carpets. Densher rejoiced in this on the occasion of his going to the station to meet the great doctor. He went after consideration, which, as he was constantly aware, was at present his imposed, his only, way of doing anything. That was where the event had landed him—where no event in his life had landed him before. He had thought, no doubt, from the day he was born, much more than he had acted; except indeed that he remembered thoughts—a few of them—which at the moment of their coming to him had thrilled him almost like adventures. But anything like his actual state he had not, as to the prohibition of impulse, accident, range—the prohibition in other words of freedom—hitherto known. The great oddity was that if he had felt his arrival, so few weeks back, especially as an adventure, nothing could now less resemble one than the fact of his staying. It would be an adventure to break away, to depart, to go back, above all, to London, and tell Kate Croy he had done so; but there was something of the merely, the almost meanly, obliged and involved sort in his going on as he was. That was the effect in particular of Mrs. Stringham's visit, which had left him as with such a taste in his mouth of what he couldn't do. It had made this quantity clear to him, and yet had deprived him of the sense, the other sense, of what, for a refuge, he possibly *could*.

It was but a small make-believe of freedom, he knew, to go to the station for Sir Luke. Nothing equally free, at all events, had he yet turned over so long. What then was his odious position but that again and again he was afraid? He stiffened himself under this consciousness as if it had been a tax levied by a tyrant. He hadn't at any time proposed to himself to live long enough for fear to preponderate in his life. Such was simply the advantage it had actually got of him. He was afraid for instance that an advance to his distinguished friend might prove for him somehow a pledge or a committal. He was afraid of it as a current that would draw him too far; yet he thought with an equal aversion of being shabby, being poor, through fear. What finally prevailed with him was the reflexion that, whatever might happen, the great man had, after that occasion at the palace, their young woman's brief sacrifice to society— and the hour of Mrs. Stringham's appeal had brought it well to the surface—shown him marked benevolence. Mrs. Stringham's comments on the relation in which Milly had placed them made him—it was unmistakeable—feel things he perhaps hadn't felt. It was in the spirit of seeking a chance to feel again adequately whatever it was he had missed—it was, no doubt, in that spirit, so far as it went a stroke for freedom, that Densher, arriving betimes, paced the platform before the train came in. Only, after it had come and he had presented himself at the door of Sir Luke's compartment with everything that followed—only, as the situation developed, the sense of an anticlimax to so many intensities deprived his apprehensions and hesitations even of the scant dignity they might claim. He could scarce have said if the visitor's manner less showed the remembrance that might have suggested expectation, or made shorter work of surprise in presence of the fact.

Sir Luke had clean forgotten—so Densher read—the rather remarkable young man he had formerly gone about with, though he picked him up again, on the spot, with one large quiet look. The young man felt himself so picked, and the thing immediately affected him as the proof of a splendid economy. Opposed to all the waste with which he was now connected the exhibition was of a nature quite nobly to admonish him. The eminent pilgrim, in the train, all the way, had used the hours as he needed, thinking not a moment in advance of what finally awaited him. An exquisite case awaited him—of which, in this queer way, the remarkable young man was an outlying part; but the single motion of his face, the motion into which

Densher, from the platform, lightly stirred its stillness, was his first renewed cognition. If, however, he had suppressed the matter by leaving Victoria he would at once suppress now, in turn, whatever else suited. The perception of this became as a symbol of the whole pitch, so far as one might one's self be concerned, of his visit. One saw, our friend further meditated, everything that, in contact, he appeared to accept—if only, for much, not to trouble to sink it: what one missed was the inward use he made of it. Densher began wondering, at the great water-steps outside, what use he would make of the anomaly of their having there to separate. Eugenio had been on the platform, in the respectful rear, and the gondola from the palace, under his direction, bestirred itself, with its attaching mixture of alacrity and dignity, on their coming out of the station together. Densher didn't at all mind now that, he himself of necessity refusing a seat on the deep black cushions beside the guest of the palace, he had Milly's three emissaries for spectators; and this susceptibility, he also knew, it was something to have left behind. All he did was to smile down vaguely from the steps—they could see him, the donkeys, as shut out as they would. "I don't," he said with a sad headshake, "go there now."

"Oh!" Sir Luke Strett returned, and made no more of it; so that the thing was splendid, Densher fairly thought, as an inscrutability quite inevitable and unconscious. His friend appeared not even to make of it that he supposed it might be for respect to the crisis. He didn't moreover afterwards make much more of anything—after the classic craft, that is, obeying in the main Pasquale's inimitable stroke from the poop, had performed the manœuvre by which it presented, receding, a back, so to speak, rendered positively graceful by the high black hump of its *felze*. Densher watched the gondola out of sight— he heard Pasquale's cry, borne to him across the water, for the sharp firm swerve into a side-canal, a short cut to the palace. He had no gondola of his own; it was his habit never to take one; and he humbly—as in Venice it *is* humble—walked away, though not without having for some time longer stood as if fixed where the guest of the palace had left him. It was strange enough, but he found himself as never yet, and as he couldn't have reckoned, in presence of the truth that was the truest about Milly. He couldn't have reckoned on the force of the difference instantly made—for it was all in the air as he heard Pasquale's cry and saw the boat disappear—by the mere visibility, on the spot, of the personage summoned to her aid. He hadn't only never been near the facts of her condition—which counted so as a blessing for him; he hadn't only, with all the world, hovered outside an impenetrable ring fence, within which there reigned a kind of expensive vagueness made up of smiles and silences and beautiful fictions and priceless arrangements, all strained to breaking; but he had also, with every one else, as he now felt, actively fostered suppressions which were in the direct interest of every one's good manner, every one's pity, every one's really quite generous ideal. It was a conspiracy of silence, as the *cliché* went, to which no one had made an exception, the great smudge of mortality across the picture, the shadow of pain and horror, finding in no quarter a surface of spirit or of speech that consented to reflect it. "The mere æsthetic instinct of mankind—!" our young man had more than once, in the connexion, said to himself; letting the rest of the proposition drop, but touching again thus sufficiently on the outrage even to taste involved in one's having to *see*. So then it had been—a general conscious fool's paradise, from which the specified had been chased like a dangerous animal. What therefore had at present befallen was that the specified, standing all the while at the gate, had now crossed the threshold as in Sir Luke Strett's person and quite on such a scale as to fill out the whole precinct. Densher's nerves, absolutely his heart-beats too, had measured the change before he on this occasion moved away.

The facts of physical suffering, of incurable pain, of the chance grimly narrowed, had been made, at a stroke, intense, and this was to be the way he was now to feel them. The clearance of the air, in short, making vision not only possible but inevitable, the one thing left to be thankful for was the breadth of Sir Luke's shoulders, which, should one be able to keep in line with them, might in some degree interpose. It was, however, far from plain to Densher for the first day or two that he was again to see his distinguished friend at all. That he couldn't, on any basis actually serving, return to the palace—this was as solid to him, every whit, as the other feature of his case, the fact of the publicity attaching to his proscription through his not having taken himself off. He had been seen often enough in the Leporelli gondola. As, accordingly, he was not on any presumption destined to meet Sir Luke about the town, where the latter would have neither time nor taste to lounge, nothing more would occur between them unless the great man should surprisingly wait upon him. His doing that, Densher further reflected, wouldn't even simply depend on Mrs. Stringham's having decided to—as they might say—turn him on. It would depend as well—for there would be practically some difference to her—on her actually attempting it; and it would depend above all on what Sir Luke would make of such an overture. Densher had for that matter his own view of the amount, to say nothing of the particular sort, of response it might expect from him. He had his own view of the ability of such a personage even to understand such an appeal. To what extent could he be prepared, and what importance in fine could he attach? Densher asked himself these questions, in truth, to put his own position at the worst. He should miss the great man completely unless the great man should come to see him, and the great man could only come to see him for a purpose unsupposable. Therefore he wouldn't come at all, and consequently there was nothing to hope.

It wasn't in the least that Densher invoked this violence to all probability; but it pressed on him that there were few possible diversions he could afford now to miss. Nothing in his predicament was so odd as that, incontestably afraid of himself, he was not afraid of Sir Luke. He had an impression, which he clung to, based on a previous taste of the visitor's company, that *he* would somehow let him off. The truth about Milly perched on his shoulders and sounded in his tread, became by the fact of his presence the name and the form, for the time, of everything in the place; but it didn't, for the difference, sit in his face, the face so squarely and easily turned to Densher at the earlier season. His presence on the first occasion, not as the result of a summons, but as a friendly whim of his own, had had quite another value; and though our young man could scarce regard that value as recoverable he yet reached out in imagination to a renewal of the old contact. He didn't propose, as he privately and forcibly phrased the matter, to be a hog; but there was something he after all did want for himself. It was something—this stuck to him—that Sir Luke would have had for him if it hadn't been impossible. These were his worst days, the two or three; those on which even the sense of the tension at the palace didn't much help him not to feel that his destiny made but light of him. He had never been, as he judged it, so down. In mean conditions, without books, without society, almost without money, he had nothing to do but to wait. His main support really was his original idea, which didn't leave him, of waiting for the deepest depth his predicament could sink him to. Fate would invent, if he but gave it time, some re-finement of the horrible. It was just inventing meanwhile this suppression of Sir Luke. When the third day came without a sign he knew what to think. He had given Mrs. Stringham during her call on him no such answer as would have armed her faith, and the ultimatum she had described as ready for him when he should be ready was therefore—if on no other ground than her want of this power to answer for him—not to be presented. The presentation, heaven knew, was not what he desired.

That was not, either, we hasten to declare—as Densher then soon enough saw—the idea with which Sir Luke finally stood before him again. For stand before him again he finally did; just when our friend had gloomily embraced the belief that the limit of his power to absent himself from London obligations would have been reached. Four or five days, exclusive of jour-neys, represented the largest supposable sacrifice—to a head not crowned—on the part of one of the highest medical lights in the world; so that really when the personage in question, following up a tinkle of the bell, solidly rose in the doorway, it was to impose on Densher a vision that for the instant cut like a knife. It spoke, the fact, and in a single dreadful word, of the magnitude—he shrank from calling it anything else—of Milly's case. The great man had not gone then, and an immense sur-render to her immense need was so expressed in it that some effect, some help, some hope, were flagrantly part of the ex-pression. It was for Densher, with his reaction from disap-pointment, as if he were conscious of ten things at once—the foremost being that just conceivably, since Sir Luke *was* still there, she had been saved. Close upon its heels, however, and quite as sharply, came the sense that the crisis—plainly even now to be prolonged for him—was to have none of that sound simplicity. Not only had his visitor not dropped in to gossip about Milly, he hadn't dropped in to mention her at all; he had dropped in fairly to show that during the brief remainder of his stay, the end of which was now in sight, as little as possible of that was to be looked for. The demonstration, such as it was, was in the key of their previous acquaintance, and it was their previous acquaintance that had made him come. He was not to stop longer than the Saturday next at hand, but there were things of interest he should like to see again meanwhile. It was for these things of interest, for Venice and the opportunity of Venice, for a prowl or two, as he called it, and a turn about, that he had looked his young man up—producing on the latter's part, as soon as the case had, with the lapse of a further twenty-four hours, so defined itself, the most incongruous, yet most beneficent revulsion. Nothing could in fact have been more monstrous on the surface—and Densher was well aware of it—than the relief he found during this short period in the tacit drop of all reference to the palace, in neither hearing news nor asking for it. That was what had come out for him, on his visitor's entrance, even in the very seconds of suspense that were connecting the fact also directly and intensely with Milly's state. He had come to say he had saved her—he had come, as from Mrs. Stringham, to say how she might *be* saved—he had come, in spite of Mrs. Stringham, to say she was lost: the distinct throbs of hope, of fear, simultaneous for all their distinctness, merged their identity in a bound of the heart just as immediate and which remained after they had passed. It simply did wonders for him—this was the truth—that Sir Luke was, as he would have said, quiet.

The result of it was the oddest consciousness as of a blest calm after a storm. He had been trying for weeks, as we know, to keep superlatively still, and trying it largely in solitude and silence; but he looked back on it now as on the heat of fever. The real, the right stillness was this particular form of society. They walked together and they talked, looked up pictures again and recovered impressions—Sir Luke knew just what he wanted; haunted a little the dealers in old wares; sat down at Florian's for rest and mild drinks; blessed above all the grand

weather, a bath of warm air, a pageant of autumn light. Once
or twice while they rested the great man closed his eyes—
keeping them so for some minutes while his companion, the
more easily watching his face for it, made private reflexions on
the subject of lost sleep. He had been up at night with her—he
in person, for hours; but this was all he showed of it and was
apparently to remain his nearest approach to an allusion. The
extraordinary thing was that Densher could take it in perfectly
as evidence, could turn cold at the image looking out of it; and
yet that he could at the same time not intermit a throb of his
response to accepted liberation. The liberation was an experience that held its own, and he continued to know why, in spite
of his deserts, in spite of his folly, in spite of everything, he had
so fondly hoped for it. He had hoped for it, had sat in his
room there waiting for it, because he had thus divined in it,
should it come, some power to let him off. He was *being* let
off; dealt with in the only way that didn't aggravate his responsibility. The beauty was also that this wasn't on system or on
any basis of intimate knowledge; it was just by being a man of
the world and by knowing life, by feeling the real, that Sir
Luke did him good. There had been in all the case too many
women. A man's sense of it, another man's, changed the air;
and he wondered what man, had he chosen, would have been
more to his purpose than this one. He was large and easy—
that was the benediction; he knew what mattered and what
didn't; he distinguished between the essence and the shell, the
just grounds and the unjust for fussing. One was thus—if one
were concerned with him or exposed to him at all—in his
hands for whatever he should do, and not much less affected
by his mercy than one might have been by his rigour. The grand
thing—it did come to that—was the way he carried off, as one
might fairly call it, the business of making odd things natural.
Nothing, if they hadn't taken it so, could have exceeded the
unexplained oddity, between them, of Densher's now complete detachment from the poor ladies at the palace; nothing
could have exceeded the no less marked anomaly of the great
man's own abstentions of speech. He made, as he had done
when they met at the station, nothing whatever of anything;
and the effect of it, Densher would have said, was a relation
with him quite resembling that of doctor and patient. One

took the cue from him as one might have taken a dose—except that the cue was pleasant in the taking.

That was why one could leave it to his tacit discretion, why for the three or four days Densher again and again did so leave it; merely wondering a little, at the most, on the eve of Saturday, the announced term of the episode. Waiting once more on this latter occasion, the Saturday morning, for Sir Luke's reappearance at the station, our friend had to recognise the drop of his own borrowed ease, the result, naturally enough, of the prospect of losing a support. The difficulty was that, on such lines as had served them, the support was Sir Luke's personal presence. Would he go without leaving some substitute for that?—and without breaking, either, his silence in respect to his errand? Densher was in still deeper ignorance than at the hour of his call, and what was truly prodigious at so supreme a moment was that—as had immediately to appear—no gleam of light on what he had been living with for a week found its way out of him. What he had been doing was proof of a huge interest as well as of a huge fee; yet when the Leporelli gondola again, and somewhat tardily, approached, his companion, watching from the water-steps, studied his fine closed face as much as ever in vain. It was like a lesson, from the highest authority, on the subject of the relevant, so that its blankness affected Densher of a sudden almost as a cruelty, feeling it quite awfully compatible, as he did, with Milly's having ceased to exist. And the suspense continued after they had passed together, as time was short, directly into the station, where Eugenio, in the field early, was mounting guard over the compartment he had secured. The strain, though probably lasting, at the carriage-door, but a couple of minutes, prolonged itself so for our poor gentleman's nerves that he involuntarily directed a long look at Eugenio, who met it, however, as only Eugenio could. Sir Luke's attention was given for the time to the right bestowal of his numerous effects, about which he was particular, and Densher fairly found himself, so far as silence could go, questioning the representative of the palace. It didn't humiliate him now; it didn't humiliate him even to feel that that personage exactly knew how little he satisfied him. Eugenio resembled to that extent Sir Luke—to the extent of the extraordinary things with which his facial habit was compatible.

By the time, however, that Densher had taken from it all its possessor intended Sir Luke was free and with a hand out for farewell. He offered the hand at first without speech; only on meeting his eyes could our young man see that they had never yet so completely looked at him. It was never, with Sir Luke, that they looked harder at one time than at another; but they looked longer, and this, even a shade of it, might mean on his part everything. It meant, Densher for ten seconds believed, that Milly Theale was dead; so that the word at last spoken made him start.

"I shall come back."

"Then she's better?"

"I shall come back within the month," Sir Luke repeated without heeding the question. He had dropped Densher's hand, but he held him otherwise still. "I bring you a message from Miss Theale," he said as if they hadn't spoken of her. "I'm commissioned to ask you from her to go and see her."

Densher's rebound from his supposition had a violence that his stare betrayed. "*She* asks me?"

Sir Luke had got into the carriage, the door of which the guard had closed; but he spoke again as he stood at the window, bending a little but not leaning out. "She told me she'd like it, and I promised that, as I expected to find you here, I'd let you know."

Densher, on the platform, took it from him, but what he took brought the blood into his face quite as what he had had to take from Mrs. Stringham. And he was also bewildered. "Then she can receive—?"

"She can receive you."

"And you're coming back—?"

"Oh because I must. She's not to move. She's to stay. I come to her."

"I see, I see," said Densher, who indeed did see—saw the sense of his friend's words and saw beyond it as well. What Mrs. Stringham had announced, and what he had yet expected not to have to face, *had* then come. Sir Luke had kept it for the last, but there it was, and the colourless compact form it was now taking—the tone of one man of the world to another, who, after what had happened, would understand—was but the characteristic manner of his appeal. Densher was to understand remarkably much; and the great thing certainly was to show that he did. "I'm particularly obliged. I'll go to-day." He brought that out, but in his pause, while they continued to look at each other, the train had slowly creaked into motion. There was time but for one more word, and the young man chose it, out of twenty, with intense concentration. "Then she's better?"

Sir Luke's face was wonderful. "Yes, she's better." And he kept it at the window while the train receded, holding him with it still. It was to be his nearest approach to the utter reference they had hitherto so successfully avoided. If it stood for everything, never had a face had to stand for more. So Densher, held after the train had gone, sharply reflected; so he reflected, asking himself into what abyss it pushed him, even while conscious of retreating under the maintained observation of Eugenio.

I

"THEN it has been—what do you say? a whole fortnight?—
without your making a sign?"

Kate put that to him distinctly, in the December dusk of
Lancaster Gate and on the matter of the time he had been
back; but he saw with it straightway that she was as admirably
true as ever to her instinct—which was a system as well—of
not admitting the possibility between them of small resent-
ments, of trifles to trip up their general trust. That by itself, the
renewed beauty of it, would at this fresh sight of her have
stirred him to his depths if something else, something no less
vivid but quite separate, hadn't stirred him still more. It was in
seeing her that he felt what their interruption had been, and
that they met across it even as persons whose adventures, on
either side, in time and space, of the nature of perils and exiles,
had had a peculiar strangeness. He wondered if he were as different for her as she herself had immediately appeared: which
was but his way indeed of taking in, with his thrill, that—even
going by the mere first look—she had never been so handsome. That fact bloomed for him, in the firelight and lamplight that glowed their welcome through the London fog, as
the flower of her difference; just as her difference itself—part
of which was her striking him as older in a degree for which no
mere couple of months could account—was the fruit of their
intimate relation. If she was different it was because they had
chosen together that she should be, and she might now, as a
proof of their wisdom, their success, of the reality of what had
happened—of what in fact, for the spirit of each, was still happening—been showing it to him for pride. His having returned and yet kept, for numbered days, so still, had been, he
was quite aware, the first point he should have to tackle; with
which consciousness indeed he had made a clean breast of it in
finally addressing Mrs. Lowder a note that had led to his present visit. He had written to Aunt Maud as the finer way; and it

would doubtless have been to be noted that he needed no effort not to write to Kate. Venice was three weeks behind
him—he had come up slowly; but it was still as if even in London he must conform to her law. That was exactly how he was
able, with his faith in her steadiness, to appeal to her feeling for
the situation and explain his stretched delicacy. He had come
to tell her everything, so far as occasion would serve them; and
if nothing was more distinct than that his slow journey, his
waits, his delay to reopen communication had kept pace with
this resolve, so the inconsequence was doubtless at bottom but
one of the elements of intensity. He was gathering everything
up, everything he should tell her. That took time, and the
proof was that, as he felt on the spot, he couldn't have brought
it all with him before this afternoon. He *had* brought it, to the
last syllable, and, out of the quantity it wouldn't be hard—as
he in fact found—to produce, for Kate's understanding, his
first reason.

"A fortnight, yes—it was a fortnight Friday; but I've only
been keeping in, you see, with our wonderful system." He
was so easily justified as that this of itself plainly enough prevented her saying she didn't see. Their wonderful system was
accordingly still vivid for her; and such a gage of its equal
vividness for himself was precisely what she must have asked.
He hadn't even to dot his i's beyond the remark that on the
very face of it, she would remember, their wonderful system
attached no premium to rapidities of transition. "I couldn't
quite—don't you know?—take my rebound with a rush; and I
suppose I've been instinctively hanging off to minimise, for
you as well as for myself, the appearances of rushing. There's a
sort of fitness. But I knew you'd understand." It was presently
as if she really understood so well that she almost appealed from
his insistence—yet looking at him too, he was not unconscious, as if this mastery of fitnesses was a strong sign for her of
what she had done to him. He might have struck her as expert
for contingencies in the very degree of her having in Venice
struck *him* as expert. He smiled over his plea for a renewal
with stages and steps, a thing shaded, as they might say, and
graduated; though—finely as she must respond—she met the
smile but as she had met his entrance five minutes before. Her
soft gravity at that moment—which was yet not solemnity, but

the look of a consciousness charged with life to the brim and wishing not to overflow—had not qualified her welcome; what had done this being much more the presence in the room, for a couple of minutes, of the footman who had introduced him and who had been interrupted in preparing the tea-table.

Mrs. Lowder's reply to Densher's note had been to appoint the tea-hour, five o'clock on Sunday, for his seeing them. Kate had thereafter wired him, without a signature, "Come on Sunday *before* tea—about a quarter of an hour, which will help us"; and he had arrived therefore scrupulously at twenty minutes to five. Kate was alone in the room and hadn't delayed to tell him that Aunt Maud, as she had happily gathered, was to be, for the interval—not long but precious—engaged with an old servant, retired and pensioned, who had been paying her a visit and who was within the hour to depart again for the suburbs. They were to have the scrap of time, after the withdrawal of the footman, to themselves, and there was a moment when, in spite of their wonderful system, in spite of the proscription of rushes and the propriety of shades, it proclaimed itself indeed precious. And all without prejudice—that was what kept it noble—to Kate's high sobriety and her beautiful self-command. If he had his discretion she had her perfect manner, which was *her* decorum. Mrs. Stringham, he had, to finish with the question of his delay, furthermore observed, Mrs. Stringham would have written to Mrs. Lowder of his having quitted the place; so that it wasn't as if he were hoping to cheat them. They'd know he was no longer there.

"Yes, we've known it."

"And you continue to hear?"

"From Mrs. Stringham? Certainly. By which I mean Aunt Maud does."

"Then you've recent news?"

Her face showed a wonder. "Up to within a day or two I believe. But haven't *you?*"

"No—I've heard nothing." And it was now that he felt how much he had to tell her. "I don't get letters. But I've been sure Mrs. Lowder does." With which he added: "Then of course you know." He waited as if she would show what she knew; but she only showed in silence the dawn of a surprise that she couldn't control. There was nothing but for him to ask what he wanted. "Is Miss Theale alive?"

Kate's look at this was large. "Don't you *know*?"

"How should I, my dear—in the absence of everything?" And he himself stared as for light. "She's dead?" Then as with her eyes on him she slowly shook her head he uttered a strange "Not yet?"

It came out in Kate's face that there were several questions on her lips, but the one she presently put was: "Is it very terrible?"

"The manner of her so consciously and helplessly dying?" He had to think a moment. "Well, yes—since you ask me: very terrible to *me*—so far as, before I came away, I had any sight of it. But I don't think," he went on, "that—though I'll try—I *can* quite tell you what it was, what it is, for me. That's why I probably just sounded to you," he explained, "as if I hoped it might be over."

She gave him her quietest attention, but he by this time saw that, so far as telling her all was concerned, she would be divided between the wish and the reluctance to hear it; between the curiosity that, not unnaturally, would consume her and the opposing scruple of a respect for misfortune. The more she studied him too—and he had never so felt her closely attached to his face—the more the choice of an attitude would become impossible to her. There would simply be a feeling uppermost, and the feeling wouldn't be eagerness. This perception grew in him fast, and he even, with his imagination, had for a moment the quick forecast of her possibly breaking out at him, should he go too far, with a wonderful: "What horrors are you telling me?" It would have the sound—wouldn't it be open to him fairly to bring that out himself?—of a repudiation, for pity and almost for shame, of everything that in Venice had passed between them. Not that she would confess to any return upon herself; not that she would let compunction or horror give her away; but it was in the air for him—yes—that she wouldn't want details, that she positively wouldn't take them, and that, if he would generously understand it from her, she would prefer to keep him down. Nothing, however, was more definite for him than that at the same time he must remain down but so far as it suited him. Something rose strong within him against his not being free with her. She had been free enough about it all, three months before, with *him*. That was what she was at present only in the sense of treating him handsomely. "I can believe," she said with perfect consideration, "how dreadful for you much of it must have been."

He didn't however take this up; there were things about which he wished first to be clear. "There's no other possibility, by what you now know? I mean for her life." And he had just to insist—she would say as little as she could. "She *is* dying?"

"She's dying."

It was strange to him, in the matter of Milly, that Lancaster Gate could make him any surer; yet what in the world, in the matter of Milly, wasn't strange? Nothing was so much so as his own behaviour—his present as well as his past. He could but do as he must. "Has Sir Luke Strett," he asked, "gone back to her?"

"I believe he's there now."

"Then," said Densher, "it's the end."

She took it in silence for whatever he deemed it to be; but she spoke otherwise after a minute. "You won't know, unless you've perhaps seen him yourself, that Aunt Maud has been to him."

"Oh!" Densher exclaimed, with nothing to add to it.

"For real news," Kate herself after an instant added.

"She hasn't thought Mrs. Stringham's real?"

"It's perhaps only I who haven't. It was on Aunt Maud's trying again three days ago to see him that she heard at his house of his having gone. He had started I believe some days before."

"And won't then by this time be back?"

Kate shook her head. "She sent yesterday to know."

"He won't leave her then"—Densher had turned it over—"while she lives. He'll stay to the end. He's magnificent."

"I think *she* is," said Kate.

It had made them again look at each other long; and what it drew from him rather oddly was: "Oh you don't know!"

"Well, she's after all my friend."

It was somehow, with her handsome demur, the answer he had least expected of her; and it fanned with its breath, for a brief instant, his old sense of her variety. "I see. You would have been sure of it. You *were* sure of it."

"Of course I was sure of it."

And a pause again, with this, fell upon them; which Densher, however, presently broke. "If you don't think Mrs. Stringham's news 'real' what do you think of Lord Mark's?"

She didn't think anything. "Lord Mark's?"

"You haven't seen him?"

"Not since he saw her."

"You've known then of his seeing her?"

"Certainly. From Mrs. Stringham."

"And have you known," Densher went on, "the rest?"

Kate wondered. "What rest?"

"Why everything. It was his visit that she couldn't stand—it was what then took place that simply killed her."

"Oh!" Kate seriously breathed. But she had turned pale, and he saw that, whatever her degree of ignorance of these connexions, it wasn't put on. "Mrs. Stringham hasn't said *that*."

He observed none the less that she didn't ask what had then taken place; and he went on with his contribution to her knowledge. "The way it affected her was that it made her give up. She has given up beyond all power to care again, and that's why she's dying."

"Oh!" Kate once more slowly sighed, but with a vagueness that made him pursue.

"One can see now that she was living by will—which was very much what you originally told me of her."

"I remember. That was it."

"Well then her will, at a given moment, broke down, and the collapse was determined by that fellow's dastardly stroke. He told her, the scoundrel, that you and I are secretly engaged."

Kate gave a quick glare. "But he doesn't know it!"

"That doesn't matter. *She* did by the time he had left her. Besides," Densher added, "he does know it. When," he continued, "did you last see him?"

But she was lost now in the picture before her. "*That* was what made her worse?"

He watched her take it in—it so added to her sombre

beauty. Then he spoke as Mrs. Stringham had spoken. "She turned her face to the wall."

"Poor Milly!" said Kate.

Slight as it was, her beauty somehow gave it style; so that he continued consistently: "She learned it, you see, too soon—since of course one's idea had been that she might never even learn it at all. And she *had* felt sure—through everything we had done—of there not being between us, so far at least as you were concerned, anything she need regard as a warning."

She took another moment for thought. "It wasn't through anything *you* did—whatever that may have been—that she gained her certainty. It was by the conviction she got from me."

"Oh it's very handsome," Densher said, "for you to take your share!"

"Do you suppose," Kate asked, "that I think of denying it?"

Her look and her tone made him for the instant regret his comment, which indeed had been the first that rose to his lips as an effect absolutely of what they would have called between them her straightness. Her straightness, visibly, was all his own loyalty could ask. Still, that was comparatively beside the mark. "Of course I don't suppose anything but that we're together in our recognitions, our responsibilities—whatever we choose to call them. It isn't a question for us of apportioning shares or distinguishing invidiously among such impressions as it was our idea to give."

"It wasn't *your* idea to give impressions," said Kate.

He met this with a smile that he himself felt, in its strained character, as queer. "Don't go into that!"

It was perhaps not as going into it that she had another idea—an idea born, she showed, of the vision he had just evoked. "Wouldn't it have been possible then to deny the truth of the information? I mean of Lord Mark's."

Densher wondered. "Possible for whom?"

"Why for you."

"To tell her he lied?"

"To tell her he's mistaken."

Densher stared—he was stupefied; the "possible" thus glanced at by Kate being exactly the alternative he had had to face in Venice and to put utterly away from him. Nothing was stranger than such a difference in their view of it. "And to lie myself, you mean, to do it? We *are*, my dear child," he said, "I suppose, still engaged."

"Of course we're still engaged. But to save her life—!"

He took in for a little the way she talked of it. Of course, it was to be remembered, she had always simplified, and it brought back his sense of the degree in which, to her energy as compared with his own, many things were easy; the very sense that so often before had moved him to admiration. "Well, if you must know—and I want you to be clear about it—I didn't even seriously think of a denial to her face. The question of it—*as* possibly saving her—was put to me definitely enough; but to turn it over was only to dismiss it. Besides," he added, "it wouldn't have done any good."

"You mean she would have had no faith in your correction?" She had spoken with a promptitude that affected him of a sudden as almost glib; but he himself paused with the overweight of all he meant, and she meanwhile went on. "Did you try?"

"I hadn't even a chance."

Kate maintained her wonderful manner, the manner of at once having it all before her and yet keeping it all at its distance. "She wouldn't see you?"

"Not after your friend had been with her."

She hesitated. "Couldn't you write?"

It made him also think, but with a difference. "She had turned her face to the wall."

This again for a moment hushed her, and they were both too grave now for parenthetic pity. But her interest came out for at least the minimum of light. "She refused even to let you speak to her?"

"My dear girl," Densher returned, "she was miserably, prohibitively ill."

"Well, that was what she had been before."

"And it didn't prevent? No," Densher admitted, "it didn't; and I don't pretend that she's not magnificent."

"She's prodigious," said Kate Croy.

He looked at her a moment. "So are you, my dear. But that's how it is," he wound up; "and there we are."

His idea had been in advance that she would perhaps sound him much more deeply, asking him above all two or three specific things. He had fairly fancied her even wanting to know and trying to find out how far, as the odious phrase was, he and Milly had gone, and how near, by the same token, they had come. He had asked himself if he were prepared to hear her do that, and had had to take for answer that he was prepared of course for everything. Wasn't he prepared for her ascertaining if her two or three prophecies had found time to be made true? He had fairly believed himself ready to say whether or no the overture on Milly's part promised according to the boldest of them had taken place. But what was in fact blessedly coming to him was that so far as such things were concerned his readiness wouldn't be taxed. Kate's pressure on the question of what had taken place remained so admirably general that even her present enquiry kept itself free of sharpness. "So then that after Lord Mark's interference you never again met?"

It was what he had been all the while coming to. "No; we met once—so far as it could be called a meeting. I had stayed —I didn't come away."

"That," said Kate, "was no more than decent."

"Precisely"—he felt himself wonderful; "and I wanted to be no less. She sent for me, I went to her, and that night I left Venice."

His companion waited. "Wouldn't *that* then have been your chance?"

"To refute Lord Mark's story? No, not even if before her there I had wanted to. What did it signify either? She was dying."

"Well," Kate in a manner persisted, "why not just *because* she was dying?" She had however all her discretion. "But of course I know that seeing her you could judge."

"Of course seeing her I could judge. And I did see her! If I had denied you moreover," Densher said with his eyes on her, "I'd have stuck to it."

She took for a moment the intention of his face. "You mean that to convince her you'd have insisted or somehow proved—?"

"I mean that to convince *you* I'd have insisted or somehow proved—!"

Kate looked for her moment at a loss. "To convince 'me'?"

"I wouldn't have made my denial, in such conditions, only to take it back afterwards."

With this quickly light came for her, and with it also her colour flamed. "Oh you'd have broken with me to make your denial a truth? You'd have 'chucked' me"—she embraced it perfectly—"to save your conscience?"

"I couldn't have done anything else," said Merton Densher. "So you see how right I was not to commit myself, and how little I could dream of it. If it ever again appears to you that I *might* have done so, remember what I say."

Kate again considered, but not with the effect at once to which he pointed. "You've fallen in love with her."

"Well then say so—with a dying woman. Why need you mind and what does it matter?"

It came from him, the question, straight out of the intensity of relation and the face-to-face necessity into which, from the first, from his entering the room, they had found themselves thrown; but it gave them their most extraordinary moment. "Wait till she *is* dead! Mrs. Stringham," Kate added, "is to telegraph." After which, in a tone still different, "For what then," she asked, "did Milly send for you?"

"It was what I tried to make out before I went. I must tell you moreover that I had no doubt of its really being to give me, as you say, a chance. She believed, I suppose, that I *might* deny; and what, to my own mind, was before me in going to her was the certainty that she'd put me to my test. She wanted from my own lips—so I saw it—the truth. But I was with her for twenty minutes, and she never asked me for it."

"She never wanted the truth"—Kate had a high headshake. "She wanted *you*. She would have taken from you what you could give her and been glad of it, even if she had known it false. You might have lied to her from pity, and she have seen you and felt you lie, and yet—since it was all for tenderness—she would have thanked you and blessed you and clung to you but the more. For that was your strength, my dear man—that she loves you with passion."

"Oh my 'strength'!" Densher coldly murmured.

"Otherwise, since she had sent for you, what was it to ask of you?" And then—quite without irony—as he waited a moment to say: "Was it just once more to look at you?"

"She had nothing to ask of me—nothing, that is, but not to stay any longer. She did to that extent want to see me. She had

supposed at first—after he had been with her—that I had seen
the propriety of taking myself off. Then since I hadn't—seeing
my propriety as I did in another way—she found, days later,
that I was still there. This," said Densher, "affected her."

"Of course it affected her."

Again she struck him, for all her dignity, as glib. "If it was
somehow for *her* I was still staying, she wished that to end, she
wished me to know how little there was need of it. And as a
manner of farewell she wished herself to tell me so."

"And she did tell you so?"

"Face-to-face, yes. Personally, as she desired."

"And as *you* of course did."

"No, Kate," he returned with all their mutual consideration;
"not as I did. I hadn't desired it in the least."

"You only went to oblige her?"

"To oblige her. And of course also to oblige you."

"Oh for myself certainly I'm glad."

" 'Glad'?"—he echoed vaguely the way it rang out.

"I mean you did quite the right thing. You did it especially
in having stayed. But that was all?" Kate went on. "That you
mustn't wait?"

"That was really all—and in perfect kindness."

"Ah kindness naturally: from the moment she asked of you
such a—well, such an effort. That you mustn't wait—that was
the point," Kate added—"to see her die."

"That was the point, my dear," Densher said.

"And it took twenty minutes to make it?"

He thought a little. "I didn't time it to a second. I paid her
the visit—just like another."

"Like another person?"

"Like another visit."

"Oh!" said Kate. Which had apparently the effect of slightly
arresting his speech—an arrest she took advantage of to continue; making with it indeed her nearest approach to an enquiry
of the kind against which he had braced himself. "Did she receive you—in her condition—in her room?"

"Not she," said Merton Densher. "She received me just as
usual: in that glorious great *salone*, in the dress she always wears,
from her inveterate corner of her sofa." And his face for the

moment conveyed the scene, just as hers equally embraced it. "Do you remember what you originally said to me of her?"

"Ah I've said so many things."

"That she wouldn't smell of drugs, that she wouldn't taste of medicine. Well, she didn't."

"So that it was really almost happy?"

It took him a long time to answer, occupied as he partly was in feeling how nobody but Kate could have invested such a question with the tone that was perfectly right. She meanwhile, however, patiently waited. "I don't think I can attempt to say now what it was. Some day—perhaps. For it would be worth it for us."

"Some day—certainly." She seemed to record the promise. Yet she spoke again abruptly. "She'll recover."

"Well," said Densher, "you'll see."

She had the air an instant of trying to. "Did she show anything of her feeling? I mean," Kate explained, "of her feeling of having been misled."

She didn't press hard, surely; but he had just mentioned that he would have rather to glide. "She showed nothing but her beauty and her strength."

"Then," his companion asked, "what's the use of her strength?"

He seemed to look about for a use he could name; but he had soon given it up. "She must die, my dear, in her own extraordinary way."

"Naturally. But I don't see then what proof you have that she was ever alienated."

"I have the proof that she refused for days and days to see me."

"But she was ill."

"That hadn't prevented her—as you yourself a moment ago said—during the previous time. If it had been only illness it would have made no difference with her."

"She would still have received you?"

"She would still have received me."

"Oh well," said Kate, "if you know—!"

"Of course I know. I know moreover as well from Mrs. Stringham."

"And what does Mrs. Stringham know?"

"Everything."

She looked at him longer. "Everything?"

"Everything."

"Because you've told her?"

"Because she has seen for herself. I've told her nothing. She's a person who does see."

Kate thought. "That's by her liking you too. She as well is prodigious. You see what interest in a man does. It does it all round. So you needn't be afraid."

"I'm not afraid," said Densher.

Kate moved from her place then, looking at the clock, which marked five. She gave her attention to the tea-table, where Aunt Maud's huge silver kettle, which had been exposed to its lamp and which she had not soon enough noticed, was hissing too hard. "Well, it's all most wonderful!" she exclaimed as she rather too profusely—a sign her friend noticed—ladled tea into the pot. He watched her a moment at this occupation, coming nearer the table while she put in the steaming water. "You'll have some?"

He hesitated. "Hadn't we better wait—?"

"For Aunt Maud?" She saw what he meant—the deprecation, by their old law, of betrayals of the intimate note. "Oh you needn't mind now. We've done it!"

"Humbugged her?"

"Squared her. You've pleased her."

Densher mechanically accepted his tea. He was thinking of something else, and his thought in a moment came out. "What a brute then I must be!"

"A brute—?"

"To have pleased so many people."

"Ah," said Kate with a gleam of gaiety, "you've done it to please *me*." But she was already, with her gleam, reverting a little. "What I don't understand is—won't you have any sugar?"

"Yes, please."

"What I don't understand," she went on when she had helped him, "is what it was that had occurred to bring her round again. If she gave you up for days and days, what brought her back to you?"

She asked the question with her own cup in her hand, but it

found him ready enough in spite of his sense of the ironic odd-ity of their going into it over the tea-table. "It was Sir Luke Strett who brought her back. His visit, his presence there did it."

"He brought her back then to life."

"Well, to what I saw."

"And by interceding for you?"

"I don't think he interceded. I don't indeed know what he did."

Kate wondered. "Didn't he tell you?"

"I didn't ask him. I met him again, but we practically didn't speak of her."

Kate stared. "Then how do you know?"

"I see. I feel. I was with him again as I had been before—"

"Oh and you pleased him too? That was it?"

"He understood," said Densher.

"But understood what?"

He waited a moment. "That I had meant awfully well."

"Ah, and made *her* understand? I see," she went on as he said nothing. "But how did he convince her?"

Densher put down his cup and turned away. "You must ask Sir Luke."

He stood looking at the fire and there was a time without sound. "The great thing," Kate then resumed, "is that she's satisfied. Which," she continued, looking across at him, "is what I've worked for."

"Satisfied to die in the flower of her youth?"

"Well, at peace with you."

"Oh 'peace'!" he murmured with his eyes on the fire.

"The peace of having loved."

He raised his eyes to her. "Is *that* peace?"

"Of having *been* loved," she went on. "That is. Of having," she wound up, "realised her passion. She wanted nothing more. She has had *all* she wanted."

Lucid and always grave, she gave this out with a beautiful authority that he could for the time meet with no words. He could only again look at her, though with the sense in so doing that he made her more than he intended take his silence for assent. Quite indeed as if she did so take it she quitted the table and came to the fire. "You may think it hideous that I should now, that I should *yet*"—she made a point of the word —"pretend to draw conclusions. But we've not failed."

"Oh!" he only again murmured.

She was once more close to him, close as she had been the day she came to him in Venice, the quickly returning memory of which intensified and enriched the fact. He could practically deny in such conditions nothing that she said, and what she said was, with it, visibly, a fruit of that knowledge. "We've succeeded." She spoke with her eyes deep in his own. "She won't have loved you for nothing." It made him wince, but she insisted. "And you won't have loved *me*."

II

He was to remain for several days under the deep impression of this inclusive passage, so luckily prolonged from moment to moment, but interrupted at its climax, as may be said, by the entrance of Aunt Maud, who found them standing together near the fire. The bearings of the colloquy, however, sharp as they were, were less sharp to his intelligence, strangely enough, than those of a talk with Mrs. Lowder alone for which she soon gave him—or for which perhaps rather Kate gave him—full occasion. What had happened on her at last joining them was to conduce, he could immediately see, to her desiring to have him to herself. Kate and he, no doubt, at the opening of the door, had fallen apart with a certain suddenness, so that she had turned her hard fine eyes from one to the other; but the effect of this lost itself, to his mind, the next minute, in the effect of his companion's rare alertness. She instantly spoke to her aunt of what had first been uppermost for herself, inviting her thereby intimately to join them, and doing it the more happily also, no doubt, because the fact she resentfully named gave her ample support. "Had you quite understood, my dear, that it's full three weeks—?" And she effaced herself as if to leave Mrs. Lowder to deal from her own point of view with this extravagance. Densher of course straightway noted that his cue for the protection of Kate was to make, no less, all of it he could; and their tracks, as he might have said, were fairly covered by the time their hostess had taken afresh, on his renewed admission, the measure of his scant eagerness. Kate had moved away as if no great showing were needed for her personal situation to be seen as delicate. She had been entertaining their visitor on her aunt's behalf—a visitor she had been at one time suspected of favouring too much and who had now come back to them as the stricken suitor of another person. It wasn't that the fate of the other person, her exquisite friend, didn't, in its tragic turn, also concern herself: it was only that her acceptance of Mr. Densher as a source of information could scarcely help having an awkwardness. She invented the awkwardness under Densher's eyes, and he marvelled on his side at the instant creation. It served her as the fine cloud that hangs about a goddess in an epic, and the young man was but vaguely to know at what point of the rest of his visit she had, for consideration, melted into it and out of sight.

He was taken up promptly with another matter—the truth of the remarkable difference, neither more nor less, that the events of Venice had introduced into his relation with Aunt Maud and that these weeks of their separation had caused quite richly to ripen for him. She had not sat down to her tea-table before he felt himself on terms with her that were absolutely new, nor could she press on him a second cup without her seeming herself, and quite wittingly, so to define and establish them. She regretted, but she quite understood, that what was taking place had obliged him to hang off; they had—after hearing of him from poor Susan as gone—been hoping for an early sight of him; they would have been interested, naturally, in his arriving straight from the scene. Yet she needed no reminder that the scene precisely—by which she meant the tragedy that had so detained and absorbed him, the memory, the shadow, the sorrow of it—was what marked him for unsociability. She thus presented him to himself, as it were, in the guise in which she had now adopted him, and it was the element of truth in the character that he found himself, for his own part, adopting. She treated him as blighted and ravaged, as frustrate and already bereft; and for him to feel that this opened for him a new chapter of frankness with her he scarce had also to perceive how it smoothed his approaches to Kate. It made the latter accessible as she hadn't yet begun to be; it set up for him at Lancaster Gate an association positively hostile to any other legend. It was quickly vivid to him that, were he minded, he could "work" this association: he had but to use the house freely for his prescribed attitude and he need hardly ever be out of it. Stranger than anything moreover was to be the way that by the end of a week he stood convicted to his own sense of a surrender to Mrs. Lowder's view. He had somehow met it at a point that had brought him on—brought him on a distance that he couldn't again retrace. He had private hours of wondering what had become of his sincerity; he had others of simply reflecting that he had it all in use. His only want of candour was Aunt Maud's wealth of sentiment.

She was hugely sentimental, and the worst he did was to take it from her. He wasn't so himself—everything was too real; but it was none the less not false that he *had* been through a mill.

It was in particular not false for instance that when she had said to him, on the Sunday, almost cosily, from her sofa behind the tea, "I want you not to doubt, you poor dear, that I'm *with* you to the end!" his meeting her halfway had been the only course open to him. She was with him to the end—or she might be—in a way Kate wasn't; and even if it literally made her society meanwhile more soothing he must just brush away the question of why it shouldn't. Was he professing to her in any degree the possession of an aftersense that wasn't real? How in the world *could* he, when his aftersense, day by day, was his greatest reality? Such only was at bottom what there was between them, and two or three times over it made the hour pass. These were occasions—two and a scrap—on which he had come and gone without mention of Kate. Now that almost as never yet he had licence to ask for her, the queer turn of their affair made it a false note. It was another queer turn that when he talked with Aunt Maud about Milly nothing else seemed to come up. He called upon her almost avowedly for that purpose, and it was the queerest turn of all that the state of his nerves should require it. He liked her better; he was really behaving, he had occasion to say to himself, as if he liked her best. The thing was absolutely that she met *him* halfway. Nothing could have been broader than her vision, than her loquacity, than her sympathy. It appeared to gratify, to satisfy her to see him as he was; that too had its effect. It was all of course the last thing that could have seemed on the cards, a change by which he was completely *free* with this lady; and it wouldn't indeed have come about if—for another monstrosity—he hadn't ceased to be free with Kate. Thus it was that on the third time in especial of being alone with her he found himself uttering to the elder woman what had been impossible of utterance to the younger. Mrs. Lowder gave him in fact, on the ground of what he must keep from her, but one uneasy moment. That was when, on the first Sunday, after Kate had suppressed herself, she referred to her regret that he mightn't have stayed to the end. He found his reason difficult to give her, but she came after all to his help.

"You simply couldn't stand it?"

"I simply couldn't stand it. Besides you see—!" But he paused.

"Besides what?" He had been going to say more—then he saw dangers; luckily however she had again assisted him. "Besides—oh I know!—men haven't, in many relations, the courage of women."

"They haven't the courage of women."

"Kate or I would have stayed," she declared—"if we hadn't come away for the special reason that you so frankly appreciated."

Densher had said nothing about his appreciation: hadn't his behaviour since the hour itself sufficiently shown it? But he presently said—he couldn't help going so far: "I don't doubt, certainly, that Miss Croy would have stayed." And he saw again into the bargain what a marvel was Susan Shepherd. She did nothing but protect him—she had done nothing but keep it up. In copious communication with the friend of her youth she had yet, it was plain, favoured this lady with nothing that compromised him. Milly's act of renouncement she had described but as a change for the worse; she had mentioned Lord Mark's descent, as even without her it might be known, so that she mustn't appear to conceal it; but she had suppressed explanations and connexions, and indeed, for all he knew, blessed Puritan soul, had invented commendable fictions. Thus it was absolutely that he *was* at his ease. Thus it was that, shaking for ever, in the unrest that didn't drop, his crossed leg, he leaned back in deep yellow satin chairs and took such comfort as came. She asked, it was true, Aunt Maud, questions that Kate hadn't; but this was just the difference, that from her he positively liked them. He had taken with himself on leaving Venice the resolution to regard Milly as already dead to him—that being for his spirit the only thinkable way to pass the time of waiting. He had left her because it was what suited her, and it wasn't for him to go, as they said in America, behind this; which imposed on him but the sharper need to arrange himself with his interval. Suspense was the ugliest ache to him, and he would have nothing to do with it; the last thing he wished was to be unconscious of her—what he wished to ignore was her own consciousness, tortured, for all he knew, crucified by its pain. Knowingly to hang about in London while the pain went on—what would that do but make his days impossible? His scheme was accordingly to convince himself—and by some art about which he was vague—that the sense of waiting had passed. "What in fact," he restlessly reflected, "have I any further to do with it? Let me assume the thing actually over—as it at any moment may be—and I become good again for something at least to somebody. I'm good, as it is, for nothing to anybody, least of all to *her*." He consequently tried, so far as shutting his eyes and stalking grimly about was a trial; but his plan was carried out, it may well be guessed, neither with marked success nor with marked consistency. The days, whether lapsing or lingering, were a stiff reality; the suppression of anxiety was a thin idea; the taste of life itself was the taste of suspense. That he *was* waiting was in short at the bottom of everything; and it required no great sifting presently to feel that if he took so much more, as he called it, to Mrs. Lowder this was just for that reason.

She helped him to hold out, all the while that she was subtle enough—and he could see her divine it as what he wanted—not to insist on the actuality of their tension. His nearest approach to success was thus in being good for something to Aunt Maud, in default of any one better; her company eased his nerves even while they pretended together that they had seen their tragedy out. They spoke of the dying girl in the past tense; they said no worse of her than that she had *been* stupendous. On the other hand, however—and this was what wasn't for Densher pure peace—they insisted enough that stupendous was the word. It was the thing, this recognition, that kept him most quiet; he came to it with her repeatedly; talking about it against time and, in particular, we have noted, speaking of his supreme personal impression as he hadn't spoken to Kate. It was almost as if she herself enjoyed the perfection of the pathos; she sat there before the scene, as he couldn't help giving it out to her, very much as a stout citizen's wife might have sat, during a play that made people cry, in the pit or the family-circle. What most deeply stirred her was the way the poor girl must have wanted to live.

"Ah yes indeed—she did, she did: why in pity shouldn't she, with everything to fill her world? The mere *money* of her, the

darling, if it isn't too disgusting at such a time to mention
that—!"

Aunt Maud mentioned it—and Densher quite understood
—but as fairly giving poetry to the life Milly clung to: a view of
the "might have been" before which the good lady was hushed
anew to tears. She had had her own vision of these possibilities, and her own social use for them, and since Milly's spirit
had been after all so at one with her about them, what was the
cruelty of the event but a cruelty, of a sort, to herself? That
came out when he named, as *the* horrible thing to know, the
fact of their young friend's unapproachable terror of the end,
keep it down though she would; coming out therefore often,
since in so naming it he found the strangest of reliefs. He allowed it all its vividness, as if on the principle of his not at least
spiritually shirking. Milly had held with passion to her dream
of a future, and she was separated from it, not shrieking indeed, but grimly, awfully silent, as one might imagine some
noble young victim of the scaffold, in the French Revolution,
separated at the prison-door from some object clutched for resistance. Densher, in a cold moment, so pictured the case for
Mrs. Lowder, but no moment cold enough had yet come to
make him so picture it to Kate. And it was the front so presented that had been, in Milly, heroic; presented with the
highest heroism, Aunt Maud by this time knew, on the occasion of his taking leave of her. He had let her know, absolutely
for the girl's glory, how he had been received on that occasion:
with a positive effect—since she was indeed so perfectly the
princess that Mrs. Stringham always called her—of princely
state.

Before the fire in the great room that was all arabesques and
cherubs, all gaiety and gilt, and that was warm at that hour too
with a wealth of autumn sun, the state in question had been
maintained and the situation—well, Densher said for the convenience of exquisite London gossip, sublime. The gossip—for
it came to as much at Lancaster Gate—wasn't the less exquisite
for his use of the silver veil, nor on the other hand was the veil,
so touched, too much drawn aside. He himself for that matter
took in the scene again at moments as from the page of a book.
He saw a young man far off and in a relation inconceivable, saw
him hushed, passive, staying his breath, but half understanding,

yet dimly conscious of something immense and holding himself painfully together not to lose it. The young man at these
moments so seen was too distant and too strange for the right
identity; and yet, outside, afterwards, it was his own face Densher had known. He had known then at the same time what
the young man had been conscious of, and he was to measure
after that, day by day, how little he had lost. At present there
with Mrs. Lowder he knew he had gathered all—that passed
between them mutely as in the intervals of their associated
gaze they exchanged looks of intelligence. This was as far as association could go, but it was far enough when she knew the
essence. The essence was that something had happened to him
too beautiful and too sacred to describe. He had been, to his
recovered sense, forgiven, dedicated, blessed; but this he
couldn't coherently express. It would have required an explanation—fatal to Mrs. Lowder's faith in him—of the nature of
Milly's wrong. So, as to the wonderful scene, they just stood at
the door. They had the sense of the presence within—they felt
the charged stillness; after which, their association deepened
by it, they turned together away.

That itself indeed, for our restless friend, became by the end
of a week the very principle of reaction: so that he woke up
one morning with such a sense of having played a part as he
needed self-respect to gainsay. He hadn't in the least stated at
Lancaster Gate that, as a haunted man—a man haunted with
a memory—he was harmless; but the degree to which Mrs.
Lowder accepted, admired and explained his new aspect laid
upon him practically the weight of a declaration. What he
hadn't in the least stated her own manner was perpetually
stating; it was as haunted and harmless that she was constantly
putting him down. There offered itself however to his purpose
such an element as plain honesty, and he had embraced, by the
time he dressed, his proper corrective. They were on the edge
of Christmas, but Christmas this year was, as in the London of
so many other years, disconcertingly mild; the still air was soft,
the thick light was grey, the great town looked empty, and in
the Park, where the grass was green, where the sheep browsed,
where the birds multitudinously twittered, the straight walks
lent themselves to slowness and the dim vistas to privacy. He
held it fast this morning till he had got out, his sacrifice to

honour, and then went with it to the nearest post-office and fixed it fast in a telegram; thinking of it moreover as a sacrifice only because he had, for reasons, felt it as an effort. Its character of effort it would owe to Kate's expected resistance, not less probable than on the occasion of past appeals; which was precisely why he—perhaps innocently—made his telegram persuasive. It had, as a recall of tender hours, to be, for the young woman at the counter, a trifle cryptic; but there was a good deal of it in one way and another, representing as it did a rich impulse and costing him a couple of shillings. There was also a moment later on, that day, when, in the Park, as he measured watchfully one of their old alleys, he might have been supposed by a cynical critic to be reckoning his chance of getting his money back. He was waiting—but he had waited of old; Lancaster Gate as a danger was practically at hand—but she had risked that danger before. Besides it was smaller now, with the queer turn of their affair; in spite of which indeed he was graver as he lingered and looked out.

Kate came at last by the way he had thought least likely, came as if she had started from the Marble Arch; but her advent was response—that was the great matter; response marked in her face and agreeable to him, even after Aunt Maud's responses, as nothing had been since his return to London. She had not, it was true, answered his wire, and he had begun to fear, as she was late, that with the instinct of what he might be again intending to press upon her she had decided—though not with ease—to deprive him of his chance. He would have of course, she knew, other chances, but she perhaps saw the present as offering her special danger. This, in fact, Densher could himself feel, was exactly why he had so prepared it, and he had rejoiced, even while he waited, in all that the conditions had to say to him of their simpler and better time. The shortest day of the year though it might be, it was, in the same place, by a whim of the weather, almost as much to their purpose as the days of sunny afternoons when they had taken their first trysts. This and that tree, within sight, on the grass, stretched bare boughs over the couple of chairs in which they had sat of old and in which—for they really could sit down again—they might recover the clearness of their prime. It was to all intents however this very reference that showed itself in Kate's face as, with her swift motion, she came toward him. It helped him, her swift motion, when it finally brought her nearer; helped him, for that matter, at first, if only by showing him afresh how terribly well she looked. It had been all along, he certainly remembered, a phenomenon of no rarity that he had felt her, at particular moments, handsomer than ever before; one of these for instance being still present to him as her entrance, under her aunt's eyes, at Lancaster Gate, the day of his dinner there after his return from America; and another her aspect on the same spot two Sundays ago—the light in which she struck the eyes he had brought back from Venice. In the course of a minute or two now he got, as he had got it the other times, his apprehension of the special stamp of the fortune of the moment.

Whatever it had been determined by as the different hours recurred to him, it took on at present a prompt connexion with an effect produced for him in truth more than once during the past week, only now much intensified. This effect he had already noted and named: it was that of the attitude assumed by his friend in the presence of the degree of response on his part to Mrs. Lowder's welcome which she couldn't possibly have failed to notice. She *had* noticed it, and she had beautifully shown him so; wearing in its honour the finest shade of studied serenity, a shade almost of gaiety over the workings of time. Everything of course was relative, with the shadow they were living under; but her condonation of the way in which he now, for confidence, distinguished Aunt Maud had almost the note of cheer. She had so by her own air consecrated the distinction, invidious in respect to herself though it might be; and nothing, really, more than this demonstration, could have given him had he still wanted it the measure of her superiority. It was doubtless for that matter this superiority alone that on the winter noon gave smooth decision to her step and charming courage to her eyes—a courage that deepened in them when he had presently got to what he did want. He had delayed after she had joined him not much more than long enough for him to say to her, drawing her hand into his arm and turning off where they had turned of old, that he wouldn't pretend he hadn't lately had moments of not quite believing he should ever again be so happy. She answered, passing over the reasons, whatever they had been, of his doubt, that her own belief was in high happiness for them if they would only have patience; though nothing at the same time could be dearer than his idea for their walk. It was only make-believe of course, with what had taken place for them, that they couldn't meet at home; she spoke of their opportunities as suffering at no point. He had at any rate soon let her know that he wished the present one to suffer at none, and in a quiet spot, beneath a great wintry tree, he let his entreaty come sharp.

"We've played our dreadful game and we've lost. We owe it to ourselves, we owe it to our feeling *for* ourselves and for each other, not to wait another day. Our marriage will—fundamentally, somehow, don't you see?—right everything that's wrong, and I can't express to you my impatience. We've only to announce it—and it takes off the weight."

"To 'announce' it?" Kate asked. She spoke as if not understanding, though she had listened to him without confusion.

"To accomplish it then—to-morrow if you will; *do* it and announce it as done. That's the least part of it—after it nothing will matter. We shall be so right," he said, "that we shall be strong; we shall only wonder at our past fear. It will seem an ugly madness. It will seem a bad dream."

She looked at him without flinching—with the look she had brought at his call; but he felt now the strange chill of her brightness. "My dear man, what has happened to you?"

"Well, that I can bear it no longer. *That's* simply what has happened. Something has snapped, has broken in me, and here I am. It's *as* I am that you must have me."

He saw her try for a time to appear to consider it; but he saw her also not consider it. Yet he saw her, felt her, further—he heard her, with her clear voice—try to be intensely kind with him. "I don't see, you know, what has changed." She had a large strange smile. "We've been going on together so well, and you suddenly desert me?"

It made him helplessly gaze. "You call it so 'well'? You've touches, upon my soul—!"

"I call it perfect—from my original point of view. I'm just where I was; and you must give me some better reason than you do, my dear, for *your* not being. It seems to me," she continued, "that we're only right as to what has been between us so long as we do wait. I don't think we wish to have behaved like fools." He took in while she talked her imperturbable consistency; which it was quietly, queerly hopeless to see her stand there and breathe into their mild remembering air. He had brought her there to be moved, and she was only immoveable —which was not moreover, either, because she didn't understand. She understood everything, and things he refused to; and she had reasons, deep down, the sense of which nearly sickened him. She had too again most of all her strange significant smile. "Of course if it's that you really *know* something—?" It was quite conceivable and possible to her, he could see, that he did. But he didn't even know what she meant, and he only looked at her in gloom. His gloom however didn't upset her. "You do, I believe, only you've a delicacy about saying it. Your delicacy to me, my dear, is a scruple too much. I should have no delicacy in hearing it, so that if you can *tell* me you know—"

"Well?" he asked as she still kept what depended on it.

"Why then I'll do what you want. We needn't, I grant you, in that case wait; and I can see what you mean by thinking it nicer of us not to. I don't even ask you," she continued, "for a proof. I'm content with your moral certainty."

By this time it had come over him—it had the force of a rush. The point she made was clear, as clear as that the blood, while he recognised it, mantled in his face. "I know nothing whatever."

"You've not an idea?"

"I've not an idea."

"I'd consent," she said—"I'd announce it to-morrow, to-day, I'd go home this moment and announce it to Aunt Maud, for an idea: I mean an idea straight *from* you, I mean as your own, given me in good faith. There, my dear!"—and she smiled again. "I call that really meeting you."

If it *was* then what she called it, it disposed of his appeal, and he could but stand there with his wasted passion—for it was in high passion that he had from the morning acted—in his face. She made it all out, bent upon her—the idea he didn't have, and the idea he had, and his failure of insistence when it brought up *that* challenge, and his sense of her personal presence, and his horror, almost, of her lucidity. They made in him a mixture that might have been rage, but that was turning quickly to mere cold thought, thought which led to something else and was like a new dim dawn. It affected her then, and she had one of the impulses, in all sincerity, that had before this, between them, saved their position. When she had come nearer to him, when, putting her hand upon him, she made him sink with her, as she leaned to him, into their old pair of chairs, she prevented irresistibly, she forestalled, the waste of his passion. She had an advantage with his passion now.

III

HE had said to her in the Park when challenged on it that nothing had "happened" to him as a cause for the demand he there made of her—happened he meant since the account he had given, after his return, of his recent experience. But in the course of a few days—they had brought him to Christmas morning—he was conscious enough, in preparing again to seek her out, of a difference on that score. Something *had* in this case happened to him, and, after his taking the night to think of it he felt that what it most, if not absolutely first, involved was his immediately again putting himself in relation with her. The fact itself had met him there—in his own small quarters—on Christmas Eve, and had not then indeed at once affected him as implying that consequence. So far as he on the spot and for the next hours took its measure—a process that made his night mercilessly wakeful—the consequences possibly implied were numerous to distraction. His spirit dealt with them, in the darkness, as the slow hours passed; his intelligence and his imagination, his soul and his sense, had never on the whole been so intensely engaged. It was his difficulty for the moment that he was face to face with alternatives, and that it was scarce even a question of turning from one to the other. They were not in a perspective in which they might be compared and considered; they were, by a strange effect, as close as a pair of monsters of whom he might have felt on either cheek the hot breath and the huge eyes. He saw them at once and but by looking straight before him; he wouldn't for that matter, in his cold apprehension, have turned his head by an inch. So it was that his agitation was still—was not, for the slow hours, a matter of restless motion. He lay long, after the event, on the sofa where, extinguishing at a touch the white light of convenience that he hated, he had thrown himself without undressing. He stared at the buried day and wore out the time; with the arrival of the Christmas dawn moreover, late and grey, he felt himself somehow determined. The common wisdom had had its say to him—that safety in doubt was *not* action; and perhaps what most helped him was this very commonness. In his case there was nothing of *that*—in no case in his life had there ever been less: which association, from one thing to another, now worked for him as a choice. He acted, after his bath and his breakfast, in the sense of that marked element of the rare which he felt to be the sign of his crisis. And that is why, dressed with more state than usual and quite as if for church, he went out into the soft Christmas day.

Action, for him, on coming to the point, it appeared, carried with it a certain complexity. We should have known, walking by his side, that his final prime decision hadn't been to call at the door of Sir Luke Strett, and yet that this step, though subordinate, was none the less urgent. His prime decision was for another matter, to which impatience, once he was on the way, had now added itself; but he remained sufficiently aware that he must compromise with the perhaps excessive earliness. This, and the ferment set up within him, were together a reason for not driving; to say nothing of the absence of cabs in the dusky festal desert. Sir Luke's great square was not near, but he walked the distance without seeing a hansom. He had his interval thus to turn over his view—the view to which what had happened the night before had not sharply reduced itself; but the complexity just mentioned was to be offered within the next few minutes another item to assimilate. Before Sir Luke's house, when he reached it, a brougham was drawn up—at the sight of which his heart had a lift that brought him for the instant to a stand. This pause wasn't long, but it was long enough to flash upon him a revelation in the light of which he caught his breath. The carriage, so possibly at such an hour and on such a day Sir Luke's own, had struck him as a sign that the great doctor was back. This would prove something else, in turn, still more intensely, and it was in the act of the double apprehension that Densher felt himself turn pale. His mind rebounded for the moment like a projectile that has suddenly been met by another: he stared at the strange truth that what he wanted *more* than to see Kate Croy was to see the witness who had just arrived from Venice. He wanted positively to be in his presence and to hear his voice—which was the spasm of his consciousness that produced the flash. Fortunately for him, on the spot, there supervened something in which the flash went out. He became aware within this minute that the coachman

on the box of the brougham had a face known to him, whereas
he had never seen before, to his knowledge, the great doctor's
carriage. The carriage, as he came nearer, was simply Mrs.
Lowder's; the face on the box was just the face that, in coming
and going at Lancaster Gate, he would vaguely have noticed,
outside, in attendance. With this the rest came: the lady of Lancaster Gate had, on a prompting not wholly remote from his
own, presented herself for news; and news, in the house, she
was clearly getting, since her brougham had stayed. Sir Luke
was then back—only Mrs. Lowder was with him.

It was under the influence of this last reflexion that Densher
again delayed; and it was while he delayed that something else
occurred to him. It was all round, visibly—given his own new
contribution—a case of pressure; and in a case of pressure
Kate, for quicker knowledge, might have come out with her
aunt. The possibility that in this event she might be sitting in
the carriage—the thing most likely—had had the effect, before
he could check it, of bringing him within range of the window.
It wasn't there he had wished to see her; yet if she *was* there he
couldn't pretend not to. What he had however the next moment made out was that if some one was there it wasn't Kate
Croy. It was, with a sensible shock for him, the person who had
last offered him a conscious face from behind the clear plate of
a café in Venice. The great glass at Florian's was a medium less
obscure, even with the window down, than the air of the London Christmas; yet at present also, none the less, between the
two men, an exchange of recognitions could occur. Densher
felt his own look a gaping arrest—which, he disgustedly remembered, his back as quickly turned, appeared to repeat itself
as his special privilege. He mounted the steps of the house and
touched the bell with a keen consciousness of being habitually
looked at by Kate's friend from positions of almost insolent
vantage. He forgot for the time the moment when, in Venice,
at the palace, the encouraged young man had in a manner assisted at the departure of the disconcerted, since Lord Mark
was not looking disconcerted now any more than he had looked
from his bench at his café. Densher was thinking that *he* seemed
to show as vagrant while another was ensconced. He was
thinking of the other as—in spite of the difference of situation
—more ensconced than ever; he was thinking of him above all

as the friend of the person with whom his recognition had, the minute previous, associated him. The man was seated in the very place in which, beside Mrs. Lowder's, he had looked to find Kate, and that was a sufficient identity. Meanwhile at any rate the door of the house had opened and Mrs. Lowder stood before him. It was something at least that *she* wasn't Kate. She was herself, on the spot, in all her affluence; with presence of mind both to decide at once that Lord Mark, in the brougham, didn't matter and to prevent Sir Luke's butler, by a firm word thrown over her shoulder, from standing there to listen to her passage with the gentleman who had rung. "*I'll* tell Mr. Densher; you needn't wait!" And the passage, promptly and richly, took place on the steps.

"He arrives, travelling straight, to-morrow early. I couldn't not come to learn."

"No more," said Densher simply, "could I. On my way," he added, "to Lancaster Gate."

"Sweet of you." She beamed on him dimly, and he saw her face was attuned. It made him, with what she had just before said, know all, and he took the thing in while he met the air of portentous, of almost functional, sympathy that had settled itself as her medium with him and that yet had now a fresh glow. "So you *have* had your message?"

He knew so well what she meant, and so equally with it what he "*had* had" no less than what he hadn't, that, with but the smallest hesitation, he strained the point. "Yes—my message."

"Our dear dove then, as Kate calls her, has folded her wonderful wings."

"Yes—folded them."

It rather racked him, but he tried to receive it as she intended, and she evidently took his formal assent for self-control. "Unless it's more true," she accordingly added, "that she has spread them the wider."

He again but formally assented, though, strangely enough, the words fitted a figure deep in his own imagination. "Rather, yes—spread them the wider."

"For a flight, I trust, to some happiness greater—!"

"Exactly. Greater," Densher broke in; but now with a look, he feared, that did a little warn her off.

"You were certainly," she went on with more reserve, "entitled to direct news. Ours came late last night: I'm not sure otherwise I shouldn't have gone to you. But you're coming," she asked, "to *me?*"

He had had a minute by this time to think further, and the window of the brougham was still within range. Her rich "me," reaching him moreover through the mild damp, had the effect of a thump on his chest. "Squared," Aunt Maud? She was indeed squared, and the extent of it just now perversely enough took away his breath. His look from where they stood embraced the aperture at which the person sitting in the carriage might have shown, and he saw his interlocutress, on her side, understand the question in it, which he moreover then uttered. "Shall you be alone?" It was, as an immediate instinctive parley with the image of his condition that now flourished in her, almost hypocritical. It sounded as if he wished to come and overflow to her, yet this was exactly what he didn't. The need to overflow had suddenly—since the night before—dried up in him, and he had never been aware of a deeper reserve.

But she had meanwhile largely responded. "Completely alone. I should otherwise never have dreamed; feeling, dear friend, but too much!" Failing on her lips what she felt came out for him in the offered hand with which she had the next moment condolingly pressed his own. "Dear friend, dear friend!"—she was deeply "with" him, and she wished to be still more so: which was what made her immediately continue. "Or wouldn't you this evening, for the sad Christmas it makes us, dine with me *tête-à-tête?*"

It put the thing off, the question of a talk with her—making the difference, to his relief, of several hours; but it also rather mystified him. This however didn't diminish his need of caution. "Shall you mind if I don't tell you at once?"

"Not in the least—leave it open: it shall be as you may feel, and you needn't even send me word. I only *will* mention that to-day, of all days, I shall otherwise sit there alone."

Now at least he could ask. "Without Miss Croy?"

"Without Miss Croy. Miss Croy," said Mrs. Lowder, "is spending her Christmas in the bosom of her more immediate family."

He was afraid, even while he spoke, of what his face might show. "You mean she has left you?"

Aunt Maud's own face for that matter met the enquiry with a consciousness in which he saw a reflexion of events. He was made sure by it, even at the moment and as he had never been before, that since he had known these two women no confessed nor commented tension, no crisis of the cruder sort would really have taken form between them: which was precisely a high proof of how Kate had steered her boat. The situation exposed in Mrs. Lowder's present expression lighted up by contrast that superficial smoothness; which afterwards, with his time to think of it, was to put before him again the art, the particular gift, in the girl, now so placed and classed, so intimately familiar for him, as her talent for life. The peace, within a day or two—since his seeing her last—had clearly been broken; differences, deep down, kept there by a diplomacy on Kate's part as deep, had been shaken to the surface by some exceptional jar; with which, in addition, he felt Lord Mark's odd attendance at such an hour and season vaguely associated. The talent for life indeed, it at the same time struck him, would probably have shown equally in the breach, or whatever had occurred; Aunt Maud having suffered, he judged, a strain rather than a stroke. Of these quick thoughts, at all events, that lady was already abreast. "She went yesterday morning—and not with my approval, I don't mind telling you—to her sister: Mrs. Condrip, if you know who I mean, who lives somewhere in Chelsea. My other niece and her affairs—that I should have to say such things to-day!—are a constant worry; so that Kate, in consequence—well, of events!—has simply been called in. My own idea, I'm bound to say, was that with *such* events she need have, in her situation, next to nothing to do."

"But she differed with you?"

"She differed with me. And when Kate differs with you—!"

"Oh I can imagine." He had reached the point in the scale of hypocrisy at which he could ask himself why a little more or less should signify. Besides, with the intention he had had he *must* know. Kate's move, if he didn't know, might simply disconcert him; and of being disconcerted his horror was by this time fairly superstitious. "I hope you don't allude to events at all calamitous."

"No—only horrid and vulgar."

"Oh!" said Merton Densher.

Mrs. Lowder's soreness, it was still not obscure, had discovered in free speech to him a momentary balm. "They've the misfortune to have, I suppose you know, a dreadful horrible father."

"Oh!" said Densher again.

"He's too bad almost to name, but he has come upon Marian, and Marian has shrieked for help."

Densher wondered at this with intensity; and his curiosity compromised for an instant with his discretion. "Come upon her—for money?"

"Oh for that of course always. But, at *this* blessed season, for refuge, for safety: for God knows what. He's *there*, the brute. And Kate's with them. And that," Mrs. Lowder wound up, going down the steps, "is her Christmas."

She had stopped again at the bottom while he thought of an answer. "Yours then is after all rather better."

"It's at least more decent." And her hand once more came out. "But why do I talk of *our* troubles? Come if you can."

He showed a faint smile. "Thanks. If I can."

"And now—I dare say—you'll go to church?"

She had asked it, with her good intention, rather in the air and by way of sketching for him, in the line of support, something a little more to the purpose than what she had been giving him. He felt it as finishing off their intensities of expression that he found himself to all appearance receiving her hint as happy. "Why yes—I think I will": after which, as the door of the brougham, at her approach, had opened from within, he was free to turn his back. He heard the door, behind him, sharply close again and the vehicle move off in another direction than his own.

He had in fact for the time no direction; in spite of which indeed he was at the end of ten minutes aware of having walked straight to the south. That, he afterwards recognised, was, very sufficiently, because there had formed itself in his mind, even while Aunt Maud finally talked, an instant recognition of his necessary course. Nothing was open to him but to follow Kate, nor was anything more marked than the influence of the step she had taken on the emotion itself that possessed him. Her complications, which had fairly, with everything else, an awful sound—what were they, a thousand times over, but his own?

His present business was to see that they didn't escape an hour longer taking their proper place in his life. He accordingly would have held his course hadn't it suddenly come over him that he had just lied to Mrs. Lowder—a term it perversely eased him to keep using—even more than was necessary. To what church was he going, to what church, in such a state of his nerves, *could* he go?—he pulled up short again, as he had pulled up in sight of Mrs. Lowder's carriage, to ask it. And yet the desire queerly stirred in him not to have wasted his word. He was just then however by a happy chance in the Brompton Road, and he bethought himself with a sudden light that the Oratory was at hand. He had but to turn the other way and he should find himself soon before it. At the door then, in a few minutes, his idea was really—as it struck him—consecrated: he was, pushing in, on the edge of a splendid service—the flocking crowd told of it—which glittered and resounded, from distant depths, in the blaze of altar-lights and the swell of organ and choir. It didn't match his own day, but it was much less of a discord than some other things actual and possible. The Oratory in short, to make him right, would do.

IV

T<small>HE</small> difference was thus that the dusk of afternoon—dusk thick from an early hour—had gathered when he knocked at Mrs. Condrip's door. He had gone from the church to his club, wishing not to present himself in Chelsea at luncheon-time and also remembering that he must attempt independently to make a meal. This, in the event, he but imperfectly achieved: he dropped into a chair in the great dim void of the club library, with nobody, up or down, to be seen, and there after a while, closing his eyes, recovered an hour of the sleep he had lost during the night. Before doing this indeed he had written—it was the first thing he did—a short note, which, in the Christmas desolation of the place, he had managed only with difficulty and doubt to commit to a messenger. He wished it carried by hand, and he was obliged, rather blindly, to trust the hand, as the messenger, for some reason, was unable to return with a gage of delivery. When at four o'clock he was face to face with Kate in Mrs. Condrip's small drawing-room he found to his relief that his notification had reached her. She was expectant and to that extent prepared; which simplified a little—if a little, at the present pass, counted. Her conditions were vaguely vivid to him from the moment of his coming in, and vivid partly by their difference, a difference sharp and suggestive, from those in which he had hitherto constantly seen her. He had seen her but in places comparatively great; in her aunt's pompous house, under the high trees of Kensington and the storied ceilings of Venice. He had seen her, in Venice, on a great occasion, as the centre itself of the splendid Piazza: he had seen her there, on a still greater one, in his own poor rooms, which yet had consorted with her, having state and ancientry even in their poorness; but Mrs. Condrip's interior, even by this best view of it and though not flagrantly mean, showed itself as a setting almost grotesquely inapt. Pale, grave and charming, she affected him at once as a distinguished stranger—a stranger to the little Chelsea street—who was making the best of a queer episode and a place of exile.

The extraordinary thing was that at the end of three minutes he felt himself less appointedly a stranger in it than she.

A part of the queerness—this was to come to him in glimpses —sprang from the air as of a general large misfit imposed on the narrow room by the scale and mass of its furniture. The objects, the ornaments were, for the sisters, clearly relics and survivals of what would, in the case of Mrs. Condrip at least, have been called better days. The curtains that overdraped the windows, the sofas and tables that stayed circulation, the chimney-ornaments that reached to the ceiling and the florid chandelier that almost dropped to the floor, were so many me- mentoes of earlier homes and so many links with their un- happy mother. Whatever might have been in itself the quality of these elements Densher could feel the effect proceeding from them, as they lumpishly blocked out the decline of the dim day, to be ugly almost to the point of the sinister. They failed to accommodate or to compromise; they asserted their differences without tact and without taste. It was truly having a sense of Kate's own quality thus promptly to see them in ref- erence to it. But that Densher had this sense was no new thing to him, nor did he in strictness need, for the hour, to be re- minded of it. He only knew, by one of the tricks his imagina- tion so constantly played him, that he was, so far as her present tension went, very specially sorry for her—which was not the view that had determined his start in the morning; yet also that he himself would have taken it all, as he might say, less hard. *He* could have lived in such a place; but it wasn't given to those of his complexion, so to speak, to be exiled anywhere. It was by their comparative grossness that they could somehow make shift. His natural, his inevitable, his ultimate home—left, that is, to itself—wasn't at all unlikely to be as queer and im- possible as what was just round them, though doubtless in less ample masses. As he took in moreover how Kate wouldn't have been in the least the creature she was if what was just round them hadn't mismatched her, hadn't made for her a medium involving compunction in the spectator, so, by the same stroke, that became the very fact of her relation with her companions there, such a fact as filled him at once, oddly, both with assur- ance and with suspense. If he himself, on this brief vision, felt

her as alien and as ever so unwittingly ironic, how must they
not feel her and how above all must she not feel them?

Densher could ask himself that even after she had presently
lighted the tall candles on the mantel-shelf. This was all their
illumination but the fire, and she had proceeded to it with a
quiet dryness that yet left play, visibly, to her implication between them, in their trouble and failing anything better, of the
presumably genial Christmas hearth. So far as the genial went
this had in strictness, given their conditions, to be all their geniality. He had told her in his note nothing but that he must
promptly see her and that he hoped she might be able to make
it possible; but he understood from the first look at her that
his promptitude was already having for her its principal reference. "I was prevented this morning, in the few minutes," he
explained, "asking Mrs. Lowder if she had let you know,
though I rather gathered she had; and it's what I've been in
fact since then assuming. It was because I was so struck at the
moment with your having, as she did tell me, so suddenly
come here."

"Yes, it was sudden enough." Very neat and fine in the contracted firelight, with her hands in her lap, Kate considered
what he had said. He had spoken immediately of what had
happened at Sir Luke Strett's door. "She has let me know
nothing. But that doesn't matter—if it's what *you* mean."

"It's part of what I mean," Densher said; but what he went
on with, after a pause during which she waited, was apparently
not the rest of that. "She had had her telegram from Mrs.
Stringham; late last night. But to me the poor lady hasn't wired.
The event," he added, "will have taken place yesterday, and Sir
Luke, starting immediately, one can see, and travelling straight,
will get back to-morrow morning. So that Mrs. Stringham, I
judge, is left to face in some solitude the situation bequeathed
to her. But of course," he wound up, "Sir Luke couldn't stay."

Her look at him might have had in it a vague betrayal of the
sense that he was gaining time. "Was your telegram from Sir
Luke?"

"No—I've had no telegram."

She wondered. "But not a letter—?"

"Not from Mrs. Stringham—no." He failed again however

to develop this—for which her forbearance from another question gave him occasion. From whom then had he heard? He might at last, confronted with her, really have been gaining time; and as if to show that she respected this impulse she made her enquiry different. "Should you like to go out to her—to Mrs. Stringham?"

About that at least he was clear. "Not at all. She's alone, but she's very capable and very courageous. Besides—!" He had been going on, but he dropped.

"Besides," she said, "there's Eugenio? Yes, of course one remembers Eugenio."

She had uttered the words as definitely to show them for not untender; and he showed equally every reason to assent. "One remembers him indeed, and with every ground for it. He'll be of the highest value to her—he's capable of anything. What I was going to say," he went on, "is that some of their people from America must quickly arrive."

On this, as happened, Kate was able at once to satisfy him. "Mr. Someone-or-other, the person principally in charge of Milly's affairs—her first trustee, I suppose—had just got there at Mrs. Stringham's last writing."

"Ah that then was after your aunt last spoke to me—I mean the last time before this morning. I'm relieved to hear it. So," he said, "they'll do."

"Oh they'll do." And it came from each still as if it wasn't what each was most thinking of. Kate presently got however a step nearer to that. "But if you had been wired to by nobody what then this morning had taken you to Sir Luke?"

"Oh something else—which I'll presently tell you. It's what made me instantly need to see you; it's what I've come to speak to you of. But in a minute. I feel too many things," he went on, "at seeing you in this place." He got up as he spoke; she herself remained perfectly still. His movement had been to the fire, and, leaning a little, with his back to it, to look down on her from where he stood, he confined himself to his point. "Is it anything very bad that has brought you?"

He had now in any case said enough to justify her wish for more; so that, passing this matter by, she pressed her own challenge. "Do you mean, if I may ask, that *she*, dying—?" Her face, wondering, pressed it more than her words.

"Certainly you may ask," he after a moment said. "What has come to me is what, as I say, I came expressly to tell you. I don't mind letting you know," he went on, "that my decision to do this took for me last night and this morning a great deal of thinking of. But here I am." And he indulged in a smile that couldn't, he was well aware, but strike her as mechanical.

She went straighter with him, she seemed to show, than he really went with her. "You didn't want to come?"

"It would have been simple, my dear"—and he continued to smile—"if it had been, one way or the other, only a question of 'wanting.' It took, I admit it, the idea of what I had best do, all sorts of difficult and portentous forms. It came up for me really—well, not at all for my happiness."

This word apparently puzzled her—she studied him in the light of it. "You look upset—you've certainly been tormented. You're not well."

"Oh—well enough!"

But she continued without heeding. "You hate what you're doing."

"My dear girl, you simplify"—and he was now serious enough. "It isn't so simple even as that."

She had the air of thinking what it then might be. "I of course can't, with no clue, know what it is." She remained none the less patient and still. "If at such a moment she could write you one's inevitably quite at sea. One doesn't, with the best will in the world, understand." And then as Densher had a pause which might have stood for all the involved explanation that, to his discouragement, loomed before him: "You *haven't* decided what to do."

She had said it very gently, almost sweetly, and he didn't instantly say otherwise. But he said so after a look at her. "Oh yes—I have. Only with this sight of you here and what I seem to see in it for you—!" And his eyes, as at suggestions that pressed, turned from one part of the room to another.

"Horrible place, isn't it?" said Kate.

It brought him straight back to his enquiry. "Is it for anything awful you've had to come?"

"Oh that will take as long to tell you as anything *you* may have. Don't mind," she continued, "the 'sight of me here,' nor whatever—which is more than I yet know myself—may be 'in it' for me. And kindly consider too that, after all, if you're in trouble I can a little wish to help you. Perhaps I can absolutely even do it."

"My dear child, it's just because of the sense of your wish—! I suppose I'm in trouble—I suppose that's it." He said this with so odd a suddenness of simplicity that she could only stare for it—which he as promptly saw. So he turned off as he could his vagueness. "And yet I oughtn't to be." Which sounded indeed vaguer still.

She waited a moment. "Is it, as you say for my own business, anything very awful?"

"Well," he slowly replied, "you'll tell me if you find it so. I mean if you find my idea—"

He was so slow that she took him up. "Awful?" A sound of impatience—the form of a laugh—at last escaped her. "I can't find it anything at all till I know what you're talking about."

It brought him then more to the point, though it did so at first but by making him, on the hearthrug before her, with his hands in his pockets, turn awhile to and fro. There rose in him even with this movement a recall of another time—the hour in Venice, the hour of gloom and storm, when Susan Shepherd had sat in his quarters there very much as Kate was sitting now, and he had wondered, in pain even as now, what he might say and mightn't. Yet the present occasion after all was somehow the easier. He tried at any rate to attach that feeling to it while he stopped before his companion. "The communication I speak of can't possibly belong—so far as its date is concerned—to these last days. The postmark, which is legible, does; but it isn't thinkable, for anything else, that she wrote—!" He dropped, looking at her as if she'd understand.

It was easy to understand. "On her deathbed?" But Kate took an instant's thought. "Aren't we agreed that there was never any one in the world like her?"

"Yes." And looking over her head he spoke clearly enough. "There was never anyone in the world like her."

Kate, from her chair, always without a movement, raised her eyes to the unconscious reach of his own. Then when the latter again dropped to her she added a question. "And won't it further depend a little on what the communication is?"

"A little perhaps—but not much. It's a communication," said Densher.

"Do you mean a letter?"

"Yes, a letter. Addressed to me in her hand—in hers unmistakeably."

Kate thought. "Do you know her hand very well?"

"Oh perfectly."

It was as if his tone for this prompted—with a slight strangeness—her next demand. "Have you had many letters from her?"

"No. Only three notes." He spoke looking straight at her. "And very, very short ones."

"Ah," said Kate, "the number doesn't matter. Three lines would be enough if you're sure you remember."

"I'm sure I remember. Besides," Densher continued, "I've seen her hand in other ways. I seem to recall how you once, before she went to Venice, showed me one of her notes precisely *for* that. And then she once copied me something."

"Oh," said Kate almost with a smile, "I don't ask you for the detail of your reasons. One good one's enough." To which however she added as if precisely not to speak with impatience or with anything like irony: "And the writing has its usual look?"

Densher answered as if even to better that description of it. "It's beautiful."

"Yes—it *was* beautiful. Well," Kate, to defer to him still, further remarked, "it's not news to us now that she was stupendous. Anything's possible."

"Yes, anything's possible"—he appeared oddly to catch at it. "That's what I say to myself. It's what I've been believing you," he a trifle vaguely explained, "still more certain to feel."

She waited for him to say more, but he only, with his hands in his pockets, turned again away, going this time to the single window of the room, where in the absence of lamplight the blind hadn't been drawn. He looked out into the lamplit fog, lost himself in the small sordid London street—for sordid, with his other association, he felt it—as he had lost himself, with Mrs. Stringham's eyes on him, in the vista of the Grand Canal. It was present then to his recording consciousness that when he had last been driven to such an attitude the very depth of his resistance to the opportunity to give Kate away was what had so driven him. His waiting companion had on that occasion waited for him to say he *would*; and what he had meantime glowered forth at was the inanity of such a hope. Kate's attention, on her side, during these minutes, rested on the back and shoulders he thus familiarly presented—rested as with a view of their expression, a reference to things unimparted, links still missing and that she must ever miss, try to make them out as she would. The result of her tension was that she again took him up. "You received—what you spoke of—last night?"

It made him turn round. "Coming in from Fleet Street—earlier by an hour than usual—I found it with some other letters on my table. But my eyes went straight to it, in an extraordinary way, from the door. I recognised it, knew what it was, without touching it."

"One can understand." She listened with respect. His tone however was so singular that she presently added: "You speak as if all this while you *hadn't* touched it."

"Oh yes, I've touched it. I feel as if, ever since, I'd been touching nothing else. I quite firmly," he pursued as if to be plainer, "took hold of it."

"Then where is it?"

"Oh I have it here."

"And you've brought it to show me?"

"I've brought it to show you."

So he said with a distinctness that had, among his other oddities, almost a sound of cheer, yet making no movement that matched his words. She could accordingly but offer again her expectant face, while his own, to her impatience, seemed perversely to fill with another thought. "But now that you've done so you feel you don't want to."

"I want to immensely," he said. "Only you tell me nothing."

She smiled at him, with this, finally, as if he were an unreasonable child. "It seems to me I tell you quite as much as you tell me. You haven't yet even told me how it is that such explanations as you require don't come from your document itself." Then as he answered nothing she had a flash. "You mean you haven't read it?"

"I haven't read it."

She stared. "Then how am I to help you with it?"

Again leaving her while she never budged he paced five strides, and again he was before her. "By telling me *this*. It's something, you know, that you wouldn't tell me the other day."

She was vague. "The other day?"

"The first time after my return—the Sunday I came to you. What's he doing," Densher went on, "at that hour of the morning with her? What does his having been with her there mean?"

"Of whom are you talking?"

"Of that man—Lord Mark of course. What does it represent?"

"Oh with Aunt Maud?"

"Yes, my dear—and with you. It comes more or less to the same thing; and it's what you didn't tell me the other day when I put you the question."

Kate tried to remember the other day. "You asked me nothing about any hour."

"I asked you when it was you last saw him—previous, I mean, to his second descent at Venice. You wouldn't say, and as we were talking of a matter comparatively more important I let it pass. But the fact remains, you know, my dear, that you haven't told me."

Two things in this speech appeared to have reached Kate more distinctly than the others. "I 'wouldn't say'?—and you 'let it pass'?" She looked just coldly blank. "You really speak as if I were keeping something back."

"Well, you see," Densher persisted, "you're not even telling me now. All I want to know," he nevertheless explained, "is whether there was a connexion between that proceeding on his part, which was practically—oh beyond all doubt!—the shock precipitating for her what has now happened, and anything that had occurred with him previously for yourself. How in the world did he know we're engaged?"

V

KATE slowly rose; it was, since she had lighted the candles and sat down, the first movement she had made. "Are you trying to fix it on me that I must have told him?"

She spoke not so much in resentment as in pale dismay—which he showed he immediately took in. "My dear child, I'm not trying to 'fix' anything; but I'm extremely tormented and I seem not to understand. What has the brute to do with us anyway?"

"What has he indeed?" Kate asked.

She shook her head as if in recovery, within the minute, of some mild allowance for his unreason. There was in it—and for his reason really—one of those half-inconsequent sweetnesses by which she had often before made, over some point of difference, her own terms with him. Practically she was making them now, and essentially he was knowing it; yet inevitably, all the same, he was accepting it. She stood there close to him, with something in her patience that suggested her having supposed, when he spoke more appealingly, that he was going to kiss her. He hadn't been, it appeared; but his continued appeal was none the less the quieter. "What's he doing, from ten o'clock on Christmas morning, with Mrs. Lowder?"

Kate looked surprised. "Didn't she tell you he's staying there?"

"At Lancaster Gate?" Densher's surprise met it. "'Staying'? —since when?"

"Since day before yesterday. He was there before I came away." And then she explained—confessing it in fact anomalous. "It's an accident—like Aunt Maud's having herself remained in town for Christmas, but it isn't after all so monstrous. *We* stayed—and, with my having come here, she's sorry now—because we neither of us, waiting from day to day for the news you brought, seemed to want to be with a lot of people."

"You stayed for thinking of—Venice?"

"Of course we did. For what else? And even a little," Kate wonderfully added—"it's true at least of Aunt Maud—for thinking of you."

670

He appreciated. "I see. Nice of you every way. But whom," he enquired, "has Lord Mark stayed for thinking of?"

"His being in London, I believe, is a very commonplace matter. He has some rooms which he has had suddenly some rather advantageous chance to let—such as, with his confessed, his decidedly proclaimed want of money, he hasn't had it in him, in spite of everything, not to jump at."

Densher's attention was entire. "In spite of everything? In spite of what?"

"Well, I don't know. In spite, say, of his being scarcely supposed to do that sort of thing."

"To try to get money?"

"To try at any rate in little thrifty ways. Apparently however he has had for some reason to do what he can. He turned at a couple of days' notice out of his place, making it over to his tenant; and Aunt Maud, who's deeply in his confidence about all such matters, said: 'Come then to Lancaster Gate—to sleep at least—till, like all the world, you go to the country.' He was to have gone to the country—I think to Matcham—yesterday afternoon: Aunt Maud, that is, told me he was."

Kate had been somehow, for her companion, through this statement, beautifully, quite soothingly, suggestive. "Told you, you mean, so that you needn't leave the house?"

"Yes—so far as she had taken it into her head that his being there was part of my reason."

"And *was* it part of your reason?"

"A little if you like. Yet there's plenty here—as I knew there would be—without it. So that," she said candidly, "doesn't matter. I'm glad I am here: even if for all the good I do—!" She implied however that that didn't matter either. "He didn't, as you tell me, get off then to Matcham; though he may possibly, if it *is* possible, be going this afternoon. But what strikes me as most probable—and it's really, I'm bound to say, quite amiable of him—is that he has declined to leave Aunt Maud, as I've been so ready to do, to spend her Christmas alone. If moreover he has given up Matcham for her it's a *procédé* that won't please her less. It's small wonder therefore that she insists, on a dull day, in driving him about. I don't pretend to know," she wound up, "what may happen between them; but that's all I see in it."

"You see in everything, and you always did," Densher returned, "something that, while I'm with you at least, I always take from you as the truth itself."

She looked at him as if consciously and even carefully extracting the sting of his reservation; then she spoke with a quiet gravity that seemed to show how fine she found it. "Thank you." It had for him, like everything else, its effect. They were still closely face to face, and, yielding to the impulse to which he hadn't yielded just before, he laid his hands on her shoulders, held her hard a minute and shook her a little, far from untenderly, as if in expression of more mingled things, all difficult, than he could speak. Then bending his head he applied his lips to her cheek. He fell, after this, away for an instant, resuming his unrest, while she kept the position in which, all passive and as a statue, she had taken his demonstration. It didn't prevent her, however, from offering him, as if what she had had was enough for the moment, a further indulgence. She made a quiet lucid connexion and as she made it sat down again. "I've been trying to place exactly, as to its date, something that did happen to me while you were in Venice. I mean a talk with him. He spoke to me—spoke out."

"Ah there you are!" said Densher who had wheeled round.

"Well, if I'm 'there,' as you so gracefully call it, by having refused to meet him as he wanted—as he pressed—I plead guilty to being so. Would you have liked me," she went on, "to give him an answer that would have kept him from going?"

It made him a little awkwardly think. "Did you know he was going?"

"Never for a moment; but I'm afraid that—even if it doesn't fit your strange suppositions—I should have given him just the same answer if I had known. If it's a matter I haven't, since your return, thrust upon you, that's simply because it's not a matter in the memory of which I find a particular joy. I hope that if I've satisfied you about it," she continued, "it's not too much to ask of you to let it rest."

"Certainly," said Densher kindly, "I'll let it rest." But the next moment he pursued: "He saw something. He guessed."

"If you mean," she presently returned, "that he was unfortunately the one person we hadn't deceived, I can't contradict you."

"No—of course not. But *why*," Densher still risked, "was he unfortunately the one person—? He's not really a bit intelligent."

"Intelligent enough apparently to have seen a mystery, a riddle, in anything so unnatural as—all things considered and when it came to the point—my attitude. So he gouged out his conviction, and on his conviction he acted."

Densher seemed for a little to look at Lord Mark's conviction as if it were a blot on the face of nature. "Do you mean because you had appeared to him to have encouraged him?"

"Of course I had been decent to him. Otherwise where *were* we?"

" 'Where'—?"

"You and I. What I appeared to him, however, hadn't mattered. What mattered was how I appeared to Aunt Maud. Besides, you must remember that he has had all along his impression of *you*. You can't help it," she said, "but you're after all—well, yourself."

"As much myself as you please. But when I took myself to Venice and kept myself there—what," Densher asked, "did he make of that?"

"Your being in Venice and liking to be—which is never on any one's part a monstrosity—was explicable for him in other ways. He was quite capable moreover of seeing it as dissimulation."

"In spite of Mrs. Lowder?"

"No," said Kate, "not in spite of Mrs. Lowder now. Aunt Maud, before what you call his second descent, hadn't convinced him—all the more that my refusal of him didn't help. But he came back convinced." And then as her companion still showed a face at a loss: "I mean after he had seen Milly, spoken to her and left her. Milly convinced him."

"Milly?" Densher again but vaguely echoed.

"That you were sincere. That it was *her* you loved." It came to him from her in such a way that he instantly, once more, turned, found himself yet again at his window. "Aunt Maud, on his return here," she meanwhile continued, "had it from him. And that's why you're now so well with Aunt Maud."

He only for a minute looked out in silence—after which he came away. "And why *you* are." It was almost, in its extremely affirmative effect between them, the note of recrimination; or it would have been perhaps rather if it hadn't been so much more the note of truth. It was sharp because it was true, but its truth appeared to impose it as an argument so conclusive as to permit on neither side a sequel. That made, while they faced each other over it without speech, the gravity of everything. It was as if there were almost danger, which the wrong word might start. Densher accordingly at last acted to better purpose: he drew, standing there before her, a pocket-book from the breast of his waistcoat and he drew from the pocket-book a folded letter to which her eyes attached themselves. He restored then the receptacle to its place and, with a movement not the less odd for being visibly instinctive and unconscious, carried the hand containing his letter behind him. What he thus finally spoke of was a different matter. "Did I understand from Mrs. Lowder that your father's in the house?"

If it never had taken her long in such excursions to meet him it was not to take her so now. "In the house, yes. But we needn't fear his interruption"—she spoke as if he had thought of that. "He's in bed."

"Do you mean with illness?"

She sadly shook her head. "Father's never ill. He's a marvel. He's only—endless."

Densher thought. "Can I in any way help you with him?"

"Yes." She perfectly, wearily, almost serenely, had it all. "By our making your visit as little of an affair as possible for him—and for Marian too."

"I see. They hate so your seeing me. Yet I couldn't—could I?—not have come."

"No, you couldn't not have come."

"But I can only, on the other hand, go as soon as possible?"

Quickly it almost upset her. "Ah don't, to-day, put ugly words into my mouth. I've enough of my trouble without it."

"I know—I know!" He spoke in instant pleading. "It's all only that I'm as troubled *for* you. When did he come?"

"Three days ago—after he hadn't been near her for more than a year, after he had apparently, and not regrettably, ceased to remember her existence; and in a state which made it impossible not to take him in."

Densher hesitated. "Do you mean in such want—?"

"No, not of food, of necessary things—not even, so far as his appearance went, of money. He looked as wonderful as ever. But he was—well, in terror."

"In terror of what?"

"I don't know. Of somebody—of something. He wants, he says, to be quiet. But his quietness is awful."

She suffered, but he couldn't not question. "What does he do?"

It made Kate herself hesitate. "He cries."

Again for a moment he hung fire, but he risked it. "What *has* he done?"

It made her slowly rise, and they were once more fully face to face. Her eyes held his own and she was paler than she had been. "If you love me—now—don't ask me about father."

He waited again a moment. "I love you. It's because I love you that I'm here. It's because I love you that I've brought you this." And he drew from behind him the letter that had remained in his hand.

But her eyes only—though he held it out—met the offer. "Why you've not broken the seal!"

"If I had broken the seal—exactly—I should know what's within. It's for *you* to break the seal that I bring it."

She looked—still not touching the thing—inordinately grave. "To break the seal of something to you from *her*?"

"Ah precisely because it's from her. I'll abide by whatever you think of it."

"I don't understand," said Kate. "What do you yourself think?" And then as he didn't answer: "It seems to me *I* think you know. You have your instinct. You don't need to read. It's the proof."

Densher faced her words as if they had been an accusation, an accusation for which he was prepared and which there was but one way to face. "I have indeed my instinct. It came to me, while I worried it out, last night. It came to me as an effect of the hour." He held up his letter and seemed now to insist more than to confess. "This thing had been timed."

"For Christmas Eve?"

"For Christmas Eve."

Kate had suddenly a strange smile. "The season of gifts!" After which, as he said nothing, she went on: "And had been written, you mean, while she could write, and kept to *be* so timed?"

Only meeting her eyes while he thought, he again didn't reply. "What do *you* mean by the proof?"

"Why of the beauty with which you've been loved. But I won't," she said, "break your seal."

"You positively decline?"

"Positively. Never." To which she added oddly: "I know without."

He had another pause. "And what is it you know?"

"That she announces to you she has made you rich."

His pause this time was longer. "Left me her fortune?"

"Not all of it, no doubt, for it's immense. But money to a large amount. I don't care," Kate went on, "to know how much." And her strange smile recurred. "I trust her."

"Did she tell you?" Densher asked.

"Never!" Kate visibly flushed at the thought. "That wouldn't, on my part, have been playing fair with her. And I did," she added, "play fair."

Densher, who had believed her—he couldn't help it—continued, holding his letter, to face her. He was much quieter now, as if his torment had somehow passed. "You played fair with me, Kate; and that's why—since we talk of proofs—I want to give *you* one. I've wanted to let you see—and in preference even to myself—something I feel as sacred."

She frowned a little. "I don't understand."

"I've asked myself for a tribute, for a sacrifice by which I can peculiarly recognise—"

"Peculiarly recognise what?" she demanded as he dropped.

"The admirable nature of your own sacrifice. You were capable in Venice of an act of splendid generosity."

"And the privilege you offer me with that document is my reward?"

He made a movement. "It's all I can do as a symbol of my attitude."

She looked at him long. "Your attitude, my dear, is that you're afraid of yourself. You've had to take yourself in hand. You've had to do yourself violence."

"So it is then you meet me?"

She bent her eyes hard a moment to the letter, from which her hand still stayed itself. "You absolutely *desire* me to take it?"

"I absolutely desire you to take it."

"To do what I like with it?"

"Short of course of making known its terms. It must remain—pardon my making the point—between you and me."

She had a last hesitation, but she presently broke it. "Trust me." Taking from him the sacred script she held it a little while her eyes again rested on those fine characters of Milly's that they had shortly before discussed. "To hold it," she brought out, "is to know."

"Oh I *know*!" said Merton Densher.

"Well then if we both do—!" She had already turned to the fire, nearer to which she had moved, and with a quick gesture had jerked the thing into the flame. He started—but only half—as to undo her action: his arrest was as prompt as the latter had been decisive. He only watched, with her, the paper burn; after which their eyes again met. "You'll have it all," Kate said, "from New York."

VI

IT WAS after he had in fact, two months later, heard from
New York that she paid him a visit one morning at his own
quarters—coming not as she had come in Venice, under his
extreme solicitation, but as a need recognised in the first instance by herself, even though also as the prompt result of a
missive delivered to her. This had consisted of a note from
Densher accompanying a letter, "just to hand," addressed him
by an eminent American legal firm, a firm of whose high character he had become conscious while in New York as of a thing
in the air itself, and whose head and front, the principal executor of Milly Theale's copious will, had been duly identified at
Lancaster Gate as the gentleman hurrying out, by the straight
southern course, before the girl's death, to the support of
Mrs. Stringham. Densher's act on receipt of the document in
question—an act as to which and to the bearings of which his
resolve had had time to mature—constituted in strictness, singularly enough, the first reference to Milly, or to what Milly
might or might not have done, that had passed between our
pair since they had stood together watching the destruction, in
the little vulgar grate at Chelsea, of the undisclosed work of
her hand. They had at the time, and in due deference now, on
his part, to Kate's mention of her responsibility for his call, immediately separated, and when they met again the subject was
made present to them—at all events till some flare of new light
—only by the intensity with which it mutely expressed its absence. They were not moreover in these weeks to meet often,
in spite of the fact that this had, during January and a part of
February, actually become for them a comparatively easy
matter. Kate's stay at Mrs. Condrip's prolonged itself under allowances from her aunt which would have been a mystery to
Densher had he not been admitted, at Lancaster Gate, really in
spite of himself, to the esoteric view of them. "It's her idea,"
Mrs. Lowder had there said to him as if she really despised
ideas—which she didn't; "and I've taken up with my own,
which is to give her her head till she has had enough of it. She
has had enough of it, she had that soon enough; but as she's as

proud as the deuce she'll come back when she has found some reason—having nothing in common with her disgust—of which she can make a show. She calls it her holiday, which she's spending in her own way—the holiday to which, once a year or so, as she says, the very maids in the scullery have a right. So we're taking it on that basis. But we shall not soon, I think, take another of the same sort. Besides, she's quite decent; she comes often—whenever I make her a sign; and she has been good, on the whole, this year or two, so that, to be decent myself, I don't complain. She has really been, poor dear, very much what one hoped; though I needn't, you know," Aunt Maud wound up, "tell *you*, after all, you clever creature, what that was."

It had been partly in truth to keep down the opportunity for this that Densher's appearances under the good lady's roof markedly, after Christmas, interspaced themselves. The phase of his situation that on his return from Venice had made them for a short time almost frequent was at present quite obscured, and with it the impulse that had then acted. Another phase had taken its place, which he would have been painfully at a loss as yet to name or otherwise set on its feet, but of which the steadily rising tide left Mrs. Lowder, for his desire, quite high and dry. There had been a moment when it seemed possible that Mrs. Stringham, returning to America under convoy, would pause in London on her way and be housed with her old friend; in which case he was prepared for some apparent zeal of attendance. But this danger passed—he had felt it a danger, and the person in the world whom he would just now have most valued seeing on his own terms sailed away westward from Genoa. He thereby only wrote to her, having broken, in this respect, after Milly's death, the silence as to the sense of which, before that event, their agreement had been so deep. She had answered him from Venice twice, and had had time to answer him twice again from New York. The last letter of her four had come by the same post as the document he sent on to Kate, but he hadn't gone into the question of also enclosing that. His correspondence with Milly's companion was somehow already presenting itself to him as a feature—as a factor, he would have said in his newspaper—of the time whatever it might be, long or short, in store for him; but one of his

acutest current thoughts was apt to be devoted to his not
having yet mentioned it to Kate. She had put him no question,
no "Don't you ever hear?"—so that he hadn't been brought
to the point. This he described to himself as a mercy, for he
liked his secret. It was as a secret that, in the same personal
privacy, he described his transatlantic commerce, scarce even
wincing while he recognised it as the one connexion in which
he wasn't straight. He had in fact for this connexion a vivid
mental image—he saw it as a small emergent rock in the waste
of waters, the bottomless grey expanse of straightness. The fact
that he had on several recent occasions taken with Kate an out-
of-the-way walk that was each time to define itself as more remarkable for what they didn't say than for what they did—this
fact failed somehow to mitigate for him a strange consciousness of exposure. There was something deep within him that
he had absolutely shown to no one—to the companion of these
walks in particular not a bit more than he could help; but he
was none the less haunted, under its shadow, with a dire apprehension of publicity. It was as if he had invoked that ugliness in some stupid good faith; and it was queer enough that
on his emergent rock, clinging to it and to Susan Shepherd, he
should figure himself as hidden from view. That represented
no doubt his belief in her power, or in her delicate disposition
to protect him. Only Kate at all events knew—what Kate did
know, and she was also the last person interested to tell it; in
spite of which it was as if his *act*, so deeply associated with her
and never to be recalled nor recovered, was abroad on the
winds of the world. His honesty, as he viewed it with Kate, was
the very element of that menace: to the degree that he saw at
moments, as to their final impulse or their final remedy, the
need to bury in the dark blindness of each other's arms the
knowledge of each other that they couldn't undo.

Save indeed that the sense in which it was in these days a
question of arms was limited, this might have been the intimate expedient to which they were actually resorting. It had
its value, in conditions that made everything count, that thrice
over, in Battersea Park—where Mrs. Lowder now never drove
—he had adopted the usual means, in sequestered alleys, of
holding her close to his side. She could make absences, on her
present footing, without having too inordinately to account

for them at home—which was exactly what gave them for the first time an appreciable margin. He supposed she could always say in Chelsea—though he didn't press it—that she had been across the town, in decency, for a look at her aunt; whereas there had always been reasons at Lancaster Gate for her not being able to plead the look at her other relatives. It was therefore between them a freedom of a purity as yet untasted; which for that matter also they made in various ways no little show of cherishing as such. They made the show indeed in every way but the way of a large use—an inconsequence that they almost equally gave time to helping each other to regard as natural. He put it to his companion that the kind of favour he now enjoyed at Lancaster Gate, the wonderful warmth of his reception there, cut in a manner the ground from under their feet. He was too horribly trusted—they had succeeded too well. He couldn't in short make appointments with her without abusing Aunt Maud, and he couldn't on the other hand haunt that lady without tying his hands. Kate saw what he meant just as he saw what she did when she admitted that she was herself, to a degree scarce less embarrassing, in the enjoyment of Aunt Maud's confidence. It was special at present—she was handsomely used; she confessed accordingly to a scruple about misapplying her licence. Mrs. Lowder then finally had found—and all unconsciously now—the way to baffle them. It wasn't however that they didn't meet a little, none the less, in the southern quarter, to point for their common benefit the moral of their defeat. They crossed the river; they wandered in neighbourhoods sordid and safe; the winter was mild, so that, mounting to the top of trams, they could rumble together to Clapham or to Greenwich. If at the same time their minutes had never been so counted it struck Densher that by a singular law their tone—he scarce knew what to call it—had never been so bland. Not to talk of what they *might* have talked of drove them to other ground; it was as if they used a perverse insistence to make up what they ignored. They concealed their pursuit of the irrelevant by the charm of their manner; they took precautions for the courtesy they had formerly left to come of itself; often, when he had quitted her, he stopped short, walking off, with the aftersense of their change. He would have described their change—had he so far faced it as to describe it—by their being so damned civil. That had even, with the intimate, the familiar at the point to which they had brought them, a touch almost of the droll. What danger had there ever been of their becoming rude—after each had long since made the other so tremendously tender? Such were the things he asked himself when he wondered what in particular he most feared.

Yet all the while too the tension had its charm—such being the interest of a creature who could bring one back to her by such different roads. It was her talent for life again; which found in her a difference for the differing time. She didn't give their tradition up; she but made of it something new. Frankly moreover she had never been more agreeable nor in a way—to put it prosaically—better company: he felt almost as if he were knowing her on that defined basis—which he even hesitated whether to measure as reduced or as extended; as if at all events he were admiring her as she was probably admired by people she met "out." He hadn't in fine reckoned that she would still have something fresh for him; yet this was what she had—that on the top of a tram in the Borough he felt as if he were next her at dinner. What a person she would be if they *had* been rich—with what a genius for the so-called great life, what a presence for the so-called great house, what a grace for the so-called great positions! He might regret at once, while he was about it, that they weren't princes or billionaires. She had treated him on their Christmas to a softness that had struck him at the time as of the quality of fine velvet, meant to fold thick, but stretched a little thin; at present, however, she gave him the impression of a contact multitudinous as only the superficial can be. She had throughout never a word for what went on at home. She came out of that and she returned to it, but her nearest reference was the look with which, each time, she bade him good-bye. The look was her repeated prohibition: "It's what I *have* to see and to know—so don't touch it. That but wakes up the old evil, which I keep still, in my way, by sitting by it. I go now—leave me alone!—to sit by it again. The way to pity me—if that's what you want—is to believe in me. If we could really *do* anything it would be another matter."

He watched her, when she went her way, with the vision

of what she thus a little stiffly carried. It was confused and obscure, but how, with her head high, it made her hold herself! He really in his own person might at these moments have been swaying a little aloft as one of the objects in her poised basket. It was doubtless thanks to some such consciousness as this that he felt the lapse of the weeks, before the day of Kate's mounting of his stair, almost swingingly rapid. They contained for him the contradiction that, whereas periods of waiting are supposed in general to keep the time slow, it was the wait, actually, that made the pace trouble him. The secret of that anomaly, to be plain, was that he was aware of how, while the days melted, something rare went with them. This something was only a thought, but a thought precisely of such freshness and such delicacy as made the precious, of whatever sort, most subject to the hunger of time. The thought was all his own, and his intimate companion was the last person he might have shared it with. He kept it back like a favourite pang; left it behind him, so to say, when he went out, but came home again the sooner for the certainty of finding it there. Then he took it out of its sacred corner and its soft wrappings; he undid them one by one, handling them, handling *it*, as a father, baffled and tender, might handle a maimed child. But so it was before him —in his dread of who else might see it. Then he took to himself at such hours, in other words, that he should never, never know what had been in Milly's letter. The intention announced in it he should but too probably know; only that would have been, but for the depths of his spirit, the least part of it. The part of it missed for ever was the turn she would have given her act. This turn had possibilities that, somehow, by wondering about them, his imagination had extraordinarily filled out and refined. It had made of them a revelation the loss of which was like the sight of a priceless pearl cast before his eyes—his pledge given not to save it—into the fathomless sea, or rather even it was like the sacrifice of something sentient and throbbing, something that, for the spiritual ear, might have been audible as a faint far wail. This was the sound he cherished when alone in the stillness of his rooms. He sought and guarded the stillness, so that it might prevail there till the inevitable sounds of life, once more, comparatively coarse and harsh, should smother and deaden it—doubtless by the same process with which they would officiously heal the ache in his soul that was somehow one with it. It moreover deepened the sacred hush that he couldn't complain. He had given poor Kate her freedom.

The great and obvious thing, as soon as she stood there on the occasion we have already named, was that she was now in high possession of it. This would have marked immediately the difference—had there been nothing else to do it—between their actual terms and their other terms, the character of their last encounter in Venice. That had been *his* idea, whereas her present step was her own; the few marks they had in common were, from the first moment, to his conscious vision, almost pathetically plain. She was as grave now as before; she looked around her, to hide it, as before; she pretended, as before, in an air in which her words at the moment itself fell flat, to an interest in the place and a curiosity about his "things"; there was a recall in the way in which, after she had failed a little to push up her veil symmetrically and he had said she had better take it off altogether, she had acceded to his suggestion before the glass. It was just these things that were vain; and what was real was that his fancy figured her after the first few minutes as literally now providing the element of reassurance which had previously been his care. It was she, supremely, who had the presence of mind. She made indeed for that matter very prompt use of it. "You see I've not hesitated this time to break your seal."

She had laid on the table from the moment of her coming in the long envelope, substantially filled, which he had sent her enclosed in another of still ampler make. He had however not looked at it—his belief being that he wished never again to do so; besides which it had happened to rest with its addressed side up. So he "saw" nothing, and it was only into her eyes that her remark made him look, declining any approach to the object indicated. "It's not 'my' seal, my dear; and my intention—which my note tried to express—was all to treat it to you as not mine."

"Do you mean that it's to that extent mine then?"

"Well, let us call it, if we like, theirs—that of the good people in New York, the authors of our communication. If the seal is broken well and good; but we *might*, you know," he presently added, "have sent it back to them intact and inviolate. Only accompanied," he smiled with his heart in his mouth, "by an absolutely kind letter."

Kate took it with the mere brave blink with which a patient of courage signifies to the exploring medical hand that the tender place is touched. He saw on the spot that she was prepared, and with this signal sign that she was too intelligent not to be, came a flicker of possibilities. She was—merely to put it at that—intelligent enough for anything. "Is it what you're proposing we *should* do?"

"Ah it's too late to do it—well, ideally. Now, with that sign that we *know*—!"

"But you don't know," she said very gently.

"I refer," he went on without noticing it, "to what would have been the handsome way. Its being dispatched again, with no cognisance taken but one's assurance of the highest consideration, and the proof of this in the state of the envelope—*that* would have been really satisfying."

She thought an instant. "The state of the envelope proving refusal, you mean, not to be based on the insufficiency of the sum?"

Densher smiled again as for the play, however whimsical, of her humour. "Well yes—something of that sort."

"So that if cognisance *has* been taken—so far as I'm concerned—it spoils the beauty?"

"It makes the difference that I'm disappointed in the hope —which I confess I entertained—that you'd bring the thing back to me as you had received it."

"You didn't express that hope in your letter."

"I didn't want to. I wanted to leave it to yourself. I wanted —oh yes, if that's what you wish to ask me—to see what you'd do."

"You wanted to measure the possibilities of my departure from delicacy?"

He continued steady now; a kind of ease—from the presence, as in the air, of something he couldn't yet have named— had come to him. "Well, I wanted—in so good a case—to test you."

She was struck—it showed in her face—by his expression. "It *is* a good case. I doubt whether a better," she said with her eyes on him, "has ever been known."

"The better the case then the better the test!"

"How do you know," she asked in reply to this, "what I'm capable of?"

"I don't, my dear! Only with the seal unbroken I should have known sooner."

"I see"—she took it in. "But I myself shouldn't have known at all. And you wouldn't have known, either, what I do know."

"Let me tell you at once," he returned, "that if you've been moved to correct my ignorance I very particularly request you not to."

She just hesitated. "Are you afraid of the effect of the corrections? Can you only do it by doing it blindly?"

He waited a moment. "What is it that you speak of my doing?"

"Why the only thing in the world that I take you as thinking of. Not accepting—what she has done. Isn't there some regular name in such cases? Not taking up the bequest."

"There's something you forget in it," he said after a moment. "My asking you to join with me in doing so."

Her wonder but made her softer, yet at the same time didn't make her less firm. "How can I 'join' in a matter with which I've nothing to do?"

"How? By a single word."

"And what word?"

"Your consent to my giving up."

"My consent has no meaning when I can't prevent you."

"You can perfectly prevent me. Understand that well," he said.

She seemed to face a threat in it. "You mean you won't give up if I *don't* consent?"

"Yes. I do nothing."

"That, as I understand, is accepting."

Densher paused. "I do nothing formal."

"You won't, I suppose you mean, touch the money."

"I won't touch the money."

It had a sound—though he had been coming to it—that made for gravity. "Who then in such an event *will*?"

"Any one who wants or who can."

Again a little she said nothing: she might say too much. But by the time she spoke he had covered ground. "How can I touch it but *through* you?"

"You can't. Any more," he added, "than I can renounce it except through you."

"Oh ever so much less! There's nothing," she explained, "in my power."

"I'm in your power," Merton Densher said.

"In what way?"

"In the way I show—and the way I've always shown. When have I shown," he asked as with a sudden cold impatience, "anything else? You surely must feel—so that you needn't wish to appear to spare me in it—how you 'have' me."

"It's very good of you, my dear," she nervously laughed, "to put me so thoroughly up to it!"

"I put you up to nothing. I didn't even put you up to the chance that, as I said a few moments ago, I saw for you in forwarding that thing. Your liberty is therefore in every way complete."

It had come to the point really that they showed each other pale faces, and that all the unspoken between them looked out of their eyes in a dim terror of their further conflict. Something even rose between them in one of their short silences— something that was like an appeal from each to the other not to be too true. Their necessity was somehow before them, but which of them must meet it first? "Thank you!" Kate said for his word about her freedom, but taking for the minute no further action on it. It was blest at least that all ironies failed them, and during another slow moment their very sense of it cleared the air.

There was an effect of this in the way he soon went on. "You must intensely feel that it's the thing for which we worked together."

She took up the remark, however, no more than if it were commonplace; she was already again occupied with a point of her own. "Is it absolutely true—for if it is, you know, it's tremendously interesting—that you haven't so much as a curiosity about what she has done for you?"

"Would you like," he asked, "my formal oath on it?"

"No—but I don't understand. It seems to me in your place—!"

"Ah," he couldn't help breaking in, "what do you know of my place? Pardon me," he at once added; "my preference is the one I express."

She had in an instant nevertheless a curious thought. "But won't the facts be published?"

"'Published'?"—he winced.

"I mean won't you see them in the papers?"

"Ah never! I shall know how to escape that."

It seemed to settle the subject, but she had the next minute another insistence. "Your desire is to escape everything?"

"Everything."

"And do you need no more definite sense of what it is you ask me to help you to renounce?"

"My sense is sufficient without being definite. I'm willing to believe that the amount of money's not small."

"Ah there you are!" she exclaimed.

"If she was to leave me a remembrance," he quietly pursued, "it would inevitably not be meagre."

Kate waited as for how to say it. "It's worthy of her. It's what she was herself—if you remember what we once said *that* was."

He hesitated—as if there had been many things. But he remembered one of them. "Stupendous?"

"Stupendous." A faint smile for it—ever so small—had flickered in her face, but had vanished before the omen of tears, a little less uncertain, had shown themselves in his own. His eyes filled—but that made her continue. She continued gently. "I think that what it really is must be that you're afraid. I mean," she explained, "that you're afraid of *all* the truth. If you're in love with her without it, what indeed can you be more? And you're afraid—it's wonderful!—to be in love with her."

"I never was in love with her," said Densher.

She took it, but after a little she met it. "I believe that now—for the time she lived. I believe it at least for the time you were there. But your change came—as it might well—the day you last saw her; she died for you then that you might understand her. From that hour you *did*." With which Kate slowly rose. "And I do now. She did it *for* us." Densher rose to

face her, and she went on with her thought. "I used
in my stupidity—for want of anything better—a do
stretched out her wings, and it was to *that* they reacheu. ...
cover us."

"They cover us," Densher said.

"That's what I give you," Kate gravely wound up. "That's
what I've done for you."

His look at her had a slow strangeness that had dried, on the
moment, his tears. "Do I understand then—?"

"That I do consent?" She gravely shook her head. "No—for
I see. You'll marry me without the money; you won't marry
me with it. If I don't consent *you* don't."

"You lose me?" He showed, though naming it frankly, a sort
of awe of her high grasp. "Well, you lose nothing else. I make
over to you every penny."

Prompt was his own clearness, but she had no smile this
time to spare. "Precisely—so that I must choose."

"You must choose."

Strange it was for him then that she stood in his own rooms
doing it, while, with an intensity now beyond any that had
ever made his breath come slow, he waited for her act. "There's
but one thing that can save you from my choice."

"From your choice of my surrender to you?"

"Yes"—and she gave a nod at the long envelope on the
table—"your surrender of that."

"What is it then?"

"Your word of honour that you're not in love with her
memory."

"Oh—her memory!"

"Ah"—she made a high gesture—"don't speak of it as if you
couldn't be. *I* could in your place; and you're one for whom it
will do. Her memory's your love. You *want* no other."

He heard her out in stillness, watching her face but not
moving. Then he only said: "I'll marry you, mind you, in an
hour."

"As we were?"

"As we were."

But she turned to the door, and her headshake was now the
end. "We shall never be again as we were!"

CHRONOLOGY

NOTE ON THE TEXTS

NOTES

Chronology

1843   Born April 15 at 21 Washington Place, New York City, the second child (after William, born January 11, 1842, N.Y.C.) of Henry James of Albany and Mary Robertson Walsh of New York. Father lives on inheritance of $10,000 a year, his share of litigated $3,000,000 fortune of his Albany father, William James, an Irish immigrant who came to the U.S. immediately after the Revolution.

1843–45   Accompanied by mother's sister, Catharine Walsh, and servants, the James parents take infant children to England and later to France. Reside at Windsor, where father has nervous collapse ("vastation") and experiences spiritual illumination. He becomes a Swedenborgian (May 1844), devoting his time to lecturing and religious-philosophical writings. James later claimed his earliest memory was a glimpse, during his second year, of the Place Vendôme in Paris with its Napoleonic column.

1845–47   Family returns to New York. Garth Wilkinson James (Wilky) born July 21, 1845. Family moves to Albany at 50 N. Pearl St., a few doors from grandmother Catharine Barber James. Robertson James (Bob or Rob) born August 29, 1846.

1847–55   Family moves to a large house at 58 W. 14th St., New York. Alice James born August 7, 1848. Relatives and father's friends and acquaintances—Horace Greeley, George Ripley, Charles Anderson Dana, William Cullen Bryant, Bronson Alcott, and Ralph Waldo Emerson ("I knew he was great, greater than any of our friends")—are frequent visitors. Thackeray calls during his lecture tour on the English humorists. Summers at New Brighton on Staten Island and Fort Hamilton on Long Island's south shore. On steamboat to Fort Hamilton August 1850, hears Washington Irving tell his father of Margaret Fuller's drowning in shipwreck off Fire Island. Frequently visits Barnum's American Museum on free days. Taken to art shows and theaters; writes and draws stage scenes. Described by father as "a devourer of libraries." Taught in assorted private schools and by tutors in lower Broadway and Greenwich Village. But father claims in 1848 that American schooling fails to provide "sensuous education" for his children and plans to take them to Europe.

1855–58   Family (with Aunt Kate) sails for Liverpool, June 27. James is intermittently sick with malarial fever as they travel to Paris, Lyon, and Geneva. After Swiss summer, leaves for London where Robert Thomson (later Robert Louis Stevenson's tutor) is engaged. Early summer 1856, family moves to Paris. Another tutor engaged and children attend experimental Fourierist school. Acquires fluency in French. Family goes to Boulogne-sur-mer in summer, where James contracts typhoid. Spends late October in Paris, but American crash of 1857 returns family to Boulogne where they can live more cheaply. Attends public school (fellow classmate is Coquelin, the future French actor).

1858–59   Family returns to America and settles in Newport, Rhode Island. Goes boating, fishing, and riding. Attends the Reverend W. C. Leverett's Berkeley Institute, and forms friendship with classmate Thomas Sergeant Perry. Takes long walks and sketches with the painter John La Farge.

1859–60   Father, still dissatisfied with American education, returns family to Geneva in October. James attends a pre-engineering school, Institution Rochette, because parents, with "a flattering misconception of my aptitudes," feel he might benefit from less reading and more mathematics. After a few months withdraws from all classes except French, German, and Latin, and joins William as a special student at the Academy (later the University of Geneva) where he attends lectures on literary subjects. Studies German in Bonn during summer 1860.

1860–62   Family returns to Newport in September where William studies with William Morris Hunt, and James sits in on his classes. La Farge introduces him to works of Balzac, Merimée, Musset, and Browning. Wilky and Bob attend Frank Sanborn's experimental school in Concord with children of Hawthorne and Emerson and John Brown's daughter. Early in 1861, orphaned Temple cousins come to live in Newport. Develops close friendship with cousin Mary (Minnie) Temple. Goes on a week's walking tour in July in New Hampshire with Perry. William abandons art in autumn 1861 and enters Lawrence Scientific School at Harvard. James suffers back injury in a stable fire while serving as a volunteer fireman. Reads Hawthorne ("an American could be an artist, one of the finest").

1862–63   Enters Harvard Law School (Dane Hall). Wilky enlists in the Massachusetts 44th Regiment, and later in Colonel Robert Gould Shaw's 54th, one of the first black regiments. Summer 1863, Bob joins the Massachusetts 55th, another black regiment, under Colonel Hollowell. James withdraws from law studies to try writing. Sends unsigned stories to magazines. Wilky is badly wounded and brought home to Newport in August.

1864   Family moves from Newport to 13 Ashburton Place, Boston. First tale, "A Tragedy of Error" (unsigned), published in *Continental Monthly* (Feb. 1864). Stays in Northampton, Massachusetts, early August–November. Begins writing book reviews for *North American Review* and forms friendship with its editor, Charles Eliot Norton, and his family, including his sister Grace (with whom he maintains a long-lasting correspondence). Wilky returns to his regiment.

1865   First signed tale, "The Story of a Year," published in *Atlantic Monthly* (March 1865). Begins to write reviews for the newly founded *Nation* and publishes anonymously in it during next fifteen years. William sails on a scientific expedition with Louis Agassiz to the Amazon. During summer James vacations in the White Mountains with Minnie Temple and her family; joined by Oliver Wendell Holmes Jr. and John Chipman Gray, both recently demobilized. Father subsidizes plantation for Wilky and Bob in Florida with black hired workers. (The idealistic but impractical venture fails in 1870.)

1866–68   Continues to publish reviews and tales in Boston and New York journals. William returns from Brazil and resumes medical education. James has recurrence of back ailment and spends summer in Swampscott, Massachusetts. Begins friendship with William Dean Howells. Family moves to 20 Quincy St., Cambridge. William, suffering from nervous ailments, goes to Germany in spring 1867. "Poor Richard," James's longest story to date, published in *Atlantic Monthly* (June–Aug. 1867). William begins intermittent criticism of Henry's story-telling and style (which will continue throughout their careers). Momentary meeting with Charles Dickens at Norton's house. Vacations in Jefferson, New Hampshire, summer 1868. William returns from Europe.

1869–70   Sails in February for European tour. Visits English towns and cathedrals. Through Nortons meets Leslie Stephen, William Morris, Dante Gabriel Rossetti, Edward Burne-Jones, John Ruskin, Charles Darwin, and George Eliot (the "one marvel" of his stay in London). Goes to Paris in May, then travels in Switzerland in summer and hikes into Italy in autumn, where he stays in Milan, Venice (Sept.), Florence, and Rome (Oct. 30–Dec. 28). Returns to England to drink the waters at Malvern health spa in Worcestershire because of digestive troubles. Stays in Paris en route and has first experience of Comédie Française. Learns that his beloved cousin, Minnie Temple, has died of tuberculosis.

1870–72   Returns to Cambridge in May. Travels to Rhode Island, Vermont, and New York to write travel sketches for *The Nation*. Spends a few days with Emerson in Concord. Meets Bret Harte at Howells' home April 1871. *Watch and Ward*, his first novel, published in *Atlantic Monthly* (Aug.–Dec. 1871). Serves as occasional art reviewer for the *Atlantic* January–March 1872.

1872–74   Accompanies Aunt Kate and sister Alice on tour of England, France, Switzerland, Italy, Austria, and Germany from May through October. Writes travel sketches for *The Nation*. Spends autumn in Paris, becoming friends with James Russell Lowell. Escorts Emerson through the Louvre. (Later, on Emerson's return from Egypt, will show him the Vatican.) Goes to Florence in December and from there to Rome, where he becomes friends with actress Fanny Kemble, her daughter Sarah Butler Wister, and William Wetmore Story and his family. In Italy sees old family friend Francis Boott and his daughter Elizabeth (Lizzie), expatriates who have lived for many years in Florentine villa on Bellosguardo. Takes up horseback riding on the Campagna. Encounters Matthew Arnold in April 1873 at Story's. Moves from Rome hotel to rooms of his own. Continues writing and now earns enough to support himself. Leaves Rome in June, spends summer in Bad Homburg. In October goes to Florence, where

William joins him. They also visit Rome, William returning to America in March. In Baden-Baden June–August and returns to America September 4, with *Roderick Hudson* all but finished.

1875   *Roderick Hudson* serialized in *Atlantic Monthly* from January (published by Osgood at the end of the year). First book, *A Passionate Pilgrim and Other Tales*, published January 31. Tries living and writing in New York, in rooms at 111 E. 25th Street. Earns $200 a month from novel installments and continued reviewing, but finds New York too expensive. *Transatlantic Sketches,* published in April, sells almost 1,000 copies in three months. In Cambridge in July decides to return to Europe; arranges with John Hay, assistant to the publisher, to write Paris letters for the *New York Tribune.*

1875–76   Arriving in Paris in November, he takes rooms at 29 Rue de Luxembourg (since renamed Cambon). Becomes friend of Ivan Turgenev and is introduced by him to Gustave Flaubert's Sunday parties. Meets Edmond de Goncourt, Émile Zola, G. Charpentier (the publisher), Catulle Mendès, Alphonse Daudet, Guy de Maupassant, Ernest Renan, Gustave Doré. Makes friends with Charles Sanders Peirce, who is in Paris. Reviews (unfavorably) the early Impressionists at the Durand-Ruel gallery. By midsummer has received $400 for *Tribune* pieces, but editor asks for more Parisian gossip and James resigns. Travels in France during July, visiting Normandy and the Midi, and in September crosses to San Sebastian, Spain, to see a bullfight ("I thought the bull, in any case, a finer fellow than any of his tormentors"). Moves to London in December, taking rooms at 3 Bolton Street, Piccadilly, where he will live for the next decade.

1877   *The American* published. Meets Robert Browning and George du Maurier. Leaves London in midsummer for visit to Paris and then goes to Italy. In Rome rides again in Campagna and hears of an episode that inspires "Daisy Miller." Back in England, spends Christmas at Stratford with Fanny Kemble.

1878   Publishes first book in England, *French Poets and Novelists* (Macmillan). Appearance of "Daisy Miller" in *Cornhill Magazine*, edited by Leslie Stephen, is international success, but by publishing it abroad loses American copyright and story is pirated in U.S. *Cornhill* also prints "An International Episode." *The Europeans* is serialized in *Atlantic*. Now a celebrity, he dines out often, visits country houses, gains weight, takes long walks, fences, and does weight-lifting to reduce. Elected to Reform Club. Meets Tennyson, George Meredith, and James McNeill Whistler. William marries Alice Howe Gibbens.

1879   Immersed in London society (". . . dined out during the past winter 107 times!"). Meets Edmund Gosse and Robert Louis Stevenson, who will later become his close friends. Sees much of Henry Adams and his wife, Marian (Clover), in London and later in Paris. Takes rooms in Paris, September–December. *Confidence* is serialized in *Scribner's* and published by Chatto & Windus. *Hawthorne* appears in Macmillan's "English Men of Letters" series.

1880–81 Stays in Florence March–May to work on *The Portrait of a Lady*. Meets Constance Fenimore Woolson, American novelist and grandniece of James Fenimore Cooper. Returns to Bolton Street in June, where William visits him. *Washington Square* serialized in *Cornhill Magazine* and published in U.S. by Harper & Brothers (Dec. 1880). *The Portrait of a Lady* serialized in *Macmillan's Magazine* (Oct. 1880–Nov. 1881) and *Atlantic Monthly*, published by Macmillan and Houghton, Mifflin (Nov. 1881). Publication both in United States and in England yields him the then-large income of $500 a month, though book sales are disappointing. Leaves London in February for Paris, the south of France, the Italian Riviera, and Venice, and returns home in July. Sister Alice comes to London with her friend Katharine Loring. James goes to Scotland in September.

1881–83 In November revisits America after absence of six years. Lionized in New York. Returns to Quincy Street for Christmas and sees ailing brother Wilky for the first time in ten years. In January visits Washington and the Henry Adamses and meets President Chester A. Arthur. Summoned to Cambridge by mother's death January 29 ("the sweetest, gentlest, most beneficent human being I have ever known"). All four brothers are together for the first time in fifteen years at her funeral. Alice and father move from Cambridge to Boston. Prepares a stage version of "Daisy Miller" and returns to England in May. William, now a Harvard professor, comes to Europe in September. Proposed by Leslie Stephen, James becomes member, without the usual red tape, of the Atheneum Club. Travels in France in October to write *A Little Tour in France* (published 1884) and has last visit with Turgenev, who is dying. Returns to England in December and learns of father's illness. Sails for America but Henry James Sr. dies December 18, 1882, before his arrival. Made executor of father's will. Visits brothers Wilky and Bob in Milwaukee in January. Quarrels with William over division of property—James wants to restore Wilky's share. Macmillan publishes a collected pocket edition of James's novels and tales in fourteen volumes. *Siege of London* and *Portraits of Places* published. Returns to Bolton Street in September. Wilky dies in November. Constance Fenimore Woolson comes to London for the winter.

1884–86   Goes to Paris in February and visits Daudet, Zola, and Goncourt. Again impressed with their intense concern with "art, form, manner" but calls them "mandarins." Misses Turgenev, who had died a few months before. Meets John Singer Sargent and persuades him to settle in London. Returns to Bolton Street. Sargent introduces him to young Paul Bourget. During country visits encounters many British political and social figures, including W. E. Gladstone, John Bright, and Charles Dilke. Alice, suffering from nervous ailment, arrives in England for visit in November but is too ill to travel and settles near her brother. *Tales of Three Cities* ("The Impressions of a Cousin," "Lady Barberina," "A New England Winter") and "The Art of Fiction" published 1884. Alice goes to Bournemouth in late January. James joins her in May and becomes an intimate of Robert Louis Stevenson, who resides nearby. Spends August at Dover and is visited by Paul Bourget. Stays in Paris for the next two months. Moves into a flat at 34 De Vere Gardens in Kensington early in March 1886. Alice takes rooms in London. *The Bostonians* serialized in *Century* (Feb. 1885–Feb. 1886; published 1886), *The Princess Casamassima* serialized in *Atlantic Monthly* (Sept. 1885–Oct. 1886; published 1886).

1886–87   Leaves for Italy in December for extended stay, mainly in Florence and Venice. Sees much of Constance Fenimore Woolson and stays in her villa. Writes "The Aspern Papers" and other tales. Returns to De Vere Gardens in July and begins work on *The Tragic Muse.* Pays several country visits. Dines out less often ("I know it all—all that one sees by 'going out'—today, as if I had made it. But if I had, I would have made it better!").

1888   *The Reverberator, The Aspern Papers, Louisa Pallant, The Modern Warning,* and *Partial Portraits* published. Elizabeth Boott Duveneck dies. Robert Louis Stevenson leaves for the South Seas. Engages fencing teacher to combat "symptoms of a portentous corpulence." Goes abroad in October to Geneva (where he visits Woolson), Genoa, Monte Carlo, and Paris.

1889–90   Catharine Walsh (Aunt Kate) dies March 1889. William comes to England to visit Alice in August. James goes to Dover in September and then to Paris for five weeks. Writes account of Robert Browning's funeral in Westminster Abbey. Dramatizes *The American* for the Compton Comedy Company. Meets and becomes close friends with American journalist William Morton Fullerton and young American publisher Wolcott Balestier. Goes to Italy for the summer, staying in Venice and Florence, and takes a brief walking tour in Tuscany with W. W. Baldwin, an American physician practicing in Florence. Miss Woolson moves to Cheltenham, England, to be near James. *Atlantic Monthly* rejects his story "The Pupil," but it appears in England. Writes series of drawing-room comedies for theater. Meets Rudyard Kipling. *The Tragic Muse* serialized in *Atlantic Monthly* (Jan. 1889–May 1890; published 1890). *A London Life* (including "The Patagonia," "The Liar," "Mrs. Temperly") published 1889.

1891   *The American* produced at Southport is a success during road tour. After residence in Leamington, Alice returns to London, cared for by Katharine Loring. Doctors discover she has breast cancer. James circulates comedies (*Mrs. Vibert,* later called *Tenants,* and *Mrs. Jasper,* later named *Disengaged*) among theater managers who are cool to his work. Unimpressed at first by Ibsen, writes an appreciative review after seeing a performance of *Hedda Gabler* with Elizabeth Robins, a young Kentucky actress; persuades her to take the part of Mme. de Cintré in the London production of *The American.* Recuperates from flu in Ireland. James Russell Lowell dies. *The American* opens in London, September 26, and runs for seventy nights.

Wolcott Balestier dies, and James attends his funeral in Dresden in December.

1892 Alice James dies March 6. James travels to Siena to be near the Paul Bourgets, and Venice, June–July, to visit the Daniel Curtises, then to Lausanne to meet William and his family, who have come abroad for sabbatical. Attends funeral of Tennyson at Westminster Abbey. Augustin Daly agrees to produce *Mrs. Jasper*. *The American* continues to be performed on the road by the Compton Company. *The Lesson of the Master* (with a collection of stories including "The Marriages," "The Pupil," "Brooksmith," "The Solution," and "Sir Edmund Orme") published.

1893 Fanny Kemble dies in January. Continues to write unproduced plays. In March goes to Paris for two months. Sends Edward Compton first act and scenario for *Guy Domville*. Meets William and family in Lucerne and stays a month, returning to London in June. Spends July completing *Guy Domville* in Ramsgate. George Alexander, actor-manager, agrees to produce the play. Daly stages first reading of *Mrs. Jasper*, and James withdraws it, calling the rehearsal a mockery. *The Real Thing and Other Tales* (including "The Wheel of Time," "Lord Beaupré," "The Visit") published.

1894 Constance Fenimore Woolson dies in Venice, January. Shocked and upset, James prepares to attend funeral in Rome but changes his mind on learning she is a suicide. Goes to Venice in April to help her family settle her affairs. Receives one of four copies, privately printed by Miss Loring, of Alice's diary. Finds it impressive but is concerned that so much gossip he told Alice in private has been included (later burns his copy). Robert Louis Stevenson dies in the South Pacific. *Guy Domville* goes into rehearsal. *Theatricals: Two Comedies* and *Theatricals: Second Series* published.

1895 *Guy Domville* opens January 5 at St. James's Theatre. At play's end James is greeted by a fifteen-minute roar of boos, catcalls, and applause. Horrified and depressed, abandons the theater. Play earns him $1,300 after five-week run. Feels he can salvage something useful from playwriting for his fiction ("a key that, working in the same *general* way fits the complicated chambers of *both* the dramatic and the narrative lock"). Writes scenario for *The*

Spoils of Poynton. Visits Lord Wolseley and Lord Houghton in Ireland. In the summer goes to Torquay in Devonshire and stays until November while electricity is being installed in De Vere Gardens flat. Friendship with W. E. Norris, who resides at Torquay. Writes a one-act play ("Mrs. Gracedew") at request of Ellen Terry. *Terminations* (containing "The Death of the Lion," "The Coxon Fund," "The Middle Years," "The Altar of the Dead") published.

1896–97 Finishes *The Spoils of Poynton* (serialized in *Atlantic Monthly* April–Oct. 1896 as *The Old Things*; published 1897). *Embarrassments* ("The Figure in the Carpet," "Glasses," "The Next Time," "The Way It Came") published. Takes a house on Point Hill, Playden, opposite the old town of Rye, Sussex, August–September. Ford Madox Hueffer (later Ford Madox Ford) visits him. Converts play *The Other House* into novel and works on *What Maisie Knew* (published Sept. 1897). George du Maurier dies early in October. Because of increasing pain in wrist, hires stenographer William MacAlpine in February and then purchases a typewriter; soon begins direct dictation to MacAlpine at the machine. Invites Joseph Conrad to lunch at De Vere Gardens and begins their friendship. Goes to Bournemouth in July. Serves on jury in London before going to Dunwich, Suffolk, to spend time with Temple-Emmet cousins. In late September 1897 signs a twenty-one-year lease for Lamb House in Rye for £70 a year ($350). Takes on extra work to pay for setting up his house—the life of William Wetmore Story ($1,250 advance) and will furnish an "American Letter" for new magazine *Literature* (precursor of *Times Literary Supplement*) for $200 a month. Howells visits.

1898 "The Turn of the Screw" (serialized in *Collier's* Jan.–April; published with "Covering End" under the title *The Two Magics*) proves his most popular work since "Daisy Miller." Sleeps in Lamb House for first time June 28. Soon after is visited by William's son, Henry James Jr. (Harry), followed by a stream of visitors: future Justice Oliver Wendell Holmes, Mrs. J. T. Fields, Sarah Orne Jewett, the Paul Bourgets, the Edward Warrens, the Daniel Curtises, the Edmund Gosses, and Howard Sturgis. His witty friend Jonathan Sturges, a young, crippled

New Yorker, stays for two months during autumn. *In the Cage* published. Meets neighbors Stephen Crane and H. G. Wells.

1899 Finishes *The Awkward Age* and plans trip to the Continent. Fire in Lamb House delays departure. To Paris in March and then visits the Paul Bourgets at Hyères. Stays with the Curtises in their Venice palazzo, where he meets and becomes friends with Jessie Allen. In Rome meets young American-Norwegian sculptor Hendrik C. Andersen; buys one of his busts. Returns to England in July and Andersen comes for three days in August. William, his wife, Alice, and daughter, Peggy, arrive at Lamb House in October. First meeting of brothers in six years. William now has confirmed heart condition. James B. Pinker becomes literary agent and for first time James's professional relations are systematically organized; he reviews copyrights, finds new publishers, and obtains better prices for work ("the germ of a new career"). Purchases Lamb House for $10,000 with an easy mortgage.

1900 Unhappy at whiteness of beard which he has worn since the Civil War, he shaves it off. Alternates between Rye and London. Works on *The Sacred Fount*. Works on and then sets aside *The Sense of the Past* (never finished). Begins *The Ambassadors*. *The Soft Side*, a collection of twelve tales, published. Niece Peggy comes to Lamb House for Christmas.

1901 Obtains permanent room at the Reform Club for London visits and spends eight weeks in town. Sees funeral of Queen Victoria. Decides to employ a typist, Mary Weld, to replace the more expensive overqualified shorthand stenographer, MacAlpine. Completes *The Ambassadors* and begins *The Wings of the Dove*. *The Sacred Fount* published. Has meeting with George Gissing. William James, much improved, returns home after two years in Europe. Young Cambridge admirer Percy Lubbock visits. Discharges his alcoholic servants of sixteen years (the Smiths). Mrs. Paddington is new housekeeper.

1902 In London for the winter but gout and stomach disorder force him home earlier. Finishes *The Wings of the Dove* (published in August). William James Jr. (Billy) visits in October and becomes a favorite nephew. Writes "The Beast in the Jungle" and "The Birthplace."

1903   *The Ambassadors, The Better Sort* (a collection of eleven
            tales), and *William Wetmore Story and His Friends* pub-
            lished. After another spell in town, returns to Lamb House
            in May and begins work on *The Golden Bowl*. Meets and
            establishes close friendship with Dudley Jocelyn Persse, a
            nephew of Lady Gregory. First meeting with Edith Whar-
            ton in December.

1904–05   Completes *The Golden Bowl* (published Nov. 1904). Rents
            Lamb House for six months, and sails in August for
            America after twenty-year absence. Sees new Manhattan
            skyline from New Jersey on arrival and stays with Colonel
            George Harvey, president of Harper's, in Jersey shore
            house with Mark Twain as fellow guest. Goes to William's
            country house at Chocorua in the White Mountains, New
            Hampshire. Re-explores Cambridge, Boston, Salem, New-
            port, and Concord, where he visits brother Bob. In
            October stays with Edith Wharton in the Berkshires and
            motors with her through Massachusetts and New York.
            Later visits New York, Philadelphia (where he delivers lec-
            ture "The Lesson of Balzac"), and then Washington, D.C.,
            as a guest in Henry Adams' house. Meets (and is critical
            of) President Theodore Roosevelt. Returns to Philadel-
            phia to lecture at Bryn Mawr. Travels to Richmond,
            Charleston, Jacksonville, Palm Beach, and St. Augustine.
            Then lectures in St. Louis, Chicago, South Bend, Indi-
            anapolis, Los Angeles (with a short vacation at Coronado
            Beach near San Diego), San Francisco, Portland, and
            Seattle. Returns to explore New York City ("the terrible
            town"), May–June. Lectures on "The Question of Our
            Speech" at Bryn Mawr commencement. Elected to newly
            founded American Academy of Arts and Letters (William
            declines). Returns to England in July; lectures had more
            than covered expenses of his trip. Begins revision of nov-
            els for the New York Edition.

1906–08   Writes "The Jolly Corner" and *The American Scene* (pub-
            lished 1907). Writes eighteen prefaces for the New York
            Edition (twenty-four volumes published 1907). Visits
            Paris and Edith Wharton in spring 1907 and motors with
            her in Midi. Travels to Italy for the last time, visiting
            Hendrik Andersen in Rome, and goes on to Florence and
            Venice. Engages Theodora Bosanquet as his typist in au-
            tumn. Again visits Edith Wharton in Paris, spring 1908.
            William comes to England to give a series of lectures at

Oxford and receives an honorary Doctor of Science degree. James goes to Edinburgh in March to see a tryout by the Forbes-Robertsons of his play *The High Bid*, a rewrite in three acts of the one-act play originally written for Ellen Terry (revised earlier as the story "Covering End"). Play gets only five special matinees in London. Shocked by slim royalties from sales of the New York Edition.

1909   Growing acquaintance with young writers and artists of Bloomsbury, including Virginia and Vanessa Stephen and others. Meets and befriends young Hugh Walpole in February. Goes to Cambridge in June as guest of admiring dons and undergraduates and meets John Maynard Keynes. Feels unwell and sees doctors about what he believes may be heart trouble. They reassure him. Late in year burns forty years of his letters and papers at Rye. Suffers severe attacks of gout. *Italian Hours* published.

1910   Very ill in January ("food-loathing") and spends much time in bed. Nephew Harry comes to be with him in February. In March is examined by Sir William Osler, who finds nothing physically wrong. James begins to realize that he has had "a sort of nervous breakdown." William, in spite of now severe heart trouble, and his wife, Alice, come to England to give him support. Brothers and Alice go to Bad Nauheim for cure, then travel to Zurich, Lucerne, and Geneva, where they learn Robertson (Bob) James has died in America of heart attack. James's health begins to improve but William is failing. Sails with William and Alice for America in August. William dies at Chocorua soon after arrival, and James remains with the family for the winter. *The Finer Grain* and *The Outcry* published.

1911   Honorary degree from Harvard in spring. Visits with Howells and Grace Norton. Sails for England July 30. On return to Lamb House, decides he will be too lonely there and starts search for a London flat. Theodora Bosanquet obtains two work rooms adjoining her flat in Chelsea and he begins autobiography, A *Small Boy and Others*. Continues to reside at the Reform Club.

1912   Delivers "The Novel in *The Ring and the Book*," on the 100th anniversary of Browning's birth, to the Royal Society of Literature. Honorary Doctor of Letters from Oxford University June 26. Spends summer at Lamb House.

Sees much of Edith Wharton ("the Firebird"), who spends summer in England. (She secretly arranges to have Scribner's put $8,000 into James's account.) Takes 21 Carlyle Mansions, in Cheyne Walk, Chelsea, as London quarters. Writes a long admiring letter for William Dean Howells' seventy-fifth birthday. Meets André Gide. Contracts bad case of shingles and is ill four months, much of the time not able to leave bed.

1913   Moves into Cheyne Walk flat. Two hundred and seventy friends and admirers subscribe for seventieth birthday portrait by Sargent and present also a silver-gilt Charles II porringer and dish ("golden bowl"). Sargent turns over his payment to young sculptor Derwent Wood, who does a bust of James. Autobiography *A Small Boy and Others* published. Goes with niece Peggy to Lamb House for the summer.

1914   *Notes of a Son and Brother* published. Works on "The Ivory Tower." Returns to Lamb House in July. Niece Peggy joins him. Horrified by the war ("this crash of our civilisation," "a nightmare from which there is no waking"). In London in September participates in Belgian Relief, visits wounded in St. Bartholomew's and other hospitals; feels less "finished and useless and doddering" and recalls Walt Whitman and his Civil War hospital visits. Accepts chairmanship of American Volunteer Motor Ambulance Corps in France. *Notes on Novelists* (essays on Balzac, Flaubert, Zola) published.

1915–16   Continues work with the wounded and war relief. Has occasional lunches with Prime Minister Asquith and family, and meets Winston Churchill and other war leaders. Discovers that he is considered an alien and has to report to police before going to coastal Rye. Decides to become a British national and asks Asquith to be one of his sponsors. Receives Certificate of Naturalization on July 26. H. G. Wells satirizes him in *Boon* ("leviathan retrieving pebbles") and James, in the correspondence that follows, writes: "Art *makes* life, makes interest, makes importance." Burns more papers and photographs at Lamb House in autumn. Has a stroke December 2 in his flat, followed by another two days later. Develops pneumonia and during delirium gives his last confused dictation (dealing with the Napoleonic legend) to Theodora Bosanquet, who types it on the familiar typewriter. Mrs. William James arrives December 13 to care for him. On New Year's Day, George V confers the Order of Merit. Dies February 28. Funeral services held at the Chelsea Old Church. The body is cremated and the ashes are buried in Cambridge Cemetery family plot.

Note on the Texts

This volume collects two novels by Henry James, *The Sacred Fount* (1901) and *The Wings of the Dove* (1902).

James recorded "2 little ideas" in a notebook on February 18, 1894, one of which would provide the basic concept for *The Sacred Fount*. He further developed his idea for a story concerning "the *liaison* that betrays itself by the *transfer* of qualities" in a notebook entry dated February 15, 1899. James began dictating *The Sacred Fount* to his stenographer-typist William MacAlpine in the winter of 1900. Although he initially planned to write a story of 7,000 to 10,000 words, the work eventually expanded into a novel. James sent the completed typescript to his agent James B. Pinker on July 25 along with a letter in which he described the novel as "impossible" to serialize. Pinker quickly sold the work to Methuen & Co., earning James £225, and then reached an agreement with Scribners for its publication in the United States. *The Sacred Fount* was published in New York by Charles Scribner's Sons on February 6, 1901, in a printing of 3,000 copies, and in London by Methuen & Co. on February 15, 1901, in a printing of 3,500 copies.

Collation of the American and English editions shows that both adopt English spellings, e.g., "candour," "colour," and "splendour." Although there are no variations in wording between the editions, there are some minor differences in spelling. For example, "news-paper-man" in the American edition appears as "newspaperman" in the English edition (95.24); "everyone" appears as "every one" (106.31); and "any one" appears as "anyone" (183.38). James did not include *The Sacred Fount* in the 1907–9 New York Edition of his collected works. This volume prints the text of the 1901 Methuen & Co. edition of *The Sacred Fount*.

James first recorded his idea for a story about a young woman "suddenly condemned to death" by "the voice of the physician" in a notebook on November 3, 1894, and he further developed the concept in another notebook entry written four days later. Although he initially considered using the story as the basis for a three-act play, James included it, under the title *La Mourante*, in a list of possible subjects for novels he wrote in a notebook on December 21, 1895. He began work on the novel in 1900 and agreed on September 12, 1900, to submit a manuscript to Archibald Constable & Co. by September 1, 1901, in return for an advance of £300. Pinker subsequently made arrangements with Scribners for its publication in the United States, but no attempt was made to have the novel serialized, and James did not resume work on it until after he completed *The Ambassadors* in July 1901. (*The Ambassadors* was not published until 1903 because of a delay in its serialization.) He then began to dictate the novel to Mary Weld, his new typist, and on July 18 informed William Meredith, his editor at Constable, that he had decided to use *The Wings of the Dove* for its title. Although he had hoped to complete the work by the end of the year, James did not send the last portion of the typescript to Constable until May 20, 1902, and then corrected and revised duplicate sets of proof sheets, returning one set to Constable and sending the other to Scribners in New York. *The Wings of the Dove* was published in New York in two volumes by Charles Scribner's Sons on August 21, 1902, in a printing of 3,000 copies, and in London in one volume by Archibald Constable & Co. on August 30, 1902, in a printing of 4,000 copies. There are numerous minor variations in wording between the English and American editions. For example, "thought him an idiot" in the English edition appears as "thought him a humbug" in the American edition (332.27); "a greater fraud" appears as "a greater brute" (333.16); and "all melted memories and harmonies" appears as "a cluster of pleasant memories" (575.15–16).

James made further revisions in *The Wings of the Dove* in 1908 while preparing the work for inclusion in *The Novels and Tales of Henry James* (commonly known as the New York Edition), published by Scribners in 24 volumes between December 14, 1907, and July 31, 1909. Using a pasted-up copy of the 1902 Scribners edition, James made hundreds of changes in the wording of the novel. Some of these alterations were minor; for example, "a sensible value" became "a tangible value" (221.23); "hesitated" was changed to "debated" (303.6); and "quick walk" was replaced by "swift motion" (649.1 and 649.2). Other revisions involved more extensive verbal changes. For example, "was there any thing but the senseless shifting tumble, like that of some great greasy sea in mid-Channel, of an overwhelming melted mixture?" became "was there anything but the groping and pawing, that of the vague billows of some great greasy sea in mid-Channel, of masses of bewildered people trying to 'get' they didn't know what or where?" (313.31–34); and "The view was a vulgar one for Densher because it was but the view that might have been taken of another man" was replaced by "These interpretations were odious to Densher for the simple reason that they might have been so true of the attitude of an inferior man" (590.27–30). He also revised punctuation, making lighter use of commas than in both of the 1902 editions, and changed the numbering of the chapters, so that what had been Book Second, chapter III, in both of the previous editions became Book Second, chapter I.

The Wings of the Dove was published by Scribners as volumes XIX and XX of *The Novels and Tales of Henry James* in the spring of 1909 in a printing of 1,000 copies. This volume prints the New York Edition text of *The Wings of the Dove* because it represents James' final revision of the novel and because both the initial composition of the novel and its later revision reflect the same period in the evolution of his style. James wrote prefaces to each of the novels and collections of stories included in the New York Edition, and he commissioned Alvin Langdon Coburn to take a series of photographs for use as frontispieces in each volume in the edition. The present volume includes the preface to *The Wings of the Dove* and reproduces the frontispiece to volume XIX of the New York Edition on page 215 and to volume XX on page 509.

This volume presents the texts of the original printings chosen for inclusion here, but it does not attempt to reproduce nontextual features of their typographic design. The texts are presented without change, except for the correction of typographical errors. Spelling, punctuation, and capitalization are often expressive features and are not altered, even when inconsistent or irregular. The following is a list of typographical errors corrected, cited by page and line number: 33.24, 'Oh; 46.17, her;; 124.29, cherish *Mon*; 173.39, sympath.y"; 197.7, a of young; 286.24, Burlington Vermont; 337.12, "Only,'; 416.1, facts; 498.37, companions; 502.14, like,"she; 542.21, it call; 625.2, obliged,; 625.11, everything;; 628.30, Mrs,.

Notes

In the notes below, the reference numbers denote page and line of this volume (the line count includes chapter headings). No note is made for material included in standard desk-reference books. For further background, see *Henry James Letters*, edited by Leon Edel (4 vols., Cambridge: The Belknap Press of Harvard University Press, 1974–84) and *The Complete Notebooks of Henry James*, edited by Leon Edel and Lyall H. Powers (New York and Oxford: Oxford University Press, 1987).

THE SACRED FOUNT

20.37   *Quoi donc?*]   What then?

21.31   *Intimissima*]   Most intimate.

33.12   *plus belle fille du monde*]   Most beautiful girl in the world.

59.39   *écrin*]   Jewelry box.

68.30   *à plus forte raison*]   So much the more.

124.1–4   'black plume . . . hath spoken!']   Cf. Edgar Allan Poe, "The Raven" (1845), l. 99.

124.29–30   *Mon siège est fait*]   My residence is established.

149.27   *s'être sauvé*]   To have escaped.

167.24   *Voyons*]   Let's see.

THE WINGS OF THE DOVE

215.1   *The Doctor's Door*]   This photograph by Alvin Langdon Coburn appeared in the New York Edition of James' collected works as the frontispiece to volume XIX, which contained Book First through Book Fifth of *The Wings of the Dove*.

221.13   *n'en parlons plus*]   Let's talk no more about it.

276.17   the car of Juggernaut]   The giant wooden car used to carry an idol of Jagannath, an avatar of Krishna, during an annual festival held in Puri in eastern India.

278.3   "Murray."]   One in a series of guidebooks published by the British publishing house John Murray.

287.31   *Transcript*] The Boston *Evening Transcript*, a daily newspaper published from 1830 to 1941.

289.34–35   Marbot and Gregorovius] Jean Baptiste Antoine Marcelin, Baron de Marbot (1782–1854), a Napoleonic general whose memoirs were published in 1891; Ferdinand Gregorovius (1821–1891), a German historian whose works included a history of medieval Rome.

295.6   cycles of Cathay] Cf. Alfred Lord Tennyson, "Locksley Hall" (1842), l. 184: "Better fifty years of Europe than a cycle of Cathay."

297.28   Tauchnitz volume] The Leipzig firm Tauchnitz published inexpensive editions of British and American writers for sale on the European continent.

299.5   *à bientôt!*] See you soon!

328.14   *Punch*] An illustrated comic periodical published weekly in London since 1841.

342.16   "The Newcomes,"] A novel (1853–55) by William Makepeace Thackeray.

342.21–23   Mrs. Nickleby . . . Mrs. Micawber] Characters in *Nicholas Nickleby* (1838–39) and *David Copperfield* (1849–50), novels by Charles Dickens.

348.37   *volage*] Inconstant, fickle.

354.11   *insupportables*] Insufferable, disagreeable people.

355.1   *beaux yeux*] Beautiful eyes.

358.38   Bronzino] Agnolo Bronzino (1503–1572), a Venetian portrait painter.

359.14   *à peu près*] More or less, just about.

361.11   "Les grands esprits se rencontrent!"] Great minds think alike.

400.10   *inespérées*] Unexpected, unhoped for.

505.25   *pourparlers*] Negotiations.

507.40–508.1   Empress Catherine's . . . steppes of Russia] In 1787 Catherine II (1729–1796) made a tour of Ukraine, southern Russia, and the Crimea, during which her adviser Prince Grigory Potemkin (1739–1791) allegedly had fake villages built in order to impress the empress with the progress of settlement in the region.

509.1   *The Venetian Palace*] This photograph by Alvin Langdon Coburn appeared as the frontispiece to volume XX in the New York Edition, which contained Book Sixth through Book Tenth of *The Wings of the Dove*. It depicts the Palazzo Barbaro, where James stayed for five weeks in 1887.

518.32   sala]   Room, hall.

525.23   *moyens*]   Resources, abilities.

533.24   *quartiere*]   Lodgings.

533.30   traghetto]   Ferry.

536.22–23   *bon prince*]   A good fellow.

537.39   padrona]   Landlady.

538.20   Gianbellini]   The Venetian painter Giovanni Bellini (c. 1430–1516).

541.20   *campi*]   Spaces.

572.33   *justesse*]   Precision, exactness.

577.23   *portone*]   Front door, front gate.

589.30   *poco bene*]   Not so well.

590.19   *piano nobile*]   Main floor.

590.21   *tanto bello*]   So very handsome.

592.10–11   *fondamenta*]   A stone walkway along a canal.

617.32   *felze*]   Gondola cabin.

636.38   *salone*]   Drawing room.

671.36   *procédé*]   Proceeding.

Library of Congress Cataloging-in-Publication Data

James, Henry, 1843–1916.
    [Novels. Selections]
    Novels, 1901–1902 / Henry James.
        p. cm.—(The Library of America ; 162)
    Includes bibliographical references.
    Contents: The sacred fount—The wings of the dove.
    ISBN 1–931082–88–X (alk. paper)
        I. Title: Sacred fount. II. Title: Wings of the dove.
    III. Title. IV. Series.

PS2112 2006
813'.4—dc22   2005049443

THE LIBRARY OF AMERICA SERIES

The Library of America fosters appreciation and pride in America's literary heritage by publishing, and keeping permanently in print, authoritative editions of America's best and most significant writing. An independent nonprofit organization, it was founded in 1979 with seed money from the National Endowment for the Humanities and the Ford Foundation.

*This book is set in 10 point Linotron Galliard,
a face designed for photocomposition by Matthew Carter
and based on the sixteenth-century face Granjon. The paper
is acid-free Domtar Literary Opaque and meets the requirements
for permanence of the American National Standards Institute. The
binding material is Brillianta, a woven rayon cloth made by
Van Heek-Scholco Textielfabrieken, Holland. Composition
by Dedicated Business Services. Printing and
binding by Courier Companies, Inc.
Designed by Bruce Campbell.*